OXFORD WORLD'S CLASSICS

THE VICOMTE DE BRAGELONNE

ALEXANDRE DUMAS was born at Villers-Cotterêts in 1802, the son of an innkeeper's daughter and of one of Napoleon's most remarkable generals. He moved to Paris in 1823 to make his fortune in the theatre. By the time he was 28, he was one of the leading literary figures of his day, a star of the Romantic Revolution, and known for his many mistresses and taste for high living. He threw himself recklessly into the July Revolution of 1830, which he regarded as a great adventure. Quickly wearying of politics, he returned to the theatre and then moved on to fiction. By the early 1840s he was producing vast historical novels at a stupendous rate and in prodigious quantities for the cheap newspapers which paid enormous sums of money to authors who could please the public. A master story-teller, he became the best-known Frenchman of his age. He earned several fortunes which he gave away, or spent on women and travel, or wasted on grandiose follies like the 'Château de Monte Cristo' which he built to symbolize his success. In 1848 he stood unsuccessfully in the elections for the new Assembly. By 1850 his creditors began to catch up with him and, partly to escape them and partly to find new material for his novels, plays, and travel books, he lived abroad for long periods, travelling through Russia, where his fame had preceded him, and Italy, where he ran guns in support of Garibaldi's libertarian cause. Without guile and without enemies, the 'great' Dumas was a man of endless fascination. He died of a stroke at Puys, near Dieppe, in 1870.

DAVID COWARD is Senior Fellow and Emeritus Professor of French Literature at the University of Leeds. He is the author of studies of Marivaux, Marguerite Duras, Marcel Pagnol, and Restif de La Bretonne. For Oxford World's Classics, he has edited eight novels by Alexandre Dumas, including the whole of the Musketeer saga, and translated Dumas *fils' La Dame aux Camélias*, two selections of Maupassant short stories, Sade's *Misfortunes of Virtue and Other Early Tales* and Diderot's *Jacques the Fatalist*. Winner of the 1996 Scott-Moncrieff prize for translation, he reviews regularly for the *Times Literary Supplement*.

OXFORD WORLD'S CLASSICS

*For over 100 years Oxford World's Classics have brought
readers closer to the world's great literature. Now with over 700
titles—from the 4,000-year-old myths of Mesopotamia to the
twentieth century's greatest novels—the series makes available
lesser-known as well as celebrated writing.*

*The pocket-sized hardbacks of the early years contained
introductions by Virginia Woolf, T. S. Eliot, Graham Greene,
and other literary figures which enriched the experience of reading.
Today the series is recognized for its fine scholarship and
reliability in texts that span world literature, drama and poetry,
religion, philosophy and politics. Each edition includes perceptive
commentary and essential background information to meet the
changing needs of readers.*

OXFORD WORLD'S CLASSICS

ALEXANDRE DUMAS

The Vicomte de Bragelonne

Edited with an Introduction and Notes by
DAVID COWARD

OXFORD
UNIVERSITY PRESS

OXFORD
UNIVERSITY PRESS

Great Clarendon Street, Oxford OX2 6DP

Oxford University Press is a department of the University of Oxford.
It furthers the University's objective of excellence in research, scholarship,
and education by publishing worldwide in

Oxford New York

Athens Auckland Bangkok Bogotá Buenos Aires Cape Town
Chennai Dar es Salaam Delhi Florence Hong Kong Istanbul Karachi
Kolkata Kuala Lumpur Madrid Melbourne Mexico City Mumbai Nairobi
Paris São Paulo Shanghai Singapore Taipei Tokyo Toronto Warsaw

with associated companies in Berlin Ibadan

Oxford is a registered trade mark of Oxford University Press
in the UK and in certain other countries

Published in the United States
by Oxford University Press Inc., New York

British Library Cataloguing in Publication Data

Data available

Library of Congress Cataloging in Publication Data

Dumas, Alexandre, 1802–1870.
[Vicomte de Bragelonne. English]
The Vicomte de Bragelonne / Alexandre Dumas; edited with an
introduction by David Coward.
p. cm.—(Oxford world's classics)
Includes bibliographical references.
1. France—History—Louis XIV, 1643–1715—
Fiction. I. Coward, David. II. Title. III. Series.
PQ2229.V413 1995 843′.7—dc20 94–43756

ISBN 0-19-283463-0

8

Printed in Great Britain by
Clays Ltd, St Ives plc

CONTENTS

INTRODUCTION

ALEXANDRE DUMAS was 27 when he made his name in the theatre, where the young Turks of the Romantic movement prefaced the July Revolution of 1830 by staging a literary revolt of their own against the stifling, conservative mood of Restoration France. In 1789 the French had been governed by an absolute king. In the forty intervening years they had lived under governments of varying republican hues, had welcomed Napoleon, first as Consul and then as Emperor, and had looked on uncertainly when, after Waterloo, the restored monarchy proceeded, as liberal opinion believed, to turn back the clock. Napoleonic glory became a memory. The power of the Church and the wealthy landed classes revived and, though the democratic gains of 1789 were not entirely lost, the regime became increasingly repressive, especially in its attitude towards the expression of opinion. As the 1820s drew to a close, the political temperature rose dramatically as an ultra-conservative establishment set its face against the attacks and taunts of a new generation which believed in heroism, energy, freedom, and youth. The embattled climate of the times could not have been better tailored for Dumas, ever a man to relish a fight.

He was born in 1802 at Villers-Cotterêts, fifty miles northeast of Paris. His mother was an innkeeper's daughter and his father one of Napoleon's most pugnacious soldiers. General Dumas had risen through the ranks. The mulatto son of a West Indian slave and a French nobleman who had prudently left France for Santo Domingo in the middle of the eighteenth century, he had fallen from Napoleon's favour for speaking his mind during the Egyptian campaign in 1798. He returned to France broken in health and died in 1806, leaving his family with little more than his name. Alexandre received a modicum of schooling and was happy: even as a boy, Dumas, who always took his own sunshine with him wherever he went, seemed permanently insulated against life's disappointments. However, his infectious good spirits were sorely tested in the lawyer's office where he was put to work when he was 14. He decided that his future lay elsewhere. With a friend, he began writing unperformable plays with which they hoped to take Paris by storm. Their first forays were unsuccessful, but in 1823, undaunted, Dumas moved to the capital, where, on the strength more of his clear handwriting than of any claim to efficiency, he became a minor secretary to the Duke of Orléans. He haunted the theatres of the capital, scribbled furiously in his spare time, and fell in love with a seamstress, Catherine Labay, by whom he had a son, also called Alexandre, who was to become famous as the author of *La Dame aux camélias*. Success continued to elude him until 1829, when *Henri III and his Court*, a passionate romantic drama, brought applause and fame, both of which he enjoyed hugely.

Cast as the most ebullient of the new school of dramatists, he turned out a steady stream of hot-blooded, melodramatic plays full of movement, excitement, and high passion which struck an immediate chord with a public hungry for sensation. In literary terms, his dramas are less finished than those of Victor Hugo or Alfred de Musset, but he possessed a far greater sense of stage-craft than either, and had that unteachable, intuitive grasp of what pleases audiences: strong characters, even stronger situations, sharp attacks on the proprieties, and a capacity to surprise: Lamartine once remarked that Dumas manufactured 'perpetual astonishment'. Soon, however, the fashion for excess faded and Fanny Trollope, in her *Paris and the Parisians* (1836; letter 46), was not alone in welcoming the passing of 'the outrageous school of dramatic extravagance which had taken possession of all the theatres in Paris'.

She was particularly incensed by the 'hideous' exhibition of 'low, grovelling brutal vice' projected by *La Tour de Nesle* (1832), which had been perpetrated by 'MM. Gaillardet et ——': 'thus the authors announce themselves'. That an observer as well-informed as Fanny Trollope should be unaware of Dumas's part in the venture is highly significant, for it helps to give the lie to the charge, still frequently made, that he was as casual with literary property as he was with money. Frédéric Gaillardet, an ambitious but unsuccessful author, had asked Dumas's opinion of a play, set in the fourteenth century, about Marguerite de Bourgogne, who, it was said, was in the habit of having discarded

lovers thrown from a tower into the Seine. Dumas liked the
subject but disliked the play, which he rewrote almost entirely.
Though, as Fanny Trollope testifies, he gave his collaborator
first billing to the point of self-effacement, Gaillardet nevertheless accused him of plagiarism, and the matter was settled, according to the fashion of the times, by a duel in 1834. It is true
that Dumas, who always needed copy in a hurry, begged and
borrowed and indeed stole ideas with cheerful abandon and did
not always acknowledge the contribution of his collaborators.
Yet this was done largely at the behest of his publishers, who,
knowing that anything signed by 'Alexandre Dumas' could not
fail to sell, insisted on exploiting his name. However, rumours
continued to circulate, and in 1845 a journalist named Jacquot
published a brochure accusing Dumas of running a 'fiction fac-
tory' which paid menial hacks to turn out novels which he
merely signed. Dumas took him to court and won his case. Only
Gaillardet ever publicly accused him of literary theft, for the
ever-genial Dumas always treated his collaborators fairly, though,
it must be admitted, within the limits of his spectacularly disorganized accounting procedures. At the height of his fame and
earning power, he kept money in a tobacco-jar on his mantel-
piece. Those who asked (and not all bothered to observe the
niceties) were welcome to help themselves, just as Dumas on
occasion borrowed money for his cab-fare which he promptly
forgot to repay.

Because of the publicity generated by the affair and Gaillardet's
subsequent failure to follow 'his' play with any others as powerful, *La Tour de Nesle* was eventually, and not unreasonably,
credited to Dumas alone. Indeed, it was to be revived many
times and proved to be one of his most durable successes. But
by the middle 1830s, he was already turning away from the
theatre (though *Kean* was rapturously received in 1836) towards
prose. He visited the south of France, Switzerland, and Italy
and published the first of his vastly entertaining travelogues.
But he also began to wonder how his interest in history, on
which he had drawn in a number of plays, could be redirected.

History was a passion he shared with his contemporaries, who
had been thrilled to the core by Walter Scott. They devoured
home-grown historical novels, like de Vigny's *Cinq-Mars* and

Hugo's *Notre-Dame*, but also the works of serious historians like Guizot and Michelet who wrote strong narratives and had an eye for the drama of Great Moments. Publishers saw their chance and issued huge collections, some running to hundreds of volumes, of journals, correspondence, and memoirs which served up the past in its rawest and most immediate form. Dumas was addicted to them and built up a vast picture in his mind of the men, women, and manners that had helped shape the destiny of France. He was drawn to four major periods: the sixteenth century, marred by the wars of religion; the emergence of the French nation-state under Richelieu and Louis XIV (the subject of his well-documented history of *Le Siècle de Louis XIV* (1844)); the early eighteenth century; and the run-up to the French Revolution. Though he also wrote of his own age—*The Count of Monte Cristo* (1844–5) is as 'contemporary' as Balzac's *Human Comedy*—his historical novels reflected his interests and played to his strengths; the large number of explanatory notes at the end of this volume bears ample testimony to his detailed knowledge of the times of which he wrote.

But even as Dumas began to turn away from the theatre, there occurred an event which was to give him new impetus and bring him lasting fame: the newspaper war inaugurated in 1836. The proprietors of *La Presse* and *Le Siècle* began accepting advertisements, which allowed them to reduce their cover price significantly. It was the beginning of the cheap, popular press, and the effects were immediate. In 1835, there were 70,000 regular subscriptions to newspapers; in 1836, there were 200,000 in Paris alone, and the figure rose steadily. In the battle for circulation, it quickly became obvious that serialized fiction had a key role to play: the magic words 'To be continued . . .' virtually guaranteed that readers would rush out to buy the next number. Authors who could deliver, to tight deadlines, exciting, dramatic copy, were richly rewarded. Balzac tried his hand at the newspaper serial (the *roman-feuilleton*) but failed, whereas Frédéric Soulié (*Les Mémoires du diable* (1837–8)) and Eugène Sue (*Les Mystères de Paris* (1842–3), *Le Juif errant* (1844–5)) proved to be masters of the genre. But it was Dumas who was to be crowned King of Romance

He had several times tried his hand at shorter fiction without great enthusiasm. But in 1838 he met Auguste Maquet (1813–88), a former history teacher, who brought him a play which Dumas reworked and insisted should be performed under Maquet's name. It was to be the beginning of a long and fruitful collaboration. In 1842, Dumas rewrote a novel by Maquet and published it as his own as *Le Chevalier d'Harmental*. Thereafter, he fell into the habit of discussing plans and plots with Maquet, asked him to fill specific gaps in his historical knowledge, and on occasion issued panic-stricken appeals for ideas and suggestions when deadlines loomed. Dumas regularly over-committed himself and usually kept several serials running at the same time. Maquet was involved in the composition of Dumas's most celebrated fictions: *The Count of Monte Cristo* (1844–5), *The Memoirs of a Physician*, and the whole of the Musketeer cycle. It is quite clear that on occasions whole chapters were sent directly to the printer, unaltered and probably unread by the hard-pressed Dumas. Yet he remained the undisputed major partner It was he who decided that *The Count of Monte Cristo* should start not obliquely, with flashbacks, but with the dramatic imprisonment and escape of Edmond Dantès from the Château d'If. It was he alone who was responsible for adding the flourish, the unique Dumas touch of magic, drama, and excitement to Maquet's wooden outline for *The Three Musketeers*, which he expanded beyond recognition. The name 'Dumas' was not a cover for a committee, nor is there a case for believing that he was the merely the director of 'Dumas Enterprises'. The 'Dumas touch' is a reality. It means not just dash, suspense, and unflagging invention, for however unerring his dramatic sense may be, others too have possessed it in generous measure. For Dumas was not just a story-teller. He is unmistakable, because readers for a century and a half have felt the power of the irresistible personality that lies behind his tales, the generous spirit of the man with his contagious lust for life, his verve and perennial good humour. We may admire Balzac. We may revere Baudelaire and Flaubert But we care about Dumas.

Eternally chained to deadlines and capable of remaining at his desk for fourteen hours at a stretch, Dumas nevertheless found time to spend his huge earnings on travel, socializing, and women. He was known as a great lover before his short-lived marriage to

Ida Ferrier in 1840, and almost to the end of his life he rarely lived alone. He drank little, was a cook of genius, could manage on a few hours sleep, and was lionized by high society He thought of himself as a liberal, and indeed had a strongly developed social conscience But he enjoyed the flattery of lords and princes and had a boyish taste for decorations and insignia, which he collected with glee. He enjoyed his success immensely. In 1847 he built the extravagant and ornately vulgar Château de Monte Cristo at Marly-le-Roi and launched the 'Théâtre historique' where he hoped to stage his own plays. But his ventures were overtaken by the Revolution of 1848, and soon a new tax on newspapers decimated his income. He was forced to close his theatre and sell his house. He wrote more plays and more novels, and floated newspapers. In 1851 he fled to Belgium to escape his creditors. Meanwhile, his love affairs continued, much to the chagrin of his son, on whom he had exerted an overpowering influence but whom he loved dearly. In 1858 he set out on a tour of Russia. Two years later he threw himself energetically into the struggle for Italian independence led by Garibaldi. By the end of the 1860s, both his star and his powers were waning. For *La Terreur prussienne* (1867) he recreated a d'Artagnan figure through whom he warned France of the mood of German aggression then building against France. But it was to be the last characteristic flourish of his talent He continued to launch newspapers and write plays, but the complacent mood of the Second Empire was against him and his strength at last ebbed, undermined perhaps by an over-active thyroid or by diabetes. After a series of minor strokes which left him listless and depressed, he died in his sleep on 5 December 1870 at Puys, near Dieppe, in the house of his son. His death went almost unreported: the war he had predicted with Prussia had happened and Paris was under siege. He had been crowded off the front pages by history.

It has been estimated that Dumas wrote nearly 650 novels and plays, which feature 4,056 main characters, 8,872 minor characters, and 24,339 walk-on parts. No one knows how many copies of his books were sold during his lifetime, nor in how many newspapers his stories appeared. Nor is it possible even to guess at the number of unauthorized, pirated reprints which were published in Belgium and elsewhere, or to put a figure on the colossal sales of translations which had flooded the New World and the Old by the end of the century. But in 1893, Dumas *fils* claimed that in France alone, in the twenty or so years since his father's death, 600 of his books had been re-serialized in newspapers, 2,840,000 volumes had been sold, and 80 million instalments had been printed of titles reissued in cheap, illustrated parts. Such statistics should not surprise. Dumas, who Hugo said was 'universal', was a force of nature and much larger than life. It was with his sales and his huge gallery of characters as it was with his personality, girth, appetites, and imagination: the standards used to measure mortal men are entirely inadequate when applied to Dumas the Titan.

His overflowing, operatic inventiveness explains why the Musketeer saga is one of the great epics of world literature, not only by virtue of its size (it runs to a million and a quarter words) but in its scope and values. Here is a tale of heroes Conflict is its heart. The stakes are high and the odds are stacked in favour of those who are fit only for treasons, stratagems, and spoils. But men of principle rise up against them to defend honour, loyalty, and right. They are red-blooded, hot-headed men who will not brook an insult nor tolerate a bully. They have short fuses and, when spurred to action by the spectacle of injustice and intrigue, leap promptly and joyfully to the challenge, displaying enough wit, daring, and panache to win over the most sceptical hearts. They are the muscular champions of Good in a world eternally at the mercy of Evil.

Even those who have never read a word of their adventures know them. Where is the group of friends who have not at one time or other christened themselves 'Musketeers' and made the cry 'All for one and one for all' their very own? Within a few years of their first appearance, d'Artagnan, Athos, Aramis, and Porthos had travelled the world in translation and made their creator the most famous Frenchman of his age. When he arrived in Russia in 1858, he discovered that the name of the *grand Dumas* was as well known as that of Napoleon. On the other side of the world, Tom Sawyer would soon take his lead from Dumas's books, and by the end of the century the whole Anglo-Saxon world had succumbed to Dumas-mania. His heroes sallied forth in English in astonishing numbers of new editions, some cheap and nasty, others handsome and illustrated, and they carried all before them. By the First War, Dumas's stock was beginning to fall, but it rose again when his doughty heroes stepped from the printed page on to the silver screen. They survived the silent cinema, where Douglas Fairbanks wore the face of d'Artagnan for a whole generation, and they slipped effortlessly into the talkies, where they proceeded to outwit the wily Richelieu and the steely Milady in most of the languages of the world. Their story has been told, adapted, and rewritten. Their adventures have been played for laughs and set to music (Don Ameche was *The Singing Musketeer* in 1939). They have been turned into cartoon characters. There is no reason to think that they will not swashbuckle their way into the cyberspace of the third millennium. For though they have been regularly restyled and repackaged to fit the taste of passing generations, they have never lost their hearts of oak and wrists of steel. They symbolize friendship, adventure, and the spirit of youth, and are to be ranked with the likes of Tarzan and James Bond among the great manufactured (as opposed to folk) myths of modern times

But if they were to become legends, Dumas did not invent them out of nothing. The preface to *The Three Musketeers* explains that, while researching his historical survey *Louis XIV and his Century* (1844), he chanced upon *The Memoirs of Monsieur d'Artagnan*, written by Courtilz de Sandras and published in 1700, which purported to be a true account of the eventful life of a dashing and very resourceful Musketeer whom he may have met and who has a minor place in history. Charles de Batz-Castelmore, sieur d'Artagnan, was a Gascon, born at Tarbes in about 1615. He joined Richelieu's Guards in 1635, fought in the king's wars, and became a Musketeer in 1644. When the Musketeers were disbanded two years later, he was employed by Mazarin, who used him as a trusted courier. After the civil wars of the Fronde he saw further active service, was almost killed at the battle of Stenay in 1654, and, when the Musketeers were reformed in 1657, was appointed second in command to the absentee Captain-Lieutenant. He married in 1659, produced two sons, and separated from his wife in 1665. He appeared at court (he is mentioned in Mme de Sévigné's letters) and was given the difficult task of arresting Fouquet in 1661. He became Captain-Lieutenant of Musketeers in 1667 and, when Louis invaded the Dutch Republic in 1672, was briefly acting governor of Lille. He was killed at the siege of Maastricht in March 1673. A few of his letters survive and they suggest that he was neither dashing nor resourceful but rather unimaginative and a respecter of authority.

If the character and exploits of Courtilz's d'Artagnan were the trigger which released Dumas's imagination, he was was no less taken with his companions. That they featured only in Courtilz's first chapters and thereafter disappeared mattered little to Dumas, who was fascinated by their names. He assumed that 'Athos', 'Aramis', and 'Porthos' were *noms de guerre* which perhaps concealed the identities of 'illustrious persons'. He was wrong on both counts. They were real names, but they belonged to three Gascons, cousins of sorts, who left no mark on public events. They were also related to the Comte de Tréville, Captain-Lieutenant of Musketeers between 1634 and 1642, a fact which doubtless explains their presence in his company. Armand de Sillègue d'Athos d'Auteville was born in the valley of the Oloron in about 1615, became a Musketeer when he was 25, and died in Paris in 1643. Henri d'Aramitz, a Béarnais, joined the Musketeers in 1640, married in 1654, fathered four children, and died perhaps in 1674. Isaac de Portau, born at Pau in 1617, transferred from Richelieu's Guards to the Musketeers in 1643 and thereafter left no trace. Dumas, who did not possess even these few and unhelpful facts, simply hung characters and adventures onto their names. There is far more Dumas than history in them, and this doubtless helps to explain why, from the start, he saw them so clearly.

Written at a furious pace between 1844 and 1850—when Dumas also completed *Monte Cristo*, *The Memoirs of a Physician*, the chronicles of Chicot the Jester, a series of plays and children's books, and numerous other long commissions—the saga spans thirty-five years of the seventeenth century. It begins with *The Three Musketeers* (1844). The year is 1625. D'Artagnan is not yet 20 and fears nothing. Like many Gascons who had supported the cause of Henri IV, he travels from his native

Béarn to Paris, where he hopes to find fame and fortune as a Royal Musketeer. He is soon embroiled in mighty matters. With Athos, Aramis, and Porthos, he foils the plot hatched by the redoubtable Milady to discredit the Queen of France, who loves the dashing Duke of Buckingham. The four friends proceed gaily to frustrate the shabby schemes of the ruthless Cardinal Richelieu, who governs France with a rod of iron. At every turn, they detect intrigues which spell danger to the throne of France and threaten to give victory to the unrighteous. They are the perfect team, for their qualities are complementary. D'Artagnan is impetuous and acts before he thinks. But it scarcely matters, since Athos, a man of unimpeachable honour, thinks for him. Aramis, secretive and well connected, obtains information from high-placed sources which allows marches to be stolen over the enemy. And Porthos, the most lovable of the quartet, a slow-witted giant with vast appetites and colossal strength, is a rock on which they all depend in a crisis. Against them is pitted the viperish Milady, who is bent on revenge, not for profit or advantage, but because she hates everything that is good and clean. During the siege of La Rochelle in 1628, where the comrades acquit themselves with nonchalant courage, she sends them a gift of poisoned wine. Her villainy is uncovered, but she eludes them and travels to England, where, using all her female wiles, she persuades the Puritan Felton to assassinate Buckingham at Portsmouth in August 1628. She returns to France, hotly pursued, but succeeds in foully murdering Constance, the only woman d'Artagnan will ever love. But she cannot escape the reckoning and is beheaded by the executioner of Béthune in a sombre, atmospheric climax which is a perfect example of what Dumas's generation took to be 'Shakespearian'. With bad grace, Richelieu, outwitted at last, signs the paper which admits d'Artagnan to the ranks of the Musketeers.

The second instalment, *Twenty Years After*, is set in 1648, at the time of the Fronde, the civil war which in its various phases was to divide France for four years. The comrades now wear the grey of middle age and only d'Artagnan is still a Musketeer. Athos has retired to a small estate near Blois where he lives in philosophical retreat, far from the shabby intrigues of court, and brings up his son, Raoul, to respect monarchs and love honour.

Still keeping his own counsel, Aramis, now the abbé d'Herblay, is rising through the ecclesiastical hierarchy and has his sights set on high office. Porthos, who married the rich Widow Coquenard, has acquired estates and titles and lives in great, if ridiculous style as M. du Vallon de Bracieux de Pierrefonds. When Mazarin summons d'Artagnan for a secret mission of vital concern to the throne of France, he proceeds to round up his old friends. But time has hardened the differences between them. Athos is occupied in his plans to free the gallant Duke of Beaufort who has been jailed for opposing the dour Mazarin, Aramis is engaged in mysterious affairs and dark political intrigues, and Porthos is fully occupied in promoting his image as a gentleman. Yet though they are older and more cautious and see the world differently, the call to arms ignites the old spark. They travel to England and fail by a whisker to save the life of Charles I. They are foiled at the last moment less by the inevitability of history than by the vile Mordaunt, the son of Milady and, like her, the embodiment of evil. They return to France just in time to put a large spoke in Mazarin's wheel and ensure that the throne of the French kings remains firmly anchored in justice, honour, and right.

The final phase is chronicled in the 268 chapters of *Le Vicomte de Bragelonne*, which appeared in serial form between 1847 and 1850. It is by far the longest segment and is usually published in English in three distinct parts: *The Vicomte de Bragelonne, Louise de la Vallière*, and *The Man in the Iron Mask*. It is now 1660 and the friends seem further apart than ever. D'Artagnan, the youngest, is well into his fifties, and still a Musketeer. He may have day-to-day command of his men, but does not have the rank to which he believes he is entitled. Still dependent on his pay, he smarts when he thinks of the many services he has rendered to his ungrateful betters who have such short memories. Athos, still at Blois, is writing his memoirs, as though to signal the end of his days of active service. But he also worries about his son, Raoul de Bragelonne, who is more sensitive than is good for him and should by now be rising in the service of his king. Aramis consorts with Fouquet, the king's extravagant finance minister, who has made him Bishop of Vannes and counts on his support and influence as Vicar-General of the Jesuits. Aramis has achieved great things but has even greater designs—on the Papacy itself. Porthos, more absurd than ever, busies himself with what he imagines are the duties of a man of substance. When the call comes yet again, d'Artagnan finds it much more difficult to unite his former comrades-in-arms. He and Athos conspire separately to restore Charles II to the throne of England, but Aramis, seconded by the amiable Porthos, schemes darkly to champion the cause of Fouquet. A shadow has fallen over the divided comrades, which does not lift until they reunite to place the mysterious masked prisoner, whom they reckon to be the true heir to the kingdom, upon the throne of France. But events take a savage toll of them. At the end of *The Man in the Iron Mask*, Athos dies and Porthos is killed in the magnificent climax which shows that even Titans are mortal. Aramis escapes to fight another day, as does d'Artagnan. However, that day inevitably dawns. On 23 March 1673 at the siege of Maastricht, he is killed by a stray musket shot just as he reads the letter which appoints him to the rank—at last—of Marshal of France.

When the story is viewed as a whole, the bones of Dumas's narrative technique are plainly visible. His yarning is based on a simple principle of conflict. Each episode has its primary villain—Milady, Mordaunt, de Wardes—who, motivated by pure hate, determines to thwart the heroic champions of right: the Musketeers, who act resolutely in the cause of the noble values of the chivalric code. The battle lines are clearly drawn, yet the war is never fought twice in the same way. Dumas did not take the easy option of writing the further (and similar) adventures of his dashing heroes in the classic manner of the sequel. On the contrary, he allows his heroes to grow old, and they age in such a way that each instalment has its own mood and character. In the first, all their plans succeed. They rise to the challenge with humour and eternal optimism and they solve all problems by prompt, virile action. In *Twenty Years After*, they are separated by their differences and, though the old spirit does return, it is obvious that age has blunted their responses, that problems are more complex now than they once were, and that a simple thrust of the sword creates more difficulties than it solves When we meet them again, in 1660, age seems not so much to have mellowed as withered them. D'Artagnan's lack of advancement has made him bitter. Athos holds the world in utter contempt, and Aramis has grown so distant and inaccessible in his scheming that we may well wonder which side he is on. Only Porthos seems unchanged, but he was always more brawn than brain, a mighty machine to be primed by his comrades. But at what target has he been pointed?

The mood grows darker, the pace slows, and action gives way to subtler manœuvrings. The dash and spring of the mountain stream turns, twenty years later, into the swirling eddies of a broad river and ends in the silt-laden delta of *Le Vicomte de Bragelonne*. It is doubtless this as much as its intimidating length which explains why readers have preferred the first two parts of Dumas's epic. This is all too understandable, and yet the last is in many ways a greater achievement. The characterization is deeper, the drama is better sustained, and over the action—of which there is no scarcity—Dumas projects a view of the world which shows that his supermen heroes are all too vulnerable: they cannot defeat time, nor can they halt the erosion of the musketeering spirit. No less heroic in death than they were in life, they acquire a sobering, human quality.

From the bright days of 1625 to the twilit denouement at Belle-Île in *Le Vicomte de Bragelonne*, the foreground is filled with the din of battle as heroes stand up to villains. But all along, in the background, a secondary and infinitely more dangerous struggle has been taking place, and it too revolves on the principle of conflict The role of Richelieu in *The Three Musketeers* is inherited, in 1648, by Mazarin, who survives into *Bragelonne*, where he is succeeded by the grim Colbert. Though Dumas distinguishes between them and may even at times write generously of their part in creating the modern French state, it is clear that he disliked them intensely for what they collectively represent. They are mean-spirited and cunning, and their methods are covert and underhanded. They have none of the fine spirit of Buckingham, Beaufort, and Fouquet, who, in succeeding episodes, possess flair, physical courage, and a zest for life The first are Roundheads, implacable and practical; the second are Cavaliers, who care more for freedom than for life The Musketeers are irresistible and win battles, which must always be fought again; but the Roundheads regroup, and it is they

who, by sheer persistence, slow patience, and their obsession
with power, threaten to win the war

Of course, this clash of styles and values—between those who
plot and those who cheerfully throw caution to the winds—is a
staple ingredient of all heroic literature. It is also a reflection of
Dumas's personality. Instinctively drawn to high-profile, free-
booting mavericks who give life a tang of excitement, he despised those who intrude, rule-book in hand, into private lives
and disapprove when they see money kept in tobacco-jars. But
the saga, especially in its later stages, has a clear philosophical
edge Most obviously, it is a meditation on the passage of time,
which hardens arteries and stiffens joints but also eats the heart
out of friendship and idealism. Time was, when danger threatened, the comrades threw a saddle on a horse and sallied forth
to fight wickedness. But now they are old, they think before they
act and the spontaneity which gave them their charm is replaced
by calculation.

Yet there is more. D'Artagnan and his comrades are older:
the times in which they live have changed. Youth is not what it
was. Raoul is too sensitive to be reckless. Buckingham, the shrill
lover of Henrietta of England, is nothing like his father, who, in
1626, was prepared to set Europe alight for one smile from Anne
of Austria. Even de Wardes seems a second-rate villain, a pale
reflection of Milady and Mordaunt. For in the thirty-five years
spanned by the story, the rousing, mettlesome court of France
has been tamed and the power of the monarchy over individuals
has been asserted. Richelieu, Mazarin, and Colbert between them
have unified the nation, broken the aristocracy, and replaced
freedom with constraint, action with calculation. It takes little
effort of the imagination to see a parallel with Dumas's own
times. The heady days of 1830 had led the young to believe that
at last France would become a land where justice and freedom
reigned. In the event, the monarchy under Louis-Philippe developed a bourgeois character which, while it promoted France's
industrial revolution well enough, lacked flair, style, and vision
By 1848, when Dumas brought his heroes out of retirement, his
own bold, musketeering generation had been overtaken by men
who were even duller and more prudent now than they had been
when d'Artagnan and company had first crossed swords with

self-interest and intrigue: the spirit of Mazarin had prevailed. The autumnal note does not simply reflect the nostalgia common in the middle-aged, though Dumas shows that grand passion is now subject more to self-interest and self-assertion than to spontaneous feeling: whereas d'Artagnan loved and lost and suffered in silence, Raoul loves, suffers, but is unable to disentangle himself from feelings which weaken and humble him. The final adventure enshrines Dumas's disappointed hopes for the France in which he lived. *Le Vicomte de Bragelonne* is a politically charged novel.

Of course, its politics—which amount to a liberal defence of an élite of enterprising spirits—are odd and have more to do with values than with doctrines or action. Indeed, Dumas's own political activities were as histrionic as they were intermittent. When unrest turned into revolution in July 1830, he prowled through the barricaded streets of Paris with a loaded gun on his arm and, eager to make his mark, set out for Soissons, proposing to capture the arms depot located there. Armed to the teeth, he faced its rather sceptical commanding officer, who was, according to Dumas's later, self-mocking account, persuaded to yield by his wife. She had lived in Santo Domingo, and on hearing Dumas's 'slight trace of a creole accent' and seeing his 'crinkly hair' and face 'blackened by three days of travelling in the sun', believed she was in the middle of a slave revolt and begged her husband to surrender. It is an instance of the bravado which was to also to mark his electoral campaign in 1848: at the hustings, Dumas shouted down objectors and was not above pitching hecklers into rivers. His political enthusiasms were brief and shallow. Paradoxically, he who stood up for fair play and justice for the people of France, was a spectacular spender who took a childish delight in associating with the great and the powerful. Yet, champagne socialist though he may have been, he honestly hated the materialism of his times, the creeping power of state control, and the meanness of spirit which characterized both the reign of Louis-Philippe and the even more complacent Second Empire which followed it. The individual had been shackled and there was neither idealism nor gallantry, merely money and sordid alliances. No wonder he took the opportunity, when it arose, to run guns for Garibaldi.

He was not alone in expressing his dismay. Stendhal found the antidote to the cramping, acquisitive spirit of the age in the more expansive idea of Italy. Balzac chronicled the demoralizing effects of money with fascinated horror. Eugène Sue earned Marx's approval for showing how the profit motive exploited the poor. Baudelaire and Flaubert made 'bourgeois' a dirty word. Dumas's answer was different and characteristic. He reminded France of the values of nobility and chivalry which had freed men's spirits in a way no amount of money and business and industry will ever match. An opponent of the petty-mindedness of the France of his day, he skewered it on the point of d'Artagnan's flashing blade.

SELECT BIBLIOGRAPHY

Le Vicomte de Bragelonne was serialized in *Le Siècle* between 20 October 1847 and, with a few breaks, 12 January 1850, and was published in France in book form by Michel Lévy (Paris, 26 vols., 1848–50). The standard French text fills volumes 2 and 3 of the edition of the complete Musketeer saga edited by Claude Schopp (Paris, Laffont, 3 vols., 1991). The first section, *Bragelonne, the Son of Athos*, was instantly translated by Thomas Williams (New York, W. E. Dean, 1848) and the complete text appeared in a version by Thomas Pederson (Philadelphia, T. E. Pederson) in 1850–1. Subsequently, nearly all 'new' translations published in the USA and in Great Britain, either in full or as three distinct parts (*The Vicomte de Bragelonne, Louise de la Vallière*, and *The Man in the Iron Mask*) have been adaptations of the first American texts. The version reproduced in this edition is taken from the classic translation, many times reprinted, of the complete text issued by Routledge in 1857. It has been lightly revised, corrected, and modernized

Readers wishing to follow the complex printing history of Dumas's voluminous writings in French may usefully consult Frank W. Reed's *A Bibliography of Dumas père* (London, 1933) and Douglas Munro's *Dumas: A Bibliography of Works Published in French, 1825–1900* (New York and London, 1981). *Alexandre Dumas père: A Bibliography of Works Translated into English to 1910* (New York and London, 1978), also by Douglas Munro, is the best guide to British and American editions.

Courtilz de Sandras's *Mémoires de M. d'Artagnan* (1700) has been edited by Gilbert Sigaux (Paris, 1965); the English translation by Ralph Nevill (London, 1899) still makes lively reading. The *Histoire de Madame Henriette d'Angleterre* (1720), which first revealed Raoul to Dumas, is included in Mme de la Fayette's *Œuvres complètes* (ed. Roger Duchêne, Paris, 1990). The most detailed account of the historical Musketeer, Charles de Batz-Castelmore, is still Charles Samaran's *D'Artagnan* (Paris, 1912).

Dumas's autobiography, *Mes mémoires* (1852–5) (ed. Claude Schopp, Paris, 1989; English trans., London, 1907–9) is an entertaining but highly romanticized account of his life to 1832. The best French biographies are by Henri Clouard, *Alexandre Dumas* (Paris, 1955); André Maurois, *Les Trois Dumas* (Paris, 1957; English trans., London, 1958); Claude Schopp, *Dumas, le génie de la vie* (Paris, 1985; English trans., New York and Toronto, 1988); and, most recently, Daniel Zimmerman, *Alexandre Dumas le Grand* (Paris, 1993).

Among the many books in English devoted to Dumas, very readable introductions are provided by Ruthven Todd, *The Laughing Mulatto* (London, 1940), A. Craig Bell, *Alexandre Dumas* (London, 1950), and Richard Stowe, *Dumas* (Boston, 1976). Michael Ross's *Alexandre Dumas* (Newton Abbot, 1981) gives a sympathetic account of Dumas's life. The most balanced and comprehensive guide, however, is F. W. J. Hemmings's excellent *The King of Romance* (London, 1979).

CHRONOLOGY

1762   25 March: Birth at Santo Domingo of Thomas-Alexandre, son of the French-born Marquis Davy de la Pailleterie and Marie-Cessette Dumas After returning to France in 1780, he enlists in 1786 and rises rapidly through the ranks during the Revolution

1802   24 July: Birth at Villers-Cotterêts of Alexandre Dumas, second child of General Dumas and Marie-Louise-Elizabeth Labouret, an innkeeper's daughter

1806   26 February: Death of General Dumas. Alexandre is brought up in straitened circumstances by his mother He attends local schools and has a happy childhood

1819   Dumas, now a lawyer's office-boy, falls in love with Adèle Dalvin, who rejects him Meets Adolphe de Leuven, with whom he collaborates in writing unsuccessful plays

1822   Visits Leuven in Paris, meets Talma, the leading actor of the day, and resolves to become a playwright.

1823   Moves to Paris Enters the service of the Duke of Orléans Falls in love with a seamstress, Catherine Labay

1824   27 July: Birth of Alexandre Dumas *fils*, author of *La Dame aux camélias*

1825   22 September: Dumas's first performed play, written in collaboration with Leuven and Rousseau, makes no impact

1826   Publication of a collection of short stories, Dumas's first solo composition, which sells four copies

1827   A company of English actors, which includes Kean, Kemble, and Mrs Smithson, performs Shakespeare in English to enthusiastic Paris audiences: Dumas is deeply impressed Liaison with Mélanie Waldor

1828–9   Dumas enters Parisian literary circles through Charles Nodier

1829   11 February: First of about 50 performances of *Henri III and his Court*, which makes Dumas famous and thrusts him into the front ranks of the Romantic revolution in literature Dumas meets Victor Hugo. He consolidates his reputation as a dramatist with *Antony* (1831), *La Tour de Nesle* (1832), and *Kean* (1836), which are all landmarks in the history of Romantic drama

1830   May: Start of an affair with the actress Belle Krelsamer, Active in the July Revolution: Dumas single-handedly

captures a gunpowder magazine at Soissons Sent by Lafayette
to promote the National Guard in the Vendée, he visits Blois
and locations in Brittany which will figure in *Le Vicomte de
Bragelonne*

1831   5 March: Birth of Marie, his daughter by Belle Krelsamer
        17 March: Dumas acknowledges Alexandre, his son by
        Catherine Labay

1832   6 February: Start of his affair with the actress Ida Ferrier
        15 April: Dumas succumbs to the cholera which kills 20,000
        Parisians
        29 May: First performance of *La Tour de Nesle*: Gaillardet
        accuses Dumas of plagiarism
        July: Suspected of republican sympathies, Dumas leaves Paris
        for Switzerland After the spectacular failure of his next
        play, he begins to take a systematic interest in the literary
        possibilities of French history

1833   Serialization of a book of impressions of Switzerland, the
        first of his travelogues

1834–5 October: Dumas travels in the Midi From the Riviera, he
        embarks on the first of many journeys to Italy

1836   31 August: Dumas returns triumphantly to the theatre with
        Kean

1838   Death of Dumas's mother Travels along the Rhine with
        Gérard de Nerval, who introduces him to Auguste Maquet
        in December

1840   1 February: Dumas marries Ida Ferrier, travels to Italy, and
        publishes *Le Capitaine Pamphile*, the best of his children's
        books

1840–2 Dividing his time between Paris and Italy, Dumas increas-
        ingly abandons the theatre for the novel

1842   June: Publication of *Le Chevalier d'Harmental*, the first of
        many romances written in association with Maquet

1844   March–July: Serialization of *The Three Musketeers* in *Le Siècle*
        August: First episode of *The Count of Monte Cristo* pub-
        lished in *Le Journal des débats*
        15 October: Amicable separation from Ida Ferrier.
        Summer–autumn: Publication of *Louis XIV and his Century*

1845   21 January–2 August: Serialization of the second d'Artagnan
        story, *Twenty Years After*, in *Le Siècle*
        February: He wins his libel suit against the journalist Jacquot,
        author of *A Fiction Factory The Firm of Alexandre Dumas
        and Company*, in which he was accused of publishing other
        men's work under his own name.

27 October: First performance of *Les Mousquetaires*, an adaptation of *Twenty Years After*

1846   Final break with Ida Ferrier Brief liaison with Lola Montès November–January 1847: Travels with his son to Spain and North Africa

1847   30 January: Loses a lawsuit brought by newspaper proprietors for failure to deliver copy for which he had accepted large advances

11 February: Questions are asked in the National Assembly about Dumas's appropriation of the Navy vessel, *Le Véloce*, during his visit to North Africa.

20 February: Opening of the 'Théâtre Historique'

7 March: Completion of the 'Château de Monte Cristo' at Marly-le-Roi

20 October–12 January 1850: Serialization of the final Musketeer adventure, *Le Vicomte de Bragelonne*, in *Le Siècle*

1848   Dumas stands unsuccessfully as a parliamentary candidate and votes for Louis-Napoleon in the December elections

1849   17 February: First performance at the Théâtre Historique of *La Jeunesse des Mousquetaires*, based on *The Three Musketeers*

1850   20 March: The Théâtre Historique is declared bankrupt The Château de Monte Cristo is sold off for 30,000 francs

1851   Michel Lévy begins to bring out the first volumes of Dumas's complete works

December 7: Dumas flees to Belgium to avoid his creditors

1852   Publication of the first volumes of *My Memoirs* Dumas declared bankrupt with debts of 100,000 francs

1853   November: Returns to Paris and founds a periodical, *Le Mousquetaire* (last issue 7 February 1857), for which he writes most of the copy himself

1857   23 April: Founds a literary weekly, *Le Monte Cristo*, which, with one break, survives until 1862

1858   15 June: Dumas leaves for a tour of Russia and returns in March 1859

1859   11 March: Death of Ida Ferrier Beginning of a liaison with Émilie Cordier which lasts until 1864

1860   Meets Garibaldi at Turin and just misses the taking of Sicily (June) He returns to Marseilles, where he buys guns for the Italian cause, and is in Naples just after the city falls in September Garibaldi stands, by proxy, as godfather to Dumas's daughter by Émilie Cordier

11 October: Founds *L'Indipendente*, a literary and political periodical published half in French and half in Italian.

THE VICOMTE
DE BRAGELONNE

CONTENTS

I

TOWARDS the middle of the month of May, in the year 1660, at nine o'clock in the morning, when the sun, already high in the heavens, was fast absorbing the dew from the ramparts of the castle of Blois,* a little cavalcade, composed of three men and two pages, re-entered the city by the bridge, without producing any other effect upon the strollers of the river bank beyond a first movement of the hand to the head, as a salute, and a second movement of the tongue to express, in the purest French then spoken in France: 'There is Monsieur* returning from hunting.' And that was all.

Whilst, however, the horses were climbing the steep slope which leads from the river to the castle, several shop-boys approached the last horse, from whose saddle-bow a number of birds were suspended by the beak.

On seeing this, the inquisitive youths manifested with rustic freedom their contempt for such paltry sport, and, after a dissertation among themselves upon the disadvantages of hawking, they returned to their occupations; one only of the curious party, a stout, stubby, cheerful lad, having demanded how it was that Monsieur, who, from his great revenues, had it in his power to amuse himself so much better, could be satisfied with such mean diversions.

'Do you not know,' one of the standers-by replied, 'that Monsieur's principal amusement is to be bored?'

The light-hearted boy shrugged his shoulders with a gesture which said as clear as day: 'In that case I would rather be plain Jack than a prince.' And all resumed their labours.

In the meanwhile, Monsieur continued his route with an air at once so melancholy and so majestic, that he certainly would have attracted the attention of spectators, if spectators there had been; but the good citizens of Blois could not pardon Monsieur for having chosen their gay city for an abode in which to indulge melancholy at his ease, and as often as they caught a glimpse of the illustrious melancholic, they stole away gaping, or drew back their heads into the interior of their dwellings, to escape the soporific influence of that long pale face, of those watery eyes, and that languid bearing; so that the worthy prince was almost certain to find the streets deserted whenever he chanced to pass through them.

Now, on the part of the citizens of Blois this was a culpable piece of disrespect, for Monsieur was, after the king—nay, even, perhaps, before the king—the greatest noble of the kingdom. In fact, God, who had granted to Louis XIV,* then reigning, the honour of being son of Louis XIII, had granted to Monsieur the honour of being son of Henry IV. It was not then, or, at least, it ought not to have been, a trifling source of pride for the city of Blois, that Gaston of Orléans had chosen it as his residence, and held his court in the ancient Castle of the States.*

But it was the destiny of this great prince to excite the attention and admiration of the public in a very modified degree wherever he might be. Monsieur had fallen into this situation by habit.

It was not, perhaps, this which gave him that air of listlessness. Monsieur had been tolerably busy in the course of his life. A man cannot allow the heads of a dozen of his best friends to be cut off without feeling a little excitement;* and as, since the accession of Mazarin* to power, no heads had been cut off, Monsieur's occupation was gone, and his spirits with it.

The life of the poor prince was then very dull. After his little morning hawking-party on the banks of the Beuvron, or in the woods of Cheverny, Monsieur crossed the Loire, went to breakfast at Chambord,* with or without an appetite, and the city of Blois heard no more of its sovereign lord and master till the next hawking-day.

So much for the ennui *extra muros*; of the ennui of the interior we will give the reader an idea if he will with us follow the cavalcade to the majestic porch of the Castle of the States.

Monsieur rode a little steady-paced horse, equipped with a large saddle of red Flemish velvet, with stirrups in the shape of buskins;* the horse was of a bay colour; Monsieur's doublet of crimson velvet corresponded with the cloak of the same shade and the horse's equipment, and it was only by this red appearance of the whole that the prince could be known from his two companions, the one dressed in violet, the other in green. He on the left, in violet, was his equerry; he on the right, in green, was the Master of the Royal Hunt.

One of the pages carried two gerfalcons upon a perch, the other a hunting-horn, which he blew with a careless note at twenty paces from the castle. Every one about this listless prince did what he had to do listlessly.

At this signal, eight guards, who were lounging in the sun in the square court, ran to their halberds,* and Monsieur made his solemn entry into the castle.

When he had disappeared under the shades of the porch, three or four idlers, who had followed the cavalcade to the castle, after pointing out the hanging birds to each other, dispersed with comments upon what they saw: and, when they were gone, the street, the place, and the court, all remained deserted.

Monsieur dismounted without speaking a word, went straight to his apartments, where his valet changed his dress, and as Madame* had not yet sent orders respecting breakfast, Monsieur stretched himself upon a *chaise longue*, and was soon as fast asleep as if it had been eleven o'clock at night.

The eight guards, who concluded their service for the day was over, laid themselves down very comfortably in the sun upon some stone benches; the grooms disappeared with their horses into the stables, and, with the exception of a few joyous birds, startling each other with their sharp chirping in the tufted shrubberies, it might have been thought that the whole castle was as soundly asleep as Monsieur was.

All at once, in the midst of this delicious silence, there resounded a clear ringing laugh, which caused several of the halberdiers in the enjoyment of their siesta to open at least one eye.

This burst of laughter proceeded from a window of the castle, visited at this moment by the sun, that embraced it in one of those large angles which the profiles of the chimneys mark out upon the walls before midday.

The little balcony of wrought iron which advanced in front of this window was furnished with a pot of red gilliflowers, another pot of primroses, and an early rose-tree, the foliage of which, beautifully green, was variegated with numerous red specks announcing future roses.

In the chamber lighted by this window, was a square table, covered with an old large-flowered Haarlem tapestry; in the centre of this table was a long-necked stone bottle, in which were irises and lilies of the valley; at each end of this table was a young girl.

The position of these two young people was singular; they might have been taken for two boarders escaped from a convent. One of them, with both elbows on the table, and a pen in her hand, was tracing characters upon a sheet of fine Dutch paper; the other, kneeling upon a chair, which allowed her to advance her head and bust over the back of it to the middle of the table, was watching her companion as she wrote, or rather hesitated to write.

Thence the thousand cries, the thousand railleries, the thousand laughs, one of which, more brilliant than the rest, had startled the birds in the gardens, and disturbed the slumbers of Monsieur's guards.

We are taking portraits now; we shall be allowed, therefore, we hope, to sketch the final two of this chapter.

The one who was leaning in the chair—that is to say, the joyous, the laughing one—was a beautiful girl of from eighteen to twenty, with brown complexion and brown hair, splendid, from eyes which sparkled beneath strongly-marked brows, and particularly from her teeth, which seemed to shine like pearls between her red coral lips. Her every movement seemed the accent of a sunny nature; she did not walk—she bounded.

The other, she who was writing, looked at her turbulent companion with an eye as limpid, as pure, and as blue as the azure of the day. Her hair, of a shaded fairness, arranged with exquisite taste, fell in silky curls over her lovely mantling cheeks; she passed across the paper a delicate hand, whose thinness announced her extreme youth. At each burst of laughter that proceeded from her friend, she raised, as if annoyed, her white shoulders in a poetical and mild manner, but they were wanting in that rich bloom which was likewise to be wished in her arms and hands.

'Montalais! Montalais!'* said she at length, in a voice soft and caressing as a melody, 'you laugh too loud—you laugh like a man! You will not only draw the attention of messieurs the guards, but you will not hear Madame's bell when Madame rings.'

This admonition did not make the young girl called Montalais cease to laugh and gesticulate She only replied: 'Louise, you do not speak as you think, my dear; you know that messieurs the guards, as you call them, have only just commenced their sleep, and that a cannon would not waken them; you know that Madame's bell can be heard on the bridge of Blois, and that consequently I shall hear it when my services are required by Madame. What annoys you, my child, is that I laugh while you are writing; and what you are afraid of is that Madame de Saint-Rémy, your mother, should come up here, as she does sometimes when we laugh too loud, that she should surprise us, and that she should see that enormous sheet of paper upon which, in a quarter of an hour, you have only traced the words *Monsieur Raoul*.* Now, you are right, my dear Louise, because after these words, "Monsieur Raoul", others may be put so significant and so incendiary as to cause Madame de Saint-Rémy to burst out into fire and flames! Aha! is not that true now?—say.'

And Montalais redoubled her laughter and noisy provocations.

The fair girl at length became quite angry; she tore the sheet of paper on which, in fact, the words 'Monsieur Raoul' were written in a fair hand; and crushing the paper in her trembling fingers, she threw it out of the window

'There! there!' said Mademoiselle de Montalais; 'there is our little lamb, our gentle dove, angry! Don't be afraid, Louise—Madame de Saint-Rémy will not come; and if she should, you know I have a quick ear. Besides, what can be more permissible than to write to an old friend of twelve years' standing, particularly when the letter begins with the words "Monsieur Raoul"?'

'It is all very well—I will not write to him at all,' said the young girl.

'Ah, ah! in good sooth, Montalais is properly punished,' cried the jeering brunette, still laughing. 'Come, come! let us try another sheet of paper, and finish our dispatch. Good! there is the bell ringing now. By my faith, so much the worse! Madame must wait, or else do without her first maid of honour this morning.'

A bell, in fact, did ring; it announced that Madame had finished her toilette, and waited for Monsieur to give her his hand, and conduct her from the salon to the dining-room.

This formality being accomplished with great ceremony, the husband and wife breakfasted, and then separated till the hour of dinner, invariably fixed at two o'clock.

The sound of this bell caused a door to be opened in the offices on the left hand of the court, from which filed two major-domos followed by eight scullions bearing a kind of hand-barrow loaded with dishes under silver covers.

One of the major-domos, the first in rank, touched one of the guards, who was snoring on his bench, slightly with his wand; he even carried his kindness so far as to place the halberd which stood against the wall in the hands of the man, stupid with sleep, after which the soldier, without explanation, escorted the vict-uals of Monsieur to the dining-room, preceded by a page and the two major-domos.

Wherever the victuals passed, the soldiers sloped arms.

Mademoiselle de Montalais and her companion had watched from their window the details of this ceremony, to which, by the by, they must have been pretty well accustomed. But they did not look so much from curiosity as to be assured they should not be disturbed. So guards, scullions, major-domos, and pages hav-ing passed, they resumed their places at the table; and the sun, which, through the window-frame, had for an instant fallen upon those two charming countenances, now only shed its light upon the gilliflowers, primroses, and rose-tree.

'Bah!' said Mademoiselle de Montalais, taking her place again; 'Madame will breakfast very well without me!'

'Oh! Montalais, you will be punished!' replied the other girl, sitting down quietly in hers

'Punished, indeed!—that is to say, deprived of a ride! That is just the way in which I wish to be punished. To go out in the grand coach, perched upon a doorstep; to turn to the left, twist round to the right, over roads full of ruts, where we cannot exceed a league in two hours; and then to come back straight towards the wing of the castle in which is the window of Mary de Medici,* so that Madame never fails to say: "Could one believe it possible that Mary de Medici should have escaped from that window—forty-seven feet high? The mother of two princes and three princesses!" If you call that relaxation, Louise, all I ask is to be punished every day; particularly when my punishment is to remain with you and write such interesting letters as we write!'

'Montalais! Montalais! there are duties to be performed.'

'You talk of them very much at your ease, dear child!—you, who are left quite free amidst this tedious court. You are the only person who reaps the advantages of them without incurring the trouble—you, who are really more one of Madame's maids of honour than I am, because Madame makes her affection for your father-in-law glance off upon you; so that you enter this dull house as the birds fly into yonder court, inhaling the air, pecking the flowers, picking up the grain, without having the least service to perform, or the least annoyance to undergo. And you talk to me of duties to be performed! In sooth, my pretty idler, what are your own proper duties, unless to write to the handsome Raoul? And even that you don't do; so that it looks to me as if you likewise were rather negligent of your duties!'

Louise assumed a serious air, leant her chin upon her hand, and, in a tone full of candid remonstrance, 'And do you reproach me with my good fortune?' said she. 'Can you have the heart to do it? You have a future; you belong to the court; the king, if he should marry, will require Monsieur to be near his person; you will see splendid balls; you will see the king, who they say is so handsome, so agreeable!'

'Ay, and still more, I shall see Raoul, who attends upon M. le Prince,'* added Montalais, maliciously.

'Poor Raoul!' sighed Louise.

'Now is the time to write to him, my pretty dear! Come, begin again, with that famous "Monsieur Raoul" which figures at the top of the poor torn sheet.'

She then held the pen toward her, and with a charming smile encouraged her hand, which quickly traced the words she named.

'What next?' asked the younger of the two girls.

'Why, now write what you think, Louise,' replied Montalais

'Are you quite sure I think of anything?'

'You think of somebody, and that amounts to the same thing, or rather even more.'

'Do you think so, Montalais?'

'Louise, Louise, your blue eyes are as deep as the sea I saw at Boulogne last year! No, no, I mistake—the sea is perfidious: your eyes are as deep as the azure yonder—look!—over our heads!'

'Well, since you can read so well in my eyes, tell me what I am thinking about, Montalais.'

'In the first place, you don't think, *Monsieur Raoul*; you think *My dear Raoul*.'

'Oh!——'

'Never blush for such a trifle as that! "My dear Raoul," we will say—"You implore me to write to you at Paris, where you are detained by your attendance on M. le Prince. As you must be very dull there, to seek amusement in the remembrance of an innocent girl who lives in the country——"'

Louise rose up suddenly. 'No, Montalais,' said she, with a smile; 'I don't think a word of that. Look, this is what I think;' and she seized the pen boldly, and traced, with a firm hand, the following words:

'I should have been very unhappy if your entreaties to obtain a remembrance of me had been less warm. Everything here reminds me of our early days, which so quickly passed away, which flew by so delightfully, that no others will ever replace the charm of them in my heart.'

Montalais, who watched the flying pen, and read, the wrong way upwards, as fast as her friend wrote, here interrupted by clapping her hands. 'Capital!' cried she; 'there is frankness—there is heart—there is style! Show these Parisians, my dear, that Blois is the city for fine language!'

'He knows very well that Blois was a Paradise to me,' replied the girl.

'That is exactly what you mean to say; and you speak like an angel.'

'I will finish, Montalais,' and she continued as follows: 'You often think of me, you say, Monsieur Raoul: I thank you; but that does not surprise me, when I recollect how often our hearts have beaten close to each other.'

'Oh! oh!' said Montalais. 'Beware, my lamb! You are scattering your wool, and there are wolves about.'

Louise was about to reply, when the gallop of a horse resounded under the porch of the castle.

'What is that?' said Montalais, approaching the window. 'A handsome rider, by my faith!'

'Oh!—Raoul!' exclaimed Louise, who had made the same movement as her friend, and, becoming pale as death, sunk back beside her unfinished letter.

'Now, he is a clever lover, upon my word!' cried Montalais; 'he arrives just at the right moment.'

'Come in, come in, I implore you!' murmured Louise.

'Bah! he does not know me. Let me see what he has come here for.'

II

THE MESSENGER

MADEMOISELLE DE MONTALAIS was right; the young rider was a sight for sore eyes.

He was a young man* of from twenty-four to twenty-five years of age, tall and slender, wearing gracefully the picturesque military costume of the period. His large boots contained a foot which Mademoiselle de Montalais might not have disowned if she had been transformed into a man. With one of his delicate but nervous hands he checked his horse in the middle of the court, and with the other raised his hat, whose long plumes shaded his at once serious and ingenuous countenance.

The guards, roused by the steps of the horse, awoke, and were on foot instantly. The young man waited till one of them was close to his saddle-bow: then, stooping towards him, in a clear, distinct voice, which was perfectly audible at the window where the two girls were concealed, he said 'A message for his royal highness.'

'Ah, ah!' cried the soldier. 'Officer, a messenger!'

But this brave guard knew very well that no officer would appear, seeing that the only one who could have appeared dwelt at the other side of the castle, in an apartment looking into the gardens. So he hastened to add: 'The officer, monsieur, is on his rounds; but, in his absence, M. de Saint-Rémy,* the major-domo, shall be informed.'

'M. de Saint-Rémy?' repeated the horseman, slightly blushing 'Do you know him?'

'Why, yes; but request him, if you please, that my visit be announced to his royal highness as soon as possible.'

'It appears to be pressing,' said the guard, as if speaking to himself, but really in the hope of obtaining an answer.

The messenger made an affirmative sign with his head.

'In that case,' said the guard, 'I will go and seek the major-domo myself.'

The young man, in the meantime, dismounted; and whilst the others were closely observing the movements of the fine horse he rode, the soldier returned.

'Your pardon, young gentleman; but your name, if you please?'

'The Vicomte de Bragelonne, with news from his highness M. le Prince de Condé.'

The soldier made a profound bow, and, as if the name of the conqueror of Rocroi and Lens* had given him wings, he stepped lightly up the steps leading to the antechamber.

M. de Bragelonne had not had time to fasten his horse to the iron railings of the main steps, when M. de Saint-Rémy came running, out of breath, supporting his capacious body with one hand, whilst with the other he cut the air as a fisherman cleaves the waves with his oar.

'Ah, Monsieur le Vicomte! You at Blois!' cried he. 'Well, that is a wonder. Good-day to you—good-day, Monsieur Raoul.'

'I offer you a thousand respects, M. de Saint-Rémy.'

'How Madame de la Vall—I mean, how delighted Madame de Saint-Rémy will be to see you! But come in. His royal highness is at breakfast—must he be interrupted? Is the matter serious?'

'Yes and no, Monsieur de Saint-Rémy. A moment's delay, however, would be disagreeable to his royal highness.'

'If that is the case, we will countermand the sentry, Monsieur le Vicomte. Come in. Besides, Monsieur is in an excellent humour to-day. And then you bring news, do you not?'

'Great news, Monsieur de Saint-Rémy.'

'And good, I presume?'

'Excellent.'

'Come quickly, come quickly then!' cried the worthy man, putting his dress to rights as he went along.

Raoul followed him, hat in hand, and a little disconcerted at the noise made by his spurs in these immense salons.

As soon as he had disappeared in the interior of the palace, the window of the court was repeopled, and an animated whispering betrayed the emotion of the two girls. They soon appeared to have formed a resolution, for one of the two faces disappeared from the window. This was the brunette; the other remained behind the balcony, concealed by the flowers, watching attentively through the branches of the trees shading the steps by which M. de Bragelonne had entered the castle.

In the meantime the object of so much laudable curiosity continued his route, following the steps of the major-domo. The noise of quick steps, an odour of wine and viands, a clinking of crystal and plates, warned them that they were coming to the end of their course.

The pages, valets, and officers, assembled in the office which led up to the dining-hall, welcomed the new-comer with the proverbial politeness of the country; some of them were acquainted with Raoul, and all knew that he came from Paris. It might be said that his arrival for a moment suspended the service. In fact, a page, who was pouring out wine for his royal highness, on hearing the jingling of spurs in the next chamber, turned round like a child, without perceiving that he was continuing to pour out, not into the glass, but upon the table-cloth.

Madame who was not so preoccupied as her glorious spouse was, remarked this distraction of the page.

'Well?' exclaimed she.

'Well!' repeated Monsieur; 'what is going on then?'

M. de Saint-Rémy, who had just introduced his head through the doorway, took advantage of the moment.

'Why am I to be disturbed?' said Gaston, helping himself to a thick slice of one of the largest salmon that had ever ascended the Loire to be captured between Paimbœuf and Saint-Nazaire.*

'There is a messenger from Paris. Oh! but after monseigneur has breakfasted will do; there is plenty of time.'

'From Paris!' cried the prince, letting his fork fall. 'A messenger from Paris, do you say? And from whom does this messenger come?'

'From M. le Prince,' said the major-domo promptly.

Every one knows that the Prince de Condé was so called.

'A messenger from M. le Prince!' said Gaston, with an inquietude that escaped none of the assistants, and consequently redoubled the general curiosity.

Monsieur, perhaps, fancied himself brought back again to the happy times when the opening of a door gave him an emotion, in which every letter might contain a state secret—in which every message was connected with a dark and complicated intrigue. Perhaps, likewise, the great name of M. le Prince expanded itself, beneath the roofs of Blois, to the proportions of a phantom.

Monsieur pushed away his plate.

'Shall I tell the envoy to wait?' asked M. de Saint-Rémy.

A glance from Madame emboldened Gaston, who replied: 'No, no; let him come in at once, on the contrary. By the by, who is he?'

'A gentleman of this country, M. le Vicomte de Bragelonne.'

'Ah, very well! Show him in, Saint-Rémy—show him in.'

And when he had let fall these words, with his accustomed gravity, Monsieur turned his eyes, in a certain manner, upon the people of his suite, so that all, pages, officers, and equerries, quitted the service, knives, and goblets, and made towards the second chamber a retreat as rapid as it was disorderly.

This little army had dispersed in two files when Raoul de Bragelonne, preceded by M. de Saint-Rémy, entered the dining-hall.

The short interval of solitude which this retreat had left him, permitted Monsieur the time to assume a diplomatic countenance. He did not turn round, but waited till the major-domo should bring the messenger face to face with him.

Raoul stopped at a level with the lower end of the table, so as to be exactly between Monsieur and Madame. From this place he made a profound bow to Monsieur, and a very humble one to Madame; then, drawing himself to attention, he waited for Monsieur to address him.

On his part the prince waited till the doors were hermetically closed; he would not turn round to ascertain the fact, as that would have been derogatory to his dignity, but he listened with all his ears for the noise of the lock, which would promise him at least an appearance of secrecy.

The doors being closed, Monsieur raised his eyes towards the vicomte, and said, 'It appears that you come from Paris, monsieur?'

'This minute, monseigneur.'

'How is the king?'

'His majesty is in perfect health, monseigneur.'

'And my sister-in-law?'*

'Her majesty the queen-mother still suffers from the complaint in her chest, but for the last month she has been rather better.'

'Somebody told me you came from M. le Prince. They must have been mistaken, surely?'

'No, monseigneur; M. le Prince has charged me to convey this letter to your royal highness, and I am to wait for an answer to it.'

Raoul had been a little annoyed by this cold and cautious reception, and his voice insensibly sank to a low key.

The prince forgot that he was the cause of this apparent mystery, and his fears returned.

He received the letter from the Prince de Condé with a haggard look, unsealed it as he would have unsealed a suspicious packet, and in order to read it so that no one should remark the effects of it upon his countenance, he turned round.

Madame followed, with an anxiety almost equal to that of the prince, every manœuvre of her august husband.

Raoul, impassible, and a little disengaged by the attention of his hosts, looked from his place through the open window at the gardens and the statues which peopled them.

'Well!' cried Monsieur, all at once, with a cheerful smile; 'here is an agreeable surprise, and a charming letter from M. le Prince. Look, Madame!'

The table was too large to allow the arm of the prince to reach the hand of Madame; Raoul sprang forward to be their intermediary, and did it with so good a grace as to procure a flattering acknowledgement from the princess.

'You know the contents of this letter, no doubt?' said Gaston to Raoul.

'Yes, monseigneur; M. le Prince at first gave me the message verbally, but upon reflection his highness took up his pen.'

'It is beautiful writing,' said Madame, 'but I cannot read it.'

'Will you read it to Madame, M. de Bragelonne?' said the duke.

'Yes; read it, if you please, monsieur.'

Raoul began to read, Monsieur giving again all his attention. The letter was conceived in these terms:

MONSEIGNEUR—The king is about to set out for the frontiers * You are aware that the marriage of his majesty is concluded upon The king has done me the honour to appoint me his quartermaster for this journey, and as I knew with what joy his majesty would pass a day at Blois, I venture to ask your royal highness's permission to mark the house you inhabit as our quarters If, however, the suddenness of this request should create to your royal highness any embarrassment, I entreat you to say so by the messenger I send, a gentleman of my suite, M le Vicomte de Bragelonne My itinerary will depend upon your royal highness's determination, and instead of passing through Blois, we shall settle on either Vendôme or Romorantin * I venture to hope that your royal highness will be pleased with my arrangement, it being the expression of my boundless desire to make myself agreeable to you.

'Nothing can be more gracious towards us,' said Madame, who had more than once consulted the looks of her husband during the reading of the letter. 'The king here!' exclaimed she, in a rather louder tone than would have been necessary to preserve secrecy.

'Monsieur,' said his royal highness in his turn, 'you will offer my thanks to M. de Condé, and express to him my gratitude for the honour he has done me.' Raoul bowed.

'On what day will his majesty arrive?' continued the prince.

'The king, monseigneur, will in all probability arrive this evening.'

'But how, then, could he have known my reply if it had been in the negative?'

'I was desired, monseigneur, to return in all haste to Beaugency,* to give counter-orders to the courier, who was himself to go back immediately with counter-orders to M. le Prince.'

'His majesty is at Orléans, then?'

'Much nearer, monseigneur; his majesty must by this time have arrived at Meung.'*

'Does the court accompany him?'

'Yes, monseigneur.'

'By the by, I forgot to ask you after M. le Cardinal.'*

'His eminence appears to enjoy good health, monseigneur '

'His nieces accompany him, no doubt?'

'No, monseigneur; his eminence has ordered the Mesdemoiselles de Mancini to set out for Brouage.* They will follow the left bank of the Loire, while the court will come by the right.'

'What! Mademoiselle Mary de Mancini quit the court in that manner?' asked Monsieur, his reserve beginning to diminish.

'Mademoiselle Mary de Mancini in particular,' replied Raoul discreetly.

A fugitive smile, an imperceptible vestige of his ancient spirit of intrigue, shot across the pale face of the prince.

'Thanks, M. de Bragelonne,' then said Monsieur. 'You would, perhaps, not be willing to carry M. le Prince the commission with which I would charge you, and that is, that his messenger has been very agreeable to me; but I will tell him so myself '

Raoul bowed his thanks to Monsieur for the honour he had done him.

Monsieur made a sign to Madame, who struck a bell which was placed at her right hand; M. de Saint-Rémy entered, and the room was soon filled with people.

'Messieurs,' said the prince, 'his majesty is about to pay me the honour of passing a day at Blois; I depend upon the king, my nephew, not having to repent of the favour he does my house.'

'*Vive le Roi!*' cried all the officers of the household with frantic enthusiasm, and M. de Saint-Rémy louder than the rest.

Gaston hung down his head with evident chagrin. He had all his life been obliged to hear, or rather to undergo, this cry of '*Vive le Roi!*'* which passed over him. For a long time, being unaccustomed to hear it, his ear had had rest, and now a younger, more vivacious, and more brilliant royalty rose up before him, like a new and more painful provocation.

Madame perfectly understood the sufferings of that timid, gloomy heart; she rose from the table, Monsieur imitated her mechanically, and all the domestics, with a buzzing like that of several bee-hives, surrounded Raoul for the purpose of questioning him.

Madame saw this movement, and called M. de Saint-Rémy. 'This is not the time for gossiping, but working,' said she, with the tone of an angry housekeeper.

M. de Saint-Rémy hastened to break the circle formed by the officers round Raoul, so that the latter was able to gain the antechamber.

'Care will be taken of that gentleman, I hope,' added Madame, addressing M. de Saint-Rémy.

The worthy man immediately hastened after Raoul. 'Madame desires refreshments to be offered to you,' said he; 'and there is, besides, a lodging for you in the castle.'

'Thanks M. de Saint-Rémy,' replied Raoul; 'but you know how anxious I must be to pay my duty to M. le Comte, my father.'*

'That is true, that is true, Monsieur Raoul; present him, at the same time, my humble respects, if you please.'

Raoul thus once more got rid of the old gentleman, and pursued his way. As he was passing under the porch, leading his horse by the bridle, a soft voice called him from the depths of an obscure path.

'Monsieur Raoul!' said the voice.

The young man turned round, surprised, and saw a dark complexioned girl, who, with a finger on her lip, held out her other hand to him. This young lady was an utter stranger.

III

THE INTERVIEW

RAOUL made one step towards the girl who thus called him.

'But my horse, madame?' said he.

'Yes, you had better do something with it. Try over there—

there is a shed in the outer court: fasten your horse, and return quickly!'

'I obey, madame.'

Raoul was not four minutes in performing what he had been directed to do; he returned to the little door, where, in the gloom, he found his mysterious guide waiting for him, on the first steps of a winding staircase.

'Are you brave enough to follow me, monsieur knight errant?' asked the girl, laughing at the momentary hesitation Raoul had manifested.

The latter replied by springing up the dark staircase after her. They thus climbed up three flights, he behind her, touching with his hands, when he felt for the banister, a silk dress which rubbed against each side of the staircase. At every false step made by Raoul, his conductress cried, 'Hush!' and held out to him a soft and perfumed hand.

'One would mount thus to the belfry of the castle without being conscious of fatigue,' said Raoul.

'All of which means, monsieur, that you are very much perplexed, very tired, and very uneasy. But be of good cheer, monsieur; here we are, at our destination.'

The girl threw open a door, which immediately, without any transition, filled with a flood of light the landing of the staircase, at the top of which Raoul appeared, holding fast by the balustrade.

The girl continued to walk on—he followed her; she entered a chamber—he did the same.

As soon as he was fairly in the net he heard a loud cry, and, turning round, saw at two paces from him, with her hands clasped and her eyes closed, that beautiful fair girl with blue eyes and white shoulders, who, recognizing him, called him Raoul.

He saw her, and divined at once so much love and so much joy in the expression of her countenance, that he sank on his knees in the middle of the chamber, murmuring, on his part, the name of Louise.

'Ah! Montalais!—Montalais!' she sighed, 'it is very wicked to deceive me so.'

'Who, I? I have deceived you?'

'Yes; you told me you would go down to inquire the news, and you have brought up monsieur!'

'Well, I was obliged to do so—how else could he have received the letter you wrote him?' And she pointed with her finger to the letter which was still upon the table.

Raoul made a step to take it; Louise, quicker, although she had sprung forward with a noticeable awkwardness of movement,* reached out her hand to stop him. Raoul came in contact with that trembling hand, took it within his own, and carried it so respectfully to his lips, that he might be said to have deposited a sigh upon it rather than a kiss.

In the meantime, Mademoiselle de Montalais had taken the letter, folded it carefully, as women do, in three folds, and slipped it into her bosom.

'Don't be afraid, Louise,' said she; 'monsieur will no more venture to take it hence than the late king Louis XIII ventured to take billets from the corsage of Mademoiselle de Hautefort.'*

Raoul blushed at seeing the smile of the two girls; and he did not remark that the hand of Louise remained in his.

'There!' said Montalais, 'you have pardoned me, Louise, for having brought monsieur to you; and you, monsieur, bear me no malice for having followed me to see mademoiselle. Now, then, peace being made, let us chat like old friends. Present me, Louise, to M. de Bragelonne.'

'Monsieur le Vicomte,' said Louise, with her quiet grace and ingenuous smile, 'I have the honour to present to you Mademoiselle Aure de Montalais, maid of honour to her royal highness Madame, and moreover my friend—my excellent friend.'

Raoul bowed ceremoniously.

'And me, Louise,' said he—'will you not present me also to mademoiselle?'

'Oh, she knows you—she knows everything!'

This unguarded expression made Montalais laugh and Raoul sigh with happiness, for he interpreted it thus: '*She knows how deeply we are in love.*'

'The ceremonies being over, Monsieur le Vicomte,' said Montalais, 'take a chair, and tell us quickly the news you bring flying thus.'

'Mademoiselle, it is no longer a secret; the king, on his way to Poitiers,* will stop at Blois, to visit his royal highness.'

'The king here!' exclaimed Montalais, clapping her hands. 'What! are we going to see the court? Only think, Louise—the real court from Paris! Oh, good heavens! But when will this happen, monsieur?'

'Perhaps this evening, mademoiselle; at latest, tomorrow.'

Montalais lifted her shoulders in sign of vexation.

'No time to get ready! No time to prepare a single dress! We are as far behind the fashions as the Poles. We shall look like portraits of the time of Henry IV. Ah, monsieur! this is sad news you bring us!'

'But, mesdemoiselles, you will be still beautiful!'

'That's no news! Yes, we shall be always beautiful, because nature has made us passable; but we shall be ridiculous, because the fashion will have passed us by. Alas! ridiculous! I shall be thought ridiculous—I!'

'And by whom?' said Louise, innocently.

'By whom? You are a strange girl, my dear. Is that a question to put to me? I mean everybody; I mean the courtiers, the nobles; I mean the king.'

'Pardon me, my good friend; but as here every one is accustomed to see us as we are——'

'Granted; but that is about to change, and we shall be ridiculous, even for Blois; for close to us will be seen the fashions from Paris, and they will perceive that we are in the fashion of Blois! It is enough to make one despair!'

'Console yourself, mademoiselle.'

'Well, so let it be! After all, so much the worse for those who do not find me to their taste!' said Montalais, philosophically.

'They would be very difficult to please,' replied Raoul, faithful to his customary gallantry.

'Thank you, Monsieur le Vicomte. We were saying, then, that the king is coming to Blois?'

'With all the court.'

'Mesdemoiselles de Mancini,* will they be with them?'

'No, certainly not.'

'But as the king, it is said, cannot do without Mademoiselle Mary?'

'Mademoiselle, the king must do without her. M. le Cardinal will have it so. He has exiled his nieces to Brouage.'

'He!—the hypocrite!'

'Hush!' said Louise, pressing a finger on her friend's rosy lips.

'Bah! nobody can hear me. I say that old Mazarino Mazarini* is a hypocrite, who burns impatiently to make his niece Queen of France.'

'That cannot be, mademoiselle, since M. le Cardinal, on the contrary, has brought about the marriage of his majesty with the Infanta Maria Theresa.'

Montalais looked Raoul full in the face, and said, 'And do you Parisians believe in these tales? Well! we are a little more knowing than you, at Blois.'

'Mademoiselle, if the king goes beyond Poitiers and sets out for Spain; if the articles of the marriage contract are agreed upon by Don Luis de Haro* and his eminence, you must plainly perceive that it is not child's play.'

'All very fine! but the king is king, I suppose?'

'No doubt, mademoiselle; but the cardinal is the cardinal.'

'The king is not a man, then! And he does not love Mary Mancini?'

'He adores her.'

'Well, he will marry her then. We shall have war with Spain. M. Mazarin will spend a few of the millions he has put away; our gentlemen will perform prodigies of valour in their encounters with the proud Castilians, and many of them will return crowned with laurels, to be recrowned by us with myrtles. Now, that is my view of politics.'

'Montalais, you are wild!' said Louise, 'and every exaggeration attracts you as light does a moth.'

'Louise, you are so extremely reasonable, that you will never know how to love.'

'Oh!' said Louise, in a tone of tender reproach, 'don't you see, Montalais? The queen-mother desires to marry her son to the Infanta; would you wish him to disobey his mother? Is it for a royal heart like his to set such a bad example? When parents forbid love, love must be banished.'

And Louise sighed: Raoul cast down his eyes, with an expression of constraint. Montalais on her part, laughed aloud.

'Well, I have no parents!' said she.

'You are acquainted, without doubt, with the state of health of M. le Comte de la Fère?' said Louise, after breathing that sigh which had revealed so many griefs in its eloquent utterance.

'No, mademoiselle,' replied Raoul, 'I have not yet paid my respects to my father; I was going to his house when Mademoiselle de Montalais so kindly stopped me. I hope the comte is well. You have heard nothing to the contrary, have you?'

'No, M. Raoul—nothing, thank God!'

Here, for several instants, ensued a silence, during which two spirits, which followed the same idea, communicated perfectly, without even the assistance of a single glance.

'Oh, heavens!' exclaimed Montalais in a fright; 'there is somebody coming up.'

'Who can it be?' said Louise, rising in great agitation.

'Mesdemoiselles, I inconvenience you very much. I have, without doubt, been very indiscreet,' stammered Raoul, very ill at ease.

'It is a heavy step,' said Louise.

'Ah! if it is only M. Malicorne,'* added Montalais, 'do not disturb yourselves.'

Louise and Raoul looked at each other to inquire who M. Malicorne could be.

'There is no occasion to mind him,' continued Montalais; 'he is not jealous.'

'But, mademoiselle——' said Raoul.

'Yes, I understand. Well, he is as discreet as I am.'

'Good heavens!' cried Louise, who had applied her ear to the door, which had been left ajar; 'it is my mother's step!'

'Madame de Saint-Rémy! Where shall I hide myself?' exclaimed Raoul, catching at the dress of Montalais, who looked quite bewildered.

'Yes,' said she; 'yes, I know the clicking of those heels! It is our excellent mother. M. le Vicomte, what a pity it is the window looks upon a stone pavement which lies fifty paces below it.'

Raoul glanced at the balcony in despair. Louise seized his arm, and held it tight.

'Oh, how silly I am!' said Montalais; 'I'm forgetting the closet where we hang our court clothes. It looks as if it were made on purpose.'

It was quite time to act; Madame de Saint-Rémy was coming up at a quicker pace than usual. She reached the landing at the moment when Montalais, as in all scenes of surprises, shut the closet by leaning with her back against the door.

'Ah!' cried Madame de Saint-Rémy, 'you are here, are you, Louise?'

'Yes, madame,' replied she, more pale than if she had committed a great crime.

'Well, well!'

'Pray be seated, madame,' said Montalais, offering her a chair, which she placed so that the back was towards the closet.

'Thank you, Mademoiselle Aure—thank you. Come my child, be quick.'

'Where do you wish me to go, madame?'

'Why, home, to be sure; have you not to prepare your toilette?'

'What did you say?' cried Montalais, hastening to affect surprise, so fearful was she that Louise would in some way commit herself.

'You don't know the news, then?' said Madame de Saint-Rémy.

'What news, madame, is it possible for two girls to learn up in this dove-cote?'

'What! have you seen nobody?'

'Madame, you talk in enigmas, and you torment us at a slow fire!' cried Montalais, who, terrified at seeing Louise become paler and paler, was at her wits' end.

At length she caught an eloquent look of her companion's, one of those looks which would convey intelligence to a brick wall. Louise directed her attention to a hat—Raoul's unlucky hat, which was set out in all its feathery splendour upon the table.

Montalais sprang towards it, and, seizing it with her left hand, passed it behind her into the right, concealing it as she was speaking.

'Well,' said Madame de Saint-Rémy, 'a courier has arrived, announcing the approach of the king. There, mesdemoiselles; there is something to make you put on your best looks.'

'Quick, quick!' cried Montalais. 'Follow Madame your mother, Louise; and leave me to get ready my court dress.'

Louise arose; her mother took her by the hand, and led her out on to the landing.

'Come along,' said she; then adding in a low voice, 'When I forbid you to come to the apartment of Montalais, why do you do so?'

'Madame, she is my friend. Besides, I had but just come.'

'Did you see nobody concealed while you were there?'

'Madame!'

'I saw a man's hat, I tell you—the hat of that fellow, that good-for-nothing!'

'Madame!' repeated Louise

'Of that do-nothing Malicorne! A maid of honour to have such company—fie! fie!' And their voices were lost in the depths of the narrow staircase.

Montalais had not missed a word of this conversation, which echo conveyed to her as if through a tunnel. She shrugged her shoulders on seeing Raoul, who had listened likewise, issue from the closet.

'Poor Montalais!' said she, 'the victim of friendship! Poor Malicorne, the victim of love!'

She stopped on viewing the tragic-comic face of Raoul, who was vexed at having, in one day, surprised so many secrets.

'Oh, mademoiselle!' said he; 'how can we repay your kindness?'

'Oh, we will balance accounts some day,' said she. 'For the present, begone, M. de Bragelonne, for Madame de Saint-Rémy is not over indulgent; and any indiscretion on her part might lead to a rather closer search, which would be disagreeable to all parties.'

'But, Louise—how shall I know——'

'Begone! begone! King Louis XI knew very well what he was about when he invented the post.'*

'Alas!' sighed Raoul.

'And am I not here—I, who am worth all the posts in the kingdom? Quick, I say, to horse! so that if Madame de Saint-Rémy should return for the purpose of preaching me a lesson on morality, she may not find you here.'

'She would tell my father, would she not?' murmured Raoul.

'And you would be scolded. Ah, vicomte, it is very plain you come from court; you are as timid as the king. Fiddlesticks! at

Blois we contrive better than that, to do without papa's consent.
Ask Malicorne!'

And at these words the girl pushed Raoul out of the room by
the shoulders. He glided swiftly down to the porch, regained his
horse, mounted, and set off as if he had had Monsieur's guards
at his heels.

IV

FATHER AND SON

RAOUL followed the well-known road, so dear to his memory,
which led from Blois to the residence of the Comte de la Fère.

The reader will dispense with a second description of that
habitation: he, perhaps, has been with us there before, and knows
it.* Only, since our last journey thither, the walls had taken a
greyer tint, and the brick-work assumed a more harmonious
copper tone; the trees had grown, and many that then only
stretched their slender branches along the tops of the hedges,
now, bushy, strong, and luxuriant, cast around, beneath boughs
swollen with sap, great shadows of blossoms or fruit for the
benefit of the traveller.

Raoul perceived, from a distance, the two little turrets, the
dove-cote in the elms, and the flights of pigeons, which wheeled
incessantly around that brick cone, seemingly without power to
quit it, like the sweet memories which hover round a spirit at
peace.

As he approached, he heard the noise of the pulleys which
grated under the weight of their heavy pails; he also fancied he
heard the melancholy moaning of the water which falls back
again into the wells—a sad, funereal, solemn sound, which strikes
the ear of the child and the poet—both dreamers—which the
English call *splash*; Arabian poets, *gasgachau*; and which we
Frenchmen, who would be poets, can only translate by a para-
phrase—*the noise of water falling into water*.

It was more than a year since Raoul had been to visit his
father. He had passed the whole time in the household of M. le
Prince. In fact, after all the commotions of the Fronde, of the

early period of which we formerly attempted to give a sketch, Louis de Condé had made a public, solemn, and frank reconciliation with the court.* During all the time that the rupture between the king and the prince had lasted, the prince, who had long entertained a great regard for Bragelonne, had in vain offered him advantages of the most dazzling kind for a young man. The Comte de la Fère, still faithful to his principles of loyalty, and royalty, one day developed before his son in the vaults of Saint-Denis*—the Comte de la Fère, in the name of his son, had always declined them. Moreover, instead of following M. de Condé in his rebellion, the vicomte had followed M. de Turenne,* fighting for the king. Then when M. de Turenne, in his turn, had appeared to abandon the royal cause, he had quitted M. de Turenne, as he had quitted M. de Condé. It resulted from this invariable line of conduct, that, as Condé and Turenne had never been conquerors of each other except under the standard of the king, Raoul, however young, had ten victories inscribed on his list of services, and not one defeat from which his bravery or conscience had to suffer.

Raoul, therefore, had, in compliance with the wish of his father, served obstinately and passively the fortunes of Louis XIV, in spite of the tergiversations which were endemic, and, it might be said, inevitable, at that period.

M. de Condé, on being restored to favour, had at once availed himself of all the privileges of the amnesty, to ask for many things back again which had been granted him before, and among others, Raoul. M. de la Fère, with his invariable good sense, had immediately sent him again to the prince.

A year, then, had passed away since the separation of the father and son; a few letters had softened, but not removed, the pains of absence. We have seen that Raoul had left at Blois another love in addition to filial love. But let us do him this justice—if it had not been for chance and Mademoiselle de Montalais, two great temptations, Raoul, after delivering his message, would have galloped off towards his father's house, turning his head round, perhaps, but without stopping for a single instant, even if Louise had held out her arms to him.

So the first part of the journey was given by Raoul to regretting the past which he had been forced to quit so quickly, that is to say, his lady-love; and the other part to the father he was about to join, so much too slowly for his wishes.

Raoul found the garden-gate open, and rode straight in, without regarding the long arms, raised in anger, of an old man dressed in a jacket of violet-coloured wool, and a large cap of faded velvet.

The old man, who was weeding with his hands a bed of dwarf roses and marguerites, was indignant at seeing a horse thus traversing his sanded and nicely-raked walks. He even ventured a vigorous 'Humph!' which made the rider turn round. Then there was a change of scene; for no sooner had he caught sight of Raoul's face, than the old man sprang up and set off in the direction of the house, amidst intermittent growlings, which appeared to be paroxysms of wild delight.

When arrived at the stables, Raoul gave his horse to a little lackey, and sprang up the steps with an ardour that would have delighted the heart of his father.

He crossed the antechamber, the dining-room, and the salon, without meeting with any one; at length, on reaching the door of M. de la Fère's apartment, he rapped impatiently, and entered almost without waiting for the word 'Enter!' which was vouchsafed him by a voice at once sweet and serious. The comte was seated at a table covered with papers and books; he was still the noble, handsome gentleman of former days, but time had given to this nobleness and beauty a more solemn and distinct character. A brow white and void of wrinkles, beneath his long hair, now more white than black; an eye piercing and mild, under the lids of a young man; his moustache, fine but slightly grizzled, waved over lips of a pure and delicate model, as if they had never been curled by mortal passions; a form straight and supple; an irreproachable but thin hand—this was what remained of the illustrious gentleman whom so many illustrious mouths had praised under the name of Athos.* He was engaged in correcting the pages of a manuscript book, entirely filled by his own hand.

Raoul seized his father by the shoulders, by the neck, and embraced him so tenderly and so rapidly, that the comte had neither strength nor time to disengage himself, or to overcome his paternal emotions.

'What! you here, Raoul—you! Is it possible?' said he.

'Oh, monsieur, monsieur, what joy to see you once again!'

'But you don't answer me, vicomte. Have you leave of absence, or has some misfortune happened at Paris?'

'Thank God, monsieur,' replied Raoul, calming himself by degrees, 'nothing has happened but what is fortunate. The king is going to be married, as I had the honour of informing you in my last letter, and, on his way to Spain, he will pass through Blois.'

'To pay a visit to Monsieur?'

'Yes, monsieur le comte. So, fearing to find him unprepared, or wishing to be particularly polite to him, monsieur le prince sent me forward to have the lodgings ready.'

'You have seen Monsieur?' asked the vicomte, eagerly.

'I have had that honour.'

'At the castle?'

'Yes, monsieur,' replied Raoul, casting down his eyes, because, no doubt, he had felt there was something more than curiosity in the comte's inquiries.

'Ah, indeed, vicomte? Accept my congratulations.'

Raoul bowed.

'But you have seen some one else at Blois?'

'Monsieur, I saw her royal highness, Madame.'

'That's very well: but it is not Madame that I mean.'

Raoul coloured deeply, but made no reply.

'You do not appear to understand me, monsieur le vicomte,' persisted M. de la Fère, without accenting his words more strongly, but with a rather severer look.

'I understand you quite plainly, monsieur,' replied Raoul, 'and if I hesitate a little in my reply, you are well assured I am not trying to evade the truth.'

'No, you cannot tell a lie; and that makes me so astonished you should be so long in saying yes or no.'

'I cannot answer you without understanding you very well; and, if I have understood you, you will take my first words in ill part. You will be displeased, no doubt, monsieur le comte, because I have seen——'

'Mademoiselle de la Vallière—have you not?'

'It was of her you meant to speak, I know very well, monsieur,' said Raoul, with inexpressible sweetness.

'And I asked you, if you have seen her.'

'Monsieur, I was ignorant, when I entered the castle, that Mademoiselle de la Vallière was there; it was only on my return, after I had performed my mission, that chance brought us together. I have had the honour of paying my respects to her.'

'But what do you call the chance that led you into the presence of Mademoiselle de la Vallière?'

'Mademoiselle de Montalais, monsieur.'

'And who is Mademoiselle de Montalais?'

'A young lady I did not know before, whom I had never seen. She is maid of honour to Madame.'

'Monsieur le vicomte, I will push my interrogation no further, and reproach myself with having carried it so far. I had desired you to avoid Mademoiselle de la Vallière, and not to see her without my permission. Oh, I am quite sure you have told me the truth, and that you took no measures to approach her. Chance has done me this injury; I do not accuse you of it. I will be content, then, with what I formerly said to you concerning this young lady. I do not reproach her with anything—God is my witness! only it is not my intention or wish that you should frequent her place of residence. I beg you once more, my dear Raoul, to understand that.'*

It was plain the limpid eyes of Raoul were troubled at this speech.

'Now, my friend,' said the comte, with his soft smile, and in his customary tone, 'let us talk of other matters. You are returning, perhaps to your duty?'

'No, monsieur, I have no duty for today, except the pleasure of remaining with you. The prince kindly appointed me no other: which was so much in accord with my wish.'

'Is the king well?'

'Perfectly.'

'And monsieur le prince also?'

'As usual, monsieur.'

The comte forgot to inquire after Mazarin; that was an old habit.

'Well, Raoul, since you are entirely mine, I will give up my whole day to you. Embrace me—again, again! You are at home, vicomte! Ah, here is our old Grimaud! Come in, Grimaud;* monsieur le vicomte wishes to embrace you.'

The good old man did not require to be told twice; he rushed in with open arms, Raoul meeting him half-way.

'Now, if you please, we will go into the garden, Raoul. I will show you the new lodging I have had prepared for you during your leave of absence; and whilst examining the last winter's plantations, and two saddle-horses I have just acquired, you will give me all the news of our friends in Paris.'

The comte closed his manuscript, took the young man's arm, and went out into the garden with him.

Grimaud looked at Raoul with a melancholy air as the young man passed out; observing that his head nearly touched the top of the door-frame, stroking his white *royale*,* he slowly murmured:

'How he has grown!'

V

IN WHICH SOMETHING WILL BE SAID OF CROPOLI*— OF CROPOLI AND OF A GREAT UNKNOWN PAINTER

WHILST the Comte de la Fère with Raoul visits the new buildings he has had erected, and the new horses he has bought, with the reader's permission we will lead him back to the city of Blois, and make him a witness of the unaccustomed activity which pervades that city.

It was in the hotels that the surprise of the news brought by Raoul was most keenly felt.

In fact, the king and the court at Blois, that is to say, a hundred horsemen, ten carriages, two hundred horses, as many lackeys as masters—where was this crowd to be housed? Where were to be lodged all the gentry of the neighbourhood, who would gather in two or three hours after the news had enlarged the circle of its report, like the increasing circumferences produced by a stone thrown into a placid lake?

Blois, as peaceful in the morning, as we have seen, as the calmest lake in the world, at the announcement of the royal arrival, was suddenly filled with the tumult and buzzing of a swarm of bees

All the servants of the castle, under the inspection of the

officers, were sent into the city in quest of provisions, and ten horsemen were dispatched to the preserves of Chambord to seek for game, to the fisheries of Beuvron for fish, and to the gardens of Cheverny for fruits and flowers.

Precious tapestries, and chandeliers with great gilt chains, were drawn from the cupboards; an army of the poor were engaged in sweeping the courts and washing the stone fronts, whilst their wives went in droves to the meadows beyond the Loire, to gather green boughs and field-flowers. The whole city, not to be behind in this orgy of cleanliness, assumed its best toilette with the help of brushes, brooms, and water.

The gutters of the upper town, swollen by these continued waterings, became rivers at the bottom of the city, and the streets, generally very muddy, it must be allowed, took a clean face, and absolutely shone in the friendly rays of the sun.

Next the music was to be provided; drawers were emptied; the shop-keepers did a glorious trade in wax, ribbons, and sword-knots; housekeepers laid in stores of bread, meat, and spices. Already numbers of the citizens whose houses were furnished as if for a siege, having nothing more to do, donned their festive clothes, and directed their course towards the city gate, in order to be the first to signal or see the procession. They knew very well that the king would not arrive before night, perhaps not before the next morning. Yet what is expectation but a kind of folly, and what is that folly but an excess of hope?

In the lower city, at scarcely a hundred paces from the Castle of the States,* between the mall and the castle, in a tolerably handsome street, then called Rue Vieille, and which must, in fact, have been very old, stood a venerable edifice, with pointed gables, of squat but large dimensions, ornamented with three windows looking into the street on the first floor, with two in the second, and with a little *œil-de-bœuf* in the third.

On the sides of this triangle had recently been constructed a parallelogram of considerable size, which encroached upon the street remorselessly, according to the familiar uses of the building of that period. The street was narrowed by a quarter by it, but then the house was enlarged by a half; and was not that a sufficient compensation?

Tradition said that this house with the pointed gables was

inhabited, in the time of Henry III, by a councillor of state whom Queen Catherine came, some say to visit, and others to strangle.* However that may be, the good lady must have stepped with a circumspect foot over the threshold of this building.

After the councillor had died—whether by strangulation or naturally is of no consequence—the house had been sold, then abandoned, and lastly isolated from the other houses of the street. Towards the middle of the reign of Louis XIII only, an Italian, named Cropoli, escaped from the kitchens of the Maréchal d'Ancre,* came and took possession of this house. There he established a little hostelry, in which was fabricated a macaroni so delicious that people came from miles round to fetch it or eat it.

So famous had the house become for it, that when Mary de Medici* was a prisoner, as we know, in the castle of Blois, she once sent for some.

It was precisely on the day she had escaped by the famous window. The dish of macaroni was left upon the table, only just tasted by the royal mouth.

This double favour, of a strangulation and a macaroni, conferred upon the triangular house, gave poor Cropoli a fancy to grace his hostelry with a pompous title. But his Italian origins were no recommendation in these times, and his small, well-concealed fortune forbade attracting too much attention.

When he found himself about to die, which happened in 1643, just after the death of Louis XIII, he called to him his son, a young cook of great promise, and with tears in his eyes, he recommended him to preserve carefully the secret of the macaroni, to Frenchify his name, and at length, when the political horizon should be cleared of the clouds which obscured it—this was practiced then as in our day—to order of the nearest smith a handsome sign, upon which a famous painter, whom he named, should design two queens' portraits, with these words as a legend: 'The Medici.'

The worthy Cropoli, after these recommendations, had only sufficient time to point out to his young successor a chimney, under the slab of which he had hidden a thousand ten-franc pieces, and then expired

Cropoli the younger, like a man of good heart, supported the loss with resignation, and the gain without insolence. He began by accustoming the public to sound the final *i* of his name so little, that by the aid of general complaisance, he soon came to be known as M. Cropole, which passes as a French name. He then married, having had in his eye a little French girl, from whose parents he extorted a reasonable dowry by showing them what there was beneath the slab of the chimney.

These two points accomplished, he went in search of the painter who was to paint the sign; and he was soon found. He was an old Italian, a rival of the Raphaels and the Caracci,* but an unfortunate rival. He said he was of the Venetian school, doubtless from his fondness for colour. His works, of which he had never sold one, attracted the eye at a distance of a hundred paces; but they so formidably displeased the citizens, that he had finished by painting no more.

He boasted of having painted a bathroom for Madame la Maréchale d'Ancre,* and moaned because this chamber had been burnt at the time of the maréchal's disaster.

Cropoli, in his character of a compatriot, was indulgent towards Pittrino, which was the name of the artist. Perhaps he had seen the famous pictures of the bathroom. Be this as it may, he held in such esteem, we may say in such friendship, the famous Pittrino, that he took him in his own house.

Pittrino, grateful, and fed with macaroni, set about propagating the reputation of this national dish, and from the time of its founder, he had rendered, with his indefatigable tongue, signal services to the house of Cropoli.

As he grew old he attached himself to the son as he had done to the father, and by degrees became a kind of steward of a house in which his remarkable integrity, his acknowledged sobriety, and a thousand other virtues useless to enumerate, gave him an eternal place by the fireside, with a right of inspection over the domestics. Besides this, it was he who tasted the macaroni, to maintain the pure flavor of the ancient tradition; and it must be allowed that he never permitted a grain of pepper too much, or an atom of parmesan too little. His joy was at its height on that day when called upon to share the secret of Cropoli the younger, and to paint the famous sign.

He was seen at once rummaging with ardour in an old box, in

which he found some brushes, a little gnawed by the rats, but still passable; some colours in leather pouches, almost dried up; some linseed-oil in a bottle, and a palette which had formerly belonged to Bronzino,* that *dieu de la pittoure*, as the ultramontane artist, in his ever young enthusiasm, always called him.

Pittrino was puffed up with all the joy of a rehabilitation.

He did as Raphael had done—he changed his style, and painted, in the fashion of Albani,* two goddesses rather than two queens. These illustrious ladies appeared so lovely on the sign—they presented to the astonished eyes such an assemblage of lilies and roses, the enchanting result of the change of style in Pittrino—they assumed the poses of sirens so Anacreontically*— that the principal *échevin*,* when admitted to view this capital piece in Cropole's best parlour, at once declared that these ladies were too handsome, of too animated a beauty, to figure as a sign in the eyes of passers-by.

To Pittrino he added, 'His royal highness Monsieur, who often comes into our city, will not be much pleased to see his illustrious mother so slightly clothed, and he will send you to the oubliettes* of the state; for, remember, the heart of that glorious prince is not always tender. You must efface either the two sirens or the legend, without which I forbid the exhibition of the sign. I say this for your sake, Master Cropole, as well as for yours, Signor Pittrino.'

What answer could be made to this? It was necessary to thank the *échevin* for his kindness, which Cropole did. But Pittrino remained downcast and said he felt assured of what was about to happen.

The visitor was scarcely gone when Cropole, crossing his arms, said: 'Well, master, what is to be done?'

'We must efface the legend,' said Pittrino, in a melancholy tone. 'I have some excellent ivory-black; it will be done in a moment, and we will replace the Medici by the nymphs or the sirens, whichever you prefer.'

'No,' said Cropole, 'the will of my father must be carried out. My father considered——'

'He considered the figures of the most importance,' said Pittrino.

'He thought most of the legend,' said Cropole.

'The proof of the importance in which he held the figures,' said Pittrino, 'is that he desired they should be likenesses, and they are so.'

'Yes; but if they had not been so, who would have recognized them without the legend? Even today, when the memory of the people of Blois begins to be faint with regard to these two celebrated persons, who would recognize Catherine and Mary without the words "The Medici"?'

'But the figures?' said Pittrino, in despair; for he felt that young Cropole was right. 'I should not like to lose the fruit of my labour.'

'And I should not wish you to be thrown into prison, and myself into the oubliettes.'

'Let us efface "Medici",' said Pittrino, supplicatingly.

'No,' replied Cropole, firmly. 'I have an idea, a sublime idea—your picture shall appear, and my legend likewise. Does not "Medici" mean doctor, or physician, in Italian?'

'Yes, in the plural.'

'Well, then, you shall order another sign-frame of the smith; you shall paint six physicians, and write underneath "The Medici" which makes a very pretty play upon words '

'Six physicians! impossible! And the composition?' cried Pittrino.

'That is your business—but so it shall be—I insist upon it—it must be so—my macaroni is burning.'

This reasoning was peremptory—Pittrino obeyed. He composed the sign of six physicians, with the legend; the *échevin* applauded and authorized it.

The sign produced an extravagant success in the city, which proves that poetry has always been in the wrong in the eyes of the crowd, as Pittrino said.

Cropole, to make amends to his painter-in-ordinary, hung up the nymphs of the preceding sign in his bedroom, which made Madame Cropole blush every time she looked at it, when she was undressing at night.

This is the way in which the pointed-gable house got a sign; and this is how the hostelry of the Medici, making a fortune, was found to be enlarged by a quarter, as we have described. And this is how there was at Blois a hostelry of that name, and had for painter-in-ordinary Master Pittrino.

VI

THUS founded and recommended by its sign, the inn of Monsieur Cropole held its way steadily on towards a solid prosperity.

It was not an immense fortune that Cropole had in view; but he might hope to double the thousand louis d'or left by his father, to make another thousand louis by the sale of his house and stock, and at length to live happily like a retired citizen.

Cropole was anxious for gain, and was half-crazy with joy at the news of the arrival of Louis XIV.

Himself, his wife, Pittrino, and two cooks, immediately laid hands upon all the denizens of dove-cote, poultry-yard, and rabbit-hutch; so that as many lamentations and cries resounded in the yards of the inn of the Medici as were formerly heard in Rama.*

Cropole had, at the time, but one single traveller in his house.

This was a man of scarcely thirty years of age, handsome, tall, austere, or rather melancholy, in all his gestures and looks.

He was dressed in black velvet with jet trimmings; a white collar, as plain as that of the severest Puritan, set off the whiteness of his youthful neck; a small dark-coloured moustache scarcely covered his curled, disdainful lip.

He spoke to people looking them full in the face, without affectation, it is true, but without scruple; so that the brilliancy of his black eyes became so unbearable, that more than one look had sunk beneath his, like the weaker sword in a single combat.

At this time, in which men, all created equal by God, were divided, thanks to prejudices, into two distinct castes, the gentleman and the commoner, as they are really divided into two races, the black and the white*—at this time, we say, he whose portrait we have just sketched could not fail of being taken for a gentleman, and of the best class. To ascertain this, there was no necessity to consult anything but his hands, long, slender, and white, of which every muscle, every vein, became apparent through the skin at the least movement, and eloquently spoke of good descent.

This gentleman, then, had arrived alone at Cropole's house.

He had taken, without hesitation, without reflection even, the principal apartment which the innkeeper had pointed out to him with an eye to profit, very praiseworthy, some will say, very reprehensible will say others, if they admit that Cropole was a physiognomist,* and judged people at first sight.

This apartment was that which composed the whole front of the ancient triangular house; a large sitting-room, lighted by two windows on the first stage, a small chamber by the side of it, and another above it.

Now, from the time he had arrived, this gentleman had scarcely touched any of the meals that had been served up to him in his chamber. He had spoken but two words to the host, to warn him that a traveller of the name of Parry would arrive, and to desire that, when he did, he should be shown up to him immediately.

He afterwards preserved so profound a silence, that Cropole was almost offended, so much did he prefer people who were good company.

This gentleman had risen early the morning of the day on which this history begins, and had placed himself at the window of his sitting-room, seated upon the ledge, and leaning upon the rail of the balcony, gazing sadly but persistently on both sides of the street, watching, no doubt, for the arrival of the traveller he had mentioned to the host.

In this way he had seen the little party of Monsieur return from hunting, then had again partaken of the profound tranquillity of the street, absorbed in his own expectations.

All at once the movement of the crowd going to the meadows, couriers setting out, washers of streets, purveyors of the royal household, gabbling, scampering shop-boys, chariots in motion, hair-dressers on the run, and pages toiling along, this tumult and bustle had surprised him, but without unsettling any of that impassible and supreme majesty which gives to the eagle and the lion that serene and contemptuous glance amidst the hurrahs and shouts of hunters or the curious.

Soon the cries of the victims slaughtered in the poultry-yard, the hasty steps of Madame Cropole up that little wooden staircase, so narrow and so echoing; the bounding pace of Pittrino, who only that morning was smoking at the door with all the phlegm of a Dutchman; all this communicated something like surprise and agitation to the traveller.

As he was rising to make inquiries, the door of his chamber opened. The stranger concluded they were about to introduce the impatiently expected traveller, and made three precipitate steps to meet him.

But, instead of the person he expected, it was Monsieur Cropole who appeared, and behind him, in the half-dark staircase the pleasant face of Madame Cropole, inflamed by curiosity. She gave one furtive glance at the handsome gentleman, and disappeared.

Cropole advanced, cap in hand, rather bent than bowing.

A gesture of the stranger interrogated him, without a word being pronounced.

'Monsieur,' said Cropole, 'I come to ask how—what ought I to say: your lordship, monsieur le comte, or monsieur le marquis?'

'Say *monsieur*, and speak quickly,' replied the stranger, with that haughty accent which admits of neither discussion nor reply.

'I came then, to inquire how monsieur had passed the night, and if monsieur intended to keep this apartment?'

'Yes.'

'Monsieur, something has happened upon which we could not reckon.'

'What?'

'His majesty Louis XIV will enter our city to-day, and will remain here one day, perhaps two.'

Great astonishment was painted on the countenance of the stranger.

'The King of France coming to Blois?'

'He is on the road, monsieur.'

'Then there is the stronger reason for my remaining,' said the stranger.

'Very well; but will monsieur keep all the apartments?'

'I do not understand you. Why should I require less to-day than yesterday?'

'Because, monsieur, your lordship will permit me to say, yesterday I did not think proper, when you chose your lodging, to fix any price that might have made your lordship believe that I prejudged your resources; whilst today——'

The stranger coloured; the idea at once struck him that he was supposed to be poor, and was being insulted.

'Whilst today,' replied he, coldly, 'you have other ideas.'

'Monsieur, I am a well-meaning man, thank God! and simple innkeeper as I am, there is in me the blood of a gentleman. My father was a servant and officer of the late Maréchal d'Ancre. God rest his soul!'

'I do not contest that point with you; I only wish to know, and that quickly, where your questions are leading?'

'You are too reasonable, monsieur, not to comprehend that our city is small, that the court is about to invade it, that the houses will be overflowing with inhabitants, and that lodgings will consequently obtain considerable prices.'

Again the stranger coloured. 'Name your terms,' said he.

'I name them with scruple, monsieur, because I seek an honest profit, and that I wish to carry on my business without being uncivil or extravagant in my demands. Now the room you occupy is large, and you are alone.'

'That is my business.'

'Oh! certainly. I do not mean to turn monsieur out.'

The blood rushed to the temples of the stranger; he darted at poor Cropole, the descendant of one of the officers of the Maréchal d'Ancre, a glance that would have crushed him down to beneath that famous chimney-slab, if Cropole had not been nailed to the spot by the question of his own proper interests.

'Do you desire me to go?' said he. 'Explain yourself—but quickly.'

'Monsieur, monsieur, you do not understand me. What I am doing is very delicate—I know. I express myself badly, or perhaps, as monsieur is a foreigner, which I perceive by his accent——'

In fact, the stranger spoke with that impetuosity which is the principal character of English accentuation, even among men who speak the French language with the greatest purity.

'As monsieur is a foreigner, I say, it is perhaps he who does not catch my exact meaning. I wish for monsieur to give up one or two of the rooms he occupies, which would diminish his expenses and ease my conscience. Indeed, it is hard to increase unreasonably the price of the chambers, when one has had the honour to let them at a reasonable price.'

'How much does the rent amount to since yesterday?'

'Monsieur, to one louis, with refreshments and the charge for the horse.'

'Very well; and that of to-day?'

'Ah! there is the difficulty. This is the day of the king's arrival; if the court comes to sleep here, the charge of the day is reckoned. From that it results that three chambers, at two louis each, makes six louis. Two louis, monsieur, are not much; but six louis make a great deal.'

The stranger, from red, as we have seen him, became very pale.

He drew from his pocket, with heroic bravery, a purse embroidered with a coat-of-arms, which he carefully concealed in the hollow of his hand. This purse was of a thinness, a flabbiness, a hollowness, which did not escape the eye of Cropole.

The stranger emptied the purse into his hand. It contained three double louis, which amounted to the six louis demanded by the host.

But it was seven that Cropole had required.

He looked, therefore, at the stranger, as much as to say, 'And the balance?'

'There remains one louis, does there not, master innkeeper?'

'Yes, monsieur, but——'

The unknown plunged his hand into the pocket of his breeches, and emptied it. It contained a small pocket-book, a gold key, and some silver. With this change he made up a louis.

'Thank you, monsieur,' said Cropole. 'It now only remains for me to ask whether monsieur intends to occupy his apartments to-morrow, in which case I will reserve them for him; whereas, if monsieur does not mean to do so, I will promise them to some of the king's retinue who are coming.'

'That is but right,' said the stranger, after a long silence; 'but as I have no more money, as you have seen, and as I yet must retain the apartments, you must either sell this diamond in the city, or hold it in pledge.'

Cropole looked at the diamond so long, that the stranger said, hastily.

'I prefer your selling it, monsieur; for it is worth three hundred pistoles.* A Jew*—are there any Jews in Blois?—would give you two hundred or a hundred and fifty for it—take whatever may be offered for it, if it be no more than the price of your lodging. Begone!'

'Oh! monsieur,' replied Cropole, ashamed of the sudden inferiority which the stranger reflected upon him by this noble and disinterested confidence, as well as by the unalterable patience opposed to so many suspicions and evasions. 'Oh, monsieur, I hope people are not so dishonest at Blois as you seem to think; and that the diamond, being worth what you say——'

The stranger here again darted at Cropole one of his withering glances

'I really do not understand diamonds, monsieur, I assure you,' cried he.

'But the jewellers do: ask them,' said the stranger. 'Now I believe our accounts are settled, are they not, master innkeeper?'

'Yes, monsieur, and to my profound regret; for I fear I have offended monsieur.'

'Not at all!' replied the stranger, with ineffable majesty.

'Or have appeared to be extortionate with a noble traveller. Consider, monsieur, the peculiarity of the circumstances.'

'Say no more about it, I desire; and leave me to myself.'

Cropole bowed profoundly, and left the room looking somewhat at a loss, which announced that he had a good heart, and felt genuine remorse.

The stranger himself shut the door after him, and, when left alone, looked mournfully at the bottom of the purse, from which he had taken a small silken bag containing the diamond, his last resource.

He dwelt likewise upon the emptiness of his pockets, turned over the papers in his pocket-book, and convinced himself of the state of absolute destitution in which he was about to be plunged.

He raised his eyes towards heaven, with a sublime emotion of despairing calmness, brushed off with his hand some drops of sweat which trickled over his noble brow, and then cast down upon the earth a look which just before had been impressed with almost divine majesty.

The storm had passed far from him; perhaps he had prayed in the bottom of his soul.

He drew near to the window, resumed his place in the

balcony, and remained there, motionless, annihilated, dead, till the moment when, the heavens beginning to darken, the first flambeaux traversed the enlivened street, and gave the signal for illumination to all the windows of the city.

VII

PARRY*

WHILST the stranger was viewing these lights with interest, and lending an ear to the various noises, Monsieur Cropole entered his apartment, followed by two attendants, who laid the cloth for his meal.

The stranger did not pay them the least attention; but Cropole approaching him respectfully, whispered, 'Monsieur, the diamond has been valued.'

'Ah!' said the traveller 'Well?'

'Well, monsieur, His Royal Highness's jeweller gives two hundred and eighty pistoles for it.'

'Have you them?'

'I thought it best to take them, monsieur; nevertheless, I made it a condition of the bargain, that if monsieur wished to keep his diamond, it should be held till monsieur was again in funds.'

'Oh, no, not at all; I told you to sell it.'

'Then I have obeyed, or nearly so, since, without having definitely sold it, I have received the money.'

'Pay yourself,' added the stranger.

'I will do so, monsieur, since you so positively require it.'

A sad smile passed over the lips of the gentleman.

'Place the money on that trunk,' said he, turning round and pointing to the piece of furniture.

Cropole deposited a tolerably large bag as directed, after having taken from it the amount of his reckoning.

'Now,' said he, 'I hope monsieur will not give me the pain of not taking any supper. Dinner has already been refused; this is affronting to the house of the Medici. Look, monsieur, the supper is on the table, and I venture to say that it is not a bad one.'

The stranger asked for a glass of wine, broke off a morsel of bread, and did not stir from the window whilst he ate and drank.

Shortly after was heard a loud flourish of trumpets; cries arose in the distance, a confused buzzing filled the lower part of the city, and the first distinct sound that struck the ears of the stranger was the tramp of advancing horses.

'The king! the king!' shouted a noisy and eager crowd.

'The king!' cried Cropole, abandoning his guest and his ideas of delicacy, to satisfy his curiosity.

With Cropole were mingled, and jostled, on the staircase, Madame Cropole, Pittrino, and the waiters and scullions

The procession advanced slowly, lighted by a thousand flambeaux, in the streets and from the windows.

After a company of musketeers,* a closely ranked troop of gentlemen, came the litter of monsieur le cardinal, drawn like a carriage by four black horses. The pages and attendants of the cardinal marched behind.

Next came the carriage of the queen-mother,* with her maids of honour at the doors, her gentlemen on horseback at both sides.

The king then appeared, mounted upon a splendid horse of Saxon breed, with a flowing mane. The young prince exhibited, when bowing to some windows from which issued the most animated acclamations, a noble and handsome countenance, illumined by the torches of his pages.

By the side of the king, though a little in the rear, the Prince de Condé, M. Dangeau,* and twenty other courtiers, followed by their people and their baggage, closed this veritably triumphant march. The pomp was of a military character.

Some of the courtiers—the elder ones, for instance—wore travelling garb; but all the rest were clothed in warlike panoply. Many wore the gorget and buff-coat* of the times of Henry IV and Louis XIII.

When the king passed before him, the stranger, who had leant forward over the balcony to obtain a better view, and who had concealed his face by leaning on his arm, felt his heart swell and overflow with a bitter jealousy

The noise of the trumpets excited him—the popular acclamations deafened him: for a moment he allowed his reason to be absorbed in this flood of lights, tumult, and brilliant images.

'He is a king!' murmured he, in an accent of despair.

Then, before he had recovered from his sombre reverie, all the noise, all the splendour, had passed away. At the angle of the street there remained nothing beneath the stranger but a few hoarse, discordant voices, shouting at intervals '*Vive le Roi!*'

There remained likewise the six candles held by the inhabitants of the inn of the Medici; that is to say, two for Cropole, two for Pittrino, and one for each scullion. Cropole never ceased repeating, 'How good-looking the king is! How strongly he resembles his illustrious father!'

'A handsome likeness!' said Pittrino.

'And what a lofty bearing he has!' added Madame Cropole, already gossiping chattily with her neighbours of both sexes.

Cropole was feeding their gossip with his own personal remarks, without observing that an old man on foot, but leading a small Irish horse by the bridle, was endeavouring to push through the crowd of men and women which blocked up the entrance to the Medici But at that moment the voice of the stranger was heard from the window.

'Make way, master innkeeper, to the entrance of your house!'

Cropole turned around, and, on seeing the old man, cleared a passage for him.

The window was instantly closed.

Pittrino pointed out the way to the newly-arrived guest, who entered without uttering a word.

The stranger waited for him on the landing; he opened his arms to the old man, and led him to a seat.

'Oh, no, no, my lord!' said he. 'Sit down in your presence?—never!'

'Parry,' cried the gentleman, 'I beg you will; you come from England—you come so far. Ah! it is not for your age to undergo the fatigues my service requires. Rest yourself.'

'I have my reply to give your lordship, in the first place.'

'Parry, I conjure you to tell me nothing; for if your news had been good, you would not have begun in such a manner; but you hesitate, which proves that the news is bad.'

'My lord,' said the old man, 'do not hasten to alarm yourself; all is not lost, I hope. You must employ energy, but more particularly resignation.'

'Parry,' said the young man, 'I have reached this place through a thousand snares and after a thousand difficulties; can you doubt my energy? I have meditated this journey ten years,* in spite of all counsels and all obstacles—have you faith in my perseverance? I have this evening sold the last of my father's diamonds; for I had nothing wherewith to pay for my lodging and my host was about to turn me out.'

Parry made a gesture of indignation, to which the young man replied by a pressure of the hand and a smile.

'I have still two hundred and seventy-four pistoles left and I feel rich. I do not despair, Parry; have you faith in my resignation?'

The old man raised his trembling hands towards heaven.

'Let me know,' said the stranger—'hide nothing from me—what has happened?'

'My report will be short, my lord; but in the name of Heaven do not tremble so.'

'It is impatience, Parry. Come, what did the general* say to you?'

'At first the general would not receive me.'

'He took you for a spy?'

'Yes, my lord; but I wrote him a letter.'

'Well?'

'He read it, and received me, my lord.'

'Did that letter thoroughly explain my position and my views?'

'Oh, yes!' said Parry, with a sad smile; 'it painted your thoughts very faithfully.'

'Well—then, Parry?'

'Then the general sent me back the letter by an aide-de-camp, informing me that if I were found the next day within the limits of his command, he would have me arrested.'

'Arrested!' murmured the young man. 'What! arrest you, my most faithful servant?'

'Yes, my lord.'

'And notwithstanding you had signed the name *Parry*?'

'To all my letters, my lord; and the aide-de-camp had known

me at St. James's and at Whitehall, too,' added the old man with a sigh.

The young man leaned forward, thoughtful and sad.

'He did that in front of his people,' said he, endeavouring to cheat himself with hopes. 'But, privately—between you and him—what did he do? Answer!'

'Alas! my lord, he sent to me four mounted men, who gave me the horse with which you just now saw me come back. These men conducted me, in great haste, to the little port of Tenby,* threw me, rather than embarked me, into a fishing-boat, about to sail for Brittany, and here I am.'

'Oh!' sighed the young man, clasping his neck convulsively with his hand, and with a sob. 'Parry, is that all?—is that all?'

'Yes, my lord; that is all.'

After this brief reply ensued a long interval of silence, broken only by the convulsive beating of the heel of the young man on the floor.

The old man endeavoured to change the conversation; it was leading to thoughts much too sinister.

'My lord,' said he, 'what is the meaning of all the noise which preceded me? Why are these people crying "*Vive le Roi!*"? What king do they mean? and what are all these lights for?'

'Ah! Parry,' replied the young man ironically, 'don't you know that this is the King of France visiting his good city of Blois? All those trumpets are his, all those gilded housings are his, all those gentlemen wear swords that are his. His mother precedes him in a carriage magnificently encrusted with silver and gold. Happy mother! His minister* heaps up millions, and conducts him to a rich bride. Then all these people rejoice; they love their king, they hail him with their acclamations, and they cry, "*Vive le Roi! Vive le Roi!*"'

'Well, well, my lord,' said Parry, more uneasy at the turn the conversation had taken than at the other.

'You know,' resumed the stranger, 'that *my* mother and *my* sister, whilst all this is going on in honour of the king of France, have neither money nor bread; you know that I myself shall be poor and degraded within a fortnight, when all Europe will become acquainted with what you have told me. Parry, are there not examples in which a man of my condition should himself——'

'My lord, in the name of Heaven——'

'You are right, Parry; I am a coward, and if I do nothing for myself, what will God do? No, no; I have two arms, Parry, and I have a sword.' And he struck his arm violently with his hand, and took down his sword, which hung against the wall.

'What are you going to do, my lord?'

'What am I going to do, Parry? What every one in my family does. My mother lives on public charity,* my sister begs for my mother; I have, somewhere or other, brothers who equally beg for themselves; and I, the eldest, will go and do as all the rest do—I will go and ask charity!'

And at these words, which he finished sharply with a nervous and terrible laugh, the young man girded on his sword, took his hat from the trunk, fastened to his shoulder a black cloak, which he had worn during all his journey, and pressing the two hands of the old man, who watched his proceedings with a look of anxiety—

'My good Parry,' said he, 'order a fire, drink, eat, sleep, and be happy; let us both be happy, my faithful friend, my only friend. We are rich, as rich as kings!'

He struck the bag of pistoles with his clenched hand as he spoke, and it fell heavily to the ground. He resumed that dismal laugh that had so alarmed Parry; and whilst the whole household was screaming, singing, and preparing to install the travellers who had been preceded by their lackeys, he glided out by the principal entrance into the street, where the old man, who had gone to the window, lost sight of him in a moment.

VIII

WHAT HIS MAJESTY KING LOUIS XIV WAS AT
THE AGE OF TWENTY-TWO

IT has been seen, by the account we have endeavoured to give of it, that the entry of King Louis XIV into the city of Blois had been noisy and brilliant; his young majesty had therefore appeared perfectly satisfied with it.

On arriving beneath the porch of the Castle of the States, the king met, surrounded by his guards and gentlemen, with His Royal Highness the duke, Gaston of Orléans, whose physiognomy, naturally rather majestic, had borrowed on this solemn occasion a fresh lustre and a fresh dignity. On her part, Madame, dressed in her robes of ceremony, awaited, in the interior balcony, the entrance of her nephew. All the windows of the old castle, so deserted and dismal on ordinary days, were resplendent with ladies and lights.

It was then to the sound of drums, trumpets, and *vivat*s, that the young king crossed the threshold of that castle in which, seventy-two years before, Henry III had called in the aid of assassination and treachery* to keep upon his head and in his house a crown which was already slipping from his brow, to fall into another family.

All eyes, after having admired the young king, so handsome and so agreeable, sought for that other king of France, much otherwise king than the former, and so old, so pale, so bent, whose name was Cardinal Mazarin.

Louis was at this time endowed with all the natural gifts which make the perfect gentleman; his eye was brilliant, mild, and of a clear azure blue. But the most skilful physiognomists, those divers into the soul, on fixing their looks upon it, if it had been possible for a subject to sustain the glance of the king—the most skilful physiognomists, we say, would never have been able to fathom the depths of that abyss of mildness. It was with the eyes of the king as with the immense depths of the azure heavens, or with those more terrific, and almost as sublime, which the Mediterranean reveals under the keels of its ships in a clear summer day, a gigantic mirror in which heaven delights to reflect sometimes its stars, sometimes its storms.

The king was short of stature—he was scarcely five feet two inches:* but his youth made up for this defect, set off likewise by great nobleness in all his movements, and by considerable address in all bodily exercises.

In truth, he was already very much a king, and it was a great thing to be a king in that period of traditional devotedness and respect; but as, up to that time, he had been but seldom and always poorly shown to the people, as they to whom he was shown saw him by the side of his mother, a tall woman, and monsieur le cardinal, a man of commanding presence, many found him so little of a king as to say:

'Why, the king is not so tall as monsieur le cardinal!'

Whatever may be thought of these physical observations, which were principally made in the capital, the young king was welcomed as a god by the inhabitants of Blois, and almost like a king by his uncle and aunt, Monsieur and Madame, the inhabitants of the castle.

It must, however, be allowed, that when he saw, in the great hall of the castle, chairs of equal height placed for himself, his mother, the cardinal, and his uncle and aunt, a disposition artfully concealed by the semi-circular form of the assembly, Louis XIV became red with anger, and looked around him to ascertain by the countenances of those present if this humiliation had been prepared for him. But as he saw nothing upon the impassive visage of the cardinal, nothing on that of his mother, nothing on those of the assembly, he resigned himself, and sat down, taking care to be seated before anybody else.

The gentlemen and ladies were presented to their majesties and monsieur le cardinal.

The king remarked that his mother and he scarcely knew the names of any of the persons who were presented to them; whilst the cardinal, on the contrary, never failed, with an admirable memory and presence of mind, to talk to every one about his estates, his ancestors, or his children, some of whom he named, which enchanted those worthy country gentlemen, and confirmed them in the idea that he alone is truly king who knows his subjects, from the same reason that the sun has no rival, because the sun alone warms and lightens.

The study of the young king, which had begun a long time before, without anybody suspecting it, was continued then, and he looked around him attentively, to endeavour to make out something in the physiognomies which had at first appeared the most insignificant and trivial.

A collation was served. The king, without daring to call upon the hospitality of his uncle, had waited for it impatiently. This time, therefore, he had all the honours due, if not to his rank, at least to his appetite.

As to the cardinal, he contented himself with touching with

his withered lips a broth served in a gold cup. The all-powerful minister, who had taken her regency from the queen, and his royalty from the king, had not been able to take a good stomach from nature.*

Anne of Austria, already suffering from the cancer which six or eight years after caused her death, ate very little more than the cardinal.

For Monsieur, already puffed up with the great event which had taken place in his provincial life, he ate nothing whatever.

Madame alone, like a true Lorrainer,* kept pace with his majesty; so that Louis XIV, who, without this partner, might have eaten nearly alone, was at first much pleased with his aunt, and afterwards with M. de Saint-Rémy, her major-domo, who had really distinguished himself.

The collation over, at a sign of approbation from M. de Mazarin, the king arose, and, at the invitation of his aunt, walked about among the ranks of the assembly.

The ladies then observed—there are certain things for which women are as good observers at Blois as at Paris—the ladies then observed that Louis XIV had a prompt and bold look, which premised a distinguished appreciator of beauty. The men, on their part, observed that the prince was proud and haughty, that he loved to stare down those who fixed their eyes upon him too long or too earnestly, which gave presage of a master.

Louis XIV had accomplished about a third of his review when his ears were struck with a word which his eminence pronounced whilst conversing with Monsieur.

This word was the name of a woman.

Scarcely had Louis XIV heard this word than he heard, or rather listened to, nothing else; and neglecting the arc of the circle which awaited his visit, his object seemed to be to come as quickly as possible to the extremity of the curve.

Monsieur, like a good courtier, was inquiring of monsieur le cardinal after the health of his nieces; he regretted, he said, not having the pleasure of receiving them at the same time with their uncle; they must certainly have grown in stature, beauty, and grace, as they had promised to do the last time Monsieur had seen them.

What had first struck the king was a certain contrast in the voices of the two speakers. The voice of Monsieur was calm and natural while he spoke thus; while that of M. de Mazarin jumped by a note and a half to reply above the diapason of his usual voice. It might have been said that he wished that voice to strike, at the end of the room, any ear that was too distant.

'Monseigneur,' replied he, 'Mesdemoiselles de Mazarin have still to finish their education: they have duties to fulfil, and a position to make. An abode in a young and brilliant court would dissipate them a little.'

Louis, at this last sentence, smiled sadly. The court was young, it was true, but the avarice of the cardinal had taken good care that it should not be brilliant.

'You have nevertheless no intention,' replied Monsieur, 'to cloister them or turn them into good middle-class girls?'

'Not at all,' replied the cardinal, forcing his Italian pronunci-ation in such a manner that, from soft and velvety as it was, it became sharp and vibrating; 'not at all: I have a full and fixed intention to find husbands for them, and that as well as I shall be able.'

'Suitors will not be wanting, monsieur le cardinal,' replied Monsieur, with a *bonhomie* worthy of one tradesman congratu-lating another.

'I hope not, monseigneur, and with reason, as God has been pleased to give them grace, intelligence, and beauty.'

During this conversation, Louis XIV, conducted by Madame, accomplished, as we have described, the circle of presentations.

'Mademoiselle Auricule,'* said the princess, presenting to his majesty a fat, fair girl of two-and-twenty, who at a village fête might have been taken for a peasant in Sunday finery—'the daughter of my music mistress.'

The king smiled. Madame had never been able to extract four correct notes from either viol or harpsichord.

'Mademoiselle Aure de Montalais,' continued Madame; 'a young lady of rank, and my good attendant.'

This time it was not the king that smiled; it was the young lady presented, because, for the first time in her life, she heard, given to her by Madame, who generally showed no tendency to spoil her, such an honourable qualification.

Our old acquaintance Montalais, therefore, made his majesty

a profound courtesy, the more respectful from the necessity she was under of concealing certain contractions of her laughing lips, which the king might not have attributed to their real cause.

It was just at this moment that the king caught the word which startled him.

'And the name of the third?' asked Monsieur.

'Mary, monseigneur,' replied the cardinal.

There was doubtless some magical influence in that word,* for, as we have said, the king started at hearing it, and drew Madame towards the middle of the circle, as if he wished to put some confidential question to her, but, in reality, for the sake of getting nearer to the cardinal.

'My dear aunt,' said he, laughing, and in a suppressed voice, 'my geography master did not teach me that Blois was at such an immense distance from Paris.'

'What do you mean, nephew?' asked Madame.

'Why, because it would appear that it requires several years, as regards fashion, to travel the distance!—Look at those young ladies!'

'Well; I know them all.'

'Some of them are pretty.'

'Don't say that too loud, nephew; you will drive them wild.'

'Hold hard, dear aunt!' said the king, smiling; 'for the second part of my sentence will serve as a corrective to the first. Well, my dear aunt, some of them appear old and others ugly, thanks to their ten-year-old fashions.'*

'But, sire, Blois is only five days' journey from Paris.'

'Yes, that is it,' said the king: 'two years behind for each day.'

'Indeed! do you really think so? Well, that is strange! It never struck me.'

'Now, look, aunt,' said Louis XIV, drawing still nearer to Mazarin, under the pretext of gaining a better point of view, 'look at that simple white dress by the side of those antiquated specimens of finery, and those pretentious coiffures. She is probably one of my mother's maids of honour, though I don't know her.'

'Ah! ah! my dear nephew!' replied Madame, laughing; 'per-mit me to tell you that your divinatory science is at fault for once. The young lady you honour with your praise is not a Parisian, but hails from Blois.'

'Oh, aunt!' replied the king with a look of doubt.

'Come here, Louise,' said Madame.

And the fair girl, already known to you under that name, approached them, timid, blushing, and almost bent beneath the royal glance.

'Mademoiselle Louise Françoise de la Beaume le Blanc, the daughter of the Marquis de la Vallière,'* said Madame, ceremoniously.

The young girl bowed with so much grace, mingled with the profound timidity inspired by the presence of the king, that the latter lost, while looking at her, a few words of the conversation of Monsieur and the cardinal.

'Daughter-in-law,' continued Madame, 'of M. de Saint-Rémy, my major-domo, who presided over the confection of that excellent *daube truffée** which your majesty seemed so much to appreciate.'

No grace, no youth, no beauty, could stand out against such a presentation. The king smiled. Whether the words of Madame were a pleasantry, or uttered in all innocence, they proved the pitiless immolation of everything that Louis had found charming or poetic in the young girl. Mademoiselle de la Vallière, for Madame and by rebound, for the king, was, for a moment, no more than the daughter of a man of superior talent in the matter of *dindes truffées*.

But princes are thus constituted. The gods, too, were just like this in Olympus. Diana and Venus, no doubt, abused the beautiful Alcmena and poor Io, when they condescended, for distraction's sake, to speak, amidst nectar, and ambrosia, of mortal beauties, at the table of Jupiter.*

Fortunately, Louise was so bent in her reverential salute, that she did not catch either Madame's words or the king's smile. In fact, if the poor child, who had so much good taste as alone to have chosen to dress herself in white amidst all her companions—if that dove's heart so easily accessible to painful emotions, had been touched by the cruel words of Madame, or the egotistical cold smile of the king, it would have annihilated her.

And Montalais herself, the girl of ingenious ideas, would not have attempted to recall her to life; for ridicule kills even beauty.

But fortunately, as we have said, Louise, whose ears were buzzing, and her eyes veiled by timidity—Louise saw nothing and heard nothing; and the king, who still had his attention directed to the conversation of the cardinal and his uncle, hastened to return to them.

He came up just at the moment Mazarin concluded by saying: 'Mary, as well as her sisters, has just set off for Brouage. I make them follow the opposite bank of the Loire to that along which we have travelled; and if I calculate their progress correctly, according to the orders I have given, they will to-morrow be opposite Blois.'

These words were pronounced with that tact—that measure, that distinctness of tone, of intention, and reach—which made *del Signor Giulio Mazarini* the foremost actor in the whole world.

It resulted that they went straight to the heart of Louis XIV, and the cardinal, on turning round at the simple noise of the approaching footsteps of his majesty, saw the immediate effect of them upon the countenance of his pupil, an effect betrayed to the keen eyes of his eminence by a slight increase of colour. But what was the spilling of such a secret to him whose craft had for twenty years deceived all the diplomats of Europe?

From the moment the young king heard these last words, he appeared as if he had received a poisoned arrow in his heart. He could not remain quiet in a place, but cast around an uncertain, dead, and aimless look over the assembly. He looked questioningly at his mother more than twenty times: but she, given up to the pleasure of conversing with her sister-in-law, and likewise constrained by the glance of Mazarin, did not appear to comprehend any of the supplications conveyed by the looks of her son.

From this moment, music, lights, flowers, beauties, all became odious and insipid to Louis XIV. After he had a hundred times bitten his lips, stretched his legs and his arms like a well-brought-up child, who, without daring to gape, exhausts all the modes of evincing his weariness—after having uselessly again implored his mother and the minister, he turned a despairing look towards the door, that is to say, towards liberty.

At this door, in the embrasure of which he was leaning, he saw, standing out strongly, a figure with a brown and lofty countenance, an aquiline nose, a stern but brilliant eye, long grey hair, a black moustache, the true type of military beauty, whose gorget, more sparkling than a mirror, broke all the reflected lights which concentrated upon it, and sent them back as lightning. This officer wore his grey hat with its long red plumes upon his head, a proof that he was called there by his duty, and not by his pleasure. If he had been brought thither by his pleasure—if he had been a courtier instead of a soldier, as pleasure always has its price—he would have held his hat in his hand.

That which proved still better that this officer was upon duty, and was accomplishing a task to which he was accustomed, was, that he watched, with folded arms, remarkable indifference, and supreme apathy, the joys and tedium of the occasion. Above all, he appeared, like a philosopher, and all old soldiers are philosophers—he appeared above all to comprehend the tedium infinitely better than the joys; but in the one he took his part, knowing very well how to do without the other.

Now, he was leaning, as we have said, against the carved door-frame when the melancholy, weary eyes of the king, by chance, met his.

It was not the first time, it seemed, that the eyes of the officer had met those eyes, and he was perfectly acquainted with the expression of them; for, as soon as he had cast his own look upon the countenance of Louis XIV, and had read by it what was passing in his heart—that is to say, all the tedium that oppressed him—all the timid desire to leave which agitated him—he perceived he must render the king a service without his commanding it—almost in spite of himself. Boldly, therefore, as if he had given the word of command to cavalry in battle, 'On the king's service!' cried he, in a clear, sonorous voice.

As these words which produced the effect of a peal of thunder, prevailing over the orchestra, the singing and the buzz of the promenaders, the cardinal and the queen-mother looked at each other with surprise.

Louis XIV, pale, but resolved, supported as he was by that intuition of his own thought which he had found in the mind

of the officer of musketeers, and which he had just manifested
by the order given, arose from his chair, and took a step towards
the door.

'Are you going, my son?' said the queen, whilst Mazarin
satisfied himself with interrogating by a look which might have
appeared mild if it had not been so piercing.

'Yes, madame,' replied the king; 'I am fatigued, and, besides,
wish to write this evening.'

A smile stole over the lips of the minister, who appeared, by
a nod of the head, to give the king permission.

Monsieur and Madame hastened to give orders to the officers
who presented themselves.

The king bowed, crossed the hall, and gained the door, where
a hedge of twenty musketeers awaited him. At the extremity of
this hedge stood the officer, impassive, with his drawn sword in
his hand. The king passed, and all the crowd stood on tip-toe, to
have one more look at him.

Ten musketeers, opening the crowd of the antechambers and
the steps, made way for his majesty. The other ten surrounded
the king and Monsieur, who had insisted upon accompanying
his majesty. The domestics walked behind. This little procession escorted the king to the chamber destined for him. The
apartment was the same that had been occupied by Henry III
during his sojourn in the States.*

Monsieur had given his orders. The musketeers, led by their
officer, took possession of the little passage by which one wing
of the castle communicates with the other. This passage began
with a small square antechamber, dark even in the finest days.
Monsieur stopped Louis XIV.

'You are passing now, sire,' said he, 'the very spot where the
Duc de Guise received the first stab of the poniard.'*

The king was ignorant of all historical matters; he had heard
of the fact, but he knew nothing of the localities or the details.

'Ah!' said he with a shudder.

And he stopped. The rest, both behind him and before him,
stopped likewise.

'The duc, sire,' continued Gaston, 'was nearly where I stand:
he was walking in the same direction as your majesty; M. de
Loignac was exactly where your lieutenant of musketeers is;

M. de Saint-Maline and his majesty's guards were behind him and around him. It was here that he was struck.'

The king turned towards his officer, and saw something like a cloud pass over his martial and daring countenance.

'Yes, from behind!' murmured the lieutenant, with a gesture of supreme disdain. And he endeavoured to resume the march, as if ill at ease at being between walls formerly defiled by treachery.

But the king, who appeared to wish to be informed, was disposed to give another look at this dismal spot.

Gaston perceived his nephew's desire.

'Look, sire,' said he, taking a torch from the hands of M. de Saint-Rémy, 'this is where he fell. There was a bed there, the curtains of which he tore with catching at them.'

'Why does the floor seem hollowed out at this spot?' asked Louis.

'Because it was here the blood flowed,' replied Gaston; 'the blood penetrated deeply into the oak, and it was only by cutting it out that they succeeded in making it disappear. And even then,' added Gaston, pointing the flambeau to the spot, 'even then this red stain resisted all the attempts made to destroy it.'

Louis XIV raised his head. Perhaps he was thinking of that bloody trace that had once been shown him at the Louvre, and which, as a pendant to that of Blois, had been made there one day by the king his father with the blood of Concini.*

'Let us go on,' said he.

The march was resumed promptly; for emotion, no doubt, had given to the voice of the young prince a tone of command which was not customary with him.* When arrived at the apartment destined for the king, which communicated not only with the little passage we have passed through, but further with the great staircase leading to the court—

'Will your majesty,' said Gaston, 'condescend to occupy this apartment, unworthy as it is to receive you?'

'Uncle,' replied the young king, 'I render you my thanks for your cordial hospitality.'

Gaston bowed to his nephew, embraced him, and then went out.

Of the twenty musketeers who had accompanied the king, ten

escorted Monsieur back to the reception-rooms, which were not yet empty, notwithstanding the king had retired.

The ten others were posted by their officer, who himself explored, in five minutes, all the localities, with that cold and certain glance which not even habit gives unless that glance belong to genius.

Then, when all were placed, he chose as his headquarters the antechamber, in which he found a large armchair, a lamp, some wine, some water, and some dry bread.

He refreshed his lamp, drank half a glass of wine, curled his lip with a smile full of expression, installed himself in his large armchair, and made preparations for sleeping.

IX

IN WHICH THE STRANGER AT THE INN OF THE MEDICI LOSES HIS INCOGNITO

THIS officer, who was sleeping, or preparing to sleep, was, notwithstanding his careless air, charged with a serious responsibility.

Lieutenant* of the king's musketeers, he commanded all the company which came from Paris, and that company consisted of a hundred and twenty men; but, with the exception of the twenty of whom we have spoken, the other hundred were engaged in guarding the queen-mother, and more particularly the cardinal.

Monsignor Giulio Mazarini economized the travelling expenses of his guards;* he consequently used the king's, and that largely, since he took fifty of them for himself—a peculiarity which would not have failed to strike any one unacquainted with the usages of that court.

That which would still further, have appeared, if not inconvenient, at least extraordinary, to a stranger, was, that the side of the castle destined for monsieur le cardinal was brilliant, light and cheerful. The musketeers there mounted guard at every door, and allowed no one to enter, except the couriers, who, even while he was travelling, followed the cardinal for the carrying on of his correspondence.

Twenty men were on duty with the queen-mother; thirty rested, in order to relieve their companions the next day.

On the king's side, on the contrary, were darkness, silence, and solitude. When once the doors were closed, there was no longer an appearance of royalty. All the attendants had by degrees retired. Monsieur le Prince had sent to know if his majesty required his attendance; and on the customary 'No' of the lieutenant of musketeers, who was accustomed to the question and the reply, all appeared to sink into the arms of sleep, as if in the dwelling of a good citizen.

And yet it was possible to hear from the side of the house occupied by the young king the music of the banquet, and to see the windows of the great hall richly illuminated.

Ten minutes after his installation in his apartment, Louis XIV had been able to learn, by a commotion much more distinguished than marked his own leaving, the departure of the cardinal, who, in his turn, sought his bedroom, accompanied by a large escort of ladies and gentlemen.

Besides, to perceive this movement, all he had to do was to look out at his window, the shutters of which had not been closed.

His eminence crossed the court, conducted by Monsieur, who himself held a torch; then followed the queen-mother, to whom Madame familiarly gave her arm; and both walked chatting away, like two old friends.

Behind these two couples filed nobles, ladies, pages and officers; the torches gleamed over the whole court, like the moving reflections of a conflagration. Then the noise of footsteps and voices became lost in the upper floors of the castle.

No one was then thinking of the king, who, leaning on his elbow at his window, had sadly seen pass away all that light, and heard that noise die off—no, not one, if it was not that stranger of the hostelry of the Medici, whom we have seen go out, enveloped in his cloak.

He had come straight up to the castle, and had, with his melancholy countenance, wandered round and round the palace, from which the people had not yet departed; and finding that no one guarded the great entrance, or the porch, seeing that the soldiers of Monsieur were fraternizing with the royal soldiers—

that is to say, swallowing Beaugency at discretion, or rather indiscretion—the stranger penetrated through the crowd, then crossed the courtyard, and came to the landing of the staircase leading to the cardinal's apartment.

What, according to all probability, induced him to direct his steps that way, was the splendour of the torches, and the busy air of the pages and domestics. But he was stopped short by a presented musket* and the cry of the sentinel.

'Where are you going, my friend?' asked the soldier.

'I am going to the king's apartment,' replied the stranger, haughtily, but coolly.

The soldier called one of his eminence's officers, who, in the tone in which a youth in office directs a petitioner to a minister, let fall these words: 'The other staircase, across the way.'

And the officer, without further notice of the stranger, resumed his interrupted conversation.

The stranger, without reply, directed his steps towards the staircase pointed out to him. On this side there was no noise, there were no more torches.

Obscurity, through which a sentinel glided like a shadow; silence, which permitted him to hear the sound of his own footsteps, accompanied with the jingling of his spurs upon the stone slabs.

This guard was one of the twenty musketeers appointed for attendance upon the king, and he mounted guard with the stiffness and consciousness of a statue.

'Who goes there?' said the guard.

'A friend,' replied the unknown.

'What do you want?'

'To speak to the king.'

'Do you, my dear monsieur? That's not possible.'

'Why not?'

'Because the king has gone to bed.'

'Gone to bed already?'

'Yes.'

'No matter: I must speak to him.'

'And I tell you that is impossible.'

'But . . .'

'Turn and go!'

'Do you need the pass-word?'

'I don't have to tell you anything. Stand back!'

And this time the soldier accompanied his word with a threatening gesture; but the stranger stirred no more than if his feet had taken root.

'Monsieur le mousquetaire,' said he, 'are you a gentleman?'

'I have that honour.'

'Very well! I also am one; and between gentlemen some consideration ought to be observed.'

The soldier lowered his arms, overcome by the dignity with which these words were pronounced.

'Speak, monsieur,' said he; 'and if you ask me anything in my power——'

'Thank you. You have an officer, have you not?'

'Our lieutenant? Yes, monsieur.'

'Well, I wish to speak to him.'

'Oh, that's a different matter. Come up, monsieur.'

The stranger saluted the soldier in a lofty fashion, and ascended the staircase; whilst a cry, 'Lieutenant, a visit!' transmitted from sentinel to sentinel, preceded the stranger, and disturbed the slumbers of the officer.

Dragging on his boot, rubbing his eyes, and fastening his cloak, the lieutenant took three steps towards the stranger.

'What can I do to serve you, monsieur?' asked he.

'You are the officer on duty, lieutenant of the musketeers, are you?'

'I have that honour,' replied the officer.

'Monsieur, I must absolutely speak to the king.'

The lieutenant looked attentively at the stranger, and in that look, however rapid, he saw all he wished to see—that is to say, a person of high distinction in an ordinary dress.

'I do not suppose you to be mad,' replied he; 'and yet you seem to me to be in a condition to know, monsieur, that people do not enter a king's apartments in this manner without his consent.'

'He will consent.'

'Monsieur, permit me to doubt that. The king has retired this quarter of an hour; he must be now undressing. Besides, the word is given.'

'When he knows who I am, he will recall the word.'

The officer was more and more surprised, more and more subdued.

'If I consent to announce you, may I at least know whom to announce, monsieur?'

'You will announce His Majesty Charles II, King of England, Scotland, and Ireland.'

The officer uttered a cry of astonishment, drew back, and there might be seen upon his pallid countenance one of the most poignant emotions that ever an energetic man endeavoured to drive back to his heart.

'Oh, yes, sire; in fact,' said he, 'I ought to have recognized you.'

'You have seen my portrait, then?'

'No, sire.'

'Or else you have seen me formerly at court, before I was driven from France?'

'No, sire, it is not even that.'

'How then could you have recognized me, if you have never seen my portrait or my person?'

'Sire, I saw his majesty your father at a terrible moment.'

'The day——'*

'Yes.'

A dark cloud passed over the brow of the prince; then, dashing his hand across it, 'Do you still see any difficulty in announcing me?' said he.

'Sire, pardon me,' replied the officer, 'but I could not imagine a king under so simple an exterior; and yet I had the honour to tell your majesty just now that I had seen Charles I. But pardon me, monsieur; I will go and inform the king.'

But returning after going a few steps, 'Your majesty is desirous, without doubt, that this interview should be a secret?' said he.

'I do not require it; but if it were possible to preserve it——'

'It is possible, sire, for I can dispense with informing the first gentleman on duty; but, for that, your majesty must please to consent to give up your sword.'

'True, true; I had forgotten that no one armed is permitted to enter the chamber of a king of France.'

'Your majesty will form an exception, if you wish it; but then I shall discharge my responsibility by informing the king's attendant.'

'Here is my sword, monsieur. Will you now please to announce me to his majesty?'

'Instantly, sire.' And the officer immediately went and knocked at the communicating door, which the valet opened to him.

'His Majesty the King of England!' said the officer.

'His Majesty the King of England!' replied the *valet de chambre*.

At these words a gentleman opened the folding-doors of the king's apartment, and Louis XIV was seen, without hat or sword, and his doublet open, advancing with signs of the greatest surprise.

'You, my brother—you at Blois!' cried Louis XIV, dismissing with a gesture both the gentleman and the *valet de chambre*, who passed out into the next apartment.

'Sire,' replied Charles II, 'I was going to Paris, in the hope of seeing your majesty, when report informed me of your approaching arrival in this city. I therefore prolonged my abode here, having something very particular to communicate to you.'

'Will this closet suit you, my brother?'

'Perfectly well, sire; for I think no one can hear us here.'

'I have dismissed my gentleman and my watcher; they are in the next chamber. There, behind that partition, is a solitary closet, looking into the antechamber, and in that antechamber you found nobody but a solitary officer, did you?'

'No, sire.'

'Well, then, speak, my brother; I listen to you.'

'Sire, I commence, and entreat your majesty to have pity on the misfortunes of our house.'*

The King of France coloured, and drew his chair closer to that of the King of England.

'Sire,' said Charles II, 'I have no need to ask if your majesty is acquainted with the details of my deplorable history.'

Louis XIV blushed, this time more strongly than before; then, stretching forth his hand to that of the King of England, 'My brother,' said he, 'I am ashamed to say so, but the cardinal scarcely ever speaks of political affairs before me. Still more, formerly I used to get Laporte*, my *valet de chambre*, to read historical subjects to me; but he put a stop to these readings, and took away Laporte from me. So that I beg my brother Charles to tell me all those matters as to a man who knows nothing.'

'Well, sire, I think that by taking things from the beginning I shall have a better chance of touching the heart of your majesty.'

'Speak on, my brother—speak on.'

'You know, sire, that being called in 1650 to Edinburgh, during Cromwell's expedition into Ireland, I was crowned at Scone.* A year after, wounded in one of the provinces he had usurped, Cromwell returned upon us. To meet him was my object; to leave Scotland was my wish.'*

'And yet,' interrupted the young king, 'Scotland is almost your native country, is it not, my brother?'

'Yes; but the Scots were cruel compatriots for me, sire; they had forced me to forsake the religion of my fathers; they had hung Lord Montrose,* the most devoted of my servants, because he was not a Covenanter: and as the poor martyr, to whom they had offered a favour when dying, had asked that his body might be cut into as many pieces as there are cities in Scotland, in order that evidence of his fidelity might be met with everywhere, I could not leave one city, or go into another, without passing under some fragments of a body which had acted, fought, and breathed for me.

'By a bold, almost desperate march, I passed through Cromwell's army, and entered England.* The Protector* set out in pursuit of this strange flight, which had a crown for its object. If I had been able to reach London before him, without doubt the prize of the race would have been mine; but he overtook me at Worcester.

'The genius of England was no longer with us, but with him. On the 3rd of September, 1651, sire, the anniversary of the other battle of Dunbar, so fatal to the Scots, I was conquered. Two thousand men fell around me before I thought of retreating a step. At length I was obliged to fly.

'From that moment my history became a romance.* Pursued with persistent inveteracy, I cut off my hair, I disguised myself as a woodman. One day spent amidst the branches of an oak gave to that tree the name of the royal oak, which it bears to this day. My adventures in the county of Stafford, whence I escaped with the daughter of my host on a pillion behind me, still fill the tales of the country firesides, and would furnish matter for ballads. I will some day write all this, sire, for the instruction of my brother kings.

'I will first tell how, on arriving at the residence of Mr Norton, I met with a court chaplain, who was looking on at a party playing at skittles, and an old servant who named me, bursting into tears, and who was as near and as certainly killing me by his fidelity as another might have been by treachery. Then I will tell of my terrors—yes, sire, of my terrors—when, at the house of Colonel Windham, a farrier who came to shoe our horses declared they had been shod in the north.'

'How strange!' murmured Louis XIV. 'I never heard anything of all this; I was only told of your embarkation at Brighelmsted* and your landing in Normandy.'

'Oh!' exclaimed Charles, 'if Heaven permits kings to be thus ignorant of the histories of each other, how can they render assistance to their brothers who need it?'

'But tell me,' continued Louis XIV, 'how, after being so roughly received in England, you can still hope for anything from that unhappy country and that rebellious people?'

'Oh, sire! since the battle of Worcester, everything is changed there.* Cromwell is dead, after having signed a treaty with France, in which his name was placed above yours. He died on the 3rd of September, 1658, a fresh anniversary of the battles of Dunbar and Worcester.'

'His son has succeeded him.'

'But certain men have a family, sire, and no heir. The inheritance of Oliver was too heavy for Richard. Richard was neither a republican nor a royalist; Richard allowed his guards to eat his dinner, and his generals to govern the republic; Richard abdicated the protectorate on the 22nd of April, 1659, more than a year ago, sire.

'From that time England is nothing but a gambling den, in which the players throw dice for the crown of my father. The two most eager players are Lambert and Monk.* Well, sire, I, in my turn, wish to take part in this game, where the stakes are thrown upon my royal mantle. Sire, it only requires a million to corrupt one of these players and make an ally of him, or two hundred of your gentlemen to drive them out of my palace at Whitehall, as Christ drove the money-changers from the temple.'

'You come, then,' replied Louis XIV, 'to ask me———'

'For your assistance; that is to say, not only for that which kings owe to each other, but that which simple Christians owe to each other—your assistance, sire, either in money or men. Your assistance, sire, and within a month, whether I oppose Lambert to Monk, or Monk to Lambert, I shall have re-conquered my paternal inheritance, without having cost my country a guinea, or my subjects a drop of blood, for they are now all drunk with revolutions, protectorates, and republics, and ask nothing better than to fall staggering to sleep in the arms of royalty.* Your assistance, sire, and I shall owe you more than I owe my father—my poor father, who bought at so dear a rate the ruin of our house! You may judge, sire, whether I am unhappy, whether I am in despair, for I accuse my own father!'

And the blood mounted to the pale face of Charles II, who remained for an instant with his head between his hands, and as if blinded by that blood which appeared to revolt against the filial blasphemy.

The young king was not less affected than his elder brother; he threw himself about in his armchair, and could not find a single word of reply.

Charles II, to whom ten years in age gave a superior strength to master his emotions, recovered his speech the first.

'Sire,' said he, 'your reply? I wait for it as a criminal waits for his sentence. Must I die?'

'My brother,' replied the French prince, 'you ask me for a million—me, who was never possessed of a quarter of that sum! I possess nothing.* I am no more king of France than you are king of England. I am a name, a cipher dressed in fleur-de-lised velvet—that is all. I am upon a visible throne; that is my only advantage over your majesty. I have nothing—I can do nothing.'

'Can it be so?' exclaimed Charles II.

'My brother,' said Louis, sinking his voice, 'I have undergone miseries with which my poorest gentlemen are unacquainted. If my poor Laporte were here, he would tell you that I have slept in ragged sheets, through the holes of which my legs have passed;

he would tell you that afterwards, when I asked for carriages, they brought me conveyances half-eaten by the rats of the coach-houses; he would tell you that when I asked for my dinner, the servants went to the cardinal's kitchen to inquire if there were any dinner for the king. And look! to-day, this very day even, when I am twenty-two years old—to-day, when I have attained the age of the majority of kings—to-day, when I ought to have the key of the treasury, the direction of policy, the supremacy in peace and war—cast your eyes around me, see how I am left! Look at this abandonment—this disdain—this silence!—Whilst yonder—look yonder! View the bustle, the lights, the homage! There!—there you see the real king of France, my brother!'

'In the cardinal's apartments?'

'Yes, in the cardinal's apartments.'

'Then I am doomed, sire?'

Louis XIV made no reply.

'Doomed is the word; for I will never solicit him who left my mother and sister to die of cold and hunger—the daughter and grand-daughter of Henry IV—as they surely would have if M. de Retz* and the parliament had not sent them wood and bread.'

'To die?' murmured Louis XIV.

'Well!' continued the king of England, 'poor Charles II, grandson of Henry IV,* just as you are, sire, having neither parliament nor Cardinal de Retz to apply to, will die of hunger, as his mother and sister nearly did.'

Louis knitted his brow, and violently twisted the lace of his ruffles.

This prostration, this immobility, serving as a mark to an emotion so visible, struck Charles II, and he took the young man's hand.

'Thanks!' said he, 'my brother. You pity me, and that is all I can require of you in your present situation.'

'Sire,' said Louis XIV, with a sudden impulse, and raising his head, 'it is a million you require, or two hundred gentlemen, I think you say?'

'Sire, a million would be quite sufficient.'

'That is very little.'

'Offered to a single man it is a great deal. Convictions have been purchased at a much lower price; and I should have nothing to do but with venalities.'

'Two hundred gentlemen! Reflect!—that is little more than a single company.'

'Sire, there is in our family a tradition, and that is, that four men, four French gentlemen,* devoted to my father, were near saving my father, though condemned by a parliament, guarded by an army and surrounded by a nation.'

'Then if I can procure you a million, or two hundred gentlemen, you will be satisfied; and you will consider me your well-affectioned brother?'

'I shall consider you as my saviour; and if I recover the throne of my father, England will be, as long as I reign at least, a sister to France, as you will have been a brother to me.'

'Well, my brother,' said Louis, rising, 'what you hesitate to ask for, I will myself demand; that which I have never done on my own account, I will do on yours. I will go and find the king of France—the other—the rich, the powerful one, I mean. I will myself solicit this million, or these two hundred gentlemen; and—we will see.'

'Oh!' cried Charles; 'you are a noble friend, sire—a heart created by God! You save me, my brother; and if you should ever stand in need of the life you restore me, demand it.'

'Silence, my brother—silence!' said Louis, in a hushed voice. 'Take care that no one hears you! We have not obtained our end yet. To ask money of Mazarin—that is worse than traversing the enchanted forest, each tree of which enclosed a demon. It is more than setting out to conquer a world.'

'But yet, sire, when you ask it——'

'I have already told you that I have never asked,' replied Louis with a haughtiness* that made the king of England turn pale.

And as the latter, like a wounded man, flinched—'Pardon me, my brother,' replied he. 'I have neither a mother nor a sister who are suffering. My throne is hard and naked, but I am firmly seated on my throne. Pardon me that expression, my brother; it was that of an egotist. I will retract it, therefore, by a sacrifice—I will go to monsieur le cardinal. Wait for me, if you please—I will return.'

WHILST the king was directing his course rapidly towards the wing of the castle occupied by the cardinal, taking nobody with him but his *valet de chambre*, the officer of musketeers came out, breathing like a man who has for a long time been forced to hold his breath, from the little closet of which we have already spoken, and which the king believed to be deserted. This little closet had formerly been part of the chamber, from which it was only separated by a thin partition. It resulted that this partition, which was only for the eye, permitted the least inquisitive ear to hear every word spoken in the chamber.

There was no doubt then, that this lieutenant of musketeers had heard all that passed in his majesty's apartment.

Warned by the last words of the young king, he came out just in time to salute him on his passage, and to follow him with his eyes till he had disappeared in the corridor.

Then as soon as he had disappeared, he shook his head after a fashion peculiarly his own, and in a voice which forty years' absence from Gascony had not deprived of its Gascon accent,* 'A melancholy service,' said he, 'and a melancholy master!'

These words pronounced, the lieutenant resumed his place in his armchair, stretched his legs, and closed his eyes, like a man who either sleeps or meditates.

During this short monologue and the actions that had accompanied it, whilst the king, through the long corridors of the old castle, proceeded to the apartment of M. de Mazarin, a scene of another sort was being enacted in those apartments.

Mazarin was in bed, suffering a little from the gout. But as he was a man of order, who utilized even pain, he forced his wakefulness to be the humble servant of his labour. He had consequently ordered Bernouin,* his *valet de chambre*, to bring him a little travelling-desk, so that he might write in bed. But the gout is not an adversary that allows itself to be conquered so easily; therefore, at each movement he made, the pain from dull became sharp.

'Is Brienne* there?' asked he of Bernouin.

'No, monseigneur,' replied the *valet de chambre*; 'M. de Brienne, with your permission, is gone to bed. But, if it is the wish of your eminence, he can speedily be called.'

'No, it is not worth while. Let us see, however. Figures!'

And the cardinal began to think, counting on his fingers the while.

'Oh! figures is it?' said Bernouin. 'Very well! if your eminence attempts calculations, I will promise you a pretty headache tomorrow! And with that please to remember M. Guénaud* is not here.'

'You are right, Bernouin. You must take Brienne's place, my friend. Indeed, I ought to have brought M. Colbert* with me. That young man goes on very well, Bernouin, very well; a very orderly youth.'

'I do not know,' said the *valet de chambre*, 'but I don't like the countenance of your young man who goes on so well.'

'Well, well, Bernouin! We don't need your advice. Place yourself there: take the pen, and write.'

'I am ready, monseigneur; what am I to write?'

'There, that's the place: after the two lines already traced.'

'I am there.'

'Write seven hundred and sixty thousand livres.'

'That is written.'

'Upon Lyons——' The cardinal appeared to hesitate.

'Upon Lyons,' repeated Bernouin.

'Three millions nine hundred thousand livres.'

'Well, monseigneur?'

'Upon Bordeaux, seven millions.'

'Seven?' repeated Bernouin.

'Yes,' said the cardinal, pettishly, 'seven.' Then, recollecting himself, 'You understand, Bernouin,' added he, 'that all this money is to be spent?'

'Eh! monseigneur; whether it be to be spent or put away is of very little consequence to me, since none of these millions are mine.'

'These millions are the king's; it is the king's money I am reckoning. Well, what were we saying? You always interrupt me!'

'Seven millions upon Bordeaux.'

'Ah! yes; that's right. Upon Madrid four millions. I give you to understand plainly whom this money belongs to, Bernouin, seeing that everybody has the stupidity to believe me rich in millions. I repel the silly idea. A minister, besides, has nothing of his own. Come, go on. General receipts, seven millions; properties, nine millions. Have you written that, Bernouin?'

'Yes, monseigneur.'

'The Change, six hundred thousand livres; various property, two millions. Ah! I forgot—the furniture of the different châteaux——'

'Must I put of the crown?' asked Bernouin.

'No, no; it is of no use doing that—that is understood. Have you written that, Bernouin?'

'Yes, monseigneur.'

'And the figures?'

'Stand straight under one another.'

'Add them up, Bernouin.'

'Thirty-nine millions two hundred and sixty thousand livres, monseigneur.'

'Ah!' cried the cardinal, in a tone of vexation; 'there are not yet forty millions!'

Bernouin recommenced the addition.

'No, monseigneur; there want seven hundred and forty thousand livres.'

Mazarin asked for the account, and checked it carefully.

'Yes, but,' said Bernouin, 'thirty-nine millions two hundred and sixty thousand livres make a good round sum.'

'Ah, Bernouin; I wish the king had it.'

'Your eminence told me that this money was his majesty's.'

'Of course, it's clear, as transparent as possible. These thirty-nine millions are bespoken, and much more.'

Bernouin smiled after his own fashion—that is like a man who believes no more than he is willing to believe—whilst preparing the cardinal's night draught, and putting his pillow to rights.

'Oh!' said Mazarin, when the valet had gone out; 'Not yet forty millions! I must, however, attain that sum on which I have set my sights. But who knows whether I shall have time? I sink, I am going, I shall never reach it! And yet, who knows that I may not find two or three millions in the pockets of my good friends the Spaniards? They discovered Peru, those people did, and—what the devil! they must have something left.'

As he was speaking thus, entirely occupied with his figures, and thinking no more of his gout, which was banished by a preoccupation which, with the cardinal, was the most powerful of all preoccupations, Bernouin rushed into the chamber in a state of agitation.

'Well!' asked the cardinal, 'what is the matter now?'

'The king, monseigneur—the king!'

'What?—the king!' said Mazarin, quickly concealing his paper. 'The king here! the king at this hour! I thought he was in bed long ago. What is the matter now?'

The king could hear these last words, and see the terrified gesture of the cardinal rising up in his bed, for he entered the chamber at that moment.

'It is nothing, monsieur le cardinal, or at least nothing which can alarm you. It is an important communication which I wish to make to your eminence to-night—that is all.'

Mazarin immediately thought of that marked attention which the king had given to his words concerning Mademoiselle de Mancini, and the communication appeared to him probably to refer to this source. He recovered his serenity then instantly, and assumed his most agreeable air, a change of countenance which inspired the king with the greatest joy; and when Louis was seated,

'Sire,' said the cardinal, 'I ought certainly to listen to your majesty standing, but the violence of my complaint——'

'No ceremony between us, my dear monsieur le cardinal,' said Louis kindly: 'I am your pupil, and not the king, you know very well, and this evening in particular, as I come to you as a petitioner, as a solicitor, and one very humble, and desirous to be kindly received, too.'

Mazarin, seeing the heightened colour of the king, was confirmed in his first idea; that is to say, that love thoughts were hidden under all these fine words. This time, political cunning, keen as it was, made a mistake; this colour was not caused by the bashfulness of a juvenile passion, but only by the painful contraction of royal pride.

Like a good uncle, Mazarin felt disposed to facilitate the confidence.

'Speak, sire,' said he, 'and since your majesty is willing for an instant to forget that I am your subject, and call me your master and instructor, I promise your majesty my most devoted and tender consideration.'

'Thanks, monsieur le cardinal,' answered the king; 'what I have to ask of your eminence has but little to do with myself.'

'Too bad!' replied the cardinal; 'too bad! Sire, I should wish your majesty to ask of me something of importance, even a sacrifice; but whatever it may be that you ask me, I am ready to set your heart at rest by granting it, my dear sire.'

'Well, this is what brings me here,' said the king, with a beating of the heart that had no equal except the beating of the heart of the minister; 'I have just received a visit from my brother, the king of England.'

Mazarin bounded in his bed as if he had been put in relation with a Leyden jar or a voltaic battery,* at the same time that a surprise, or rather a manifest disappointment, inflamed his features with such a blaze of anger, that Louis XIV, inexperienced diplomat as he was, saw that the minister had hoped to hear something else.

'Charles II?' exclaimed Mazarin, with a hoarse voice and a disdainful curl of his lips. 'You have received a visit from Charles II?'

'From King Charles II,' replied Louis, according in a marked manner to the grandson of Henry IV the title which Mazarin had forgotten to give him. 'Yes, monsieur le cardinal, that unhappy prince has touched my heart with the relation of his misfortunes. His distress is great, monsieur le cardinal, and it has appeared painful to me, who have seen my own throne disputed, who have been forced in times of upheaval to quit my capital—to me, in short, who am acquainted with misfortune—to leave a deposed and fugitive brother without assistance.'

'Eh!' said the cardinal, sharply; 'why had he not as you have, a Jules Mazarin by his side? His crown would then have remained intact.'

'I know all that my house owes to your eminence,' replied the king, haughtily, 'and you may believe well that I, on my part, shall never forget it. It is precisely because my brother the king of England has not about him the powerful genius who has saved me, it is for that, I say, that I wish to call on the aid of that same genius, and beg you to extend your arm over his head, well assured, monsieur le cardinal, that your hand, by touching him only, would know how to replace upon his brow the crown which fell at the foot of his father's scaffold.'

'Sire,' replied Mazarin, 'I thank you for your good opinion with regard to myself, but we have nothing to do yonder: they are a set of madmen who deny God, and cut off the heads of their kings. They are dangerous, note well, sire, and filthy to the touch after having wallowed in royal blood and covenantal murder. That policy has never suited me—I scorn it and reject it.'

'Therefore you ought to assist in establishing a better.'

'What is that?'

'The restoration of Charles II for example.'

'Good heavens!' cried Mazarin, 'does the poor prince flatter himself with that pipe-dream?'

'Yes, he does,' replied the young king, alarmed by the difficulties opposed to this project, which he fancied he could perceive in the infallible eye of his minister; 'he only asks for a million to carry out his purpose.'

'Is that all—a little million, if you please!' said the cardinal, ironically, with an effort to conquer his Italian accent. 'A little million, if you please, brother! Bah! a family of mendicants!'

'Cardinal,' said Louis, raising his head, 'that family of mendicants is a branch of my family.'

'Are you rich enough to give millions to other people, sire? Have you millions to throw away?'

'Oh!' replied Louis XIV, with great pain, which he, however, by a strong effort, prevented from appearing on his countenance; 'oh! yes, monsieur le cardinal, I am well aware I am poor, and yet the crown of France is worth a million, and to perform a good action I would pledge my crown if it were necessary. I could find Jews* who would be willing to lend me a million.'

'So, sire, you say you want a million?' said Mazarin.

'Yes, monsieur, I say so.'

'You are mistaken, greatly mistaken, sire; you want much

more than that. Bernouin!—you shall see, sire, how much you really want.'

'What, cardinal!' said the king, 'are you going to consult a lackey about my affairs?'

'Bernouin!' cried the cardinal again, without appearing to remark the humiliation of the young prince. 'Come here, Bernouin, and tell me the figures I gave you just now.'

'Cardinal, cardinal! did you not hear me?' said Louis, turning pale with anger.

'Do not be angry, sire; I deal openly with the affairs of your majesty. Every one in France knows that; my books are as open as day. What did I tell you to do just now, Bernouin?'

'Your eminence commanded me to draw up an account.'

'You did it, did you not?'

'Yes, my lord.'

'To verify the amount of which his majesty, at this moment, stands in need. Did I not tell you so? Be frank, my friend.'

'Your eminence said so.'

'Well, what sum did I say I wanted?'

'Forty-five millions, I think.'

'And what sum could we find, after collecting all our resources?'

'Thirty-nine millions two hundred and sixty thousand.'

'That is correct, Bernouin; that is all I wanted to know. Leave us now,' said the cardinal, fixing his brilliant eye upon the young king, who sat mute with stupefaction.

'But——' stammered the king.

'What, do you still doubt, sire?' said the cardinal. 'Well, here is a proof of what I said.'

And Mazarin drew from under his bolster the paper covered with figures, which he presented to the king, who turned away his eyes, his vexation was so deep.

'Therefore, as it is a million you want, sire, and that million is not set down here, it is forty-six millions your majesty stands in need of. Well I don't think that any Jews in the world would lend such a sum, even upon the crown of France.'

The king, clenching his hands beneath his ruffles, pushed away his chair.

'So it must be then!' said he; 'my brother the king of England will die of hunger.'

'Sire,' replied Mazarin, in the same tone, 'remember this proverb, which I give you as the expression of the soundest policy: "Rejoice at being poor when your neighbour is poor likewise." '

Louis meditated for a few moments, with an inquisitive glance at the paper, one end of which remained under the bolster.

'Then,' said he, 'it is impossible to comply with my demand for money, my lord cardinal, is it?'

'Absolutely, sire.'

'Remember, this will secure me a future enemy, if he succeed in recovering his crown without my assistance.'

'If your majesty only fears that, you may be quite at ease,' replied Mazarin, eagerly.

'Very well, I say no more about it,' exclaimed Louis XIV.

'Have I at least convinced you, sire?' placing his hand upon that of the young king.

'Perfectly.'

'If there be anything else, ask it, sire; I shall be most happy to grant it to you, having refused this.'

'Anything else, my lord?'

'Why, yes; am I not devoted body and soul to your majesty? Halloa! Bernouin!—lights and guards for his majesty! His majesty is returning to his own chamber.'

'Not yet, monsieur: since you place your good-will at my disposal, I will take advantage of it.'

'For yourself, sire?' asked the cardinal, hoping that his niece was at length about to be named.

'No, monsieur, not for myself,' replied Louis, 'but still for my brother Charles.'

The brow of Mazarin again became clouded, and he muttered a few words that the king could not catch.

INSTEAD of the hesitation with which he had accosted the cardinal a quarter of an hour before, there might be read in the eyes of the young king that will against which a struggle might be maintained, and which might be crushed by its own impotence, but which, at least, would preserve, like a wound in the depth of the heart, the memory of its defeat.

'This time, my lord cardinal, we have to deal with something more easily found than a million.'

'Do you think so, sire?' said Mazarin, looking at the king with that penetrating eye which was accustomed to read to the bottom of hearts.

'Yes, I think so; and when you know the object of my request——'

'And do you think I do not know it, sire?'

'You know what remains for me to say to you?'

'Listen, sire; these are King Charles's own words——'

'Oh, impossible!'

'Listen. "And if that miserly, beggarly Italian," said he——'

'My lord cardinal!'

'That is the sense, if not the words. Eh! Good heavens! I wish him no ill on that account; one is biased by passion. He said to you: "If that vile Italian refuses the million we ask of him, sire—if we are forced, for want of money, to renounce diplomacy, well, then, we will ask him to grant us five hundred gentlemen."'

The king started, for the cardinal was only mistaken in the number.

'Is not that it, sire,' cried the minister, with a triumphant accent. 'And then he added some fine words: he said, "I have friends on the other side of the channel, and these friends only want a leader and a banner. When they see me, when they behold the banner of France, they will rally round me, for they will comprehend that I have your support. The colours of the French uniform will be worth as much to me as the million M. de Mazarin refuses us"—for he was pretty well assured I should refuse him that million. "I shall conquer with these five hundred gentlemen, sire, and all the honour will be yours." Now, that is what he said, or to that purpose, was it not?—turning those plain words into brilliant metaphors and pompous images, for they are fine talkers, in that family! The father talked even on the scaffold.'*

The perspiration of shame stood upon the brow of Louis. He felt that it was inconsistent with his dignity to hear his brother thus insulted, but he did not yet know how to act with him to whom every one yielded, even his mother. At last he made an effort.

'But,' said he, 'my lord cardinal, it is not five hundred men, it is only two hundred.'

'Well, but you see I guessed what he wanted.'

'I never denied that you had a penetrating eye, and that was why I thought you would not refuse my brother Charles a thing so simple and so easy to grant him as what I ask of you in his name, my lord cardinal, or rather in my own.'

'Sire,' said Mazarin, 'I have studied politics these thirty years; first, under M. le Cardinal de Richelieu; and then alone. Our policy has not always been over-honest, it must be allowed, but it has never been unskilful. Now that which is proposed to your majesty is dishonest and unskilful at the same time.'

'Dishonest, monsieur!'

'Sire, you entered into a treaty with Cromwell.'*

'Yes, and in that very treaty Cromwell signed his name above mine.'

'Why did you sign yours so low down, sire? Cromwell found a good place, and he took it; that was his custom. I return, then, to M. Cromwell. You have a treaty with him, that is to say, with England, since when you signed that treaty M. Cromwell was England.'

'M. Cromwell is dead.'

'Do you think so, sire?'

'No doubt he is, since his son Richard has succeeded him, and has abdicated.'

'Yes, that is it exactly. Richard inherited after the death of his father, and England at the abdication of Richard. The treaty formed part of the inheritance, whether in the hands of M.

Richard or in the hands of England. The treaty is, then, still as good, as valid as ever. Why should you evade it, sire? What is changed? Charles wants to-day what we were not willing to grant him ten years ago; but that was foreseen and provided against. You are the ally of England, sire, and not of Charles II. It was doubtless wrong, from a family point of view, to sign a treaty with a man who had cut off the head of the brother-in-law* of the king, your royal father, and to contract an alliance with a parliament which they call yonder the Rump Parliament;* it was unbecoming, I acknowledge, but it was not unskilful from a political point of view, since, thanks to that treaty, I saved your majesty, then a minor, the trouble and danger of a foreign war, which the Fronde—you remember the Fronde, sire?'—the young king hung his head—'which the Fronde might have fatally complicated. And thus I prove to your majesty, that to change our plan now, without warning our allies, would be at once unskilful and dishonest. We should make war with the aggression on our side; we should make it, deserving to have it made against us; and we should have the appearance of fearing it whilst provoking it, for a permission granted to five hundred men, to two hundred men, to fifty men, to ten men, is still a permission. One Frenchman, that is the nation; one uniform, that is the army. Suppose, sire, for example, that you should have war with Holland,* which, sooner or later, will certainly happen; or with Spain, which will perhaps ensue if your marriage fails' (Mazarin stole a furtive glance at the king), 'and there are a thousand causes that might yet make your marriage fail—well, would you approve of England's sending to the United Provinces or to the Infanta a regiment, a company, a squadron even, of English gentlemen? Would you think that they kept within the limits of their treaty of alliance?'

Louis listened; it seemed so strange to him that Mazarin should invoke good faith, and he the author of so many political tricks, called Mazarinades.* 'And yet,' said the king, 'without any manifest authorization, I cannot prevent gentlemen of my states from passing over into England, if such should be their good pleasure.'

'You should compel them to return, sire, or at least protest against their presence as enemies in an allied country.'

'But come, my lord cardinal, you who are so profound a genius, try if you cannot find means to assist this poor king, without compromising ourselves.'

'And that is exactly what I am not willing to do, my dear sire,' said Mazarin. 'If England were to act exactly according to my wishes, she could not act better than she does; if I directed the policy of England from this place, I should not direct it otherwise. Governed as she is governed, England is an eternal nest of contention for all Europe. Holland protects Charles II, let Holland do so;* they will quarrel, they will fight. They are the only two maritime powers. Let them destroy each other's navies; we can construct ours with the wrecks of their vessels if we ever have money enough to buy nails.'

'Oh, how paltry and mean is all this that you are telling me, monsieur le cardinal!'

'Yes, but nevertheless it is true, sire; you must confess that. Still further. Suppose I admit, for a moment, the possibility of breaking your word, and evading the treaty—such a thing sometimes happens, but that is when some great interest is to be promoted by it, or when the treaty is found to be too troublesome—well, you will authorize the engagement asked of you: France—her banner, which is the same thing—will cross the Channel and will fight; France will be conquered.'

'Why so?'

'*Ma foi!* we have a pretty general to fight under,—this Charles II! Worcester gave us good proofs of that.'

'But he will no longer have to deal with Cromwell, Monsieur.'

'But he will have to deal with Monk, who is quite as dangerous. The brave brewer* of whom we speak, was a visionary; he had moments of exaltation, of inflation during which he ran over like an over-filled cask; and from the chinks there always escaped some drops of his thoughts, and by the sample the whole of his thought was to be made out. Cromwell has thus allowed us more than ten times to penetrate into his very soul, when one would have conceived that soul to be enveloped in triple brass,* as Horace has it. But Monk! Oh, sire, God defend you from ever having anything to transact politically with Monk. It is he who has given me, in one year, all the grey hairs I have. Monk is no fanatic; unfortunately he is a politician; he does not overflow, he keeps close together. For ten years he has had his eyes fixed upon one object, and nobody has yet been able to ascertain what. Every morning, as Louis XI advised, he burns his nightcap.* Therefore, on the day when this plan, slowly and solitarily ripened, shall break forth, it will break forth with all the conditions of success which always accompany an unforeseen event. That is Monk, sire, of whom, perhaps, you have never heard—of whom, perhaps, you did not even know the name, before your brother, Charles II, who knows what he is, pronounced it before you. He is a marvel of depth and tenacity,* the two only things against which intelligence and ardour are blunted. Sire, I had ardour when I was young: I always was intelligent. I may safely boast of it, because I am reproached with it. I have done very well with these two qualities, since, from the son of a fisherman of Piscina,* I have become prime minister to the king of France; and in that position your majesty will perhaps acknowledge I have rendered some service to the throne of your majesty. Well, sire, if I had met with Monk on my way, instead of Monsieur de Beaufort, Monsieur de Retz, or Monsieur le Prince*—well, we should have been ruined. If you engage yourself rashly, sire, you will fall into the talons of this politic soldier. The helmet of Monk, sire, is an iron coffer, in the recesses of which he shuts up his thoughts, and no one has the key of it. Therefore, near him, or rather before him, I bow, sire, for I have nothing but a velvet cap.'*

'What do you think Monk wishes to do, then?'

'Eh! sire, if I knew that, I would not tell you to mistrust him, for I should be stronger than he; but with him, I am afraid to guess—to guess!—you understand my word?—for if I thought I had guessed, I should stop at an idea, and, in spite of myself, should pursue that idea. Since that man has been in power yonder, I am like one of the damned in Dante whose neck Satan has twisted,* and who walk forward, looking behind them. I am travelling towards Madrid, but I never lose sight of London. To guess, with that devil of a man, is to deceive oneself and to deceive oneself is to ruin oneself. God keep me from ever seeking to guess what he aims at; I confine myself to watching what he does, and that is well enough. Now I believe—you observe the meaning of the word *I believe*?—*I believe*, with respect to

Monk, ties one to nothing—I believe that he has a strong inclination to succeed Cromwell. Your Charles II has already caused
proposals to be made to him by ten persons; he has satisfied
himself with driving these ten meddlers from his presence, without saying anything to them but, "Begone, or I will have you
hung." That man is a whited sepulchre! At this moment Monk
is affecting devotion to the Rump Parliament; of this devotion,
observe, I am not the dupe. Monk has no wish to be assassinated—an assassination would stop him in the midst of his operations; and his work must be accomplished; so I believe—but do
not believe what I believe, sire: for I say I believe from habit—
I believe, that Monk is keeping on friendly terms with the parliament till the day comes for dispersing it.* You are asked for
swords, but they are to fight against Monk. God preserve you
from fighting against Monk, sire; for Monk would beat us, and
I should never console myself after being beaten by Monk. I
should say to myself, Monk has foreseen that victory ten years.
For God's sake, sire, out of friendship for you, if not out of
consideration for himself, let Charles II keep quiet. Your majesty will give him a little income here; give him one of your
châteaux. Yes, yes—wait awhile. But I forgot the treaty—that
famous treaty of which we were just now speaking. Your majesty has not even the right to give him a château.'

'How is that?'

'Yes, yes; your majesty is bound not to grant hospitality to
King Charles, and even to compel him to leave France.* It was
on this account we forced him to quit you, and yet here he is
again. Sire, I hope you will give your brother to understand that
he cannot remain with us; that it is impossible he should be
allowed to compromise us; or I myself——'

'Enough, my lord,' said Louis XIV, rising. 'In refusing me a
million, perhaps, you may be right; your millions are your own.
In refusing me two hundred gentlemen, you are still further in
the right; for you are prime minister, and you have, in the eyes
of France, the responsibility of peace and war. But that you
should pretend to prevent me, who am king, from extending my
hospitality to the grandson of Henry IV, to my cousin-german,
to the companion of my childhood*—there your power stops,
and there begins my will.'

'Sire,' said Mazarin, delighted at being let off so cheaply, and having, besides, only fought so earnestly to arrive at that—'sire, I shall always bend before the will of my king. Let my king, then, keep near him, or in one of his châteaux, the king of England; let Mazarin know it, but let not the minister know it.'

'Good-night, my lord,' said Louis XIV, 'I go in despair.'

'But convinced, and that is all I desire, sire,' replied Mazarin.

The king made no answer, and retired quite pensive, convinced, not of all Mazarin had told him, but of one thing which he took care not to mention to him; and that was, that it was necessary for him to study seriously both his own affairs and those of Europe, for he found them very difficult and very obscure. Louis found the king of England seated in the same place where he had left him. On perceiving him, the English prince arose; but at the first glance he saw discouragement written in dark letters upon his cousin's brow. Then, speaking first, as if to facilitate the painful avowal that Louis had to make to him—

'Whatever it may be,' said he, 'I shall never forget all the kindness, all the friendship, you have exhibited towards me.'

'Alas!' replied Louis, in a melancholy tone, 'only barren goodwill, my brother.'

Charles II became extremely pale; he passed his cold hand over his brow, and struggled for a few instants against a faintness that made him tremble. 'I understand,' said he at last; 'no more hope!'

Louis seized the hand of Charles II. 'Wait, my brother,' said he; 'precipitate nothing; everything may change; hasty resolutions ruin all causes; add another year of trial, I implore you, to the years you have already undergone. You have, to induce you to act now rather than at another time, neither occasion nor opportunity. Come with me, my brother; I will give you one of my residences, whichever you prefer, to inhabit. I, with you, will keep my eyes upon events; we will prepare. Come, then, my brother, have courage!'

Charles II withdrew his hand from that of the king, and drawing back, to salute him with more ceremony, 'With all my heart, thanks!' replied he, 'sire; but I have prayed without success to the greatest king on earth; now I will go and ask a miracle of God.' And he left, refusing to hear any more, his head carried loftily, his hand trembling, with a painful contraction of his noble countenance, and that profound gloom which, finding no more hope in the world of men, appeared to go beyond it, and ask it in worlds unknown. The officer of musketeers, on seeing him pass by thus pale, bowed almost to his knees as he saluted him. He then took a torch, called two musketeers, and descended the deserted staircase with the unfortunate king, holding in his left hand his hat, the plume of which swept the steps. At the door, the musketeer asked the king which way he was going, that he might direct the musketeers.

'Monsieur,' replied Charles II, in a subdued voice, 'you who have known my father, say, did you ever pray for him? If you have done so, do not forget me in your prayers. Now, I go alone, and beg of you not to accompany me, or have me accompanied any further.'

The officer bowed, and sent away the musketeers into the interior of the palace. But he himself remained an instant under the porch watching the departing Charles II, till he was lost at the corner of the next street. 'To him, as to his father formerly,' murmured he, 'Athos, if he were here, would say with reason, "Salute fallen majesty!" ' Then, reascending the staircase: 'Oh! the vile service that I follow!' said he at every step. 'Oh! my pitiful master! Life thus carried on is no longer tolerable, and it is high time that I should do something! No more generosity, no more energy! The master has succeeded, the pupil is starved forever. *Mordioux!* I will not resist. Come, you men,' continued he, entering the antechamber, 'why are you all looking at me so? Extinguish these torches and return to your posts. Ah! you were guarding me? Yes, you watch over me, do you not, worthy fellows? Brave fools! I am not the Duc de Guise.* Begone! They will not assassinate me in the little passage. Besides,' added he, in a low voice, 'that would be a resolution, and no resolutions have been formed since Monsieur le Cardinal de Richelieu died. Now, with all his faults, that was a man! It is settled: to-morrow I will hang up my uniform for good.'

Then, reflecting: 'No,' said he, 'not yet! I have one great trial to make, and I will make it; but that, and I swear it, shall be the last, *Mordioux!*'

He had not finished speaking, when a voice issued from the king's chamber. 'Monsieur le lieutenant!' said this voice.

'Here am I,' replied he.

'The king desires to speak to you.'

'Humph!' said the lieutenant; 'perhaps of what I was thinking about.' And he went into the king's apartment.

XII

THE KING AND THE LIEUTENANT

As soon as the king saw the officer enter, he dismissed his *valet de chambre* and his gentleman. 'Who is on duty to-morrow, monsieur?' asked he.

The lieutenant bowed his head with military politeness, and replied, 'I am, sire.'

'What! still you?'

'Always I, sire.'

'How can that be, monsieur?'

'Sire, when travelling, the musketeers supply all the posts of your majesty's household; that is to say, yours, her majesty the queen's, and monsieur le cardinal's, the latter of whom borrows of the king the best part, or rather the most numerous part, of the royal guard.'

'But in the interims?'

'There are no interims, sire, but for twenty or thirty men who rest out of a hundred and twenty. At the Louvre* it is very different, and if I were at the Louvre, I should rely upon my brigadier; but, when travelling, sire, no one knows what may happen, and I prefer doing my duty myself.'

'Then you are on guard every day?'

'And every night. Yes, sire.'

'Monsieur, I cannot allow that—I will have you rest.'

'That is very kind, sire; but I will not.'

'What do you say?' said the king, who did not at first comprehend the full meaning of this reply.

'I say, sire, that I will not expose myself to the chance of a fault. If the devil had a trick to play on me, you understand, sire, as he knows the man with whom he has to deal, he would choose the moment when I should not be there. My duty and the peace of my conscience before everything, sire.'

'But such duty will kill you, monsieur.'

'Eh! sire, I have performed it for over thirty years,* and in all France and Navarre there is not a man in better health than I am. Moreover, I entreat you, sire, not to trouble yourself about me. That would appear very strange to me, seeing that I am not accustomed to it.'

The king cut short the conversation by a fresh question. 'Shall you be here, then, to-morrow morning?'

'As at present? yes, sire.'

The king walked several times up and down his chamber; it was very plain that he burned with a desire to speak, but that he was restrained by some fear or other. The lieutenant, standing motionless, hat in hand, watched him making these evolutions, and, whilst looking at him, grumbled to himself, biting his moustache:

'He has not half a crown worth of resolution! Upon my soul! I would lay a wager he does not speak at all!'

The king continued to walk about, casting from time to time a side glance at the lieutenant. 'He is the very image of his father,' continued the latter, in his secret soliloquy, 'he is at once proud, avaricious, and timid. The devil take his master, say I.'

The king stopped. 'Lieutenant,' said he.

'I am here, sire.'

'Why did you cry out this evening, down below in the salons—"The king's service! His majesty's musketeers!"'

'Because you gave me the order, sire.'

'I?'

'Yourself.'

'Indeed, I did not say a word, monsieur.'

'Sire, an order is given by a sign, by a gesture, by a glance, as intelligibly, as freely, and as clearly as by word of mouth. A servant who has nothing but ears is not half a good servant.'

'Your eyes are very penetrating, then, monsieur.'

'How is that, sire?'

'Because they see what is not.'

'My eyes are good, though, sire, although they have served their master long and much: when they have any thing to see, they seldom miss the opportunity. Now, this evening, they saw that your majesty coloured with endeavouring to conceal the inclination to yawn, that your majesty looked with eloquent supplications, first at his eminence, and then at her majesty the queen-mother, and at length to the entrance door, and they so thoroughly remarked all I have said, that they saw your majesty's lips articulate these words: "Who will get me out of this?"'

'Monsieur!'

'Or something to this effect, sire—"My musketeers!" I could then no longer hesitate. That look was for me—the order was for me. I cried out instantly, "His majesty's musketeers!" And, besides, that was showed to be true, sire, not only by your majesty's not saying I was wrong, but proving I was right by going out at once.'

The king turned away to smile; then, after a few seconds, he again fixed his limpid eye upon that countenance, so intelligent, so bold, and so firm, that it might have been said to be the proud and energetic profile of the eagle facing the sun.* 'That is all very well,' said he, after a short silence, during which he tried, in vain, to make his officer lower his eyes.

But seeing the king said no more, the latter pirouetted on his heels, and took three steps towards the door, muttering, 'He will not speak! *Mordioux!* he will not speak!'

'Thank you, monsieur,' said the king at last.

'Humph!' continued the lieutenant; 'there was only wanting that. Blamed for having been less of a fool than another might have been.' And he went to the door, allowing his spurs to jingle in true military style. But when he was on the threshold, feeling that the king's desire drew him back, he returned.

'Has your majesty told me everything?' asked he, in a tone we cannot describe, but which, without appearing to solicit the royal confidence, contained so much persuasive frankness, that the king immediately replied:

'Yes; but draw near, monsieur.'

'Now then,' murmured the officer, 'he is coming to it at last.'

'Listen to me.'

'I shall not miss a word, sire.'

'You will mount on horseback to-morrow, at about half-past four in the morning, and you will have a horse saddled for me.'

'From your majesty's stables?'

'No; one of your musketeers' horses.'

'Very well, sire. Is that all?'

'And you will accompany me.'

'Alone?'

'Alone.'

'Shall I come to seek your majesty, or shall I wait?'

'You will wait for me.'

'Where, sire?'

'At the little park-gate.'

The lieutenant bowed, understanding that the king had told him all he had to say. In fact, the king dismissed him with a gracious wave of the hand. The officer left the chamber of the king, and returned to place himself philosophically in his arm-chair, where, far from sleeping, as might have been expected, considering how late it was, he began to reflect more deeply than he had ever reflected before. The result of these reflections was not so melancholy as the preceding ones had been.

'Come, he has begun,' said he. 'Love urges him on, and he goes forward—he goes forward! The king is nobody in his own palace; but the man perhaps may prove to be worth something. Well, we shall see to-morrow morning. Oh! oh!' cried he, all at once starting up, 'that is a gigantic idea, *mordioux!* and perhaps my fortune depends, at least, upon that idea!' After this ex-clamation, the officer arose and marched, with his hands in the pockets of his jerkin, around the immense antechamber that served him as an apartment. The wax-light flamed furiously under the effects of a fresh breeze which stole in through the chinks of the door and the window, and cut the room diagonally. It threw out a reddish, unequal light, sometimes brilliant, some-times dull, and the tall shadow of the lieutenant was seen marching on the wall, in profile, like a figure by Callot,* with his long sword and feathered hat.

'Certainly!' said he, 'I am mistaken if Mazarin is not laying a snare for this amorous boy. Mazarin, this evening, gave an ad-dress, and made an appointment as complacently as M. Dangeau himself could have done—I heard him, and I know the meaning of his words. "To-morrow morning," said he, "they will pass opposite the bridge of Blois." *Mordioux!* that is clear enough, and particularly for a lover. That is the cause of this embarrassment; that is the cause of this hesitation; that is the cause of this order—"Monsieur the lieutenant of my musketeers, be on horseback to-morrow at four o'clock in the morning." Which is as clear as if he had said: "Monsieur the lieutenant of my musketeers, to-morrow, at four, at the bridge of Blois—do you understand?" Here is a state secret, then, which I, humble as I am, have presently in my possession. And how did I get it? Because I have good eyes, as his majesty just now said. They say he loves this little Italian doll furiously. They say he threw himself at his mother's feet, to beg her to allow him to marry her. They say the queen went so far as to consult the court of Rome, whether such a marriage, contracted against her will, would be valid.* Oh, if I were but twenty-five! If I had by my side those I no longer have! If I did not despise the whole world most profoundly, I would embroil Mazarin with the queen-mother, France with Spain, and I would make a queen after my own fashion. But let that pass.' And the lieutenant snapped his fingers in disdain.

'This miserable Italian—this poor creature—this sordid wretch—who has just refused the king of England a million, would not perhaps give me a thousand pistoles for the news I could carry him. *Mordioux!* I am falling into second childhood: I am becoming stupid indeed! The idea of Mazarin giving anything! ha! ha! ha!' and he laughed in a subdued voice.

'Well, let us go to sleep—let us go to sleep; and the sooner the better. My mind is wearied with my evening's work, and will see things to morrow more clearly than to-day.'

And upon this recommendation, made to himself, he folded his cloak around him, with disdainful thoughts for his royal neighbour. Five minutes after this he was asleep, with his hands clenched and his lips apart, giving escape, not to his secret, but to a sonorous sound, which rose and spread freely beneath the majestic roof of the antechamber.

XIII

MARY DE MANCINI

THE sun had scarcely shed its first beams on the majestic trees of the park and the lofty turrets of the castle, when the young king, who had been awake more than two hours, possessed by the sleeplessness of love, opened his shutters himself, and cast an inquiring look into the courts of the sleeping palace. He saw that it was the hour agreed upon: the great court clock pointed to a quarter-past four. He did not disturb his *valet de chambre*, who was sleeping soundly at some distance; he dressed himself, and the valet, in a great fright, sprang up, thinking he had been deficient in his duty; but the king sent him back again, commanding him to preserve the most absolute silence. He then descended the little staircase, went out at a side door, and perceived at the end of the wall a mounted horseman, holding another horse by the bridle. This horseman could not be recognized in his cloak and broad-brimmed hat. As to the horse, saddled like that of a rich citizen, it offered nothing remarkable to the most experienced eye. Louis took the bridle: the officer held the stirrup without dismounting, and asked his majesty's orders in a low voice.

'Follow me,' replied the king.

The officer put his horse to the trot, behind that of his master, and they descended the hill towards the bridge. When they reached the other side of the Loire,

'Monsieur,' said the king, 'you will please to ride on till you see a carriage coming; then return and inform me. I will wait here.'

'Will your majesty deign to give me some description of the carriage I am charged to discover?'

'A carriage in which you will see two ladies, and probably their attendants likewise.'

'Sire, I should not wish to make a mistake; is there no other sign by which I may know this carriage?'

'It will bear, in all probability, the arms of monsieur le cardinal.'

'That is sufficient, sir,' replied the officer, fully instructed in the object of his search. He put his horse to the trot, and rode sharply on in the direction pointed out by the king. But he had scarcely gone five hundred paces when he saw four mules, and then a carriage, loom up from behind a little hill. Behind this carriage came another. It required only one glance to assure him that these were the equipages he was in search of; he therefore turned his bridle, and rode back to the king.

'Sire,' said he, 'here are the carriages. The first, as you said, contains two ladies with their ladies-in-waiting; the second contains the footmen, provisions, and necessaries.'

'That is well,' replied the king, in an agitated voice. 'Please to go and tell those ladies that a cavalier of the court wishes to pay his respects to them alone.'

The officer set off at a gallop. '*Mordioux!*' said he, as he rode on, 'here is a new and an honourable employment, I hope! I complained of being nobody. I am the king's confidant: that is enough to make a musketeer burst with pride.'

He approached the carriage, and delivered his message, gallantly and intelligently. There were two ladies in the carriage: one of great beauty, although rather thin; the other less favoured by nature, but lively, graceful, and uniting in the delicate lines of her brow all the signs of a strong will. Her eyes, animated and piercing, in particular, spoke more eloquently than all the amorous phrases in fashion in those days of gallantry. It was to her D'Artagnan addressed himself, without fear of being mistaken, although the other was, as we have said, the more handsome of the two.

'Madame,' said he, 'I am the lieutenant of the musketeers, and there is on the road a horseman who awaits you, and is desirous of paying his respects to you.'

At these words, the effect of which he watched closely, the lady with the black eyes uttered a cry of joy, leant out of the carriage window, and seeing the cavalier approaching, held out her arms, exclaiming:

'Ah, my dear sire!' and the tears gushed from her eyes.

The coachman stopped his team; the women rose in confusion from the back of the carriage, and the second lady made a slight curtsy, terminated by the most ironical smile that jealousy ever imparted to the lips of woman.

'Marie, dear Marie,' cried the king, taking the hand of the black-eyed lady in both his. And opening the heavy door himself, he drew her out of the carriage with so much ardour, that she was in his arms before she touched the ground. The lieutenant, posted on the other side of the carriage, saw and heard all without being observed.

The king offered his arm to Mademoiselle de Mancini, and made a sign to the coachman and lackeys to proceed. It was nearly six o'clock; the road was fresh and pleasant; tall trees, with their foliage still enclosed in the golden down of their buds, let the dew of morning filter from their trembling branches, like liquid diamonds; the grass was bursting at the foot of the hedges; the swallows, having returned only a few days since, described their graceful curves between the heavens and the water; a breeze, laden with the perfumes of the blossoming woods, sighed along the road, and wrinkled the surface of the waters of the river; all these beauties of the day, all these perfumes of the plants, all these aspirations of the earth towards heaven, intoxicated the two lovers, walking side by side, leaning upon each other, eyes fixed upon eyes, hand clasping hand, and who, lingering as by a common desire, did not dare to speak, they had so much to say.*

The officer saw that the king's horse, in wandering this way and that, annoyed Mademoiselle de Mancini. He took advantage of the pretext of securing the horse to draw near them, and dismounting walked between the two horses he led; he did not miss a single word or gesture of the lovers. It was Mademoiselle de Mancini who at length began.

'Ah, my dear sire!' said she, 'you do not abandon me, then?'

'No, Marie,' replied the king; 'you see I do not.'

'I had so often been told, though, that as soon as we should be separated you would no longer think of me.'

'Dear Marie, is it then only to-day that you have discovered we are surrounded by people interested in deceiving us?'

'But then, sire, this journey, this alliance with Spain? They are going to marry you off!'

Louis hung his head. At the same time the officer could see the eyes of Marie de Mancini shine in the sun with the brilliancy of a dagger starting from its sheath. 'And you have done nothing in favour of our love?' asked the girl, after a silence of a moment.

'Ah! mademoiselle, how could you believe that? I threw myself at the feet of my mother; I begged her, I implored her; I told her all my hopes of happiness were in you; I even threatened——'

'Well?' asked Marie, eagerly.

'Well, the queen-mother wrote to the court of Rome, and received as answer, that a marriage between us would have no validity, and would be dissolved by the holy father. At length, finding there was no hope for us, I requested to have my marriage with the infanta at least delayed.'

'And yet that does not prevent your being on the road to meet her?'

'How can I help it? To my prayers, to my supplications, to my tears, I received no answer but reasons of state.'

'Well, well?'

'Well, what is to be done, mademoiselle, when so many wills are leagued against me?'

It was now Marie's turn to hang her head. 'Then I must bid you adieu for ever,' said she. 'You know that I am being exiled; you know that I am going to be buried alive; you know still more that they want to marry me off too.'

Louis became very pale, and placed his hand upon his heart.

'If I had thought that only my life was at stake, I have been so persecuted that I might have yielded; but I thought yours was concerned, my dear sire, and I stood out for the sake of preserving your happiness.'

'Oh, yes! my happiness, my treasure!' murmured the king, more gallantly than passionately, perhaps.

'The cardinal might have yielded,' said Marie, 'if you had addressed yourself to him, if you had pressed him. For the cardinal to call the king of France his nephew! do you not see, sire? He would have made war even for that honour; the cardinal, assured of governing alone, under the double pretext of having brought up the king and given his niece to him in marriage—the cardinal would have fought all enemies, overcome all obstacles. Oh, sire! I can answer for that. I am a woman, and I see clearly into everything where love is concerned.'

These words produced a strange effect upon the king. Instead of heightening his passion, they cooled it. He stopped, and said hastily—

'What is to be said, mademoiselle? Everything has failed.'

'Except your will, I trust, my dear sire?'

'Alas!' said the king, colouring, 'have I a will?'

'Oh!' said Mademoiselle de Mancini mournfully, wounded by that expression.

'The king has no will but that which policy dictates, except that which reasons of state impose upon him.'

'Oh! it is because you have no love,' cried Mary; 'if you loved, sire, you would have a will.'

On pronouncing these words, Mary raised her eyes to her lover, whom she saw more pale and more cast down than an exile who is about to quit his native land forever. 'Accuse me,' murmured the king, 'but do not say I do not love you.'

A long silence followed these words, which the young king had pronounced with a perfectly true and profound feeling. 'I am unable to think that to-morrow, and after to-morrow, I shall see you no more; I cannot think that I am going to end my sad days far from Paris; that the lips of an old man, of an stranger, should touch that hand which you hold in yours; no, in truth, I cannot think of all that, my dear sire, without having my poor heart burst with despair.'

And Marie de Mancini did shed floods of tears. On his part, the king, much affected, carried his handkerchief to his mouth, and stifled a sob.

'See,' said she, 'the carriages have stopped, my sister waits for me, the time is come; what you are about to decide upon, will be decided for life. Oh, sire! you are willing then that I should lose you? You are willing then, Louis, that she to whom you have said, "I love you," should belong to another than to her king, to her master, to her lover? Oh! courage, Louis! courage! One word, a single word! Say "I will!" and all my life is enchained to yours, and all my heart is yours for ever.'

The king made no reply. Mary then looked at him as Dido looked at Æneas in the Elysian fields, fierce and disdainful.*

'Farewell then,' said she; 'farewell life! love! heaven!'

And she took a step away. The king detained her, seized her hand, which he pressed to his lips, and despair prevailing over the resolution he appeared to have inwardly formed, he let fall upon that beautiful hand a burning tear of regret, which made Mary start, so really had that tear burnt her. She saw the damp eyes of the king, his pale brow, his convulsed lips, and cried, with an accent that cannot be described,

'Oh, sire! you are a king, you weep, and yet I depart!'*

As his sole reply, the king hid his face in his handkerchief. The officer uttered something so like a roar that it frightened the horses. Mademoiselle de Mancini, quite indignant, quitted the king's arm, hastily entered the carriage, crying to the coachman, 'Go on, go on, and quick!'

The coachman obeyed, flogged his mules, and the heavy carriage rocked upon its creaking axle, whilst the king of France, alone, cast down, annihilated, did not dare to look either behind or before him.

XIV

IN WHICH THE KING AND THE LIEUTENANT EACH GIVE PROOFS OF MEMORY

WHEN the king, like all the people in the world who are in love, had long and attentively watched disappear in the distance the carriage which bore away his mistress; when he had turned and turned again a hundred times to stare after her and had at length succeeded in somewhat calming the agitation of his heart and thoughts, he recollected that he was not alone. The officer still held the horse by the bridle, and had not lost all hope of seeing the king recover his resolution. He could still mount his horse and ride after the carriage; they would have lost nothing by waiting a little. But the imagination of the lieutenant of the musketeers was too rich and too brilliant; it left far behind it that of the king, who took care not to allow himself to be carried away to any such excess. He contented himself with approaching the officer, and in a doleful voice, 'Come,' said he, 'let us be gone; all is ended. To horse!'

The officer imitated his manner, his slowness, his sadness, and leisurely mounted his horse. The king pushed on sharply, the lieutenant followed him. At the bridge Louis turned around for the last time. The lieutenant, patient as a god who has eternity behind and before him, still hoped for a return of energy.* But it was groundless, nothing appeared. Louis gained the street which led to the castle, and entered as seven was striking. As the king returned, and the musketeer, who missed nothing, had seen a corner of the tapestry over the cardinal's window lifted up, he breathed a profound sigh, like a man unloosed from the tightest bonds, and said in a low voice:

'Now then, my officer, I hope that it is over.'

The king summoned his gentleman. 'Please understand I shall receive nobody before two o'clock,' said he.

'Sire,' replied the gentleman, 'there is, however, some one who requests admittance.'

'Who is that?'

'Your lieutenant of musketeers.'

'He who accompanied me?'

'Yes, sire.'

'Ah,' said the king, 'let him come in.'

The officer entered. The king made a sign, and the gentleman and the valet retired. Louis followed them with his eyes until they had shut the door, and when the tapestries had fallen behind them: 'You remind me by your presence, monsieur, of something I had forgotten to recommend to you, that is to say, the most absolute discretion.'

'Oh! sire, why does your majesty give yourself the trouble of making me such a recommendation? It is plain you do not know me.'

'Yes, monsieur, that is true. I know that you are discreet; but as I had prescribed nothing——'

The officer bowed. 'Has your majesty nothing else to say to me?'

'No, monsieur; you may retire.'

'Shall I obtain permission not to do so till I have spoken to the king, sire?'

'What have you to say to me? Explain yourself, monsieur.'

'Sire, a thing without importance to you, but which interests me greatly. Pardon me then for speaking of it. Without urgency, without necessity, I never would have done it, and I would have disappeared, mute and insignificant as I always have been.'

'How! Disappeared! I do not understand you, monsieur.'

'Sire, in a word,' said the officer, 'I am come to ask for my discharge from your majesty's service.'

The king made a movement of surprise, but the officer remained as motionless as a statue.

'Your discharge—yours, monsieur? and for how long a time, I pray?'

'Why, for ever, sire.'

'What, you are desirous of quitting my service, monsieur?' said Louis, with an expression that revealed something more than surprise.

'Sire, I regret to say that I am.'

'Impossible!'

'It is so, however, sire. I am getting old; I have been in harness now thirty-five years; my poor shoulders are tired; I feel that I must give place to the young. I don't belong to this age; I have still one foot in the old one;* it results that everything is strange in my eyes, everything astonishes and bewilders me. In short, I have the honour to ask your majesty for my discharge.'

'Monsieur,' said the king, looking at the officer, who wore his uniform with an ease that would have caused envy in a young man, 'you are stronger and more vigorous than I am.'

'Oh!' replied the officer, with an air of false modesty, 'your majesty says so because I still have a good eye and a tolerably firm foot—because I can still ride a horse, and my moustache is black; but, sire, vanity of vanities all that—illusions all that—appearance, smoke, sire! I have still a youthful air, it is true, but I feel old, and within six months I am certain I shall be broken down, gouty, impotent. Therefore, then, sire——'

'Monsieur,' interrupted the king, 'remember your words of yesterday. You said to me in this very place where you now are, that you were endowed with the best health of any man in France; that fatigue was unknown to you! that you did not mind spending whole days and nights at your post. Did you tell me that, monsieur, or not? Try and recall, monsieur.'

The officer sighed. 'Sire,' said he, 'old age is boastful; and it is pardonable for old men to praise themselves when others no longer do it. It is very possible I said that; but the fact is, sire, I am very much fatigued, and request permission to retire.'

'Monsieur,' said the king, advancing towards the officer with a gesture full of majesty, 'you are not telling me the true reason. You wish to quit my service, it may be true, but you disguise from me the motive of your retreat.'

'Sire, believe that——'

'I believe what I see, monsieur; I see a vigorous, energetic man, full of presence of mind, the best soldier in France, perhaps; and this man cannot persuade me the least in the world that he stands in need of rest.'

'Ah! sire,' said the lieutenant, with bitterness, 'what praise! Indeed, your majesty confounds me! Energetic, vigorous, brave, intelligent, the best soldier in the army! But, sire, your majesty exaggerates my small portion of merit to such a point, that however good an opinion I may have of myself, I do not recognize myself; in truth I do not. If I were vain enough to believe only half of your majesty's words, I should consider myself a valuable, indispensable man. I should say that a servant possessed of such brilliant qualities was a treasure beyond all price. Now, sire, I have been all my life—I feel bound to say it— except at the present time appreciated, in my opinion, much below my value.* I therefore repeat, your majesty exaggerates.'

The king knitted his brow, for he saw a bitter raillery beneath the words of the officer. 'Come, monsieur,' said he, 'let us meet the question frankly. Are you dissatisfied with my service, say? No evasions; speak boldly, frankly—I command you to do so.'

The officer who had been twisting his hat about in his hands, with an embarrassed air, for several minutes, raised his head at these words. 'Oh! sire,' said he, 'that puts me a little more at my ease. To a question put so frankly, I will reply frankly. To tell the truth is a good thing, as much from the pleasure one feels in relieving one's heart, as on account of its rarity. I will speak the truth, then, to my king, at the same time imploring him to excuse the frankness of an old soldier.'

Louis looked at his officer with anxiety which he manifested by the agitation of his gesture. 'Well, then, speak,' said he, 'for I am impatient to hear the truths you have to tell me.'

The officer threw his hat upon a table, and his countenance, always so intelligent and martial, assumed, all at once, a strange character of grandeur and solemnity. 'Sire,' said he, 'I quit the king's service because I am dissatisfied. The valet, in these times, can approach his master as respectfully as I do, can give him an account of his labour, bring back his tools, return the funds that have been entrusted to him, and say, "Master, my day's work is done. Pay me, if you please, and let us part."'

'Monsieur! monsieur!' exclaimed the king, crimson with rage.

'Ah! sire,' replied the officer, bending his knee for a moment, 'never was servant more respectful than I am before your majesty; only you commanded me to tell the truth. Now I have begun to tell it, it must come out, even if you command me to hold my tongue.'

There was so much resolution expressed in the deep sunk muscles of the officer's countenance, that Louis XIV had no occasion to tell him to continue; he continued, therefore, whilst the king looked at him with a curiosity mingled with admiration.

'Sire, I have, as I have said, now served the house of France thirty-five years; few people have worn out so many swords in that service as I have, and the swords I speak of were good swords, too, sire. I was a boy, ignorant of everything except courage, when the king your father guessed that there was a man in me. I was a man, sire, when the Cardinal de Richelieu, who was a judge of manhood, discovered an enemy in me. Sire, the history of that enmity between the ant and the lion may be read from the first to the last line, in the secret archives* of your family. If ever you feel an inclination to know it, do so, sire; the history is worth the trouble—it is I who tell you so. You will there read that the lion, fatigued, harassed, out of breath, at length cried for quarter, and the justice must be rendered him to say, that he gave as much as he required. Oh! those were glorious times, sire, strewed over with battles like one of Tasso's or Ariosto's epics.* The wonders of those times, to which the people of ours would refuse belief, were every-day occurrences. For five years together, I was a hero every day; at least, so I was told by persons of judgment; and that is a long period for heroism, trust me, sire, a period of five years. Nevertheless, I have faith in what these people told me, for they were good judges. They were named M. de Richelieu,* M. de Buckingham, M. de Beaufort, M. de Retz, a mighty genius himself in street warfare—in short, the king, Louis XIII, and even the queen, your noble mother, who one day condescended to say, "Thank you."

I don't know what service I had had the good fortune to render her. Pardon me, sire, for speaking so boldly; but what I relate to you, as I have already had the honour to tell your majesty, is history.'

The king bit his lips, and threw himself violently on a chair.

'I appear importunate to your majesty,' said the lieutenant. 'Well, sire, that is the fate of truth; she is a stern companion; she bristles all over with steel; she wounds those whom she attacks, and sometimes him who speaks her.'

'No, monsieur,' replied the king: 'I bade you speak—speak then.'

'After the service of the king and the cardinal, came the service of the regency,* sire; I fought pretty well in the Fronde— much less, though, than the first time. The men began to diminish in stature. I have, nevertheless, led your majesty's musketeers on some perilous occasions, which stand upon the orders of the day of the company. I could not wish for a better life than the one I led at that time. I was the favourite of M. de Mazarin. Lieutenant here! lieutenant there! lieutenant to the right! lieutenant to the left! There was not a fight in France, in which your humble servant did not have a hand; but soon France was not enough. The cardinal sent me to England on Cromwell's account; another gentleman who was not over gentle, I assure you, sire. I had the honour of knowing him, and I was well able to appreciate him. A great deal was promised me on account of that mission. So, as I did much more than I had been bidden to do, I was generously paid, for I was at length appointed captain of the musketeers; that is to say, the most envied position in court, which takes precedence over the marshals of France,* and rightly so; for who says captain of the musketeers says the flower of chivalry and king of the brave.'

'Captain, monsieur!' interrupted the king; 'you make a mistake. Lieutenant, you mean.'

'Not at all, sire—I make no mistake; your majesty may rely upon me in that respect. Monsieur le cardinal gave me the commission himself.'*

'Well!'

'But M. de Mazarin, as you know better than anybody, does not often give, and sometimes takes back what he has given; he took it back again as soon as peace was made and he was no longer in want of me. Certainly I was not worthy to replace M. de Tréville, of illustrious memory; but they had promised me, and they had given me; they ought to have stopped there.'

'Is that what dissatisfies you, monsieur? Well, I shall make inquiries. I love justice; and your claim, though made in military fashion, does not displease me.'

'Oh, sire!' said the officer, 'your majesty has ill understood me; I no longer claim anything now.'

'Excess of delicacy, monsieur; but I will keep my eye upon your affairs, and later——'

'Oh, sire! what a word!—later! Thirty years have I lived upon that promising word, which has been pronounced by so many great personages, and which your mouth has, in its turn, just pronounced. Later—that is how I have received a score of wounds, and how I have reached fifty-four years of age,* without ever having had a louis in my purse, and without ever having met with a protector on my way—I, who have protected so many people! So I change my formula, sire; and when any one says to me "Later" I reply "*Now.*" It is rest that I solicit, sire. That may be easily granted me. That will cost nobody anything.'

'I did not look for this language, monsieur, particularly from a man who has always lived among the great. You forget you are speaking to the king, to a gentleman who is, I suppose, of as good a house as yourself; and when *I* say later, I mean a certainty.'

'I do not at all doubt it, sire; but this is the end of the terrible truth I had to tell you. If I were to see upon that table a marshal's stick, the sword of constable, the crown of Poland, instead of later, I swear to you, sire, that I should still say *Now!* Oh, excuse me, sire! I am from the country of your grandfather, Henry IV.* I do not speak often: but when I do speak, I speak all.'

'The future of my reign has little interest for you, monsieur, it appears,' said Louis, haughtily.

'Forgetfulness, forgetfulness everywhere!' cried the officer, with a noble air; 'the master has forgotten the servant, so that the servant is reduced to forget his master. I live in unfortunate times, sire. I see youth full of discouragement and fear, I see it timid and despoiled, when it ought to be rich and powerful. I, yesterday evening, for example, open the door to a king of England, whose father, humble as I am, I was near saving, if God had not been against me—God, who inspired his elect, Cromwell! I open, I said, the door, that is to say, the palace of one brother to another brother, and I see—stop, sire, that is a load on my heart!—I see the minister of that king drive away the outlawed prince, and humiliate his master by condemning to poverty another king, his equal. Then I see my prince, who is young, handsome and brave, who has courage in his heart and lightning in his eye—I see him tremble before a priest, who laughs at him behind the curtain of his alcove, where he digests all the gold of France, which he afterwards stuffs into secret coffers. Yes—I understand your looks, sire. I am bold to madness; but what is to be said? I am an old man, and I tell you here, sire, to you, my king, things which I would cram down the throat of any one who should dare to pronounce them before me. You have commanded me to pour out the bottom of my heart before you, sire, and I cast at the feet of your majesty the pent-up indignation of thirty years, as I would pour out all my blood, if your majesty commanded me to do so.'

The king, without speaking a word, wiped the drops of cold and abundant perspiration which trickled from his temples. The moment of silence which followed this vehement outburst, represented for him who had spoken, and for him who had listened, ages of suffering.

'Monsieur,' said the king at length, 'you spoke the word forgetfulness. I have heard nothing but that word; I will reply then, to it alone. Others have perhaps been able to forget, but I have not, and the proof is, that I remember that one day of riot, that one day when the furious people, raging and roaring as the sea, invaded the royal palace; that one day when I feigned sleep in my bed, one man alone, naked sword in hand, concealed behind my curtain, watched over my life, ready to risk his own for me, as he had before risked it twenty times for the lives of my family.* Was not the gentleman, whose name I then demanded, called M. d'Artagnan? say, monsieur.'

'Your majesty has a good memory,' replied the officer, coldly.

'You see, then,' continued the king, 'if I have such

remembrances of my childhood, what an amount I may gather in the age of reason.'

'Your majesty has been richly endowed by God,' said the officer, in the same tone.

'Come, Monsieur d'Artagnan,' continued Louis, with feverish agitation, 'ought you not to be as patient as I am? Ought you not to do as I do? Come!'

'And what do you do, sire?'

'I wait.'

'Your majesty may do so, because you are young; but I, sire, have not time to wait; old age is at my door, and death is behind it,* looking into the very depths of my house. Your majesty is beginning life, its future is full of hope and fortune; but I sire, I am on the other side of the horizon, and we are so far from each other, that I should never have time to wait till your majesty came up to me.'

Louis made another turn in his apartment, still wiping the moisture from his brow, in a manner that would have terrified his physicians, if his physicians had witnessed the state his majesty was in.

'Very well, monsieur,' said Louis XIV, in a sharp voice; 'you are desirous of having your discharge, and you shall have it. You offer me your resignation of the rank of lieutenant of the musketeers?'

'I deposit it humbly at your majesty's feet, sire.'

'That is sufficient. I will order your pension.'

'I shall have a thousand obligations to your majesty.'

'Monsieur,' said the king, with a violent effort, 'I think you are losing a good master.'

'And I am sure of it, sire.'

'Shall you ever find such another?'

'Oh, sire! I know that your majesty is alone in the world; therefore will I never again take service with any king upon earth, and will never again have other master than myself.'

'You say so?'

'I swear so, your majesty.'

'I shall remember that word, monsieur.'

D'Artagnan bowed.

'And you know I have a good memory,' said the king.

'Yes, sire; and yet I should desire that that memory should fail your majesty in this instance, in order that you might forget all the miseries I have been forced to spread before your eyes. Your majesty is so much above the poor and the mean, that I hope——'

'My majesty, monsieur, will act like the sun, which looks upon all, great and small, rich and poor, giving lustre to some, warmth to others, and life to all. Adieu, Monsieur d'Artagnan—adieu: you are free.'

And the king, with a hoarse sob, which was lost in his throat, passed quickly into the next room. D'Artagnan took up his hat from the table upon which he had thrown it, and left.

XV

THE PROSCRIBED

D'ARTAGNAN had not reached the bottom of the staircase, when the king called his gentleman. 'I have a commission to give you, monsieur,' said he.

'I am at your majesty's commands.'

'Wait, then.' And the young king began to write the following letter, which cost him more than one sigh, although, at the same time, something like a feeling of triumph glittered in his eyes:

MY LORD CARDINAL—Thanks to your good counsels, and, above all, thanks to your firmness, I have succeeded in overcoming a weakness unworthy of a king. You have so ably arranged my destiny that gratitude stopped my hand at the moment when I was about to destroy your work. I felt I was wrong to wish to make my life turn from the course you had marked out for it. Certainly it would have been a misfortune to France and my family if a misunderstanding had taken place between me and my minister. This, however, would certainly have happened if I had made your niece my wife. I am perfectly aware of this, and will henceforth oppose nothing to the accomplishment of my destiny. I am prepared, then, to wed the infanta, Maria Theresa. You may at once open the conference. Your affectionate

LOUIS.

The king, after re-perusing the letter, sealed it himself. 'This letter for my lord cardinal,' said he.

The gentleman took it. At Mazarin's door he found Bernouin waiting with anxiety.

'Well?' asked the minister's *valet de chambre.*

'Monsieur,' said the gentleman, 'here is a letter for his eminence.'

'A letter! Ah! we expected one after the little journey of the morning.'

'Oh! you know then that his majesty——'

'As first minister, it belongs to the duties of our charge to know everything. And his majesty prays and implores, I presume.'

'I don't know, but he sighed frequently whilst he was writing.'

'Yes, yes, yes; we understand all that; people sigh sometimes from happiness as well as from grief, monsieur.'

'And yet the king did not look very happy when he returned, monsieur.'

'You did not see clearly. Besides, you only saw his majesty on his return, for he was only accompanied by the lieutenant of the guards. But I had his eminence's telescope; I looked through it when he was tired, and I am sure they both wept.'

'Well! was it for happiness they wept?'

'No, but for love, and they vowed to each other a thousand tendernesses, which the king asks no better than to keep. Now this letter is a beginning of the execution.'

'And what does his eminence think of this love, which is, by the by, no secret to anybody?'

Bernouin took the gentleman by the arm, and whilst ascending the staircase, 'In confidence,' said he, in a low voice, 'his eminence looks for success in the affair. I know very well we shall have war with Spain; but, bah! war will please the nobles. My lord cardinal, besides, can endow his niece royally, nay, more than royally. There will be money, festivities, and fireworks—everybody will be delighted.'

'Well, for my part,' replied the gentleman, shaking his head, 'it appears to me that this letter is very light to contain all that.'

'My friend,' replied Bernouin, 'I am certain of what I tell you. M. d'Artagnan related all that passed to me.'

'Ay, ay! and what did he tell you? Let us hear.'

'I accosted him by asking him, on the part of the cardinal, if there were any news, without discovering my designs, observe, for M. d'Artagnan is a cunning hand. "My dear Monsieur Bernouin," he replied, "the king is madly in love with Mademoiselle de Mancini, that is all I have to tell you." And then I asked him: "Do you think, to such a degree that it will urge him to act contrary to the designs of his eminence?" "Ah! don't ask me," said he; "I think the king capable of anything; he has a will of iron, and what he wills he wills in earnest. If he takes it into his head to marry Mademoiselle de Mancini, he will marry her, depend upon it." And thereupon he left me and went straight to the stables, took a horse, saddled it himself, jumped upon its back, and set off as if the devil were at his heels.'

'So that you believe, then——'

'I believe that monsieur the lieutenant of the guards knew more than he was willing to say.'

'In your opinion, then, M. d'Artagnan——'

'Is gone, according to all probability, after the exiles,* to carry out all that can facilitate the success of the king's love.'

Chatting thus, the two confidants arrived at the door of his eminence's apartment. His eminence's gout had left him; he was walking about his chamber in a state of great anxiety, listening at doors and looking out of windows. Bernouin entered, followed by the gentleman, who had orders from the king to place the letter in the hands of the cardinal himself. Mazarin took the letter, but before opening it, he got up a ready smile, a smile of circumstance, able to throw a veil over emotions of whatever sort they might be. So prepared, whatever was the impression received from the letter, no reflection of that impression was allowed to transpire upon his countenance.

'Well,' said he, when he had read and re-read the letter, 'very well, monsieur. Inform the king that I thank him for his obedience to the wishes of the queen-mother, and that I will do everything for the accomplishment of his will.'

The gentleman left the room. The door had scarcely closed before the cardinal, who had no mask for Bernouin, took off that which had so recently covered his face, and with a most dismal expression, 'Call M. de Brienne,' said he. Five minutes afterward the secretary entered.

'Monsieur,' said Mazarin, 'I have just rendered a great service to the monarchy, the greatest I have ever rendered it. You will carry this letter, which proves it, to her majesty the queen-mother, and when she shall have returned it to you, you will lodge it in portfolio B, which is filled with documents and papers relative to my ministry.'

Brienne went as desired, and, as the letter was unsealed, did not fail to read it on his way. There is likewise no doubt that Bernouin, who was on good terms with everybody, approached so near to the secretary as to be able to read the letter over his shoulder; so that the news spread with such speed through the castle, that Mazarin might have feared it would reach the ears of the queen-mother before M. de Brienne could convey Louis XIV's letter to her. A moment after, orders were given for departure, and M. de Condé having been to pay his respects to the king on his pretended rising, inscribed the city of Poitiers upon his tablets, as the place of sojourn and rest for their majesties.

Thus in a few instants was unravelled an intrigue which had covertly occupied all the diplomacies of Europe. It had nothing, however, very clear as a result, but to make a poor lieutenant of musketeers lose his commission and his fortune. It is true, that in exchange he gained his liberty. We shall soon know how M. d'Artagnan profited by this. For the moment, if the reader will permit us, we shall return to the hostelry of the Medici, of which one of the windows opened at the very moment the orders were given for the departure of the king.

The window that opened was that of one of the rooms of Charles II. The unfortunate prince had passed the night in bitter reflections, his head resting on his hands, and his elbows on the table, whilst Parry, infirm and old, wearied in body and in mind, had fallen asleep in a corner. A singular fortune was that of this faithful servant, who saw beginning for the second generation the fearful series of misfortunes which had weighed so heavily on the first. When Charles II had well thought over the fresh defeat he had experienced, when he perfectly comprehended the complete isolation into which he had just fallen, on seeing his fresh hope left behind him, he was seized as with a vertigo, and sank back in the large armchair in which he was seated. Then God took pity on the unhappy prince, and to console him sent sleep, the innocent brother of death. He did not wake till half-past six, that is to say, till the sun shone brightly into his chamber, and Parry, motionless with fear of waking him, was observing with profound grief the eyes of the young man already red with wakefulness, and his cheeks pale with suffering and privations.

At length the noise of some heavy carts descending towards the Loire awakened Charles. He arose, looked around him like a man who has forgotten everything, perceived Parry, shook him by the hand, and commanded him to settle the reckoning with Monsieur Cropole. Monsieur Cropole, being called upon to settle his account with Parry, acquitted himself, it must be allowed, like an honest man; he only made his customary remark, that the two travellers had eaten nothing, which had the double disadvantage of being humiliating for his kitchen, and of forcing him to ask payment for a meal not consumed, but not the less lost. Parry had nothing to say to the contrary, and paid.

'I hope,' said the king, 'it has not been the same with the horses. I don't see that they have eaten at your expense, and it would be a misfortune for travellers like us, who have a long journey to make, to have our horses fail us.'

But Cropole, at this doubt, assumed his majestic air, and replied that the stables of the Medici were not less hospitable than its refectory.

The king mounted his horse; his old servant did the same, and both set out towards Paris, without meeting a single person on their road, in the streets or the outskirts of the city. For the prince the blow was the more severe, as it was a fresh exile. The unfortunate cling to the smallest hopes, as the happy do to the greatest good; and when they are obliged to quit the place where that hope has soothed their hearts, they experience the mortal regret which the banished man feels when he places his foot upon the vessel which is to bear him into exile. It appears that the heart already wounded so many times suffers from the least scratch; it appears that it considers as a good the momentary absence of evil, which is nothing but the absence of pain; and that God, into the most terrible misfortunes, has thrown hope as the drop of water which the rich sinner in hell entreated of Lazarus.*

For one instant even the hope of Charles II had been more than a passing joy—that was when he found himself so kindly welcomed by his brother king; then it had taken a form that had become a reality; then, all at once, the refusal of Mazarin had reduced the fictitious reality to the state of a dream. This promise of Louis XIV, so soon retracted, had been nothing but a mockery; a mockery like his crown—like his sceptre—like his friends—like all that had surrounded his royal childhood, and which had abandoned his proscribed youth. Mockery! everything was a mockery for Charles II except the cold, black repose promised by death.

Such were the ideas of the unfortunate prince while sitting listlessly upon his horse, to which he abandoned the reins: he rode slowly along beneath the warm May sun, in which the sombre misanthropy of the exile perceived a last insult to his grief.

XVI

'REMEMBER!'

A HORSEMAN going rapidly along the road leading towards Blois, which he had left nearly half an hour before, passed the two travellers, and, though apparently in haste, raised his hat as he passed them. The king scarcely observed this young man, who was about twenty-five years of age, and who turning round several times, made friendly signals to a man standing before the gate of a handsome white-and-red house; that is to say, built of brick and stone, with a slated roof, situated on the left hand of the road the prince was travelling.

This man, old, tall, and thin, with white hair,—we speak of the one standing by the gate;—this man replied to the farewell signals of the young one by signs of parting as tender as could have been made by a father. The young man disappeared at the first turn of the road, bordered by fine trees, and the old man was preparing to return to the house, when the two travellers, arriving in front of the gate, attracted his attention.

The king, we have said, was riding with his head cast down, his arms inert, leaving his horse to go what pace he liked, whilst Parry behind him, the better to imbibe the genial influence of the sun, had taken off his hat, and was looking about right and left. His eyes encountered those of the old man leaning against the gate; the latter, as if struck by some strange spectacle, uttered an exclamation, and made one step towards the two travellers. From Parry his eyes immediately turned towards the king, upon whom they rested for an instant. This examination, however rapid, was instantly reflected in a visible manner upon the features of the tall old man. For scarcely had he recognized the younger of the travellers—and we say recognized, for nothing but a perfect recognition could have explained such an act—scarcely, we say, had he recognized the younger of the two travellers, than he clapped his hands together, with respectful surprise, and, raising his hat from his head, bowed so profoundly that it might have been said he was kneeling. This demonstration, however absent, or rather, however absorbed was the king in his reflections, attracted his attention instantly; and checking his horse, and turning towards Parry, he exclaimed, 'Good God, Parry, who is that man who salutes me in such a marked manner? can he know me, think you?'

Parry, much agitated and very pale, had already turned his horse towards the gate. 'Ah, sire!' said he, stopping suddenly at five or six paces' distance from the still bending old man: 'sire, I am seized with astonishment, for I think I recognize that brave man. Yes, it must be he! Will your majesty permit me to speak to him?'

'Certainly.'

'Can it be you, Monsieur Grimaud?' asked Parry.

'Yes, it is I,' replied the tall old man, drawing himself up, but without losing his respectful demeanour.

'Sire,' then said Parry, 'I was not deceived. This good man is the servant of the Count de la Fère, and the Count de la Fère, if you remember, is the worthy gentleman of whom I have so often spoken to your majesty that the his memory must remain, not only in your mind, but in your heart.'

'He who assisted my father at his last moments?'* asked Charles, evidently affected at the remembrance.

'The same, sire.'

'Alas!' said Charles; and then addressing Grimaud, whose penetrating and intelligent eyes seemed to search and divine his thoughts, 'My friend,' said he, 'does your master, Monsieur le Comte de la Fère, live in this neighbourhood?'

'There,' replied Grimaud, pointing with his outstretched arm to the white-and-red house behind the gate.

'And is Monsieur le Comte de la Fère at home at present?'

'At the back, under the chestnut-trees.'

'Parry,' said the king, 'I will not miss this opportunity, so precious for me, to thank the gentleman to whom our house is indebted for such a noble example of devotedness and generosity. Hold my horse, my friend, if you please.' And, throwing the bridle to Grimaud, the king entered the abode of Athos, quite alone, as one equal enters the dwelling of another. Charles had been informed by the concise explanation of Grimaud, 'At the back, under the chestnut-trees'; he left, therefore, the house on the left, and went straight down the path indicated. The thing was easy; the tops of those noble trees, already covered with leaves and flowers, rose above all the rest.

On arriving under the lozenges, by turns luminous and dark, which dappled the ground of this path according as the trees were more or less in leaf, the young prince saw a gentleman walking with his arms behind him, apparently plunged in a deep meditation. Without doubt he had often had this gentleman described to him, for, without hesitating, Charles II walked straight up to him. At the sound of his footsteps, the Comte de la Fère raised his head, and seeing an unknown man of noble and elegant bearing coming towards him, he raised his hat and waited. At some paces from him, Charles II likewise took off his hat. Then, as if in reply to the count's mute interrogation,

'Monsieur le Comte,' said he, 'I come to discharge a duty towards you. I have, for a long time, had the expression of a profound gratitude to bring you. I am Charles II, son of Charles Stuart, who reigned in England, and died on the scaffold.'

On hearing this illustrious name, Athos felt a kind of shudder creep through his veins, but at the sight of the young prince standing uncovered before him, and stretching out his hand towards him, two tears, for an instant, dimmed his brilliant eyes. He bent respectfully, but the prince took him by the hand.

'See how unfortunate I am, my lord count; it is only due to chance that I have met with you. Alas! I ought to have people around me whom I love and honour, whereas I am reduced to preserve their services in my heart, and their names in my memory: so that if your servant had not recognized mine, I should have passed by your door as by that of a stranger.'

'It is but too true,' said Athos, replying with his voice to the first part of the king's speech, and with a bow to the second; 'it is but too true, indeed, that your majesty has seen many evil days.'

'And the worst, alas!' replied Charles, 'are perhaps still to come.'

'Sire, let us hope.'

'Count', continued Charles, shaking his head, 'I entertained hope till last night, and that of a good Christian, I swear.'

Athos looked at the king as if to interrogate him.

'Oh, the history is soon related,' said Charles. 'Proscribed, despoiled, disdained, I resolved in spite of all my repugnance, to tempt fortune one last time. Is it not written above, that, for our family, all good fortune and all bad fortune shall eternally come from France? You know something of that, monsieur—you, who are one of the Frenchmen whom my unfortunate father found at the foot of his scaffold, on the day of his death, after having found them at his right hand on the day of battle.'

'Sire,' said Athos modestly, 'I was not alone. My companions and I did, under the circumstances, our duty as gentlemen, and that was all. Your majesty was about to do me the honour to relate——'

'That is true. I had the protection—pardon my hesitation, count, but, for a Stuart, you, who understand everything, you will comprehend that the word is hard to pronounce—I had, I say, the protection of my cousin the stadtholder of Holland;* but without the intervention, or at least without the authorization of France, the stadtholder would not take the initiative. I came, then, to ask this authorization of the king of France, who has refused me.'

'The king has refused you, sire!'

'Oh, not he; all justice must be rendered to my younger brother Louis; but Monsieur de Mazarin——'

Athos bit his lips.

'You perhaps think I should have expected this refusal?' said the king who had noticed the movement.

'That was, in truth, my thought, sire,' replied Athos, respectfully; 'I know that Italian of old.'

'Then I determined to come to the test, and know at once the last word of my destiny. I told my brother Louis, that, not to compromise either France or Holland, I would tempt fortune myself in person, as I had already done, with two hundred gentlemen, if he would give them to me; and a million, if he would lend it me.'

'Well, sire?'

'Well, monsieur, I am suffering at this moment something strange, and that is, the satisfaction of despair. There is in certain souls—and I have just discovered that mine is of the number—a real satisfaction in the assurance that all is lost, and the time is come to yield.'

'Oh, I hope,' said Athos, 'that your majesty is not come to that extremity.'

'To say so, my lord count, to endeavour to revive hope in my heart, you must have ill understood what I have just told you. I came to Blois to ask of my brother Louis the alms of a million, with which I had the hopes of re-establishing my affairs; and my brother Louis has refused me. You see, then, plainly that all is lost.'

'Will your majesty permit me to express a contrary opinion?'

'How is that, count? Do you think my heart of so low an order that I do not know how to face my position?'

'Sire, I have always seen that it was in desperate positions that suddenly the great turns of fortune have taken place.'

'Thank you, count; it is some comfort to meet with a heart like yours; that is to say, sufficiently trustful in God and in monarchy, never to despair of a royal fortune, however low it may be fallen. Unfortunately, my dear count, your words are like those remedies they call "sovereign," and which though able to cure curable wounds or diseases, fail against death. Thank you for your perseverance in consoling me, count, thanks for your devoted remembrance, but I know in what I must trust—nothing will save me now. And see, my friend, I was so convinced of it, that I was taking the route to exile,* with my old Parry; I was returning to devour my poignant griefs in the little hermitage offered me by Holland. There, believe me, count, all will soon be over, and death will come quickly; it is called so often by this body, eaten up by its soul, and by this soul, which aspires to heaven.'

'Your majesty has a mother, a sister, and brothers; your majesty is the head of the family, and ought, therefore, to ask a long life of God, instead of imploring him for a prompt death. Your majesty is an exile, a fugitive, but you have right on our side; you ought to aspire to combats, dangers, business, and not to rest in heavens.'

'Count,' said Charles II, with a smile of indescribable sadness, 'have you ever heard of a king who re-conquered his kingdom with one servant of the age of Parry, and with three hundred crowns which that servant carried in his purse?'

'No, sire; but I have heard—and that more than once—that a dethroned king has recovered his kingdom with a firm will, perseverance, some friends, and a million skilfully employed.'

'But you cannot have understood me. The million I asked of my brother Louis was refused me.'

'Sire,' said Athos, 'will your majesty grant me a few minutes, and listen attentively to what remains for me to say to you?'

Charles II looked earnestly at Athos. 'Willingly, monsieur,' said he.

'Then I will show your majesty the way,' resumed the count directing his steps towards the house. He then conducted the king to his study, and begged him to be seated. 'Sire,' said he, 'your majesty just now told me that, in the present state of England, a million would suffice for the recovery of your kingdom.'

'To attempt it at least, monsieur; and to die as a king if I should not succeed.'

'Well, then, sire, let your majesty, according to the promise you have made me, have the goodness to listen to what I have to say.' Charles made an affirmative sign with his head. Athos walked straight up to the door, the bolts of which he drew, after looking to see if anybody was near, and then returned. 'Sire,' said he, 'your majesty has kindly remembered that I lent assistance to the very noble and very unfortunate Charles I, when his executioners conducted him from St. James's to Whitehall.'

'Yes, certainly I do remember it, and always shall remember it.'

'Sire, it is a dismal history to be heard by a son who no doubt has had it related to him many times; and yet I ought to repeat it to your majesty without omitting one detail.'

'Speak on, monsieur.'

'When the king your father ascended the scaffold,* or rather when he passed from his chamber to the scaffold, on a level with his window, everything was prepared for his escape. The executioner was got out of the way; a hole contrived under the floor of his apartment; I myself was beneath the funeral vault, which I heard all at once creak beneath his feet.'

'Parry has related to me all these terrible details, monsieur.'

Athos bowed, and resumed. 'But here is something he has not related to you, sire, for what follows passed between God, your father, and myself; and never has the revelation of it been made even to my dearest friends. "Go a little further off," said the royal prisoner to the executioner; "it is but for an instant, and I know that I belong to you; but remember not to strike till I give the signal. I wish to offer up my prayers in freedom." '

'Pardon me,' said Charles II, turning very pale, 'but you, count, who know so many details of this melancholy event—details which, as you said just now, have never been revealed to any one—do you know the name of that infernal executioner, of that base wretch who concealed his face that he might assassinate a king with impunity?'

Athos became slightly pale. 'His name?'* said he: 'yes, I know it, but cannot tell it.'

'And what is become of him, for nobody in England knows his destiny?'

'He is dead.'

'But he did not die in his bed; he did not die a calm and peaceful death; he did not die the death of the good?'

'He died a violent death, in a terrible night, rendered so by the passions of man and a tempest from God. His body, pierced by a dagger, sank to the depths of the ocean. God pardon his murderer!'

'Proceed, then,' said Charles II, seeing that the count was unwilling to say more.

'The king of England, after having, as I have said, spoken thus to the masked executioner, added, "Observe, you will not strike till I shall stretch out my arms, saying—REMEMBER!"'

'I was aware,' said Charles, in an agitated voice, 'that that was the last word pronounced by my unfortunate father. But why and for whom?'

'For the French gentleman placed beneath his scaffold.'

'For you, then, monsieur?'

'Yes, sire; and every one of the words which he spoke to me, through the planks of the scaffold covered with a black cloth, still sounds in my ears. The king knelt down on one knee: "Comte de la Fère," said he, "are you there?" "Yes, sire," replied I. Then the king stooped towards the boards.'

Charles II, also, palpitating with interest, burning with grief, stooped towards Athos, to catch, one by one, every word that escaped from him. His head touched that of the count.

'Then,' continued Athos, 'the king stooped. "Comte de la Fère," said he, "I could not be saved by you: it was not to be. Now, even though I commit a sacrilege, I must speak to you. Yes, I have spoken to men—yes, I have spoken to God, and I speak to you the last. To sustain a cause which I thought sacred, I have lost the throne of my fathers and the heritage of my children."'

Charles II concealed his face in his hands, and a bitter tear glided between his white and slender fingers.

'"I have still a million in gold," continued the king. "I buried it in the vaults of the castle of Newcastle,* a moment before I left that city."' Charles raised his head with an expression of such painful joy that it would have drawn tears from any one acquainted with his misfortunes.

'A million!' murmured he, 'Oh, count!'

'"You alone know that this money exists: employ it when you think it can be of the greatest service to my eldest son. And now, Comte de la Fère, bid me adieu!"'

'"Adieu, adieu, sire!" cried I.'

Charles arose, and went and leant his burning brow against the window.

'It was then,' continued Athos, 'that the king pronounced the word "REMEMBER!" addressed to me. You see, sire, that I have remembered.'

The king could not resist or conceal his emotion. Athos beheld the movement of his shoulders, which heaved convulsively; he heard the sobs which burst from his overcharged breast. He was silent himself, suffocated by the flood of bitter memories he had just poured upon that royal head. Charles II, with a violent effort, left the window, devoured his tears, and came and sat by Athos. 'Sire,' said the latter, 'I thought till today that the time had not yet arrived for the employment of that last resource; but, with my eyes fixed upon England, I felt it was approaching. To-morrow I meant to go and inquire in what part of the world your majesty was, and then I purposed going to you. You come to me, sire; that is an indication that God is with us.'

'My lord,' said Charles, in a voice choked by emotion, 'you are, for me, what an angel sent from heaven would be,—you are a preserver, sent to me from the tomb of my father himself; but, believe me, for ten years' civil war has passed over my country, striking down men, tearing up the soil, it is no more probable that gold should remain in the entrails of the earth, than love in the hearts of my subjects.'

'Sire, the spot in which his majesty buried the million is well known to me, and no one, I am sure, has been able to discover it. Besides, is the castle of Newcastle quite destroyed? Have they demolished it stone by stone, and uprooted the soil to the last tree?'

'No, it is still standing: but at this moment General Monk occupies it, and is encamped there.* The only spot from which I could look for succour, where I possess a single resource, you see, is invaded by my enemies.'

'General Monk, sire, cannot have discovered the treasure which I speak of.'

'Yes, but can I go and deliver myself up to Monk, in order to recover this treasure? Ah! count, you see plainly I must yield to destiny, since it strikes me to the earth every time I rise. What can I do with Parry as my only servant, with Parry, whom Monk has already driven from his presence? No, no, no, count, we must yield to this last blow.'

'But what your majesty cannot do, and what Parry can no more attempt, do you not believe that I could succeed in accomplishing?'

'You—you, count—you would go?'

'If it please your majesty,' said Athos, bowing to the king, 'yes, I will go, sire.'

'What! you so happy here, count?'

'I am never happy when I have a duty left to accomplish, and it is an imperative duty which the king your father left me to watch over your fortunes, and make a royal use of his money. So, if your majesty honours me with a sign I will go with you.'

'Ah, monsieur!' said the king, forgetting all royal etiquette and throwing his arms round the neck of Athos, 'you prove to me that there is a God in heaven, and that this God sometimes sends messengers to the unfortunate who groan on the earth.'

Athos, exceedingly moved by this burst of feeling of the young man, thanked him with profound respect, and approached the window. 'Grimaud!' cried he, 'bring out my horses.'

'What, now—immediately!' said the king. 'Ah, monsieur, you are indeed a wonderful man!'

'Sire,' said Athos, 'I know nothing more pressing than your majesty's service. Besides,' added he, smiling, 'it is a habit contracted long since, in the service of the queen your aunt,* and of the king your father. How is it possible for me to lose it at the moment your majesty's service calls for it?'

'What a man!' murmured the king.

Then, after a moment's reflection, 'But no, count, I cannot expose you to such privations. I have no means of rewarding such services.'

'Bah!' said Athos, laughing. 'Your majesty is joking; have you not a million? Ah! why am I not possessed of half such a sum! I would already have raised a regiment. But, thank God! I have still a few rolls of gold and some family diamonds left. Your majesty will, I hope, deign to share with a devoted servant.'

'With a friend—yes, count, but on condition that, in his turn, that friend will share with me hereafter!'

'Sire!' said Athos, opening a casket, from which he drew both gold and jewels, 'you see, sire, we are too rich. Fortunately, there are four of us, in the event of our meeting with thieves.'

Joy made the blood rush to the pale cheeks of Charles II, as he saw Athos's two horses, led by Grimaud, who was already booted for the journey, advance towards the porch.

'Blaisois, this letter for the Vicomte de Bragelonne. For everybody else I am gone to Paris. I confide the house to you, Blaisois.' Blaisois bowed, shook hands with Grimaud, and shut the gate.

XVII

IN WHICH ARAMIS IS SOUGHT, AND ONLY BAZIN IS FOUND

TWO hours had scarcely elapsed since the departure of the master of the house, who, in Blaisois's sight, had taken the road to Paris, when a horseman, mounted on a sturdy piebald, stopped before the gate, and with a sonorous 'halloo!' called the stable-boys, who, with the gardeners, had formed a circle round Blaisois, the historian-in-ordinary to the household of the château. This 'halloo', doubtless well known to Master Blaisois, made him turn his head and exclaim—'Monsieur d'Artagnan! look lively, men, run and open the gate.'

A swarm of eight brisk lads flew to the gate, which was opened as if it had been made of feathers; and every one loaded him with attentions, for they knew the welcome this friend was accustomed to receive from their master; and for such remarks the eye of the valet may always be depended upon.

'Ah!' said M. d'Artagnan, with an agreeable smile balancing himself upon his stirrup to jump to the ground 'where is the dear count?'

'Ah! how unfortunate you are, monsieur!' said Blaisois: 'and how unfortunate will monsieur le comte, our master, think himself when he hears of your coming! As ill luck will have it, monsieur le comte left home two hours ago.'

D'Artagnan did not trouble himself about such trifles. 'Well said!' he smiled. 'You always speak the best French in the world;

you shall give me a lesson in grammar and correct language, whilst I wait the return of your master.'

'That is impossible, monsieur,' said Blaisois; 'you would have to wait too long.'

'Will he not come back to-day, then?'

'No, nor to-morrow, nor the day after to-morrow. Monsieur le comte has gone on a journey.'

'A journey!' said D'Artagnan, surprised; 'is this some yarn you are spinning me, Master Blaisois?'

'Monsieur, it is no more than the truth. Monsieur has done me the honour to give me the house in charge; and he added with his voice so full of authority and kindness—that is all one to me: "You will say I have gone to Paris." '

'Well!' cried D'Artagnan, 'since he is gone towards Paris, that is all I wanted to know! you should have told me so at first, booby! He is then two hours in advance?'

'Yes, monsieur.'

'I shall soon overtake him. Is he alone?'

'No, monsieur.'

'Who is with him, then?'

'A gentleman whom I don't know, an old man, and M. Grimaud.'

'Such a party cannot travel as fast as I can—I will start immediately.'

'Will monsieur listen to me an instant?' said Blaisois, laying his hand gently on the reins of the horse.

'Yes, if you don't favour me with fine speeches, and make haste.'

'Well, then, monsieur, that word Paris appears to me to be only an excuse.'

'Oh, oh!' said D'Artagnan, seriously, 'an excuse, eh?'

'Yes, monsieur: and monsieur le comte is not going to Paris I will swear.'

'What makes you think so?'

'This—M. Grimaud always knows where our master is going; and he had promised me that the first time he went to Paris, he would take a little money for me to my wife.'

'What, have you a wife, then?'

'I had one—she was from these parts; but monsieur thought

her a noisy scold, and I sent her to Paris: it is sometimes incon-venient, but very agreeable at others.'

'I understand; but go on. You do not believe the count has gone to Paris?'

'No, monsieur; for then M. Grimaud would have broken his word; he would have perjured himself, and that is impossible.'

'That is impossible,' repeated D'Artagnan, thoughtfully, because he was quite convinced. 'Well, my brave Blaisois, many thanks to you.'

Blaisois bowed.

'Come, you know I am not curious—I have serious business with your master. Could you not, by a little bit of a word—you, who speak so well—give me to understand—one syllable only—I will guess the rest.'

'Upon my word, monsieur, I cannot. I am quite ignorant of where monsieur le comte is gone. As to listening at doors, that is contrary to my nature; and besides, it is forbidden here.'

'My dear fellow,' said D'Artagnan, 'this is a very bad begin-ning for me. Never mind; you know when monsieur le comte will return, at least?'

'As little, monsieur, as the place of his destination.'

'Come, Blaisois, come, search.'

'Monsieur doubts my sincerity? Ah, monsieur, that grieves me much.'

'The devil take his gilded tongue!' grumbled D'Artagnan. 'A fool with a careless word would be worth a dozen of him. Adieu!'

'Monsieur, I have the honour to present you my respects.'

'Pedant!' said D'Artagnan to himself, 'the fellow is unbear-able.' He gave another look up to the house, turned his horse's head, and set off like a man who has nothing either annoying or embarrassing in his mind. When he reached the end of the wall, and was out of sight—'Well now, I wonder,' said he, breathing quickly, 'whether Athos was at home. No; all those idlers, stand-ing with their arms crossed, would have been at work if the eye of the master was near. Athos gone a journey?—that is incom-prehensible. Bah! it is all devilish mysterious! And then—no—he is not the man I want. I want one of a cunning, patient mind. My business is at Melun,* in a certain clergy-house I am ac-quainted with. Forty-five leagues—four days and a half! Well, it is fine weather, and I am free. Never mind the distance!'

And he put his horse into a trot, directing his course towards Paris. On the fourth day* he alighted at Melun, as he had intended.

D'Artagnan was never in the habit of asking any one on the road for any common information. For these sorts of details, unless in very serious circumstances, he confided in his perspicacity, which was so seldom at fault, in his experience of thirty years, and in a great habit of reading the physiognomies of houses, as well as those of men. At Melun, D'Artagnan immediately found the presbytery—a charming house, plastered over red brick, with vines climbing along the gutters, and a cross, in carved stone, surmounting the ridge of the roof. From the ground-floor of this house came a noise, or rather a confusion of voices, like the chirping of young birds when the brood is just hatched under the down. One of these voices was spelling the alphabet distinctly. A voice thick, yet pleasant, at the same time scolded the talkers and corrected the faults of the reader. D'Artagnan recognized that voice, and as the window of the ground-floor was open, he leant down from his horse under the branches and red fibres of the vine, and cried, 'Bazin,* my dear Bazin! good-day to you.'

A short fat man, with a flat face, a cranium ornamented with a crown of grey hairs, cut short, in imitation of a tonsure, and covered with an old black velvet cap, arose as soon as he heard D'Artagnan—we ought not to say *arose*, but *bounded up*. In fact, Bazin bounded up, carrying with him his little low chair, which the children tried to take away, with battles more fierce than those of the Greeks endeavouring to recover the body of Patroclus from the hands of the Trojans.* Bazin did more than bound; he let fall both his alphabet and his cane. 'You!' said he; 'you, Monsieur d'Artagnan?'

'Yes, myself! Where is Aramis—no, M. le Chevalier d'Herblay*—no, I am still mistaken—Monsieur le Vicaire-Général?'

'Ah, monsieur,' said Bazin, with dignity, 'monseigneur is at his diocese.'

'What did you say?' said D'Artagnan. Bazin repeated the sentence.

'Ah, ah! but has Aramis a diocese?'

'Yes, monsieur. Why not?'

'Is he a bishop, then?'

'Why, where can you come from,' said Bazin, rather irreverently, 'that you don't know that?'

'My dear Bazin, we pagans, we men of the sword, know very well when a man is made a colonel, or battalion commander, or marshal of France; but if he be made a bishop, archbishop, or pope—devil take me, if the news reaches us before three quarters of the population have had the advantage of it!'

'Hush! hush!' said Bazin, opening his eyes: 'do not spoil these poor children, in whom I am endeavouring to inculcate good habits.' In fact, the children had surrounded D'Artagnan, whose horse, long sword, spurs, and martial air they very much admired. But above all, they admired his strong voice; so that, when he uttered his oath, the whole school cried out, 'The devil take me!' with fearful bursts of laughter, shouts, and bounds which delighted the musketeer, and bewildered the old pedagogue.

'There!' said he, 'hold your tongues, you brats! You have come, M. d'Artagnan, and all my good principles fly out of the window. With you, as usual, comes disorder. Babel is revived. Ah! good Lord! Ah! the wild little wretches!' And the worthy Bazin distributed right and left blows which increased the cries of his scholars by changing the nature of them.

'At least,' said he, 'you will no longer lead any one astray here.'

'Do you think so?' said D'Artagnan, with a smile which made a shudder creep over the shoulders of Bazin.

'He is capable of it,' murmured he.

'Where is your master's diocese?'

'Monseigneur René is bishop of Vannes.'*

'Who had him nominated?'

'Why, the Superintendent of the King's finances, who lives nearby.'

'What! Monsieur Fouquet?'*

'To be sure he did.'

'Is Aramis on good terms with him, then?'

'Monseigneur preached every Sunday at the house of monsieur le surintendant at Vaux; then they hunted together.'

'Ah!'

'And monseigneur composed his homilies—no, I mean his sermons—with monsieur le surintendant.'

'Bah! he preached in verse,* then, this worthy bishop?'

'Monsieur, for the love of heaven, do not jest with sacred things.'

'There, Bazin, there! So then Aramis is at Vannes?'

'At Vannes, in Brittany.'

'You are a deceitful old liar, Bazin; that is not true.'

'See, monsieur, if you please; the apartments of the clergy-house are empty.'

'He is right there,' said D'Artagnan, looking attentively at the house, the aspect of which announced solitude.

'But monseigneur must have written you an account of his promotion.'

'When did it take place?'

'A month back.'

'Oh! then there is no time lost. Aramis cannot yet have wanted me. But how is it, Bazin, you do not follow your master?'

'Monsieur, I cannot; I have duties here.'

'Your alphabet?'

'And my penitents.'

'What, do you confess, then? Are you a priest?'

'As good as. I have such a call.'

'But are you ordained?'

'Oh,' said Bazin, without hesitation, 'now that monseigneur is a bishop, I shall soon have my ordination, or at least my dispensations.' And he rubbed his hands.

'Decidedly,' said D'Artagnan to himself, 'there will be no means of uprooting these people. Get me some supper, Bazin.'

'With pleasure, monsieur.'

'A fowl, some soup, and a bottle of wine.'

'This is Saturday, monsieur—it is a day of abstinence.'

'I have a dispensation,' said D'Artagnan.

Bazin looked at him suspiciously.

'Ah, ah, master hypocrite!' said the musketeer, 'who do you take me for? If you, who are the valet, hope for dispensation to commit a crime, shall not I, the friend of your bishop, have dispensation for eating meat at the call of my stomach? Make yourself agreeable with me, Bazin, or, by heavens! I will complain to the king, and you shall never confess a sinner. Now you know that the nomination of bishops rests with the king—I have the king, I am the stronger.'

Bazin smiled hypocritically. 'Ah, but we have monsieur le surintendant,' said he.

'And you laugh at the king, then?'

Bazin made no reply; his smile was sufficiently eloquent.

'My supper,' said D'Artagnan, 'it is getting towards seven o'clock.'

Bazin turned round and ordered the oldest pupil to inform the cook. In the meantime, D'Artagnan surveyed the clergy-house.

'Phew!' said he, disdainfully, 'monseigneur lodged his grandeur very meanly here.'

'We have the Château de Vaux,' said Bazin.

'Which is perhaps equal to the Louvre?' said D'Artagnan, jeeringly.

'Which is better,' replied Bazin, with the greatest coolness imaginable.

'Ah, ah!' said D'Artagnan.

He would perhaps have prolonged the discussion, and maintained the superiority of the Louvre, but the lieutenant perceived that his horse was still hitched to the bars of a gate.

'The devil!' said he. 'Get my horse looked after; your master the bishop has none like him in his stables.'

Bazin cast a sidelong glance at the horse, and replied, 'Monsieur le surintendant gave him four from his own stables; and each of the four is worth four of yours.'

The blood mounted to the face of D'Artagnan. His hand itched, and his eye glanced over the head of Bazin, to select the place upon which he should discharge his anger. But it passed away; reflection came, and D'Artagnan contented himself with saying—

'Hell's teeth! I have done well to quit the service of the king. Tell me, worthy Master Bazin,' added he, 'how many musketeers does monsieur le surintendant retain in his service?'

'He could have all there are in the kingdom with his money,' replied Bazin, closing his book, and dismissing the boys with some kindly blows with his cane.

'Hell's teeth!' repeated D'Artagnan, once more, as if to annoy the pedagogue. But as supper was now announced, he followed the cook, who introduced him into the refectory, where it awaited him. D'Artagnan placed himself at the table, and began a hearty attack upon his fowl.

'It appears to me,' said D'Artagnan, biting with all his might at the tough fowl they had served up to him, and which they had evidently forgotten to fatten, 'it appears that I have done wrong in not seeking service with this other master. A powerful noble this superintendent it seems! In truth, we poor fellows know nothing at the court, and the rays of the sun prevent our seeing the large stars, which are also suns, at a little greater distance from our earth—that is the fact of it.'

As D'Artagnan delighted, both from pleasure and system, in making people talk about things which interested him, he fenced in his best style with Master Bazin, but it was a waste of time; beyond the tiresome and hyperbolical praises of monsieur le surintendant, Bazin, who, on his side, was on his guard, afforded nothing but platitudes to the curiosity of D'Artagnan, so that our musketeer, in a tolerably bad humour, desired to go to bed as soon as he had supped. D'Artagnan was introduced by Bazin into a bare chamber, in which there was a poor bed; but D'Artagnan was not fastidious in that respect. He had been told that Aramis had taken away the key of his own private apartment, and as he knew Aramis was a very particular man, and had generally many things to conceal in his apartment, he had not been surprised. He, therefore, although it appeared comparatively even harder, attacked the bed as bravely as he had done the fowl; and, as he had as great an inclination to sleep as he had had to eat, he took scarcely longer time to be snoring harmoniously than he had employed in picking the last bones of the bird.

Since he was no longer in the service of any one, D'Artagnan had promised himself to indulge in sleeping as soundly as he had formerly slept lightly; but with whatever good faith D'Artagnan had made himself this promise, and whatever desire he might have to keep it religiously, he was awakened in the middle of the night by a loud noise of carriages, and servants on horseback. A sudden illumination flashed over the walls of his chamber; he jumped out of bed and ran to the window in his shirt.

'Can the king be coming this way?' he thought, rubbing his eyes; 'in truth, such a suite can only be attached to royalty.'

'*Vive monsieur le surintendant!*' cried, or rather vociferated, from a window on the ground-floor, a voice which he recognized as Bazin's, who at the same time waved a handkerchief with one hand, and held a large candle in the other. D'Artagnan then saw something like a brilliant human form leaning out of the principal carriage; at the same time loud bursts of laughter, caused no doubt by the strange figure of Bazin, and issuing from the same carriage, left, as it were, a train of joy upon the passage of the fast-moving retinue.

'I might easily see it was not the king,' said D'Artagnan; 'people don't laugh so heartily when the king passes. Ho, Bazin!' cried he to his neighbour, three quarters of whose body still hung out of the window, to follow the carriage with his eyes as long as he could. 'What is all that about?'

'It is M. Fouquet,' said Bazin, in a patronizing tone.

'And all those people?'

'That is the court of M. Fouquet.'

'Oh, oh!' said D'Artagnan; 'what would M. Mazarin say to that if he heard it?' And he returned to his bed, asking himself how Aramis always contrived to be protected by the most powerful personages in the kingdom.* 'Is it that he has more luck than I, or that I am a greater fool than he? Bah!' That was the concluding word by the aid of which D'Artagnan, having become wise, now terminated every thought and every cadence of his style. Formerly he said, '*Mordioux!*' which was a prick of the spur, but now he had become older, and he murmured that philosophical '*Bah!*' which served as a bridle to all the passions.

XVIII

IN WHICH D'ARTAGNAN SEEKS PORTHOS, AND ONLY FINDS MOUSQUETON

WHEN D'Artagnan was quite sure that the absence of the Vicar-General d'Herblay* was real, and that his friend was not to be found at Melun or in the vicinity, he left Bazin without regret, cast an ill-natured glance at the magnificent Château de Vaux, which was beginning to shine with that splendour which was to be its ruin,* and, compressing his lips like a man full of mistrust and suspicion, he put spurs to his piebald horse, saying, 'Well, well! I have still Pierrefonds* left, and there I shall find the best man and the best filled coffer. And that is all I want, for I have an idea of my own.'

We will spare our readers the prosaic incidents of D'Artagnan's journey, which terminated on the morning of the third day within sight of Pierrefonds. D'Artagnan came by way of Nanteuil-le-Haudouin and Crépy.* At a distance he perceived the Castle of Louis of Orléans,* which, having become part of the crown domain, was looked after by an old *concierge*. This was one of those marvellous medieval manors, with walls twenty feet thick and a hundred high.

D'Artagnan rode slowly past its walls, measured its towers with his eye and descended into the valley. From afar he looked down upon the château of Porthos, situated on the shores of a small lake, and contiguous to a magnificent forest. It was the same place we have already had the honour of describing to our readers;* we shall therefore satisfy ourselves with naming it. The first thing D'Artagnan saw after the fine trees, the May sun gilding the sides of the green hills, the long rows of feather-topped trees which stretched out towards Compiègne, was a sort of large box on wheels, pushed by two servants and pulled by two others. In this box there was an enormous green-and-gold object, which went along the smiling glades of the park, thus pushed and pulled. This object, at a distance, could not be made out, and signified absolutely nothing; nearer, it was a hogshead wrapped in gold-bound green cloth; when close, it was a man, or rather a *poussa*,* the inferior extremity of which spreading over the interior of the box, entirely filled it; when still closer, the man turned out to be Mousqueton*—Mousqueton, with grey hair and a face as red as Punchinello's.

'Zounds!' cried D'Artagnan; 'why, it's my dear Monsieur Mousqueton!'

'Ah!' cried the fat man—'ah! what happiness! what joy! There's M. d'Artagnan. Stop, you rascals!' These last words were addressed to the lackeys who pushed and pulled him. The box stopped, and the four lackeys, with military precision, took off their laced hats and ranged themselves behind it.

'Oh, Monsieur d'Artagnan!' said Mousqueton, 'why can I not embrace your knees? But I have become weak and helpless, as you see.'

'Hell's teeth, my dear Mousqueton, it's age.'

'No, monsieur, it is not age; it is infirmities—troubles.'

'Troubles! you, Mousqueton?' said D'Artagnan, walking round of the box; 'are you out of your mind, my dear friend? Thank God! you are as hearty as a three-hundred-year-old oak.'

'Ah! but my legs, monsieur, my legs!' groaned the faithful servant.

'What's the matter with your legs?'

'Oh, they will no longer bear me!'

'Ah, the ungrateful things! And yet you feed them well, Mousqueton, apparently.'

'Alas, yes! They can reproach me with nothing in that respect,' said Mousqueton, with a sigh; 'I have always done what I could for my poor body; I am not selfish.' And Mousqueton sighed afresh.

'I wonder whether Mousqueton wants to be a baron too, as he seems to?' thought D'Artagnan.

'*Mon Dieu*, monsieur!' said Monsqueton, as if rousing himself from a painful revery; 'how happy monseigneur will be that you have thought of him!'

'Kind Porthos!' cried D'Artagnan, 'I am anxious to embrace him.'

'Oh!' said Mousqueton, much affected, 'I shall certainly write to him.'

'What!' cried D'Artagnan, 'you will write to him?'

'This very day; I shall not delay it an hour.'

'Is he not here, then?'

'No, monsieur.'

'But is he near at hand?—is he far off?'

'Oh, can I tell, monsieur, can I tell?'

'*Mordioux!*' cried the musketeer, stamping with his foot, 'I am unfortunate. Porthos is such a stay-at-home!'

'Monsieur, there is not a more sedentary man than monseigneur, but——'

'But what?'

'When a friend presses you——'

'A friend?'

'Doubtless—the worthy M. d'Herblay.'

'What, has Aramis pressed Porthos?'

'This is how the thing happened, Monsieur d'Artagnan. M. d'Herblay wrote to monseigneur——'

'Indeed!'

'A letter, monsieur, such a pressing letter that it threw us all into a bustle.'

'Tell me all about it, my dear friend,' said D'Artagnan; 'but send these people a little further off first.'

Mousqueton shouted, 'Fall back, you knaves,' with such powerful lungs that the breath, without the words, would have been sufficient to disperse the four lackeys. D'Artagnan seated himself on the shaft of the box and opened his ears. 'Monsieur,' said Mousqueton, 'monseigneur, then, received a letter from M. le Vicaire-Général d'Herblay, eight or nine days ago; it was the day of the rustic pleasures, yes, it must have been Wednesday.'

'What do you mean?' said D'Artagnan. 'The day of rustic pleasures?'

'Yes, monsieur; we have so many pleasures to take in this delightful country, that we were encumbered by them; so much so, that we have been forced to put them on a more orderly footing.'

'How easily do I recognize Porthos's love of order in that! Now, that idea would never have occurred to me; but then I am not encumbered with pleasures.'

'We were, though,' said Mousqueton.

'And how did you regulate the matter, let me know?' said D'Artagnan.

'It is rather long, monsieur.'

'Never mind, we have plenty of time; and you speak so well, my dear Mousqueton, that it is really a pleasure to hear you.'

'It is true,' said Mousqueton, with a sigh of satisfaction, which emanated evidently from the justice which had been done him, 'it is true I have made great progress in the company of monseigneur.'

'I am waiting for the distribution of the pleasures, Mousqueton, and with impatience. I want to know if I have arrived on a lucky day.'

'Oh, Monsieur d'Artagnan,' said Mousqueton in a melancholy tone, 'since monseigneur's departure all the pleasures have gone too!'

'Well, my dear Mousqueton, refresh your memory.'

'With what day shall I begin?'

'Dammit! begin with Sunday; that is the Lord's day.'

'Sunday, monsieur?'

'Yes.'

'Sunday pleasures are religious: monseigneur goes to mass, makes the bread-offering, and has discourses and instructions made to him by his resident almoner. He's rather on the dull side, but we expect a Carmelite* from Paris who will do the duty of our almonry, and who, we are assured, speaks very well, which will keep us awake, whereas our present almoner always sends us to sleep. These are Sunday religious pleasures. On Monday, worldly pleasures.'

'Ah, ah!' said D'Artagnan, 'what do you mean by that? Let us have a glimpse at your worldly pleasures.'

'Monsieur, on Monday we see society; we pay and receive visits, we play on the lute, we dance, we make verses, and burn a little incense in honour of the ladies.'

'Hell's teeth! that is the height of gallantry,' said the musketeer, who was obliged to call to his aid all the strength of his facial muscles to suppress an enormous inclination to laugh.

'Tuesday, scholarly pleasures.'

'Good!' cried D'Artagnan. 'What are they? Detail them, my dear Mousqueton.'

'Monseigneur has bought a sphere or globe, which I shall show you; it fills all the perimeter of the great tower, except a gallery which he has had built over the sphere: there are little strings and brass wires to which the sun and moon are hooked. It all turns; and that is very beautiful. Monseigneur points out to me seas and distant countries. We don't intend to visit them, but it is very interesting.'

'Interesting! yes, that's the word,' repeated D'Artagnan. 'And Wednesday?'

'Rustic pleasures, as I have had the honour to tell you, monsieur le chevalier. We look over monseigneur's sheep and goats; we make the shepherds dance to pipes and reeds, as is written in a book monseigneur has in his library, which is called "Bergeries." The author died about a month ago.'

'Monsieur Racan,* perhaps,' said D'Artagnan.

'Yes, that was his name—Racan. But that is not all: we angle in the little canal, after which we dine, crowned with flowers. That is Wednesday.'

'Zounds!' said D'Artagnan; 'you don't divide your pleasures badly. And Thursday?—what can be left for poor Thursday?'

'It is not too bad, monsieur,' said Mousqueton smiling. 'Thursday, Olympian pleasures. Ah, monsieur, that is superb! We get together all monseigneur's young vassals, and we make them throw the discus, wrestle, and run races. Monseigneur can't run now, no more can I; but monseigneur throws the discus as nobody else can throw it. And when he does deal a punch, his opponent knows it!'

'How so?'

'Yes, monsieur, we were obliged to give up the cestus.* He cracked heads; he broke jaws—beat in ribs. It was charming sport; but nobody was willing to play with him.'

'Then his wrist——'

'Oh, monsieur, firmer than ever. Monseigneur gets a trifle weaker in his legs—he confesses that himself; but his strength has all taken refuge in his arms, so that——'

'So that he can knock down bullocks, as he used formerly?'

'Monsieur, better than that—he beats in walls. Lately, after having supped with one of our farmers—you know how popular and kind monseigneur is—after supper, as a joke, he struck the wall a blow. The wall crumbled away beneath his hand, the roof fell in, and three men and an old woman were crushed.'

'Good God, Mousqueton! And your master?'

'Oh, monseigneur, a little skin was rubbed off his head. We bathed the wounds with some water which the monks gave us. But there was nothing the matter with his hand.'

'Nothing?'

'No, nothing, monsieur.'

'Devil take the Olympic pleasures! They must cost your master too dear; for widows and orphans——'

'They all had pensions, monsieur; a tenth of monseigneur's revenue was spent in that way.'

'Then pass on to Friday,' said D'Artagnan.

'Friday, noble and warlike pleasures. We hunt, we fence, we train falcons and break horses. Then, Saturday is the day for intellectual pleasures: we adorn our minds; we look at monseigneur's pictures and statues; we write even, and trace plans: and then we fire monseigneur's cannon.'

'You draw plans, and fire cannon?'

'Yes, monsieur.'

'Why, my friend,' said D'Artagnan, 'M. du Vallon,* in truth, possesses the most subtle and amiable mind that I know. But there is one kind of pleasure you have forgotten, it appears to me.'

'What is that, monsieur?' asked Mousqueton, with anxiety.

'The material pleasures.'

Mousqueton coloured. 'What do you mean by that, monsieur?' said he, casting down his eyes.

'I mean the table—good wine—evenings occupied in passing the bottle.'

'Ah, monsieur, we don't reckon those pleasures—we practise them every day.'

'My brave Mousqueton,' resumed D'Artagnan, 'pardon me, but I was so absorbed in your charming recital that I have forgotten the principal object of our conversation, which was to learn what M. le Vicaire-Général d'Herblay could have to write to your master about.'

'That is true, monsieur,' said Mousqueton; 'the pleasures have misled us. Well, monsieur, this is how it was.'

'I am all ears, Mousqueton.'

'On Wednesday——'

'The day of the rustic pleasures?'

'Yes—a letter arrived; he received it from my hands. I recognized the writing.'

'Well?'

'Monseigneur read it and cried out, "Quick, my horses! my arms!"'

'Oh, good Lord! then it was for some duel?' said D'Artagnan.

'No, monsieur, there were only these words; "Dear Porthos, set out, if you would wish to arrive before the Equinox.* I expect you."'

'*Mordioux!*' said D'Artagnan, thoughtfully, 'that was pressing apparently.'

'I think so; therefore,' continued Mousqueton, 'monseigneur set out the very same day with his secretary, in order to try and arrive in time?'

'And did he arrive in time.'

'I hope so. Monseigneur, who is hasty, as you know, monsieur, repeated incessantly "Thunder! What can this mean? Who is this Equinox? Never mind, a fellow must be well mounted to arrive before I do"'

'And you think Porthos will have arrived first, do you?' asked D'Artagnan.

'I am sure of it. This Equinox, however rich he may be, has certainly no horses so good as monseigneur's.'

D'Artagnan repressed his inclination to laugh, because the brevity of Aramis's letter gave rise to reflection. He followed Mousqueton, or rather Mousqueton's chariot, to the castle. He sat down to a sumptuous table, of which they did him the honours as to a king. But he could draw nothing from Mousqueton—the faithful servant seemed to shed tears at will, but that was all.

D'Artagnan, after a night passed in an excellent bed, reflected much upon the meaning of Aramis's letter; puzzled himself as to the relation of the Equinox with the affairs of Porthos; and being unable to make anything out unless it concerned some *amour* of the bishop's, for which it was necessary that the days and nights should be equal; D'Artagnan left Pierrefonds as he had left Melun, as he had left the château of the Comte de la Fère. It was not, however, without melancholy, which might in all truth pass for one of the most dismal of D'Artagnan's moods. His head cast down, his eyes fixed, he suffered his legs to hang on each side of his horse, and said to himself, in that vague sort of reverie which ascends sometimes to the sublimest eloquence:

'No more friends! no more future! no more anything! My energies are broken like the bonds of our ancient friendship. Oh, old age is coming, cold and inexorable; it envelops in its funereal crêpe all that was brilliant, all that was embalming in my youth; then it throws that sweet burden on its shoulders and carries it away with the rest into the fathomless gulf of death.'

A shudder crept through the heart of the Gascon, so brave and so strong against all the misfortunes of life; and for some moments, the clouds appeared black to him, the earth slippery and full of pits as that of cemeteries.

'Where am I going?' said he to himself. 'What am I going to do! Alone, quite alone—without family, without friends! Bah!' cried he all at once. And he clapped spurs to his horse, which, having found nothing melancholy in the heavy oats of Pierrefonds, profited by this permission to show his spirits in a gallop which absorbed two leagues. 'To Paris!' said D'Artagnan to himself. And on the morrow he alighted in Paris. He had spent ten days on this journey.

XIX

WHAT D'ARTAGNAN WENT TO PARIS FOR

THE lieutenant dismounted before a shop in the Rue des Lombards,* at the sign of the Golden Pestle. A man of good appearance, wearing a white apron, and stroking his grey moustache with a large hand, uttered a cry of joy on perceiving the piebald horse. 'Monsieur le chevalier,' said he, 'ah, is that you?'

'Good day, Planchet,'* replied D'Artagnan, stooping to enter the shop.

'Quick, somebody,' cried Planchet, 'to look after Monsieur d'Artagnan's horse—somebody to get his room ready—somebody to prepare his supper.'

'Thanks, Planchet. Good-day, my children,' said D'Artagnan to the eager boys.

'Allow me to send off this coffee, this treacle, and these raisins,' said Planchet; 'they are for the store room of monsieur le surintendant.'

'Send them off, send them off!'

'It will take only a moment, then we shall sup.'

'Arrange it that we may sup alone; I want to speak to you.'

Planchet looked at his old master in a significant manner.

'Oh, don't be uneasy, it is nothing unpleasant,' said D'Artagnan.

'So much the better—so much the better!' And Planchet breathed freely again, whilst D'Artagnan seated himself quietly down in the shop, upon a bale of corks, and made a survey of the premises. The shop was well stocked; there was a mingled perfume of ginger, cinnamon, and ground pepper, which made D'Artagnan sneeze. The shop-boy, proud of being in company with so renowned a warrior, a lieutenant of musketeers, who approached the person of the king, began to work with an enthusiasm which was akin to frenzy, and to serve the customers with a disdainful haste that was noticed by several.

Planchet put away his money, and made up his accounts, amidst civilities addressed to his former master. Planchet had with his equals the short speech and the haughty familiarity of the rich shopkeeper who serves everybody and waits for nobody. D'Artagnan observed this habit with a pleasure which we shall analyse presently. He saw night come on by degrees, and at length Planchet conducted him to a chamber on the first floor, where, amidst bales and chests, a table very nicely set out awaited the two guests.

D'Artagnan took advantage of a moment's pause to examine Planchet, whom he had not seen for a year. The shrewd Planchet had acquired a slight protuberance in front, but his countenance was not puffed. His keen eye still played with facility in its deep-sunk orbit; and fat, which levels all the characteristic features of the human face, had not yet touched either his high cheek-bones, the sign of cunning and cupidity, or his pointed chin, the sign of acuteness and perseverance. Planchet reigned with as much majesty in his dining-room as in his shop. He set before his master a frugal, but typically Parisian repast: roast meat, cooked at the baker's, with vegetables, salad, and a dessert which came from the shop itself. D'Artagnan was pleased that the grocer had drawn from his private store a bottle of that Anjou wine which during all his life, had been D'Artagnan's favourite wine.

'Formerly, monsieur,' said Planchet, with a smile full of *bonhomie*, 'it was I who drank your wine; now you do me the honour to drink mine.'

'And, thank God, friend Planchet, I shall drink it for a long time to come, I hope; for at present I am free.'

'Free? You have leave of absence, monsieur?'

'Unlimited.'

'You are leaving the service?' said Planchet, stupefied.

'Yes, I am resting.'

'And the king?' cried Planchet, who could not suppose it possible that the king could do without the services of such a man as D'Artagnan.

'The king will try his fortune elsewhere. But we have supped well, you are disposed to enjoy yourself; you invite me to confide in you. Open your ears, then.'

'They are open.' And Planchet, with a laugh more frank than cunning, opened a bottle of white wine.

'Leave me my reason, at least.'

'Oh, as to you losing your head—you, monsieur!'

'Now my head is my own, and I mean to take better care of it than ever. In the first place, we shall talk business. How fares our money-box?'

'Wonderfully well, monsieur. The twenty thousand livres I had of you are still employed in my trade, in which they bring me nine per cent. I give you seven, so I gain two by you.'

'And you are still satisfied?'

'Delighted. Have you brought me any more?'

'Better than that. But do you need any?'

'Oh! not at all. Every one is willing to trust me now. I am extending my business.'

'That was your intention.'

'I play the banker a little. I buy goods of my needy brethren; I lend money to those who are not ready for their payments.'

'Without usury?'*

'Oh! monsieur, in the course of the last week I have had two meetings* on the boulevards, on account of the word you have just pronounced.'

'What?'

'You shall see: it concerned a loan. The borrower gives me in pledge some raw sugars, on condition that I should sell if repayment were not made within a fixed period. I lend a thousand livres. He does not pay me, and I sell the sugars for thirteen hundred livres. He learns this and claims a hundred crowns. Of course I refused, pretending that I could not sell them for more than nine hundred livres. He accused me of usury. I begged him to repeat that word to me behind the boulevards. He was an old guard, and he came: and I passed your sword through his left thigh.'

'My God, what a pretty sort of banker you make!' said D'Artagnan.

'For above thirteen per cent I fight,' replied Planchet; 'that is my character.'

'Take only twelve,' said D'Artagnan, 'and call the rest premium and brokerage.'

'You are right, monsieur; but to your business.'

'Ah! Planchet, it is very long and very hard to tell.'

'Do tell it, nevertheless.'

D'Artagnan twisted his moustache like a man embarrassed with the confidence he is about to make and mistrustful of his confidant.

'Is it an investment?' asked Planchet.

'Why, yes.'

'At good profit?'

'A capital profit—four hundred per cent, Planchet.'

Planchet gave such a blow with his fist upon the table, that the bottles bounded as if they had been frightened.

'Good heavens! is it possible?'

'I think it will be more,' replied D'Artagnan coolly; 'but I like to lay it at the lowest!'

'The devil!' said Planchet, drawing nearer. 'Why, monsieur, that is magnificent! Can one put much money in it?'

'Twenty thousand livres each, Planchet.'

'Why, that is all you have, monsieur. For how long a time?'

'For a month.'

'And that will give us——'

'Fifty thousand livres each, profit.'

'It is monstrous! It is worth while to fight for such interest as that!'

'In fact, I believe it will be necessary to fight not a little,' said D'Artagnan, with the same tranquillity; 'but this time there are two of us, Planchet, and I shall take all the blows myself.'

'Oh! monsieur, I will not allow that.'

'Planchet, you cannot be concerned in it; you would be obliged to leave your business and your family.'

'The affair is not in Paris, then.'

'No.'

'Abroad?'

'In England.'

'A country that thrives on enterprise, that is true,' said Planchet—'a country that I know well. What sort of an affair, monsieur, without too much curiosity?'

'Planchet, it is a restoration.'

'Of monuments?'

'Yes, of monuments; we shall restore Whitehall.'

'Ah! now that is indeed a large undertaking. And in a month, you think?'

'I shall undertake it.'

'That is your business, monsieur, and when once you are engaged——'

'Yes, it is my business. I know what I am about; nevertheless, I will freely consult with you.'

'You do me great honour; but I know very little about architecture.'

'Planchet, you are wrong; you are an excellent architect, quite as good as I am, for the case in question.'

'Thanks, monsieur. But what of your old friends of the musketeers?'

'I have been, I confess, tempted to speak of the thing to those gentlemen, but they are all absent from their houses. It is vexatious, for I know none more bold or more able.'

'Ah! then it appears there will be an opposition, and the enterprise will be disputed?'

'Oh, yes, Planchet, yes.'

'I burn to know the details, monsieur.'

'Here they are Planchet—close all the doors tight.'

'Yes, monsieur.' And Planchet double-locked them.

'That is well; now draw near.' Planchet obeyed.

'And open the window, because the noise of the passers-by and the carts will deafen all who might hear us.' Planchet opened the window as desired, and the gust of tumult which filled the room with cries, wheels, barkings, and steps deafened D'Artagnan himself, as he had wished. He then swallowed a glass of white wine, and began in these terms: 'Planchet, I have an idea.'

'Ah! monsieur,' replied Planchet, panting with emotion, 'That's just like you!'

XX

OF THE FIRM WHICH WAS FORMED IN THE RUE DES LOMBARDS, AT THE SIGN OF THE GOLDEN PESTLE, TO CARRY OUT M. D'ARTAGNAN'S IDEA

AFTER a moment's silence, in which D'Artagnan appeared to be collecting, not one idea, but all his ideas, 'It cannot be, my dear Planchet,' said he, 'that you have not heard of his majesty Charles I of England?'

'Alas! yes, monsieur, since you left France in order to assist him, and that, in spite of that assistance, he fell, and was near dragging you down in his fall.'

'Exactly so; I see you have a good memory, Planchet.'

'The astonishing thing would be, if I could have lost that memory, however bad it might have been. When one has heard Grimaud, who, you know, is not given to talking, relate how the head of King Charles fell, how you sailed the half of a night in a scuttled vessel, and saw floating on the water that good M. Mordaunt* with a certain gold-hafted dagger buried in his breast, one is not very likely to forget such things.'

'And yet there are people who forget them, Planchet.'

'Yes, such as have not seen them, or have not heard Grimaud relate them.'

'Well, it is all the better that you recollect all that; I shall only have to remind you of one thing, and that is that Charles I had a son.'

'Without contradicting you, monsieur, he had two,' said Planchet; 'for I saw the second one in Paris, M. the Duke of York,* one day, as he was going to the Palais Royal, and I was told that he was not the eldest son of Charles I. As to the eldest, I have the honour of knowing him by name, but not personally.'

'That is exactly the point, Planchet, we must come to: it is to this eldest son, formerly called the Prince of Wales, and who is now styled* Charles II, king of England.'

'A king without a kingdom, monsieur,' replied Planchet sententiously.

'Yes, Planchet, and you may add an unfortunate prince, more unfortunate than the poorest man of the people lost in the worst quarter of Paris.'

Planchet made a gesture full of that sort of compassion which we grant to strangers with whom we think we can never possibly find ourselves in contact. Besides, he did not see in this politico-sentimental conversation any sign of the commercial idea of M. d'Artagnan, and it was in this idea that D'Artagnan, who was, from habit, pretty well acquainted with men and things, had principally interested Planchet.

'I am coming to our business. This young Prince of Wales, a king without a kingdom, as you have so well said, Planchet, has interested me. I, D'Artagnan, have seen him begging assistance of Mazarin, who is a miser, and the aid of Louis, who is a child, and it appeared to me, who am acquainted with such things, that in the intelligent eye of the fallen king, in the nobility of his whole person, a nobility apparent above all his miseries, I could discern the stuff of a man and the heart of a king.'*

Planchet tacitly approved of all this; but it did not at all, in his eyes at least, throw any light upon D'Artagnan's idea. The latter continued: 'This, then, is the reasoning which I made with myself. Listen attentively, Planchet, for we are coming to the conclusion.'

'I am listening.'

'Kings are not so thickly sown upon the earth, that people can find them whenever they want them. Now, this king without a kingdom is, in my opinion, a grain of seed which will blossom in some season or other, provided a skilful, discreet, and vigorous hand sow it duly and truly, selecting soil, sky, and time.'

Planchet still approved by a nod of his head, which showed that he did not perfectly comprehend all that was said.

'"Poor little seed of a king," said I to myself, and really I was saddened, Planchet, which leads me to think I am entering upon a foolish business. And that is why I wished to consult you, my friend.'

Planchet coloured with pleasure and pride.

'"Poor little seed of a king! I will pick you up and cast you into good ground."'

'Good God!' said Planchet, looking earnestly at his old master, as if in doubt as to the state of his reason.

'Well, what is it?' said D'Artagnan; 'what ails you?'

'Me! nothing, monsieur.'

'You said, "Good God!"'

'Did I?'

'I am sure you did. Can you already understand?'

'I confess, M. d'Artagnan, that I am afraid——'

'To understand?'

'Yes.'

'To understand that I wish to replace upon his throne this King Charles II, who has no throne? Is that it?'

Planchet made a prodigious bound in his chair. 'Ah, ah!' said he, in evident terror, 'that is what you call a restoration!'

'Yes, Planchet; is it not the proper term for it?'

'Oh, no doubt, no doubt! But have you reflected seriously?'

'Upon what?'

'Upon what is going on over there.'

'Where?'

'In England.'

'And what is that? Tell me, Planchet.'

'In the first place, monsieur, I ask your pardon for meddling in these things, which have nothing to do with my trade; but since you are putting a proposition to me—for you are putting a proposition, are you not?——'

'A superb one, Planchet.'

'But as it is business you propose to me, I have the right to discuss it.'

'Discuss it, Planchet; out of discussion is born light.'

'Well, then, since I have monsieur's permission, I will tell him that in the first place, there is the parliament.'

'And next?'

'The army.'

'Good! Do you see anything else?'

'Why, then the nation.'

'Is that all?'

'The nation which consented to the overthrow and death of the late king, the father of this one, and which will not be willing to disown its actions.'

'Planchet,' said D'Artagnan, 'you argue like a cheese! The nation—the nation is tired of these gentlemen who give themselves such barbarous names, and who sing songs to it. Singing for singing's sake, my dear Planchet; I have remarked that nations prefer singing merry tunes to the plain chant. Remember the Fronde; what did they sing in those times? Well, those were good times.'

'Good? I was near being hung in those times.'

'Well, but you were not.'

'No.'

'And you laid the foundation of your fortune in the midst of all those songs?'

'That is true.'

'Then you have nothing to say against them.'

'Well, I return, then, to the army and parliament.'

'I say that I borrow twenty thousand livres of M. Planchet, and that I put twenty thousand livres of my own to it; and with these forty thousand livres I raise an army.'

Planchet clasped his hands; he saw that D'Artagnan was in earnest, and, in truth, he believed his master had lost his senses.

'An army!—ah, monsieur,' said he, with his most agreeable smile, for fear of irritating the madman, and rendering him furious, 'an army!—how many?'

'Of forty men,' said D'Artagnan.

'Forty against forty thousand! that is not enough. I know very well that you, M. d'Artagnan, alone, are equal to a thousand men; but where are we to find thirty-nine men equal to you?

Or, if we could find them, who would furnish you with money to pay them?'

'Not bad, Planchet. Ah, the devil! you speak like a courtier.'

'No, monsieur, I speak what I think, and that is exactly why I say that, in the first pitched battle you fight with your forty men, I am very much afraid——'

'Which is why I shall fight no pitched battles, my dear Planchet,' said the Gascon, laughing. 'We have very fine examples in antiquity of skilful retreats and marches, which consisted in avoiding the enemy instead of attacking them. You should know that, Planchet, you who commanded the Parisians the day on which they ought to have fought against the musketeers, and who so well calculated marches and countermarches, that you never left the Palais Royal.'*

Planchet could not help laughing. 'It is plain,' replied he, 'that if your forty men conceal themselves, and are not unskilful, they may hope not to be beaten: but you propose obtaining some result, do you not?'

'No doubt. This then, in my opinion, is the plan to be proceeded upon in order quickly to replace his majesty Charles II on his throne.'

'Good!' said Planchet, increasing his attention; 'let us see your plan. But in the first place it seems to me we are forgetting something.'

'What is that?'

'We have set aside the nation which prefers merry songs to psalms, and the army which we will not fight: but the parliament remains, and that seldom sings.'

'Nor does it fight. How is it, Planchet, that an intelligent man like you should take any heed of a set of brawlers who call themselves Rumps and Barebones?* The parliament does not trouble me at all, Planchet.'

'Since it does not trouble you, monsieur, let us pass on.'

'Yes, and arrive at the result. You remember Cromwell, Planchet?'

'I have heard a great deal of talk about him.'

'He was a rough soldier.'

'And a terrible eater, moreover.'

'What do you mean by that?'

'Why, at one gulp he swallowed all England.'

'Well, Planchet, the evening before the day on which he swallowed England, what if someone had swallowed M. Cromwell?'

'Oh! monsieur, it is one of the axioms of mathematics that the container must be greater than the contained.'

'Very well! That is our affair, Planchet.'

'But M. Cromwell is dead, and his container is now the tomb.'

'My dear Planchet, I see with pleasure that you have not only become a mathematician, but a philosopher.'

'Monsieur, in my grocery business I use newspapers for wrapping, and that instructs me.'

'Bravo! You know then, in that case—for you have not learnt mathematics and philosophy without a little history—that after this Cromwell so great, there came one who was very little.'

'Yes; he was named Richard, and he has done as you have, M. d'Artagnan—he has tendered his resignation.'

'Very well said—very well! After the great man who is dead, after the little one who tendered his resignation, there came a third. This one is named Monk; he is an able general, considering he has never fought a battle; he is a skilful diplomat, considering that he never speaks in public, and that having to say "good-day" to a man, he thinks for twelve hours, and ends by saying "good-night"; which makes people exclaim "a miracle!" seeing that he turns out to be right.'

'That is rather strong,' said Planchet; 'but I know another political man who resembles him very much.'

'M. Mazarin you mean?'

'Himself.'

'You are right, Planchet; only Mazarin does not aspire to the throne of France; and that changes everything. Do you see? Well, this Monk, who has England ready-roasted in his plate, and who is already opening his mouth to swallow it—this Monk, who says to the people of Charles II, and to Charles II himself, "*Nescio vos*"*——'

'I don't understand English,' said Planchet.

'Yes, but I understand it,' said D'Artagnan. '"*Nescio vos*" means "I do not know you." This M. Monk, the most important man in England, when he shall have swallowed it——'

'Well?' asked Planchet.

'Well, my friend, I shall go there, and with my forty men I shall carry him off, pack him up, and bring him into France, where two modes of proceeding present themselves to my dazzled eyes.'

'Oh! and to mine too,' cried Planchet, transported with enthusiasm. 'We will put him in a cage and show him for money.'

'Well, Planchet, that is a third plan, of which I had not thought.'

'Do you think it a good one?'

'Yes, certainly; but I think mine better.'

'Let us see yours, then.'

'In the first place, I shall set a ransom on him.'

'Of how much?'

'Hell's teeth! a fellow like that must be well worth a hundred thousand crowns.'

'Yes, yes!'

'You see, then—in the first place, a ransom of a hundred thousand crowns.'

'Or else——'

'Or else, what is much better, I deliver him up to King Charles, who, having no longer either a general or an army to fear, or a diplomat to trick him, will restore himself, and when once restored, will pay down to me the hundred thousand crowns in question. That is the idea I have formed; what do you say to it, Planchet?'

'Magnificent, monsieur!' cried Planchet trembling with emotion. 'How did you conceive that idea?'

'It came to me one morning on the banks of the Loire, whilst our beloved king, Louis XIV, was pretending to weep upon the hand of Mademoiselle de Mancini.'

'Monsieur, I declare the idea is sublime. But——'

'Ah! is there a but?'

'Permit me! But this is a little like the skin of that fine bear—you know—that they were about to sell, but which it was necessary to take from the back of the living bear.* Now, to take M. Monk, there will be a bit of scuffle, I should think.'

'No doubt; but as I shall raise an army to——'

'Yes, yes—I understand, a surprise attack. Yes, then,

monsieur, you will triumph, for no one equals you in such sorts of encounters.'

'I certainly am lucky in them,' said D'Artagnan, with a proud simplicity. 'You know that if for this affair I had my dear Athos, my brave Porthos, and my cunning Aramis, the business would be settled; but they are all lost, as it appears, and nobody knows where to find them. I will do it, then, alone. Now, do you find the business good, and the investment advantageous?'

'Too much so—too much so.'

'How can that be?'

'Because fine things never reach the expected point.'

'This is infallible, Planchet, and the proof is that I undertake it. It will be for you a tolerably pretty gain, and for me a very pretty piece of business. It will be said, "Such was the old age of M. d'Artagnan," and I shall hold a place in tales and even in history itself, Planchet. I am hungry for honour.'

'Monsieur,' cried Planchet, 'when I think that it is here, in my home, in the midst of my sugar, my prunes, and my cinnamon, that this gigantic project is ripened, my shop seems a palace to me.'

'Beware, beware, Planchet! If the least report of this escapes, there is the Bastille for both of us. Beware, my friend; for this is a plot we are hatching. M. Monk is the ally of M. Mazarin—beware!'

'Monsieur, when a man has had the honour to serve you, he knows nothing of fear; and when he has the advantage of being bound up in business with you, he holds his tongue.'

'Very well; that is more your affair than mine, seeing that in a week I shall be in England.'

'Depart, monsieur, depart—the sooner the better.'

'Is the money then ready?'

'It will be to-morrow; to-morrow you shall receive it from my own hands. Will you have gold or silver?'

'Gold; that is the most convenient. But how are we going to arrange this? Let us see.'

'Oh, good Lord! in the simplest way possible. You shall give me a receipt, that is all.'

'No, no,' said D'Artagnan, warmly; 'we must preserve order in all things.'

'That is likewise my opinion; but with you, M. d'Artagnan——'

'And if I should die yonder—if I should be killed by a musket-ball—if I should burst from drinking beer?'

'Monsieur, I beg you to believe that in that case I should be so much afflicted at your death, that I should not think about the money.'

'Thank you, Planchet; but no matter. We shall, like two lawyers' clerks, draw up together an agreement, a sort of act, which may be called a deed of association.'

'Willingly, monsieur.'

'I know it is difficult to draw such a thing up, but we can try.'

'Let us try, then.' And Planchet went in search of pens, ink, and paper. D'Artagnan took the pen and wrote: 'Between Messire d'Artagnan, ex-lieutenant of the king's musketeers, at present residing in the Rue Tiquetonne,* Hotel de la Chevrette; and the Sieur Planchet, grocer, residing in the Rue des Lombards, at the sign of the Golden Pestle, it has been agreed as follows: A company, with a capital of forty thousand livres, and formed for the purpose of carrying out an idea conceived by M. d'Artagnan, and the said Planchet approving of it in all points, will place twenty thousand livres in the hands of M. d'Artagnan. He will require neither repayment nor interest before the return of M. d'Artagnan from a journey he is about to take into England. On his part, M. d'Artagnan undertakes to find twenty thousand livres, which he will join to the twenty thousand already laid down by the Sieur Planchet. He will employ the said sum of forty thousand livres according to his judgment in an undertaking which is described below. On the day when M. d'Artagnan shall have re-established, by whatever means, his majesty King Charles II upon the throne of England, he will pay into the hands of M. Planchet the sum of——'

'The sum of a hundred and fifty thousand livres,' said Planchet, innocently, perceiving that D'Artagnan hesitated.

'Oh, the devil, no!' said D'Artagnan, 'the division cannot be made by half; that would not be just.'

'And yet, monsieur, we each lay down half,' objected Planchet, timidly.

'Yes; but listen to this clause, my dear Planchet, and if you do not find it equitable in every respect, when it is written, well, we can scratch it out again: "Nevertheless, as M. d'Artagnan brings to the association, besides his capital of twenty thousand livres, his time, his idea, his industry, and his skin—things which he appreciates strongly, particularly the last—M. d'Artagnan will keep, of the three hundred thousand livres, two hundred thousand livres for himself, which will make his share two-thirds"'

'Very well,' said Planchet.

'Is that fair?' asked D'Artagnan.

'Perfectly fair, monsieur.'

'And you will be contented with a hundred thousand livres?'

'The devil I do! A hundred thousand for twenty thousand!'

'And in a month, understand.'

'What, in a month?'

'Yes, I only ask one month.'

'Monsieur,' said Planchet, generously, 'I give you six weeks.'

'Thank you,' replied the musketeer politely; after which the two partners re-perused their deed.

'That is perfect, monsieur,' said Planchet; 'and the late M. Coquenard,* the first husband of Madame la Baronne du Vallon could not have done it better.'

'Do you find it so? Let us sign it, then.' And both affixed their signatures.

'This way,' said D'Artagnan, 'I shall be under obligations to no one.'

'But I shall be under obligations to you,' said Planchet.

'No; for whatever store I set by it, Planchet, I may lose my skin yonder, and you will lose everything. By the by, that makes me think of the principal, an indispensable clause. I shall write it: "In the case of M. d'Artagnan dying in this enterprise, liquidation will be considered made, and the Sieur Planchet will give quittance from that moment to the shade of Messire d'Artagnan for the twenty thousand livres paid by him into the hands of the said company."'

This last clause made Planchet knit his brows a little; but when he saw the brilliant eye, the muscular hand, the supple and strong back of his associate, he regained his courage, and, without regret, he at once added another stroke to his signature. D'Artagnan did the same. This was how the first known company contract was written; perhaps such things have been abused a little since, both in form and principle.*

'Now,' said Planchet, pouring out the last glass of Anjou wine for D'Artagnan, 'now go to sleep, my dear master.'

'No,' replied D'Artagnan; 'for the most difficult part now remains to be done, and I will think over that difficult part.'

'Bah!' said Planchet; 'I have such great confidence in you, M. d'Artagnan, that I would not give my hundred thousand livres for ninety thousand livres down.'

'And devil take me if I don't think you are right!' Upon which D'Artagnan took a candle and went up to his bedroom.

XXI

IN WHICH D'ARTAGNAN PREPARES TO TRAVEL FOR THE FIRM OF PLANCHET & CO.

D'ARTAGNAN reflected to such good purpose during the night, that his plan was settled by morning. 'This is it,' said he, sitting up in bed, supporting his elbow on his knee, and his chin in his hand; 'this is it. I shall seek out forty steady, firm men, recruited among people who are a little compromised, but have habits of discipline. I shall promise them five hundred livres for a month if they return; nothing if they do not return, or half for their families. As to food and lodging, that concerns the English, who have cattle in their pastures, bacon in their bacon-racks, fowls in their poultry-yards, and corn in their barns. I will present myself to General Monk with my little body of troops. He will receive me. I shall win his confidence, and take advantage of it, as soon as possible.'

But without going farther, D'Artagnan shook his head and interrupted himself. 'No,' said he; 'I should not dare to relate this to Athos; the way is therefore not honourable. I must use violence,' continued he, 'very certainly, I must, but without compromising my loyalty. With forty men I will traverse the country as a partisan. But if I fall in with, not forty thousand English, as Planchet said, but with just four hundred, I shall be beaten. Supposing that among my forty warriors there should be

found at least ten stupid ones—ten who will allow themselves to
be killed one after the other, from mere folly? No; it is, in fact,
impossible to find forty men to be depended upon—they do not
exist. I must learn how to be contented with thirty. With ten
men less I should have the right to avoid any armed encounter,
on account of the small number of my men; and if the encounter
should take place, my chance is better with thirty men than
forty. Besides I should save five thousand francs; that is to say,
an eighth of my capital; that is worth the trial. This being so, I
should have thirty men. I shall divide them into three bands,—
we will spread ourselves about over the country, with orders to
reunite at a given moment; in this fashion, ten by ten, we should
excite no suspicion—we should go unnoticed. Yes, yes, thirty—
that is a magic number. There are three tens—three, that divine
number! And then, truly, a company of thirty men, when all
together, will look rather imposing. Ah! stupid wretch that I
am!' continued D'Artagnan, 'I want thirty horses. That is ruin-
ous. Where the devil was my head when I forgot the horses? We
cannot however, think of striking such a blow without horses.
Well, so be it, that sacrifice must be made; we can get the horses
there—they are not bad, besides. But I forgot—Hell's teeth!
Three bands—that necessitates three leaders; there is the difficulty. Of the three commanders I have already one—that is
myself; yes, but the two others will of themselves cost almost as
much money as all the rest of the troop. No; positively I must
have but one lieutenant. In that case, then, I should reduce my
troop to twenty men. I know very well that twenty men is but
very little; but since with thirty I was determined not to seek to
come to blows, I should do so more carefully still with twenty.
Twenty—that is a round number; that, besides, reduces the
number of the horses by ten, which is a consideration; and then,
with a good lieutenant—— *Mordioux!* what things patience and
calculation are! Was I not going to embark with forty men, and
I have now reduced them to twenty for an equal success? Ten
thousand livres saved at one stroke, and more safety; that is all
to the good! Now, then, let us see; we have nothing to do but to
find this lieutenant—let him be found, then; and after——
That is not so easy; he must be brave and good, a second myself.
Yes, but a lieutenant must have my secret, and as that secret is

worth a million, and I shall only pay my man a thousand livres, fifteen hundred at the most, my man will sell the secret to Monk. *Mordioux!* no lieutenant. Besides, this man, were he as mute as a disciple of Pythagoras*—this man would be sure to have in the troop some favourite soldier, whom he would make his sergeant; the sergeant would find out the secret of the lieutenant, in case the latter should be honest and unwilling to sell it. Then the sergeant, less honest and less ambitious, will give up the whole for fifty thousand livres. Come, come! that is impossible. The lieutenant is impossible. But then I must have no fractions; I cannot divide my troop into two, and act upon two points, at once, without another self, who—— But what is the use of acting upon two points as we have only one man to take? What can be the good of weakening a corps by placing the right here, and the left there? A single corps, *Mordioux!* a single one, and that commanded by D'Artagnan. Very well. But twenty men marching in one band are suspected by everybody; twenty horsemen must not be seen marching together, or a company will be detached against them, and the pass-word will be required; the which company, upon seeing them embarrassed to give it, would shoot M. d'Artagnan and his men like so many rabbits. I reduce myself then to ten men; in this fashion I shall act simply and with unity; I shall be forced to be prudent, which is half the success in an affair of the kind I am undertaking, a greater number might, perhaps, have drawn me into some folly. Ten horses are not many either to buy or take. A capital idea; it puts my mind to rest! No more suspicions—no pass-words—no more dangers! Ten men, they are valets or clerks. Ten men, leading ten horses laden with merchandise of whatever kind, are tolerated, well received everywhere. Ten men travel on account of the firm of Planchet & Co., of France; nothing can be said against that. These ten men, clothed like manufacturers, have a good cutlass or a good musket at their saddle-bow, and a good pistol in the holster. They never allow themselves to be uneasy, because they have no evil designs. They are perhaps, in truth, a little disposed to be smugglers, but what harm is in that? Smuggling is not, like polygamy, a hanging offence.* The worst that can happen to us is the confiscation of our merchandise. Our merchandise confiscated—so what! Come, come! it is a superb plan. Ten men only—ten men, whom I will engage for my service; ten men who shall be as resolute as forty who would cost me four times as much, and to whom, for greater security, I will never open my mouth as to my designs, and to whom I shall only say, "My friends, there is a blow to be struck." Things being after this fashion, Satan will be very malicious if he plays me one of his tricks. Fifteen thousand livres saved—that's superb—out of twenty!'

Thus fortified by his laborious calculations, D'Artagnan stopped at this plan, and determined to change nothing in it. He had already on a list furnished by his inexhaustible memory, ten men illustrious amongst the seekers of adventures, ill-treated by fortune, and not on good terms with justice. Upon this D'Artagnan rose, and instantly set off on the search, telling Planchet not to expect him to breakfast, and perhaps not to dinner. A day and a half spent in rummaging amongst certain dens of Paris sufficed for his recruiting; and, without allowing his adventurers to communicate with each other, he had picked up and got together, in less than thirty hours, a charming collection of ill-looking faces, speaking a French less pure than the English they were about to attempt. These men were, for the most part, guards,* whose merit D'Artagnan had had an opportunity of appreciating in various encounters, whom drunkenness, unlucky sword-thrusts, unexpected winnings at play, or the economical reforms of Mazarin, had forced to seek shade and solitude, those two great consolers of irritated and chafing spirits. They bore upon their countenances and in their vestments the traces of the heartaches they had undergone. Some had their faces scarred—all had their clothes in rags. D'Artagnan comforted the most needy of these brotherly miseries by a prudent distribution of the money of the company; then having taken care that this money should be employed in the physical improvement of the troop, he appointed a meeting place in the north of France, between Bergues and Saint Omer.* Six days were allowed to the deadline, and D'Artagnan was sufficiently acquainted with the good-will, the good humour, and the relative probity of these illustrious recruits, to be certain that not one of them would fail in his appointment. These orders given, this rendezvous fixed, he went to bid farewell to Planchet, who asked news of his army. D'Artagnan did not think proper to inform him of the reduction he had made in his recruitment. He feared that the confidence of his associate would be shaken by such an admission. Planchet was delighted to learn that the army was raised, and that he (Planchet) found himself a kind of half-king, who, from his throne-counter, kept in pay a body of troops destined to make war against perfidious Albion, that enemy of all true French hearts.* Planchet paid down, in double-louis, twenty thousand livres to D'Artagnan, on the part of himself (Planchet) and twenty thousand livres, still in double-louis, in account with D'Artagnan. D'Artagnan placed each of the twenty thousand francs in a bag, and weighing a bag in each hand, 'This money is very cumbersome, my dear Planchet,' said he. 'Do you know it weighs thirty pounds?'

'Bah! your horse will carry that like a feather.'

D'Artagnan shook his head. 'Don't tell me such things, Planchet: a horse overloaded with thirty pounds, in addition to the rider and his portmanteau, cannot cross a river so easily—cannot leap over a wall or ditch so lightly; and the horse failing, the horseman fails. It is true that you, Planchet, who have served in the infantry, may not be aware of all that.'

'Then what is to be done, monsieur?' said Planchet, greatly embarrassed.

'Listen to me,' said D'Artagnan. 'I will pay my army on its return home. Keep my half of twenty thousand livres, which you can use during that time.'

'And my half?' said Planchet.

'I shall take that with me.'

'Your confidence does me honour,' said Planchet; 'but supposing you should not return?'

'That is possible, though not very probable. Then, Planchet, in case I should not return—give me a pen; I will make my will.' D'Artagnan took a pen and some paper, and wrote upon a clean sheet, 'I, D'Artagnan, possess twenty thousand livres, laid up sou by sou during the thirty years that I have been in the service of his majesty the king of France. I leave five thousand to Athos, five thousand to Porthos, and five thousand to Aramis, that they may give the said sums in my name and their own to my young friend Raoul, Vicomte de Bragelonne. I give the remaining five thousand to Planchet, that he may distribute the fifteen thousand with less regret among my friends. With which purpose I sign these presents. D'ARTAGNAN.'

Planchet appeared very curious to know what D'Artagnan had written.

'Here,' said the musketeer, 'read it.'

On reading the last lines the tears came into Planchet's eyes. 'You think then, that I would not have given the money without that? Then I will have none of your five thousand francs.'

D'Artagnan smiled. 'Accept it, accept it, Planchet; and in that way you will only lose fifteen thousand francs instead of twenty thousand, and you will not be tempted to disregard the signature of your master and friend, by losing nothing at all.'

How well that dear Monsieur d'Artagnan knew the hearts of men and grocers! They who have pronounced Don Quixote* mad because he rode out to the conquest of an empire with nobody but Sancho his squire, and they who have pronounced Sancho mad because he accompanied his master in his attempt to conquer that empire—they certainly will have no hesitation in extending the same judgment to D'Artagnan and Planchet. And yet the first passed for one of the most subtle spirits among the astute spirits of the court of France. As to the second, he had acquired by good right the reputation of having one of the longest heads among the grocers in the Rue des Lombards; consequently in Paris, and consequently in France. Now, to consider these two men from the point of view from which you would consider other men, and the means with which they contemplated to restore a monarch to his throne, compared with other means, the shallowest brains of the country where brains are most shallow must have recoiled from the presumptuous madness of the lieutenant and the stupidity of his associate. Fortunately, D'Artagnan was not a man to listen to the idle talk of those around him, or to the comments that were made on himself. He had adopted the motto, 'Act well, and let people talk.' Planchet on his part had adopted this, 'Act, and say nothing.' It resulted from this, that, according to the custom of all superior geniuses, these two men flattered themselves, *intra pectus*,* with being in the right against all who found fault with them.

As a beginning, D'Artagnan set out in the finest of possible weather, without a cloud in the heavens—without a cloud on his mind, joyous and strong, calm and decided, great in his resolution, and consequently carrying with him a tenfold dose of that potent fluid* which the shocks of mind cause to spring from the nerves, and which procure for the human machine a force and an influence of which future ages will render, according to all probability, a more arithmetical account than we can possibly do at present. He was again, as in times past, on that same road of adventures which had led him to Boulogne, and which he was now travelling for the fourth time.* It appeared to him that he could almost recognize the trace of his own steps upon the road, and that of his fist upon the doors of the hostelries; his memory, always active and present, brought back that youth which neither thirty years later his great heart nor his wrist of steel would have belied. What a rich nature was that of this man! He had all the passions, all the defects, all the weaknesses, and a constitutional spirit of contradiction which changed all these imperfections into corresponding qualities. D'Artagnan, thanks to his ever active imagination, was afraid of a shadow, and ashamed of being afraid, he marched straight up to that shadow, and then became extravagant in his bravery, if the danger proved to be real. Thus everything in him was emotion, and therefore enjoyment. He loved the company of others, but never became tired of his own; and more than once, if he could have been heard when he was alone, he might have been seen laughing at the jokes he told to himself, or the tricks his imagination created where five minutes before boredom might have been expected. D'Artagnan was not perhaps so gay this time as he would have been with the prospect of finding some good friends at Calais, instead of joining the ten knaves there; melancholy, however, did not visit him more than once a day,* and it was about five visits that he received from that sombre deity before he got sight of the sea at Boulogne, and then these visits were indeed but short. But when once D'Artagnan found himself near the field of action, all other feelings but that of confidence disappeared never to return. From Boulogne he followed the coast to Calais. Calais was the place of general rendezvous, and at Calais he had named to each of his recruits the Mighty Monarch tavern, where living was not extravagant, where sailors messed, and where men of the sword, with sheath of leather, be it understood, found lodging, table, food, and all the comforts of life, for thirty sous per diem. D'Artagnan proposed to himself to take them by surprise *in flagrante delicto* of wandering life, and to judge by the first appearance if he could count on them as trusty companions.

He arrived at Calais at half-past four in the afternoon.

XXII

D'ARTAGNAN TRAVELS FOR THE FIRM OF PLANCHET & CO.

THE Mighty Monarch tavern was situated in a little street parallel to the quayside without looking out on the quay itself. Some lanes cut—as steps cut the two uprights of a ladder—the two great straight lines of the quayside and the street. By these lanes, passengers came suddenly from the quayside into the street, or from the street on to the quayside. D'Artagnan, arrived at the quay, took one of these lanes, and came out in front of the Mighty Monarch. The moment was well chosen and might remind D'Artagnan of his start in life at the inn of the Jolly Miller at Meung.* Some sailors who had been playing at dice had started a quarrel, and were threatening each other furiously. The host, hostess, and two lads were watching with anxiety the circle of these angry gamblers, from the midst of which war seemed ready to break forth, bristling with knives and hatchets. The play, nevertheless, was continued. A stone bench was occupied by two men, who appeared thence to watch the door; four tables, placed at the back of the common chamber, were occupied by eight other individuals. Neither the men at the door, nor those at the tables took any part in the play or the quarrel. D'Artagnan recognized his ten men in these cold, indifferent spectators. The quarrel went on increasing. Every passion has, like the sea, its tide which ascends and descends. Reaching the climax of passion, one sailor overturned the table and the money which was upon it. The table fell, and the money rolled about. In an instant all belonging to the hostelry threw themselves upon the stakes, and many a piece of silver was picked up by people who stole away whilst the sailors were scuffling with each other.

The two men on the bench and the eight at the tables, although they seemed perfect strangers to each other, these ten men alone, we say, appeared to have agreed to remain impassive amidst the cries of fury and the chinking of money. Two only contented themselves with pushing with their feet combatants who came under their table. Two others, rather than take part in this disturbance, buried their hands in their pockets; and another two jumped upon the table they occupied, as people do to avoid being submerged by overflowing water.

'Come, come,' said D'Artagnan to himself, not having missed one of the details we have related, 'this is a very fair gathering—circumspect, calm, accustomed to disturbance, acquainted with blows! Hell's teeth! I have been lucky.'

All at once his attention was called to a particular part of the room. The two men who had pushed the strugglers with their feet, were assailed with abuse by the sailors, who had become reconciled. One of them, half-drunk with passion, and quite drunk with beer, came, in a menacing manner, to demand of the shorter of these two sages, by what right he had touched with his foot creatures of the good God, who were not dogs. And whilst putting this question, in order to make it more direct, he applied his great fist to the nose of D'Artagnan's recruit.

This man became pale, without its being to be discerned whether his pallor arose from anger or from fear; seeing which, the sailor concluded it was from fear, and raised his fist with the manifest intention of letting it fall upon the head of the stranger. But though the threatened man did not appear to move, he dealt the sailor such a severe blow in the stomach that he sent him rolling and howling to the other side of the room. At the same instant, rallied by the *esprit de corps*, all the comrades of the conquered man fell upon the conqueror.

The latter, with the same coolness of which he had given proof, without committing the imprudence of touching his weapons, took up a beer-pot with a pewter-lid, and knocked down two or three of his assailants; then, as he was about to yield to numbers, the seven other silent men at the tables, who had not stirred, perceived that their cause was at stake, and came to the rescue. At the same time, the two indifferent spectators at the door turned round with frowning brows, indicating their evident intention of taking the enemy in the rear, if the enemy did not cease their aggressions.

The host, his helpers and two watchmen who were passing, and who from curiosity, had penetrated too far into the room, were mixed up in the tumult and showered with blows. The Parisians hit like Cyclops,* with a spirit and tactics delightful to behold. At length, obliged to beat a retreat before superior numbers, they formed an entrenchment behind the large table, which they raised by main force; whilst the two others, arming themselves each with a trestle, and using it like a great sledge-hammer, knocked down at a blow eight sailors upon whose heads they had brought their monstrous weapon. The floor was already strewn with wounded, and the room filled with cries and dust, when D'Artagnan, satisfied with the test, advanced, sword in hand, and striking with the pommel every head that came in his way, he uttered a vigorous 'Halt!' which put an instantaneous end to the conflict. A great back-flood directly took place from the centre to the sides of the room, so that D'Artagnan found himself isolated and commanding.

'What is all this about?' he then demanded of the assembly, with the majestic tone of Neptune pronouncing the *Quos ego* . . .*

At the very instant, at the first sound of his voice, to carry on the Virgilian metaphor, D'Artagnan's recruits, recognizing each his sovereign lord, discontinued their plank-fighting and trestle blows. On their side, the sailors, seeing that long naked sword, that martial air, and the agile arm which came to the rescue of their enemies, in the person of a man who seemed accustomed to command—the sailors picked up their wounded and their pitchers. The Parisians wiped their brows, and viewed their leader with respect. D'Artagnan was loaded with thanks by the host of Mighty Monarch. He received them like a man who knows that nothing is being offered that does not belong to him, and then said he would go and walk upon the quayside till supper was ready. Immediately each of the recruits, who understood the summons, took his hat, brushed the dust off his clothes, and followed D'Artagnan. But D'Artagnan, whilst walking and observing, took care not to stop; he directed his course towards the dunes, and the ten men—surprised at finding themselves going in the track of each other, uneasy at seeing on their right, on their left, and behind them, companions upon whom they had not reckoned—followed him, casting furtive glances at each other. It was not till he had arrived at the hollow part of the deepest dune that D'Artagnan, smiling to see them outdone, turned towards them, making a friendly sign with his hand.

'Eh! come, come, gentlemen,' said he, 'let us not devour each other; you are made to live together, to understand each other in all respects; and not to quarrel.'

Instantly all hesitation ceased; the men breathed as if they had been taken out of a coffin, and examined each other with complaisance. After this examination they turned their eyes towards their leader, who had long been acquainted with the art of speaking to men of that class, and who improvised the following little speech, pronounced with an energy truly Gascon:

'Gentlemen, you all know who I am. I have engaged you from knowing you to be brave, and willing to associate you with me in a glorious enterprise. Imagine that in labouring for me you labour for the king. I only warn you that if you allow anything of this supposition to appear, I shall be forced to crack your skulls immediately, in the manner most convenient to me. You are not ignorant, gentlemen, that state secrets are like a mortal poison: as long as that poison is in its box and the box is closed, it is not injurious; out of the box, it kills. Now draw near, and you shall know as much of this secret as I am able to tell you.' All drew close to him with an expression of curiosity. 'Approach,' continued D'Artagnan, 'and let not the bird which passes over our heads, the rabbit which sports on the dunes, the fish which bounds from the waters, hear us. Our business is to learn and to report to monsieur le surintendant to what extent English smuggling is injurious to French merchants. I shall enter every place, and see everything. We are poor Picard fishermen, thrown upon the coast by a storm. It is certain that we must sell fish, neither more or less, like true fishermen. Only people might guess who we are, and might molest us; it is therefore necessary that we should be in a condition to defend ourselves. And this is why I have selected men of spirit and courage. We shall lead a steady life, and not incur much danger, seeing that we have behind us a powerful protector, thanks to whom no embarrassment is possible. One thing worries me, though; but I hope that after a short explanation, you will relieve me of that difficulty. The thing that worries me is having to take with us a crew of stupid fishermen, who will certainly turn out to be a confounded nuisance. But if, by chance, there were among you any who have seen the sea——'

'Oh! don't let that trouble you,' said one of the recruits; 'I was a prisoner among the pirates of Tunis* three years, and can manœuvre a boat like an admiral.'

'See,' said D'Artagnan, 'what an admirable thing chance is!' D'Artagnan pronounced these words with an indefinable tone of feigned bonhomie, for he knew very well that the victim of pirates was an old corsair, and had engaged him in consequence of that knowledge. But D'Artagnan never said more than there was need to say, in order to leave people wondering. He paid himself with the explanation, and welcomed the effect, without appearing to be preoccupied with the cause.

'And I,' said a second, 'I, by chance, had an uncle who directed the works of the port of La Rochelle. As a boy, I played about the boats, and I know how to handle an oar or a sail as well as the best Ponantais* sailor.' The latter did not lie much more than the first, for he had rowed on board his majesty's galleys* six years, at Ciotat. Two others were more frank: they confessed honestly that they had served on board a vessel as soldiers on punishment, and did not blush for it. D'Artagnan found himself, then, the leader of ten fighting men including four sailors, having at once a land army and a sea force, which would have carried the pride of Planchet to its height, if Planchet had known the details.

Nothing was now left but arranging the general orders, and D'Artagnan gave them with precision. He enjoined his men to be ready to set out for the Hague, some following the coast which leads to Breskens,* others the road to Antwerp. The rendezvous was given, by calculating each day's march, a fortnight from that time, upon the chief place at the Hague. D'Artagnan recommended his men to go in couples, as they liked best, from sympathy. He himself selected from among those with the least disreputable look, two guards whom he had formerly known, and whose only faults were being drunkards and gamblers. These men had not entirely lost all ideas of civilization, and under proper garments, their hearts would beat again. D'Artagnan, not to create any jealousy with the others, made the rest go forward. He kept his two selected ones, clothed them from his own wardrobe, and set out with them.

It was to these two, whom he seemed to honour with absolute confidence, that D'Artagan imparted a false secret, destined to secure the success of the expedition. He confessed to them that the object was not to learn to what extent French merchants were injured by English smuggling, but to learn how far French smuggling could disrupt English trade. These men appeared convinced; they were effectively so. D'Artagnan was quite sure that at the first debauch, when thoroughly drunk, one of the two would divulge the secret to the whole band. His game appeared infallible.

A fortnight after all we have said had taken place at Calais, the whole troop assembled at the Hague.

Then D'Artagnan perceived that all his men, with remarkable intelligence, had already disguised themselves as sailors, more or less ill-treated by the sea. D'Artagnan left them to sleep in a den in Newkerke Street,* whilst he lodged comfortably upon the Grand Canal. He learned that the king of England had come back to his old ally, William II of Nassau, stadtholder of Holland.* He learned also that the refusal of Louis XIV had a little cooled the protection afforded him up to that time, and in consequence he had gone to reside in a little village house at Scheveningen,* situated in the dunes, on the sea-shore, about a league from the Hague.

There, it was said, the unfortunate banished king consoled himself in his exile, by looking, with the melancholy peculiar to the princes of his race, at that immense North Sea, which separated him from his England, as it had formerly separated Mary Stuart from France. There, behind the trees of the beautiful wood of Scheveningen, on the fine sand upon which grows the golden broom of the dunes, Charles II vegetated just as it did, though he was more unfortunate, for he had life and thought, and he hoped and despaired by turns.

D'Artagnan went once as far as Scheveningen, in order to be certain that all was true that was said of the king. He beheld Charles II, pensive and alone, coming out of a little door opening into the wood, and walking on the beach in the setting sun, without even attracting the attention of the fishermen, who, on their return in the evening, drew, like the ancient mariners of the Archipelago,* their barks up upon the sand of the shore.

D'Artagnan recognized the king; he saw him fix his melancholy look upon the immense extent of the waters, and absorb upon his pale countenance the red rays of the sun already cut by the black line of the horizon. Then Charles returned to his isolated abode, always alone, slow and sad, amusing himself with making the friable and moving sand creak beneath his feet.

That very evening D'Artagnan hired for a thousand livres a fishing-boat worth four thousand. He paid a thousand livres down, and deposited the three thousand with a Burgomaster, after which he brought on board without their being seen, the six men who formed his land army; and with the rising tide, at three o'clock in the morning, he got into the open sea, manœuvring with no attempt at secrecy with the four others, and depending upon the science of his galley slave as upon that of the first pilot of the port.

XXIII

IN WHICH THE AUTHOR, VERY UNWILLINGLY, IS FORCED TO WRITE A LITTLE HISTORY

While kings and men were thus occupied with England, which governed itself quite alone, and which, it must be said in its praise, had never been so badly governed,* a man upon whom God had fixed his eye, and placed his finger, a man predestined to write his name in brilliant letters upon the page of history, was pursuing in the face of the world a work full of mystery and audacity. He went on, and no one knew whither he meant to go, although not only England, but France, and Europe, watched him marching with a firm step and head held high. All that was known of this man we are about to tell.

Monk had just declared himself in favour of the liberty of the Rump Parliament, a parliament which General Lambert, imitating Cromwell, whose lieutenant he had been, had just blocked up so closely, in order to bring it to his will, that no member, during all the blockade, was able to go out, and only one, Peter Wentworth,* had been able to get in.

Lambert and Monk—everything was summed up in these two men; the first representing military despotism, the second pure republicanism. These men were the two sole political representatives of that revolution in which Charles I had first lost his crown, and afterwards his head. As regarded Lambert, he did not dissemble his views; he sought to establish a military government, and to be himself the head of that government.

Monk, a rigid republican, some said, wished to maintain the Rump Parliament, that visible though degenerated representative of the republic. Monk, artful and ambitious, said others, wished simply to make of this parliament, which he affected to protect, a solid step by which to mount the throne which Cromwell had left empty, but upon which he had never dared to take his seat.*

Thus Lambert by persecuting the parliament, and Monk by declaring for it, had mutually proclaimed themselves enemies of each other.* Monk and Lambert, therefore, had at first thought of creating an army each for himself: Monk in Scotland, where were the Presbyterians and the royalists, that is to say, the malcontents; Lambert in London, where was found, as is always the case, the strongest opposition to the existing power which it had beneath its eyes.

Monk had pacified Scotland,* he had there formed for himself an army, and found an asylum. The one watched the other. Monk knew that the day was not yet come, the day marked by the Lord for a great change: his sword, therefore, appeared glued to the sheath. Inexpugnable in his wild and mountainous Scotland, an absolute general, king of an army of eleven thousand old soldiers,* whom he had more than once led on to victory; as well informed, nay, even better, of the affairs of London, than Lambert, who held garrison in the city—such was the position of Monk, when, at a hundred leagues from London, he declared himself for the parliament. Lambert, on the contrary, as we have said, lived in the capital. That was the centre of all his operations, and he there collected around him all his friends, and all the people of the lower class, eternally inclined to cherish the enemies of constituted power.*

It was then in London that Lambert learnt the support that, from the frontiers of Scotland, Monk lent to the parliament. He judged there was no time to be lost, and that the Tweed was not so far distant from the Thames that an army could not march from one river to the other, particularly when it was well commanded. He knew, besides, that as fast as the soldiers of Monk penetrated into England, they would form on their route that snowball, the emblem of the globe of fortune, which is for the ambitious nothing but a step growing unceasingly higher to conduct him to his object. He got together, therefore, his army, formidable at the same time for its composition and its numbers, and hastened to meet Monk, who, on his part, like a prudent navigator sailing amidst rocks, advanced by very short marches, listening to the reports and scenting the air which came from London.

The two armies came in sight of each other near Newcastle;* Lambert, arriving first, encamped in the city itself. Monk, always circumspect, stopped where he was, and placed his general quarters at Coldstream, on the Tweed. The sight of Lambert spread joy through Monk's army, whilst, on the contrary, the sight of Monk threw disorder into Lambert's army. It might have been thought that these intrepid warriors, who had made such a noise in the streets of London, had set out with the hopes of meeting no one, and that now seeing that they had met an army, and that that army hoisted before them not only a standard, but still further, a cause and a principle—it might have been believed, we say, that these intrepid warriors had begun to reflect that they were less good republicans than the soldiers of Monk, since the latter supported the parliament; whilst Lambert supported nothing, not even himself.

As to Monk, if he had had to reflect, or if he did reflect, it must have been after a sad fashion, for history relates—and that modest dame, it is well known, never lies*—history relates, that the day of his arrival at Coldstream search was made in vain throughout the place for a single sheep.

If Monk had commanded an English army, that was enough

to have brought about a general desertion. But it is not with the Scots as it is with the English, to whom that fluid flesh which is called blood is a paramount necessity; the Scots, a poor and sober race, live upon a little oats crushed between two stones, diluted with the water of the fountain, and cooked upon another stone, heated.

The Scots, their distribution of oats being made, cared very little whether there was or was not any meat in Coldstream. Monk, little accustomed to oatcakes, was hungry, and his staff, at least as hungry as himself, looked with anxiety right and left, to know what was being prepared for supper.

Monk ordered search to be made; his scouts had on arriving in the place found it deserted and the cupboards empty; upon butchers and bakers it was of no use depending in Coldstream. The smallest morsel of bread, then, could not be found for the general's table.

As accounts succeeded each other, all equally unsatisfactory, Monk, seeing terror and discouragement upon every face, declared that he was not hungry; besides, they should eat on the morrow, since Lambert was there probably with the intention of giving battle, and consequently would give up his provisions, if he were forced from Newcastle, or for ever to relieve Monk's soldiers from hunger if he conquered.

This consolation was only efficacious upon a very small number; but of what importance was that to Monk? for Monk was very absolute, under the appearance of the most perfect mildness. Every one, therefore, was obliged to be satisfied, or at least to appear so. Monk, quite as hungry as his people, but affecting perfect indifference for the absent mutton, cut a fragment of tobacco,* half an inch long, from the plug of a sergeant who formed part of his suite, and began to masticate the said fragment, assuring his lieutenants that hunger was an illusion, and that, besides, people were never hungry when they had something to chew.

This joke satisfied some of those who had resisted Monk's first deduction drawn from the neighbourhood of Lambert's army; the number of the dissentients diminished greatly; the guard took their posts, the patrols began, and the general continued his frugal repast beneath his open tent.

Between his camp and that of the enemy stood an old abbey,

of which, at the present day, there only remain some ruins, but which then was in existence, and was called Newcastle Abbey.* It was built upon a vast site, independent at once of the plain and of the river, because it was almost a marsh fed by springs and kept up by rains. Nevertheless, in the midst of these pools of water, covered with long grass, rushes, and reeds, were seen solid islands of ground, formerly used as the kitchen-garden, the park, the pleasure-gardens, and other dependencies of the abbey, looking like one of those great sea-spiders, whose body is round, whilst the claws go diverging round from this circumference.

The kitchen-garden, one of the longest claws of the abbey, extended to Monk's camp. Unfortunately it was, as we have said, early in June,* and the kitchen-garden, being abandoned, offered no resources.

Monk had ordered this spot to be guarded, as most subject to surprises. The fires of the enemy's general were plainly to be perceived on the other side of the abbey. But between these fires and the abbey extended the Tweed, unfolding its luminous scales beneath the thick shade of tall green oaks. Monk was perfectly well acquainted with this position, Newcastle and its environs having already more than once been his head-quarters. He knew that by day his enemy might without doubt throw a few scouts into these ruins and promote a skirmish, but that by night he would take care to abstain from such a risk. He felt himself, therefore, secure.

Thus his soldiers saw him, after what he boastingly called his supper—that is to say, after the exercise of mastication reported by us at the commencement of this chapter—like Napoleon on the eve of Austerlitz,* seated asleep in his rush chair, half beneath the light of his lamp, half beneath the reflection of the moon, commencing its ascent in the heavens, which denoted that it was nearly half-past nine in the evening. All at once Monk was roused from his half-sleep, fictitious perhaps, by a troop of soldiers, who came with joyous cries, and kicked the poles of his tent with a humming noise as if on purpose to wake him. There was no need of so much noise; the general opened his eyes quickly.

'Well, my children, what is going on now?' asked the general.

'General!' replied several voices at once, 'General! you shall have some supper.'

'I have had my supper, gentlemen,' replied he quietly, 'and was comfortably digesting it, as you see. But come in, and tell me what brings you hither.'

'Good news, general.'

'Bah! Has Lambert sent us word that he will fight to-morrow!'

'No; but we have just captured a fishing-boat conveying fish to Newcastle.'

'And you have done very wrong, my friends. These gentlemen from London are delicate, must have their first course; you will put them sadly out of humour this evening, and to-morrow they will be pitiless. It would really be in good taste to send back to Lambert both his fish and his fishermen, unless——' and the general reflected an instant.

'Tell me,' continued he, 'what are these fishermen, if you please?'

'Some Picard* seamen who were fishing on the coasts of France or Holland, and who have been thrown upon ours by a gale of wind.'

'Do any among them speak our language?'

'The leader spoke some few words of English.'

The mistrust of the general was awakened in proportion as fresh information reached him. 'That is well,' said he. 'I wish to see these men; bring them to me.'

An officer immediately went to fetch them.

'How many are there of them?' continued Monk; 'and what is their vessel?'

'There are ten or twelve of them, general, and they were aboard of a kind of lugger, as they call it—Dutch-built, apparently.'

'And you say they were carrying fish to Lambert's camp?'

'Yes, general, and they seem to have had good luck in their fishing.'

'Humph! We shall see that,' said Monk.

At this moment the officer returned, bringing the leader of the fishermen with him. He was a man from fifty to fifty-five years old, but good-looking for his age. He was of middle height, and wore a jerkin of coarse wool and a cap pulled down over his eyes; a cutlass hung from his belt, and he walked with the hesitation peculiar to sailors, who, never knowing, thanks to the movement of the vessel, whether their foot will be placed upon the plank or upon nothing, give to every one of their steps a fall as firm as if they were driving a pile. Monk, with an acute and penetrating look, examined the fisherman for some time, while the latter smiled, with that smile, half cunning, half silly, peculiar to French peasants.

'Do you speak English?' asked Monk, in excellent French.

'Ah! but badly, my lord,'* replied the fisherman.

This reply was made much more with the lively and sharp accentuation of the people beyond the Loire, than with the slightly-drawling accent of the countries of the west and north of France.

'But you do speak it?' persisted Monk, in order to examine his accent once more.

'Eh! we men of the sea,' replied the fisherman, 'speak a little of all languages.'

'Then you are a sea fisherman?'

'I am at present, my lord—a fisherman, and a famous fisherman too. I have taken a barbel that weighs at least thirty pounds, and more than fifty mullets; I have also some little whitings that will fry beautifully.'

'You appear to me to have fished more frequently in the Gulf of Gascony than in the Channel,' said Monk, smiling.

'Well, I am from the south; but does that prevent me from being a good fisherman, my lord?'

'Oh! not at all; I shall buy your fish. And now speak frankly; for whom did you intend them?'

'My lord, I will conceal nothing from you. I was going to Newcastle, following the coast, when a party of horsemen who were passing along in an opposite direction made a sign to my bark to turn back to your honour's camp, under penalty of a discharge of musketry. As I was not armed for fighting,' added the fisherman, smiling, 'I was forced to submit.'

'And why did you go to Lambert's camp in preference to mine?'

'My lord, I will be frank; will your lordship permit me?'

'Yes, and even if need be shall command you to be so.'

'Well, my lord, I was going to M. Lambert's camp because those gentlemen from the city pay well—whilst your Scotchmen,

Puritans, Presbyterians, Covenanters, or whatever you choose to call them, eat but little, and pay for nothing.'

Monk shrugged his shoulders, without, however, being able to refrain from smiling at the same time. 'How is it that, being from the south, you come to fish on our coasts?'

'Because I have been fool enough to marry in Picardy.'

'Yes; but even Picardy is not England.'

'My lord, man shoves his boat into the sea, but God and the wind do the rest, and drive the boat where they please.'

'You had, then, no intention of landing on our coasts?'

'Never.'

'And what route were you steering?'

'We were returning from Ostend, where some mackerel had already been seen, when a sharp wind from the south drove us from our course; then, seeing that it was useless to struggle against it, we let it drive us. It then became necessary, not to lose our fish, which were good, to go and sell them at the nearest English port, and that was Newcastle. We were told the market was good, as there was an increase of population in the camp, an increase of population in the city; both we were told were full of gentlemen, very rich and very hungry. So we steered our course towards Newcastle.'

'And your companions, where are they?'

'Oh! my companions have remained on board; they are poor, ignorant sailors.'

'Whilst you——' said Monk.

'Who, me?' said the captain, laughing; 'I have sailed about with my father; and I know what a sou, a crown, a pistole, a louis, and a double-louis are called in all the languages of Europe; my crew, therefore, listen to me as they would to an oracle, and obey me as if I were an admiral.'

'Then it was you who preferred M. Lambert as the best customer?'

'Yes, certainly. And, to be frank, my lord, was I wrong?'

'You will see that by and by.'

'At all events, my lord, if there is a fault, the fault is mine; and my comrades should not be dealt hardly with on that acount.'

'This is decidedly an intelligent, sharp fellow,' thought Monk. Then, after a few minutes' silence employed in scrutinizing the fisherman, 'You come from Ostend, did you not say?' asked the general.

'Yes, my lord, in a straight line.'

'You have then heard of the affairs of the day; for I have no doubt that both in France and Holland they excite interest. What is he doing who calls himself king of England?'

'Oh, my lord!' cried the fisherman, with loud and expansive frankness, 'that is a lucky question, and you could not put it to anybody better than to me, for in truth I can make you a famous reply. Imagine, my lord, that when putting into Ostend to sell the few mackerel we had caught, I saw the ex-king walking on the dunes waiting for his horses which were to take him to the Hague. He is a rather tall, pale man, with black hair, and somewhat hard-featured.* He looks ill, and I don't think the air of Holland agrees with him.'

Monk followed with the greatest attention the rapid, excited, and diffuse conversation of the fisherman, in a language which was not his own, but which, as we have said, he spoke with great facility.* The fisherman, on his part, employed sometimes a French word, sometimes an English word, and sometimes a word which appeared not to belong to any language, but was, in truth, pure Gascon. Fortunately his eyes spoke for him, and that so eloquently, that it was possible to lose a word from his mouth, but not a single intention from his eyes. The general appeared more and more satisfied with his examination. 'You must have heard that this ex-king, as you call him, was going to the Hague for some purpose?'

'Oh, yes,' said the fisherman, 'I heard that.'

'And what was his purpose?'

'Always the same,' said the fisherman. 'Must he not always entertain the fixed idea of returning to England?'

'That is true,' said Monk, pensively.

'Without reckoning,' added the fisherman, 'that the stadtholder—you know, my lord, William II?——'

'Well?'

'He will assist him with all his power.'

'Ah! did you hear that said?'

'No, but I think so.'

'You are quite a politician, apparently,' said Monk.

'Why, we sailors, my lord, who are accustomed to study the water and the air—that is to say, the two most changeable things in the world—are seldom deceived as to the rest.'

'Now, then,' said Monk, changing the conversation, 'I am told you are going to provision us.'

'I shall do my best, my lord.'

'How much do you ask for your fish in the first place?'

'Not such a fool as to name a price, my lord.'

'Why not?'

'Because my fish is yours.'

'By what right?'

'By that of the strongest.'

'But my intention is to pay you for it.'

'That is very generous of you, my lord.'

'And the worth of it——'

'My lord, I fix no price.'

'What do you ask, then?'

'I only ask to be permitted to go away.'

'Where?—to General Lambert's camp?'

'I!' cried the fisherman; 'what should I go to Newcastle for, now I have no longer any fish?'

'At all events, listen to me.'

'I do, my lord.'

'I shall give you some advice.'

'How, my lord!—pay me and give me good advice likewise! You overwhelm me, my lord.'

Monk looked more earnestly than ever at the fisherman, about whom he still appeared to entertain some suspicion. 'Yes, I shall pay you, and give you a piece of advice; for the two things are connected. If you return, then, to General Lambert——'

The fisherman made a movement of his head and shoulders, which signified, 'If he persists in it, I won't contradict him.'

'Do not cross the marsh,' continued Monk: 'you will have money in your pocket, and there are in the marsh some Scottish ambuscaders I have placed there. Those people are very intractable; they understand but very little of the language which you speak, although it appears to me to be composed of three languages. They might take from you what I had given you, and, on your return to your country, you would not fail to say that

General Monk has two hands, the one Scottish, and the other English; and that he takes back with the Scottish hand what he has given with the English hand.'

'Oh! general, I shall go where you like, be sure of that,' said the fisherman, with a fear too expressive not to be exaggerated. 'I only wish to remain here, if you will allow me to remain.'

'I readily believe you,' said Monk, with an imperceptible smile, 'but I cannot, nevertheless, keep you in my tent.'

'I have no such wish, my lord, and desire only that your lordship should point out where you will have me posted. Do not trouble yourself about us—with us a night soon passes.'

'You shall be conducted to your ship.'

'As your lordship pleases. Only, if your lordship would allow me to be taken back by a carpenter, I should be extremely grateful.'

'Why so?'

'Because the gentlemen of your army, in dragging my boat up the river with a cable pulled by their horses, have battered it a little upon the rocks of the shore, so that I have at least two feet of water in my hold, my lord.'

'The greater reason why you should watch your boat, I think.'

'My lord, I am quite at your orders,' said the fisherman, 'I shall empty my baskets where you wish; then you will pay me, if you please to do so; and you will send me away, if it appears right to you. You see I am very easily managed and pleased, my lord.'

'Come, come, you are a very good sort of a fellow,' said Monk, whose scrutinizing glance had not been able to find a single shade in the clear eye of the fisherman. 'Holloa, Digby!'* An aide-de-camp appeared. 'You will conduct this good fellow and his companions to the little tents of the canteens, in front of the marshes, so that they will be near their ship, and yet will not sleep on board to-night. What is the matter, Spithead?'

Spithead was the sergeant from whom Monk had borrowed a piece of tobacco for his supper. Spithead having entered the general's tent without being sent for, had drawn this question from Monk.

'My lord,' said he, 'a French gentleman has just presented himself at the outposts, and wishes to speak to your honour.'

All this was said, be it understood, in English; but, notwith-standing, it produced a slight emotion in the fisherman, which Monk, occupied with his sergeant, did not notice.

'Who is the gentleman?' asked Monk.

'My lord,' replied Spithead, 'he told it me; but those devils of French names are so difficult to pronounce for a Scottish throat, that I could not retain it. I believe, however, from what the guards say, that it is the same gentleman who presented himself yesterday at the halt, and whom your honour would not receive.'

'That is true; I was holding a council of officers.'

'Will your honour give any orders respecting this gentleman?'

'Yes, let him be brought here.'

'Must we take any precautions?'

'Such as what?'

'Binding his eyes, for instance?'

'To what purpose? He can only see what I desire should be seen; that is to say, that I have around me eleven thousand brave men, who ask no better than to have their throats cut in honour of the parliament of Scotland and England.'

'And this man, my lord?' said Spithead, pointing to the fisher-man, who, during this conversation, had remained standing and motionless, like a man who sees but does not understand.

'Ah, that is true,' said Monk. Then turning towards the fisherman, 'I shall see you again, my brave fellow,' said he; 'I have selected a lodging for you. Digby, take him to it. Fear nothing: your money shall be sent to you presently.'

'Thank you, my lord,' said the fisherman, and after having bowed, he left the tent, accompanied by Digby. Before he had gone a hundred paces he found his companions, who were whispering with a volubility which did not appear exempt from uneasiness, but he made them a sign which seemed to reassure them. 'Hey there, you fellows!' said the captain, 'come this way. His lordship, General Monk, has the generosity to pay us for our fish, and the goodness to give us hospitality for to-night.'

The fishermen gathered round their leader, and, conducted by Digby, the little troop proceeded towards the canteens, the quarters, as may be remembered, which had been assigned them. As they went along in the dark, the fishermen passed close to the

guards who were conducting the French gentleman to General
Monk. This gentleman was on horseback and enveloped in a
large cloak, which prevented the captain from seeing him, however great his curiosity might be. As to the gentleman, ignorant
that he was elbowing compatriots, he did not pay any attention
to the little troop.

The aide-de-camp settled his guests in a tolerably comfortable tent, from which was dislodged an Irish canteen woman,
who went, with her six children, to sleep where she could. A
large fire was burning in front of this tent, and threw its purple
light over the grassy pools of the marsh, rippled by a fresh
breeze. The arrangements made, the aide-de-camp wished the
fishermen good-night, calling to their notice that they might see
from the door of the tent the masts of their boat, which was
tossing gently on the Tweed, a proof that it had not yet sunk.
The sight of this appeared to delight the leader of the fishermen
greatly.

XXIV

THE TREASURE

THE French gentleman whom Spithead had announced to Monk,
and who, closely wrapped in his cloak, had passed by the
fishermen who left the general's tent five minutes before he
entered it—the French gentleman went through the various
posts without even casting his eyes around him, for fear of
appearing indiscreet. As the order had been given, he was conducted to the tent of the general. The gentleman was left alone
in a sort of antechamber in front of the principal body of the
tent, where he awaited Monk, who only delayed till he had
heard the report of his people, and observed through the opening of the canvas the countenance of the person who solicited an
audience.

Without doubt, the report of those who had accompanied
the French gentleman established the discretion with which he
had behaved, for the first impression the stranger received of the
welcome made him by the general was more favourable than he

could have expected at such a moment, and from so suspicious a man. Nevertheless, according to his custom, when Monk found himself in the presence of a stranger, he fixed upon him his penetrating eyes, which scrutiny the stranger, on his part, sustained without embarrassment or notice. At the end of a few seconds, the general made a gesture with his hand and head in sign of attention.

'My lord,' said the gentleman, in excellent English, 'I have requested an interview with your honour, for an affair of importance.'

'Monsieur,' replied Monk, in French, 'you speak our language well for a son of the continent. I ask your pardon—for doubtless the question is indiscreet—do you speak French with the same purity?'

'There is nothing surprising, my lord, in my speaking English tolerably; I resided for some time in England in my youth, and since then I have made two voyages to this country.' These words were spoken in French, and with a purity of accent that bespoke not only a Frenchman, but a Frenchman from the vicinity of Tours.

'And what part of England have you resided in, monsieur?'

'In my youth, London, my lord; then, about 1635, I made a pleasure trip to Scotland; and lastly, in 1648, I lived for some time at Newcastle,* particularly in the abbey, the gardens of which are now occupied by your army.'

'Excuse me, monsieur; but you must comprehend that these questions are necessary on my part—do you not?'

'It would astonish me, my lord, if they were not asked.'

'Now, then, monsieur, what can I do to serve you? What do you wish?'

'This, my lord—but, in the first place, are we alone?'

'Perfectly so, monsieur, except, of course, for the sentry who guards us.' So saying, Monk pulled open the canvas with his hand, and pointed to the soldier placed at ten paces from the tent, and who, at the first call, could have rendered assistance in a second.

'In that case, my lord,' said the gentleman, in as calm a tone as if he had been for a length of time in habits of intimacy with his interlocutor, 'I have made up my mind to address myself to you, because I believe you to be an honest man. Indeed, the communication I am about to make to you will prove to you the esteem in which I hold you.'

Monk, astonished at this language, which established between him and the French gentleman equality at least, raised his piercing eye to the stranger's face, and with a perceptible irony conveyed by the inflection of his voice alone, for not a muscle of his face moved, 'I thank you, monsieur,' said he; 'but, in the first place, to whom have I the honour of speaking?'

'I sent you my name by your sergeant, my lord.'

'Excuse him, monsieur, he is a Scotsman—he could not retain it.'

'I am called the Comte de la Fère, monsieur,' said Athos, bowing.

'The Comte de la Fère?' said Monk, endeavouring to recollect the name. 'Pardon me, monsieur, but this appears to be the first time I have ever heard that name. Do you fill any post at the court of France?'

'None; I am a simple gentleman.'

'What dignity?'

'King Charles I made me a knight of the Garter, and Queen Anne of Austria has given me the cordon of the Holy Ghost.* These are my only dignities.'

'The Garter! the Holy Ghost! Are you a knight of those two orders, monsieur?'

'Yes.'

'And on what occasions have such favours been bestowed upon you?'

'For services rendered to their majesties.'

Monk looked with astonishment at this man, who appeared to him so simple and so great at the same time. Then, as if he had given up trying to penetrate this mystery of a simplicity and grandeur upon which the stranger did not seem disposed to give him any other information than that which he had already received—'Did you present yourself yesterday at our advanced posts?'

'And was sent back? Yes, my lord.'

'Many officers, monsieur, would permit no one to enter their camp, particularly on the eve of a probable battle. But I differ from my colleagues, and like to leave nothing behind me. All advice is good to me; all danger is sent to me by God, and I weigh it in my hand with the energy He has given me. So, yesterday, you were only sent back on account of the council I was holding. To-day I am at liberty—speak.'

'My lord, you have done much better in receiving me, for what I have to say has nothing to do with the battle you are about to fight with General Lambert, or with your camp; and the proof is, that I turned away my head that I might not see your men, and closed my eyes that I might not count your tents. No, I come to speak to you, my lord, on my own account.'

'Speak then, monsieur,' said Monk.

'Just now,' continued Athos, 'I had the honour of telling your lordship that for a long time I lived in Newcastle; it was in the time of Charles I, and when the king was given up to Cromwell by the Scots.'*

'I know,' said Monk, coldly.

'I had at that time a large sum in gold, and on the eve of the battle, from a presentiment perhaps of the turn which things would take on the morrow, I concealed it in the principal vault of Newcastle Abbey, in the tower whose summit you now see silvered by the moonbeams. My treasure has then remained interred there, and I have come to entreat your honour to permit me to withdraw it before, perhaps, the battle turning that way, a mine or some other war engine has destroyed the building and scattered my gold, or exposed it to view so that the soldiers will take possession of it.'

Monk was well acquainted with mankind; he saw in the physiognomy of this gentleman all the energy, all the reason, all the circumspection possible; he could therefore only attribute to a magnanimous confidence the revelation the Frenchman had made him, and he showed himself profoundly touched by it.

'Monsieur,' said he, 'you have augured well of me. But is the sum worth the trouble to which you expose yourself? Do you even believe that it can be in the place where you left it?'

'It is there, monsieur, I do not doubt.'

'That is a reply to one question; but to the other. I asked you if the sum was so large as to warrant your exposing yourself thus.'

'It is really large; yes, my lord, for it is a million I enclosed in two barrels.'

'A million!' cried Monk, at whom this time, in turn, Athos looked earnestly and long. Monk perceived this, and his mistrust returned.

'Here is a man who is laying a snare for me,' he said to himself. 'So,' he replied, 'you wish to withdraw this money, monsieur, as I understand?'

'If you please, my lord.'

'To-day?'

'This very evening, and that on account of the circumstances I have named.'

'But, monsieur,' objected Monk, 'General Lambert is as near the abbey where you have to act as I am. Why, then, have you not addressed yourself to him?'

'Because, my lord, when one acts in important matters, it is best to consult one's instinct before everything. Well, General Lambert does not inspire me with so much confidence as you do.'

'Be it so, monsieur. I shall assist you in recovering your money, if, however, it can still be there; for that is far from likely. Since 1648 twelve years have rolled away, and many events have taken place.' Monk dwelt upon this point, to see if the French gentleman would seize the evasions that were open to him, but Athos did not hesitate.

'I assure you, my lord,' he said firmly, 'that my conviction is, that the two barrels have neither changed place nor master.' This reply had removed one suspicion from the mind of Monk, but it had suggested another. Without doubt this Frenchman was some emissary sent to entice into error the protector of the parliament; the gold was nothing but a lure; and by the help of this lure they thought to excite the cupidity of the general. This gold might not exist. It was Monk's business, then, to seize the Frenchman in the act of falsehood and deception, and to draw from the false step itself in which his enemies wished to trap him, a triumph for his renown. When Monk was determined how to act,

'Monsieur,' said he to Athos, 'without doubt you will do me the honour to share my supper this evening?'

'Yes, my lord,' replied Athos, bowing; 'for you do me an honour of which I feel myself worthy, by the inclination which drew me towards you.'

'It is so much the more gracious on your part to accept my invitation with such frankness, as my cooks are but few and inexperienced, and my providers have returned this evening empty-handed; so that if it had not been for a fisherman of your nation who strayed into our camp, General Monk would have gone to bed without his supper to-day; I have then some fresh fish to offer you, as the vendor assures me.'

'My lord, it is principally for the sake of having the honour to spend another hour with you.'

After this exchange of civilities, during which Monk had lost nothing of his circumspection, the supper, or what was to serve for one, had been laid upon a deal table. Monk invited the Comte de la Fère to be seated at this table, and took his place opposite to him. A single dish of boiled fish, set before the two illustrious guests, was more tempting to hungry stomachs than to delicate palates.

Whilst supping, that is, while eating the fish, washed down with bad ale, Monk got Athos to relate to him the last events of the Fronde, the reconciliation of M. de Condé with the king, and the probable marriage of the infanta of Spain; but he avoided, as Athos himself avoided it, all allusion to the political interests which united, or rather which disunited at this time, England, France and Holland.

Monk, in this conversation, convinced himself of one thing, which he must have remarked after the first words exchanged: that was, that he had to deal with a man of high distinction. He could not be an assassin, and it was repugnant to Monk to believe him to be a spy; but there was sufficient finesse and at the same time firmness in Athos to lead Monk to fancy he was a conspirator. When they had quitted table, 'You still believe in your treasure, then, monsieur?' asked Monk.

'Yes, my lord.'

'Seriously?'

'Quite seriously.'

'And you think you can find the place again where it was buried?'

'At the first inspection.'

'Well, monsieur, from curiosity I shall accompany you. And it is so much the more necessary that I should accompany you, that you would find great difficulties in passing through the camp without me or one of my lieutenants.'

'General, I would not suffer you to inconvenience yourself if I did not, in fact, stand in need of your company: but, as I recognize that this company is not only honourable, but necessary, I accept it.'

'Do you desire we should take any men with us?' asked Monk.

'General, I believe that would be useless, if you yourself do not see the necessity for it. Two men and a horse will suffice to transport the two casks on board the felucca* which brought me hither.'

'But it will be necessary to pick, dig, and remove the earth, and split stones; you don't intend doing this work yourself, monsieur, do you?'

'General, there is no picking or digging required. The treasure is buried in the sepulchral vault of the convent, under a stone in which is fixed a large iron ring, and under which are four steps leading down. The two casks are there, placed end to end, covered with a coat of plaster in the form of a bier. There is besides an inscription, which will enable me to recognize the stone; and as I am not willing, in an affair of delicacy and confidence, to keep the secret from your honour, here is the inscription: "*Hic jacet venerabilis, Petrus Gulielmus Scott, Canon Honorab. Conventûs Novi Castelli. Obiit quartâ et decimâ Feb. ann. Dom.* MCCVIII. *Requiescat in pace.*" '*

Monk did not miss a single word. He was astonished either at the amazing duplicity of this man and the superior style in which he played his part, or at the good faith with which he presented his request, in a situation in which concerning a million of money, risked against the blow from a dagger, amidst an army that would have looked upon the theft as a restitution.

'Very well,' said he; 'I shall accompany you; and the adventure appears to me so extraordinary, that I shall carry the torch myself.' And saying these words, he girded on a short sword, and placed a pistol in his belt, disclosing in this movement, which opened his doublet a little, the fine rings of a coat of mail, destined to protect him from the first dagger-thrust of an assassin. After which he took a Scottish dirk in his left hand, and then turning to Athos, 'Are you ready, monsieur?' said he.

'I am.'

Athos, as if in opposition to what Monk had done, unfastened his poniard, which he placed upon the table; unhooked his sword-belt, which he laid close to his poniard; and, without affectation, opening his doublet as if to look for his handkerchief, showed beneath his fine cambric shirt his naked breast, without weapons either offensive of defensive.

'This is truly a singular man,' said Monk; 'he is without any arms; he has an ambush placed somewhere yonder.'

'General,' said he, as if he had divined Monk's thought, 'you wish we should be alone; that is very right, but a great captain ought never to expose himself with temerity. It is night, the passage of the marsh may present dangers; be accompanied.'

'You are right,' replied he, calling Digby. The aide-de-camp appeared. 'Fifty men, with swords and muskets,' said he, looking at Athos.

'That is too few if there is danger, too many if there is not.'

'I will go alone,' said Monk; 'I want nobody. Come, monsieur.'

XXV

THE MARSH

ATHOS and Monk passed over in going from the camp towards the Tweed that part of the ground which Digby had traversed with the fishermen coming from the Tweed to the camp. The aspect of this place, the aspect of the changes man had wrought in it, was of a nature to produce a great effect upon a lively and delicate imagination like that of Athos. Athos looked at nothing but these desolate spots; Monk looked at nothing but Athos—at Athos, who, with his eyes sometimes directed towards heaven, and sometimes towards the earth, sought, thought, and sighed.

Digby, whom the last orders of the general, and particularly the accent with which he had given them, had at first a little excited—Digby followed the pair at about twenty paces, but the

general having turned round as if astonished to find his orders
had not been obeyed, the aide-de-camp perceived his indiscretion, and returned to his tent.

He supposed that the general wished to make, incognito, one
of those reviews of vigilance which every experienced captain
never fails to make on the eve of a decisive engagement: he
explained to himself the presence of Athos in this case as an
inferior explains all that is mysterious on the part of his leader.
Athos might be, and, indeed, in the eyes of Digby, must be, a
spy, whose information was to enlighten the general.

At the end of a walk of about ten minutes among the tents
and posts, which were closer together near the head-quarters,
Monk entered upon a little causeway which diverged into three
branches. That on the left led to the river, that in the middle to
Newcastle Abbey on the marsh, that on the right crossed the
first lines of Monk's camp; that is to say, the lines nearest to
Lambert's army. Beyond the river was an advanced post, belonging to Monk's army, which watched the enemy; it was composed of one hundred and fifty Scots. They had swum across
the Tweed, and, in case of attack, were to re-cross it in the same
manner, giving the alarm; but as there was no post at that spot,
and as Lambert's soldiers were not so prompt at taking to the
water as Monk's were, the latter appeared not to have much
uneasiness on that side. On this side of the river, at about five
hundred paces from the old abbey, the fishermen had taken up
their abode amidst a crowd of small tents raised by the soldiers
of the neighbouring clans, who had with them their wives and
children. All this confusion, seen by the moon's light, presented
a striking sight; the half-shadow enlarged every detail, and the
light, that flatterer which only attaches itself to the polished
side of things, caught every musket barrel that was not rusty
and picked out the whitest and cleanest part of every rag of
canvas.

Monk arrived then with Athos, crossing this spot, illumined
with a double light, the silver splendour of the moon, and the
red blaze of the fires at the meeting of the three causeways; there
he stopped, and addressing his companion, 'Monsieur,' said he,
'do you know the way?'

'General, if I am not mistaken, the middle causeway leads
straight to the abbey.'

'That is right; but we shall want lights to guide us in the vaults.' Monk turned round.

'Ah! I thought Digby was following us!' said he. 'So much the better; he will procure us what we want.'

'Yes, general, there is a man yonder who has been walking behind us for some time.'

'Digby!' cried Monk. 'Digby! come here, if you please.'

But, instead of obeying, the shadow made a motion of surprise, and, retreating instead of advancing, it bent down and disappeared along the jetty on the left, directing its course towards the lodging of the fishermen.

'It appears not to be Digby,' said Monk.

Both had followed the shadow which had vanished. But it was not so rare a thing for a man to be wandering about at eleven o'clock at night, in a camp of ten or eleven thousand men, as to give Monk and Athos any alarm at his disappearance.

'Still,' said Monk, 'we must have a light, a lantern, a torch, or something by which we may see where to set our feet; let us seek this light.'

'General, the first soldier we meet will light us.'

'No,' said Monk in order to discover if there were not any connivance between the Comte de la Fère and the fisherman. 'No, I should prefer one of these French sailors who came this evening to sell me their fish. They leave to-morrow, and the secret will be better kept by them; whereas, if a report should be spread in the Scottish army, that treasures are to be found in the abbey of Newcastle, my Highlanders will believe there is a million concealed beneath every slab; and they will not leave stone upon stone in the building.'

'Do as you think best, general,' replied Athos, in a natural tone of voice, making evident that soldier or fisherman was the same to him, and that he had no preference.

Monk approached the causeway behind which had disappeared the person he had taken for Digby, and met a patrol who, making the tour of the tents, was going towards head-quarters; he was stopped with his companion, gave the pass-word, and went on. A soldier, roused by the noise, unrolled his plaid, and looked up to see what was going forward. 'Ask him,' said Monk to Athos, 'where the fishermen are; if I were to speak to him, he would know me.'

Athos went up to the soldier, who pointed out the tent to him; immediately Monk and Athos turned towards it. It appeared to the general that at the moment they came up, a shadow like that they had already seen, glided into this tent; but on drawing nearer he perceived he must have been mistaken, for all of them were asleep higgledy-piggledy, and nothing was seen but arms and legs joined, crossed, and mixed. Athos, fearing lest he should be suspected of connivance with some of his compatriots, remained outside the tent.

'Wake up here!' said Monk, in French. 'On your feet!' Two or three of the sleepers got up.

'I want a man to light me,' continued Monk.

'Your honour may depend upon us,' said a voice which made Athos start. 'Where do you wish us to go?'

'You shall see. A light! come, quickly!'

'Yes, your honour. Does it please your honour that I should accompany you?'

'You or another, it is of very little consequence, provided I have a light.'

'It is strange!' thought Athos; 'what a singular voice* that man has!'

'Some fire, you fellows!' cried the fisherman; 'come, make haste!'

Then addressing his companion nearest to him in a low voice: 'Get a light, Menneville,'* said he, 'and hold yourself ready for anything.'

One of the fishermen struck light from a stone, set fire to some tinder, and by the aid of a match lit a lantern. The light immediately spread all over the tent.

'Are you ready, monsieur?' said Monk to Athos, who had turned away, not to expose his face to the light.

'Yes, general,' replied he.

'Ah! the French gentleman!' said the leader of the fishermen to himself. 'Hell's teeth! I have a great mind to charge you with the commission, Menneville; he may know me. Light! light!' This dialogue was pronounced at the back of the tent, and in so low a voice that Monk could not hear a syllable of it; he was, besides, talking with Athos. Menneville got himself ready in the meantime, or rather received the orders of his leader.

'Well?' said Monk.

'I am ready, general,' said the fisherman.

Monk, Athos, and the fisherman left the tent.

'It is impossible!' thought Athos. 'What dream could put that into my head?'

'Go forward; follow the middle causeway, and stretch out your legs,' said Monk to the fisherman.

They were not twenty paces on their way, when the same shadow that had appeared to enter the tent came out of it again, crawled along as far as the piles, and, protected by a sort of parapet placed along the causeway, carefully observed the progress of the general. All three disappeared in the night haze. They were walking towards Newcastle, the white stones of which appeared to them like sepulchres. After standing for a few seconds under the porch, they penetrated into the interior. The door had been broken open by axes. A detail of four men slept in safety in a corner; so certain were they that the attack would not take place on that side.

'Will not these men be in your way?' said Monk to Athos.

'On the contrary, monsieur, they will assist in rolling out the casks, if your honour will permit them.'

'You are right.'

The sentries, though fast asleep, roused up at the first steps of the three visitors amongst the briars and grass that invaded the porch. Monk gave the pass-word, and penetrated into the interior of the abbey, preceded by the light. He walked last, watching the least movement of Athos, his naked dirk in his sleeve, and ready to plunge it into the back of the gentleman at the first suspicious gesture he should see him make. But Athos, with a firm and sure step, crossed the chambers and courts.

Not a door, not a window was left in this building. The doors had been burnt, some on the spot, and the charcoal of them was still jagged from the action of the fire, which had gone out of itself, powerless, no doubt, to get to the heart of those massive joints of oak fastened together with iron nails. As to the windows, all the panes having been broken, night birds, alarmed by the torch, flew away through their holes. At the same time, gigantic bats began to trace their vast, silent circles around the intruders, whilst the light of the torch made their shadows

tremble on the high stone walls. Monk concluded there could be
no man in the abbey, since wild beasts and birds were there still,
and fled away at his approach.

After having passed the debris, and torn away more than one
branch of ivy that had made itself a guardian of the solitude,
Athos arrived at the vaults situated beneath the great hall, but
the entrance of which was from the chapel. There he stopped.
'Here we are, general,' said he.

'This, then, is the slab?'

'Yes.'

'Ay, and here is the ring—but the ring is sealed into the
stone.'

'We must have a lever.'

'That's a thing very easy to find.'

Whilst looking round them, Athos and Monk saw a little ash
tree about three inches in diameter, which had shot up in an
angle of the wall, reaching a window, concealed by its branches.

'Have you a knife?' said Monk to the fisherman.

'Yes, Monsieur.'

'Cut down this tree, then.'

The fisherman obeyed, but not without notching his cutlass.
When the ash was cut and fashioned into the shape of a lever,
the three men penetrated into the vault.

'Stop where you are,' said Monk to the fisherman. 'We are
going to dig up some powder; your light may be dangerous.'

The man drew back in a sort of terror, and faithfully stayed
at his post, whilst Monk and Athos turned behind a column at
the foot of which, penetrating through a crack, was a moon-
beam, reflected exactly on the stone which the Comte de la Fère
had come so far to find.

'This is it,' said Athos, pointing out to the general the Latin
inscription.

'Yes,' said Monk.

Then, as if still willing to leave the Frenchman one way out—

'Do you not observe that this vault has already been broken
into,' continued he, 'and that several statues have been knocked
down?'

'My lord, you have, without doubt, heard that the religious
respect of your Scots loves to confide to the statues of the dead

the valuable objects they have possessed during their lives. Therefore the soldiers had reason to think that under the pedestals of
the statues which ornament most of these tombs, a treasure was
hidden. They have consequently broken down pedestal and statue:
but the tomb of the venerable canon, with which we have to do,
is not distinguised by any monument. It is quite plain, and as
a result it has been protected by the superstitious fear which
your puritans have always had of sacrilege. Not a morsel of the
masonry of this tomb has been chipped off.'

'That is true,' said Monk.

Athos seized the lever.

'Shall I help you?' said Monk.

'Thank you, my lord; but I am not willing that your honour
should lend your hand to a work of which, perhaps, you would
not take the responsibility if you knew the probable consequences
of it.'

Monk raised his head.

'What do you mean by that, monsieur?'

'I mean—but that man back there——'

'Stop,' said Monk; 'I see what you are afraid of. I shall test
him.' Monk turned towards the fisherman, the whole of whose
profile was thrown upon the wall.

'Come here, friend!' said he in English, and in a tone of
command.

The fisherman did not stir.

'That is well,' continued he: 'he does not know English. Speak
to me, then, in English, if you please, monsieur.'

'My lord,' replied Athos, 'I have frequently seen men in
certain circumstances have sufficient command over themselves
not to reply to a question put to them in a language they understood. The fisherman is perhaps more learned than we believe
him to be. Send him away, my lord, I beg you.'

'Decidedly,' said Monk, 'he wishes to have me alone in this
vault. Never mind, we shall go through with it; one man should
be a match for another; and we are alone. My friend,' said Monk
to the fisherman, 'go back up the stairs we have just descended,
and watch that nobody comes to disturb us.' The fisherman
made a sign of obedience. 'Leave your torch,' said Monk; 'it
would betray your presence, and might earn you a musket-ball.'

The fisherman appeared to appreciate the advice; he laid down the light, and disappeared under the vault of the stairs. Monk took the torch, and brought it to the foot of the column.

'Ah, ah!' said he; 'money, then, is concealed under this tomb?'

'Yes, my lord; and in five minutes you will no longer doubt it.'

At the same time Athos struck a violent blow upon the plaster, which split, presenting a chink for the point of the lever. Athos introduced the bar into this crack, and soon large pieces of plaster yielded, rising up like rounded slabs. Then the Comte de la Fère seized the stones and threw them away with a force that hands so delicate as his might not have been supposed capable of having.

'My lord,' said Athos, 'this is plainly the masonry of which I told your honour.'

'Yes; but I do not yet see the casks,' said Monk.

'If I had a dagger,' said Athos, looking round him, 'you should soon see them, monsieur. Unfortunately I left mine in your tent.'

'I would willingly offer you mine,' said Monk, 'but the blade is too thin for such work.'

Athos appeared to look around him for a thing of some kind that might serve as a substitute for the weapon he desired. Monk did not miss one of the movements of his hands, or one of the expressions of his eyes. 'Why do you not ask the fisherman for his cutlass?' said Monk; 'he has a cutlass.'

'Ah! that is true,' said Athos; 'for he cut the tree down with it.' And he advanced towards the stairs.

'Friend,' said he to the fisherman, 'throw me down your cutlass, if you please; I want it.'

The noise of the falling weapon sounded on the steps.

'Take it,' said Monk; 'it is a solid instrument, as I have seen, and a strong hand might make good use of it.'

Athos only appeared to give to the words of Monk the natural and simple sense under which they were to be heard and understood. Nor did he notice, or at least appear to notice, that when he returned with the weapon, Monk drew back, placing his left hand on the stock of his pistol; in the right he already held his dirk. He went to work then, turning his back to Monk, placing his life in his hands, without possible defence. He then struck, during several seconds, so skilfully and sharply upon the intermediary plaster, that it separated into two parts, and Monk was able to discern two barrels placed end to end, and which their weight maintained motionless in their chalky envelope.

'My lord,' said Athos, 'you see that my presentiments have not been disappointed.'

'Yes, monsieur,' said Monk, 'and I have good reason to believe you are satisfied; are you not?'

'To be sure, I am; the loss of this money would have been inexpressibly great to me; but I was certain that God, who protects the good cause, would not have permitted this gold, which should procure its triumph, to be diverted to baser purposes.'

'You are, upon my honour, as mysterious in your words as in your actions, monsieur,' said Monk. 'Just now I did not perfectly understand you when you said that you were not willing to throw upon me the responsibility of the work we were accomplishing.'

'I had reason to say so, my lord.'

'And now you speak to me of the good cause. What do you mean by the words "the good cause"? We are defending at this moment, in England, five or six causes, which does not prevent every one from considering his own not only as the good cause, but as the best. What is yours, monsieur? Speak boldly that we may see if, upon this point, to which you appear to attach a great importance, we are of the same opinion.'

Athos fixed upon Monk one of those penetrating looks which seem to convey to him to whom they were directed a challenge to conceal a single one of his thoughts; then, taking off his hat, he began in a solemn voice, while his interlocutor, with one hand upon his visage, allowed that long and nervous hand to compress his moustache and beard, while his vague and melancholy eye wandered about the recesses of the vaults.

XXVI

HEART AND MIND

'My lord,' said the Comte de la Fère, 'you are a noble English-man, you are a loyal man; you are speaking to a noble French-man, to a man of heart. The gold contained in these two casks before us, I have told you was mine. I was wrong—it is the first lie I have pronounced in my life, a temporary lie, it is true. This gold is the property of King Charles II, exiled from his country, driven from his palaces, the orphan at once of his father and his throne, and deprived of everything, even of the melancholy happiness of kissing on his knees the stone upon which the hands of his murderers have written that simple epitaph which will eternally cry out for vengeance upon them: "Here lies Charles I." '*

Monk grew slightly pale, and an imperceptible shudder crept over his skin and raised his grey moustache.

'I,' continued Athos, 'I, Comte da la Fère, the last, only faithful friend the poor abandoned prince has left, I have offered him to come hither to find the man upon whom now depends the fate of royalty and of England; and I have come, and placed myself under the eye of this man, and have placed myself naked and unarmed in his hands, saying: "My lord, here are the last resources of a prince whom God made your master, whom his birth made your king; upon you, and you alone, depend his life and his future. Will you employ this money in consoling Eng-land for the evils it has had to suffer from anarchy; that is to say, will you aid, and if not aid, will you allow King Charles II to act? You are master, you are king, all-powerful master and king, for chance sometimes defeats the work of time and God. I am here alone with you, my lord: if divided success alarms you, if my loyalties anger you, you are armed, my lord, and here is a grave ready dug; if, on the contrary, the enthusiasm of your cause carries you away, if you are what you appear to be, if your hand in what it undertakes obeys your mind, and your mind your heart, here are the means of ruining for ever the cause of your enemy, Charles Stuart. Kill, then, the man you have before you, for that man will never return to him who has sent him without bearing with him the deposit which Charles I, his father, confided to him, and keep the gold which may assist in carrying on the civil war. Alas! my lord, it is the fate of this unfortunate prince. He must either corrupt or kill, for everything resists him, everything rejects him, everything is hostile to him; and yet he is marked with the divine seal, and he must, not to belie his blood, reascend the throne, or die upon the sacred soil of his country."

'My lord, you have heard me. To any other but the illustrious man who listens to me, I would have said: "My lord, you are poor; my lord, the king offers you this million as an earnest of an immense bargain; take it, and serve Charles II as I served Charles I, and I feel assured that God who listens to us, who sees us, who alone reads in your heart, shut up from all human eyes—I am assured God will give you a happy eternal life after a happy death." But to General Monk, to the illustrious man of whose standard I believe I have taken the measure, I say: "My lord, there is for you in the history of peoples and kings a brilliant place, an immortal, imperishable glory, if alone, without any other interest but the good of your country and the interests of justice, you become the supporter of your king. Many others have been conquerors and proud usurpers; you, my lord, you will be content with being the most virtuous, the most honest, and the most incorruptible of men: you will have held a crown in your hand, and instead of placing it upon your own brow, you will have deposited it upon the head of him for whom it was made. Oh, my lord, act thus, and you will leave to posterity the most enviable of names, in which no human creature can rival you."'

Athos stopped. During the whole time that the noble gentleman was speaking, Monk had not given one sign of either approbation or disapprobation; scarcely even, during this vehement appeal, had his eyes been animated with that fire which bespeaks intelligence. The Comte de la Fère looked at him sorrowfully, and on seeing that melancholy countenance, felt discouragement penetrate to his very heart. At length Monk appeared to recover, and broke the silence.

'Monsieur,' said he, in a mild, calm tone, 'in reply to you, I will make use of your own words. To any other but yourself I would reply by expulsion, imprisonment, or still worse, for, in fact, you tempt me and you force me at the same time. But you are one of those men, monsieur, to whom it is impossible to refuse the attention and respect they merit; you are a brave gentleman, monsieur—I say so, and I am a judge. You just now spoke of a sacred pledge which the late king transmitted through you to his son—are you, then, one of those Frenchmen who, as I have heard, endeavoured to carry off Charles I from White-hall?'

'Yes, my lord; it was I who was beneath the scaffold during the execution; I, who had not been able to redeem it, received upon my brow the blood of the martyred king. I received at the same time, the last word of Charles I; it was to me he said, "Remember!", and in saying "Remember!" he alluded to the money at your feet, my lord.'

'I have heard much of you, monsieur,' said Monk, 'but I am happy to have, in the first place, appreciated you by my own observations, and not by my recollection. I will give you, then, explanations that I have given to no other, and you will appreciate what a distinction I make between you and the persons who have hitherto been sent to me.'

Athos bowed, and prepared to absorb greedily the words which fell, one by one, from the mouth of Monk—those words rare and precious as the dew in the desert.

'You spoke to me,' said Monk, 'of Charles II; but pray, monsieur, of what consequence to me is that phantom of a king? I have grown old in a war and in a policy which are nowadays so closely linked together, that every man of the sword must fight in virtue of his rights or his ambition with a personal interest, and not blindly behind an officer, as in ordinary wars. For myself, I perhaps desire nothing, but I fear much. In the war of to-day rests the liberty of England, and, perhaps, that of every Englishman. How can you expect that I, free in the position I have made for myself, should go willingly and hold out my hands to the shackles of a stranger? That is all Charles is to me. He has fought battles here which he has lost, he is therefore a bad captain; he has succeeded in no negotiation, he is therefore a bad diplomat; he has paraded his needs and his miseries in all the courts of Europe, he has therefore a weak and pusillanimous heart. Nothing noble, nothing great, nothing strong has hitherto emanated from that genius which aspires to govern one of the greatest kingdoms of the earth. I know this Charles, then, in none but a bad light, and you would wish me, a man of good sense, to go and make myself gratuitously the slave of a creature who is inferior to me in military capacity, in politics, and in dignity! No, monsieur. When some great and noble action shall have taught me to value Charles, I shall perhaps recognize his rights to a throne from which we have cast the father because he lacked the virtues which his son has hitherto lacked, but, in the matter of rights, I only recognize my own; the revolution made me a general, my sword will make me protector, if I wish it. Let Charles show himself, let him present himself, let him enter the competition open to talent, and, above all, let him remember that he is of a race from whom more will be expected than from any other. Therefore, monsieur, say no more about him. I neither refuse nor accept: I reserve myself—I wait.'

Athos knew Monk to be too well informed of all concerning Charles to venture to urge the discussion further; it was neither the time nor the place. 'My lord,' then said he, 'I have nothing to do but to thank you.'

'And why, monsieur? Because you have formed a correct opinion of me, or because I have acted according to your judgment? Is that, in truth, worthy of thanks? This gold which you are about to carry to Charles, will serve me as a test for him, by seeing the use he will make of it. I shall have an opinion which now I have not.'

'And yet does not your honour fear to compromise yourself by allowing such a sum to be carried away for the service of your enemy?'

'My enemy, say you? Eh, monsieur, I have no enemies. I am in the service of the parliament, which orders me to fight General Lambert and Charles Stuart—its enemies, and not mine. I fight them. If the parliament, on the contrary, ordered me to unfurl my standards on the port of London, to assemble my soldiers on the banks to receive Charles II——'

'You would obey?' cried Athos, joyfully.

'Pardon me,' said Monk, smiling, 'I was going—I, a grey-headed man—in truth, how could I forget myself? was going to speak like a foolish young man.'

'Then you would not obey?' said Athos.

'I do not say that either, monsieur. The welfare of my country before everything. God who has given me the power, has, no doubt, willed that I should have that power for the good of all, and He has given me, at the same time, discernment. If the parliament were to order such a thing, I should reflect.'

The brow of Athos became clouded. 'Then I may positively say that your honour is not inclined to favour King Charles II?'

'You continue to question me, Monsieur le Comte; allow me to do so in turn, if you please.'

'Do, monsieur; and may God inspire you with the idea of replying to me as frankly as I shall reply to you.'

'When you shall have taken this money back to your prince, what advice will you give him?'

Athos fixed upon Monk a proud and resolute look.

'My lord,' said he, 'with this million, which others would perhaps employ in negotiating, I would advise the king to raise two regiments, to enter Scotland, which you have just pacified: to give to the people the freedoms which the revolution promised them, and in which it has not, in all cases, kept its word. I should advise him to command in person this little army, which would, believe me, increase, and to die, standard in hand, and sword in its sheath, saying, "Englishmen! I am the third king of my race* you have killed; beware of the justice of God!"'

Monk hung down his head, and mused for an instant. 'If he succeeded,' said he, 'which is very improbable, but not impossible—for everything is possible in this world—what would you advise him to do?'

'To think that by the will of God he lost his crown, but by the good will of men he recovered it.'

An ironical smile passed over the lips of Monk.

'Unfortunately, monsieur,' said he, 'kings do not know how to follow good advice.'

'Ah, my lord, Charles II is not a king,' replied Athos, smiling in his turn, but with a very different expression from Monk.

'Let us terminate this, Monsieur le Comte—that is your desire, is it not?'

Athos bowed.

'I shall give orders to have these two casks transported whither you please. Where are you lodging, monsieur?'

'In a little hamlet at the mouth of the river, your honour.'

'Oh, I know the hamlet; it consists of five or six houses, does it not?'

'Exactly. Well, I inhabit the first—two net-makers occupy it with me; it is their boat which brought me ashore.'

'But your own vessel, monsieur?'

'My vessel is at anchor, a quarter of a mile out to sea, and waits for me.'

'You do not think, however, of setting out immediately?'

'My lord, I shall try once more to convince your honour.'

'You will not succeed,' replied Monk; 'but it is of consequence that you should depart from Newcastle without leaving of your passage the least suspicion that might prove injurious to me or you. To-morrow my officers think Lambert will attack me. I, on the contrary, am convinced that he will not stir; it is in my opinion impossible. Lambert leads an army divided in its loyalties, and a divided army is no army at all. I have taught my soldiers to consider my authority subordinate to another, therefore, after me, round me, and beneath me, they still look for something. It would result, that if I were dead, whatever might happen, my army would not be demoralized all at once; it results, that if I chose to absent myself, for instance, as it does please me to do sometimes, there would not be in the camp the shadow of uneasiness or disorder. I am the magnet—the sympathetic and natural strength of the English. All those scattered Ironsides that will be sent against me I shall attract to myself. Lambert, at this moment, commands eighteen thousand deserters; but I have never mentioned that to my officers, you may easily suppose. Nothing is more useful to an army than the expectation of a coming battle; everybody is alert—everybody is on guard. I tell you this that you may live in perfect security. Do not be in a hurry, then, to cross the seas; within a week there will be something fresh, either a battle or an accommodation. Then, as you have judged me to be an honourable man, and confided your secret to me, I have to thank you for this confidence, and I shall come and pay you a visit or send for you. Do not go before I send you word. I repeat the request.'

'I promise you, general,' cried Athos, with a joy so great, that in spite of all his circumspection, he could not prevent its sparkling in his eyes.

Monk surprised this flash, and immediately extinguished it by one of those silent smiles which always caused his interlocutors to know they had made no inroad on his mind.

'Then, my lord, it is a week that you desire me to wait?'

'A week? yes, monsieur.'

'And during these days what shall I do?'

'If there should be a battle, keep at a distance from it, I beseech you. I know the French delight in such amusements; you might take a fancy to see how we fight, and you might receive some chance shot. Our Scotsmen are very bad marksmen, and I do not wish that a worthy gentleman like you should return to France wounded. Nor should I like to be obliged, myself, to send to your prince his million left here by you; for then it would be said, and with some reason, that I paid the Pretender to enable him to make war against the parliament. Go, then, monsieur, and let it be done as has been agreed upon.'

'Ah, my lord,' said Athos, 'what joy it would give me to be the first that penetrated to the noble heart which beats beneath that cloak!'

'You think, then, that I have secrets,' said Monk, without changing the half-cheerful expression of his countenance. 'Why, monsieur, what secret can you expect to find in the hollow head of a soldier? But it is getting late, and our torch is almost out; let us call our man.'

'Holà!' cried Monk in French, approaching the stairs; 'holà! fisherman!'

The fisherman, benumbed by the cold night air, replied in a hoarse voice, asking what they wanted of him.

'Go to the post,' said Monk, 'and order a sergeant, in the name of General Monk, to come here immediately.'

This was a commission easily performed; for the sergeant, uneasy at the general's being in that desolate abbey, had drawn nearer by degrees, and was not much further off than the fisherman. The general's order was therefore heard by him, and he hastened to obey it.

'Get a horse and two men,' said Monk.

'A horse and two men?' repeated the sergeant.

'Yes,' replied Monk. 'Have you any means of getting a horse with a pack-saddle or two panniers?'

'No doubt, at a hundred paces off, in the Scottish camp.'

'Very well.'

'What shall I do with the horse, general?'

'Look here.'

The sergeant descended the three steps which separated him from Monk, and came into the vault.

'You see,' said Monk, 'that gentleman yonder?'

'Yes, general.'

'And you see these two casks?'

'Yes.'

'They are two casks, one containing powder, and the other cannon-balls; I wish these casks to be transported to the little hamlet at the mouth of the river, and which I intend to occupy to-morrow with two hundred muskets. You understand that the commission is a secret one, for it is a movement that may decide the fate of the battle.'

'Oh, general!' murmured the sergeant.

'Mind, then! Let these casks be fastened on to the horse, and have them escorted by two men and you to the residence of this gentleman, who is my friend. But take care that nobody knows it.'

'I would go by the marsh if I knew the road,' said the sergeant.

'I know one myself,' said Athos; 'it is not wide, but it is firm, having been made upon piles; and with care we shall get over safely enough.'

'Do everything this gentleman shall order you to do.'

'Oh! oh! the casks are heavy,' said the sergeant, trying to lift one.

'They weigh four hundred pounds each, if they contain what they ought to contain, do they not, monsieur?'

'Thereabouts,' said Athos.

The sergeant went in search of the two men and the horse. Monk, left alone with Athos, affected to speak to him on nothing but indifferent subjects while examining the vault in a cursory manner. Then, hearing the horse's steps——

'I leave you with your men, monsieur,' said he, 'and return to the camp. You are perfectly safe.'

'I shall see you again, then, my lord?' asked Athos.

'That is agreed upon, monsieur, and with much pleasure.'

Monk held out his hand to Athos.

'Ah! my lord, if you would!' murmured Athos.

'Hush! monsieur, it is agreed that we shall speak no more of that.' And bowing to Athos he went up the stairs, meeting about half-way his men, who were coming down. He had not gone twenty paces, when a faint but prolonged whistle was heard at a distance. Monk listened, but seeing nothing and hearing nothing, he continued his route. Then he remembered the fisherman, and looked about for him; but the fisherman had disappeared. If he had, however, looked with more attention, he might have seen that man, bent double, gliding like a serpent along the stones and losing himself in the mist that floated over the surface of the marsh. He might have equally seen, had he attempted to pierce that mist, a spectacle that might have attracted his attention; and that was the rigging of the vessel, which had moved anchor, and was now nearer the shore. But Monk saw nothing; and thinking he had nothing to fear he entered the deserted causeway which led to his camp. It was then that the disappearance of the fisherman appeared strange, and that a real suspicion began to take possession of his mind. He had just placed at the orders of Athos the only soldiers who could protect him. He had a mile of causeway to traverse before he could regain his camp. The fog increased with such intensity that he could scarcely distinguish objects at ten paces' distance. Monk then thought he heard the sound of an oar over the marsh on the right. 'Who goes there?' said he.

But nobody answered; then he cocked his pistol, took his sword in his hand, and quickened his pace, without, however, being willing to call anybody. Such a summons, for which there was no absolute necessity, appeared unworthy of him.

XXVII

THE NEXT DAY

IT was seven o'clock in the morning, the first rays of day lightened the pools of the marsh, in which the sun was reflected like a red ball, when Athos awaking and opening the window of his bed-chamber, which looked out upon the banks of the river, saw, at fifteen paces' distance from him, the sergeant and the men who had accompanied him the evening before, and who, after having deposited the casks at his house, had returned to the camp by the causeway on the right.

Why had these men come back after having returned to the camp? That was the question which first presented itself to Athos. The sergeant, with his head raised, appeared to be watching the moment when the gentleman should appear, to address him. Athos, surprised to see these men, whom he had seen depart the night before, could not refrain from expressing his astonishment to them.

'There is nothing surprising in that, monsieur,' said the sergeant; 'for yesterday the general commanded me to watch over your safety, and I thought it right to obey that order.'

'Is the general at the camp?' asked Athos.

'No doubt he is, monsieur; as when he left you he was going back.'

'Well, wait for me a moment; I am going thither to render an account of the fidelity with which you fulfilled your duty, and to retrieve my sword, which I left upon the table in the tent.'

'That is good news, monsieur,' said the sergeant, 'for we were about to request you to do so.'

Athos fancied he could detect an odd look on the countenance of the sergeant; but the adventure of the vault might have excited the curiosity of the man, and it was not surprising that he allowed some of the feelings which agitated his mind to appear in his face. Athos closed the doors carefully, confiding the keys to Grimaud, who had chosen his lodging beneath the shed itself, which led to the cellar where the casks had been deposited. The sergeant escorted the Count de la Fère to the camp. There a fresh guard awaited him, and relieved the four men who had conducted Athos.

This fresh guard was commanded by the aide-de-camp Digby, who, on their way, fixed upon Athos looks so unfriendly, that the Frenchman asked himself, whence arose such vigilance and severity, when the evening before he had been left perfectly free. He nevertheless continued his way to the head-quarters, keeping to himself the observations which men and things forced him to make. He found in the general's tent, to which he had been introduced the evening before, three superior officers: these were Monk's lieutenant and two colonels. Athos perceived his sword; it was still on the table where he left it. Neither of the officers had seen Athos, consequently neither of them knew him. Monk's lieutenant asked, at the appearance of Athos, if that were the same gentleman with whom the general had left the tent.

'Yes, your honour,' said the sergeant; 'it is the same.'

'But,' said Athos, haughtily, 'I do not deny it; and now, gentlemen, in turn, permit me to ask you to what purpose these questions are asked, and particularly some explanation upon the tone in which you ask them?'

'Monsieur,' said the lieutenant, 'if we address these questions to you, it is because we have a right to do so, and if we make them in a particular tone, it is because that tone, believe me, agrees with the circumstances.'

'Gentlemen,' said Athos, 'you do not know who I am; but I must tell you I acknowledge no one here but General Monk as my equal. Where is he? Let me be conducted to him, and if he has any questions to put to me, I will answer him and to his satisfaction, I hope. I repeat, gentlemen, where is the general?'

'Eh! good God! you know better than we do where he is,' said the lieutenant.

'I?'

'Yes, you.'

'Monsieur,' said Athos, 'I do not understand you.'

'You will understand me—and, in the first place, do not speak so loud.'

Athos smiled disdainfully.

'We don't ask you to smile,' said one of the colonels warmly; 'we require you to answer.'

'And I, gentlemen, declare to you that I will not reply until I am in the presence of the general.'

'But,' replied the same colonel who had already spoken, 'you know very well that is impossible.'

'This is the second time I have received this strange reply to the wish I express,' said Athos. 'Is the general absent?'

This question was made with such apparent good faith, and the gentleman wore an air of such natural surprise, that the three officers exchanged a meaning look. The lieutenant, by a tacit convention with the other two, was spokesman.

'Monsieur, the general left you last night outside the abbey.'

'Yes, monsieur.'

'And you went——'

'It is not for me to answer you, but for those who accompanied me. They were your soldiers, ask them.'

'But if we please to question you?'

'Then it will please me to reply, monsieur, that I do not recognize any one here, that I know no one here but the general, and that it is to him alone I will reply.'

'So be it, monsieur; but as we are the masters, we constitute ourselves a council of war, and when you are before judges you must reply.'

The countenance of Athos expressed nothing but astonishment and disdain, instead of the fear the officers expected to read in it at this threat.

'Scottish or English judges upon me, a subject of the king of France; upon me, placed under the safeguard of British honour! You are mad, gentlemen!' said Athos, shrugging his shoulders.

The officers looked at each other. 'Then, monsieur,' said one of them, 'do you claim you do not know where the general is?'

'To that, monsieur, I have already given an answer.'

'Yes, but you have already given an incredible answer.'

'It is true, nevertheless, gentlemen. Men of my rank are not generally liars. I am a gentleman, I have told you, and when I have at my side the sword which, by an excess of delicacy, I left last night upon the table whereon it still lies, believe me, no man says that to me which I am unwilling to hear. I am at this moment disarmed; if you pretend to be my judges, try me; if you are but my executioners, kill me.'

'But, monsieur——' asked the lieutenant, in a more courteous voice, struck with the lofty coolness of Athos.

'Sir, I came to speak confidentially with your general about affairs of importance. It was not an ordinary welcome that he gave me. The accounts your soldiers can give you may convince you of that. If, then, the general received me in that manner, he knew my titles to his esteem. Now, you do not suspect, I should think, that I should reveal my secrets to you, and still less his.'

'But these casks, what do they contain?'

'Have you not put that question to your soldiers? What was their reply?'

'That they contained powder and ball.'

'From whom had they that information? They must have told you that.'

'From the general; but we are not dupes.'

'Beware, gentlemen; it is not to me you are now accusing of lying, it is to your leader.'

The officers again looked at each other. Athos continued: 'In front of your soldiers the general told me to wait a week, and at the expiration of that week he would give me the answer he had to make me. Have I fled away? No; I wait.'

'He told you to wait a week!' cried the lieutenant.

'He told me that so clearly, sir, that I have a sloop at the mouth of the river, which I could with ease have joined yesterday, and embarked. Now, if I have remained, it was only in compliance with the desire of your general; his honour having requested me not to depart without a last audience, which he fixed at a week hence. I repeat to you then, I am waiting.'

The lieutenant turned towards the other officers, and said, in a low voice: 'If this gentleman speaks truth, there may still be some hope. The general may be carrying out some negotiations so secret, that he thought it imprudent to inform even us. Then the time reasonably allowable for his absence would be a week.' Then, turning towards Athos: 'Monsieur,' said he, 'your declaration is of the greatest importance; are you willing to repeat it under the seal of an oath?'

'Sir,' replied Athos. 'I have always lived in a world where my simple word was regarded as the most sacred of oaths.'

'This time, however, monsieur, the circumstance is more grave than any you may have been placed in. The safety of the whole army is at stake. Reflect; the general has disappeared, and our search for him has been vain. Is this disappearance natural? Has a crime been committed? Are we not bound to carry our investigations to their farthest point? Have we any right to wait patiently? At this moment, everything, monsieur, depends upon the words you are about to pronounce.'

'Thus questioned, gentlemen, I no longer hesitate,' said Athos. 'Yes, I came hither to converse confidentially with General Monk, and ask him for an answer regarding certain interests; yes, the general being, doubtless, unable to pronounce before the expected battle, begged me to remain a week in the house I inhabit, promising me that in a week I should see him again. Yes, all this is true, and I swear it, by the God who is the absolute master of my life and yours.' Athos pronounced these words with so much grandeur and solemnity, that the three officers were almost convinced. Nevertheless, one of the colonels made a last attempt.

'Monsieur,' said he, 'although we may be now persuaded of the truth of what you say, there is yet a strange mystery in all this. The general is too prudent a man to have thus abandoned his army on the eve of a battle without having at least given notice of it to one of us. As for myself, I cannot believe but that some strange event has been the cause of this disappearance. Yesterday some foreign fishermen came to sell their fish here; they were lodged yonder among the Scots; that is to say, on the road the general took with this gentleman, to go to the abbey, and to return from it. It was one of those fishermen that accompanied the general with a light. And this morning, boat and fishermen have all disappeared, carried away by the night's tide.'

'For my part,' said the lieutenant, 'I see nothing in that that is not quite natural, for these people were not prisoners.'

'No; but I repeat it was one of them who lighted the general and this gentleman to the abbey, and Digby assures us that the general had strong suspicions concerning those men. Now, who can say whether they were not connected with this gentleman; and that, the blow being struck, the gentleman, who is evidently brave, did not remain to reassure us by his presence, and to prevent our researches being made in a right direction?'

This speech made an impression upon the other two officers.

'Sir,' said Athos, 'permit me to tell you, that your reasoning, though seemingly well-founded, nevertheless lacks consistency, as regards me. I have remained, you say, to divert suspicion. Well! on the contrary, suspicions arise in me as well as in you; and I say, it is impossible, gentlemen, that the general, on the eve of a battle, should leave his army without saying anything to, at least, one of his officers. Yes, there is some strange event connected with this; instead of being idle and waiting, you must display all the activity and all the vigilance possible. I am your prisoner, gentlemen, upon parole or otherwise. My honour is concerned in ascertaining what has become of General Monk, and to such a point, that if you were to say to me, "Depart!" I should reply: "No, I will remain!" And if you were to ask my opinion, I should add: "Yes, the general is the victim of some conspiracy, for, if he had intended to leave the camp he would have told me so." Seek then, search the land, search the sea; the general has not gone of his own free will.'

The lieutenant made a sign to the other two officers.

'No, monsieur,' said he, 'no; in your turn you go too far. The general has nothing to suffer from these events, and, no doubt, has directed them. What Monk is now doing he has often done before. We are wrong in alarming ourselves; his absence will, doubtless, be of short duration; therefore, let us beware, lest by a pusillanimity which the general would consider a crime, of making his absence public, and by that means demoralize the army. The general gives a striking proof of his confidence in us; let us show ourselves worthy of it. Gentlemen, let the most profound silence cover all this with an impenetrable veil; we will detain this gentleman, not from mistrust of him with regard to the crime, but to assure more effectively the secret of the general's absence by keeping among ourselves; therefore, until fresh orders, the gentleman will remain at head-quarters.'

'Gentlemen,' said Athos, 'you forget that last night the general confided to me a trust over which I am bound to watch. Give me whatever guard you like, chain me if you like, but leave me the house I inhabit for my prison. The general, on his return, would reproach you, I swear on the honour of a gentleman, for having displeased him in this.'

'So be it, monsieur,' said the lieutenant; 'return to your abode.'

Then they placed over Athos a guard of fifty men, who surrounded his house, without losing sight of him for a minute.

The secret remained secure, but hours, days passed away without the general's returning, and without anything being heard of him.

XXVIII

SMUGGLING

TWO days after the events we have just related, and while General Monk was expected every minute in the camp to which he did not return, a little Dutch felucca, manned by eleven men, cast anchor upon the coast of Scheveningen, nearly within cannon-shot of the port. It was night, the darkness was intense, the tide rose in the darkness; it was a capital time to land passengers and merchandise.

The roadstead of Scheveningen forms a vast crescent; it is not very deep and not very safe; therefore, nothing is seen stationed there but large Flemish hoys,* or some of those Dutch flat-bottomed boats which fishermen draw up on the sand on rollers, as the ancients did, according to Virgil.* When the tide is rising, and advancing on land, it is not prudent to bring the vessels too close in shore, for, if the wind is fresh, the prows are buried in the sand; and the sand of that coast is spongy; it receives easily, but does not yield so well. It was on this account, no doubt, that a boat was detached from the ship, as soon as the latter had cast anchor, and came with eight sailors, amidst whom was to be seen an object of an oblong form, a sort of large pannier or bale.

The shore was deserted; the few fishermen inhabiting the down were gone to bed. The only sentinel that guarded the coast (a coast very badly guarded, seeing that a landing from large ships was impossible), without having been able to follow the example of the fishermen, who were gone to bed, imitated them so far, that he slept at the back of his watch-box as soundly as they slept in their beds. The only noise to be heard, then, was the whistling of the night-breeze among the bushes and the brambles of the dunes. But the men who were approaching were doubtless suspicious by nature, for this real silence and apparent solitude did not satisfy them. Their boat, therefore, scarcely visible as a dark speck upon the ocean, glided along noiselessly, avoiding the use of their oars for fear of being heard, and reached the nearest land.

Scarcely had it touched the ground when a single man jumped out of the boat, after having given a brief order, in a manner which denoted the habit of commanding. In consequence of this order, several muskets immediately glittered in the feeble light reflected from that mirror of the heavens, the sea; and the oblong bale of which we spoke, containing no doubt some contraband object, was transported to land, with infinite precautions. Immediately after that, the man who had landed first, set off at a rapid pace diagonally towards the village of Scheveningen, directing his course to the nearest point of the wood. When there, he sought for that house already described as the temporary residence—and a very humble residence—of him who was styled by courtesy king of England.*

All were asleep there, as everywhere else, only a large dog, of the race of those which the fishermen of Scheveningen harness to little carts to carry fish to the Hague, began to bark loudly as soon as the stranger's steps were audible beneath the windows. But the watchfulness, instead of alarming the newly-landed man, appeared on the contrary, to give him great joy, for his voice might perhaps have proved insufficient to rouse the people of the house, whilst, with an auxiliary of that sort, his voice became almost useless. The stranger waited, then, till these reiterated and sonorous barkings should, according to all probability, have produced their effect, and then he ventured a summons. On hearing his voice, the dog began to roar with such violence that another voice was soon heard from the interior, quieting the dog. When the dog was quieted,

'What do you want?' asked that voice, at the same time weak, broken, and civil.

'I want his majesty King Charles II, king of England,' said the stranger.

'What do you want with him?'

'I want to speak to him.'

'Who are you?'

'Ah! *mordioux!* you ask too much; I don't like talking through doors.'

'Only tell me your name.'

'I don't like to declare my name in the open air, either; besides, you may be sure I shall not eat your dog, and I hope to God he will be as reserved with me.'

'You bring news, perhaps, monsieur, do you not?' replied the voice, patient and querulous as that of an old man.

'I will answer for it, I bring you news you little expect. Open the door, then, if you please!'

'Monsieur,' persisted the old man, 'do you believe, upon your soul and conscience, that your news is worth waking the king?'

'For God's sake, my dear monsieur, draw your bolts; you will not be sorry, I swear, for the trouble it will give you. I am worth my weight in gold, you have my word on it!'

'Monsieur, I cannot open the door till you have told me your name.'

'Must I, then?'

'It is by the order of my master, monsieur.'

'Well, my name is—but, I warn you, my name will tell you absolutely nothing.'

'Never mind, tell it, notwithstanding.'

'Well, I am the Chevalier d'Artagnan.'

The voice uttered an exclamation.

'Oh! good heavens!' said the voice on the other side of the door, 'Monsieur d'Artagnan. What happiness! I could not help thinking I knew that voice.'

'Humph!' said D'Artagnan. 'My voice is known here! That's flattering.'

'Oh! yes, we know it,' said the old man, drawing the bolts; 'and here is the proof.' And at these words he let in D'Artagnan, who, by the light of the lantern he carried in his hand, recognized his obstinate interlocutor.

'Ah! *mordioux!*' cried he: 'why, it is Parry! I should to have known it.'

'Parry, yes, my dear Monsieur d'Artagnan, it is I. What joy to see you once again!'

'You are right there, what joy!' said D'Artagnan, pressing the old man's hand. 'There, now you'll go and inform the king, will you not?'

'But the king is asleep, my dear monsieur.'

'*Mordioux!* then wake him. He won't scold you for having disturbed him, I promise you.'

'You come from the count, do you not?'

'The Comte de la Fère?'

'From Athos?'

'Hell's teeth! no; I come from no one but myself. Come, Parry, quick! The king—I want the king.'

Parry did not think it his duty to resist any longer; he knew D'Artagnan of old; he knew that, although a Gascon, his words never promised more than they could deliver. He crossed a court and a little garden, appeased the dog, that seemed most anxious to taste of the musketeer's flesh, and went to knock at the window of a chamber forming the ground-floor of a little pavilion. Immediately a little dog inhabiting that chamber answered the large dog inhabiting the court.

'Poor king!' said D'Artagnan to himself, 'these are his body-guards. It is true he is not the worse guarded on that account.'

'What is wanted with me?' asked the king, from the back of the chamber.

'Sire, it is M. le Chevalier d'Artagnan, who brings you some news.'

A noise was immediately heard in the chamber, a door was opened, and a flood of light inundated the corridor and the garden. The king was working by the light of a lamp. Papers were lying about upon his desk, and he had commenced the first draft of a letter which showed, by the numerous erasures, the trouble he had had in writing it.

'Come in, monsieur le chevalier,' said he, turning around. Then perceiving the fisherman, 'What do you mean, Parry? Where is M. le Chevalier d'Artagnan?' asked Charles.

'He is before you, sire,' said M. d'Artagnan.

'What, in that costume?'

'Yes; look at me, sire; do you not remember having seen me at Blois, in the antechambers of king Louis XIV?'

'Yes, monsieur, and I remember I was much pleased with you.'

D'Artagnan bowed. 'It was my duty to behave as I did, the moment I knew that I had the honour of being near your majesty.'

'You bring me news, do you say?'

'Yes, sire.'

'From the king of France?'

'No, sire,' replied D'Artagnan. 'Your majesty must have observed that the king of France is only occupied with his own majesty?'

Charles raised his eyes towards heaven.

'No, sire, no,' continued D'Artagnan. 'I bring news entirely composed of personal facts. Nevertheless, I hope your majesty will listen to the facts and news with some favour.'

'Speak, monsieur.'

'If I am not mistaken, sire, your majesty spoke a great deal at Blois, of the embarrassed state of the affairs of England.'

Charles coloured. 'Monsieur,' said he, 'it was to the king of France I related——'

'Oh! your majesty is mistaken,' said the musketeer, coolly; 'I know how to speak to kings in misfortune. It is only when they are in misfortune that they speak to me; once fortunate, they look upon me no more. I have, then, for your majesty, not only the greatest respect, but, still more, the most absolute devotion; and that, believe me, with me, sire, means something. Now, hearing your majesty complain of fate, I found that you were noble and generous, and bore misfortune well.'

'In truth!' said Charles, much astonished, 'I do not know which I ought to prefer, your freedoms or your respects.'

'You will choose presently, sire,' said D'Artagnan. 'Then your majesty complained to your brother, Louis XIV, of the difficulty you experienced in returning to England and regaining your throne, for want of men and money.'

Charles allowed a movement of impatience to escape him.

'And the principal object your majesty found in your way,' continued D'Artagnan, 'was a certain general commanding the armies of the parliament, and who was playing yonder the part of another Cromwell. Did not your majesty say so?'

'Yes; but I repeat to you, monsieur, those words were for the king's ears alone.'

'And you will see, sire, that it is very fortunate that they fell into those of his lieutenant of musketeers. That man so troublesome to your majesty was one General Monk, I believe, did I not hear his name correctly, sire?'

'Yes, monsieur, but once more, to what purpose are all these questions?'

'Oh! I know very well, sir, that etiquette will not allow kings to be questioned. I hope, however, presently you will pardon my want of etiquette. Your majesty added that, notwithstanding, if you could see him, confer with him, and meet him face to face, you would triumph, either by force or persuasion, over that obstacle—the only serious one, the only insurmountable one, the only real one you met with on your road.'

'All that is true, monsieur: my destiny, my future, my obscurity, or my glory depend upon that man; but what do you draw from that?'

'One thing alone, that if this General Monk is troublesome to the point your majesty describes it would be expedient to get rid of him or to make an ally of him.'

'Monsieur, a king who has neither army nor money, as you have heard my conversation with my brother Louis, has no means of acting against a man like Monk.'

'Yes, sire, that was your opinion, I know very well: but, fortunately for you, it was not mine.'

'What do you mean by that?'

'That, without an army and without a million, I have done— I, myself—what your majesty thought could alone be done with an army and a million.'

'How! What do you say? What have you done?'

'What have I done? Eh! well, sir, I went yonder to capture this man who is so troublesome to your majesty.'

'In England?'

'Exactly, sire.'

'You went to capture Monk in England?'

'Should I by chance have done wrong, sire?'

'In truth you are mad, monsieur!'

'Not the least in the world, sire.'

'You have captured Monk?'

'Yes, sire.'

'Where?'

'In the midst of his camp.'

The king trembled with impatience.

'And having captured him on the causeway of Newcastle, I bring him to your majesty,' said D'Artagnan, simply.

'You bring him to me!' cried the king, almost indignant at what he considered a mystification.

'Yes, sire,' replied D'Artagnan, in the same tone, 'I bring him to you; he is yonder, in a large chest pierced with holes, so as to allow him to breathe.'

'Good God!'

'Oh! don't be uneasy, sire, we have taken the greatest possible care of him. He comes in good state, and in perfect condition. Would your majesty please to see him, to talk with him, or to have him thrown into the sea?'

'Oh, heavens!' repeated Charles, 'oh, heavens! do you speak the truth, monsieur? Are you not insulting me with some unseemly jest? You have accomplished this unheard-of act of audacity and genius—impossible!'

'Will your majesty permit me to open the window?' said D'Artagnan, opening it.

The king had not time to reply, yes or no. D'Artagnan gave a shrill and prolonged whistle, which he repeated three times through the silence of the night.

'There!' said he, 'he will be brought to your majesty.'

XXIX

IN WHICH D'ARTAGNAN BEGINS TO FEAR HE HAS INVESTED HIS MONEY AND THAT OF PLANCHET VERY UNWISELY

THE king could not overcome his surprise, and looked now at the smiling face of the musketeer, and now at the dark window which opened into the night. But before he had fixed his ideas, eight of D'Artagnan's men, for two had remained to take care of the boat, brought to the house, where Parry received him, that object of an oblong form, which, for the moment, enclosed the destinies of England. Before he left Calais, D'Artagnan had had made in that city a sort of coffin, large and deep enough for a man to turn in it at his ease. The bottom and sides, properly upholstered, formed a bed sufficiently soft to prevent the rolling of the ship turning this kind of cage into a rat-trap. The little grating, of which D'Artagnan had spoken to the king, like the visor of a helmet, was placed opposite the man's face. It was so constructed that, at the least cry, a sudden pressure would stifle that cry, and, if necessary, him who had uttered that cry.

D'Artagnan was so well acquainted with his crew and his prisoner, that during the whole voyage he had been in dread of two things: either that the general would prefer death to this sort of imprisonment, and would smother himself by endeavouring to speak, or that his guards would allow themselves to be tempted by the offers of the prisoner, and put him, D'Artagnan, into the box instead of Monk.

D'Artagnan, therefore, had passed the two days and the two nights of the voyage close to the coffin, alone with the general, offering him wine and food, which the latter had refused, and constantly endeavouring to reassure him upon the destiny which awaited him at the end of this singular captivity. Two pistols on the table and his naked sword made D'Artagnan easy with regard to indiscretions from without.

When once at Scheveningen he had felt completely reassured. His men greatly dreaded any conflict with the lords of the soil. He had, besides, interested in his cause him who had faithfully served him as lieutenant, and whom we have seen reply to the name of Menneville. The latter, not being a vulgar spirit, had more to risk than the others, because he had more conscience. He believed in a future in the service of D'Artagnan, and consequently would have allowed himself to be cut to pieces, rather than violate the order given by his leader. Thus it was that, once landed, it was to him D'Artagnan had confided the care of the chest and the general's breathing. It was he, too, he had ordered to have the chest brought by the seven men as soon as he should hear the triple whistle. We have seen that the lieutenant obeyed. The coffer once in the house, D'Artagnan dismissed his men with a gracious smile, saying, 'Messieurs, you have rendered a great service to King Charles II, who in less than six weeks* will be king of England. Your gratification will then be doubled. Return to the boat and wait for me.' Upon which they departed with such shouts of joy as terrified even the dog himself.

D'Artagnan had caused the coffer to be brought as far as the king's antechamber. He then, with great care, closed the door of this antechamber, after which he opened the coffer, and said to the general,

'General, I have a thousand excuses to make to you; my manner of acting has not been worthy of such a man as you, I know very well; but I wished you to take me for the captain of a fishing boat. And then England is a very inconvenient country for transporting goods. I hope, therefore, you will take all that into consideration. But now, general, you are at liberty to get up and walk.' This said, he cut the bonds which fastened the arms and hands of the general. The latter got up, and then sat down with the countenance of a man who expects death. D'Artagnan opened the door of Charles's study, and said, 'Sire, here is your enemy, M. Monk; I promised myself to perform this service for your majesty. It is done; now order as you please. M. Monk,' added he, turning towards the prisoner, 'you are in the presence of his majesty Charles II, sovereign lord of Great Britain.'

Monk raised towards the prince his coldly stoical look, and replied: 'I know no king of Great Britain; I recognize even here no one worthy of bearing the name of gentleman: for it is in the name of King Charles II that an emissary, whom I took for an honest man, came and laid an infamous snare for me. I have fallen into that snare; so much the worse for me. Now, you the tempter,' said he to the king; 'you the executor,' said he to D'Artagnan; 'remember what I am about to say to you: you have my body, you may kill it, and I advise you to do so, for you shall never have my mind or my will. And now, ask me not a single word, as from this moment I will not open my mouth even to cry out. I have spoken.'

And he pronounced these words with the savage, invincible resolution of the most mortified Puritan. D'Artagnan looked at his prisoner like a man who knows the value of every word, and who fixes that value according to the accent with which it has been pronounced.

'The fact is,' said he, in a whisper to the king, 'the general is an obstinate man; he would not take a mouthful of bread, nor swallow a drop of wine, during the two days of our voyage. But as from this moment it is your majesty who must decide his fate, I wash my hands of him.'

Monk, erect, pale, and resigned, waited with his eyes fixed and his arms folded. D'Artagnan turned towards him. 'You will please understand perfectly,' said he, 'that your speech, otherwise very fine, does not suit anybody, not even yourself. His majesty wished to speak to you, you refused him an interview; why, now that you are face to face, that you are here by a force independent of your will, why do you submit to rigours which I consider useless and absurd? Speak! what the devil! speak, if only to say "No."'

Monk did not unclose his lips; Monk did not turn his eyes; Monk stroked his moustache with a thoughtful air, which announced that matters were going badly.

During all this time Charles II had fallen into a profound reverie. For the first time he found himself face to face with Monk; with the man he had so much desired to see; and, with that peculiar glance which God has given to eagles and kings, he had fathomed the abyss of his heart. He beheld Monk, then, resolved positively to die rather than speak, which was not to be wondered at in so considerable a man, the wound in whose mind must at the moment have been cruel. Charles II formed, on the instant, one of those resolutions upon which an ordinary man risks his life, a general his fortune, and a king his kingdom.* 'Monsieur,' said he to Monk, 'you are perfectly right upon certain points; I do not, therefore, ask you to answer me, but to listen to me.'

There was a moment's silence, during which the king looked at Monk, who remained impassive.

'You have made me just now a painful reproach, monsieur,' continued the king; 'you said that one of my emissaries had been to Newcastle to lay a snare for you, and that, let it be said, cannot be understood by M. d'Artagnan here, and to whom, before everything, I owe sincere thanks for his generous, his heroic devotion.'

D'Artagnan bowed with respect; Monk took no notice.

'For M. d'Artagnan—and observe, M. Monk, I do not say

this to excuse myself—for M. d'Artagnan,' continued the king, 'went to England of his free will, without interest, without orders, without hope, like a true gentleman as he is, to render a service to an unfortunate king, and to add to the illustrious actions of an existence, already so well filled, one glorious deed more.'

D'Artagnan coloured a little, and coughed to keep his countenance. Monk did not stir.

'You do not believe what I tell you, M. Monk,' continued the king. 'I can understand that—such proofs of devotion are so rare, that their reality may well be put in doubt.'

'Monsieur would do wrong not to believe you, sire,' cried D'Artagnan: 'for what your majesty has said is the exact truth, and the truth so exact that it seems, in going to fetch the general, I have done something which sets everything wrong. In truth, if it be so, I am in despair.'

'Monsieur d'Artagnan,' said the king, pressing the hand of the musketeer, 'you have obliged me as much as if you had promoted the success of my cause, for you have revealed to me an unknown friend, to whom I shall ever be grateful, and whom I shall always love.' And the king pressed his hand cordially. 'And,' continued he, bowing to Monk, 'an enemy whom I shall henceforth esteem at his proper value.'

The eyes of the Puritan flashed, but only once, and his countenance, for an instant illuminated by that flash, resumed its sombre impassivity.

'Then, Monsieur d'Artagnan,' continued Charles, 'this is what was about to happen: M. le Comte de la Fère, whom you know, I believe, has set out for Newcastle.'

'What, Athos!' exclaimed D'Artagnan.

'Yes, that was his *nom de guerre*,* I believe. The Comte de la Fère had then set out for Newcastle, and was going, perhaps, to bring the general to hold a conference with me or with those of my party, when you violently, as it appears, interfered with the negotiation.'

'*Mordioux!*' replied D'Artagnan, 'he entered the camp the very evening in which I succeeded in getting into it with my fishermen——'

An almost imperceptible frown on the brow of Monk told D'Artagnan that he had surmised rightly.

'Yes, yes,' muttered he; 'I thought I knew his person; I even fancied I knew his voice. Unlucky wretch that I am! Oh! sire, pardon me! I thought I had so successfully steered my course.'

'There is nothing ill in it, sir,' said the king, 'except that the general accuses me of having laid a snare for him, which is not the case. No, general, those are not the arms which I contemplated employing with you, as you will soon see. In the meanwhile, when I give you my word upon the honour of a gentleman, believe me, sir, believe me! Now, Monsieur d'Artagnan, a word with you, if you please.'

'I listen on my knees, sire.'

'You are truly at my service, are you not?'

'Your majesty has seen I am, too much so.'

'That is well; from a man like you one word suffices. In addition to that word you bring actions. General, have the goodness to follow me. Come with us, M. d'Artagnan.'

D'Artagnan, considerably surprised, prepared to obey. Charles II went out, Monk followed him, D'Artagnan followed Monk. Charles took the path by which D'Artagnan had come to his abode; the fresh sea breezes soon caressed the faces of the three nocturnal travellers, and, at fifty paces from the little gate which Charles opened, they found themselves upon the dune facing the ocean, which, having ceased to rise, reposed upon the shore like a wearied monster. Charles II walked pensively along, his head hanging down and his hand beneath his cloak. Monk followed him, with crossed arms and an uneasy look. D'Artagnan came last, with his hand on the hilt of his sword.

'Where is the boat in which you came, gentlemen?' said Charles to the musketeer.

'Yonder, sire; I have seven men and an officer waiting me in that little smack which is lighted by a fire.'

'Yes, I see; the boat is drawn upon the sand; but you certainly did not come from Newcastle in that frail bark?'

'No, sire; I chartered a felucca, at my own expense, which is at anchor within cannon-shot of the dunes. It was in that felucca we made the voyage.'

'Sir,' said the king to Monk, 'you are free.'

However firm his will, Monk could not suppress an exclamation. The king added an affirmative motion of his head, and

continued: 'We shall waken a fisherman of the village, who will
put his boat to sea immediately, and will take you back to any
place you may command him. M. d'Artagnan here will escort
your honour. I place M. d'Artagnan under the safeguard of your
loyalty, M. Monk.'

Monk allowed a murmur of surprise to escape him, and
D'Artagnan a profound sigh. The king, without appearing to
notice either, knocked against the deal trellis which enclosed the
hut belonging to the principal fisherman inhabiting the dune.

'Hey! Keyser!' cried he, 'awake!'

'Who calls me?' asked the fisherman.

'I, Charles the king.'

'Ah, my lord!' cried Keyser, rising ready dressed from the sail
in which he slept, as people sleep in a hammock. 'What can I do
to serve you?'

'Captain Keyser,' said Charles, 'you must set sail immediately. Here is a traveller who wishes to charter your boat, and
will pay you well; serve him well.' And the king drew back a few
steps to allow Monk to speak to the fisherman.

'I wish to cross over into England,' said Monk, who spoke
Dutch enough to make himself understood.

'This minute,' said the captain, 'this very minute, if you wish
it.'

'But will that be long?' said Monk.

'Not half an hour, your honour. My eldest son is at this
moment preparing the boat, as we were going out fishing at
three o'clock in the morning.'

'Well, is all arranged?' asked the king drawing near.

'All but the price,' said the fisherman; 'yes, sire.'

'That is my affair,' said Charles, 'the gentleman is my friend.'

Monk started and looked at Charles, on hearing this word.

'Very well, my lord,' replied Keyser. And at that moment
they heard Keyser's eldest son, signalling from the shore with
the blast of a bull's horn.

'Now, gentlemen,' said the king, 'depart.'

'Sire,' said D'Artagnan, 'will it please your majesty to grant
me a few minutes? I have engaged men, and I am going without
them, I must give them notice.'

'Whistle to them,' said Charles, smiling.

D'Artagnan, accordingly, whistled, whilst Captain Keyser replied to his son; and four men, led by Menneville, attended the first summons.

'Here is some money on account,' said D'Artagnan, putting into their hands a purse containing two thousand five hundred livres in gold. 'Go and wait for me at Calais, you know where.' And D'Artagnan heaved a profound sigh, as he let the purse fall into the hands of Menneville.

'What, are you leaving us?' cried the men.

'For a short time,' said D'Artagnan, 'or for a long time, who knows? But with 2,500 livres, and the 2,500 you have already received, you are paid according to our agreement. We are quits, then, my friend.'

'But the boat?'

'Do not trouble yourself about that.'

'Our things are on board the felucca.'

'Go and seek them, and then set off immediately.'

'Yes, captain.'

D'Artagnan returned to Monk, saying—'Monsieur, I await your orders, for I understand we are to go together, unless my company be disagreeable to you.'

'On the contrary, monsieur,' said Monk.

'Come, gentlemen, on board,' cried Keyser's son.

Charles bowed to the general with grace and dignity, saying—'You will pardon me this unfortunate accident, and the violence to which you have been subjected, when you are convinced that I was not the cause of them.'

Monk bowed profoundly without replying. On his side, Charles affected not to say a word to D'Artagnan in private, but aloud—'Once more, thanks, monsieur le chevalier,' said he, 'thanks for your services. They will be repaid you by the Lord God, who, I hope, reserves trials and troubles for me alone.'

Monk followed Keyser and his son embarked with them. D'Artagnan came after, muttering to himself—'Poor Planchet! poor Planchet! I am very much afraid we can say goodbye to our investment.'

XXX

THE SHARES OF PLANCHET & CO. RISE
AGAIN TO PAR

DURING the passage, Monk only spoke to D'Artagnan in cases
of urgent necessity. Thus, when the Frenchman hesitated to
come and take his meals, poor meals, composed of salt fish,
biscuit, and Hollands gin*, Monk called him, saying—'To table,
monsieur, to table!'

This was all. D'Artagnan, from being himself on all great
occasions extremely concise, did not draw from the general's
conciseness a favourable augury of the result of his mission.
Now, as D'Artagnan had plenty of time for reflection, he racked
his brains during this time in endeavouring to find out how
Athos had seen King Charles, how he had conspired his departure with him, and lastly, how he had entered Monk's camp;
and the poor lieutenant of musketeers plucked a hair from
his moustache every time he reflected that the horseman who
accompanied Monk on the night of the famous abduction must
have been Athos.

At length, after a passage of two nights and two days, Captain
Keyser touched at the point where Monk, who had given all the
orders during the voyage, had commanded they should land. It
was exactly at the mouth of the little river, near which Athos
had chosen his abode.

Daylight was waning, a splendid sun, like a red steel buckler,
was plunging the lower edge of its disc beneath the blue line of
the sea. The felucca was making fair way up the river, tolerably
wide in that part, but Monk, in his impatience, desired to be
landed, and Keyser's boat set him and D'Artagnan upon the
muddy bank, amidst the reeds. D'Artagnan, resigned to obedience, followed Monk exactly as a chained bear follows his master; but the position humiliated him not a little, and he grumbled
to himself that the service of kings was a bitter one, and that the
best of them was good for nothing. Monk walked with long,
rapid strides; it might be thought that he did not yet feel certain
of having reached English land. They had already begun to

make out a few of the cottages of the sailors and fishermen spread over the little quay of this humble port, when, all at once, D'Artagnan cried out, 'God pardon me, there is a house on fire!'

Monk raised his eyes, and saw that there was, in fact, a house which the flames were beginning to consume. It had begun at a little shed belonging to the house, the roof of which had caught. The fresh evening breeze agitated the fire. The two travellers quickened their steps, hearing loud cries, and seeing, as they drew nearer, soldiers with their glittering arms pointing towards the house on fire. It was doubtless this menacing occupation which had made them neglect to signal the felucca. Monk stopped short for an instant, and, for the first time, formulated his thoughts into words. 'Eh! but,' said he, 'perhaps they are not my soldiers, but Lambert's.'

These words contained at once a sorrow, an apprehension, and a reproach perfectly intelligible to D'Artagnan. In fact, during the general's absence, Lambert might have given battle, conquered, and dispersed the parliament's army, and taken with his own the place of Monk's army, deprived of its strongest support. At this doubt, which passed from the mind of Monk to his own, D'Artagnan reasoned in this manner: 'One of two things is going to happen; either Monk has spoken correctly, and there are no longer any but Lambertists in the country— that is to say, enemies who would receive me wonderfully well, since it is to me they owe their victory; or nothing is changed, and Monk, transported with joy at finding his camp still in the same place, will not prove too severe in his settlement with me.' Whilst thinking thus, the two travellers advanced, and began to mingle with a little knot of sailors, who looked on with dismay at the burning house, but did not dare to say anything, on account of the threats of the soldiers. Monk addressed one of these sailors: 'What is going on here?' asked he.

'Sir,' replied the man, not recognizing Monk as an officer, under the thick cloak which enveloped him, 'that house was inhabited by a foreigner and this foreigner became suspected by the soldiers. They wanted to get into his house under pretence of taking him to the camp; but he, without being frightened by their number, threatened death to the first who should cross the threshold of his door; and as there was one who did venture, the Frenchman stretched him on the earth with a pistol-shot.'

'Ah! he is a Frenchman, is he?' said D'Artagnan, rubbing his hands. 'Good!'

'What do you mean, good?' replied the fisherman.

'No, I don't mean that. A slip of the tongue. And what happened next?'

'What happened next, sir?—why, the other men became as enraged as so many lions: they fired more then a hundred shots at the house; but the Frenchman was sheltered by the wall, and every time they tried to enter by the door they met with a shot from his lackey, whose aim is deadly, d'ye see? Every time they threatened the window, they met with a pistol-shot from the master. Look and count—there are seven men down.'

'Ah! my brave countryman,' cried D'Artagnan, 'wait a little, wait a little. I will be with you; and we will settle with this rabble.'

'One instant, sir,' said Monk, 'wait.'

'Long?'

'No; only the time to ask a question.' Then, turning towards the sailor, 'My friend,' asked he, with an emotion which, in spite of all his self-command, he could not conceal, 'whose soldiers are these, pray tell me?'

'Whose should they be but that madman, Monk's?'

'There has been no battle, then?'

'A battle, ah yes! for what purpose? Lambert's army is melting away like snow in April. All come to Monk, officers and soldiers. In a week Lambert won't have fifty men left.'

The fisherman was interrupted by a fresh discharge directed against the house, and by another pistol-shot which replied to the discharged and struck down the most daring of the aggressors. The rage of the soldiers was at its height. The fire still continued to increase, and a crest of flame and smoke whirled and spread over the roof of the house. D'Artagnan could no longer contain himself. '*Mordioux!*' said he to Monk, glancing at him sideways: 'you are a general, and allow your men to burn houses and murder people, while you look on and warm your hands at the blaze of the conflagration? *Mordioux!* you are not a man.'

'Patience, sir, patience!' said Monk, smiling.

'Patience! yes, until that brave gentleman is roasted—is that what you mean?' And D'Artagnan rushed forward.

'Remain where you are, sir,' said Monk, in a tone of command. And he advanced towards the house, just as an officer had approached it, saying to the besieged: 'The house is burning, you will be roasted within an hour! There is still time—come, tell us what you know of General Monk, and we will spare your life. Reply, or by Saint Patrick*——'

The besieged made no answer; he was no doubt reloading his pistol.

'A reinforcement is expected,' continued the officer; 'in a quarter of an hour there will be a hundred men round your house.'

'I reply to you,' said the Frenchman. 'Let your men be sent away; I will come out freely and repair to the camp alone, or else I will be killed here!'

'Hell's teeth!' shouted D'Artagnan; 'why that's the voice of Athos! you knaves!' and the sword of D'Artagnan flashed from its sheath. Monk stopped him and advanced himself, exclaiming, in a sonorous voice: 'Hold hard! what is going on here? Digby, whence this fire? why these cries?'

'The general!' cried Digby, letting the point of his sword fall.

'The general!' repeated the soldiers.

'Well, what is there so astonishing in that?' said Monk, in a calm tone. Then, silence being re-established—'Now,' said he, 'who lit this fire?'

The soldiers hung their heads.

'What! do I ask a question, and nobody answers me?' said Monk. 'What! do I find a fault, and nobody repairs it? The fire is still burning, I believe.'

Immediately the twenty men rushed forward, seizing pails, buckets, jars, barrels, and extinguishing the fire with as much ardour as they had, an instant before, employed in promoting it. But already, and before all the rest, D'Artagnan had applied a ladder to the house, crying, 'Athos! it is I, D'Artagnan! Do not kill me, my dearest friend!' And in a moment the count was clasped in his arms.

In the meantime, Grimaud, preserving his calmness, dismantled the fortification of the ground floor, and after having opened the door, stood, with his arms folded, quietly on the threshold. Only, on hearing the voice of D'Artagnan, he uttered an exclamation of surprise. The fire being extinguished, the soldiers presented themselves, Digby at their head.

'General,' said he, 'excuse us; what we have done was for love of your honour, whom we thought lost.'

'You are mad, gentlemen. Lost! Is a man like me to be lost? Am I not permitted to be absent, according to my pleasure, without giving formal notice? Do you, by chance, take me for an ordinary citizen? Is a gentleman, my friend, my guest, to be besieged, entrapped, and threatened with death, because he is suspected? What signifies that word, suspected? Curse me if I don't have every one of you shot like dogs, that the brave gentleman has left alive!'

'General,' said Digby, piteously, 'there were twenty-eight of us, and see, there are eight on the ground.'

'I authorize M. le Comte de la Fère to send the twenty to join the eight,' said Monk, stretching out his hand to Athos. 'Let them return to camp. Digby, you will consider yourself under arrest for a month.'

'General——'

'That is to teach you, sir, not to act, another time, without orders.'

'I had those of the lieutenant, general.'

'The lieutenant has no such orders to give you, and he shall be placed under arrest, instead of you, if he has really commanded you to burn this gentleman.'

'He did not command that, general; he commanded us to bring him to the camp; but the count was not willing to follow us.'

'I was not willing that they should enter and plunder my house,' said Athos to Monk, with a significant look.

'And you were quite right. To the camp, I say.' The soldiers departed with dejected looks. 'Now we are alone,' said Monk to Athos, 'have the goodness to tell me, monsieur, why you persisted in remaining here, whilst you had your felucca——'

'I waited for you, general,' said Athos. 'Had not your honour appointed to meet me in a week?'

An eloquent look from D'Artagnan made it clear to Monk that these two men, so brave and so loyal, had not acted in concert for his abduction. He knew already it could not be so.

'Monsieur,' said he to D'Artagnan, 'you were perfectly right. Have the kindness to allow me a moment's conversation with M. le Comte de la Fère?'

D'Artagnan took advantage of this to go and ask Grimaud how he was. Monk requested Athos to conduct him to the chamber he lived in.

This chamber was still full of smoke and rubbish. More than fifty musket-balls had passed through the windows and scarred the walls. They found a table, inkstand, and materials for writing. Monk took up a pen, wrote a single line, signed it, folded the paper, sealed the letter with the seal of his ring, and handed over the missive to Athos, saying, 'Monsieur, carry, if you please, this letter to King Charles II, and set out immediately, if nothing detains you here any longer.'

'And the casks?' said Athos.

'The fisherman who brought me hither will assist you in transporting them on board. Depart, if possible, within an hour.'

'Yes, general,' said Athos.

'Monsieur d'Artagnan!' cried Monk, from the window. D'Artagnan ran up precipitately.

'Embrace your friend and bid him adieu, sir; he is returning to Holland.'

'To Holland!' cried D'Artagnan; 'and I?'

'You are at liberty to follow him, monsieur; but I request you to remain,' said Monk. 'Will you refuse me?'

'Oh no, general; I am at your orders.'

D'Artagnan embraced Athos, and only had time to bid him adieu. Monk watched them both. Then he took upon himself the preparations for the departure, the transportation of the casks on board, and the embarking of Athos; then, taking D'Artagnan by the arm who was quite amazed and agitated, he led him towards Newcastle. Whilst going along, the general leaning on his arm, D'Artagnan could not help murmuring to himself, 'Come, come, it seems to me that the shares of the firm of Planchet & Co. are rising.'

XXXI

MONK REVEALS HIMSELF

D'ARTAGNAN, although he flattered himself with better success, had, nevertheless, not too well comprehended his situation.
It was a strange and grave subject for him to reflect upon—this
voyage of Athos into England; this league of the king with
Athos, and that extraordinary combination of his design with
that of the Comte de la Fère. The best way was to let things
follow their course. An imprudence had been committed, and,
whilst having succeeded, as he had promised, D'Artagnan found
that he had gained no advantage by his success. Since everything was lost, he could risk no more.

D'Artagnan followed Monk through his camp. The return of
the general had produced a marvellous effect, for his people had
thought him lost. But Monk, with his austere look and icy
demeanour, appeared to ask of his eager lieutenants and delighted soldiers the cause of all this joy. Therefore, to the lieutenants who had come to meet him, and who expressed the
uneasiness with which they had learnt his departure,

'Why is all this?' said he; 'am I obliged to give you an account
of myself?'

'But, your honour, the sheep tremble when the shepherd is
absent.'

'Tremble!' replied Monk, in his calm and powerful voice; 'ah,
monsieur, what a word! Curse me, if my sheep have not both
teeth and claws, I renounce being their shepherd. Ah, you tremble, gentlemen, do you?'

'Yes, general, for you.'

'Oh! pray meddle with your own concerns. If I have not the
wit God gave to Oliver Cromwell, I have that which he has sent
to me: I am satisfied with it, however little it may be.'

The officer made no reply; and, Monk having imposed silence
on his people, all remained persuaded that he had accomplished
some important work or had been testing them in some way.
This was to take a very poor idea of his patience and scrupulous
genius. Monk, if he had the good faith of the Puritans, his allies,

must have returned fervent thanks to the patron saint* who had
taken him out of the box of M. d'Artagnan. Whilst these things
were going on, our musketeer could not help constantly repeating,

'God grant that M. Monk may not have as much pride as I
have; for I declare if any one had put me into a coffer with that
grating over my mouth, and carried me packed up, like a calf,
across the seas, I should cherish such a memory of my piteous
looks in that coffer, and such an ugly animosity against him who
had enclosed me in it, I should dread so greatly to see a sarcastic
smile on the face of the malicious wretch, or in his attitude any
grotesque imitation of my position in the box, that, *Mordioux!* I
should plunge a good dagger into his throat in compensation for
the grating, and would nail him down in a real bier, in remembrance of the false coffin in which I had been left to moulder for
two days.'

And D'Artagnan spoke honestly when he spoke thus; for the
skin of our Gascon was a very thin one. Monk, fortunately,
entertained other ideas. He never opened his mouth to his timid
conqueror concerning the past; but he admitted him very near
to his person in his labours, took him with him to several
reconnoitrings, in such a way as to obtain that which he evidently warmly desired—to restore D'Artagnan's spirits. The latter conducted himself like a past-master in the art of flattery: he
admired all Monk's tactics, and the ordering of his camp; he
joked very pleasantly upon the circumvallations* of Lambert's
camp, who had, he said, unnecessarily given himself the trouble
to enclose a camp for twenty thousand men, whilst an acre of
ground would have been quite sufficient for the corporal and
fifty guards who would perhaps remain faithful to him.

Monk, immediately after his arrival, had accepted the proposition made by Lambert the evening before, for an interview,
which Monk's lieutenants had refused, under the pretext that
the general was indisposed. This interview was neither long nor
interesting: Lambert demanded a profession of faith from his
rival. The latter declared he had no other opinion than that of
the majority. Lambert asked if it would not be more expedient
to terminate the quarrel by an alliance than by a battle. Monk
hereupon demanded a week for consideration.* Now, Lambert
could not refuse this: and Lambert, nevertheless, had come

saying that he should devour Monk's army. Therefore, at the end of the interview, which Lambert's party watched with impatience, nothing was decided—neither treaty nor battle—the rebel army, as D'Artagnan had foreseen, began to prefer the good cause to the bad one, and the parliament, *rumpish* as it was, to the pompous nothings of Lambert's designs.

They remembered, likewise, the good times in London—the profusion of ale and sherry with which the citizens of London paid their friends the soldiers; they looked with terror at the black war bread, at the troubled waters of the Tweed—too salt for the glass, not enough so for the pot; and they said to themselves, 'Are not the roast meats kept warm for Monk in London?' From that time nothing was heard of but desertion in Lambert's army. The soldiers allowed themselves to be drawn away by the force of principles, which are, like discipline, the obligatory tie in every body constituted for any purpose. Monk defended the parliament—Lambert attacked it. Monk had no more inclination to support parliament than Lambert, but he had it inscribed on his standards, so that all those of the contrary party were reduced to write upon theirs, 'Rebellion', which sounded ill to puritan ears. They flocked then from Lambert to Monk,* as sinners flock from Baal to God.

Monk made his calculations; at a thousand desertions a day Lambert had men enough to last twenty days; but there is in sinking things such a growth of weight and swiftness, which combine with each other, that a hundred left the first day, five hundred the second, a thousand the third. Monk thought he had obtained his rate. But from one thousand the deserters increased to two thousand, then to four thousand, and, a week after, Lambert, perceiving that he had no longer the possibility of accepting battle, if it were offered to him, took the wise resolution of decamping during the night, returning to London, and being beforehand with Monk in constructing a power out of the wreckage of the military party.*

But Monk, free and without uneasiness, marched towards London as a conqueror, augmenting his army with all the floating parties on his way. He encamped at Barnet,* that is to say, within four leagues from the capital, cherished by the parliament, which thought it beheld in him a protector, and awaited by the people, who were anxious to see him reveal himself that they might judge him. D'Artagnan himself had not been able to fathom his tactics; he observed—he admired. Monk could not enter London with a settled determination without bringing about civil war. He temporized for a short time.

Suddenly, when least expected, Monk drove the military party out of London, and installed himself in the city amidst the citizens, by order of the parliament; then, at the moment when the citizens were crying out against Monk—at the moment when the soldiers themselves were accusing their leader—Monk, finding himself certain of a majority, declared to the Rump Parliament that it must abdicate—be dissolved—and yield its place to a government which would not be a joke. Monk pronounced this declaration, supported by fifty thousand swords, to which, that same evening, were united, with shouts of delirious joy, the five hundred thousand inhabitants of the good city of London. At length, at the moment when the people, after their triumphs and celebrations in the open streets, were looking about for a master, it was affirmed that a vessel had left the Hague, bearing Charles II and his fortunes.

'Gentlemen,' said Monk to his officers, 'I am going to meet the legitimate king. He who loves me will follow me.' A burst of acclamations welcomed these words, which D'Artagnan did not hear without the greatest delight.

'*Mordioux!*' said he to Monk, 'this is bold, monsieur.'

'You will accompany me, will you not?' said Monk.

'Gladly, general. But tell me, I beg, what you wrote by Athos, that is to say, the Comte de la Fère—you know—the day of our arrival?'

'I have no secrets from you now,' replied Monk. 'I wrote those words: "Sire, I expect your majesty in six weeks* at Dover."'

'Ah!' said D'Artagnan, 'I no longer say it is bold; I say it is well played: it is a fine stroke!'

'You are something of a judge in such matters,' replied Monk.

And this was the only time the general had ever made an allusion to his voyage to Holland.

XXXII

ATHOS AND D'ARTAGNAN MEET ONCE MORE AT THE HARTSHORN TAVERN

THE king of England made his entrance into Dover with great pomp, as he afterwards did in London. He had sent for his brothers; he had brought over his mother and sister.* England had been for so long a time given up to herself—that is to say, to tyranny, mediocrity and nonsense,* that this return of Charles II, whom the English only knew as the son of the man whose head they had cut off, was a festival of rejoicing for the three kingdoms. Consequently, all the good wishes, all the acclamations, which accompanied his return, struck the young king so forcibly that he stooped and whispered in the ear of James of York, his younger brother, 'In truth, James, it seems to have been our own fault that we were so long absent from a country where we are so much beloved!' The pageant was magnificent. Beautiful weather favoured the solemnity. Charles had regained all his youth, all his good-humour; he appeared to be transfigured; hearts seemed to smile on him like the sun. Amongst this noisy crowd of courtiers and worshippers, who did not appear to remember they had led to the scaffold at Whitehall the father of the new king, a man, in the garb of a lieutenant of musketeers, looked, with a smile upon his thin, intellectual lips, sometimes at the people vociferating their blessings, and sometimes at the prince, who appeared duly pleased and bowed most particularly to the women, whose bouquets fell beneath his horse's feet.

'What a fine thing it is to be a king!' said this man, so completely absorbed in contemplation that he stopped in the middle of his road, leaving the procession to file past. 'Now, there is, in truth, a prince all bespangled over with gold and diamonds, strewn with flowers like a spring meadow; he is about to plunge his empty hands into the immense coffer in which his now faithful—but so lately unfaithful—subjects have amassed one or two cart-loads of ingots of gold. They threw enough bouquets upon him to smother him; and yet, if he had presented himself to them two months ago, they would have sent as many bullets and balls at him as they now throw flowers. Decidedly it is worth something to be born in a certain sphere, with due respect to the lowly, who pretend that it is of very little advantage to them to be born lowly.' The procession continued to file on, and, with the king, the acclamations began to die away in the direction of the palace, which, however, did not prevent our officer from being pushed about.

'*Mordioux!*' continued the reasoner, 'these people tread upon my toes and look upon *me* as of very little consequence, or rather of none at all, seeing that they are Englishmen and I am a Frenchman. If all these people were asked—"Who is M. d'Artagnan?" they would reply, "*Nescio vos.*" But let any one say to them, "There is the king going by," "There is M. Monk going by," they would run away, shouting—"*Vive le roi! Vive M. Monk!*" till their lungs were exhausted. And yet,' continued he, surveying, with that look sometimes so keen and sometimes so proud, the diminishing crowd—'and yet, reflect a little, my good people, on what your king has done, on what M. Monk has done, and then think what has been done by this poor unknown, who is called D'Artagnan! It is true you do not know him, since he is here unknown, and that prevents your thinking about the matter. But, bah! what does it matter! All that does not prevent Charles II from being a great king, although he has been exiled twelve years, or M. Monk from being a great captain, although he did make a voyage to Holland in a box. Well, then, since it is admitted that one is a great king and the other a great captain— "*Hurrah for King Charles II!—Hurrah for General Monk!*"' And his voice mingled with the voices of the hundreds of spectators, over which it sounded for a moment. Then, the better to play the devoted man, he took off his hat and waved it in the air. Some one seized his arm in the very height of his expansive loyalism. (In 1660 that was the word for what we now call royalism.)

'Athos!' cried D'Artagnan, 'you here!' And the two friends seized each other's hands.

'You here!—and being here,' continued the musketeer; 'you are not in the midst of all those courtiers, my dear comte! What! you, the hero of the hour, you are not prancing on the left hand of the king, as M. Monk is prancing on the right? In truth, I cannot comprehend your character, nor that of the prince who owes you so much!'

'Always scornful, my dear D'Artagnan!' said Athos. 'Will you never correct yourself of that vile habit?'

'But, you do not form part of the pageant?'

'I do not, because I was not willing to do so.'

'And why were you not willing?'

'Because I am neither envoy nor ambassador, nor representative of the king of France; and it does not become me to exhibit myself thus near the person of another king than the one God has given me for a master.'

'*Mordioux!* you came very near to the person of the king, his father.'

'That was another thing, my friend; he was about to die.'

'And yet that which you did for him——'

'I did it because it was my duty to do it. But you know I hate all ostentation. Let King Charles II then, who no longer stands in need of me, leave me to my rest, and in the shadow, that is all I claim of him.'

D'Artagnan sighed.

'What is the matter with you?' said Athos. 'One would say that this happy return of the king to London saddens you, my friend; you who have done at least as much for his majesty as I have.'

'Have I not,' replied D'Artagnan, with his Gascon laugh, 'have I not done much for his majesty, without any one suspecting it?'

'Yes, yes, but the king is well aware of it, my friend,' cried Athos.

'He is aware of it!' said the musketeer bitterly, 'by my faith! I did not suspect so, and I was even a moment ago trying to forget it myself.'

'But he, my friend, will not forget it, I will answer for him.'

'You tell me that to console me a little, Athos.'

'For what?'

'*Mordioux!* for all the expense I incurred. I have ruined myself, my friend, ruined myself for the restoration of this young prince who has just passed, riding on his bay horse.'

'The king does not know you have ruined yourself, my friend; but he knows he owes you much.'

'But, Athos, does that advance me in any respect; for to do you justice, you have laboured nobly. But I—I, who in appearance marred your plans, it was I who really made them succeed. Follow my calculations closely; you might not have, by persuasions or mildness, convinced General Monk, whilst I so roughly treated this dear general, that I furnished your prince with an opportunity of showing himself generous: this generosity was inspired in him by the fact of my fortunate mistake, and Charles is paid by the restoration which Monk has brought about.'

'All that, my dear friend, is strikingly true,' replied Athos.

'Well, strikingly true as it may be, it is not less true, my friend, that I shall return—greatly beloved by M. Monk, who calls me *dear captain* all day long, although I am neither dear to him nor a captain; and much appreciated by the king, who has already forgotten my name—it is not less true, I say, that I shall return to my beautiful country, cursed by the soldiers I had raised with the hopes of large pay, cursed by the brave Planchet, of whom I borrowed a part of his fortune.'

'How is that? What the devil had Planchet to do in all this?'

'Ah, yes, my friend; but this king, so spruce, so smiling, so adored, M. Monk fancies he has recalled him, you fancy you have supported him, I fancy I have brought him back, the people fancy they have re-conquered him, he himself fancies he has negotiated his restoration; and yet, nothing of all this is true, for Charles II, king of England, Scotland, and Ireland, has been replaced upon the throne by a French grocer, who lives in the Rue des Lombards, and is named Planchet. And such is grandeur! Vanity! says the Scripture, vanity, all is vanity.'*

Athos could not help laughing at this whimsical outbreak of his friend.

'My dear D'Artagnan,' said he, pressing his hand affectionately, 'should you not exercise a little more philosophy? Is it not some further satisfaction to you to have saved my life as you did by arriving so fortunately with Monk, when those damned parliamentarians wanted to burn me alive?'

'Well, but you, in some degree, deserved a little burning, my friend.'

'How so? What, for having saved King Charles's million?'

'What million?'

'Ah, that is true! you never knew that, my friend; but you must not be angry, for it was not my secret. That word "Remember" which the king pronounced upon the scaffold.'

'And which means do not forget?'

'Exactly. It meant: "Remember there is a million buried in the vaults of Newcastle Abbey, and that that million belongs to my son."'

'Ah! very well, I understand. But what I understand likewise, and what is very frightful, is, that every time his majesty Charles II will think of me, he will say to himself: "There is the man who came very near making me lose my crown. Fortunately I was generous, great, full of presence of mind." That will be said by the young gentleman in a shabby black doublet, who came to the château of Blois, hat in hand, to ask me if I would give him access to the king of France.'

'D'Artagnan! D'Artagnan!' said Athos, laying his hand on the shoulder of the musketeer, 'you are unjust.'

'I have a right to be so.'

'No—for you are ignorant of the future.'

D'Artagnan looked his friend full in the face, and began to laugh. 'In truth, my dear Athos,' said he, 'you have some sayings so superb, that they only belong to you and M. le Cardinal Mazarin.'

Athos frowned slightly.

'I beg your pardon,' continued D'Artagnan, laughing, 'I beg your pardon, if I have offended you. The future! what pretty words are words that promise, and how well they fill the mouth in default of other things! *Mordioux!* After having met with so many who promised, when shall I find one who will give? But, let that pass!' continued D'Artagnan. 'What are you doing here, my dear Athos? Are you the king's treasurer?'

'How—why the king's treasurer?'

'Well, since the king possesses a million, he must want a treasurer. The king of France, although he is not worth a sou, has still a superintendent of finance, M. Fouquet. It is true, that, in exchange, M. Fouquet, they say, has a good number of millions of his own.'

'Oh! our million was spent, long ago,' said Athos, laughing in his turn.

'I understand; it was frittered away in satin, precious stones, velvet, and feathers of all sorts and colours. All these princes and princesses stood in great need of tailors and dress-makers. Eh! Athos, do you remember what we fellows spent in equipping ourselves for the campaign of La Rochelle,* and to make our appearance on horseback? Two or three thousand livres, by my faith! But a king's robe is more ample; it would require a million to purchase the stuff. At least, Athos, if you are not treasurer, you are on a good footing at court.'

'By the faith of a gentleman, I know nothing of all that,' said Athos, simply.

'What! you know nothing of it?'

'No! I have not seen the king since we left Dover.'

'Then he has forgotten you, too! *Mordioux!* That is shameful!'

'His majesty has had so much business to transact.'

'Oh!' cried D'Artagnan, with one of those intelligent grimaces which he alone knew how to make, 'that is enough to make me recover my love for Monseigneur Giulio Mazarini. What, Athos! the king has not seen you since then?'

'No.'

'And you are not furious?'

'I! why should I be? Do you imagine, my dear D'Artagnan, that it was on the king's account I acted as I have done? I did not know the young man. I defended the father, who represented a principle sacred in my eyes, and I allowed myself to be drawn towards the son from sympathy for this same principle. Besides, he was a worthy knight, a noble creature, that father; do you remember him?'

'Yes; that is true; he was a brave, an excellent man, who led a sad life, but made a fine end.'

'Well; my dear D'Artagnan, understand this: to that king, to that man of heart, to that friend of my thoughts, if I durst venture to say so, I swore at the last hour, to preserve faithfully a secret trust which was to be transmitted to his son, to assist him in his hour of need. This young man came to me; he described his destitution; he was ignorant that he was anything to me save a living memory of his father. I have accomplished towards Charles II what I promised Charles I; that is all! Of what consequence is it to me, then, whether he be grateful or not! It is to myself I have rendered a service, by relieving myself of this responsibility, and not to him.'

'Well, I have always said,' replied D'Artagnan, with a sigh, 'that disinterestedness was the finest thing in the world.'

'Well, and you, my friend,' resumed Athos, 'are you not in the same situation as myself? If I have properly understood your words, you allowed yourself to be affected by the misfortunes of this young man; that, on your part, was much greater than it was upon mine, for I had a duty to fulfil; whilst you were under no obligation to the son of the martyr. You had not, on your part, to pay him the price of that precious drop of blood which he let fall upon my brow, through the planks of his scaffold. That which made you act was heart alone—the noble and good heart which you possess beneath your apparent scepticism and sarcasm; you have engaged the fortune of a servant, and your own, I suspect, my benevolent miser! and your sacrifice is not acknowledged! Of what consequence is it? You wish to repay Planchet his money. I can comprehend that, my friend: for it is not becoming in a gentleman to borrow from his inferior, without returning to him principal and interest. Well, I will sell La Fère* if necessary, and if not, some little farm. You shall pay Planchet, and there will be enough, believe me, of corn left in my granaries for us two and Raoul. In this way, my friend, you will be under obligations to nobody but yourself; and, if I know you well, it will not be a small satisfaction to your mind to be able to say, "I have made a king!" Am I right?'

'Athos! Athos!' murmured D'Artagnan, thoughtfully, 'I have told you more than once that the day on which you will preach I shall attend the sermon; the day on which you will tell me there is a hell, *mordioux!* I shall be afraid of the gridiron and the pitch-forks. You are better than I, or rather, better than anybody, and I only acknowledge the possession of one quality, and that is, of not being jealous. Except that defect, damme, as the English say, if I have not all the rest.'

'I know no one equal to D'Artagnan,' replied Athos; 'but here we are having quietly reached the house I inhabit. Will you come in, my friend?'

'Eh! why this is the Hartshorn Tavern, I think?' said D'Artagnan.

'I confess I chose it on purpose. I like old acquaintances; I like to sit down on that place, whereon I sank, overcome by fatigue, overwhelmed with despair, when you returned on the 31st of January.'*

'After having discovered the abode of the masked executioner? Yes, that was a terrible day!'

'Come in, then,' said Athos, interrupting him.

They entered the large apartment, formerly the common one. The tavern, in general, and this room in particular, had undergone great changes; the ancient host of the musketeers having become tolerably rich for an innkeeper, had closed his shop, and made of this room of which we were speaking, a storeroom for colonial provisions. As for the rest of the house, he let it ready furnished to strangers. It was with unspeakable emotion D'Artagnan recognized all the furniture of the chamber of the first story; the wainscoting, the tapestries, and even that geographical chart which Porthos had so fondly studied in his moments of leisure.

'It is eleven years ago,' cried D'Artagnan. '*Mordioux!* it appears to me a century!'

'And to me but a day,' said Athos. 'Imagine the joy I experience, my friend, in seeing you there, in pressing your hand, in casting from me sword and dagger, and tasting without mistrust this glass of sherry. And, oh! what still further joy it would be, if our two friends were there, at the two corners of the tables, and Raoul, my beloved Raoul, on the threshold, looking at us with his large eyes, at once so brilliant and so gentle!'

'Yes, yes,' said D'Artagnan, much affected, 'that is true. I approve particularly of the first part of your thought; it is very pleasant to smile there where we have so legitimately shuddered in thinking that from one moment to another M. Mordaunt might appear upon the landing.'

At this moment the door opened, and D'Artagnan, brave as he was, could not restrain a slight movement of fright. Athos understood him, and smiling,

'It is our host,' said he, 'bringing me a letter.'

'Yes, my lord,' said the good man; 'here is a letter for your honour.'

'Thank you,' said Athos, taking the letter without looking at it. 'Tell me, my dear host, if you do not remember this gentleman?'

The old man raised his head, and looked attentively at D'Artagnan.

'No,' said he.

'It is,' said Athos, 'one of those friends of whom I have spoken to you, and who lodged here with me eleven years ago.'

'Oh! but,' said the old man, 'so many strangers have lodged here!'

'But we lodged here on the 30th of January, 1649,' added Athos, believing he should stimulate the lazy memory of the host by this remark.

'That is very possible,' replied he, smiling; 'but it is so long ago!' and he bowed, and went out.

'Thank you,' said D'Artagnan—'perform exploits, accomplish revolutions, endeavour to engrave your name in stone or bronze with strong swords! there is something more rebellious, more hard, more forgetful than iron, bronze, or stone, and that is, the brain of a lodging-house keeper who has grown rich in the trade—he does not know me! Well, I should have known him though.'

Athos, smiling at his friend's philosophy, unsealed his letter.

'Ah!' said he, 'a letter from Parry.'

'Oh! oh!' said D'Artagnan, 'read it, my friend, read it! No doubt it contains news.'

Athos shook his head, and read:

MONSIEUR LE COMTE—The king has experienced much regret at not seeing you to-day beside him, at his entrance. His majesty commands me to say so, and to recall him to your memory. His majesty will expect you this evening, at the palace of St. James, between nine and ten o'clock.

I am, respectfully, Monsieur le Comte, your honour's very humble and very obedient servant,

PARRY.

'You see, my dear D'Artagnan,' said Athos, 'we must not despair of the hearts of kings.'

'Not despair! you are right to say so!' replied D'Artagnan.

'Oh! my dear, very dear friend,' resumed Athos, whom the

almost imperceptible bitterness of D'Artagnan had not escaped. 'Pardon me! can I have unintentionally wounded my best comrade?'

'You are mad, Athos, and to prove it I shall conduct you to the palace; or at least as far as the gate; the walk will do me good.'

'You shall go in with me, my friend, I will speak to his majesty.'

'No, no!' replied D'Artagnan, with true, unalloyed pride; 'if there is anything worse than begging yourself, it is making others beg for you. Come, let us go, my friend, the walk will be pleasant; on the way I shall show you the house of M. Monk, who has detained me with him. A beautiful house, by my faith. Being a general in England is better than being a marshal in France, please to know.'

Athos allowed himself to be led along, quite saddened by D'Artagnan's forced attempts at gaiety. The whole city was in a state of joy; the two friends were jostled at every moment by enthusiasts who required them, in their intoxication, to cry out, 'Long live good King Charles!' D'Artagnan replied by a grunt, and Athos by a smile. They arrived thus at Monk's house, before which, as we have said, they had to pass on their way to St. James's.

Athos and D'Artagnan said but little on the road, for the very reason that they would have had so many things to talk about if they had spoken. Athos thought that by speaking he should evince satisfaction, and that might wound D'Artagnan. The latter feared that in speaking he should allow some little bitterness to steal into his words which would render his company unpleasant to his friend. It was a singular emulation of silence between contentment and ill-humour. D'Artagnan gave way first to that itching at the tip of his tongue which he so habitually experienced.

'Do you remember, Athos,' said he, 'the passage of the "Mémoires de D'Aubigny," in which that devoted servant, a Gascon like myself, poor as myself, and, I was going to add, brave as myself, relates instances of the meanness of Henry IV?* My father always told me, I remember, that D'Aubigny was a liar. But, nevertheless, examine how all the princes, the male descendants of the great Henry, keep up the character of the race.'

'Nonsense!' said Athos, 'the kings of France misers? You are mad, my friend.'

'Oh! you are so perfect yourself, you never see the faults of others. But, in reality, Henry IV was covetous, Louis XIII, his son, was so likewise; we know something of that, don't we? Gaston* carried this vice to exaggeration, and has made himself, in this respect, hated by all who surround him. Henriette, poor woman, might well be avaricious, she who did not eat every day, and could not warm herself every winter; and that is an example she has given to her son Charles II, grandson of the great Henry IV, who is as covetous as his mother and his grandfather. See if I have well traced the genealogy of the misers?'

'D'Artagnan, my friend,' cried Athos, 'you are very rude towards that eagle race called the Bourbons.'

'Eh! and I have forgotten the best instance of all—the other grandson of the Béarnais, Louis XIV, my ex-master. Well, I hope he is miserly enough, he who would not lend a million to his brother Charles! Good! I see you are beginning to be angry. Here we are, by good luck, close to my house, or rather to that of my friend, M. Monk.'

'My dear D'Artagnan, you do not make me angry, you make me sad; it is cruel, in fact, to see a man of your deserts out of the position his services ought to have acquired; it appears to me, my dear friend, that your name is as radiant as the greatest names in war and diplomacy. Tell me if the Luynes, the Bellegardes, and the Bassompierres* have merited, as we have, fortunes and honours? You are right, my friend, a hundred times right.'

D'Artagnan sighed, and preceded his friend through the porch of the mansion Monk inhabited, at the extremity of the city. 'Permit me,' said he, 'to leave my purse at home; for if in the crowd those clever pickpockets of London, who are much boasted of, even in Paris, were to steal from me the remainder of my poor crowns, I should not be able to return to France. Now, content I left France, and wild with joy I should return to it, seeing that all my prejudices of former days against England have returned, accompanied by many others.'

Athos made no reply.

'So then, my dear friend, one second, and I will follow you,' said D'Artagnan. 'I know you are in a hurry to go yonder to receive your reward, but, believe me, I am not less eager to partake of your joy, although from a distance. Wait for me.' And D'Artagnan was already passing through the vestibule, when a man, half servant, half soldier, who filled in Monk's establishment the double functions of porter and guard, stopped our musketeer, saying to him, in English:

'I beg your pardon, my Lord d'Artagnan!'

'Well,' replied the latter: 'what is it? Is the general going to dismiss me? I only needed to be expelled by him.'

These words, spoken in French, made no impression upon the person to whom they were addressed, and who himself only spoke an English mixed with the rudest Scots. But Athos was grieved at them, for he began to think D'Artagnan was not wrong.

The Englishman showed D'Artagnan a letter: 'From the general,' said he.

'Aye! that's it, my dismissal!' replied the Gascon. 'Must I read it, Athos?'

'You must be deceived,' said Athos, 'or I know no more honest people in the world but you and myself.'

D'Artagnan shrugged his shoulders and unsealed the letter, while the impassive Englishman held for him a large lantern, by the light of which he was able to read it.

'Well, what is the matter?' said Athos, seeing the countenance of the reader change.

'Read it yourself,' said the musketeer.

Athos took the paper and read:

MONSIEUR D'ARTAGNAN—The king regrets very much you did not come to St. Paul's with his procession. He missed you as I also have missed you, my dear captain. There is but one means of repairing all this. His majesty expects me at nine o'clock at the palace of St. James's: will you be there at the same time with me? His gracious majesty appoints that hour for an audience he grants you.

This letter was from Monk.

XXXIII

'WELL?' cried Athos, with a mild look of reproach, when D'Artagnan had read the letter addressed to him by Monk.

'Well!' said D'Artagnan, red with pleasure, and a little with shame, at having so hastily accused the king and Monk. 'This is a courtesy—which leads to nothing, it is true, but yet it is a courtesy.'

'I had great difficulty in believing the young prince ungrateful,' said Athos.

'The fact is, that his present is still too near his past,' replied D'Artagnan; 'after all, everything to the present moment proved me right.'

'I acknowledge it, my dear friend, I acknowledge it. Ah! there is your cheerful look returned. You cannot think how delighted I am.'

'Thus you see,' said D'Artagnan, 'Charles II receives M. Monk at nine o'clock; he will receive me at ten; it is a grand audience, of the sort which at the Louvre are called "distributions of holy court water".* Come, let us go and place ourselves under the spout, my dear friend! Come along.'

Athos replied nothing; and both directed their steps, at a quick pace, towards the palace of St. James's, which the crowd still surrounded, to catch, through the windows, the shadows of the courtiers, and the reflection of the royal person. Eight o'clock was striking, when the two friends took their places in the gallery filled with courtiers and politicians. Every one looked at these simply-dressed men in foreign costumes, at these two noble heads so full of character and meaning. On their side, Athos and D'Artagnan, having with two glances taken the measure of the whole assembly, resumed their chat.

A great noise was suddenly heard at the extremity of the gallery—it was General Monk, who entered, followed by more than twenty officers, all eager for a smile, as only the evening before he was master of all England, and a glorious morrow was looked to, for the restorer of the Stuart family.

'Gentlemen,' said Monk, turning round, 'henceforward I beg you to remember that I am no longer anything. Lately I commanded the principal army of the republic; now that army is the king's, into whose hands I am about to surrender, at his command, my power of yesterday.'

Great surprise was painted on all the countenances, and the circle of adulators and suppliants which surrounded Monk an instant before steadily grew larger, and ended by merging into the general swell of the crowd. Monk was going into the antechamber as others did. D'Artagnan could not help remarking this to the Comte de la Fère, who frowned on beholding it. Suddenly the door of the royal apartment opened, and the young king appeared, preceded by two officers of his household.

'Good evening, gentlemen,' said he. 'Is General Monk here?'

'I am here, sire,' replied the old general.

Charles stepped hastily towards him, and seized his hand with the warmest demonstration of friendship. 'General,' said the king, aloud, 'I have just signed your patent—you are Duke of Albemarle;* and my intention is that no one shall equal you in power and fortune in this kingdom, where—the noble Montrose excepted—no one has equalled you in loyalty, courage, and talent. Gentlemen, the duke is commander of our armies of land and sea, pay him your respects, if you please, in that character.'

Whilst every one was pressing round the general, who received all this homage without losing his impassivity for an instant, D'Artagnan said to Athos: 'When one thinks that this duchy, this commander of the land and sea forces, all these grandeurs, in a word, have been shut up in a box six feet long and three feet wide——'

'My friend,' replied Athos, 'much more imposing grandeurs are confined in boxes still smaller—and remain there for ever.'

All at once, Monk perceived the two gentlemen, who held themselves aside until the crowd had diminished; he made himself a passage towards them, so that he surprised them in the midst of their philosophical reflections. 'You were speaking of me!' said he, with a smile.

'My lord,' replied Athos, 'we were speaking likewise of God.'

Monk reflected for a moment, and then replied gaily;

'Gentlemen, let us speak a little of the king likewise, if you please; for you have, I believe, an audience of his majesty.'

'At nine o'clock,'* said Athos.

'At ten o'clock,' said D'Artagnan.

'Let us go into this closet at once,' replied Monk, making a sign to his two companions to precede him; but to that neither would consent.

The king during this discussion so characteristic of the French had returned to the centre of the gallery.

'Oh! my Frenchmen!' said he, in that tone of careless gaiety which in spite of so much grief and so many crosses, he had never lost. 'My Frenchmen! my consolation!' Athos and D'Artagnan bowed.

'Duke, conduct these gentlemen into my study. I am at your service, messieurs,' added he in French. And he promptly dismissed his court, to return to his Frenchmen, as he called them. 'Monsieur d'Artagnan,' said he, as he entered his closet, 'I am glad to see you again.'

'Sire, my joy is at its height, at having the honour to salute your majesty in your own palace of St. James's.'

'Monsieur, you have been willing to render me a great service, and I owe you my gratitude for it. If I did not fear to intrude upon the rights of our commanding general I would offer you some post worthy of you near our person.'

'Sire,' replied D'Artagnan, 'I have quitted the service of the king of France, making a promise to my prince not to serve any other king.'

'Humph!' said Charles, 'I am sorry to hear that; I should like to do much for you; I like you very much.'

'Sire——'

'But, let us see,' said Charles, with a smile, 'if we cannot make you break your word. Duke, assist me. If you were offered, that is to say, if I offered you the chief command of my musketeers?' D'Artagnan bowed lower than before.

'I should have the regret to refuse what your gracious majesty would offer me,' said he; 'a gentleman has but his word, and that word, as I have had the honour to tell your majesty, is engaged to the king of France.'

'We shall say no more about it, then,' said the king, turning towards Athos, and leaving D'Artagnan plunged in the deepest pangs of disappointment.

'Ah! I said so!' muttered the musketeer. 'Words! words! Court holy water! Kings have always a marvellous talent for offering us that which they know we will not accept, and in appearing generous without risk. So be it!—triple fool that I was to have hoped for a moment!'

During this time, Charles took the hand of Athos. 'Comte,' said he, 'you have been to me a second father; the services you have rendered me are above all price. I have nevertheless thought of a recompense. You were created by my father a Knight of the Garter—that is an order which all the kings of Europe cannot bear; by the queen regent, Knight of the Holy Ghost—which is an order not less illustrious; I join to it that of the Golden Fleece* sent me by the king of France, to whom the king of Spain, his father-in-law, gave two on the occasion of his marriage;* but in return, I have a service to ask of you.'

'Sire,' said Athos, with confusion, 'the Golden Fleece for me! when the king of France is the only person in my country who enjoys that distinction?'

'I wish you to be in your country and all others the equal of all those whom sovereigns have honoured with their favour,' said Charles, drawing the chain from his neck; 'and I am sure, count, my father smiles on me from his grave.'

'It is unaccountably strange,' said D'Artagnan to himself, whilst his friend, on his knees, received the eminent order which the king conferred on him—'It is almost incredible that I have always seen showers of prosperity fall upon all who surrounded me, and that not a drop ever reached me! If I were a jealous man, it would be enough to make me tear my hair, I'll be damned if it wouldn't!'

Athos rose from his knees, and Charles embraced him tenderly. 'General!' said he to Monk—then stopping, with a smile, 'Pardon me, duke I mean. No wonder if I make a mistake; the word duke is too short for me, I always seek some title to lengthen it. I should wish to see you so near my throne, that I might say to you, as to Louis XIV, my brother! I have it; and you will be almost my brother, for I make you viceroy of Ireland and of Scotland,* my dear duke. So, after that fashion, henceforward I shall not make a mistake.'

The duke seized the hand of the king, but without enthusiasm, without joy, as he did everything. His heart, however, had been moved by this last favour. Charles, by skilfully husbanding his generosity, had given the duke time to wish, although he might not have wished for so much as was given him.

'*Mordioux!*' grumbled D'Artagnan, 'there is the shower beginning again! Oh! it is enough to turn one's brain!' and he turned away with an air so sorrowful and so comically piteous, that the king, who caught it, could not restrain a smile. Monk was preparing to leave the room to take leave of Charles.

'What! my trusty and well-beloved!' said the king to the duke, 'are you going?'

'With your majesty's permission, for in truth I am weary. The emotions of the day have worn me out; I stand in need of rest.'

'But,' said the king, 'you are not going without M. d'Artagnan, I hope.'

'Why not, sire?' said the old warrior.

'Well! you know very well why,' said the king.

Monk looked at Charles with astonishment.

'Oh! it may be possible; but if you forget, you, M. d'Artagnan, do not.'

Astonishment was painted on the face of the musketeer.

'Well, then, duke,' said the king, 'do you not lodge with M. d'Artagnan?'

'I had the honour of offering M. d'Artagnan a lodging; yes, sire.'

'That idea is your own, and yours solely?'

'Mine and mine only; yes, sire.'

'Well! but it could not be otherwise—the prisoner always lodges with his conqueror.'

Monk coloured in his turn. 'Ah! that is true,' said he; 'I am M. d'Artagnan's prisoner.'

'Without doubt, duke, since you are not yet ransomed; but have no care of that; it was I who took you out of M. d'Artagnan's hands, and it is I who will pay your ransom.'

The eyes of D'Artagnan regained their gaiety and their brilliancy. The Gascon began to understand. Charles advanced towards him.

'The general,' said he, 'is not rich, and cannot pay you what he is worth. I am richer, certainly; but now that he is a duke, and if not a king, almost a king, he is worth a sum I could not perhaps pay. Come, M. d'Artagnan, be moderate with me; how much do I owe you?'

D'Artagnan, delighted at the turn things were taking, but not for a moment losing his self-possession, replied, 'Sire, your majesty has no occasion to be alarmed. When I had the good fortune to take his grace, M. Monk was only a general; it is therefore only a general's ransom that is due to me. But if the general will have the kindness to deliver me his sword, I shall consider myself paid; for there is nothing in the world but the general's sword which is worth so much as himself.'

'Odds fish! as my father said,' cried Charles. 'That is a gallant proposal, and a gallant man, is he not, duke?'

'Upon my honour, yes, sire,' and he drew his sword. 'Monsieur,' said he to D'Artagnan, 'here is what you demand. Many may have handled a better blade; but however modest mine may be, I have never surrendered it to any one.'

D'Artagnan received with pride the sword which had just made a king.

'Oh! oh!' cried Charles II; 'what, a sword that has restored me to my throne—to go out of the kingdom—and not, one day, to figure among the crown jewels! No, on my soul! that shall not be! Captain d'Artagnan, I will give you two hundred thousand livres for your sword! if that is too little, say so.'

'It is too little, sire,' replied D'Artagnan, with inimitable seriousness. 'In the first place, I do not at all wish to sell it; but your majesty desires me to do so, and that is an order. I obey, then, but the respect I owe to the illustrious warrior who hears me, commands me to estimate at a third more the reward of my victory. I ask then three hundred thousand livres for the sword, or I shall give it to your majesty for nothing.' And taking it by the point he presented it to the king. Charles broke into hilarious laughter.

'A gallant man, and a merry companion! Odds fish! is he not, duke? is he not, count? He pleases me! I like him! Here, Chevalier d'Artagnan, take this.' And going to the table, he took a pen and wrote an order upon his treasurer for three hundred thousand livres.

D'Artagnan took it, and turning gravely towards Monk. 'I have still asked too little, I know,' said he, 'but believe me, your grace, I would rather have died than allow myself to be governed by avarice.'

The king began to laugh again, like the happiest cockney of his kingdom.

'You will come and see me again before you go, chevalier?' said he, 'I shall want to lay in a stock of gaiety now my French-men are leaving me.'

'Ah! sire, it will not be with the gaiety as with the duke's sword; I will give it to your majesty gratis,' replied D'Artagnan, whose feet scarcely seemed to touch the ground.

'And you, comte,' added Charles, turning towards Athos, 'come again, also; I have an important message to confide to you. Your hand, duke.' Monk pressed the hand of the king.

'Adieu! gentlemen,' said Charles, holding out each of his hands to the two Frenchmen, who carried them to their lips.

'Well,' said Athos, when they were out of the palace, 'are you satisfied?'

'Hush!' said D'Artagnan, wild with joy, 'I have not yet re-turned from the treasurer's—the sky may fall upon my head.'

XXXIV

THE BURDEN OF WEALTH

D'ARTAGNAN lost no time, and as soon as suitable and oppor-tune, he paid a visit to the lord-treasurer of his majesty. He had then the satisfaction to exchange a piece of paper, covered with very ugly writing, for a prodigious number of gold pieces, re-cently stamped with the head* of his very gracious majesty Charles II.

D'Artagnan easily controlled himself: and yet, on this occa-sion, he could not help evincing a joy which the reader will perhaps comprehand, if he deigns to have some indulgence for a man who, since his birth, had never seen so many pieces and rolls of pieces juxtaposed in an order truly agreeable to the eye.

The treasurer placed all the rolls in bags, and closed each bag with a stamp sealed with the arms of England, a favour which treasurers do not grant to everybody. Then, impassive, and just as polite as he ought to be towards a man honoured with the friendship of the king, he said to D'Artagnan:

'Take away your money, sir.' *Your money!* These words made a thousand chords vibrate in the heart of D'Artagnan, which he had never felt before. He had the bags packed in a small cart, and returned home meditating deeply. A man who possesses three hundred thousand livres can no longer expect to wear a smooth brow; a wrinkle for every hundred thousand livres is not too much.

D'Artagnan shut himself up, ate no dinner, closed his door to everybody, and, with a lighted lamp, and a loaded pistol on the table, watched all night, ruminating upon the means of preventing these lovely crowns, which from the coffers of the king had passed into his coffers, from passing from his coffers into the pockets of any thief whatever. The best means discovered by the Gascon was to enclose his treasure, for the present, under locks so solid that no wrist could break them, and so complicated that no master-key could open them. D'Artagnan remembered that the English are masters in mechanics and the security business;* and he determined to go in the morning in search of a mechanic who would sell him a strong box. He did not go far. Master Will Jobson, dwelling in Piccadilly, listened to his propositions, comprehended his wishes, and promised to make him a safety lock that should relieve him from all future fear.

'I will give you,' said he, 'a piece of mechanism entirely new. At the first serious attempt upon your lock, an invisible plate will open of itself and discharge a pretty copper bullet of the weight of a mark*—which will knock down the intruder, and not without a loud report. What do you think of it?'

'I think it very ingenious,' cried D'Artagnan; 'the little copper bullet pleases me mightily. So now, sir mechanic, the terms?'

'A fortnight for the execution, and fifteen hundred livres payable on delivery,' replied the artisan.

D'Artagnan's brow darkened. A fortnight was delay enough to allow the thieves of London time to remove all occasion for the strong box. As to the fifteen hundred livres—that would be paying too dear for what a little vigilance would procure him for nothing.

'I will think of it,' said he; 'thank you, sir.' And he returned home at full speed; nobody had yet touched his treasure. That same day, Athos paid a visit to his friend and found him so thoughtful that he could not help expressing his surprise.

'How is this?' said he, 'you are rich and not gay—you, who were so anxious for wealth!'

'My friend, the pleasures to which we are not accustomed oppress us more than the griefs with which we are familiar. Give me your opinion, if you please. I can ask you, who have always had money: when we have money, what do we do with it?'

'That depends.'

'What have you done with yours, seeing that it has not made you a miser or a prodigal? For avarice dries up the heart, and prodigality drowns it—is not that so?'

'Fabricius* could not have spoken more justly. But in truth, my money has never been a burden to me.'

'How so? Do you place it out at interest?'

'No; you know I have a tolerably handsome house; and that house composes the better part of my property.'

'I know it does.'

'So that you can be as rich as I am, and, indeed, more rich, whenever you like, by the same means.'

'But your rents—do you lay them by?'

'No.'

'What do you think of a chest concealed in a wall?'

'I never made use of such a thing.'

'Then you must have some confidant, some safe man of business, who pays you interest at a fair rate.'

'Not at all.'

'Good heavens! what do you do with it, then?'

'I spend all I have, and I only have what I spend, my dear D'Artagnan.'

'Ah! that may be. But you are something of a prince; fifteen or sixteen thousand livres melt away between your fingers; and then you have expenses and appearances——'

'Well, I don't see why you should be less of a noble than I am, my friend; your money would be quite sufficient.'

'Three hundred thousand livres! Two-thirds too much!'

'I beg your pardon—did you not tell me?—I thought I heard you say—I fancied you had a partner——'

'Ah! *Mordioux!* that's true,' cried D'Artagnan, colouring, 'there is Planchet. I had forgotten Planchet, upon my life! Well! there are my three hundred thousand livres broken into. That's a pity! it was a round sum, and sounded well. That is true, Athos; I am no longer rich. What a memory you have!'

'Tolerably good; yes, thank God!'

'The worthy Planchet!' grumbled D'Artagnan; 'his was not a bad dream! What an investment! Hell's teeth! Well! what is said is said.'

'How much are you to give him?'

'Oh!' said D'Artagnan, 'he is not a bad fellow; I shall arrange matters with him. I have had a great deal of trouble, you see, and expenses, all that must be taken into account.'

'My dear friend, I can depend upon you, and have no fear for the worthy Planchet; his interests are better in your hands than in his own. But now that you have nothing more to do here, we shall depart, if you please. You can go and thank his majesty, ask if he has any commands, and in six days* we may be able to get sight of the towers of Notre Dame.'

'My friend, I am most anxious to be off, and will go at once and pay my respects to the king.'

'I,' said Athos, 'am going to call upon some friends in the city, and shall then be at your service.'

'Will you lend me Grimaud?'

'With all my heart. What do you want to do with him?'

'Something very simple, and which will not fatigue him; I shall only beg him to take charge of my pistols, which lie there on the table near that coffer.'

'Very well!' replied Athos, imperturbably.

'And he will not stir, will he?'

'Not more than the pistols themselves.'

'Then I shall go and take leave of his majesty. *Au revoir!*'

D'Artagnan arrived at St. James's, where Charles II, who was busy writing, kept him in the antechamber a full hour. Whilst walking about in the gallery, from the door to the window, from the window to the door, he thought he saw a cloak like Athos's cross the vestibule; but at the moment he was going to ascertain if it were he, the usher summoned him to his majesty's presence. Charles II rubbed his hands while receiving the thanks of our friend.

'Chevalier,' said he, 'you are wrong to express gratitude to me; I have not paid you a quarter of the value of the story of the box into which you put the brave general—the excellent Duke of Albemarle, I mean.' And the king laughed heartily.

D'Artagnan did not think it proper to interrupt his majesty, and bowed with much modesty.

'By the by,' continued Charles, 'do you think my dear Monk has really pardoned you?'

'Pardoned me! yes, I hope so, sire!'

'Eh!—but it was a cruel trick! Odds fish! to pack up the first personage of the English revolution like a herring. In your place, I would not trust him, chevalier.'

'But, sire——'

'Yes, I know very well that Monk calls you his friend. But he has too penetrating an eye not to have a memory, and too lofty a brow not to be very proud, you know, *grande supercilium*.'*

'I shall certainly learn Latin,' said D'Artagnan to himself.

'But stop,' cried the merry monarch, 'I must manage your reconciliation; I know how to set about it; so——'

D'Artagnan bit his moustache. 'Will your majesty permit me to tell you the truth?'

'Speak, chevalier, speak.'

'Well, sire, you alarm me greatly. If your majesty undertakes the affair, as you seem inclined to do, I am a lost man; the duke will have me assassinated.'

The king burst into a fresh roar of laughter, which changed D'Artagnan's alarm into downright terror.

'Sire, I beg you to allow me to settle this matter myself, and if your majesty has no further need of my services——'

'No, chevalier. What, do you want to leave us?' replied Charles, with an hilarity that grew more and more alarming.

'If your majesty has no more commands for me.'

Charles became more serious.

'One single thing. See my sister, the Lady Henrietta.* Do you know her?'

'No, sire, but—an old soldier like me is not an agreeable spectacle for a young and gay princess.'

'Ah! but my sister must know you; she must in case of need, have you to depend upon.'

'Sire, every one that is dear to your majesty will be sacred to me.'

'Very well!—Parry! Come here, Parry!'

The side door opened, and Parry entered, his face beaming with pleasure as soon as he saw D'Artagnan.

'What is Rochester* doing?' said the king.

'He is on the canal with the ladies,' replied Parry.

'And Buckingham?'*

'He is there also.'

'That is well. You will conduct the chevalier to Villiers; that is, the Duke of Buckingham, chevalier; and beg the duke to introduce M. d'Artagnan to the Princess Henrietta.'

Parry bowed, and smiled to D'Artagnan.

'Chevalier,' continued the king, 'this is your parting audience; you can afterwards set out as soon as you please.'

'Sire, I thank you.'

'But be sure you make your peace with Monk!'

'Oh, sire——'

'You know there is one of my vessels at your disposal?'

'Sire, you overwhelm me, I cannot think of putting your majesty's officers to inconvenience on my account.'

The king slapped D'Artagnan upon the shoulder.

'Nobody will be inconvenienced on your account, chevalier, but on that of an ambassador I am about sending to France, and to whom you will willingly serve as a companion, I fancy, for you know him.'

D'Artagnan appeared astonished.

'He is a certain Comte de la Fère—whom you call Athos,' added the king; terminating the conversation, as he had begun it, by a joyous burst of laughter. 'Adieu, chevalier, adieu. Love me as I love you.' And thereupon, making a sign to Parry to ask if there were anyone waiting for him in the adjoining closet, the king disappeared into that closet, leaving the chevalier perfectly astonished by this singular audience. The old man took his arm in a friendly way, and led him towards the garden.

XXXV

ON THE CANAL

UPON the green waters of the canal bordered with marble, upon which time had already scattered black spots and tufts of mossy grass, there glided majestically a long flat boat adorned with the arms of England, surmounted by a dais, and carpeted with long damasked cloths, which trailed their fringes in the water. Eight rowers, leaning lazily to their oars, made it move upon the canal with the graceful slowness of the swans, which, disturbed in their ancient possessions by the approach of the boat, looked from a distance at this splendid and noisy pageant. We say noisy—for the boat contained four guitar and lute players, two singers, and several courtiers, all sparkling with gold and precious stones, and showing their white teeth in emulation of each other, to please the Lady Henrietta Stuart, grand-daughter of Henry IV, daughter of Charles I, and sister of Charles II, who occupied the seat of honour under the dais of the boat. We know this young princess,* we have seen her at the Louvre with her mother wanting wood, wanting bread, and fed by the coadjutor* and the parliament. She had, therefore, like her brothers, passed through an uneasy youth; then, all at once, she had just awakened from a long and horrible dream, seated on the steps of a throne, surrounded by courtiers and flatterers. Like Mary Stuart, on leaving prison, she aspired not only to life and liberty but to power and wealth.*

The Lady Henrietta, in growing, had attained remarkable beauty, which the recent restoration had made famous. Misfortune had taken from her the lustre of pride, but prosperity had restored it to her. She was resplendent, then, in her joy and her happiness—like those hot-house flowers which, forgotten during a frosty autumn night, have hung their heads, but which on the morrow, warmed once more by the atmosphere in which they were born, rise again with greater splendour than ever. Villiers, Duke of Buckingham, son of him who played so conspicuous a part in the early chapters of this history*—Villiers of Buckingham, a handsome cavalier, melancholy with women, a jester with men—and Wilmot, Lord Rochester, a jester with both sexes, were standing at this moment before the Lady Henrietta, disputing the privilege of making her smile. As to that young and beautiful princess, reclining upon a cushion of velvet bordered with gold, her hands hanging listlessly so as to dip in the water, she listened carelessly to the musicians without hearing them, and heard the two courtiers without appearing to listen to them.

This Lady Henrietta—this charming creature—this woman who joined the graces of France to the beauties of England, not having yet loved, was cruel in her coquetry. The smile, then—that innocent favour of young girls—did not even lighten her countenance; and if, at times, she did raise her eyes, it was to fasten them upon one or other of the cavaliers with such a fixity, that their gallantry, bold as it generally was, took alarm, and became timid.

In the meanwhile the boat continued its course, the musicians made a great noise, and the courtiers began, like them, to be out of breath. Besides, the excursion became doubtless monotonous to the princess, for all at once, shaking her head with an air of impatience—'Come, gentlemen—enough of this; let us land.'

'Ah, madam,' said Buckingham, 'we are very unfortunate! We have not succeeded in making the excursion agreeable to your royal highness.'

'My mother* expects me,' replied the princess; 'and I must frankly admit, gentlemen, I am bored.' And whilst uttering this cruel word, Henrietta endeavoured to console by a look each of the two young men, who appeared terrified at such frankness. The look produced its effect—the two faces brightened; but immediately, as if the royal coquette thought she had done too much for simple mortals, she made a movement, turned her back on both her adorers, and appeared plunged in a reverie in which it was evident they had no part.

Buckingham bit his lips with anger, for he was truly in love* with the Lady Henrietta, and, in that case, took everything in a serious light. Rochester bit his lips likewise; but his wit always dominated over his heart, it was purely and simply to repress a malicious smile. The princess was then allowing the eyes she turned from the young nobles to wander over the green and flowery turf of the park, when she perceived Parry and D'Artagnan at a distance.

'Who is coming yonder?' said she.

The two young men turned round with the rapidity of lightning.

'Parry,' replied Buckingham; 'nobody but Parry.'

'I beg your pardon,' said Rochester, 'but I think he has a companion.'

'Yes,' said the princess, at first with languor, but then—'What mean those words, "Nobody but Parry"; say, my lord?'

'Because, madam,' replied Buckingham, piqued, 'because the faithful Parry, the wandering Parry, the eternal Parry, is not, I believe, of much consequence.'

'You are mistaken, duke. Parry—the wandering Parry, as you call him—has always wandered in the service of my family, and the sight of that old man always gives me satisfaction.'

The Lady Henrietta followed the usual progress of pretty women, particularly coquettish women; she passed from caprice to contradiction—the gallant had undergone the caprice, the courtier must bend beneath the contradictory humour. Buckingham bowed, but made no reply.

'It is true, madam,' said Rochester, bowing in his turn, 'that Parry is the model of servants; but, madam, he is no longer young, and we laugh only when we see cheerful objects. Is an old man a gay object?'

'Enough, my lord,' said the princess, coolly; 'the subject of conversation is unpleasant to me.'

Then, as if speaking to herself, 'It is really unaccountable,' said she, 'how little regard my brother's friends have for his servants.'

'Ah, madam,' cried Buckingham, 'your royal highness pierces my heart with a dagger forged by your own hands.'

'What is the meaning of that speech, which is turned so like a French madrigal, duke? I do not understand it.'

'It means, madam, that you yourself, so good, so charming, so sensible, you have laughed sometimes—smiled, I should say—at the idle prattle of that good Parry, for whom your royal highness to-day entertains such an astonishing susceptibility.'

'Well, my lord, if I have forgotten myself so far,' said Henrietta, 'you do wrong to remind me of it.' And she made a sign of impatience. 'The good Parry wants to speak to me, I believe: please order them to row to the shore, my Lord Rochester.'

Rochester hastened to repeat the princess's command: and a moment later the boat touched the bank.

'Let us land, gentlemen,' said Henrietta, taking the arm which Rochester offered her, although Buckingham was nearer to her, and had presented his. Then Rochester, with an ill-dissembled pride, which pierced the heart of the unhappy Buckingham through and through, led the princess across the little bridge which the rowers had cast from the royal boat to the shore.

'Which way will your royal highness go?' asked Rochester.

'You see, my lord, towards that good Parry, who is wandering, as my lord of Buckingham says, and seeking me with eyes weakened by the tears he has shed over our misfortunes.'

'Good heavens!' said Rochester, 'how sad your royal highness is to-day; in truth we seem ridiculous fools to you, madam.'

'Speak for yourself, my lord,' interrupted Buckingham with vexation; 'for my part, I displease her royal highness to such a degree, that I appear absolutely nothing to her.'

Neither Rochester nor the princess made any reply; Henrietta only urged her companion more quickly on. Buckingham remained behind, and took advantage of this isolation to give himself up to his anger; he bit his handkerchief so furiously that it was soon in shreds.

'Parry, my good Parry,' said the princess, with her gentle voice, 'come hither. I see you are seeking me, and I am waiting for you.'

'Ah, madam,' said Rochester, coming charitably to the help of his companion, who had remained, as we have said, behind, 'if Parry cannot see your royal highness, the man who follows him is a sufficient guide, even for a blind man; for he has eyes of flame. That man is a double-lamped lantern.'

'Lighting a very handsome martial countenance,' said the princess, determined to be as contrary as possible. Rochester bowed. 'One of those vigorous soldiers' heads seen nowhere but in France,' added the princess, with the perseverance of a woman sure of impunity.

Rochester and Buckingham looked at each other, as much as to say, 'What can be the matter with her?'

'See, my lord of Buckingham, what Parry wants,' said Henrietta, 'go!'

The young man, who considered this order as a favour, resumed his courage, and hastened to meet Parry, who, followed by D'Artagnan, advanced slowly on account of his age. D'Artagnan walked slowly but nobly, as D'Artagnan, doubled by the third of a million, ought to walk, that is to say, without conceit or swagger, but without timidity. When Buckingham, very eager to comply with the desire of the princess, who had seated herself on a marble bench, as if fatigued with the few steps she had gone—when Buckingham, we say, was at a distance of only a few paces from Parry, the latter recognized him.

'Ah! my lord!' cried he, quite out of breath, 'will your grace obey the king?'

'In what, Mr. Parry?' said the young man, with a kind of coolness tempered by a desire to make himself agreeable to the princess.

'Well, his majesty begs your grace to present this gentleman to her royal highness the Princess Henrietta.'

'In the first place, what is the gentleman's name?' said the duke, haughtily.

D'Artagnan, as we know, was easily affronted, and the Duke of Buckingham's tone displeased him. He surveyed the courtier from head to foot, and two flashes beamed from beneath his bent brows. But, after a struggle, 'Monsieur le Chevalier d'Artagnan, my lord,' replied he, quietly.

'Pardon me, sir, that name teaches me your name, but nothing more.'

'You mean——'

'I mean I do not know you.'

'I am more fortunate than you, sir,' replied D'Artagnan, 'for I have had the honour of knowing your family, and particularly my lord Duke of Buckingham, your illustrious father.'

'My father?' said Buckingham. 'Well, I think I now remember. Monsieur le Chevalier d'Artagnan, do you say?'

D'Artagnan bowed. 'In person,' said he.

'Pardon me, but are you one of those Frenchmen who had secret relations with my father?'

'Exactly, my lord duke, I am one of those Frenchmen.'

'Then, sir, permit me to say that it was strange my father never heard of you during his lifetime.'

'No, monsieur, but he heard of me at the moment of his death: it was I who sent to him, through the hands of the *valet de chambre* of Anne of Austria, notice of the dangers which threatened him; unfortunately, it came too late.'*

'Never mind, monsieur,' said Buckingham. 'I understand now, that, having had the intention of rendering a service to the father, you have come to claim the protection of the son.'

'In the first place, my lord,' replied D'Artagnan, phlegmatically, 'I claim the protection of no man. His Majesty Charles II, to whom I have had the honour of rendering some service—I may tell you, my lord, my life has been passed in such occupations—King Charles II, then, who wishes to honour me with some kindness, desires me to be presented to her royal highness the Princess Henrietta, his sister, to whom I shall, perhaps, have the good fortune to be of service hereafter. Now, the king knew that you, at this moment, were with her royal highness, and sent me to you. There is no other mystery, I ask absolutely nothing of you; and if you will not present me to her royal highess, I shall be compelled to do without you, and present myself.'

'At least, sir,' said Buckingham, determined to have the last word, 'you will not refuse me an explanation provoked by yourself.'

'I never refuse, my lord,' said D'Artagnan.

'As you have had relations with my father, you must be acquainted with some private details?'

'These relations are already far removed from us, my lord—for you were not then born—and for some unfortunate diamond studs, which I received from his hands and carried back to France, it is really not worth while awakening so many remembrances.'

'Ah! sir,' said Buckingham, warmly, going up to D'Artagnan, and holding out his hand to him, 'it is you, then—you whom my father sought everywhere and who had a right to expect so much from us.'

'To expect, my lord, in truth, that is my *forte*; all my life I have expected.'

At this moment, the princess, who was tired of not seeing the stranger approach her, arose and came towards them.

'At least, sir,' said Buckingham, 'you shall not wait for the presentation you claim of me.'

Then turning towards the princess and bowing; 'Madam,' said the young man, 'the king your brother desires me to have the honour of presenting to your royal highness, Monsieur le Chevalier d'Artagnan.'

'In order that your royal highness may have in case of need, a firm support and a sure friend,' added Parry. D'Artagnan bowed.

'You have still something to say, Parry,' replied Henrietta, smiling upon D'Artagnan, while addressing the old servant.

'Yes, madam, the king desires you to preserve religiously in your memory the name and merit of M. d'Artagnan, to whom his majesty owes, he says, the recovery of his kingdom.' Buckingham, the princess, and Rochester looked at each other.

'That,' said D'Artagnan, 'is another little secret, of which, in all probability, I shall not boast to his majesty's son, as I have done to you with respect to the diamond studs.'

'Madam,' said Buckingham, 'monsieur has just, for the second time, recalled to my memory an event which excites my curiosity to such a degree, that I shall venture to ask your permission to take him to one side for a moment, to converse in private.'

'Do, my lord,' said the princess; 'but restore to the sister, as quickly as possible, this friend so devoted to the brother.' And she took the arm of Rochester, whilst Buckingham took that of D'Artagnan.

'Oh! tell me, chevalier,' said Buckingham, 'all that affair of the diamonds, which nobody knows in England, not even the son of him who was the hero of it.'

'My lord, one person alone had a right to relate all that affair, as you call it, and that was your father; he thought proper to be silent, I must beg you to allow me to be so likewise.' And D'Artagnan bowed like a man upon whom it was evident no entreaties could prevail.

'Since it is so, sir,' said Buckingham, 'pardon my indiscretion, I beg you; and, if at any time, I should go into France——' and he turned round to take a last look at the princess, who took but little notice of him, totally occupied as she was, or appeared to be, with Rochester. Buckingham sighed.

'Well?' said D'Artagnan.

'I was saying that if, any day, I were to go to France——'

'You will go, my lord,' said D'Artagnan, 'I shall answer for that.'

'And how so?'

'Oh, I have strange powers of prediction; if I do predict anything I am seldom mistaken. If, then, you do come to France?'

'Well, then, monsieur, you, of whom kings ask that valuable friendship which restores crowns to them, I will venture to beg of you a little of that great interest you took in my father.'

'My lord,' replied D'Artagnan, 'believe me, I shall deem myself highly honoured if, in France, you remember having seen me here. And now, if you will permit——'

Then, turning towards the princess: 'Madam,' said he, 'your royal highness is a daughter of France; and in that quality I hope to see you again in Paris. One of my happy days will be that on which your royal highness shall give me any command whatever, thus proving to me that you have not forgotten the recommendations of your august brother.' And he bowed respectfully to the young princess, who gave him her hand to kiss with a right royal grace.

'Ah! madam,' said Buckingham, in a subdued voice, 'what can a man do to obtain a similar favour from your royal highness?'

'Why, my lord,' replied Henrietta, 'ask Monsieur d'Artagnan; he will tell you.'

XXXVI

HOW D'ARTAGNAN DREW, AS A FAIRY WOULD HAVE DONE, A COUNTRY SEAT FROM A WOODEN BOX

THE king's words regarding the wounded pride of Monk had inspired D'Artagnan with no small degree of apprehension. The lieutenant had had, all his life, the great art of choosing his enemies; and when he had found them implacable and invincible, it was when he had not been able, under any pretence, to make them otherwise. But points of view change greatly in the course of a life. It is a magic lantern, of which the eye of man every year changes the aspects. It results that from the last day of a year on which we saw white, to the first day of the year on which we shall see black, there is but the interval of a single night.

Now, D'Artagnan, when he left Calais with his ten mercenaries, would have hesitated as little in attacking a Goliath, a Nebuchadnezzar, or a Holofernes,* as he would in crossing swords with a recruit or arguing with a landlady. Then he resembled the sparrow-hawk, which, when fasting, will attack a ram. Hunger is blind. But D'Artagnan satisfied—D'Artagnan rich—D'Artagnan a conqueror—D'Artagnan proud of so difficult a triumph—D'Artagnan had too much to lose not to reckon, figure by figure, with probable misfortune.

His thoughts were employed, therefore, all the way on the road from his presentation, with one thing, and that was, how he should handle a man like Monk, a man whom Charles himself, king as he was, handled with difficulty; for, scarcely established, the protected might again stand in need of the protector, and would, consequently, not refuse him, such being the case, the petty satisfaction of transporting M. d'Artagnan, or of confining him in one of the Middlesex prisons, or drowning him a little on his passage from Dover to Boulogne.* Such sorts of satisfaction kings are accustomed to render to viceroys without disagreeable consequences.

It would not be at all necessary for the king to be active in that sequel to the play in which Monk should take his revenge. The part of the king would be confined to simply pardoning the viceroy of Ireland all he should undertake against D'Artagnan. Nothing more was necessary to place the conscience of the Duke of Albemarle at rest than a *te absolvo** said with a laugh, or the scrawl of 'Charles the King,' traced at the foot of a parchment; and with these two words pronounced, and these two words written, poor D'Artagnan was forever crushed beneath the ruins of his imagination.

And then, a thing sufficiently disquieting for a man with such foresight as our musketeer, he found himself alone; and even the friendship of Athos could not restore his confidence. Certainly if the affair had only involved a free distribution of sword-thrusts, the musketeer would have counted upon his companion; but in delicate dealings with a king, when the *perhaps* of an unlucky chance should arise in justification of Monk or of Charles of England, D'Artagnan knew Athos well enough to be sure he would give the best possible colouring to the loyalty of the survivor, and would content himself with shedding floods of tears on the tomb of the dead man, if he was his friend, and afterwards composing his epitaph in the most pompous superlatives.

'Decidedly,' thought the Gascon; and this thought was the result of the reflections which he had just whispered to himself and which we have repeated aloud—'decidedly, I must be reconciled with M. Monk, and acquire a proof of his perfect indifference to the past. If, and God forbid it should be so! he is still sulky and reserved in the expression of this sentiment, I shall give my money to Athos to take away with him, and remain in England just long enough to unmask him, then, as I have a quick eye and a light foot, I shall notice the first hostile sign; to decamp, or conceal myself at the residence of my lord of Buckingham, who seems a good sort of devil at bottom, and to whom, in return for his hospitality, I shall relate all that history of the diamonds, which can now compromise nobody but an elderly queen, who need not be ashamed, after being the wife of a miserly creature like Mazarin, of having formerly been the mistress of a handsome nobleman like Buckingham.* *Mordioux!* that is the thing, and this Monk shall not get the better of me. Eh? and besides, I have an idea!'

We know that, in general, D'Artagnan was not wanting in ideas; and during his soliloquy, he buttoned his jerkin up to the chin, and nothing excited his imagination like this preparation for a combat of any kind, called *accinction** by the Romans. He was quite heated when he reached the mansion of the Duke of Albemarle. He was introduced to the viceroy with a promptitude which proved that he was considered as one of the household. Monk was in his business-closet.

'My lord,' said D'Artagnan, with that expression of frankness which the Gascon knew so well how to assume, 'my lord, I have come to ask your grace's advice!'

Monk, as closely buttoned up morally as his antagonist was physically, replied: 'Ask, my friend;' and his countenance presented an expression not less open than that of D'Artagnan.

'My lord, in the first place, promise me secrecy and indulgence.'

'I promise you all you wish. What is the matter? Speak!'

'It is, my lord, that I am not quite pleased with the king.'

'Indeed! And on what account, my dear lieutenant?'

'Because his majesty gives way sometimes to jests very compromising for his servants; and jesting, my lord, is a weapon that seriously wounds men of the sword, as we are.'

Monk did all in his power not to betray his thought, but D'Artagnan watched him with too close an attention not to detect an almost imperceptible flush upon his face. 'Well, now, for my part,' said he, with the most natural air possible, 'I am not an enemy of jesting, my dear Monsieur d'Artagnan; my soldiers will tell you that even many times in camp, I listened very indifferently, and with a certain pleasure, to the satirical songs which the army of Lambert passed into mine, and which, certainly, would have caused the ears of a general more susceptible than I am to tingle.'

'Oh, my lord,' said D'Artagnan, 'I know you are a complete man; I know you have been, for a long time, placed above human miseries; but there are jests and jests, and a certain kind have the power of irritating me beyond expression.'

'May I inquire what kind, my friend?'

'Such as are directed against my friends, or against people I respect, my lord!'

Monk made a slight movement, which D'Artagnan perceived. 'Eh? but how,' asked Monk, 'how can the pin which pricks another prick you? Answer me that.'

'My lord, I can explain it to you in one single sentence; it concerns you.'

Monk advanced a single step towards D'Artagnan. 'Concerns me?' said he.

'Yes, and this is what I cannot explain; though it derives, perhaps, from my lack of knowledge of his character. How can the king have the heart to jest about a man who has rendered him so many and such great services? How can one understand that he should amuse himself in setting by the ears a lion like you with a gnat like me?'*

'I cannot conceive that in any way,' said Monk.

'But so it is. The king, who owed me a reward, might have rewarded me as a soldier, without contriving that history of the ransom, which affects you, my lord.'

'No,' said Monk, laughing: 'it does not affect me in any way, I can assure you.'

'Not as regards me, I can understand; you know me, my lord, I am so discreet, that the grave would appear a babbler compared to me; but—do you understand, my lord?'

'No,' replied Monk, with persistent obstinacy.

'If another knew the secret which I know——'

'What secret?'

'Eh! my lord, why that unfortunate secret of Newcastle.'

'Oh! the million of M. le Comte de la Fère?'

'No, my lord, no; the enterprise made upon your grace's person.'

'It was well played, chevalier, that is all, and no more is to be said about it: you are a soldier, both brave and wily, which proves that you unite the qualities of Fabius and Hannibal.* You employed your means, force and cunning: there is nothing to be said against that. I ought to have been on guard.'

'Ah! yes; I know, my lord, and I expected nothing less from your partiality; so that if it were only the abduction in itself, *mordioux!* that would be nothing; but there are——'

'What?'

'The circumstances of that abduction.'

'What circumstances?'

'Oh! you know very well what I mean, my lord.'

'No, curse me if I do.'

'There is—in truth, it is difficult to speak it.'

'There is?'

'Well, there is that devil of a box!'

Monk coloured visibly. 'Well, I have forgotten it.'

'A wooden box,' continued D'Artagnan, 'with holes for the nose and mouth. In truth, my lord, all the rest was well; but the box, the box! that was really a tasteless joke.' Monk fidgeted about in his chair. 'And yet,' resumed D'Artagnan, 'the fact that

I, a soldier of fortune, perpetrated the deed is not important, since apart from that one action, which was, I concede, rather inconsiderate but which might be excused by the seriousness of the situation, I am circumspect and reserved.'

'Oh!' said Monk, 'believe me, I know you well, Monsieur d'Artagnan, and I appreciate you at your worth.'

D'Artagnan never took his eyes off Monk; studying all which passed in the mind of the general, as he followed his train of thought through. 'But it does not concern me,' resumed he.

'Well, then, whom does it concern?' said Monk, who began to grow a little impatient.

'It relates to the king, who will never restrain his tongue.'

'Well! and suppose he should say all he knows?' said Monk, with a degree of hesitation.

'My lord,' replied D'Artagnan, 'do not dissemble, I implore you, with a man who speaks so frankly as I do. You have a right to feel your susceptibility excited, however tolerant it may be. What, the devil! it is not the place for a man like you, a man who plays with crowns and sceptres as a gypsy juggles with oranges; it is not the place of a serious man, I said, to be shut up in a box like some freak of nature; for you must understand it would make all your enemies ready to burst with laughter, and you are so great, so noble, so generous, that you must have many enemies. This secret is enough to set half the human race laughing, if you were represented in that box. It is not decent to have the second personage in the kingdom laughed at.'

Monk was quite out of countenance at the idea of seeing himself represented in his box. Ridicule, as D'Artagnan had judiciously foreseen, acted upon him in a manner which neither the chances of war, the aspirations of ambition, nor the fear of death had been able to do.

'Good,' thought the Gascon, 'he is frightened: I am safe.'

'Oh! as to the king,' said Monk, 'fear nothing, my dear Monsieur d'Artagnan, the king will not jest with Monk, I assure you!'

The momentary flash of his eye was noticed by D'Artagnan. Monk lowered his tone immediately: 'The king,' continued he, 'is of too noble a nature, the king's heart is too high to allow him to wish ill to those who serve him well.'

'Oh! certainly,' cried D'Artagnan. 'I am entirely of your grace's opinion with regard to his heart, but not as to his head—it is good, but it is trifling.'

'The king will not trifle with Monk, be assured.'

'Then you are quite at ease, my lord?'

'In that respect, at least! yes, perfectly.'

'Oh! I understand you, you are at ease as far as the king is concerned?'

'I have told you I was.'

'But you are not so much so on my account?'

'I thought I had told you that I had faith in your loyalty and discretion.'

'No doubt, no doubt, but you must remember one thing——'

'What is that?'

'That I was not alone, that I had companions; and what companions!'

'Oh! yes, I know them,'

'And, unfortunately, my lord, they know you, too!'

'Well?'

'Well; they are yonder, at Boulogne,* waiting for me.'

'And you fear——'

'Yes, I fear that in my absence——Zounds! if I were near them, I could answer for their silence.'

'Was I not right in saying that the danger, if there was any danger, would not come from his majesty, however disposed he may be to jest, but from your companions, as you say—— To be laughed at by a king may be tolerable, but by the ostlers and riff-raff of the army! Damn it!'

'Yes, I understand, that would be unbearable; that is why, my lord, I came to say—do you not think it would be better for me to set out for France as soon as possible?'

'Certainly, if you think your presence——'

'Would impose silence upon those scoundrels? Oh! I am sure of that, my lord.'

'Your presence will not prevent the report from spreading, if the tale has already been put about.'

'Oh! it has not been put about, my lord, I will wager. At all events, be assured I am determined upon one thing.'

'What is that?'

'To blow out the brains of the first man who propagated that report, and of the first who has heard it. After which I shall return to England to seek asylum, and perhaps employment with your grace.'

'Oh, come back! come back!'

'Unfortunately, my lord, I am acquainted with nobody here but your grace, and if I should no longer find you, or if you should have forgotten me in your greatness?'

'Listen to me, Monsieur d'Artagnan,' replied Monk; 'you are a superior man, full of intelligence and courage; you deserve all the good fortune this world can bring you; come with me into Scotland, and, I swear to you, I shall arrange for you a fate which all may envy.'

'Oh! my lord, that is impossible. At present I have a sacred duty to perform; I have to watch over your good name, I have to prevent a low jester from tarnishing in the eyes of our contemporaries—who knows? in the eyes of posterity—the splendour of your name.'

'Of posterity, Monsieur d'Artagnan?'

'Doubtless. It is necessary, as regards posterity, that all the details of this story should remain a mystery; for, admit that this unfortunate story of the wooden box should spread, and it should be asserted that you had not re-established the king loyally, and of your own free-will, but in consequence of a compromise entered into at Scheveningen between you two. It would be vain for me to declare how the thing came about, for though I know I should not be believed, it would be said that I had received my part of the cake, and was eating it.'

Monk knitted his brow. 'Glory, honour, probity!' said he, 'you are but empty words.'

'Smoke!' replied D'Artagnan; 'just smoke, through which nobody can see clearly.'

'Well, then, go to France, my dear Monsieur d'Artagnan,' said Monk; 'go, and to render England more attractive and agreeable to you, accept a remembrance of me.'

'What now?' thought D'Artagnan.

'I have on the banks of the Clyde,' continued Monk, 'a little house in a grove, a cottage as it is called here. To this house are attached a hundred acres of land. Accept it as a souvenir.'

'Oh, my lord!——'

'Faith! you will be there in your own home, and that will be the place of refuge you spoke of just now.'

'For me to be obliged to your lordship to such an extent! Really, your grace, I am ashamed.'

'Not at all, not at all, monsieur,' replied Monk, with an arch smile; 'it is I who shall be obliged to you. And,' pressing the hand of the musketeer, 'I shall go and draw up the deed of gift'—and he left the room.

D'Artagnan looked at him as he went out with something of a pensive and even an agitated air.

'After all,' said he, 'he is a brave man. It is only a sad reflection that it is from fear of me, and not affection that he acts thus. Well, I shall endeavour that affection may follow.' Then, after an instant's deeper reflection—'Bah!' said he, 'to what purpose? He is an Englishman.' And he in his turn went out, a little confused after the combat.

'So,' said he, 'I am a land-owner! But how the devil am I to share the cottage with Planchet? Unless I give him the land, and I take the château, or that he takes the house and I—nonsense! M. Monk will never allow me to share a house he has inhabited with a grocer. He is too proud for that. Besides, why should I say anything about it to him? It was not with the firm's money I have acquired that property, it was with my mother-wit alone; it is all mine, then. So, now I will go and find Athos.' And he directed his steps towards the dwelling of the Comte de la Fère.

XXXVII

HOW D'ARTAGNAN REGULATED THE 'ASSETS' OF THE COMPANY BEFORE HE ESTABLISHED ITS 'LIABILITIES'

'DECIDEDLY,' said D'Artagnan to himself, 'I have struck a good vein. That star which shines once in the life of every man, which shone for Job and Irus,* the most unfortunate of the Jews and the poorest of the Greeks, is come at last to shine on me. I will commit no folly, I will take advantage of it; it comes quite late enough to find me reasonable.'

He supped that evening, in very good humour, with his friend Athos; he said nothing to him about the expected donation, but he could not forbear questioning his friend, while eating, about country produce, sowing, and planting. Athos replied agreeably, as he always did. His idea was that D'Artagnan wished to become a land-owner, only he could not help regretting, more than once, the absence of the lively humour and amusing sallies of the cheerful companion of former days. In fact, D'Artagnan was so absorbed, that, with his knife, he took advantage of the grease left at the bottom of his plate, to trace figures and make additions of gratifying roundness.

The order, or rather licence, for their embarkation, arrived at Athos's lodgings that evening. While this paper was remitted to the comte, another messenger brought to D'Artagnan a little bundle of parchments, adorned with all the seals which adorn property deeds in England. Athos surprised him turning over the leaves of these different acts which establish the transfer of property. The prudent Monk—others would say the generous Monk—had commuted the donation into a sale, and acknowledged the receipt of the sum of fifteen thousand crowns as the price of the property ceded. The messenger was gone. D'Artagnan still continued reading, Athos watched him with a smile. D'Artagnan, surprising one of those smiles over his shoulder, put the bundle in its wrapper.

'I beg your pardon,' said Athos.

'Oh! not at all, my friend,' replied the lieutenant, 'I shall tell you——'

'No, don't tell me anything, I beg you; orders are things so sacred, that to one's brother, one's father, the person charged with such orders should never open his mouth. Thus I, who speak to you, and love you more tenderly than brother, father, or all the world——'

'Except your Raoul?'

'I shall love Raoul still better when he is a man, and have seen him develop himself in all the phases of his character and actions—as I have seen you, my friend.'

'You said, then, that you had an order likewise, and that you would not communicate it to me.'

'Yes, my dear D'Artagnan.'

The Gascon sighed. 'There was a time,' said he, 'when you would have placed that order open upon the table, saying, "D'Artagnan, read this scrawl to Porthos, Aramis, and to me."'

'That is true. Oh! that was the time of youth, confidence, the generous season when the blood commands, when it is warmed by feeling!'

'Well! Athos, will you allow me to tell you something?'

'Speak, my friend!'

'That delightful time, that generous season, that ruling by warm blood, were all very fine things, no doubt: but I do not regret them at all. It is absolutely like the period of studies. I have constantly met with fools who would boast of the days of hard lessons, canings, and crusts of dry bread. It is odd, but I never loved all that; for my part, however active and sober I might be (you know if I was so, Athos), however simple I might appear in my clothes, I would not the less have preferred the braveries and embroideries of Porthos to my little torn school cloak, which gave passage to the wind in winter and the sun in summer. I should always, my friend, mistrust him who would pretend to prefer evil to good. Now, in times past all went wrong with me, and every month found a fresh hole in my cloak and in my skin, a gold crown less in my poor purse; of that execrable time of small beer and ups and downs, I regret absolutely nothing, nothing, nothing, save our friendship; for within me I have a heart, and it is a miracle that heart has not been dried up by the wind of poverty which passed through the holes of my cloak, or pierced by the swords of all shapes which passed through the holes in my poor flesh.'

'Do not regret our friendship,' said Athos, 'that will only die with ourselves. Friendship is composed, above all things, of memories and habits, and if you have just now made a little satire upon mine, because I hesitate to tell you the nature of my mission into France——'

'Who! I?—Oh! heavens! if you knew, my dear friend, how indifferent all the missions of the world will henceforth become to me!' And he laid his hand upon the parchment in his jerkin pocket.

Athos rose from the table and called the host in order to pay the reckoning.

'Since I have known you, my friend,' said D'Artagnan, 'I have never paid the reckoning. Porthos often did, Aramis sometimes, and you, you almost always drew out your purse with the dessert. I am now rich, and should like to see if it is heroic to pay.'

'Do so,' said Athos, returning his purse to his pocket.

The two friends then directed their steps towards the port, not, however, without D'Artagnan's frequently turning round to watch the transportation of his precious crowns. Night had just spread her thick veil over the yellow waters of the Thames; they heard those noises of casks and pulleys, the preliminaries of preparing to sail which had so many times made the hearts of the musketeers beat when the dangers of the sea were the least of those they were going to face. This time they were to embark on board a large vessel which awaited them at Gravesend, and Charles II, always delicate in small matters, had sent one of his yachts, with twelve men of his Scots guard, to do honour to the ambassador he was sending to France. At midnight the yacht had deposited its passengers on board the vessel, and at eight o'clock in the morning, the vessel landed the ambassador and his friend on the wharf at Boulogne. Whilst the comte, with Grimaud, was busy procuring horses to go straight to Paris, D'Artagnan hastened to the hostelry where, according to his orders, his little army was to wait for him. These gentlemen were at breakfast upon oysters, fish, and spiced brandy, when D'Artagnan appeared. They were all very cheerful, but not one of them had yet exceeded the bounds of reason. A hurrah of joy welcomed the general. 'Here I am,' said D'Artagnan, 'the campaign is ended. I am come to bring to each his supplement of pay, as agreed.'— Their eyes sparkled. 'I will lay a wager there are not, at this moment, a hundred crowns remaining in the purse of the richest among you.'

'That is true!' cried they in chorus.

'Gentlemen,' said D'Artagnan, 'then, this is the last order. The commercial treaty has been concluded, thanks to our bold stroke which made us masters of the most skilful financier of England, for now I am at liberty to confess to you that the man we had to carry off was the treasurer of General Monk.'

This word treasurer produced a certain effect on his army.

D'Artagnan observed that the eyes of Menneville alone did not evince perfect faith. 'This treasurer,' he continued, 'I conveyed to a neutral territory, Holland, I forced him to sign the treaty; I even escorted him back to Newcastle, and as he was obliged to be satisfied with our proceedings towards him—the deal coffer being always carried without jolting, and being softly padded, I asked for a gratuity for you. Here it is.' He threw a respectable-looking purse upon the cloth; and all, involuntarily, stretched out their hands. 'One moment, my lambs,' said D'Artagnan; 'if there are profits there are also charges.'

'Oh! oh!' murmured they.

'We are about to find ourselves, my friends, in a position that would not be tenable for people without brains. I speak plainly: we are between the gallows and the Bastille.'

'Oh! oh!' said the chorus.

'That is easily understood. It was necessary to explain to General Monk the disappearance of his treasurer. I waited for that purpose, till the very unlooked-for moment of the restoration of King Charles II, who is one of my friends.'

The army exchanged a glance of satisfaction in reply to the sufficiently proud look of D'Artagnan. 'The king being restored, I restored to Monk his man of business, a little plucked, it is true, but, in short, I restored him. Now, General Monk, when he pardoned me, for he has pardoned me, could not help repeating these words to me, which I charge every one of you to engrave deeply there, between the eyes, under the vault of the cranium: "Monsieur, the joke has been a good one, but I don't naturally like jokes; if ever a word of what you have done" (you understand me, Menneville) "escapes from your lips, or the lips of your companions, I have, in my government of Scotland and Ireland, seven hundred and forty-one wooden gibbets, of strong oak, clamped with iron, and freshly greased every week. I will make a present of one of these gibbets to each of you, and observe well, M. d'Artagnan," added he (observe it also, M. Menneville), "I shall still have seven hundred and thirty left for my private pleasure. And still further——" '

'Ah! ah!' said the auxiliaries, 'is there more still?'

'A mere trifle. "Monsieur d'Artagnan, I send to the king of France the treaty in question, with a request that he will cast into the Bastille provisionally, and then send to me, all who have taken part in this expedition; and that is a request with which the king will certainly comply." '

A cry of terror broke from all corners of the table.

'There! there! there!' said D'Artagnan, 'this brave M. Monk has forgotten one thing, and that is he does not know the name of any one of you; I alone know you, and it is not I, you may well believe, who will betray you. Why should I? As for you, I cannot suppose you will be foolish enough to give yourselves away, for then the king, to spare himself the expense of feeding and lodging you, will send you off to Scotland, where the seven hundred and forty-one gibbets are to be found. That is all, messieurs; I have not another word to add to what I have had the honour to tell you. I am sure you have understood me perfectly well, have you not, M. Menneville?'

'Perfectly,' replied the latter.

'Now the crowns!' said D'Artagnan. 'Shut the doors,' he cried, and opened the bag upon the table, from which rolled several fine gold crowns. Every one made a movement towards the floor.

'Gently!' cried D'Artagnan. 'Let no one stoop, and then I shall not be out in my reckoning.' He found it all right, gave fifty of those splendid crowns to each man, and received as many benedictions as he bestowed pieces. 'Now,' said he, 'if it were possible for you to reform a little, if you could become good and honest citizens——'

'That is rather difficult,' said one of the troop.

'What if we did, captain?' said another.

'Because I might be able to find you again, and, who knows what other good fortune?' He made a sign to Menneville, who listened to all he said with a composed air. 'Menneville,' said he, 'come with me. Adieu, my brave fellows! I need not warn you to be discreet.'

Menneville followed him, whilst the salutations of the auxiliaries were mingled with the sweet sound of the money clinking in their pockets.

'Menneville,' said D'Artagnan, when they were once in the street, 'you were not my dupe; beware of being so. You did not appear to me to have any fear of the gibbets of Monk, or the

Bastille of his majesty King Louis XIV, but you will do me the favour of being afraid of me. So listen; at the smallest word that shall escape you, I will kill you as I would a chicken. I have absolution from our holy father the pope in my pocket.'

'I assure you I know absolutely nothing, my dear M. d'Artagnan, and that your words have all been to me so many articles of faith.'

'I was quite sure you were an intelligent fellow,' said the musketeer; 'I have tried you for a length of time. These fifty gold crowns which I give you above the rest will prove the esteem I have for you. Take them.'

'Thanks, Monsieur d'Artagnan,' said Menneville.

'With that sum you can really become an honest man,' replied D'Artagnan, in the most serious tone possible. 'It would be disgraceful for a mind like yours, and a name you no longer dare to bear, to sink for ever under the rust of an evil life. Become a gallant man, Menneville, and live for a year upon those hundred gold crowns: it is a good provision; twice the pay of a high officer. In a year come to me, and, *mordioux!* I will make something of you.'

Menneville swore, as his comrades had sworn, that he would be as silent as the grave. And yet some one must have spoken; and as, certainly, it was not one of the nine companions, and quite as certainly, it was not Menneville, it must have been D'Artagnan, who in his quality of a Gascon, had his tongue very near to his lips. For, in short, if it were not he who could it be? And how can it be explained that the secret of the wooden coffer pierced with holes should come to our knowledge, and in so complete a fashion that we have, as has been seen, related the history of it in all its most minute details; details which, besides, throw a light as new as unexpected upon all that portion of the history of England which has been left, up to the present day, completely in darkness by the historians of our neighbours?*

XXXVIII

IN WHICH IT IS SEEN THAT THE FRENCH GROCER HAD ALREADY BEEN ESTABLISHED IN THE SEVENTEENTH CENTURY

His accounts once settled, and his recommendations made, D'Artagnan thought of nothing but returning to Paris as soon as possible. Athos, on his part, was anxious to reach home and to rest a little. However whole the character and the man may remain after the fatigues of a voyage, the traveller perceives with pleasure, at the close of the day—even though the day has been a fine one—that night is approaching, and will bring a little sleep with it. So, from Boulogne to Paris, jogging on, side by side, the two friends, in some degree absorbed each in his individual thoughts, conversed of nothing sufficiently interesting for us to repeat to our readers. Each of them given up to his personal reflections, and constructing his future after his own fashion, was, above all, anxious to abridge the distance by speed. Athos and D'Artagnan arrived at the gates of Paris on the evening of the fourth day* after leaving Boulogne.

'Where are you going, my friend?' asked Athos. 'I shall direct my course straight to my hotel.'

'And I straight to my partner's.'

'To Planchet's?'

'Yes; the Golden Pestle.'

'Well, but shall we not meet again?'

'If you remain in Paris, yes; for I shall stay here.'

'No: after having embraced Raoul, with whom I have appointed a meeting at my hotel, I shall set out immediately for La Fère.'

'Well, adieu, then, dear and true friend.'

'*Au revoir!* I should rather say, for why can you not come and live with me at Blois? You are free, you are rich, I shall purchase for you, if you like, a handsome estate in the vicinity of Cheverny or of Bracieux.* On the one side you will have the finest woods in the world, which join those of Chambord; on the other, admirable marshes. You who love sporting, and who, whether you admit it or not, are a poet, my dear friend, you will find enough pheasants, rail, and teal, not to mention the sunsets and ample opportunities for excursions on the water, to make you think you are Nimrod and Apollo* rolled into one. While awaiting the purchase, you can live at La Fère, and we shall go together to fly our hawks among the vines, as Louis XIII* used to do. That is a quiet amusement for old fellows like us.'

D'Artagnan took the hands of Athos in his own. 'Dear count,' said he 'I shall say neither "Yes" nor "No". Let me spend in Paris the time necessary for settling my affairs, and accustom myself, by degrees, to the heavy and glittering idea which is beating in my brain and dazzles me. I am rich, you see, and from this moment until the time when I shall have acquired the habit of being rich, I know myself, and I shall be an unbearable animal. Now, I am not enough of a fool to wish to appear to have lost my wits before a friend like you, Athos. The cloak is handsome, the cloak is richly gilded, but it is new, and does not seem to fit me.'

Athos smiled. 'So be it,' said he. 'But talking of this cloak, dear D'Artagnan, will you allow me to offer you a little advice?'

'Yes, willingly.'

'You will not be angry?'

'Proceed.'

'When wealth comes to a man late in life or all at once, that man, in order not to change, must most likely become a miser—that is to say, not spend much more money than he had done before; or else become a prodigal, and contract so many debts as to become poor again.'

'Oh! but what you say looks very much like a sophism, my dear philosophical friend.'

'I do not think so. Will you become a miser?'

'No, God forbid! I was one already, having nothing. Let us change.'

'Then be prodigal.'

'Still less, *mordioux!* Debts terrify me. Creditors appear to me, by anticipation, like those devils who turn the damned upon spits, and as patience is not my dominant virtue, I am always tempted to thrash the devils.'

'You are the wisest man I know, and stand in no need of

advice from any one. Great fools must they be who think they have anything to teach you. But are we not at the Rue Saint Honoré?'*

'Yes, dear Athos.'

'Look yonder, on the left, that small, long white house is the hotel where I lodge. You may observe that it has but two stories, I occupy the first; the other is let to an officer whose duties oblige him to be absent eight or nine months in the year—so I am in that house as in my own home, without the expense.'

'Oh! how well you manage, Athos! What order and what liberality! They are what I wish to combine! But, of what use trying! that comes from birth, and cannot be acquired.'

'You are a flatterer! Well! adieu, dear friend. By the by, remember me to Master Planchet, he was always a bright fellow.'

'And a man of heart too, Athos. Adieu.'

And they separated. During all this conversation, D'Artagnan had not for a moment lost sight of a certain pack-horse, in whose panniers, under some hay, were spread the money-bags alongside the portmanteau. Nine o'clock was striking at Saint-Merri.* Planchet's assistants were shutting up his shop. D'Artagnan stopped the postilion who rode the pack-horse, at the corner of the Rue des Lombards, under an arch, and calling one of Planchet's boys, he desired him not only to take care of the two horses, but to watch the postilion; after which he entered the shop of the grocer, who had just finished supper, and who, in his little private room, was, with a degree of anxiety, consulting the calendar, on which, every evening, he scratched out the day that was past. At the moment when Planchet, according to his daily custom, with the back of his pen, erased another day, D'Artagnan kicked the door with his foot, and the blow made his steel spur jingle. 'Oh! good Lord!' cried Planchet. The worthy grocer could say no more; he had just perceived his partner. D'Artagnan entered with a bent back and a dull eye: the Gascon had an idea with regard to Planchet.

'Good God!' thought the grocer, looking earnestly at the traveller, 'he looks sad!' The musketeer sat down.

'My dear Monsieur d'Artagnan!' said Planchet, with a horrible palpitation of the heart. 'Here you are! and your health?'

'Tolerably good! Planchet, tolerably good!' said D'Artagnan, with a profound sigh.

'You have not been wounded, I hope?'

'Phew!'

'Ah, I see,' continued Planchet, more and more alarmed, 'the expedition has been a trying one?'

'Yes,' said D'Artagnan. A shudder ran down Planchet's back. 'I should like to have something to drink,' said the musketeer, raising his head piteously.

Planchet ran to the cupboard, and poured out to D'Artagnan some wine in a large glass. D'Artagnan examined the bottle.

'What wine is that?' asked he.

'The one you like, monsieur,' said Planchet; 'that good old Anjou wine, which one day nearly cost us all so dear.'*

'Ah!' replied D'Artagnan, with a melancholy smile, 'Ah! my poor Planchet, ought I still to drink good wine?'

'Come! my dear master,' said Planchet, making a superhuman effort, whilst all his contracted muscles, his pallor, and his trembling betrayed the most acute anguish. 'Come! I have been a soldier and consequently have some courage; do not make me linger, dear Monsieur d'Artagnan; our money is lost, is it not?'

Before he answered, D'Artagnan took his time and that appeared an age to the poor grocer. Nevertheless he did nothing but turn about on his chair.

'And if that were the case,' said he, slowly, moving his head up and down, 'if that were the case, what would you say, my dear friend?'

Planchet, from being pale turned yellow. It might have been thought he was going to swallow his tongue, so full became his throat, so red were his eyes!

'Twenty thousand livres!' murmured he. 'Twenty thousand livres, and yet——'

D'Artagnan, with his neck elongated, his legs stretched out, and his hands hanging listlessly, looked like a statue of discouragement. Planchet drew up a sigh from the deepest cavities of his breast.

'Well,' said he, 'I see how it is. Let us be men! It is all over, is it not? The principal thing is, monsieur, that your life is safe.'

'Doubtless! doubtless!—life is something—but I am ruined!'

'Well, monsieur!' said Planchet, 'if it is so, we must not despair for that; you shall become a grocer with me; I shall take you for my partner, we will share the profits, and if there should be no more profits, well, why then we shall share the almonds, raisins, and prunes, and we will nibble together the last quarter of Dutch cheese.'

D'Artagnan could hold out no longer. *'Mordioux!'* cried he, with great emotion, 'thou art a brave fellow, on my honour, Planchet. You have not been playing a part have you? You have not seen the pack-horse with the bags under the shed yonder?'

'What horse? What bags?' said Planchet, whose trembling heart began to suggest that D'Artagnan was mad.

'Why, the English bags, *mordioux!'* said D'Artagnan, all radiant, quite transfigured.

'Ah! good God!' articulated Planchet, drawing back before the dazzling fire of his looks.

'Imbecile!' cried D'Artagnan, 'you think me mad! *mordioux!* on the contrary, never was my head more clear, or my heart more joyous. To the bags, Planchet, to the bags!'

'But to what bags, good heavens!'

D'Artagnan pushed Planchet towards the window.

'Under the shed yonder, don't you see a horse?'

'Yes.'

'Don't you see how his back is laden?'

'Yes, yes!'

'Don't you see your lad talking with the postilion!'

'Yes, yes, yes!'

'Well, you know the name of that lad, because he is your own. Call him.'

'Abdon! Abdon!' vociferated Planchet, from the window.

'Bring the horse!' shouted D'Artagnan.

'Bring the horse!' screamed Planchet.

'Now give ten livres to the postilion,' said D'Artagnan, in the tone he would have employed in commanding a manœuvre; 'two lads to bring up the two first bags, two to bring up the two last —and, move, *mordioux!* be lively!'

Planchet rushed down the stairs, as if the devil had been at his heels. A moment later, the lads ascended the staircase, bending beneath their burden. D'Artagnan sent them off to their garrets, carefully closed the door, and addressing Planchet, who, in his turn, looked a little wild.

'Now, we are by ourselves,' said he; and he spread upon the floor a large cover, and emptied the first bag into it. Planchet did the same with the second; then D'Artagnan, all in a tremble, let out the precious bowels of the third with a knife. When Planchet heard the provoking sound of the silver and gold—when he saw bubbling out of the bags the shining crowns, which glittered like fish from the sweep-net—when he felt himself plunging his hands up to the elbow in that still rising tide of yellow and white coins, a giddiness seized him, and like a man struck by lightning, he sank heavily down upon the enormous heap, which his weight caused to roll away in all directions. Planchet, suffocated with joy, had lost his senses. D'Artagnan threw a glass of white wine in his face, which, immediately, recalled him to life.

'Ah! good heavens! good heavens ! good heavens!' said Planchet, wiping his moustache and beard.

At that time, as they do now, grocers wore a cavalier moustache and full beard, but money baths, already rare in those days, have become almost unknown now.

'*Mordioux!*' said D'Artagnan, 'there are a hundred thousand livres for you, partner. Draw your share, if you please, and I will draw mine.'

'Oh! the lovely sum! Monsieur d'Artagnan, the lovely sum!'

'I confess that, half an hour ago, I regretted that I had to give you so much; but I now no longer regret it; thou art a brave grocer, Planchet. There, let us close our accounts, for, as they say, short reckonings make long friends.'

'Oh! rather, in the first place, tell me the whole history,' said Planchet; 'that must be better than the money.'

'*Ma foi!*' said D'Artagnan, stroking his moustache, 'I can't say no; and if ever a historian turns to me for information, he will be able to say he has not dipped his bucket into a dry spring. Listen, then, Planchet, I will tell you all about it.'

'And I shall build piles of crowns,' said Planchet. 'Begin, my dear master.'

'Well, this is how it was,' said D'Artagnan, drawing breath.

'And this is how it turned out,' said Planchet, picking up his first handful of crowns.

XXXIX

MAZARIN'S GAMING PARTY

In a large chamber of the Palais Royal,* hung with a dark-coloured velvet, which threw into strong relief the gilded frames of a great number of magnificent pictures, on the evening of the arrival of the two Frenchmen, the whole court was assembled before the alcove of M. le Cardinal de Mazarin, who gave a card party to the king and queen.

A small screen separated three prepared tables. At one of these tables the king and the two queens were seated. Louis XIV, placed opposite to the young queen, his wife, smiled upon her with an expression of real happiness. Anne of Austria held the cards against the cardinal, and her daughter-in-law assisted her in the game, when she was not engaged in smiling at her husband.* As for the cardinal, who was lying on his bed with a weary and careworn face, his cards were held by the Comtesse de Soissons,* and he watched them with an incessant look of interest and cupidity.

The Cardinal's face had been rouged by Bernouin; but the rouge, which glowed only on his cheeks, threw into stronger contrast the sickly pallor of his countenance and the shining yellow of his brow. His eyes alone acquired a more brilliant lustre from this contrast, and upon those sick man's eyes were, from time to time, turned the uneasy looks of the king, the queen, and the courtiers. The fact is, that the two eyes of the Signor Mazarin were the stars more or less brilliant in which the France of the seventeenth century read its destiny every evening and every morning.

Monseigneur neither won nor lost; he was, therefore, neither cheerful nor sad. It was a stagnation in which, full of pity for him, Anne of Austria would not have willingly left him; but in order to attract the attention of the sick man by some brilliant stroke, she must have either won or lost. To win would have been dangerous, because Mazarin would have changed his indifference into a scowl; to lose would likewise have been danger-ous, because she must have cheated, and the infanta, who watched her game, would, doubtless, have exclaimed against her partiality for Mazarin. Profiting by this calm, the courtiers were chatting. When not in a bad humour, M. Mazarin was a very easy-going prince, and he, who prevented nobody from singing, provided they paid,* was not tyrant enough to prevent people from talking, provided they made up their minds to lose.

They were therefore chatting. At the first table, the king's younger brother, Philip, Duc d'Anjou,* was admiring his handsome face in the glass of a box. His favourite, the Chevalier de Lorraine, leaning over the back of the prince's chair, was listening, with secret envy, to the Comte de Guiche, another of Philip's favourites, who was relating in choice terms the various vicissitudes of fortune of the royal adventurer Charles II. He told, as so many fabulous events, all the history of his peregrinations in Scotland, and his terrors when the enemy's party was so closely on his track; of nights spent in trees, and days spent in hunger and combats. By degrees, the fate of the unfortunate king interested his listeners so greatly, that the play languished even at the royal table, and the young king, with a pensive look and downcast eye, followed, without appearing to give any attention to it, the smallest details of this Odyssey, very picturesquely related by the Comte de Guiche.

The Comtesse de Soissons interrupted the narrator, 'Confess, count, you are making it up.'

'Madame, I am repeating like a parrot all the stories related to me by different Englishmen. To my shame I am compelled to say, I am as exact as a copy.'

'Charles II would have died before he could have endured all that.'

Louis XIV raised his intelligent and proud head. 'Madame,' said he, in a grave tone, still partaking something of the timid child, 'monsieur le cardinal will tell you that during my minority, the affairs of France were in jeopardy—and that if I had been older, and obliged to take sword in hand, it would sometimes have been for the purpose of procuring the evening meal.'

'Thanks to God,' said the cardinal, who spoke for the first time, 'your majesty exaggerates, and your supper has always been ready with that of your servants.'

The king coloured.

'Oh!' cried Philip, inconsiderately, from his place, and without ceasing to admire himself—'I recollect once, at Melun, the supper was laid for nobody, and that the king ate two-thirds of a slice of bread, and abandoned to me the other third.'*

The whole assembly, seeing Mazarin smile, began to laugh. Courtiers flatter kings with the remembrance of past distresses, as with the hopes of future good fortune.

'It is not to be denied that the crown of France has always remained firm upon the heads of its kings,' Anne of Austria hastened to say, 'and that it has fallen off that of the king of England; and when by chance, that crown shook a little—for there are throne-quakes as well as earthquakes—every time, I say, that rebellion threatened it, a good victory restored tranquillity.'

'With a few gems added to the crown,' said Mazarin.

The Comte de Guiche was silent: the king composed his countenance, and Mazarin exchanged looks with Anne of Austria, as if to thank her for her intervention.

'It is of no consequence,' said Philip, smoothing his hair; 'my cousin Charles is not handsome, but he is very brave, and fought like a reiter; and if he continues to fight thus, no doubt he will finish by gaining a battle, like Rocroi*——'

'He has no soldiers,' interrupted the Chevalier de Lorraine.

'The king of Holland, his ally, will give him some. I would willingly have given him some if I had been king of France.'

Louis XIV blushed excessively. Mazarin affected to be more attentive to his game than ever.

'By this time,' resumed the Comte de Guiche, 'the fortune of this unhappy prince is decided. If he has been deceived by Monk he is ruined. Imprisonment, perhaps death, will finish what exile, battles, and privations have commenced.'

Mazarin's brow became clouded.

'Is it certain,' said Louis XIV, 'that his majesty Charles II has quitted the Hague?'

'Quite certain, your majesty,' replied the young man; 'my father has received a letter containing all the details; it is even known that the King has landed at Dover; some fishermen saw him entering the port; the rest is still a mystery.'

'I should like to know the rest,' said Philip, impetuously. 'You know—you, my brother.'

Louis XIV coloured again. That was the third time within an hour. 'Ask my lord cardinal,' replied he, in a tone which made Mazarin, Anne of Austria, and everybody else open their eyes.

'That means, my son,' said Anne of Austria, laughing, 'that the king does not like affairs of state to be talked of out of the council.'

Philip received the reprimand with good grace, and bowed, first smiling at his brother, and then at his mother. But Mazarin saw from the corner of his eye that a group was about to be formed in the corner of the room, and that the Duc d'Anjou, with the Comte de Guiche and the Chevalier de Lorraine, prevented from talking aloud, might say, in a whisper, what it was not convenient should be said. He was beginning then to dart at them glances full of mistrust and uneasiness, inviting Anne of Austria to throw perturbation in the midst of the unlawful assembly, when, suddenly, Bernouin, entering from behind the tapestry of the bedroom, whispered in the ear of Mazarin, 'Monseigneur, an envoy from his majesty, the king of England,'

Mazarin could not help exhibiting a slight emotion, which was perceived by the king. To avoid being indiscreet, rather than to appear useless, Louis XIV rose immediately, and approaching his eminence, wished him good-night. All the assembly had risen with a great noise of rolling of chairs and tables being pushed away.

'Let everybody depart by degrees,' said Mazarin in a whisper to Louis XIV, 'and be so good as to excuse me a few minutes. I am going to despatch an affair about which I wish to converse with your majesty this very evening.'

'And the queens?' asked Louis XIV.

'And M. le Duc d'Anjou,' said his eminence,

At the same time he turned round in his alcove, the curtains of which, in falling, concealed the bed. The cardinal, nevertheless, did not lose sight of the conspirators.

'M. le Comte de Guiche,' said he, in a fretful voice, whilst putting on, behind the curtain, his dressing gown, with the assistance of Bernouin.

'I am here, my lord,' said the young man, as he approached.

'Take my cards, you are lucky. Win a little money for me from these gentlemen.'

'Yes, my lord.'

The young man sat down at the table from which the king withdrew to talk with the two queens. A serious game was commenced between the comte and several rich courtiers. In the meantime Philip was discussing questions of dress with the Chevalier de Lorraine, and they had ceased to hear the rustling of the cardinal's silk robe from behind the curtain. His eminence had followed Bernouin into the closet adjoining the bedroom.

XL

AN AFFAIR OF STATE

THE cardinal, on passing into his cabinet, found the Comte de la Fère, who was waiting for him, engaged in admiring a very fine Raphael placed over a sideboard covered with plate. His eminence came in softly, lightly, and silently as a shadow, and watched the countenance of the unsuspecting comte, as he was accustomed to do, for he could tell simply by examining the face of his interlocutor what the result of the conversation would be.

But this time Mazarin was foiled in his expectation: he read nothing upon the face of Athos, not even the respect he was accustomed to see on all faces. Athos was dressed in black, with a simple lacing of silver. He wore the Holy Ghost, the Garter, and the Golden Fleece, three orders of such importance, that a king alone, or else a player, could wear them at once.

Mazarin rummaged a long time in his somewhat troubled memory to recall the name he ought to give to this icy figure, but he did not succeed. 'I am told,' said he, at length, 'you have a message from England for me.'

And he sat down, dismissing Bernouin, who, in his role as secretary, was getting his pen ready.

'From his majesty, the king of England, yes, your eminence.'

'You speak very good French for an Englishman, monsieur,' said Mazarin, graciously, looking through his fingers at the Holy

Ghost, Garter, and Golden Fleece, but more particularly at the face of the messenger.

'I am not an Englishman, but a Frenchman, monsieur le cardinal,' replied Athos.

'It is remarkable that the king of England should choose a Frenchman for his ambassador; it is an excellent augury. Your name, monsieur, if you please.'

'Comte de la Fère,' replied Athos, bowing more slightly than the ceremonial and pride of the all-powerful minister required.

Mazarin bent his shoulders, as if to say:

'I do not know that name.'

Athos did not alter his bearing.

'And you come, monsieur,' continued Mazarin, 'to tell me——'

'I come from his majesty the King of Great Britain to announce to the King of France'—Mazarin frowned—'to announce to the King of France,' continued Athos, imperturbably, 'the happy restoration of his majesty Charles II to the throne of his ancestors.'

This nuance did not escape his cunning eminence. Mazarin was too much accustomed to mankind, not to see in the cold and almost haughty politeness of Athos, an index of hostility, which was not of the temperature of that hot-house called a court.

'You have accreditation, I suppose?' asked Mazarin, in a short, querulous tone.

'Yes, monseigneur.' And the word 'monseigneur' came so painfully from the lips of Athos, that it might be said it skinned them.

Athos took from an embroidered velvet bag which he carried under his doublet a dispatch. The cardinal held out his hand for it. 'Your pardon, monseigneur,' said Athos. 'My dispatch is for the king.'

'Since you are a Frenchman, monsieur, you ought to know the position of a prime minister at the court of France.'

'There was a time,' replied Athos, 'when I occupied myself with the importance of prime ministers; but I have formed, long ago, a resolution to treat no longer with any but the king.'

'Then, monsieur,' said Mazarin, who began to be irritated, 'you will neither see the minister nor the king.'

Mazarin rose. Athos replaced his dispatch in its bag, bowed gravely, and took several steps towards the door. This coolness exasperated Mazarin. 'What strange diplomatic proceedings are these!' cried he. 'Have we returned to the times when Cromwell sent us bullies in the guise of *chargés d'affaires*? You lack nothing, monsieur, but the steel cap on your head, and a Bible at your girdle.'

'Monsieur,' said Athos, drily, 'I have never had, as you have, the advantage of treating with Cromwell; and I have only seen his *chargés d'affaires* sword in hand; I am therefore ignorant of how he treated with prime ministers. As for the king of England, Charles II, I know that when he writes to his majesty King Louis XIV, he does not write to his eminence the Cardinal Mazarin. I see no diplomacy in that distinction.'

'Ah!' cried Mazarin, raising his sickly hand, and striking his head, 'I remember now!' Athos looked at him in astonishment. 'Yes, that is it!' said the cardinal, continuing to look at his interlocutor; 'yes, that is certainly it. I know you now, monsieur. Ah! *diavolo!** I am no longer astonished.'

'In fact, I was astonished that, with your eminence's excellent memory,' replied Athos, smiling, 'you had not recognized me before.'

'Always refractory and grumbling—monsieur—monsieur— What do they call you? Stop—a name of a river—Potamos; no—the name of an island—Naxos;* no, *per Giove!*—the name of a mountain—Athos! now I have it. Delighted to see you again, and to be no longer at Rueil,* where you and your damned companions made me pay ransom. That accursed Fronde! Oh, what grudges! Why, monsieur, have your antipathies survived mine? If any one had cause to complain, I think it could not be you, who got out of the affair not only in a sound skin, but with the sash of the Holy Ghost around your neck.'

'My lord cardinal,' replied Athos, 'permit me not to enter into considerations of that kind, I have a mission to fulfil. Will you facilitate the means of my fulfilling that mission, or will you not?'

'I am astonished,' said Mazarin—quite delighted at having recovered his memory, and bristling with malice—'I am astonished, Monsieur—Athos—that a *Frondeur* like you should have accepted a mission to perfidious Mazarin, as used to be said in those good old times——' And Mazarin began to laugh, in spite of a painful cough, which cut short his sentences, converting them into sobs.

'I have only accepted a mission to the King of France, monsieur le cardinal,' retorted the count, though with less asperity, for he thought he had sufficiently the advantage to show himself moderate.

'And yet, *Monsieur le Frondeur*,' said Mazarin gaily, 'the affair which you have taken in charge must, from the king——'

'With which I am charged, monseigneur. I do not run after affairs.'

'Be it so. I say that this negotiation must pass through my hands. Let us waste no precious time, then. Tell me the conditions.'

'I have had the honour of assuring your eminence that only the letter of his majesty King Charles II contains the revelation of his wishes.'

'Pooh! you are ridiculous with your obstinacy, Monsieur Athos. It is plain you have kept company with the Puritans yonder. As to your secret, I know it better than you do; and you have done wrongly, perhaps, in not having shown some respect for a very old and suffering man, who has laboured much during his life, and fought for his ideas as bravely as you have for yours. You will not communicate your letter to me?—You will say nothing to me!—Very well! Come with me into my chamber; you shall speak to the king—and with the king. Now then, one last word: who gave you the Fleece? I recall it being said that you had the Garter; but as to the Fleece, I do not know——'

'Recently, my lord, Spain, on the occasion of the marriage of his majesty Louis XIV, sent King Charles II a blank patent of the Fleece; Charles II immediately transmitted it to me, filling up the blank with my name.'

Mazarin arose and leaning on the arm of Bernouin, he returned to his alcove at the moment the name of M. le Prince was being announced. The Prince de Condé, the first prince of the blood, the conqueror of Rocroi, Lens, and Nordlingen, was, in fact, entering the apartment of Monseigneur de Mazarin, followed by his gentlemen, and had already saluted the king, when

the prime minister raised his curtain. Athos had time to see
Raoul shaking the hand of the Comte de Guiche, and send him
a smile in return for his respectful bow. He had time, likewise,
to see the radiant countenance of the cardinal, when he perceived before him, upon the table, an enormous heap of gold,
which the Comte de Guiche had won in a run of luck, after his
eminence had confided his cards to him. So forgetting ambassador, embassy and prince, his first thought was of the gold.
'What!' cried the old man—'all that—won?'

'Some fifty thousand crowns; yes, monseigneur,' replied the
Comte de Guiche, rising. 'Must I give up my place to your
eminence, or shall I continue?'

'Give up! give up! you are mad. You would lose all you have
won. A plague on it!'

'My lord!' said the Prince de Condé bowing.

'Good-evening, monsieur le prince,' said the minister, in a
careless tone; 'it is very kind of you to visit an old sick friend.'

'A friend!' murmured the Comte de la Fère, at witnessing
with stupor this monstrous combination of words, 'friends!*
when the parties are Condé and Mazarin!'

Mazarin seemed to divine the thought of the *Frondeur*, for he
smiled upon him with triumph, and immediately, 'Sire,' said he
to the king, 'I have the honour of presenting to your majesty,
Monsieur le Comte de la Fère, an envoy from his Britannic
majesty. An affair of state, gentlemen,' added he, waving his
hand to all who filled the chamber, and who, the Prince de
Condé at their head, all disappeared at the simple gesture. Raoul,
after a last look cast at the count, followed M. de Condé. Philip of
Anjou and the queen appeared to be consulting about departing.

'A family affair,' said Mazarin, suddenly, detaining them in
their seats. 'This gentleman is the bearer of a letter in which
King Charles II, completely restored to his throne, demands an
alliance between Monsieur, the brother of the king, and Mademoiselle Henrietta, grand-daughter of Henry IV. Will you
remit your letter of credit to the king, monsieur le comte?'

Athos remained for a minute stupefied. How could the minister possibly know the contents of the letter, which had never
been out of his keeping for a single instant? Nevertheless, always
master of himself, he held out the dispatch to the young king,

Louis XIV, who took it with a blush. A solemn silence reigned in the cardinal's chamber. It was only troubled by the dull sound of the gold which Mazarin, with his yellow, dry hand, piled up in a casket, whilst the king was reading.

XLI

THE REPORT

THE wiliness of the cardinal did not leave much for the ambassador to say; nevertheless, the word 'restoration' had struck the king, who, addressing the comte, upon whom his eyes had been fixed since his entrance, 'Monsieur,' said he, 'will you have the kindness to give us some details concerning the affairs of England? You come from that country, you are a Frenchman, and the orders which I see glittering upon your person announce you to be a man of merit as well as a man of quality.'

'Monsieur,' said the cardinal, turning towards the queen-mother, 'is an ancient servant of your majesty's, Monsieur le Comte de la Fère.'

Anne of Austria was as non-committal as any queen whose life had been mingled with fine and stormy days. She looked at Mazarin, whose evil smile promised her something disagreeable; then she solicited from Athos, by another look, an explanation.

'Monsieur,' continued the cardinal, 'was a Tréville musketeer, in the service of the late king. Monsieur is well acquainted with England, whither he has made several voyages at various periods; he is a subject of the highest merit.'*

These words made allusion to all the memories which Anne of Austria trembled to evoke. England, that was her hatred of Richelieu and her love for Buckingham; a Tréville musketeer, that was the whole Odyssey of the triumphs which had made the heart of the young woman throb, and of the dangers which had been so near overturning the throne of the young queen. These words had much power, for they rendered mute and attentive all the royal personages, who, with very various sentiments, set about coming to terms with mysteries which the young had not seen, and which the old had believed to be for ever effaced.

'Speak, monsieur,' said Louis XIV, the first to escape from troubles, suspicions, and memories.

'Yes, speak,' added Mazarin, to whom the little malicious thrust directed against Anne of Austria had restored energy and gaiety.

'Sire,' said the comte, 'a sort of miracle has changed the whole destiny of Charles II. That which men, till that time, had been unable to do, God resolved to accomplish.'

Mazarin coughed, while tossing about in his bed.

'King Charles II,' continued Athos, 'left the Hague neither as a fugitive nor a conqueror, but as an absolute king, who, after a distant voyage from his kingdom, returns amidst universal benedictions.'

'A great miracle, indeed,' said Mazarin; 'for, if the news was true, King Charles II, who has just returned amidst benedictions, went away amidst musket-shots.'

The king remained impassive. Philip, younger and more frivolous, could not repress a smile, which flattered Mazarin as an applause of his pleasantry.

'It is plain,' said the king, 'there is a miracle; but God, who does so much for kings, monsieur le comte, nevertheless employs the hand of man to bring about the triumph of His designs. To what men does Charles II principally owe his re-establishment?'

'Why,' interrupted Mazarin, without any regard for the king's pride—'does not your majesty know that it is to M. Monk?'

'I ought to know it,' replied Louis XIV, resolutely; 'and yet I ask my lord ambassador, the causes of the change in this General Monk?'

'And your majesty touches precisely the question,' replied Athos; 'for without the miracle of which I have had the honour to speak, General Monk would probably have remained an implacable enemy of Charles II. God willed that a strange, bold, and ingenious idea should enter into the mind of a certain man, whilst a devoted and courageous idea took possession of the mind of another man. The combinations of these two ideas brought about such a change in the position of M. Monk, that, from an inveterate enemy, he became a friend to the deposed king.'

'These are exactly the details I asked for,' said the king. 'Who and what are the two men of whom you speak?'

'Two Frenchmen, sire.'

'Indeed! I am glad of that.'

'And the two ideas,' said Mazarin; 'I am more curious about ideas than about men, for my part.'

'Yes,' murmured the king.

'The second idea, the devoted, reasonable idea—the least important, sir—was to go and dig up a million in gold, buried by King Charles I at Newcastle, and to purchase with that gold the support of Monk.'

'Oh, oh!' said Mazarin, reanimated by the word million. 'But Newcastle was at the time occupied by Monk.'

'Yes, monsieur le cardinal, and that is why I venture to call the idea courageous as well as devoted. It was necessary, if Monk refused the offers of the negotiator, to reinstate King Charles II in possession of this million, which was to be torn, as it were, from the loyalty and not the loyalism of General Monk. This was effected, in spite of many difficulties: the general proved to be loyal, and allowed the money to be taken away.'

'It seems to me,' said the timid, thoughtful king, 'that Charles II could not have known of this million whilst he was in Paris.'

'It seems to me,' rejoined the cardinal, spitefully, 'that his majesty the king of Great Britain knew perfectly well of this million, but that he preferred having two millions to having one.'

'Sire,' said Athos, firmly, 'the king of England, whilst in France, was so poor that he had not even money to travel by public coach; so destitute of hope that he frequently thought of dying. He was so entirely ignorant of the existence of the million at Newcastle, that but for a gentleman—one of your majesty's subjects—the moral depositary of the million, who revealed the secret to King Charles II, that prince would still be vegetating in the most cruel forgetfulness.'

'Let us pass on to the strange, bold, and ingenious idea,' interrupted Mazarin, whose sagacity foresaw a check. 'What was that idea?'

'This—M. Monk formed the only obstacle to the re-establishment of the fallen king. A Frenchman imagined the idea of suppressing this obstacle.'

'Oh! oh! then that Frenchman is a scoundrel,' said Mazarin; 'and the idea is not so ingenious as to prevent its author being tied up by the neck at the Place de Grève,* by decree of the parliament.'

'Your eminence is mistaken,' replied Athos drily; 'I did not say that the Frenchman in question had resolved to assassinate M. Monk, but only to suppress him. The words of the French language have a value which the gentlemen of France know perfectly. Besides, this is an affair of war; and when men serve kings against their enemies they are not to be condemned by a parliament*—God is their judge. This French gentleman, then, formed the idea of gaining possession of the person of Monk, and he executed his plan.'

The king became animated at the recital of great actions. The king's younger brother struck the table with his hand, exclaiming, 'Ah! how splendid!'

'He carried off Monk?' said the king. 'Why, Monk was in his camp.'

'And the gentleman was alone, sire.'

'That is amazing!' said Philip.

'Amazing, indeed!' cried the king.

'Good! There are the two little lions unchained,' murmured the cardinal. And with an air of spite, which he did not dissemble, he said: 'I am unacquainted with these details, will you guarantee their authenticity, monsieur!'

'All the more easily, my lord cardinal, from having seen the events.'

'You have?'

'Yes, monseigneur.'

The king had involuntarily drawn close to the count, the Duc d'Anjou had turned sharply round, and pressed Athos on the other side.

'What next? monsieur, what next?' cried they both at the same time.

'Sire, M. Monk, being taken by the Frenchman, was brought to King Charles II, at the Hague. The king gave back his freedom to Monk and the grateful general, in return, gave Charles II the throne of Great Britain, for which so many valiant men had fought in vain.'

Philip clapped his hands with enthusiasm, Louis XIV, more reflective, turned towards the Comte de la Fère.

'Is this true,' said he, 'in all its details?'

'Absolutely true, sire.'

'That one of my gentlemen knew the secret of the million, and kept it?'

'Yes, sire.'

'The name of that gentleman?'

'It was your humble servant,' said Athos, simply, and bowing.

A murmur of admiration made the heart of Athos swell with pleasure. He had reason to be proud, at least. Mazarin, himself, had raised his arms towards heaven.

'Monsieur,' said the king, 'I shall seek, and find means to reward you.' Athos made a movement. 'Oh, not for your honesty, to be paid for that would humiliate you; but I owe you a reward for having participated in the restoration of my brother, King Charles II.'

'Certainly,' said Mazarin.

'It is the triumph of a good cause which fills the whole house of France with joy,' said Anne of Austria.

'I continue,' said Louis XIV: 'Is it also true, that a single man got to Monk, in his camp, and carried him off?'

'That man had ten others with him, taken from a very inferior rank.'

'And nothing but them?'

'Nothing more.'

'And he is named?'

'Monsieur d'Artagnan, formerly lieutenant of the musketeers of your majesty.'

Anne of Austria coloured; Mazarin became yellow with shame; Louis XIV was deeply thoughtful, and a drop of moisture fell from his pale brow. 'What men!' murmured he. And, involuntarily, he darted a glance at the minister which would have terrified him, if Mazarin, at the moment, had not concealed his head under his pillow.

'Monsieur,' said the young Duc d'Anjou, placing his hand, delicate and white as that of a woman, upon the arm of Athos, 'tell that brave man, I beg you, that Monsieur, brother of the king, will to-morrow drink his health before five hundred of the best gentlemen of France.' And, on finishing these words, the young man, perceiving that his enthusiasm had deranged one of his ruffles, set to work to put it to rights with the greatest care imaginable.

'Let us resume business, sire,' interrupted Mazarin, who never was enthusiastic, and who wore no ruffles.

'Yes, monsieur,' replied Louis XIV. 'Pursue your communication, monsieur le comte,' added he, turning towards Athos.

Athos immediately began and offered in due form the hand of the Princess Henrietta Stuart* to the young prince, the king's brother. The conference lasted an hour; after which the doors of the chamber were thrown open to the courtiers, who resumed their places, as if nothing had been kept from them in the occupations of that evening. Athos then found himself again with Raoul, and the father and son were able to clasp each other's hands.

XLII

IN WHICH MAZARIN BECOMES PRODIGAL

WHILST Mazarin was endeavouring to recover from the serious alarm he had just experienced, Athos and Raoul were exchanging a few words in a corner of the apartment. 'Well, here you are at Paris, then, Raoul?' said the comte.

'Yes, monsieur, since the return of M. le Prince.'*

'I cannot converse freely with you here, because we are observed; but I shall return home presently, and shall expect you as soon as your duty permits.'

Raoul bowed, and, at that moment, M. le Prince came up to them. The prince had that clear and keen look which distinguishes birds of prey of the noble species: his physiognomy itself presented several distinct traits of this resemblance. It is known, that in the Prince de Condé, the aquiline nose rose out sharply and incisively from a brow slightly retreating, rather low than high, and according to the railers of the court—a race without mercy even for genius—constituted rather an eagle's

beak than a human nose, in the heir of the illustrious princes
of the house of Condé. This penetrating look, this imperious
expression of the whole countenance, generally disturbed those
to whom the prince spoke, more than either majesty or regular
beauty could have done in the conqueror of Rocroi. Besides
this, the fire mounted so suddenly to his prominent eyes, that
with the prince every sort of animation resembled passion. Now,
on account of his rank, everybody at the court respected M. le
Prince, and many even, seeing only the man, carried their respect as far as fear.

Louis de Condé then advanced towards the Comte de la Fère
and Raoul, with the marked intention of being saluted by the
one, and of speaking to the other. No man bowed with more
reserved grace than the Comte de la Fère. He disdained to put
into a salutation all the shades which a courtier ordinarily borrows from the same colour—the desire to please. Athos knew
his own personal value, and bowed to the prince like a man,
correcting by something sympathetic and undefinable what might
have appeared offensive to the pride of the highest rank in the
inflexibility of his attitude. The prince was about to speak to
Raoul. Athos forestalled him. 'If M. le Vicomte de Bragelonne,'
said he, 'were not one of the humble servants of your royal
highness, I would beg him to pronounce my name before you—
mon prince.'

'I have the honour to address Monsieur le Comte de la Fère,'
said Condé, instantly.

'My protector,' added Raoul, blushing.

'One of the most honourable men in the kingdom,' continued
the prince; 'one of the first gentlemen of France, and of whom
I have heard so much that I have frequently desired to number
him among my friends.'

'An honour of which I should be unworthy,' replied Athos,
'but for the respect and admiration I entertain for your royal
highness.'

'Monsieur de Bragelonne,' said the prince, 'is a good officer,
and it is plainly seen he has been to a good school. Ah, monsieur
le comte, in your time, generals had soldiers!'

'That is true, my lord, but nowadays soldiers have generals.'

This compliment, which savoured so little of flattery, gave a thrill of joy to the man whom already Europe considered a hero; and who might be thought to be satiated with praise.

'I regret very much,' continued the prince, 'that you should have retired from the service, monsieur le comte; for it is more than probable that the king will soon have a war with Holland or England, and opportunities for distinguishing himself would not be wanting for a man who, like you, knows Great Britain as well as you do France.'

'I believe I may say, monseigneur, that I have acted wisely in retiring from the service,' said Athos, smiling. 'France and Great Britain will henceforward live like two sisters, if I can trust my presentiments.'

'Your presentiments?'

'Stop, monseigneur, listen to what is being said yonder, at the table of my lord the cardinal.'

'Where they are playing?'

'Yes, my lord.'

The cardinal had just raised himself on one elbow, and made a sign to the king's brother, who went to him.

'My lord,' said the cardinal, 'pick up, if you please, all those gold crowns.' And he pointed to the enormous pile of yellow and glittering pieces which the Comte de Guiche had raised by degrees before him by a surprising run of luck at play.

'For me?' cried the Duc d'Anjou.

'Those fifty thousand crowns; yes, monseigneur, they are yours.'

'Do you give them to me?'

'I have been playing on your account, monseigneur,' replied the cardinal, getting weaker and weaker, as if this effort of giving money had exhausted all his physical and moral faculties.

'Oh good heavens!' exclaimed Philip, wild with joy, 'what a fortunate day!' And he himself, making a rake of his fingers, drew a part of the sum into his pockets, which he filled, and still full a third remained on the table.

'Chevalier,' said Philip to his favourite, the Chevalier de Lorraine, 'come hither, chevalier.' The favourite quickly obeyed. 'Pocket the rest,' said the young prince.

This singular scene was considered by the persons present only as a touching kind of family celebration. The cardinal assumed the airs of a father with the sons of France, and the two young princes had grown up under his wing. No one then imputed to pride, or even impertinence, as would be done nowadays, this liberality on the part of the first minister. The courtiers were satisfied with envying the prince. The king turned away his head.

'I never had so much money before,' said the young prince, joyously, as he crossed the chamber with his favourite, to go to his carriage. 'No, never! What a weight these crowns are!'

'But why has monsieur le cardinal given away all this money at once?' asked monsieur le prince of the Comte de la Fère. 'He must be very ill!'

'Yes, my lord, very ill, without doubt; he looks very ill, as your royal highness may perceive.'

'But surely he will die of it. A hundred and fifty thousand livres! Oh, it is incredible! But, count, tell me a reason for it?'

'Patience, monseigneur, I beg of you. Here comes M. le Duc d'Anjou, talking with the Chevalier de Lorraine; I should not be surprised if they spared us the trouble of being indiscreet. Listen to them.'

In fact, the chevalier said to the prince in a low voice, 'My lord, it is not natural for M. Mazarin to give you so much money. Take care! you will let some of the pieces fall, my lord. What design has the cardinal upon you to make him so generous?'

'As I said,' whispered Athos, in the prince's ear; 'that, perhaps, is the best reply to your question.'

'Tell me, my lord,' repeated the chevalier impatiently, as he was calculating, by weighing them in his pocket, the quota of the sum which had fallen to his share by rebound.

'My dear chevalier, a wedding present.'

'How a wedding present?'

'Eh! yes, I am going to be married,' replied the Duc d'Anjou, without perceiving, at the moment he was passing the Prince and Athos, who both bowed respectfully.

The chevalier darted at the young duke a glance so strange, and so acute, that the Comte de la Fère quite started on beholding it.

'You! you to be married!' repeated he; 'oh! that's impossible. You would not commit such a folly!'

'Bah! I don't do it myself; I am made to do it,' replied the Duc d'Anjou. 'But come, quick! let us get rid of our money.' Thereupon he disappeared with his companion, laughing and talking, whilst all heads were bowed on his passage.

'Then,' whispered the Prince to Athos, 'that is the secret.'

'It was not I that told you so, my lord.'

'He is to marry the sister of Charles II?'

'I believe so.'

The prince reflected for a moment, and his eye shot forth one of its not unfrequent flashes. 'Humph!' said he, slowly, as if speaking to himself; 'our swords are once more to be hung on the wall—for a long time!' and he sighed.

All that sigh contained of ambition silently stifled, of extinguished illusions and disappointed hopes, Athos alone divined, for he alone had heard the sigh. Immediately after, the prince took leave and the king left the apartment. Athos, by a sign made to Bragelonne, renewed the desire he had expressed at the beginning of the scene. By degrees the chamber emptied, and Mazarin was left alone, a prey to suffering which he could no longer dissemble. 'Bernouin! Bernouin!' cried he, in a broken voice.

'What does monseigneur want?'

'Guénaud—let Guénaud be sent for,' said his eminence. 'I think I'm dying.'

Bernouin, in great terror, rushed into the closet to give the order, and the messenger, who hastened to fetch the physician, passed the king's carriage in the Rue Saint Honoré.

XLIII

GUÉNAUD

THE cardinal's order was pressing; Guénaud quickly obeyed it. He found his patient stretched on his bed, his legs swelled, his face livid, and his stomach collapsed. Mazarin had a severe attack of gout. He suffered tortures with the impatience of a man who has not been accustomed to opposition to his wishes. On seeing Guénaud: 'Ah!' said he; 'now I am saved!'

Guénaud was a very learned and circumspect man, who stood in no need of the critiques of Boileau to obtain a reputation.* When facing a disease, if it were personified in a king, he treated the patient as a Turk treats a Moor. He did not therefore reply to Mazarin as the minister expected: 'Here is the doctor; good-bye disease!' On the contrary, on examining his patient, with a very serious air:

'Oh! oh!' said he.

'Eh! what! Guénaud! Why do you look at me like that?'

'I look as I should on seeing your complaint, my lord; it is a very dangerous one.'

'The gout—oh! yes, the gout.'

'With complications, my lord.'

Mazarin raised himself upon his elbow, and, questioning by look and gesture: 'What do you mean by that? Am I worse than I believe myself to be?'

'My lord,' said Guénaud, seating himself beside the bed, 'your eminence has worked very hard during your life; your eminence has suffered much.'

'But I am not old, I fancy. The late M. de Richelieu was but seventeen months younger than I am, when he died, and died of a mortal disease. I am young, Guénaud: remember I am scarcely fifty-two.'*

'Oh! my lord, you are much more than that. How long did the Fronde last?'

'For what purpose do you put such a question to me?'

'For a medical calculation, monseigneur.'

'Well, some ten years—off and on.'

'Very well; be kind enough to reckon every year of the Fronde as three years—that makes thirty; now twenty and fifty-two make seventy-two years. You are seventy-two, my lord; and that is a great age.'

Whilst saying this, he felt the pulse of his patient. This pulse was full of such fatal indications, that the physician continued, notwithstanding the interruptions of the patient: 'Put down the years of the Fronde at four each, and you have lived eighty-two years.'

'Are you speaking seriously, Guénaud?'

'Alas! yes, monseigneur.'

'You take a roundabout way, then, to inform me that I am very ill?'

'*Ma foi!* yes, my lord, and with a man of the mind and courage of your eminence, it ought not to be necessary to do so.'

The cardinal breathed with such difficulty that he inspired pity even in a pitiless physician. 'There are diseases and diseases,' resumed Mazarin. 'From some of them people escape.'

'That is true, my lord.'

'Is it not?' cried Mazarin, almost joyously; 'for, in short, what else would be the use of power, of strength of will? What would the use of genius be—your genius, Guénaud? What would be the use of science and art, if the patient, who disposes of all that, cannot be saved from peril?'

Guénaud was about to open his mouth, but Mazarin continued,

'Remember,' said he, 'I am the most confiding of your patients; remember I obey you blindly, and that consequently——'

'I know all that,' said Guénaud.

'I shall be cured then?'

'Monseigneur, there is neither strength of will, nor power, nor genius, nor science that can resist a disease which God doubtless sends, or which he cast upon the earth at the creation, with full power to destroy and kill mankind. When the disease is fatal, it kills, and nothing can——'

'Is—my—disease—fatal?' asked Mazarin.

'Yes, my lord.'

His eminence sank down for a moment, like an unfortunate wretch who is crushed by a falling column. But the spirit of Mazarin was a strong one, or rather his mind was a firm one. 'Guénaud,' said he, recovering from his first shock, 'you will permit me to appeal against your judgment. I will call together the most learned men of Europe: I will consult them. I will live, in short, by the virtue of I care not what remedy.'

'My lord must not suppose,' said Guénaud, 'that I have the presumption to pronounce alone upon an existence so valuable as yours. I have already assembled all the good physicians and practitioners of France and Europe. There were twelve of them.'

'And they said——'

'They said that your eminence was suffering from a fatal disease; I have the consultation signed in my portfolio. If your eminence will please to see it, you will find the names of all the incurable diseases we have met with. There is first——'

'No, no!' cried Mazarin, pushing away the paper. 'No, no, Guénaud, I yield! I yield!' And a profound silence, during which the cardinal resumed his senses and recovered his strength, followed the agitation of this scene. 'There is another thing,' murmured Mazarin; 'there are empirics and charlatans. In my country, those whom physicians abandon, resort to a quack, who out of a hundred patients kills ten but cures ninety.'

'Has not your eminence observed, that during the last month I have changed my remedies ten times?'

'Yes. Well?'

'Well, I have spent fifty thousand crowns in purchasing the secrets of all these fellows: the list is exhausted, and so is my purse. You are not cured; and, but for my art, you would be dead.'

'It's the end!' murmured the cardinal; 'it's the end——' And he threw a melancholy look upon the riches which surrounded him. 'And must I quit all this?' sighed he. 'I am dying, Guénaud! I am dying!'

'Oh! not yet, my lord,' said the physician.

Mazarin seized his hand. 'When?' asked he, fixing his two large eyes upon the impassive countenance of the physician.

'My lord, we never tell that.'

'To ordinary men, perhaps not; but to me—to me, whose every minute is worth a treasure. Tell me, Guénaud, tell me!'

'No, no, my lord.'

'I insist upon it, I tell you. Oh! give me a month, and for every one of those thirty days I will pay you a hundred thousand crowns.'

'My lord,' replied Guénaud, in a firm voice, 'it is God who can give you days of grace, and not I. God only allows you a fortnight.'

The cardinal breathed a painful sigh, and sank back upon his pillow, murmuring, 'Thank you, Guénaud, thank you!'

The physician was about to depart; the dying man raising himself up: 'Silence!' said he, with flaming eyes, 'silence!'

'My lord, I have known this secret two months; you see that I have kept it faithfully.'

'Go, Guénaud; I will take care of your fortunes; go, and tell Brienne to send me a clerk called M. Colbert. Go!'

XLIV

COLBERT

COLBERT was not far off. During the whole evening he had remained in one of the corridors, chatting with Bernouin and Brienne, and commenting, with the usual skill of people of a court, upon the news which developed like air bubbles upon the water, on the surface of each event. It is doubtless time to trace, in a few words, one of the most interesting portraits of the age, and to trace it with as much truth, perhaps, as contemporary painters have been able to do. Colbert was a man to whom the historian and the moralist have an equal right.

He was thirteen years older than Louis XIV,* his future master. Of middle height, rather lean than otherwise, he had deep-set eyes, a mean appearance, his hair was coarse black and thin, which, say the biographers of his time, made him take early to the skull cap. A look of severity, of harshness even, a sort of stiffness, which, with inferiors, was pride, with superiors an affectation of superior virtue; a surly cast of countenance upon all occasions, even when looking at himself in a glass alone— such is the exterior of this personage. As to the moral part of his character, the depth of his talent for accounts, and his ingenuity in making sterility itself productive, were much boasted of. Colbert had formed the idea of forcing governors of frontier places to feed the garrisons without pay, with what they drew from contributions. Such a valuable quality made Mazarin think of replacing Joubert, his intendant, who had recently died, by M. Colbert, who had such skill in nibbling down allowances. Colbert by degrees crept into court, notwithstanding his lowly birth, for he was the son of a man who sold wine as his father had done, but who afterwards sold cloth, and then silk stuffs. Colbert, destined for trade, had been clerk in Lyons to a merchant, whom he had quitted to come to Paris in the office of a Châtelet procureur named Biterne. It was here he learnt the art of drawing up an account, and the much more valuable one of complicating it.

This stiffness of manner in Colbert had been of great service to him; it is so true that Fortune, when she has a caprice, resembles those women of antiquity, who, when they had a fancy, were disgusted by no physical or moral defects in either men or things. Colbert, placed with Michel Letellier, secretary of state in 1648, by his cousin Colbert, Seigneur de Saint-Pouange, who protected him, received one day from the minister a commission for Cardinal Mazarin. His eminence was then in the enjoyment of flourishing health, and the bad years of the Fronde had not yet counted triple and quadruple for him. He was at Sedan, very much annoyed at a court intrigue in which Anne of Austria seemed inclined to desert his cause.

Of this intrigue Letellier held the thread. He had just received a letter from Anne of Austria, a letter very valuable to him, and strongly compromising Mazarin; but, as he already played the double part which served him so well, and by which he always managed two enemies so as to draw advantage from both, either by embroiling them more and more or by reconciling them, Michel Letellier wished to send Anne of Austria's letter to Mazarin, in order that he might be acquainted with it, and consequently pleased with his having so willingly rendered him a service. To send the letter was an easy matter; to recover it again, after having communicated it, that was the difficulty. Letellier cast his eyes around him, and seeing the gaunt black-garbed clerk with the scowling brow, scribbling away in his office, he preferred him to the best gendarme for the execution of this design.

Colbert was commanded to set out for Sedan, with positive orders to carry the letter to Mazarin, and bring it back to Letellier. He listened to his orders with scrupulous attention, required the instructions to be repeated twice, and was particular in learning whether the bringing back was as necessary as the communicating, and Letellier replied sternly, 'More necessary.' Then he set out, travelled like a courier, without any care for his body, and placed in the hands of Mazarin, first a letter from Letellier, which announced to the cardinal the sending of the precious letter, and then that letter itself. Mazarin coloured greatly whilst reading Anne of Austria's letter, gave Colbert a gracious smile and dismissed him.

'When shall I have the answer, monseigneur?'

'To-morrow.'

'To-morrow morning?'

'Yes, monsieur.'

The clerk turned upon his heel, after making his very best bow. The next day he was at his post at seven o'clock. Mazarin made him wait till ten. He remained patiently in the ante-chamber; his turn having come, he entered: Mazarin gave him a sealed packet. On the envelope of this packet were these words: Monsieur Michel Letellier, etc. Colbert looked at the packet with much attention; the cardinal put on a pleasant counten-ance, and pushed him towards the door.

'And the letter of the queen-mother, my lord?' asked Colbert.

'It is with the rest, in the packet,' said Mazarin.

'Oh! very well,' replied Colbert; and placing his hat between his knees, he began to unseal the packet.

Mazarin uttered a cry. 'What are you doing?' said he, angrily.

'I am unsealing the packet, my lord.'

'You mistrust me, then, master pedant, do you? Did any one ever see such impertinence?'

'Oh! my lord, do not be angry with me! It is certainly not your eminence's word I place in doubt, God forbid!'

'What then?'

'It is the carefulness of your chancery, my lord. What is a letter? A rag. May not a rag be forgotten? And look, my lord, look if I was not right. Your clerks have forgotten the rag; the letter is not in the packet.'

'You are an insolent fellow, and you have not looked,' cried Mazarin, very angrily; 'begone and wait my pleasure.' Whilst saying these words, with perfectly Italian subtlety he snatched the packet from the hands of Colbert, and re-entered his apartments.

But this anger could not last so long as not to be replaced in time by reason. Mazarin, every morning, on opening his closet door, found the figure of Colbert like a sentinel behind the bench, and this disagreeable figure never failed to ask him hum-bly, but with tenacity, for the queen-mother's letter. Mazarin

could hold out no longer, and was obliged to give it up. He
accompanied this restitution with a most severe reprimand, during which Colbert contented himself with examining, feeling,
even smelling, as it were, the paper, the characters, and the
signature, neither more nor less than if he had to deal with the
greatest forger in the kingdom. Mazarin behaved still more rudely
to him, but Colbert, still impassive, having obtained a certainty
that the letter was the true one, went off as if he had been deaf.
This conduct obtained for him afterwards the post of Joubert;
for Mazarin, instead of bearing malice, admired him, and was
desirous of attaching so much fidelity to himself.

It may be judged by this single anecdote, what the character
of Colbert was. Events, developing themselves, by degrees allowed all the powers of his mind to act freely. Colbert was not
long in insinuating himself into the good graces of the cardinal:
he became even indispensable to him. The clerk was acquainted
with all his accounts without the cardinal's ever having spoken
to him about them. This secret between them was a powerful
tie, and this was why, when about to appear before the Master
of another world, Mazarin was desirous of taking good counsel
in disposing of the wealth he was so unwillingly obliged to leave
in this world. After the visit to Guénaud, he therefore sent for
Colbert, desired him to sit down, and said to him: 'Let us
converse, Monsieur Colbert, and seriously, for I am very ill, and
I may chance to die.'

'Man is mortal,' replied Colbert.

'I have always remembered that, M. Colbert, and I have worked
with that end in view. You know that I have amassed a little
wealth.'

'I know you have, monseigneur.'

'At how much do you estimate, as near as you can, the amount
of this wealth, M. Colbert?'

'At forty millions, five hundred and sixty thousand, two hundred livres, nine cents, eight farthings,' replied Colbert.

The cardinal heaved a deep sigh, and looked at Colbert with
wonder, but he allowed a smile to steal across his lips.

'Known money,' added Colbert, in reply to that smile.

The cardinal gave quite a start in bed. 'What do you mean by
that?' said he.

'I mean,' said Colbert, 'that besides those forty millions, five hundred and sixty thousand, two hundred livres, nine cents, eight farthings, there are thirteen millions that are not known.'

'*Ouf!*' sighed Mazarin, 'what a man!'

At this moment the head of Bernouin appeared through the embrasure of the door.

'What is it?' asked Mazarin, 'and why do you disturb me?'

'The Théatin* father, your eminence's director, was sent for this evening; and he cannot come again to my lord till after to-morrow.'

Mazarin looked at Colbert, who arose and took his hat, saying: 'I shall come again, my lord.'

Mazarin hesitated. 'No, no,' said he; 'I have as much business to transact with you as with him. Besides, you are my other confessor—and what I have to say to one, the other may hear. Remain where you are, Colbert.'

'But, my lord, if there be no secret of penitence, will the director consent to my being here?'

'Do not trouble yourself about that; come into the alcove.'

'I can wait outside, monseigneur.'

'No, no, it will do you good to hear the confession of a rich man.'

Colbert bowed, and went into the alcove.

'Introduce the Théatin father,' said Mazarin, closing the curtains.

XLV

THE CONFESSION OF A RICH MAN

THE Théatin entered deliberately, without being too much astonished at the noise and agitation which anxiety for the cardinal's health had raised in his household. 'Come in, my reverend father,' said Mazarin, after a last look at the alcove, 'come in, and console me.'

'That is my duty, my lord,' replied the Théatin.

'Begin by sitting down, and making yourself comfortable, for I am going to begin with a general confession; you will afterwards give me a good absolution, and I shall believe myself more tranquil.'

'My lord,' said the father, 'you are not so ill as to make a general confession urgent—and it will be very fatiguing—take care.'

'You suspect, then, that it may be long, father?'

'How can I think it otherwise, when a man has lived so completely as your eminence has done?'

'Ah! that is true!—yes—the recital may be long.'

'The mercy of God is great,' snuffled the Théatin.

'Stop,' said Mazarin, 'there I begin to terrify myself with having allowed so many things to pass which the Lord might reprove.'

'Is not that always so?' said the Théatin naïvely, removing further from the lamp his thin pointed face, which was like that of a mole. 'Sinners are so forgetful beforehand, and so scrupulous when it is too late.'

'Sinners?' replied Mazarin. 'Do you use that word ironically, and to reproach me with all the genealogies I have allowed to be made on my account—I—the son of a fisherman,* in fact.''

'Hum!' said the Théatin.

'That is a first sin, father; for I have allowed it to be said that I am descended from a line of Roman consuls, S. Geganius Macerinus 1st, Macerinus 2d, and Proculus Macerinus 3d, of whom the Chronicle of Haolander* speaks. Macerinus was tantalizingly close to Mazarin. But *macerinus*, the diminutive, means undernourished. Oh! reverend father! Mazarini is also close to the augmentative, *macer*, meaning as thin as Lazarus. Look!'— and he showed his fleshless arms.

'In your having been born of a family of fishermen I see nothing injurious to you; for—St. Peter was a fisherman; and if you are a prince of the church, my lord, he was the supreme head of it. Pass on, if you please.'

'So much the more for my having threatened with the Bastille a certain Bounet,* a priest of Avignon, who wanted to publish a genealogy of the Casa Mazarini much too marvellous.'

'To be probable?' replied the Théatin.

---

[1] This is quite untranslatable—it being a play upon the words *pécheur*, a sinner, and *pêcheur*, a fisherman. It is in very bad taste.—TRANS.

'Oh! if I had acted up to his idea, father, that would have been the vice of pride—another sin.'

'It was excess of wit, and a person is not to be reproached with such sorts of abuses. Pass on, pass on!'

'I was all pride. Look you, father, I will endeavour to divide this into mortal sins.'

'I like divisions, when well made.'

'I am glad of that. You must know that in 1630—alas! that is thirty-one years ago*——'

'You were then twenty-nine years old, monseigneur.'

'A hot-headed age. I was then something of a soldier, and I threw myself at Casal* into the arquebusades, to show that I rode on horseback as well as any officer. It is true, I restored peace between the French and the Spaniards.* That redeems my sin a little.'

'I see no sin in being able to ride well on horseback,' said the Théatin; 'that is in perfect good taste, and does honour to our gown. As a Christian, I approve of your having prevented the effusion of blood; as a monk, I am proud of the bravery a man of the cloth has exhibited.'

Mazarin bowed his head humbly. 'Yes,' said he, 'but the consequences?'

'What consequences?'

'Eh! that damned sin of pride has roots without end. From the time that I threw myself in that manner between two armies, that I had smelt powder and faced lines of soldiers, I have held generals a little in contempt.'

'Ah!' said the father.

'There is the evil; so that I have not found one I could stand since that time.'

'The fact is,' said the Théatin, 'that the generals we have had have not been remarkable.'

'Oh!' cried Mazarin, 'there was monsieur le prince.* I have tormented him thoroughly!'

'He is not much to be pitied: he has acquired sufficient glory, and sufficient wealth.'

'That may be, for monsieur le prince; but M. Beaufort,* for example—whom I held suffering so long in the dungeon of Vincennes?'

'Ah! but he was a rebel, and the safety of the state required that you should make a sacrifice. Pass on!'

'I believe I have exhausted pride. There is another sin which I am afraid to name.'

'I will find a name for it myself. Tell it.'

'A great sin, reverend father!'

'We shall judge, monseigneur.'

'You cannot fail to have heard of certain relations* which I have had—with her majesty the queen-mother—the malevolent——'

'The malevolent, my lord, are fools. Was it not necessary, for the good of the state and the interests of the young king, that you should live in good intelligence with the queen?—Pass on, pass on!'

'I assure you,' said Mazarin, 'you remove a terrible weight from my breast.'

'These are all trifles!—look for something serious.'

'I have had much ambition, father.'

'That is the way of great minds and things, my lord.'

'Even the longing for the tiara?'

'To be pope is to be the first of Christians. Why should you not desire that?'

'It has been written that, to gain that object, I had sold Cambrai* to the Spaniards.'

'You have, perhaps, yourself written pamphlets* without severely persecuting pamphleteers.'

'Then, reverend father, I have truly a clean breast. I feel nothing remaining but minor peccadilloes.'

'What are they?'

'Gambling.'

'That is rather worldly: but you were obliged by the duties of greatness to keep a good house.'

'I like to win.'

'No player plays to lose.'

'I cheated a little.'

'You took your advantage. Pass on.'

'Well! reverend father, I feel nothing else upon my conscience. Give me absolution, and my soul will be able, when God shall please to call it, to mount without obstacle to the throne——'

The Théatin moved neither his arms nor his lips. 'What are you waiting for, father?' said Mazarin.

'I am waiting for the end.'

'The end of what?'

'Of the confession, monsieur.'

'But I have ended.'

'Oh, no; your eminence is mistaken.'

'Not that I know of.'

'Search diligently.'

'I have searched as well as possible.'

'Then I shall assist your memory.'

'Do.'

The Théatin coughed several times. 'You have said nothing of avarice, another capital sin, nor of those millions,' said he.

'What millions, father?'

'Why, those you possess, my lord.'

'Father, that money is mine, why should I speak to you about that?'

'Because, see you, our opinions differ. You say that money is yours, whilst I—I believe it is rather the property of others.'

Mazarin lifted his cold hand to his brow, which was beaded, with perspiration. 'How so?' stammered he.

'This way. Your excellency has acquired much wealth—in the service of the king.'

'Hum! much—that is, not too much.'

'Whatever it may be, whence came that wealth?'

'From the state.'

'The state; that is the king.'

'But what do you conclude from that, father?' said Mazarin, who began to tremble.

'I cannot conclude without seeing a list of the riches you possess. Let us reckon a little, if you please. You have the bishopric of Metz?'*

'Yes.'

'The abbeys of St. Clement, St. Arnould, and St. Vincent, all at Metz?'

'Yes.'

'You have the abbey of St. Denis, in France, a magnificent property?'

'Yes, father.'

'You have the abbey of Cluny, which is rich?'

'I have.'

'That of St. Médard at Soissons, with a revenue of one hundred thousand livres!'

'I cannot deny it.'

'That of St. Victor, at Marseilles—one of the best in the south?'

'Yes, father.'

'A good million a year. With the emoluments of the cardinalship and the ministry, I say too little when I say two millions a year.'

'Eh!'

'In ten years that is twenty millions—and twenty millions put out at fifty per cent give, by progression, a further twenty millions in ten years.'

'How well you reckon* for a Théatin!'

'Since your eminence placed our order in the convent we occupy, near St. Germain des Prés, in 1644,* I have kept the accounts of the society.'

'And mine likewise, apparently, father.'

'One ought to know a little of everything, my lord.'

'Very well. Conclude, at present.'

'I conclude that your baggage is too heavy to allow you to pass through the gates of Paradise.'

'Shall I be damned?'

'If you do not make restitution, yes.'

Mazarin uttered a piteous cry. 'Restitution!—but to whom, good God?'

'To the owner of that money—to the king.'

'But it was the king who gave it all to me!'

'One moment! It is not the king who signs such papers!'

Mazarin passed from sighs to groans. 'Absolution! absolution!' cried he.

'Impossible, my lord. Restitution! restitution!' replied the Théatin.

'But you absolve me from all other sins, why not from that?'

'Because,' replied the father, 'to absolve you for that motive would be a sin from which the king would never absolve me, my lord.'

Thereupon the confessor quitted his penitent with an air full of compunction. He then went out in the same manner he had entered.

'Oh, good God!' groaned the cardinal. 'Come here, Colbert, I am very, very ill indeed, my friend.'

XLVI

THE DONATION

COLBERT reappeared beneath the curtains.

'Did you hear?' said Mazarin.

'Alas! yes, my lord.'

'Can he be right? Can all this money be ill-gotten?'

'A Théatin, monseigneur, is a bad judge in matters of finance,' replied Colbert, coolly. 'And yet it is very possible that, according to his theological ideas, your eminence has been, in a certain degree, in the wrong. People generally find they have been so— when they die.'

'In the first place, they commit the wrong of dying, Colbert.'

'That is true, my lord. Against whom however, did the Théatin make out that you had committed these wrongs? Against the king?'

Mazarin shrugged his shoulders. 'As if I had not saved both his state and his finances.'

'That admits of no contradiction, my lord.'

'Does it? Then I have received a merely legitimate salary, in spite of the opinion of my confessor?'

'That is beyond doubt.'

'And I might fairly keep for my own family, which is so needy, a good fortune—the whole, even, of which I have earned?'

'I see no impediment to that, monseigneur.'

'I felt assured that in consulting you, Colbert, I should have good advice,' replied Mazarin, greatly delighted.

Colbert resumed his pedantic look. 'My lord,' interrupted he, 'I think it would be quite as well to examine whether what the Théatin said is not a *snare*.'

'Oh! no; a snare? What for? The Théatin is an honest man.'

'He believed your eminence to be at death's door, because

your eminence consulted him. Did not I hear him say—"Distinguish that which the king has given you from that which you have given yourself." Recollect, my lord, if he did not say something a little like that to you?—it was a rather theatrical speech.'

'That is possible.'

'In which case, my lord, I should consider you as required by the Théatin to——'

'To make restitution!' cried Mazarin, with great warmth.

'Eh! I do not say no.'

'What, of everything! You cannot be serious! You speak just as the confessor did.'

'To make restitution of a part*—that is to say, his majesty's part; and that, monseigneur, may have its dangers. Your eminence is too skilful a politician not to know that, at this moment, the king does not possess a hundred and fifty thousand livres clear in his coffers.'

'That is not my affair,' said Mazarin, triumphantly; 'that is the business of M. le Surintendant Fouquet, whose accounts I gave you to verify some months ago.'

Colbert bit his lips at the name of Fouquet. 'His majesty,' said he, between his teeth, 'has no money but that which M. Fouquet collects: your money, monseigneur, would afford him a delicious banquet.'

'Well, but I am not the superintendent of his majesty's finances—I have my purse—surely I would do much for his majesty's welfare—some legacy—but I cannot disappoint my family.'

'The legacy of a part would dishonour you and offend the king. Leaving a part to his majesty, is to admit that that part has inspired you with doubts as to the lawfulness of the means of its acquisition.'

'Monsieur Colbert!'

'I thought your eminence did me the honour to ask my advice?'

'Yes, but you are ignorant of the principal details of the question.'

'I am ignorant of nothing, my lord; during ten years, all the columns of figures which there are in France, have passed in review before me; and if I have painfully nailed them into my

brain, they are there now so well riveted, that, from the office of
M. Letellier, who is sober, to the little secret largesses of M.
Fouquet, who is prodigal, I could recite figure by figure, all the
money that is spent in France, from Marseilles to Cherbourg.'

'Then, you would have me throw all my money into the
coffers of the king!' cried Mazarin, ironically; from whom, at the
same time the gout forced painful moans. 'Surely the king would
reproach me with nothing, but he would laugh at me, while
squandering my millions, and with good reason.'

'Your eminence has misunderstood me. I did not, the least in
the world, pretend that his majesty ought to spend your money.'

'You said so, clearly, it seems to me, when you advised me to
give it to him.'

'Ah,' replied Colbert, 'that is because your eminence, absorbed
as you are by your disease, entirely loses sight of the character of
Louis XIV.'

'How so?'

'That character, if I may venture to express myself thus,
resembles that which my lord confessed just now to the Théatin.'

'Go on—that is?'

'Pride! Pardon me, my lord, dignity, is rather what I meant;
kings have no pride, that is a human passion.'

'Pride—yes, you are right. Next?'

'Well, my lord, if I have divined rightly, your eminence has
but to offer all your money to the king, and that immediately.'

'But why?' said Mazarin, quite bewildered.

'Because the king will not accept the whole sum.'

'What, and he a young man, and devoured by ambition?'

'Just so.'

'A young man who is anxious for my death——'

'My lord!'

'To inherit, yes, Colbert, yes; he is anxious for my death, in
order to inherit. Triple fool that I am! I would prevent him!'

'Exactly: if the donation were made in a certain form he
would refuse it.'

'Well; but how?'

'It is plain enough. A young man who has yet done nothing—
who burns to distinguish himself—who burns to reign alone,
will never take anything ready built, he will construct for himself.

This prince, monseigneur, will never be content with the Palais Royal, which M. de Richelieu left him, nor with the Palais Mazarin, which you have had so superbly constructed, nor with the Louvre, which his ancestors inhabited; nor with St. Germain, where he was born.* All that does not proceed from himself, I predict, he will disdain.'

'And you will guarantee, that if I give my forty millions to the king——'

'Saying certain things to him at the same time, I guarantee he will refuse them.'

'But those things—what are they?'

'I will write them, if my lord will have the goodness to dictate them.'

'Well, but, after all, what advantage will that be to me?'

'An enormous one. Nobody will then be able to accuse your eminence of that unjust avarice with which pamphleteers have reproached the most brilliant mind of the present age.'

'You are right, Colbert, you are right; go, and seek the king, on my part, and take him my will.'

'Your donation, my lord.'

'But, if he should accept it; if he should even think of accepting it!'

'Then there would remain thirteen millions for your family, and that is a good round sum.'

'But then *you* would be either a fool or a traitor.'

'And I am neither the one nor the other, my lord. You appear to fear that the king will accept; you have a deal more reason to fear that he will not accept.'

'But, see you, if he does not accept, I should like to guarantee the thirteen millions I have in reserve for him—yes, I will do so—yes. But my pains are returning, I shall faint. I am very, very ill, Colbert; I am very near my end!'

Colbert started. The cardinal was indeed very ill; large drops of sweat flowed down upon his bed of agony, and the frightful pallor of a face streaming with water, was a spectacle which the most hardened practitioner could not have beheld without compassion. Colbert was, without doubt, very much affected, for he left the chamber, calling Bernouin to attend the dying man, and went into the corridor. There, walking about with a meditative expression, which almost gave nobility to his vulgar head, his shoulders thrown up, his neck stretched out, his lips half-open, to give vent to unconnected fragments of incoherent thoughts, he lashed up his courage to the pitch of the undertaking contemplated, whilst within ten paces of him, separated only by a wall, his master was being stifled by pain which drew from him lamentable cries, thinking no more of the treasures of the earth, or of the joys of Paradise, but much of all the horrors of hell. Whilst burning-hot napkins, physic, counter-irritants, and Guénaud, who was recalled, were performing their functions with increased activity, Colbert, holding his great head in both his hands, to compress within it the fever of the projects engendered by the brain, was meditating the tenor of the donation he would make Mazarin write, at the first hour of respite his disease should afford him. It would appear as if all the cries of the cardinal, and all the attacks of death upon this representative of the past, were stimulants for the genius of this thinker with the bushy eyebrows,* who was turning already towards the rising sun of a regenerated society. Colbert resumed his place at Mazarin's pillow at the first interval of pain, and persuaded him to dictate a donation thus conceived.

Being about to appear before God, the Master of mankind, I beg the king, who was my master on earth, to resume the wealth which his bounty has bestowed upon me, and which my family would be happy to see pass into such illustrious hands. The particulars of my property will be found—they are drawn up—at the first requisition of his majesty, or at the last sigh of his most devoted servant,

JULES, *Cardinal de Mazarin.*

The cardinal sighed heavily as he signed this; Colbert sealed the packet, and carried it immediately to the Louvre, whither the king had returned.

He then went back to his own home, rubbing his hands with the confidence of a workman who has done a good day's work.

XLVII

THE news of the extreme illness of the cardinal had already spread, and attracted at least as much attention among the people of the Louvre as the news of the marriage of Monsieur, the king's brother, which had already been announced as an official fact. Scarcely had Louis XIV returned home, with his thoughts fully occupied with the various things he had seen and heard in the course of the evening, when an usher announced that the same crowd of courtiers who, in the morning, had thronged his *lever*, presented themselves again at his *coucher*, a remarkable piece of respect which, during the reign of the cardinal, the court, not very discreet in its preferences, had accorded to the minister, without caring about displeasing the king.

But the minister had had, as we have said, an alarming attack of gout, and the tide of flattery was mounting towards the throne. Courtiers have a marvellous instinct in scenting the turn of events; courtiers possess a supreme kind of science; they are diplomats in throwing light upon the unravelling of complicated intrigues, captains in divining the issue of battles, and physicians in curing the sick. Louis XIV, to whom his mother had taught this axiom, together with many others, understood at once that the cardinal must be very ill.

Scarcely had Anne of Austria conducted the young queen to her apartments and taken from her brow the head-dress of ceremony, when she went to see her son in his closet, where, alone, melancholy and depressed, he was indulging, as if to exercise his will, in one of those terrible inward passions—king's passions—which create events when they break out, and with Louis XIV, thanks to his astonishing command over himself, became such benign tempests, that his most violent, his only passion, that which Saint Simon* mentions with astonishment, was that famous fit of anger which he exhibited fifty years later, on the occasion of a little concealment of the Duc de Maine's and

which had for result a shower of blows inflicted with a cane
upon the back of a poor valet who had stolen a biscuit. The
young king then was, as we have seen, a prey to a double excitement; and he said to himself as he looked in a glass, 'O king!—
king in name but not in fact! a phantom, a vain phantom! an
inert statue, which has no other power than that of provoking
salutations from courtiers, when will the time come when you
shall raise your velvet arm or brandish your fist? when shall you
open your lips for any purpose but to sigh or smile, and unchain
your tongue which is condemned to the mute stupidity of the
marble statues in your palace?'

Then, passing his hand over his brow, and feeling the want of
air, he approached a window, and looking down saw below some
horsemen talking together, and groups of diffident observers.
These horsemen were a fraction of the watch: the groups were
busy portions of the people, to whom a king is always a curious
thing, the same as a rhinoceros, a crocodile, or a serpent. He
struck his brow with his open hand, crying, 'King of France!
what a title! People of France! what a heap of creatures! I have
just returned to my Louvre; my horses, just unharnessed, are
still smoking, and I have created interest enough to induce scarcely
twenty persons to look at me as I passed. Twenty! what do I say?
no; there were not twenty anxious to see the king of France.
There are not even ten archers to guard my place or residence:
archers, people, guards, all are at the Palais Royal! Why, my
God! why have not I, the king, the right to ask that of you?'

'Because,' said a voice, replying to his, and which sounded
from the other side of the door of the cabinet, 'because at the
Palais Royal lies all the gold—that is to say, all the power of him
who desires to reign.'

Louis turned sharply round. The voice which had pronounced
these words was that of Anne of Austria. The king started, and
advanced towards her. 'I hope,' said he, 'your majesty has paid
no attention to the vain declamations which the solitude and
aversion familiar to kings, suggest to the happiest dispositions?'

'I only paid attention to one thing, my son, and that was, that
you were complaining.'

'Who! I? Not at all,' said Louis XIV; 'no, in truth, you err,
madame.'

'What were you doing then?'

'I thought I was under the stern eye of my professor, and developing and amplifying an argument.'

'My son,' replied Anne of Austria, shaking her head, 'you are wrong not to trust my word; you are wrong not to grant me your confidence. A day will come and perhaps quickly when you will have occasion to remember this axiom: Gold is universal power; and they alone are kings who are all-powerful.'

'Your intention,' continued the king, 'was not, however, to cast blame upon the rich men of this age, was it?'

'No,' said the queen, warmly; 'no, sire; they who are rich in this age, under your reign, are rich because you have been willing they should be so: and I entertain against them neither malice nor envy; they have, without doubt, served your majesty sufficiently well for your majesty to have permitted them to reward themselves. That is what I mean to say by the words for which you reproach me.'

'God forbid, madame, that I should ever reproach my mother with anything!'

'Besides,' continued Anne of Austria, 'the Lord never gives the goods of this world but for a season; the Lord—as correctives to honour and riches—the Lord has placed sufferings, sickness, and death; and no one,' added she, with a melancholy smile, which proved she made the application of the sombre precept to herself, 'no man can take his wealth or greatness with him to the grave. It results therefore that the young gather the abundant harvest prepared for them by the old.'

Louis listened with increased attention to the words which Anne of Austria, no doubt, pronounced with a view to console him. 'Madame,' said he, looking earnestly at his mother, 'one would almost say in truth that you had something else to announce to me.'

'I have absolutely nothing, my son; only you cannot have failed to remark that his eminence the cardinal is very ill.'

Louis looked at his mother, expecting some emotion in her voice, some sorrow in her countenance.* The face of Anne of Austria appeared a little changed, but that was from sufferings of quite a personal character. Perhaps the alteration was caused by the cancer which had begun to consume her breast. 'Yes, madame,' said the king; 'yes, M. de Mazarin is very ill.'

'And it would be a great loss to the kingdom if God were to summon his eminence away. Is not that your opinion as well as mine, my son?' said the queen.

'Yes, madame; yes, certainly, it would be a great loss for the kingdom,' said Louis, colouring; 'but the peril does not seem to me to be so great; besides, the cardinal is still young.' The king had scarcely ceased speaking when an usher lifted the tapestry, and stood with a paper in his hand, waiting for the king to speak to him.

'What have you there?' asked the king.

'A message from M. de Mazarin,' replied the usher.

'Give it to me,' said the king; and he took the paper. But at the moment he was about to open it, there was a great noise in the gallery, the antechamber, and the court.

'Ah, ah,' said Louis XIV, who doubtless knew the meaning of that triple noise. 'How could I say there was but one king in France! I was mistaken, there are two.'

As he spoke or thought thus, the door opened, and the superintendent of finances, Fouquet, appeared before his nominal master. It was he who made the noise in the antechamber, it was his horses that made the noise in the courtyard. In addition to all this, a loud murmur was heard at his passage, which did not die away till some time after he had passed. It was this murmur which Louis XIV regretted so deeply not hearing as he passed, and dying away behind him.

'He is not precisely a king, as you fancy,' said Anne of Austria to her son; 'he is only a man who is much too rich—that is all.'

Whilst saying these words, a bitter feeling gave to these words of the queen a most hateful expression; whereas the brow of the king, calm and self-possessed, on the contrary, was without the slightest wrinkle. He nodded, therefore, familiarly to Fouquet, whilst he continued to unfold the paper given to him by the usher. Fouquet perceived this movement, and with a politeness at once easy and respectful, advanced towards the queen, so as not to disturb the king. Louis had opened the paper, and yet he did not read it. He listened to Fouquet paying the most charming compliments to the queen as he kissed her hand and arm. Anne of Austria's frown relaxed a little, she even almost smiled. Fouquet perceived that the king, instead of reading, was looking at him; he turned half round, therefore, and while continuing his conversation with the queen, faced the king.

'You know, Monsieur Fouquet,' said Louis, 'how ill M. Mazarin is?'

'Yes, sire, I know,' said Fouquet; 'in fact, he is very ill. I was at my country house at Vaux when the news reached me; and the affair seemed so pressing that I left at once.'

'You left Vaux this evening, monsieur?'

'An hour and a half ago, yes, your majesty,' said Fouquet, consulting a watch, richly ornamented with diamonds.

'An hour and a half!' said the king, still able to restrain his anger, but not to conceal his astonishment.

'I understand you, sire. Your majesty doubts my word, and you have reason to do so; but I have really come in that time though it is wonderful! I received from England three pairs of very fast horses, as I had been assured. They were placed at distances of four leagues apart, and I tried them this evening. They really brought me from Vaux to the Louvre* in an hour and a half, so your majesty sees I have not been cheated.' The queen-mother smiled with something like secret envy. But Fouquet caught her thought. 'Thus, madame,' he promptly said, 'such horses are made for kings, not for subjects; for kings ought never to yield to any one in anything.'

The king looked up.

'And yet,' interrupted Anne of Austria, 'you are not a king, that I know of, M. Fouquet.'

'Truly not, madame; therefore the horses only await the orders of his majesty to enter the royal stables; and if I allowed myself to try them, it was only for fear of offering to the king anything that was less than magnificent.'

The king became quite red.

'You know, Monsieur Fouquet,' said the queen, 'that at the court of France it is not the custom for a subject to offer anything to his king.'

Louis started.

'I hoped, madame,' said Fouquet, much agitated, 'that my love for his majesty, my incessant desire to please him, would serve to compensate the want of etiquette. It was not so much a present that I permitted myself to offer, as the tribute I paid.'

'Thank you, Monsieur Fouquet,' said the king politely, 'and I am gratified by your intention, for I love good horses; but you know I am not very rich; you, who are my superintendent of finances, know it better than any one else. I am not able then, however willing I may be, to purchase such a valuable set of horses.'

Fouquet darted a haughty glance at the queen-mother, who appeared to triumph at the false position in which the minister had placed himself, and replied:

'Luxury is the virtue of kings, sire: it is luxury which makes them resemble God; it is by luxury they are more than other men. With luxury a king nourishes his subjects, and honours them. The benign warmth of the luxury of kings nurtures the luxury of individuals, a source of riches for the people.* His majesty, by accepting the gift of these six incomparable horses, would stimulate the pride of his own breeders, of Limousin, Perche, and Normandy;* and this emulation would have been beneficial to all. But the king is silent, and consequently I stand condemned.'

During this speech, Louis was, unconsciously, folding and unfolding Mazarin's paper, upon which he had not cast his eyes. At length he glanced upon it, and uttered a faint cry at reading the first line.

'What is the matter, my son?' asked the queen, anxiously, and going toward the king.

'From the cardinal,' replied the king, continuing to read; 'yes, yes, it is really from him.'

'Is he worse then?'

'Read!' said the king, passing the parchment to his mother, as if he thought that nothing less than reading would convince Anne of Austria of a thing so astonishing as was conveyed in that paper.

Anne of Austria read in turn, and as she read, her eyes sparkled with a joy all the greater from her useless endeavour to hide it, which attracted the attention of Fouquet.

'Oh! a regularly drawn up deed of gift,' said she.

'A gift?' repeated Fouquet.

'Yes,' said the king, replying pointedly to the superintendent of finances, 'yes, at the point of death, monsieur le cardinal makes me a donation of all his wealth.'

'Forty millions,' cried the queen. 'Oh, my son! this is very noble on the part of his eminence, and will silence all malicious rumours; forty millions scraped together slowly, coming back all in one heap to the treasury! It is the act of a faithful subject and a good Christian.' And having once more cast her eyes over the act, she restored it to Louis XIV, whom the announcement of the sum greatly agitated. Fouquet had taken some steps backwards, and remained silent. The king looked at him, and held the paper out to him, in turn. The superintendent only bestowed a haughty look of a second upon it; then bowing—'Yes, sire,' said he, 'a donation, I see.'

'You must reply to it, my son,' said Anne of Austria; 'you must reply to it, and immediately.'

'But how, madame?'

'By a visit to the cardinal.'

'Why, it is but an hour since I left his eminence,' said the king.

'Write, then, sire.'

'Write!' said the young king, with evident repugnance.

'Well!' replied Anne of Austria, 'it seems to me, my son, that a man who has just made such a present, has a good right to expect to be thanked for it with some degree of promptitude.' Then turning towards Fouquet: 'Is not that likewise your opinion, monsieur?'

'That the present is worth the trouble of saying thank you for? Yes, madame,' said Fouquet, with a lofty air that did not escape the king.

'Accept, then, and thank him,' insisted Anne of Austria.

'What says M. Fouquet?' asked Louis XIV.

'Does your majesty wish to know my opinion?'

'Yes.'

'Thank him, sire——'

'Ah!' said the queen.

'But do not accept,' continued Fouquet.

'And why not?' asked the queen.

'You have yourself said why, madame,' replied Fouquet; 'because kings cannot and ought not to receive presents from their subjects.'

The king remained silent between these two contrary opinions.

'But forty millions!' said Anne of Austria, in the same tone as that in which, at a later period, poor Marie Antoinette replied, 'You will tell me as much!'*

'I know,' said Fouquet, laughing, 'forty millions makes a good round sum—such a sum as could almost tempt a royal conscience.'

'But, monsieur,' said Anne of Austria, 'instead of persuading the king not to receive this present, recall to his majesty's mind, you, whose duty it is, that these forty millions are a fortune to him.'

'It is precisely, madame, because these forty millions would be a fortune that I will say to the king, "Sire, if it be not decent for a king to accept from a subject six horses, worth twenty thousand livres, it would be disgraceful for him to owe a fortune to another subject who was not always entirely scrupulous in the choice of the materials which contributed to the building up of that fortune."'

'It ill becomes you, monsieur, to give your king a lesson,' said Anne of Austria; 'better procure for him forty millions to replace those you prevent his having.'

'The king shall have them whenever he wishes,' said the superintendent of finances, bowing.

'Yes, by oppressing the people,' said the queen.

'And were they not oppressed, madame,' replied Fouquet, 'when they were made to sweat the forty millions given by this deed? Furthermore, his majesty has asked my opinion, I have given it; if his majesty ask my assistance in this matter, it will be the same.'

'Nonsense! accept, my son, accept,' said Anne of Austria. 'You are above reports and comment.'

'Refuse, sire,' said Fouquet. 'As long as a king lives, he has no other measure but his conscience—no other judge than his own desires; but when dead, he has posterity, which applauds or accuses.'

'Thank you, mother,' replied Louis, bowing respectfully to the queen. 'Thank you, Monsieur Fouquet,' said he dismissing the superintendent civilly.

'Do you accept?' asked Anne of Austria, once more.

'I shall consider of it,' replied he, looking at Fouquet.

XLVIII

THE day that the deed of gift had been sent to the king, the cardinal gave orders that he be transported to Vincennes.* The king and the court followed him thither. The last flashes of this torch still cast splendour enough around to absorb all other lights in its rays. Besides, as it has been seen, the faithful satellite of his minister, young Louis XIV, remained within his orbit until the very last. The disease, as Guénaud had predicted, had become worse; it was no longer an attack of gout, it was an attack of death: then there was another thing which made his suffering more agonizing still—and that was the agitation brought into his mind by the donation he had sent to the king, and which, according to Colbert, the king ought to send back unaccepted to the cardinal. The cardinal had, as we have said, great faith in the predictions of his secretary; but the sum was a large one, and whatever might be the genius of Colbert, from time to time the cardinal thought to himself that the Théatin also might possibly have been mistaken, and that there was at least as much chance of his not being damned, as there was of Louis XIV sending back his millions.

Besides, the longer the donation was in coming back, the more Mazarin thought that forty millions were worth a little risk, particularly of so hypothetical a thing as the soul. Mazarin, in his character of cardinal and prime minister, was almost an atheist, a thoroughgoing materialist.* Every time the door opened, he turned sharply round, expecting to see the return of his unfortunate donation; then deceived in his hope, he fell back again with a sigh, and found his pains so much the greater for having forgotten them for an instant.

Anne of Austria had also followed the cardinal; her heart, though age had made it selfish, could not help evincing towards the dying man a sorrow which she owed him as a wife, according to some; and as a sovereign, according to others. She had, in some sort, put on a mourning countenance beforehand, and all the court wore it was she did.

Louis, in order not to show on his face what was passing in the recesses of his heart, persisted in remaining in his own apartments, where his nurse alone kept him company; the more he saw the approach of the time when all constraint would be at an end, the more humble and patient he was, falling back upon himself, as all strong men do when they form great designs, in order to gain more spring at the decisive moment. Extreme unction had been administered to the cardinal, who, faithful to his habits of dissimulation, struggled against appearances, and even against reality, receiving company in his bed, as if he only suffered from a passing malaise.

Guénaud, on his part, preserved profound secrecy; wearied with visits and questions, he answered nothing but 'his eminence is still full of youth and strength, but God wills what he wills, and when he has decided that a man is to be laid low, he will be laid low.' These words, which he scattered with a sort of discretion, reserve, and preference, were commented upon earnestly by two persons—the king and the cardinal. Mazarin, notwithstanding the prophecy of Guénaud, still clung to a hope, or rather played his part so well, that the most cunning, when saying that he deceived himself, proved that they were his dupes.

Louis, absent from the cardinal for two days; Louis, with his eyes fixed upon that same donation which so constantly preoccupied the cardinal; Louis did not exactly know how to make out Mazarin's conduct. The son of Louis XIII, following the paternal traditions, had up to that time been so little of a king that, whilst ardently desiring royalty, he desired it with that terror which always accompanies the unknown. Thus, having formed his resolution, which, besides, he communicated to nobody, he determined to have an interview with Mazarin. It was Anne of Austria, who, constant in her attendance upon the cardinal, first heard this proposition of the king's, and transmitted it to the dying man, whom it greatly agitated. For what purpose could Louis wish for an interview? Was it to return the deed, as Colbert had said he would? Was it to keep it, after thanking him, as Mazarin thought he would? Nevertheless, as the dying man felt that the uncertainty increased his torments, he did not hesitate an instant.

'His majesty will be welcome—yes, very welcome,' cried he,

making a sign to Colbert, who was seated at the foot of the bed, which the latter understood perfectly. 'Madame,' continued Mazarin, 'will your majesty be good enough to assure the king yourself of the truth of what I have just said?'

Anne of Austria rose; she herself was anxious to have the question of the forty millions settled—the question which seemed to lie heavy on the mind of every one. Anne of Austria went out; Mazarin made a great effort, and, raising himself up towards Colbert; 'Well, Colbert,' said he, 'two days have passed away—two mortal days—and, you see, nothing has been returned from yonder.'

'Patience, my lord,' said Colbert.

'Are you mad, you wretch? You advise me to have patience! Oh, in sad truth, Colbert, you mock me. I am dying, and you call out to me to wait!'

'My lord,' said Colbert, with his habitual coolness, 'it is impossible that things should not come out as I have said. His majesty is coming to see you, and no doubt, he brings back the deed himself.'

'Do you think so? Well, I, on the contrary, am sure that his majesty is coming to thank me.'

At this moment Anne of Austria returned. On her way to the apartments of her son she had found yet another quack who promised a magical cure. It was a powder* which was said to have power to save the cardinal; and she brought a portion of this powder with her. But this was not what Mazarin expected; therefore he would not even look at it, declaring that life was not worth the pains that were taken to preserve it. But, whilst professing this philosophical axiom, his long-confined secret escaped him at last.

'That, madame,' said he, 'that is not the interesting part of my situation. I made, two days ago, a little donation to the king, up to this time, from delicacy, no doubt, his majesty has not condescended to say anything about it; but the time for explanation is come, and I implore your majesty to tell me if the king has made up his mind on that matter.'

Anne of Austria was about to reply, when Mazarin stopped her.

'The truth, madame,' said he—'in the name of Heaven, the

truth! Do not flatter a dying man with a hope that may prove vain.' There he stopped, a look from Colbert telling him that he was on a wrong tack.

'I know,' said Anne of Austria, taking the cardinal's hand, 'I know that you have generously made, not a little donation, as you modestly call it, but a magnificent gift. I know how painful it would be to you if the king——'

Mazarin listened, dying as he was, as ten living men could not have listened.

'If the king——' replied he.

'If the king,' continued Anne of Austria, 'should not freely accept what you offer so nobly.'

Mazarin allowed himself to sink back upon his pillow like Pantaloon;* that is to say, with all the despair of a man who bows before the tempest; but he still preserved sufficient strength and presence of mind to cast upon Colbert one of those looks which are well worth ten sonnets, which is to say, ten long poems.*

'Should you not,' added the queen, 'have considered the refusal of the king as a sort of insult?' Mazarin rolled his head about upon his pillow, without articulating a syllable. The queen was deceived, or feigned to be deceived, by this demonstration.

'Therefore,' resumed she, 'I have circumvented him with good counsels; and as certain minds, jealous, no doubt, of the glory you are about to acquire by this generosity, have endeavoured to prove to the king that he ought not to accept this donation, I have struggled in your favour, and so well have I struggled, that you will not have, I hope, that distress to undergo.'

'Ah!' murmured Mazarin, with languishing eyes, 'ah! that is a service I shall never forget for a single minute of the few hours I still have to live.'

'I must admit,' continued the queen, 'that it was not without trouble I rendered it to your eminence.'

'Ah really! I believe it. Oh! oh!'

'Good God! what is the matter?'

'I am burning!'

'Do you suffer much?'

'As much as one of the damned.'

Colbert would have liked to sink through the floor.

'So, then,' resumed Mazarin, 'your majesty thinks that the king——' he stopped several seconds—'that the king is coming here to offer me some small thanks?'

'I think so,' said the queen. Mazarin annihilated Colbert with his last look.

At that moment the ushers announced that the king was in the antechambers, which were filled with people. This announcement produced a stir of which Colbert took advantage to escape by the door of the alcove. Anne of Austria arose, and awaited her son, standing. Louis XIV appeared at the threshold of the door, with his eyes fixed upon the dying man, who did not even think it worth while to notice that majesty from whom he thought he had nothing more to expect. An usher placed an armchair close to the bed. Louis bowed to his mother, then to the cardinal, and sat down. The queen took a seat in her turn.

Then, as the king looked behind him, the usher understood that look, and made a sign to the courtiers who filled up the doorway to go out, which they instantly did. Silence fell upon the chamber with the velvet curtains. The king, still very young, and very timid in the presence of him who had been his master from his birth, still respected him much, particularly now, in the supreme majesty of death. He did not dare, therefore, to begin the conversation, feeling that every word must have its weight not only upon things of this world, but of the next. As to the cardinal, at that moment he had but one thought—his donation. It was not physical pain which gave him that air of despondency, and that lugubrious look; it was the expectation of the thanks that were about to issue from the king's mouth, and cut off all hope of restitution, Mazarin was the first to break the silence. 'Is your majesty come to make any stay at Vincennes?' said he.

Louis made an affirmative sign with his head.

'That is a gracious favour,' continued Mazarin, 'granted to a dying man, and which will render death less painful to him.'

'I hope,' replied the king, 'I am come to visit, not a dying man, but a sick man, susceptible of cure.'

Mazarin replied by a movement of the head.

'Your majesty is very kind; but I know more than you on that subject. The last visit, sire,' said he, 'the last visit.'

'If it were so, monsieur le cardinal,' said Louis, 'I would come a last time to ask the counsels of a guide to whom I owe everything.'

Anne of Austria was a woman; she could not restrain her tears. Louis showed himself much affected, and Mazarin still more than his two guests, but from very different motives. Here the silence returned. The queen wiped her eyes, and the king resumed his firmness.

'I was saying,' continued the king, 'that I owed much to your eminence.' The eyes of the cardinal devoured the king, for he felt the great moment had come. 'And,' continued Louis, 'the principal object of my visit was to offer you very sincere thanks for the last evidence of friendship you have kindly sent me.'

The cheeks of the cardinal became sunken, his lips partially opened, and the most lamentable sigh he had ever uttered was about to issue from his chest.

'Sire,' said he, 'I shall have despoiled my poor family; I shall have ruined all who belong to me, which may be imputed to me as an error; but, at least, it shall not be said of me that I have refused to sacrifice everything to my king.'

Anne of Austria's tears flowed afresh.

'My dear Monsieur Mazarin,' said the king, in a more serious tone than might have been expected from his youth, 'you have misunderstood me, apparently.'

Mazarin raised himself upon his elbow.

'I have no purpose to despoil your dear family, nor to ruin your servants. Oh, no, that must never be!'

'Humph!' thought Mazarin, 'he is going to restore me some scraps; let us get the largest piece we can.'

'The king is going to be foolishly affected and behave generously,' thought the queen; 'he must not be allowed to impoverish himself; such an opportunity for getting a fortune will never occur again.'

'Sire,' said the cardinal, aloud, 'my family is very numerous, and my nieces will be destitute when I am gone.'

'Oh,' interrupted the queen, eagerly, 'have no uneasiness with respect to your family, dear Monsieur Mazarin; we have no friends dearer than your friends; your nieces shall be my children, the sisters of his majesty; and if a favour be distributed in France, it shall be to those you love.'

'Humbug!' thought Mazarin, who knew better than any one the trust that can be put in the promises of kings. Louis read the dying man's thought in his face.

'Be comforted, my dear Monsieur Mazarin,' said he, with a half-smile, sad beneath its irony; 'the Mesdemoiselles de Mancini will lose, in losing you, their most precious good; but they shall none the less be the richest heiresses of France; and since you have been kind enough to give me their dowry'—the cardinal was panting—'I restore it to them,' continued Louis, drawing from his breast and holding towards the cardinal's bed the parchment which contained the donation that, during two days, had kept alive such tempests in the mind of Mazarin.

'What did I tell you, my lord?' murmured in the alcove a voice which passed away like a breath.

'Your majesty returns my donation!' cried Mazarin, so disturbed by joy as to forget his character of a benefactor.

'Your majesty rejects the forty millions!' cried Anne of Austria, so stupefied as to forget her character of an afflicted wife, or queen.

'Yes, my lord cardinal; yes, madame,' replied Louis XIV, tearing the parchment which Mazarin had not yet ventured to clutch; 'yes, I destroy this deed which despoiled a whole family. The wealth acquired by his eminence in my service is his own wealth and not mine.'

'But, sire, does your majesty reflect,' said Anne of Austria, 'that you have not ten thousand crowns in your coffers?'

'Madame, I have just performed my first royal action, and I hope it will worthily inaugurate my reign.'

'Ah! sire, you are right!' cried Mazarin; 'that is truly great—that is truly generous which you have just done.' And he looked, one after the other, at the remnants of the deed spread over his bed, to assure himself that it was the original and not a copy that had been torn. At length his eyes fell upon the fragment which bore his signature, and recognizing it, he sunk back on his bolster in a swoon. Anne of Austria, without strength to conceal her regret raised her hands and eyes towards heaven.

'Oh! sire,' cried Mazarin, 'may you be blessed! My God! May

you be beloved by all my family. *Per Baccho!* if even any of those belonging to me should cause you displeasure, sire, only frown, and I will rise from my tomb!'

This mummery did not produce all the effect Mazarin had counted upon. Louis had already passed to considerations of a higher nature, and as to Anne of Austria, unable to bear, without abandoning herself to the anger she felt burning within her, the magnanimity of her son and the hypocrisy of the cardinal, she arose and left the chamber, heedless of thus betraying the extent of her grief. Mazarin saw all this, and fearing that Louis XIV might repent his decision, in order to draw attention another way he began to cry out, as, at a later period, Scapin was to cry out, in that sublime piece of pleasantry with which the morose and grumbling Boileau dared to reproach Molière.* His cries, however, by degrees, became fainter; and when Anne of Austria left the apartment, they ceased altogether.

'Monsieur le cardinal,' said the king, 'have you any recommendations to make to me?'

'Sire,' replied Mazarin, 'you are already wisdom itself, prudence personified; of your generosity I shall not venture to speak; that which you have just done exceeds all that the most generous men of antiquity or of modern times have ever done.'

The king received this praise coldly.

'So you confine yourself,' said he, 'to your thanks—and your experience, much more extensive than my wisdom, my prudence, or my generosity, does not furnish you with a single piece of friendly advice to guide my future.' Mazarin reflected for a moment. 'You have just done much for me, sire,' said he, 'that is, for my family.'

'Say no more about that,' said the king.

'Well!' continued Mazarin, 'I shall give you something in exchange for these forty millions you have refused so royally.'

Louis XIV indicated by a movement that these flatteries were displeasing to him. 'I shall give you a piece of advice,' continued Mazarin; 'yes, a piece of advice—advice more precious than the forty millions.'

'My lord cardinal!' interrupted Louis.

'Sire, listen to this advice.'

'I am listening.'

'Come nearer, sire, for I am weak!—nearer, sire, nearer!'

The king bent over the dying man. 'Sire,' said Mazarin, in so low a tone that the breath of his words arrived only like a recommendation from the tomb in the attentive ears of the king—'Sire, never have a prime minister.'

Louis drew back astonished. The advice was a confession— but a treasure, in fact, was contained in that sincere confession of Mazarin. The legacy of the cardinal to the young king was composed of six words only, but those six words, as Mazarin had said, were worth forty millions. Louis remained for an instant bewildered. As for Mazarin, he appeared only to have said something quite natural. A little scratching was heard along the curtains of the alcove. Mazarin understood: 'Yes, yes!' cried he warmly, 'yes, sire, I recommend to you a wise man, an honest man, and a clever man.'

'Tell me his name, my lord.'

'His name is yet almost unknown, sire; it is M. Colbert, my attendant. Oh! try him,' added Mazarin, in an earnest voice; 'all that he has predicted has come to pass; he is very shrewd, he is never mistaken either in things or in men—which is more surprising still. Sire, I owe you much, but I think I acquit myself of all towards you in giving you M. Colbert.'*

'So be it,' said Louis, faintly, for, as Mazarin had said, the name of Colbert was quite unknown to him, and he thought the enthusiasm of the cardinal partook of the delirium of a dying man. The cardinal sank back on his pillows.

'For the present, adieu, sire! adieu,' murmured Mazarin. 'I am tired, and I have yet a rough journey to take before I present myself to my new Master. Adieu, sire!'

The young king felt the tears rise to his eyes; he bent over the dying man, already half a corpse, and then hastily retired.

XLIX

ENTER COLBERT

THE whole night was passed in anguish shared by the dying man and the king: the dying man expected his deliverance, the king awaited his liberty. Louis did not go to bed. An hour after leaving the chamber of the cardinal, he learned that the dying man, recovering a little strength, had insisted upon being dressed, adorned and rouged, and seeing the ambassadors. Like Augustus,* he no doubt considered the world a great stage, and was desirous of playing out the last act of the comedy. Anne of Austria reappeared no more in the cardinal's apartments; she had no further business there. Propriety was the pretext for her absence. On his part, the cardinal did not ask for her: the advice the queen had given her son rankled in his heart.

Towards midnight, while still rouged, Mazarin's mortal agony came on. He had revised his will, and as this will was the exact expression of his wishes, and as he feared that some interested influence might take advantage of his weakness to make him change something in it, he had given orders to Colbert, who walked up and down the corridor which led to the cardinal's bed-chamber, like the most vigilant of sentinels. The king, shut up in his own apartment, dispatched his nurse every hour to Mazarin's chamber, with orders to bring him back an exact bulletin of the cardinal's state. After having heard that Mazarin was dressed, rouged, and had seen the ambassadors, Louis heard that the prayers for the dying were being read for the cardinal. At one o'clock in the morning, Guénaud had administered the last remedy.* This was a relic of the old customs of that fencing age, which was about to disappear to give place to another age: to believe that death could be kept off by some good secret thrust. Mazarin, after having taken the remedy, respired freely for nearly ten minutes. He immediately gave orders that the news should be spread everywhere of a sudden improvement. The king, on learning this, felt as if a cold sweat were passing over his brow; he had had a glimpse of the light of liberty; slavery appeared to him more dark and less acceptable than ever.

But the bulletin which followed entirely changed the face of things. Mazarin could no longer breathe at all, and could scarcely follow the prayers which the curé of Saint-Nicholas-des-Champs* recited at his side. The king resumed his agitated walk about his chamber, and consulted, as he walked, several papers drawn from a casket of which he alone had the key. A third time the nurse returned. M. de Mazarin had just uttered a joke, and had ordered his 'Flora', by Titian,* to be revarnished. At length, towards two o'clock in the morning, the king could not longer resist his weariness: he had not slept for twenty-four hours. Sleep, so powerful at his age, overcame him for about an hour. But he did not go to bed for that hour; he slept in an armchair About four o'clock his nurse awoke him by entering the room.*

'Well?' asked the king.

'Well, my dear sire,' said the nurse, clasping her hands with an air of commiseration. 'Well; he is dead!'

The king arose at a bound, as if a steel spring had been applied to his legs. 'Dead!' cried he.

'Alas! yes.'

'Is it quite certain?'

'Yes.'

'Is it official?'

'Yes.'

'Has the news been made public?'

'Not yet.'

'Who told you, then, that the cardinal was dead?'

'M. Colbert.'

'M. Colbert?'

'Yes.'

'And was he sure of what he said?'

'He came out of the chamber, and had held a glass for some minutes before the cardinal's lips.'

'Ah!' said the king. 'And what is become of M. Colbert?'

'He has just left his eminence's chamber.'

'Where is he?'

'He followed me.'

'So that he is——'

'Sire, waiting at your door, till it shall be your good pleasure to receive him.'

Louis ran to the door, opened it himself, and perceived Colbert
standing waiting in the passage. The king started at sight of this
statue, all clothed in black. Colbert, bowing with profound respect, advanced two steps towards his majesty. Louis re-entered
his chamber, making Colbert a sign to follow. Colbert entered;
Louis dismissed the nurse, who closed the door as she went out.
Colbert remained modestly standing near that door.

'What do you come to announce to me, monsieur?' said Louis,
very much troubled at being thus surprised in his private
thoughts, which he could not completely conceal.

'That monsieur le cardinal has just expired, sire; and that I
bring your majesty his last adieu.'

The king remained pensive for a minute; and during that
minute he looked attentively at Colbert; it was evident that the
cardinal's last words were in his mind. 'Are you, then, M.
Colbert?' asked he.

'Yes, sire.'

'His faithful servant, as his eminence himself told me?'

'Yes, sire.'

'The depositary of many of his secrets?'

'Of all of them.'

'The friends and servants of his eminence will be dear to me,
monsieur, and I shall take care that you are well placed in my
employment.'

Colbert bowed.

'You are a financier, monsieur, I believe?'

'Yes, sire.'

'And did monsieur le cardinal employ you in his stewardship?'

'I had that honour, sire.'

'You never did anything personally for my household, I
believe?'

'Pardon me, sire, it was I who had the honour of giving
monsieur le cardinal the idea of an economy which puts three
hundred thousand livres a year into your majesty's coffers.'

'What economy was that, monsieur?' asked Louis XIV.

'Your majesty knows that the hundred Swiss* have silver lace
on each side of their ribbons?'

'Doubtless.'

'Well, sir, it was I who proposed that imitation silver lace should be placed upon these ribbons; it could not be detected, and a hundred thousand crowns feeds a regiment during six months; and is the price of ten thousand good muskets or the value of a vessel of ten guns, ready for sea.'

'That is true,' said Louis XIV, considering more attentively, 'and, zounds! that was a well placed economy; besides it was ridiculous for soldiers to wear the same lace as noblemen.'

'I am happy to be approved of by your majesty.'

'Is that the only appointment you held about the cardinal?' asked the king.

'It was I who was appointed to examine the accounts of the superintendent, sire.'

'Ah!' said Louis, who was about to dismiss Colbert, but whom that word stopped; 'ah! it was you whom his eminence had charged to monitor M. Fouquet, was it? And the result of the examination?'

'Is that there is a deficit, sire; but if your majesty will permit me——'

'Speak, M. Colbert.'

'I ought to give your majesty some explanations.'

'Not at all, monsieur, it is you who have checked these accounts; give me the result.'

'That is very easily done, sire: emptiness everywhere, money nowhere.'

'Beware, monsieur; you are roughly attacking the administration of M. Fouquet, who, nevertheless, I have heard say, is an able man.'

Colbert coloured, and then became pale, for he felt that from that minute he entered upon a struggle with a man whose power almost equalled the sway of him who had just died. 'Yes, sire, a very able man,' repeated Colbert, bowing.

'But if M. Fouquet is an able man, and, in spite of that ability, if money be wanting, whose fault is it?'

'I do not accuse, sire, I say what is.'

'That is well; make out your accounts, and present them to me. There is a deficit, you say? A deficit may be temporary; credit returns and funds are restored.'

'No, sire.'

'Upon this year, perhaps, I understand that; but upon next year?'

'Next year is eaten as bare as the current year.'

'But the year after, then?'

'Will be just like next year.'

'What do you tell me, Monsieur Colbert?'

'I say there are four years mortgaged in advance.'

'We must have a loan, then.'

'We must have three, sire.'

'I will create offices and sell them, and the salary of the posts shall be paid into the treasury.'

'Impossible, sire, for already a great many offices have been created, and patents sold which leave the duties unspecified, so that the purchasers enjoy the benefits without discharging any obligations. That is why these patents cannot be cancelled. Moreover, M. Fouquet allowed a third off for cash purchase, so that the state has been robbed without any gain to your majesty.'

The king started. 'Explain me that, M. Colbert,' he said.

'Make your meaning clear, your majesty, and tell me what you wish me to explain.'

'You are right, clarity is what you wish, is it not?'

'Yes, sire, clarity. God is God above all things, because He made light.'

'Well, for example,' resumed Louis XIV, 'if to-day, the cardinal being dead, and I being king, suppose I needed money?'

'Your majesty would not have any.'

'Oh! that is strange, monsieur! How! my superintendent would not find me any money?'

Colbert shook his large head.

'How is that?' said the king; 'is the income of the state so much mortgaged that there is no longer any revenue?'

'Yes, sire.'

The king frowned and said, 'If it be so, I will draw up orders-in-council to obtain a discharge from the holders, a liquidation at a cheap rate.'

'Impossible, for the orders-in-council have been converted into bills, which bills, for the convenience of return and facility of transaction, are divided into so many parts that the originals can no longer be recognized.'

Louis, very much agitated, walked about, still frowning. 'But, if this is as you say, Monsieur Colbert,' said he, stopping all at once, 'I shall be ruined before I begin to reign.'

'You are in fact, sire,' said the impassive adder-up of figures.

'Yet, monsieur, the money is somewhere?'

'Yes, sire, and even as a beginning, I bring your majesty a note of funds which M. le Cardinal Mazarin was not willing to set down in his testament, neither in any act whatever, but which he confided to me.'

'To you?'

'Yes, sire, with an injunction to remit it to your majesty.'

'What! besides the forty millions of the testament?'

'Yes, sire.'

'M. de Mazarin had still other funds?'

Colbert bowed.

'Why, that man was a bottomless pit!' murmured the king. 'M. de Mazarin on one side, M. Fouquet on the other—more than a hundred millions perhaps between them! No wonder my coffers should be empty!' Colbert waited without stirring.

'And is the sum you bring me worth the trouble?' asked the king.

'Yes sire, it is a round sum.'

'Amounting to how much?'

'To thirteen millions* of livres, sire.'

'Thirteen millions!' cried Louis, trembling with joy; 'do you say thirteen millions, Monsieur Colbert?'

'I said thirteen millions, yes, your majesty.'

'Of which everybody is ignorant?'

'Of which everybody is ignorant.'

'Which are in your hands?'

'In my hands, yes, sire.'

'And which I can have?'

'Within two hours, sire.'

'But where are they, then?'

'In the cellar of a house which the cardinal owned in the city, and which he was so kind as to leave me by a particular clause of his will.'

'You are acquainted with the cardinal's will, then?'

'I have a duplicate of it, signed by his hand.'

'A duplicate?'

'Yes, sire, and here it is.' Colbert drew the deed quietly from his pocket, and showed it to the king. The king read the article relative to the donation of the house.

'But,' said he, 'there is no question here but of the house, there is nothing said of the money.'

'Your pardon, sire, it is in my conscience.'

'And Monsieur Mazarin has entrusted it to you?'

'Why not, sire?'

'He! a man mistrustful of everybody?'

'He was not so of me, sire, as your majesty may perceive.'

Louis fixed his eyes with admiration upon that vulgar but expressive face. 'You are an honest man, M. Colbert,' said the king.

'That is not a virtue, it is a duty,' replied Colbert, coolly.

'But,' added Louis, 'does not the money belong to the family?'

'If this money belonged to the family it would be disposed of in the testament, as the rest of his fortune is. If this money belonged to the family, I, who drew up the deed of donation in favour of your majesty, should have added the sum of thirteen millions to that of forty millions which was offered to you.'

'How!' exclaimed Louis XIV, 'was it you who drew up the deed of donation?'

'Yes, sire.'

'And yet the cardinal trusted you?' added the king ingenuously.

'I had assured his eminence you would by no means accept the gift,' said Colbert in that same quiet manner we have described, and which, even in the common habits of life, had something solemn in it.

Louis passed his hand over his brow: 'Oh! how young I am,' murmured he, 'to have the command of men.'

Colbert waited until the king had done musing. He saw Louis raise his head. 'At what hour shall I send the money to your majesty?' asked he.

'To-night, at eleven o'clock; I desire that no one may know that I possess this money.'

Colbert made no more reply than if the thing had not been said to him.

'Is the amount in ingots, or coined gold?'

'In coined gold, sire.'

'That is well.'

'Where shall I send it?'

'To the Louvre. Thank you, M. Colbert.'

Colbert bowed and retired. 'Thirteen millions!' exclaimed Louis, as soon as he was alone. 'This must be a dream!' Then he allowed his head to sink between his hands, as if he were really asleep. But, at the end of a moment, he arose, and opening the window violently, he bathed his burning brow in the keen morning air, which brought to his senses the scent of the trees, and the perfume of flowers. A splendid dawn was gilding the horizon, and the first rays of the sun bathed in flame the young king's brow. 'This is the dawn of my reign,' murmured Louis XIV. 'It is a presage sent by the Almighty.'

L

THE FIRST DAY OF THE ROYALTY OF LOUIS XIV

IN the morning, the news of the death of the cardinal was spread through the castle, and thence speedily reached the city. The ministers Fouquet, Lyonne, and Letellier* entered the council chamber to assess the situation. The king sent for them immediately. 'Messieurs,' said he, 'as long as Monsieur le Cardinal lived, I allowed him to govern my affairs; but now, I mean to govern them myself. You will give me your advice when I ask it. You may go.'*

The ministers looked at each other with surprise. If they concealed a smile, it was with a great effort, for they knew that the prince, brought up in absolute ignorance of business, by this, took upon himself a burden much too heavy for his strength. Fouquet took leave of his colleagues upon the stairs, saying: 'Messieurs! there will be so much the less labour for us.'

And he climbed gaily into his carriage. The others, a little uneasy at the turn things had taken, went back to Paris together. Towards ten o'clock, the king repaired to the apartment of his mother, with whom he had a long and private conversation. After dinner, he got into his carriage, and went straight to the Louvre. There he received much company, and took a degree of pleasure in remarking the hesitation of each, and the curiosity of all. Towards evening, he ordered the doors of the Louvre to be closed, with the exception of one only, which opened on the quay. He placed on duty at this point two hundred Swiss, who did not speak a word of French, with orders to admit all who carried packages, but no others; and on no account to allow any one to go out. At eleven o'clock precisely, he heard the rolling of a heavy carriage under the arch, then of another, then of a third; after which the gate grated upon its hinges to be closed. Soon after, somebody scratched with his nail at the door of the cabinet. The king opened it himself, and beheld Colbert, whose first word was this: 'The money is in your majesty's cellar.'

The king then descended and went himself to see the barrels of coin, in gold and silver, which, under the direction of Colbert, four men had just rolled into a cellar of which the king had given Colbert the key in the morning. This review completed, Louis returned to his apartments, followed by Colbert, who had not apparently warmed with one ray of personal satisfaction.

'Monsieur,' said the king, 'what do you wish that I should give you, as a recompense for this devotedness and probity?'

'Absolutely nothing, sire.'

'How! nothing? Not even an opportunity of serving me?'

'If your majesty were not to furnish me with that opportunity, I should not the less serve you. It is impossible for me not to be the best servant of the king.'

'You shall be my intendant of finances, M. Colbert.'

'But there is already a superintendent, sire.'

'I know that.'

'Sire, the superintendent of the finances is the most powerful man in the kingdom.'

'Ah!' cried Louis, colouring, 'do you think so?'

'He will crush me in a week, sire. Your majesty gives me a role for which strength is indispensable. An intendant under a superintendent—that is inferiority.'

'You want support—you do not reckon upon me?'

'I had the honour of telling your majesty, that during the lifetime of M. de Mazarin, M. Fouquet was the second man in the kingdom; now M. de Mazarin is dead, M. Fouquet is become the first.'

'Monsieur, I agree to what you told me of all things up to to-day; but to-morrow, please to remember, I shall no longer suffer it.'

'Then I shall be of no use to your majesty?'

'You are already of no use, since you fear to compromise yourself in serving me.'

'I only fear to be placed so that I cannot serve your majesty.'

'What do you wish then?'

'I wish your majesty to allow me assistance in the labours of the office of intendant.'

'The post would lose its value.'

'It would gain in security.'

'Choose your colleagues.'

'Messrs. Breteuil, Marin, Hervart.'*

'To-morrow the decree shall appear.'

'Sire, I thank you.'

'Is that all you ask?'

'No, sire, one thing more.'

'What is that?'

'Allow me to compose a court of justice.'

'What would this court of justice do?'

'Try the farmers-general* and contractors, who, during ten years, have been robbing the state.'

'Well, but what would you do with them?'

'Hang two or three, and that would make the rest repay.'

'I cannot commence my reign with executions, Monsieur Colbert.'

'Oh the contrary, sire, you had better, in order not to have to end with them.'

The king made no reply. 'Does your majesty consent?' said Colbert.

'I will reflect upon it, monsieur.'

'It will be too late, when reflection has been made.'

'Why?'

'Because you have to deal with people stronger than ourselves, if they are forewarned.'

'Compose your court, monsieur.'

'I will, sire.'

'Is that all?'

'No, sire; there is still another important affair. What rights does your majesty attach to this office of intendant?'

'Well—I do not know—the customary ones.'

'Sire, I desire that this office be invested with the right of reading the correspondence with England.'

'Impossible, monsieur, for that correspondence is kept from the council; Monsieur le Cardinal himself carried it on.'

'I thought your majesty had this morning declared that there should no longer be a council?'

'Yes, I said so.'

'Let your majesty then have the goodness to read all the letters yourself, particularly those from England; I hold strongly to this article.'

'Monsieur, you shall have that correspondence, and render me an account of it.'

'Now, sire, what shall I do with respect to the finance?'

'Everything M. Fouquet will not do.'

'That is all I ask of your majesty. Thanks, sire, I depart in peace;' and at these words he took his leave. Louis watched his departure. Colbert was not yet a hundred paces from the Louvre, when the king received a courier from England. After having looked at and examined the enveloped, the king broke the seal precipitately, and found a letter from Charles II. The following is what the English prince wrote to his royal brother:

'Your majesty must be rendered very uneasy by the illness of M. le Cardinal Mazarin; but the excess of danger can only prove of service to you. The cardinal is despaired of by his physician. I thank you for the gracious reply you have made to my communication touching the Princess Henrietta, my sister, and, in a week, the princess and her court will set out for Paris.* It is gratifying to me to acknowledge the fraternal friendship you have evinced towards me, and to call you, more justly than ever, my brother. It is gratifying to me, above everything, to prove to your majesty how much I am interested in all that may please you. You are having Belle-Isle-en-Mer* secretly fortified. That is wrong. We shall never be at war with each other. That measure does not make me uneasy, it makes me sad. You are spending useless millions; tell your ministers so; and rest assured that

I am well informed; render me the same service, my brother, if occasion offers.'

The king rang his bell violently, and his *valet de chambre* appeared. 'Monsieur Colbert is just gone; he cannot be far off. Let him be called back!' exclaimed he.

The valet was about to execute the order, when the king stopped him.

'No,' said he, 'no; I see the whole scheme of that man. Belle-Isle belongs to M. Fouquet; Belle-Isle is being fortified, that is a conspiracy on the part of M. Fouquet. The discovery of that conspiracy is the ruin of the superintendent, and that discovery is the result of the correspondence with England: this is why Colbert wished to have that correspondence. Oh! but I cannot place all my dependence upon that man; he has a good head, but I must have an arm!' Louis, all at once, uttered a joyful cry. 'I had,' said he, 'a lieutenant of musketeers!'

'Yes, sire—Monsieur d'Artagnan.'

'He quitted the service for a time.'

'Yes, sire.'

'Let him be found, and be here, to-morrow the first thing in the morning.'

The *valet de chambre* bowed and went out.

'Thirteen millions in my cellar,' said the king; 'Colbert carrying my purse and D'Artagnan my sword—*I am king.*'

LI

A PASSION

THE day of his arrival, on returning from the Palais Royal, Athos, as we have seen, went straight to his hotel in the Rue Saint-Honoré. He there found the Vicomte de Bragelonne waiting for him in his chamber, chatting with Grimaud. It was not an easy thing to talk with this old servant. Two men only possessed the secret, Athos and D'Artagnan. The first succeeded, because Grimaud sought to make him speak himself; D'Artagnan on the contrary, because he knew how to make Grimaud talk. Raoul was occupied in making him describe the voyage to

England, and Grimaud had related it in all its details, with a limited number of gestures and eight words, neither more nor less. He had, at first, indicated by an undulating movement of his hand, that his master and he had crossed the sea. 'Upon some expedition?' Raoul had asked.

Grimaud by bending down his head, had answered, 'Yes.'

'When monsieur le comte incurred much danger?' asked Raoul.

'Neither too much, nor too little,' was replied by a shrug of the shoulders.

'But, still, what sort of danger?' insisted Raoul

Grimaud pointed to the sword; he pointed to the fire and to a musket that was hanging on the wall.

'Monsieur le comte had an enemy there, then?' cried Raoul.

'Monk,' replied Grimaud.

'It is strange,' continued Raoul, 'that monsieur le comte persists in considering me a novice, and not allowing me to partake the honour and danger of his adventures.'

Grimaud smiled. It was at this moment Athos came in. The host was lighting him up the stairs, and Grimaud, recognizing the step of his master, hastened to meet him, which cut short the conversation. But Raoul was launched on the sea of questions, and did not stop. Taking both hands of the comte, with warm, but respectful tenderness—'How is it, monsieur,' said he, 'that you set out upon a dangerous voyage, without bidding me adieu, without commanding the aid of my sword, of myself, who ought to be your support, now I have the strength; whom you have brought up like a man? Ah! monsieur, can you expose me to the cruel trial of never seeing you again?'

'Who told you, Raoul,' said the comte, placing his cloak and hat in the hands of Grimaud, who had unbuckled his sword, 'who told you that my voyage was a dangerous one?'

'I,' said Grimaud.

'And why did you do so?' said Athos, sternly.

Grimaud was embarrassed; Raoul came to his assistance, by answering for him. 'It is natural, monsieur, that our good Grimaud should tell me the truth in what concerns you. By whom should you be loved and supported, if not by me?'

Athos did not reply. He made a friendly motion to Grimaud,

which sent him out of the room; he then seated himself in an
armchair, whilst Raoul remained standing before him.

'But it is true,' continued Raoul, 'that your voyage was an
expedition, and that steel and fire threatened you?'

'Say no more about that, vicomte,' said Athos, mildly. 'I set
out hastily, it is true: but the service of King Charles II required
a prompt departure. As to your anxiety, I thank you for it, and
I know that I can depend upon you. You have not wanted for
anything, vicomte, in my absence, have you?'

'No, monsieur, thank you.'

'I left orders with Blaisois to pay you a hundred pistoles, if
you should stand in need of money.'

'Monsieur, I have not seen Blaisois.'

'You have been without money, then?'

'Monsieur, I had thirty pistoles left from the sale of the horses
I took in my last campaign, and M. le Prince had the kindness
to allow me to win two hundred pistoles at his play-table three
months ago.'

'Do you play? I don't like that, Raoul.'

'I never play, monsieur; it was M. le Prince who ordered me
to hold his cards at Chantilly—one night when a courier came
to him from the king. I won, and M. le Prince commanded me
to take the stakes.'

'Is that a practice in the household, Raoul?' asked Athos with
a frown.

'Yes, monsieur; every week, M. le Prince affords, upon one
occasion or another, a similar advantage to one of his gentlemen.
There are fifty gentlemen in his highness's household; it was my
turn.'

'Very well! You went into Spain,* then?'

'Yes, monsieur, I made a very delightful and interesting
journey.'

'You have been back a month, have you not?'

'Yes, monsieur.'

'And in the course of that month?'

'In that month——'

'What have you done?'

'My duty, monsieur.'

'Have you not been home, to La Fère?'

Raoul coloured. Athos looked at him with a fixed but tranquil expression.

'You would be wrong not to believe me,' said Raoul. 'I feel that I blushed, but it was in spite of myself. The question you did me the honour to ask me is of a nature to raise in me much emotion. I blushed, then, because I am agitated, not because I meditate a falsehood.'

'I know, Raoul, you never lie.'

'No, monsieur.'

'Besides, my young friend, you would be wrong; what I wanted to say——'

'I know quite well, monsieur. You would ask me if I have not been to Blois?'

'Exactly so.'

'I have not been there; I have not even seen the person to whom you allude.'

Raoul's voice trembled as he pronounced these words. Athos, a sovereign judge in all matters of delicacy, immediately added, 'Raoul, you answer with a painful feeling; you are unhappy.'

'Very, monsieur; you have forbidden me to go to Blois, or to see Mademoiselle de la Vallière again.' Here the young man stopped. That dear name, so delightful to pronounce, made his heart bleed, although so sweet upon his lips.

'And I have acted rightly, Raoul,' Athos hastened to reply. 'I am neither an unjust nor a barbarous father; I respect true love; but I look forward for you to a future—an immense future. A new reign is about to break upon us like a fresh dawn. War calls upon a young king full of chivalric spirit. What is wanting to assist this heroic ardour is a battalion of young and free lieutenants who would rush to the fight with enthusiasm, and fall, crying: "*Vive le Roi!*" instead of "Adieu, my dear wife." You understand that, Raoul. However brutal my reasoning may appear, I conjure you, then, to believe me, and to turn away your thoughts from those early days of youth in which you took up this habit of love—days of effeminate carelessness, which soften the heart and render it incapable of swallowing those strong, bitter draughts called glory and adversity. Therefore, Raoul, I repeat to you, you should see in my counsel only the desire of being useful to you, only the ambition of seeing you prosper. I believe you capable of becoming a remarkable man. March alone, and you will march better, and more quickly.'

'You have commanded, monsieur,' replied Raoul, 'and I obey.'

'Commanded!' cried Athos. 'Is it thus you reply to me? I have commanded you! Oh! you distort my words as you misconceive my intentions. I do not command you; I request you.'

'No, monsieur, you have commanded,' said Raoul, insistently; 'had you only requested me, your request is even more effective than your order. I have not seen Mademoiselle de la Vallière again.'

'But you are unhappy! you are unhappy!' insisted Athos.

Raoul made no reply.

'I find you pale; I find you low in spirit. The sentiment is strong, then?'

'It is a passion,' replied Raoul.

'No—a habit.'

'Monsieur, you know I have travelled much, that I have passed two years* far away from her. A habit would yield to an absence of two years, I believe; whereas, on my return, I loved, not more, that was impossible, but as much. Mademoiselle de la Vallière is for me the one lady above all others; but you are for me a god upon earth—to you I sacrifice everything.'

'You are wrong,' said Athos; 'I have no longer any right over you. Age has emancipated you; you no longer even stand in need of my consent. Besides, I will not refuse my consent after what you have told me. Marry Mademoiselle de la Vallière, if you like.'

Raoul was startled, but suddenly: 'You are very kind, monsieur,' said he; 'and your concession excites my warmest gratitude, but I will not accept it.'

'Then you now refuse?'

'Yes, monsieur.'

'I will not oppose you in anything, Raoul.'

'But you have at the bottom of your heart an idea against this marriage: it is not your choice.'

'That is true.'

'That is sufficient to make me resist: I will wait.'

'Beware, Raoul! What you are now saying is serious.'

'I know it is, monsieur; as I said, I will wait.'

'Until I die?' said Athos, much agitated.

'Oh! monsieur,' cried Raoul, with tears in his eyes, 'is it possible that you should wound my heart thus? I have never given you cause of complaint!'

'Dear boy, that is true,' murmured Athos, pressing his lips violently together to conceal the emotion of which he was no longer master. 'No, I will no longer afflict you; only I do not comprehend what you mean by waiting. Will you wait till you love no longer?'

'Ah! for that!—no, monsieur. I will wait till you change your opinion.'

'I should wish to put the matter to a test, Raoul; I should like to see if Mademoiselle de la Vallière will wait as you do.'

'I hope so, monsieur.'

'But, take care, Raoul! suppose she did not wait? Ah, you are so young, so confiding, so loyal! Women are changeable.'

'You have never spoken ill to me of women,* monsieur; you have never had to complain of them; why should you doubt of Mademoiselle de la Vallière?'

'That is true,' said Athos, casting down his eyes; 'I have never spoken ill to you of women; I have never had to complain of them; Mademoiselle de la Vallière never gave birth to a suspicion; but when we are looking forward, we must go even to exceptions, even to improbabilities! *If*, I say, Mademoiselle de la Vallière should not wait for you?'

'How, monsieur?'

'If she turned her eyes another way.'

'If she looked favourably upon another, do you mean, monsieur?' said Raoul, pale with agony.

'Exactly.'

'Well, monsieur, I would kill him,' said Raoul, simply, 'and all the men whom Mademoiselle de la Vallière should choose, until one of them had killed me, or Mademoiselle de la Vallière had restored me her heart.'

Athos started. 'I thought,' resumed he, in an agitated voice, 'that you called me just now your god, your law in this world.'

'Oh!' said Raoul, trembling, 'you would forbid me the duel?'

'Suppose I *did* forbid it, Raoul?'

'You would forbid me to hope, monsieur; consequently you would not forbid me to die.'

Athos raised his eyes toward the vicomte. He had pronounced these words with the most melancholy inflection, accompanied by the most melancholy look. 'Enough,' said Athos, after a long silence, 'enough of this subject, upon which we both go too far. Live as well as you are able, Raoul, perform your duties, love Mademoiselle de la Vallière; in a word, act like a man, since you have attained the age of a man; only do not forget that I love you tenderly, and that you profess to love me.'

'Ah! monsieur le comte!' cried Raoul, pressing the hand of Athos to his heart.

'Enough, dear boy, leave me; I want rest. By the way, M. d'Artagnan has returned from England with me; you owe him a visit.'

'I will pay it, monsieur, with great pleasure. I love Monsieur d'Artagnan exceedingly.'

'You are right in doing so; he is a worthy man and a brave cavalier.'

'Who loves you dearly.'

'I am sure of that. Do you know his address?'

'At the Louvre, I suppose, or wherever the king is. Does he not command the musketeers?'

'No; at present M. d'Artagnan is absent on leave; he is resting for a while. Do not, therefore, seek him at the posts of his service. You will hear of him at the house of a certain Planchet.'

'His former lackey?'

'Exactly; turned grocer.'

'I know; Rue des Lombards?'

'Somewhere thereabouts, or Rue des Arcis.'*

'I will find it, monsieur—I will find it.'

'You will say a thousand kind things to him, on my part, and ask him to come and dine with me, before I set out for La Fère.'

'Yes, monsieur.'

'Good-night, Raoul!'

'Monsieur, I see you wear an order I never saw you wear before; accept my compliments.'

'The Fleece!—that is true. A bauble, my boy, which no longer amuses an old booby like myself. Good-night, Raoul!'

LII

D'ARTAGNAN'S LESSON

RAOUL did not meet with D'Artagnan the next day, as he had hoped. He only met with Planchet, whose joy was great at seeing the young man again, and who contrived to pay him two or three little soldierly compliments, savouring very little of the grocer's shop. But as Raoul was returning the next day from Vincennes, at the head of fifty dragoons confided to him by monsieur le prince, he perceived, in la Place Baudoyer,* a man with his nose in the air, examining a house as we examine a horse we have a fancy to buy. This man, dressed in citizen costume buttoned up like a military doublet, a very small hat* on his head, but a long shagreen-mounted sword by his side, turned his head as soon as he heard the steps of the horses, and left off looking at the house to look at the dragoons. It was simply M. d'Artagnan; D'Artagnan on foot; D'Artagnan with his hands behind him, casting an eye upon the dragoons, after having reviewed the buildings. Not a man, not a tag, not a horse's hoof escaped his inspection. Raoul rode at the side of his troop; D'Artagnan perceived him the last. 'Eh!' said he, 'Eh! *mordioux!*'

'I was not mistaken!' cried Raoul, turning his horse towards him.

'Mistaken—no! Good day to you,' replied the ex-musketeer; whilst Raoul eagerly pressed the hand of his old friend. 'Take care, Raoul,' said D'Artagnan, 'the second horse of the fifth rank will cast a shoe before he gets to the Pont Marie;* he has only two nails left in his off fore-foot.'

'Wait a minute, I will come back,' said Raoul.

'Can you leave your detachment?'

'The cornet* is there to take my place.'

'Then you will come and dine with me?'

'Most willingly, Monsieur d'Artagnan.'

'Be quick, then; leave your horse, or make them give me one.'

'I prefer coming back on foot with you.'

Raoul hastened to give notice to the cornet, who took his post;

he then dismounted, gave his horse to one of the dragoons, and with great delight seized the arm of M. d'Artagnan, who had watched him during all these little operations with the satisfaction of a connoisseur.

'What, do you come from Vincennes?' said he.

'Yes, monsieur le chevalier.'

'And the cardinal?'

'Is very ill; it is even reported he is dead.'

'Are you on good terms with M. Fouquet?' asked D'Artagnan, with a disdainful shrug of the shoulders, proving that the death of Mazarin did not affect him beyond measure.

'With M. Fouquet?' said Raoul; 'I do not know him.'

'So much the worse for you! for a new king always seeks to get good men in his employment.'

'Oh! the king means no harm,' replied the young man.

'I say nothing about the crown,' cried D'Artagnan; 'I am speaking of the king—the king, that is M. Fouquet, if the cardinal is dead. You must contrive to stand well with M. Fouquet, if you do not wish to moulder away all your life as I have mouldered. It is true you have, fortunately, other protectors.'

'M. le Prince, for instance.'

'Worn out! worn out!'

'M. le Comte de la Fère?'

'Athos! Oh! that's different; yes, Athos—and if you have any wish to make your way in England, you cannot apply to a better person. I can even say, without too much vanity, that I myself have some credit at the court of Charles II. Now there is a king—God speed him!'

'Ah!' cried Raoul, with the natural curiosity of well-born young people, while listening to experience and courage.

'Yes, a king who amuses himself, it is true, but who has had a sword in his hand, and can appreciate useful men. Athos is on good terms with Charles II. Take service there, and leave these scoundrels of contractors and farmers-general, who steal as well with French hands as others have done with Italian hands; leave the little snivelling king, who is going to give us another reign of Francis II.* Do you know anything of history, Raoul?'

'Yes, monsieur le chevalier.'

'Do you know, then, that Francis II always had ear-ache?'

'No, I did not know that.'

'That Charles IV always had head-aches?'

'Indeed!'

'And Henry III always had stomach-ache?'

Raoul began to laugh.

'Well, my dear friend, Louis XIV always has heart-ache; it is deplorable to see a king sighing from morning till night without saying once in course of the day, by God's guts, or a pox on it, or anything to make a man prick up his ears.'

'Was that the reason why you quitted the service, monsieur le chevalier?'

'Yes.'

'But you yourself, M. d'Artagnan, are throwing the handle after the axe; you will not make a fortune.'

'Who? I?' replied D'Artagnan, in a casual tone; 'I am settled—I had some family property.'

Raoul looked at him. The poverty of D'Artagnan was proverbial. A Gascon, he exceeded in ill-luck all the gasconnades of France and Navarre; Raoul had a hundred times heard Job and D'Artagnan linked together, like the twins Romulus and Remus. D'Artagnan caught Raoul's look of astonishment.

'And has not your father told you I have been in England?'

'Yes, monsieur le chevalier.'

'And that I there met with very good fortune?'

'No, monsieur, I did not know that.'

'Yes, a very worthy friend of mine, a great nobleman, the viceroy of Scotland and Ireland,* has endowed me with an inheritance.'

'An inheritance'

'And a good one, too.'

'Then you are rich?'

'Bah!'

'Receive my sincere congratulation.'

'Thank you! Look, that is my house.'

'Place de Grève?'

'Yes; don't you like this quarter?'

'On the contrary, the look-out over the water is pleasant. Oh! what a pretty old house!'

'The Face of Our Lady; it is an old tavern, which I have transformed into a private house in two days.'

'But the tavern is still open?'

'Naturally!'

'And where do you lodge, then?'

'I? I lodge with Planchet.'

'You said, just now, "This is my house."'

'I said so, because, in fact, it is my house. I have bought it.'

'Ah!' said Raoul.

'It brings me ten per cent interest a year, my dear Raoul; I bought the house for thirty thousand livres; it has a garden which opens to the Rue de la Mortellerie;* the tavern lets for a thousand livres, with the first storey; the garret or second floor, for five hundred livres.'

'Indeed!'

'Yes, indeed.'

'Five hundred livres for a garret? Why, it is not habitable.'

'Therefore no one inhabits it; only, you see, this garret has two windows which look out upon the Place.'

'Yes, monsieur.'

'Well, then, every time anybody is broken on the wheel or hung, quartered, or burnt, these two windows let for twenty pistoles.'*

'Oh!' said Raoul, with horror.

'It is appalling; is it not?' said D'Artagnan.

'Oh!' repeated Raoul.

'Quite appalling, but there it is. These Parisians can get very bloodthirsty. I cannot conceive how men, Christians, can make money from such a business.'

'That is true.'

'As for myself,' continued D'Artagnan, 'if I inhabited that house, on days of execution I would shut it up and block the keyholes; but I do not live there.'

'And you let the garret for five hundred livres?'

'To the ferocious innkeeper, who sub-lets it. I said, then, fifteen hundred livres.'

'The natural interest of money,' said Raoul—'five per cent.'

'Exactly so. I then have left the side of the house at the back, storerooms, and cellars, inundated every winter, two hundred livres; and the garden, which is very fine, well planted, well shaded under the walls and the portal of Saint Gervais and Saint Protais,* thirteen hundred livres.'

'Thirteen hundred livres! why, that is royal!'

'This is the story. I strongly suspect some canon of the parish (these canons are all as rich as Croesus)*—I suspect some canon of having hired the garden to take his pleasure in. The tenant has given the name of M. Godard.* That is either a false name or a real name; if true, he is a canon; if false, he is some unknown; but of what consequence is it to me? he always pays in advance. I had also an idea just now, when I met you, of buying a house in the Place Baudoyer, the back premises of which join my garden, and would make a magnificent property. Your dragoons interrupted my calculations. But come, let us take the Rue de la Vannerie,* that will lead us straight to M. Planchet's.' D'Artagnan mended his pace, and conducted Raoul to Planchet's dwelling, a chamber of which the grocer had given up to his old master. Planchet was out, but the dinner was ready. There was a vestige of military regularity and punctuality preserved in the grocer's household. D'Artagnan returned to the subject of Raoul's future.

'Your father brings you up rather strictly?' said he.

'Justly, monsieur le chevalier.'

'Oh, yes, I know Athos is just; but close, perhaps?'

'A royal hand, Monsieur d'Artagnan.'

'Well, never want, my boy! If ever you stand in need of a few pistoles, the old musketeer is at hand.'

'My dear Monsieur d'Artagnan.'

'Do you play a little?'

'Never.'

'Successful with the ladies, then?—Oh! you little Aramis!* That, my dear friend, costs even more than losing at cards. It is true we fight when we lose; that is a compensation. Bah! that little sniveller, the king, makes winners give him his revenge. What a reign! my poor Raoul, what a reign! When we think that, in my time, the musketeers were besieged in their houses like Hector and Priam in the city of Troy;* and the women wept, and then the walls laughed, and then five hundred beggarly fellows clapped their hands, and cried, "Kill! kill!" though they did not dare lay hands on a single musketeer! *Mordioux!* you will never see anything like *that*.'

'You are very hard upon the king, my dear Monsieur d'Artagnan; and yet you scarcely know him.'

'I! Listen Raoul. Day by day, hour by hour—take note of my words—I will predict what he will do. The cardinal being dead, he will fret; very well, that is the least silly thing he will do, particularly if he does not shed a tear.'

'And then?'

'Why then he will get M. Fouquet to allow him a pension, and will go and compose verses at Fontainebleau,* upon some Mancini or other, whose eyes the queen will scratch out. She is a Spaniard, you see—this queen of ours; and she has, for mother-in-law, Madame Anne of Austria. I know something of the Spaniards of the house of Austria.'*

'And next?'

'Well, after having torn off the silver lace from the uniforms of his Swiss, because lace is too expensive, he will dismount the musketeers, because the oats and hay of a horse cost five sols* a day.'

'Oh! do not say that.'

'Of what consequence is it to *me*; I am no longer a musketeer, am I? Let them be on horseback, let them be on foot, let them carry a rolling-pin, a cooking-spit, a sword, or nothing—what is it to *me*?'

'My dear Monsieur d'Artagnan, I beseech you speak no more ill of the king. I am almost in his service, and my father would be very angry with me for having heard, even from your mouth, words injurious to his majesty.'

'Your father, eh! He is a knight in every bad cause, by God! yes, your father is a brave man, a Caesar, it is true—but a man without perception.'

'Now, my dear chevalier,' exclaimed Raoul, laughing, 'are you going to speak ill of my father, of him you call the great Athos? Truly you are in a bad mood to-day; riches make you as sour as poverty makes other people.'

'By God! you are right. I am a rascal and in my dotage; I am an unhappy wretch grown old; a tent-cord untwisted, a holed breast-plate, a boot without a sole, a spur without a rowel; but do me the pleasure to add one thing.'

'What is that, my dear Monsieur d'Artagnan?'

'Simply say: "Mazarin was a peasant."'

'Perhaps he is dead.'

'All the more reason—I say *was*; if I did not hope that he was dead, I would entreat you to say: "Mazarin *is* a peasant." Come say so, say so, for love of me.'

'Well, I will.'

'Say it!'

'Mazarin was a peasant,' said Raoul, smiling at the musketeer, who roared with laughter, as in his best days.

'A moment,' said the latter; 'you have spoken my first proposition, here is the conclusion of it—repeat, Raoul, repeat: "But I shall miss Mazarin."'

'Chevalier!'

'You will not say it? Well, then, I will say it twice for you.'

'But would you miss Mazarin?'

And they were still laughing and discussing this profession of principles, when one of the shop-boys entered. 'A letter, monsieur,' said he, 'for M. d'Artagnan.'

'Thank you; give it me,' cried the musketeer.

'The handwriting of monsieur le comte,' said Raoul.

'Yes, yes.' And D'Artagnan broke the seal.

'Dear friend,' said Athos, 'a person has just been here to beg me to seek for you, in the name of the king.'

'Seek me!' said D'Artagnan, letting the paper fall upon the table. Raoul picked it up, and continued to read aloud:

'Make haste. His majesty is very anxious to speak to you, and expects you at the Louvre.'

'Expects me?' again repeated the musketeer.

'He, he, he!' laughed Raoul.

'Oh, oh!' replied D'Artagnan. 'What the devil can this mean?'

LIII

THE KING

THE first moment of surprise over, D'Artagnan re-perused Athos's note. 'It is strange,' said he, 'that the king should send for me.'

'Why so?' said Raoul; 'do you not think, monsieur, that the king must regret such a servant as you?'

'Oh, oh!' cried the officer, laughing with all his might; 'you mock me, Master Raoul. If the king had regretted me, he would not have let me leave him. No, no; I see in it something better, or worse, if you like.'

'Worse What can that be, monsieur le chevalier?'

'You are young, you are a boy, you are admirable. Oh, how I should like to be as you are! To be but twenty-four, with an unfurrowed brow, under which the brain is void of everything but woman, love, and good intentions. Oh, Raoul, as long as you have not received the smiles of kings, the confidence of queens; as long as you have not had two cardinals killed under you, the one a tiger, the other a fox;* as long as you have not—— But what is the good of all this trifling? We must part, Raoul.'

'How you say the word! What a serious face!'

'Eh! but the occasion is worthy of it. Listen to me. I have a request to make of you.'

'I am all attention, Monsieur d'Artagnan.'

'You will go and inform your father of my departure.'

'Your departure?'

'Yes, by God!—You will tell him that I am gone into England; and that I am living in my little country-house.'

'In England, you!—And the king's orders?'

'You get more and more foolish: do you imagine that I am going to the Louvre, to place myself at the disposal of that little crowned wolf-cub?'

'The king a wolf-cub? Why, monsieur le chevalier, you are mad!'

'On the contrary, I never was so sane. You do not know what he wants to do with me, this worthy son of *Louis le Juste*!*— But, *mordioux!* that is policy. He wishes to ensconce me snugly in the Bastille—no more and no less!'

'What for?' cried Raoul, terrified at what he heard.

'On account of what I told him one day at Blois. I was angry; he remembers it.'

'You told him what?'

'That he was mean, cowardly, and a fool.'

'Good God!' cried Raoul, 'is it possible that such words should have issued from your mouth?'

'Perhaps I don't give the letter of my speech, but I give the sense of it.'

'But did not the king have you arrested immediately?'

'By whom? It was I who commanded the musketeers; he would have had to order me to convey myself to prison; I would never have consented: I would have resisted myself. And then I went into England—no more D'Artagnan. Now, the cardinal is dead, or nearly so, they learn that I am in Paris, and they lay their hands on me.'

'The cardinal was your protector?'

'The cardinal knew me; he knew certain particularities of me; I also knew some of his; we respected each other. And then, on rendering his soul to the devil, he would recommend Anne of Austria to make me the inhabitant of a safe place. Go, then, and find your father, relate the fact to him—and, adieu!'

'My dear Monsieur d'Artagnan,' said Raoul, very much agitated, after having looked out at the window, 'you cannot even flee!'

'Why not?'

'Because there is below an officer of the Swiss guards waiting for you.'

'Well?'

'Well, he will arrest you.'

D'Artagnan broke into a Homeric laugh.

'Oh! I know very well that you will resist, that you will fight even; I know very well that you will prove the conqueror; but that amounts to rebellion, and you are an officer yourself, knowing what discipline is.'

'Devil of a boy, how logical he is!' grumbled D'Artagnan.

'You agree with me, do you not?'

'Yes, instead of going into the street, where that idiot is waiting for me, I will slip quietly out at the back. I have a horse in the stable, and a good one. I will ride him to death: my means permit me to do so, and by killing one horse after another, I shall arrive at Boulogne in eleven hours; I know the road. Only tell your father one thing.'

'What is that?'

'That is—that the thing he knows about is placed at Planchet's house, except a fifth, and that——'

'But, my dear M. d'Artagnan, rest assured that if you flee, two things will be said of you.'

'What are they, my dear friend?'

'The first, that you have been afraid.'

'Ah! and who will dare to say that?'

'The king, first.'

'Well! but he will tell the truth—I am afraid.'

'The second, that you knew yourself guilty.'

'Guilty of what?'

'Why, of the crimes they wish to impute to you.'

'That is true again. So, then, you advise me to go and get myself made a prisoner in the Bastille?'

'M. le Comte de la Fère would advise you just as I do.'

'Hell's teeth! I know he would,' said D'Artagnan thoughtfully. 'You are right, I shall not escape. But if they throw me into the Bastille?'

'We will get you out again,' said Raoul, with a quiet, calm air.

'*Mordioux!* You said that after a brave fashion, Raoul,' said D'Artagnan, seizing his hand; 'that smacks of Athos, distinctly. Well, I will go, then. Do not forget my last word.'

'Except a fifth,' said Raoul.

'Yes, you are a fine boy! and I wish you to add one thing to that last word.'

'Speak, chevalier!'

'It is that if you cannot get me out of the Bastille, and I remain there—Oh! that will be so, and I shall be a detestable prisoner; I, who have been a passable man—in that case, I give three-fifths to you, and the fourth to your father.'

'Chevalier!'

'*Mordioux!* If you will have some masses said for me, you are welcome.'

That being said, D'Artagnan took his belt from its hook, girded on his sword, took a hat the feather of which was fresh, and held his hand out to Raoul, who threw himself into his arms. When in the shop, he cast a quick glance at the shop-lads, who looked upon the scene with a pride mingled with some anxiety; then plunging his hands into a chest of currants, he went straight to the officer who was waiting for him at the door.

'Those features! Can it be you, Monsieur de Friedisch?'*
cried D'Artagnan, gaily. 'Eh! eh! what, do we arrest our friends?'

'Arrest!' whispered the lads among themselves.

'Ja, it is I, Monsieur d'Artagnan! Good-day to you!' said the
Swiss, in his guttural accent.

'Must I give you up my sword? I warn you, that it is long and
heavy; you had better let me wear it to the Louvre: I feel quite
lost in the streets without a sword, and you would be more at sea
than I should, with two.'

'Ach, the king has given no orders about it,' replied the Swiss,
'so keep your sword.'

'Well, that is very polite on the part of the king. Let us go, at
once.'

Monsieur de Friedisch was not a talker, and D'Artagnan had
too many things to think about to say much. From Planchet's
shop to the Louvre was not far*—they arrived in ten minutes.
It was a dark night. M. de Friedisch wanted to enter by the side
gate. 'No,' said D'Artagnan, 'you would waste time by that; take
the little staircase.'

The Swiss did as D'Artagnan advised, and conducted him to
the vestibule of the king's closet. When arrived there, he bowed
to his prisoner, and, without saying anything, returned to his
post. D'Artagnan had not had time to ask why his sword was not
taken from him, when the door of the cabinet opened, and a
valet de chambre called, 'M. d'Artagnan!' The musketeer assumed his best parade manner, and entered, with his large eyes
wide open, his brow calm, his moustache stiff. The king was
seated at a table writing. He did not disturb himself when the
step of the musketeer resounded on the floor; he did not even
turn his head. D'Artagnan advanced as far as the middle of the
room, and seeing that the king paid no attention to him, and
suspecting, besides, that this was nothing but affectation, a sort
of tormenting preamble to the explanation that was preparing,
he turned his back on the prince, and began to examine the
frescoes on the cornices, and the cracks in the ceiling. This
manœuvre was accompanied by a little tacit monologue. 'Ah!
you want to humble me, do you?—you, whom I have seen so
young—you, whom I have served as I would my own child—
you, whom I have served as I would a God—that is to say, for

nothing. Wait awhile! wait awhile! you shall see what a man can do who has snuffed the air of the fire of the Huguenots,* under the beard of monsieur le cardinal—the true cardinal.' At this moment Louis turned round.

'Ah! are you there, Monsieur d'Artagnan?' said he.

D'Artagnan saw the movement and imitated it. 'Yes, sire,' said he.

'Very well; have the goodness to wait till I have added this up.'

D'Artagnan made no reply; he only bowed. 'That is polite enough,' thought he; 'I have nothing to say.'

Louis made a violent dash with his pen, and threw it angrily away.

'Ah! go on, work yourself up!' thought the musketeer; 'you will put me at my ease. You shall find I did not get everything off my chest, that day, at Blois.'

Louis rose from his seat, passed his hand over his brow; then, stopping opposite to D'Artagnan, he looked at him with an air at once imperious and kind. 'What the devil does he want with me? I wish he would begin!' thought the musketeer.

'Monsieur,' said the king, 'you know, without doubt, that monsieur le cardinal is dead?'

'I suspected so, sire.'

'You know that, consequently, I am master in my own kingdom?'

'That is not a thing that dates from the death of monsieur le cardinal, sire; a man is always master in his own house, when he wishes to be so.'

'Yes; but do you remember all you said to me at Blois?'

'Now we come to it,' thought D'Artagnan; 'I was not deceived. Well, so much the better, it is a sign that my scent is tolerably keen yet.'

'You do not answer me,' said Louis.

'Sire, I think I recollect.'

'You only think?'

'It is so long ago.'

'If you do not remember, I do. You said to me—listen with attention.'

'Ah! I shall listen with all my ears, sire; for it is very likely the conversation will turn in a fashion very interesting to me.'

Louis once more looked at the musketeer. The latter smoothed the feather of his hat, then his moustache, and waited bravely. Louis XIV continued: 'You quitted my service, monsieur, after having told me the whole truth?'

'Yes, sire.'

'That is, after having declared to me all you thought to be true, with regard to my mode of thinking and acting. That is always a merit. You began by telling me that you had served my family thirty years, and were weary.'

'I said so; yes, sire.'

'And you afterwards admitted that your fatigue was a pretext, and that discontent was the real cause.'

'I was discontented, in fact; but that discontent has never betrayed itself, that I know of, and if, like a man of heart, I have spoken out before your majesty, I have not even thought of the matter before anybody else.'

'Do not excuse yourself, D'Artagnan, but continue to listen to me. When making me the reproach that you were discontented, you received in reply a promise—"Wait"—is not that true?'

'Yes, sire, as true as what I told you.'

'You answered me, "Hereafter! No, now, immediately." Do not excuse yourself, I tell you. It was natural, but you had no charity for your poor prince, Monsieur d'Artagnan.'

'Sire!—charity for a king, on the part of a poor soldier!'

'You understand me very well; you knew that I stood in need of it; you knew very well that I was not master; you knew very well that my hope was in the future. Now, you answered me when I spoke of that future, "My discharge—and that directly." '

'That is true,' murmured D'Artagnan, biting his moustache.

'You did not flatter me when I was in distress,' added Louis.

'But,' said D'Artagnan, raising his head nobly, 'if I did not flatter your majesty when poor, neither did I betray you. I have shed my blood for nothing; I have watched like a dog at a door, knowing full well that neither bread nor bone would be thrown to me. I, although poor likewise, asked nothing of your majesty but the discharge you speak of.'

'I know you are a brave man, but I was a young man, and you ought to have had some indulgence for me. What had you to reproach the king with?—that he left King Charles II without assistance?—let us say further—that he did not marry Mademoiselle de Mancini?' When saying these words, the king fixed upon the musketeer a searching look.

'Ah! ah!' thought the latter, 'he is doing far more than remembering, he has guessed. The devil!'

'Your sentence,' continued Louis, 'fell upon the king and fell upon the man. But, Monsieur d'Artagnan, that weakness, for you considered it a weakness?'—D'Artagnan made no reply—'you reproached me also with regard to monsieur, the late cardinal. Now, monsieur le cardinal, did he not bring me up, did he not support me—elevating himself and supporting himself at the same time, I admit; still, I reaped the benefit of it. As an ingrate or an egotist, would you, then, have better loved or served me?'

'Sire!'

'We will say no more about it, monsieur; it would only create in you too many regrets, and me too much pain.'

D'Artagnan was not convinced. The young king, in adopting a haughty tone with him, did not forward his purpose.

'You have since reflected?' resumed Louis.

'Upon what, sire?' asked D'Artagnan, politely.

'Why, upon what I have been saying to you, monsieur.'

'Yes, sire, no doubt——'

'And you have only waited for an opportunity of retracting your words?'

'Sire!'

'You hesitate, it seems.'

'I do not understand what your majesty did me the honour to say to me.'

Louis's brow became cloudy.

'Have the goodness to excuse me, sire; my understanding is particularly thick; things do not penetrate it without difficulty; but it is true, when once they get in, they remain there.'

'Yes, yes; you appear to have a memory.'

'Almost as good as your majesty's.'

'Then give me quickly one solution. My time is valuable. What have you been dong since your discharge?'

'Making my fortune, sire.'

'The expression is crude, Monsieur d'Artagnan.'

'Your majesty takes it in bad part, certainly. I entertain nothing but the profoundest respect for the king; and if I have been impolite, which might be excused by my long sojourn in camps and barracks, your majesty is too much above me to be offended at a word that a soldier lets slip in all innocence.'

'In fact, I know you performed a brilliant action in England, monsieur. I only regret that you have broken your promise.'

'I!' cried D'Artagnan.

'Yes. You engaged your word not to serve any other prince on quitting my service. Now it was for King Charles II that you undertook the marvellous carrying off of M. Monk.'

'Pardon me, sire; it was for myself.'

'And did you succeed?'

'As did the captains of the fifteenth century, with armed fray and adventures.'

'What do you call succeeding?—a fortune?'

'A hundred thousand crowns, sire, which I now possess— that is, in one week three times as much money as I ever had in fifty years.'

'It is a handsome sum. But you are ambitious, I perceive.'

'I, sire? The quarter of that would be a treasure; and I swear to you I have no thought of augmenting it.'

'What! you contemplate remaining idle?'

'Yes, sire.'

'You mean to sheathe your sword?'

'That I have already done.'

'Impossible, Monsieur d'Artagnan!' said Louis, firmly.

'But, sire——'

'Well?'

'And why, sire?'

'Because it is *my* wish you should not!' said the young prince, in a voice so stern and imperious that D'Artagnan evinced surprise and even uneasiness.

'Will your majesty allow me one word of reply?' said he.

'Speak.'

'I formed that resolution when I was poor and destitute.'

'So be it. Go on.'

'Now, when by my energy I have acquired a comfortable means of subsistence, would your majesty despoil me of my liberty? Your majesty would condemn me to the lowest, when I have gained the highest?'

'Who gave you permission, monsieur, to fathom my designs, or to reckon with me?' replied Louis, in a voice almost angry; 'who told you what I shall do or what you will yourself do?'

'Sire,' said the musketeer, quietly, 'as far as I see, freedom is not the order of the conversation, as it was on the day we spoke plainly at Blois.'

'No, monsieur; everything is changed.'

'I tender your majesty my sincere compliments upon that, but——'

'But you don't believe it?'

'I am not a great statesman, and yet I have my eye upon affairs; it seldom fails; now, I do not see exactly as your majesty does, sire. The reign of Mazarin is over, but that of the financiers is begun. They have the money; your majesty will not often see much of it. To live under the paw of these hungry wolves is hard for a man who reckoned upon independence.'

At this moment someone scratched at the door of the cabinet; the king raised his head proudly. 'Your pardon, Monsieur d'Artagnan,' said he; 'it is M. Colbert who comes to make me a report. Come in, M. Colbert.'

D'Artagnan drew back. Colbert entered with papers in his hand, and went up to the king. There can be little doubt that the Gascon did not waste an opportunity of applying his keen, quick glance to the new figure which presented itself.

'Is the inquiry made?'

'Yes, sire.'

'And the opinion of the investigators?'

'Is that the accused merit confiscation and death.'

'Ah! ah!' said the king, without changing countenance, and casting an oblique look at D'Artagnan. 'And your own opinion, M. Colbert?' said he.

Colbert looked at D'Artagnan in his turn. That imposing countenance checked the words upon his lips. Louis perceived this. 'Do not disturb yourself,' said he; 'it is M. d'Artagnan—do you not recognize M. d'Artagnan?'

The two men looked at each other—D'Artagnan, with eyes open and bright as the day—Colbert, with his half-closed, and dim. The frank intrepidity of the one annoyed the other; the circumspection of the financier repelled the soldier. 'Ah! ah! this is the gentleman who made that brilliant stroke in England,' said Colbert. And he bowed slightly to D'Artagnan.

'Ah! ah!' said the Gascon, 'this is the gentleman who clipped off the lace from the uniform of the Swiss! A praiseworthy piece of economy.'

The financier would have liked to make a strike at the musketeer; but the musketeer ran the financier through.

'Monsieur d'Artagnan,' resumed the king, who had not remarked all the shades of which Mazarin would have missed not one, 'this concerns the tax-farmers who have robbed me, whom I am hanging, and whose death-warrants I am about to sign.'

'Oh! oh!' said D'Artagnan, starting.

'What did you say?'

'Oh! nothing, sire. This is no business of mine.'

The king had already taken up the pen, and was applying it to the paper. 'Sire,' said Colbert in a subdued voice, 'I beg to warn your majesty, that if an example be necessary, there will be difficulty in the execution of your orders.'

'What do you say?' said Louis.

'You must not conceal from yourself,' continued Colbert quietly, 'that to attack the farmers-general is to attack the superintendence. The two unfortunate guilty men in question are the particular friends of a powerful personage, and the punishment, which otherwise might be comfortably confined to the Châtelet,* will doubtless be a signal for disturbances!'

Louis coloured and turned towards D'Artagnan, who took a slight bite at his moustache, not without a smile of pity for Colbert, and for the king who had to listen to him so long. But Louis seized the pen, and with a movement so rapid, that his hand shook, he affixed his signature at the bottom of the two papers presented by Colbert—then looking the latter in the face, 'Monsieur Colbert,' said he, 'when you speak to me on business, exclude more frequently the word difficulty from your reasonings and opinions; as to the word impossibility, never pronounce it.'

Colbert bowed, much humiliated at having to undergo such a lesson before the musketeer; he was about to leave, but, jealous to repair his discomfiture: 'I forgot to announce to your majesty,' said he, 'that the confiscations amount to the sum of five million livres.'

'That's pretty well!' thought D'Artagnan.

'Which makes in my coffers?' said the king.

'Eighteen million livres, sire,' replied Colbert, bowing.

'*Mordioux!*' growled D'Artagnan, 'that's glorious!'

'Monsieur Colbert,' added the king, 'you will, if you please, go through the gallery where M. Lyonne is waiting, and will tell him to bring hither what he has drawn up—by my order.'

'Directly, sire; if your majesty wants me no more this evening?'

'No, monsieur: good-night!' And Colbert went out.

'Now, let us return to our affair, M. d'Artagnan,' said the king, as if nothing had happened. 'You see that, with respect to money, there is already a notable change.'

'Something to the tune of from zero to eighteen millions,' replied the musketeer, gaily. 'Ah! that was what your majesty wanted the day King Charles II came to Blois. The two states would not have been embroiled to-day; for I *must* say, that there also I see another stumbling-block.'

'Well, in the first place,' replied Louis, 'you are unjust, monsieur; for, if Providence had made me able to give my brother the million that day, you would not have quitted my service, and, consequently, you would not have made your fortune, as you told me just now you have done. But, in addition to this, I have had another piece of good fortune; and my difference with Great Britain need not alarm you.'

A *valet de chambre* interrupted the king by announcing M. Lyonne. 'Come in, monsieur,' said the king; 'you are punctual; that is like a good servant. Let us see your letter to my brother Charles II.'

D'Artagnan pricked up his ears. 'A moment, monsieur,' said Louis, carelessly, to the Gascon; 'I must expedite to London my consent to the marriage of my brother, M. le Duc d'Anjou, with the Princess Henrietta Stuart.'

'He is knocking me about, it seems,' murmured D'Artagnan, whilst the king signed the letter, and dismissed M. de Lyonne; 'but, Hell's teeth! the more he knocks me about in this manner, the better I like it.'

The king followed M. de Lyonne with his eyes, till the door was closed behind him; he even made three steps, as if he would follow the minister; but, after these three steps, stopping, pausing, and coming back to the musketeer, 'Now, monsieur,' said he, 'let us hasten to terminate our affair. You told me that day, at Blois, that you were not rich?'

'But I am now, sire.'

'Yes, but that does not concern me; you have your own money, not mine; *that* does not enter into my account.'

'I do not well understand what your majesty means.'

'Then, instead of making me drag words out of you, speak spontaneously. Should you be satisfied with twenty thousand livres a year as a fixed income?'

'But, sire,' said D'Artagnan, opening his eyes wide.

'Would you be satisfied with four horses furnished and kept, and with any extra funds as you might require, according to occasions and needs, or would you prefer a fixed sum which would be, for example, forty thousand livres? Answer.'

'Sire, your majesty——'

'Yes, you are surprised; that is natural, and I expected it. Answer me, come! or I shall think you have no longer that rapidity of judgment I have so much admired in you.'

'It is certain, sire, that twenty thousand livres a year make a handsome sum; but——'

'No buts! Yes or no, is it an honourable sum?'

'Oh! very certainly.'

'You will be satisfied with it? That is well. It will be better to reckon the extra expenses separately; you can arrange that with Colbert. Now let us pass to something more important.'

'But, sire, I told your majesty——'

'That you wanted rest, I know you did: only I replied that I would not allow it—I am master, I suppose?'

'Yes, sire.'

'That is well. You were formerly in the way of becoming captain of the musketeers?'*

'Yes, sire.'

'Well, here is your commission signed. I place it in this drawer. The day on which you shall return from a certain expedition which I have to confide to you, on that day you may yourself take the commission from the drawer.' D'Artagnan still hesitated, and hung down his head. 'Come, monsieur,' said the king, 'one would believe, to look at you, that you did not know that at the court of the most Christian king, the captain-general of the musketeers takes precedence of the Marshals of France.'

'Sire, I know he does.'

'Then, am I to think you do put no faith in my word?'

'Oh! sire, never—never dream of such a thing.'

'I have wished to prove to you, that you, so good a servant, had lost a good master; am I anything like the master that will suit you?'

'I begin to think you are, sire.'

'Then, monsieur, you will resume your functions. Your company has become disorganized since your departure, and the men go about drinking and rioting in the taverns, where they fight, in spite of my edicts, and those of my father.* You will reorganize the service as soon as possible.'

'Yes, sire.'

'You will not again quit my person.'

'Very well, sire.'

'You will march with me to the army, you will encamp round my tent.'

'Then, sire,' said D'Artagnan, 'if it is only to impose upon me a service like that, your majesty need not give me twenty thousand livres a year. I shall not earn it.'

'I desire that you shall keep open house; I desire that you should keep a liberal table; I desire that my captain of musketeers should be a personage.'

'And I,' said D'Artagnan, bluntly; 'I do not like easily found money; I like money won! Your majesty gives me an idle trade, which the first comer would perform for four thousand livres.'

Louis XIV began to laugh. 'You are a true Gascon, Monsieur d'Artagnan; you will draw my heart's secret from me.'

'Bah! has your majesty a secret, then?'

'Yes, monsieur.'

'Well! then I accept the twenty thousand livres, for I will keep it secret, and discretion is above all price, in these times. Will your majesty speak now?'

'Boot yourself, Monsieur d'Artagnan, and to horse!'

'Directly, sire.'

'Within two days.'

'That is well, sire: for I have my affairs to settle before I set out; particularly if it is likely there should be any fighting in the offing.'

'That *may* happen.'

'We shall give as good as we get! But, sire, you have addressed yourself to avarice, to ambition; you have addressed yourself to the heart of M. d'Artagnan, but you have forgotten one thing.'

'What is that?'

'You have said nothing to his vanity; when shall I be a knight of the king's orders?'*

'Does that interest you?'

'Why, yes, sire. My friend Athos is quite covered with orders, and that dazzles me.'

'You shall be a knight of my order a month after you have taken your commission of captain.'

'Ah! ah!' said the officer, thoughtfully, 'after the expedition.'

'Precisely.'

'Where is your majesty going to send me?'

'Are you acquainted with Brittany?'

'No, sire.'

'Have you any friends there?'

'In Brittany? No!'

'So much the better. Do you know anything about fortifications?'

'I believe I do, sire,' said D'Artagnan, smiling.

'That is to say you can readily distinguish a fortress from a simple fortification, such as is allowed to owners of Châteaux or vassals?'

'I can distinguish a fort from a rampart as easily as I can I distinguish between a breast plate and a raised pie-crust, sire. Is that sufficient?'

'Yes, monsieur. You will set out then.'

'For Brittany?'

'Yes.'

'Alone?'

'Absolutely alone. That is to say, you must not even take a lackey with you.'

'May I ask your majesty for what reason?'

'Because, monsieur, it will be necessary to disguise yourself sometimes, as the servant of a good family. Your face is very well known in France, M. d'Artagnan.'

'And then, sire?'

'And then you will travel slowly through Brittany, and will examine carefully the fortifications of that country.'

'The coasts?'

'Yes, and the isles; starting with Belle-Isle-en-Mer.'

'Ah! which belongs to M. Fouquet!' said D'Artagnan, in a serious tone, raising his intelligent eye to Louis XIV.

'I fancy you are right, monsieur, and that Belle-Isle *does* belong to M. Fouquet, in fact.'

'Then your majesty wishes me to ascertain if Belle-Isle is fortified.'

'Yes.'

'If the fortifications of it are new or old?'

'Precisely.'

'And if the vassals of M. Fouquet are sufficiently numerous to form a garrison?'

'That is what I want to know; you have placed your finger on the question.'

'And if they are not fortifying, sire?'

'You will travel about Brittany, listening and judging.'

'Then I am a king's spy?' said D'Artagnan, bluntly, twisting his moustache.

'No, monsieur.'

'Your pardon, sire; I spy on your majesty's account.'

'You start on a voyage of discovery, monsieur. Would you march at the head of your musketeers, with your sword in your hand, to observe any spot whatever, or an enemy's position?'

At this word D'Artagnan started.

'Do you,' continued the king, 'imagine yourself to be a spy?'

'No, no,' said D'Artagnan, but pensively; 'the thing changes its face when one observes an enemy: one is then a soldier. And if they are fortifying Belle-Isle?' added he, quickly.

'You will take an exact plan of the fortifications.'

'Will they permit me to enter?'

'That does not concern me; that is *your* affair. Did you not understand that I reserved for you a supplement of twenty thousand livres per annum, if you wished it?'

'Yes, sire; but if they are not fortifying?'

'You will return quietly, without fatiguing your horse.'

'Sire, I am ready.'

'You will begin to-morrow by going to monsieur le surintendant's to take the first quarter of the pension I give you. Do you know M. Fouquet?'

'Very little, sire; but I beg your majesty to observe that I don't think it immediately necessary that I *should* know him.'

'Your pardon, monsieur; for he will refuse you the money I wish you to take; and it is that refusal I look for.'

'Ah!' said D'Artagnan. 'Then, sire?'

'The money being refused, you will go and seek it at M. Colbert's. By the way, have you a good horse?'

'An excellent one, sire.'

'How much did it cost you?'

'A hundred and fifty pistoles.'

'I will buy it of you. Here is a note for two hundred pistoles.'

'But I want my horse for my journey, sire.'

'Well?'

'Well, and you take mine from me.'

'Not at all. On the contrary, I give it you. Only as it is now mine and not yours, I am sure you will not spare it.'

'Your majesty is in a hurry then?'

'A great hurry.'

'Then what compels me to wait two days?'

'Reasons known to myself.'

'That's a different matter. The horse may make up the two days, in the eight he has to travel; and then there is the post.'

'No, no, using post horses compromises, Monsieur d'Artagnan. Begone, and do not forget you are my servant.'

'Sire, it is not my duty to forget it! At what hour to-morrow shall I take my leave of your majesty?'

'Where do you lodge?'

'I must henceforward lodge at the Louvre.'*

'That must not be now—keep your lodgings in the city: I will pay for them. As to your departure, it must take place at night; you must set out without being seen by any one, or, if you are seen, it must not be known that you belong to me. Keep your mouth shut, monsieur.'

'Your majesty spoils all you have said by that single word.'

'I asked you where you lodged, for I cannot always send to M. le Comte de la Fère to seek you.'

'I lodge with M. Planchet, a grocer, Rue des Lombards, at the sign of the Golden Pestle.'

'Go out little, show yourself less, and await my orders.'

'And yet, sire, I must go for the money.'

'That is true, but, when going to the superintendence, where so many people are constantly going, you must mingle with the crowd.'

'I want the notes, sire, for the money.'

'Here they are.' The king signed them, and D'Artagnan looked on, to assure himself that they were in order.

'Adieu! Monsieur d'Artagnan,' added the king; 'I think you have perfectly understood me.'

'I? I understand that your majesty sends me to Belle-Isle-en-Mer, that is all.'

'To learn?'

'To learn how M. Fouquet's works are going on; that is all.'

'Very well: I admit you may be taken prisoner.'

'And I do not admit it,' replied the Gascon, boldly.

'I admit you may be killed,' continued the king.

'That is not probable, sire.'

'In the first case, you must not speak; in the second, there must be no papers found upon you.'

D'Artagnan shrugged his shoulders without ceremony, and took leave of the king, saying to himself:—'The English shower continues—let us remain under the spout!'

LIV

THE HOUSES OF M. FOUQUET

WHILST D'Artagnan was returning to Planchet's house, his head aching and bewildered with all that had happened to him, there was passing a scene of quite a different character, and which, nevertheless, is not foreign to the conversation our musketeer had just had with the king; only this scene took place out of Paris, in a house possessed by superintendent Fouquet in the village of Saint-Mandé.* The minister had just arrived at this country-house, followed by his principal clerk, who carried an enormous portfolio full of papers to be examined, and others waiting for signature. As it was about five o'clock in the afternoon, the masters had dined:* supper was being prepared for twenty lesser guests. The superintendent did not stop: on alighting from his carriage, he, at the same bound, sprang through the doorway, traversed the apartments and gained his closet, where he declared he would shut himself up to work, commanding that he should not be disturbed for anything but an order from the king. As soon as this order was given, Fouquet shut himself up, and two footmen were placed as sentinels at his door. Then Fouquet pushed a bolt which displaced a panel that walled up the entrance, and prevented everything that passed in this apartment from being either seen or heard. But, against all probability, it was only for the sake of shutting himself up that Fouquet shut himself up thus, for he went straight to a bureau, seated himself at it, opened the portfolio, and began to sort through the enormous mass of papers it contained. It was not more than ten minutes after he had entered, and taken all the precautions we have described, when the repeated sound of several slight equal knocks struck his ear, and appeared to fix his utmost attention. Fouquet raised his head, turned his ear, and listened.

The strokes continued. Then the worker arose with a slight movement of impatience and walked straight up to a mirror on which the blows were struck by a hand, or by some invisible mechanism. It was a large mirror let into a panel. Three other mirrors, exactly similar to it, completed the symmetry of the apartment. Nothing distinguished that one from the others. Without doubt, these reiterated knocks were a signal; for, at the moment Fouquet approached the mirror listening, the same noise was renewed, and in the same measure. 'Oh! oh!' murmured the superintendent, with surprise, 'who is there? I did not expect anybody to-day.' And without doubt to respond to that signal, he pulled out a gilded nail near the mirror, and pulled it thrice. Then returning to his place, and seating himself again, 'By God, let them wait,' said he. And plunging again into the ocean of papers unrolled before him, he appeared to think of nothing now but work. In fact, with incredible rapidity and marvellous lucidity, Fouquet deciphered the largest papers and most complicated writings, correcting them, annotating them with a pen moved as if by a fever, and the work melting under his hands, signatures, figures, references, became multiplied as if ten clerks—that is to say, a hundred fingers and ten brains had performed the duties, instead of the five fingers and single brain of this man. From time to time, Fouquet, absorbed by his work, raised his head to cast a furtive glance upon a clock placed before him. The reason of this was, Fouquet set himself a task, and when this task was once set, in one hour's work he, by himself, did what another would not have accomplished in a day; always certain, consequently, provided he was not disturbed, of arriving at the close in the time his all-consuming activity had fixed. But in the midst of his ardent labour, the soft strokes upon the little bell placed behind the mirror sounded again, hasty, and, consequently, more urgent.

'The lady appears to be impatient,' said Fouquet. 'Humph! it has stopped! It must be the comtesse; but, no, the comtesse is gone to Rambouillet for three days. The présidente, then? Oh! no, the présidente would not assume such grand airs; she would ring very humbly, then she would wait my good pleasure. The greatest certainty is, that I do not know who it can be, but that I know who it cannot be. And since it is not you, marquise, since it cannot be you, deuce take the rest!' And he went on with his work in spite of the repeated ringing of the bell. At the end of a quarter of an hour, however, impatience prevailed over Fouquet: he might be said to consume, rather than to complete the rest of his work; he thrust his papers into his portfolio, and giving a glance at the mirror, whilst the taps continued faster than ever. 'Oh! oh!' said he, 'whence comes all this racket? What has happened, and who can the Ariadne* be who expects me so impatiently. Let us see!'

He then applied the tip of his finger to the nail parallel to the one he had pulled. Immediately the glass moved like a folding-door and revealed a secret cupboard in which the superintendent disappeared as if going into a vast box. When there, he pressed another spring, which opened, not a board, but a section of the wall, and he went out through the opening, leaving the door to shut of itself. Then Fouquet descended about a score of steps which sank, winding, underground, and came to a long, subterranean passage,* lighted by imperceptible loop-holes. The walls of this vault were covered with slabs or tiles, and the floor with carpeting. This passage was under the street which separated Fouquet's house from the Park of Vincennes. At the end of the passage ascended a winding staircase parallel with that by which Fouquet had entered. He climbed these other stairs, entered by means of a spring placed in a cupboard similar to that in his closet, and from this cupboard an untenanted chamber furnished with the utmost elegance. As soon as he entered, he examined carefully whether the mirror closed without leaving any trace, and, doubtless satisfied with his observation, he opened by means of a small gold key the triple lock of a door in front of him. This time the door opened upon a handsome closet, sumptuously furnished, in which was seated upon cushions a lady of surpassing beauty, who at the sound of the lock sprang towards Fouquet. 'Ah! good Heavens!' cried the latter, starting back with astonishment. 'Madame la Marquise de Bellière,* you here?'

'Yes,' murmured la marquise. 'Yes; it is I, monsieur.'

'Marquise! dear marquise!' added Fouquet, ready to prostrate himself. 'Ah! my God! how did you come here? And I, to keep you waiting!'

'A long time, monsieur; yes, a very long time!'

'I am happy in thinking this waiting has appeared long to you, marquise!'

'Oh! an eternity, monsieur; oh! I rang more than twenty times. Did you not hear me?'

'Marquise, you are pale, you tremble.'

'Did you not hear, then, that you were summoned?'

'Oh, yes; I heard plainly enough, madame; but I could not come. After your rigours and your refusals, how could I dream it was you? If I could have had any suspicion of the happiness that awaited me, believe me, madame, I would have dropped everything to fall at your feet, as I do at this moment.'

'Are we quite alone, monsieur?' asked the marquise, looking round the room.

'Oh, yes, madame, I can assure you of that.'

'Really?' said the marquise, in a melancholy tone.

'You sigh,' said Fouquet.

'What mysteries! what precautions!' said the marquise, with a slight bitterness of expression; 'and how evident it is that you fear the least suspicion of your amours to escape.'

'Would you prefer their being made public?'

'Oh, no; you behave like a cautious man,' said the marquise, smiling.

'Come, dear marquise, punish me not with reproaches, I implore you.'

'Reproaches! Have I a right to make you any?'

'No, unfortunately, no; but tell me, you, who during a year I have loved without return or hope——'

'You are mistaken—without hope it is true, but not without return.'

'What! for me, of my love! there is but one proof, and that proof I still want.'

'I am here to bring it, monsieur.'

Fouquet wished to clasp her in his arms, but she disengaged herself with a gesture.

'You persist in deceiving yourself, monsieur, and never will accept of me the only thing I am willing to give you—devotion.'

'Ah, then, you do not love me? Devotion is but a virtue, love is a passion.'

'Listen to me, I implore you: I should not have come hither without a serious motive: you are convinced of that, are you not?'

'The motive is of very little consequence, so that you are but here—so that I see you—so that I speak to you!'

'You are right; the principal thing is that I am here without any one having seen me, and that I can speak to you.'—Fouquet sank on his knees before her. 'Speak! speak, madame!' said he, 'I am listening.'

The marquise looked at Fouquet, on his knees at her feet, and there was in the looks of the woman a strange mixture of love and melancholy. 'Oh!' at length murmured she, 'would that I were she who has the right of seeing you every minute, of speaking to you every instant! would that I were she who might watch over you, she who would have no need of mysterious springs to summon and conjure, like a sylph, the man she loves, to look at him for an hour, and then see him disappear in the darkness of a mystery, still more strange at his going out than at his coming in. Oh! that would be to live a happy woman!'

'Do you happen, marquise,' said Fouquet, smiling, 'to be speaking of my wife?'*

'Yes, certainly, of her I spoke.'

'Well, you need not envy her lot, marquise; of all the women with whom I have any contact, Madame Fouquet is the one I see the least of, and who has the least to do with me.'

'At least, monsieur, she is not reduced to place, as I have done, her hand upon the signal of a mirror to call you to her; at least you do not reply to her by the mysterious, alarming sound of a bell, the source of which comes from I don't know where; at least you have not forbidden her to attempt to discover the secret of these communications under pain of breaking off for ever your connections with her, as you have forbidden all who have come here before me, and all who will come after me.'

'Dear marquise, how unjust you are, and how little do you know what you are doing in complaining of a mystery; it is with mystery alone we can love without interference; it is only with love without interference that we can be happy. But let us return to ourselves, to that devotion of which you were speaking, or rather let me labour under a pleasant delusion, and believe that this devotion is love.'

'Just now,' repeated the marquise, passing over her eyes a hand that might have been a model for the graceful contours of antiquity; 'just now I was prepared to speak, my ideas were clear and bold; now I am confused and troubled; I fear I bring you bad news.'

'If it is to that bad news I owe your presence, marquise,

welcome be even that bad news! or rather, marquise, since you
allow that I am not quite indifferent to you, let me hear nothing
of the bad news, but speak of yourself.'

'No, no, on the contrary, demand it of me; require me to tell
it to you instantly, and not to allow myself to be turned aside by
any feeling whatever. Fouquet, my friend! it is of immense
importance!'

'You astonish me, marquise; I will even say you almost frighten
me. You, so serious, so collected; you who know the world we
live in so well. Is it then important?'

'Oh! very important.'

'In the first place, how did you get here?'

'You shall know that presently; but first to something of more
consequence.'

'Speak, marquise, speak! I implore you, have pity on my
impatience.'

'Do you know that Colbert is made intendant of finances?'

'Bah! Colbert, little Colbert.'

'Yes, Colbert, *little* Colbert.'

'Mazarin's factotum?'

'The same.'

'Well! what do you see so disturbing in that, dear marquise?
little Colbert is intendant; it is surprising, I confess, but is not
alarming.'

'Do you think the king has given, without a pressing motive,
such a place to one you call a little pedant?'

'In the first place, is it really true that the king has given it to
him?'

'It is so said.'

'Ay, but who says so?'

'Everybody.'

'Everybody, that's nobody; mention some one likely to be
well informed who says so.'

'Madame Vanel.'*

'Ah! now you begin to frighten me in earnest,' said Fouquet,
laughing; 'if any one is well informed, or ought to be well
informed, it is the person you name.'

'Do not speak ill of poor Marguerite, Monsieur Fouquet, for
she still loves you.'

'Bah! indeed? That is scarcely credible. I thought little Colbert, as you called him just now, had passed over that love, and left the impression upon it of a spot of ink or a stain of grease.'

'Fouquet! Fouquet! Is this the way you always treat the poor creatures you desert?'

'Why, you surely are not going to undertake the defence of Madame Vanel?'

'Yes, I will undertake it: for, I repeat, she loves you still, and the proof is she saves you.'

'But your interposition, marquise; that is a very cunning move on her part. No angel could be more agreeable to me, or could lead me more certainly to salvation. But, let me ask you, do you know Marguerite?'

'She was my convent friend.'

'And you say that she has informed you that Monsieur Colbert was named intendant?'

'Yes, she did.'

'Well, enlighten me, marquise; granted Monsieur Colbert is intendant—so be it. In what can an intendant, that is to say my subordinate, my clerk, give me trouble or hurt me, even if he *is* Monsieur Colbert?'

'You do not reflect, monsieur, apparently,' replied the marquise.

'Upon what?'

'This: that Monsieur Colbert hates you.'

'Hates me?' cried Fouquet; 'Good heavens! marquise, where have you been? where can you live? Hates me! why all the world hates me, he, of course, as others do.'

'He more than others.'

'More than others—let him.'

'He is ambitious.'

'Who is not, marquise?'

'Yes, but with him ambition has no bounds.'

'I am quite aware of that, since he made it a point to follow me with Madame Vanel.'

'And obtained his end; take note of that.'

'Do you mean to say he has the presumption to hope to pass from intendant to superintendent?'

'Have you not yourself already had the same fear?'

'Oh! oh!' said Fouquet, 'to succeed with Madame Vanel is one thing, to succeed me with the king is another. France is not to be purchased so easily as the wife of an accountant.'

'Eh! monsieur, everything is to be bought; if not by gold, then by intrigue.'

'Nobody knows the contrary better than you, madame, you to whom I have offered millions.'

'Instead of millions, Fouquet, you should have offered me a true, undivided, and boundless love: I might have accepted that. So you see, still, everything can be bought, if not in one way, then in another.'

'So Colbert, in your opinion, is in a fair way of bargaining for my office as superintendent. Make yourself easy on that head, my dear marquise, he is not yet rich enough to purchase it.'

'But if he should rob you of it?'

'Ah! that is another thing. Unfortunately, before he can reach me, that is to say, the head-quarters, he must destroy, must make a breach in the advanced works, and I am devilishly well fortified, marquise.'

'What you call your advanced works are your creatures, are they not—your friends?'

'Exactly so.'

'And is M. d'Eymeris* one of your creatures?'

'Yes, he is.'

'Is M. Lyodot one of your friends?'

'Certainly.'

'M. de Vanin?'

'M. de Vanin! ah! they may do what they like with him, but——'

'But——'

'But they must not touch the others.'

'Well, if you are anxious they should not touch MM. d'Eymeris and Lyodot, it is time to look about you.'

'Who threatens them?'

'Will you listen to me, now?'

'Attentively, marquise.'

'Without interrupting me?'

'Speak.'

'Well, this morning Marguerite sent for me.'

'And what did she want with you?'

'"I dare not see M. Fouquet myself," said she.'

'Bah! why should she think I would reproach her? Poor woman, she vastly deceives herself.'

'"See him yourself," said she, "and tell him to beware of M. Colbert."'

'What! she warned me to beware of her lover?'

'I have told you she still loves you.'

'Go on, marquise.'

'"M. Colbert," she added, "came to me two hours ago, to inform me he was appointed intendant."'

'I have already told you, marquise, that M. Colbert would only be the more in my power for that.'

'Yes, but that is not all: Marguerite is intimate, as you know, with Madame d'Eymeris and Madame Lyodot.'

'I know.'

'Well, M. Colbert put many questions to her, relative to the fortunes of those two gentlemen, and as to the devotion they had for you.'

'Oh, as to those two, I can answer for them; they must be killed before they will cease to be mine.'

'Then, as Madame Vanel was obliged to quit M. Colbert for an instant to receive a visitor, and as M. Colbert is industrious, scarcely was the new intendant left alone, before he took a pencil from his pocket, and, as there was paper on the table, began to make notes.'

'Notes concerning D'Eymeris and Lyodot?'

'Exactly.'

'I should like to know what those notes were about.'

'And that is just what I have brought you.'

'Madame Vanel has taken Colbert's notes and sent them to me?'

'No; but by a lucky chance, almost a miracle, she has a duplicate of those notes.'

'How could she get that?'

'Listen; I told you that Colbert found paper on the table.'

'Yes.'

'That he took a pencil from his pocket.'

'Yes.'

'And wrote upon that paper.'

'Yes.'

'Well, this pencil was a lead pencil, consequently hard; so, it marked in black upon the first sheet, and left an imprint upon the second.'

'Go on.'

'Colbert, when tearing off the first sheet, took no notice of the second.'

'Well?'

'Well, on the second was to be read what had been written on the first; Madame Vanel read it, and sent for me.'

'Yes, yes.'

'Then, when she was assured I was your devoted friend, she gave me the paper, and told me the secret of this house.'

'And this paper?' said Fouquet, in some degree of agitation.

'Here it is, monsieur—read it,' said the marquise.

Fouquet read:

'Names of the tax-farmers to be condemned by the Court of Justice: D'Eymeris, friend of M. F.; Lyodot, friend of M. F.; De Vanin, indif.'*

'D'Eymeris and Lyodot!' cried Fouquet, reading the paper eagerly again.

'Friends of M. F.,' pointed the marquise with her finger.

'But what is the meaning of these words: "To be condemned by the Court of Justice?"'

'Why!' said the marquise, 'it is clear enough, I think. Besides, that is not all. Read on, read on;' and Fouquet continued, 'The two first to death, the third to be dismissed, with MM. d'Hautemont and de la Vallette,* who will only have their property confiscated.'

'Great God!' cried Fouquet, 'to death, to death! Lyodot and D'Eymeris! But even if the Court should condemn them to death, the king will never ratify their condemnation, and they cannot be executed without the king's signature.'

'The king has made M. Colbert intendant.'

'Oh!' cried Fouquet, as if he caught a glimpse of the abyss that yawned beneath his feet, 'impossible! impossible! But who traced a pencil over the marks made by Colbert?'

'I did. I was afraid the first would be effaced.'

'Oh! I will know all.'

'You will know nothing, monsieur; you despise your enemy too much for that.'

'Pardon me, my dear marquise; excuse me; yes, M. Colbert is my enemy, I believe him to be so; yes, M. Colbert is a man to be feared, I admit. But I! I have time, and as you are here, as you have assured me of your devotion, as you have allowed me to hope for your love, as we are alone——'

'I came here to save you, Monsieur Fouquet, and not to ruin myself,' said the marquise, rising—'therefore, beware!——'

'Marquise, in truth you terrify yourself too much at least, unless this terror is but a pretext——'

'He is very, very deep, this M. Colbert: beware!'

Fouquet, in his turn, drew himself up. 'And I?' asked he.

'And you, you have only a noble heart. Beware! beware!'

'So?'

'I have done what was right, my friend, at the risk of my reputation. Adieu!'

'Not adieu, *au revoir!*'

'Perhaps,' said the marquise, giving her hand to Fouquet to kiss, and walking towards the door with so firm a step, that he did not dare to bar her passage. As to Fouquet, he retraced, with his head hanging and a fixed cloud on his brow, the path of the subterranean passage along which ran the metal wires that communicated from one house to the other, transmitting, through two mirrors, the wishes and signals of hidden correspondents.

LV

THE ABBÉ FOUQUET

FOUQUET hastened back to his apartment by the subterranean passage, and immediately closed the mirror with the spring. He was scarcely in his closet, when he heard some one knocking violently at the door, and a well-known voice crying: 'Open the door, monseigneur, I entreat you open the door!' Fouquet quickly restored a little order to everything that might have revealed either his absence or his agitation: he spread his papers over the desk, took up a pen, and, to gain time, said, through the closed door, 'Who is there?'

'What, monseigneur, do you not know me?' replied the voice.

'Yes, yes,' said Fouquet to himself, 'yes, my friend, I know you well enough.' And then, aloud: 'Is it not Gourville?'*

'Why, yes, monseigneur.'

Fouquet arose, cast a last look at one of the mirrors, went to the door, pushed back the bolt, and Gourville entered. 'Ah, monseigneur? monseigneur?' cried he, 'what cruelty!'

'In what?'

'I have been a quarter of an hour imploring you to open the door and you would not even answer me.'

'Once for all, you know that I will not be disturbed when I am busy. Now, although I might make you an exception, Gourville, I insist upon my orders being respected by others.'

'Monseigneur, at this moment, orders, doors, bolts, locks, and walls, I could have broken, forced and overthrown!'

'Ah! ah! it relates to some great event, then?' asked Fouquet.

'Oh! I assure you it does, monseigneur,' replied Gourville.

'And what is this event?' said Fouquet, a little troubled by the evident agitation of his most intimate confidant.

'There is a secret court of justice instituted, monseigneur.'

'I know there is, but do the members meet, Gourville?'

'They not only meet, but they have passed a sentence, monseigneur.'

'A sentence?' said the superintendent, with a shudder and pallor he could not conceal. 'A sentence!—and on whom?'

'Two of your best friends.'

'Lyodot and D'Eymeris, do you mean? But what sort of a sentence?'

'Sentence of death.'

'Passed? Oh! you must be mistaken, Gourville; that is impossible.'

'Here is a copy of the sentence which the king is to sign to-day, if he has not already signed it.'

Fouquet seized the paper eagerly, read it, and returned it to Gourville. 'The king will never sign that,' said he.

Gourville shook his head.

'Monseigneur, M. Colbert is a bold councillor: do not be too confident!'

'Monsieur Colbert again!' cried Fouquet. 'How is it that that name rises upon all occasions to torment my ears, during the last two or three days? You make so trifling a subject of too much importance, Gourville. Let M. Colbert appear, I will face him; let him raise his head, I will crush him; but you understand, there must be a weak spot upon which my look may fall, there must be a surface upon which my feet may be placed.'

'Patience, monseigneur; for you do not know what Colbert is—study him quickly; it is with this dark financier as it is with meteors,* which the eye never sees completely before their disastrous invasion; when we feel them we are dead.'

'Oh! Gourville, this is going too far,' replied Fouquet, smiling; 'allow me, my friend, not to be so easily frightened; M. Colbert a meteor! Take my word, we shall confront the meteor. Let us see deeds, and not words. What has he done?'

'He has ordered two gibbets of the executioner of Paris,'* answered Gourville.

Fouquet raised his head, and a flash gleamed from his eyes. 'Are you sure of what you say?' cried he.

'Here is the proof, monseigneur.' And Gourville held out to the superintendent a note communicated by a certain secretary of the Hôtel de Ville,* who was one of Fouquet's creatures.

'Yes, that is true,' murmured the minister; 'the scaffold may be prepared, but the king has not signed; Gourville, the king will not sign.'

'I shall soon know,' said Gourville.

'How?'

'If the king has signed, the gibbets will be sent this evening to the Hôtel de Ville, in order to be got up and ready by to-morrow morning.'

'Oh! no, no!' cried the superintendent, once again; 'you are all deceived, and deceive me in my turn; Lyodot came to see me only the day before yesterday; only three days ago I received a gift of some Syracuse wine from poor D'Eymeris.'

'What does that prove?' replied Gourville, 'except that the court of justice has been secretly assembled, has deliberated in the absence of the accused, and that the whole proceeding was complete when they were arrested.'

'What! are they, then, arrested?'

'They are.'

'But where, when, and how have they been arrested?'

'Lyodot, yesterday at daybreak; D'Eymeris, the day before yesterday, in the evening, as he was returning from the house of his mistress; their disappearance was noticed by nobody; but at length M. Colbert all at once raised the mask, and caused the affair to be published; it is being cried with the sound of the trumpet, at this moment in Paris, and, in truth, monseigneur, there is scarcely anybody but yourself who is ignorant of the event.'

Fouquet began to walk about his chamber with an uneasiness that became more and more serious.

'What do you resolve, monseigneur?' said Gourville.

'If it really were as you say, I would go to the king,' cried Fouquet. 'But as I go to the Louvre, I will pass by the Hôtel de Ville. We shall see if the sentence is signed.'

'Incredulity! thou art the pest of all great minds,' said Gourville, shrugging his shoulders.

'Gourville!'

'Yes,' continued he, 'and incredulity! thou ruinest, as contagion destroys the most robust health; that is to say, in an instant.'

'Let us go,' cried Fouquet; 'order the door to be opened, Gourville.'

'Be cautious,' said the latter, 'the Abbé Fouquet is there.'

'Ah! my brother,'* replied Fouquet, in a tone of annoyance; 'he is there, is he? he knows all the ill news, then, and is rejoiced to bring it to me, as usual. The devil! if my brother is there, my affairs are bad, Gourville; why did you not tell me so sooner, I should have been the more readily convinced.'

'Monseigneur slanders him,' said Gourville, laughing; 'if he is come, it is not with a bad intention.'

'What, do you excuse him?' cried Fouquet; 'a fellow without a heart, without ideas; a devourer of wealth.'

'He knows you are rich.'

'And would ruin me.'

'No, but he would like to have your purse. That is all.'

'Enough! enough! A hundred thousand crowns per month, during two years. God's blood! it is I that pay, Gourville, and I know my figures.' Gourville, laughed in a silent, sly manner.

'Yes, yes, you mean to say it is the king who pays,' said the superintendent. 'Ah, Gourville, that is a vile joke; this is not the place.'

'Monseigneur, do not be angry.'

'Well, then, send the Abbé Fouquet away, I have not a sou.' Gourville made a step towards the door. 'He has been a month without seeing me,' continued Fouquet, 'why could he not be *two* months?'

'Because he repents of living in bad company,' said Gourville, 'and prefers you to all his bandits.'

'Thanks for the preference! You make a strange advocate, Gourville, to-day—the advocate of the Abbé Fouquet!'

'Eh! but everything and every man has a good side—their useful side, monseigneur.'

'The bandits whom the abbé keeps in pay and drink have their useful side, have they? Prove that, if you please.'

'Let the circumstance arise, monseigneur, and you will be very glad to have those bandits under your hand.'

'You advise me, then, to be reconciled to the abbé?' said Fouquet, ironically.

'I advise you, monseigneur, not to quarrel with a hundred or a hundred and twenty loose fellows, who, by putting their rapiers end to end, would form a cordon of steel capable of surrounding three thousand men.'

Fouquet darted a searching glance at Gourville, and passing ahead of him, 'That is all very well; let M. l'Abbé Fouquet be introduced,' said he to the footman. 'You are right, Gourville.'

Two minutes after, the Abbé Fouquet appeared in the doorway, with profound reverences. He was a man of from forty to forty-five years of age, half churchman half soldier—a hired assassin grafted onto an abbé; if you saw him without a sword by his side, you might be sure he had pistols. Fouquet saluted him more as an elder brother than as a minister.

'What can I do to serve you, monsieur l'abbé?' said he.

'Oh! oh! how coldly you speak to me, brother!'

'I speak like a man who is in a hurry, monsieur.'

The abbé looked slyly at Gourville, and anxiously at Fouquet, and said, 'I have three hundred pistoles to pay to M. de Bregi* this evening. A gambling debt, a sacred debt.'

'What more?' said Fouquet bravely, for he comprehended that the Abbé Fouquet would not have disturbed him for such a want.

'A thousand to my butcher, who will supply no more meat.'

'And?'

'Twelve hundred to my tailor,' continued the abbé; 'the fellow has made me take back seven of my servants' suits, which compromises my liveries, and my mistress talks of replacing me by a tax-farmer, which would be a humiliation for the church.'

'What else?' said Fouquet.

'You will please take note,' said the abbé, humbly, 'that I have asked nothing for myself.'

'That is delicate, monsieur,' replied Fouquet; 'so, as you see, I wait.'

'And I ask nothing, oh! no—it is not for want of need though, I assure you.'

The minister reflected a minute. 'Twelve hundred pistoles to the tailor; that seems a great deal for clothes,' said he.

'I maintain a hundred men,' said the abbé, proudly; 'that is a charge, I believe.'

'Why a hundred men?' said Fouquet. 'Are you a Richelieu or a Mazarin, to require a hundred men as a guard? What use do you make of these men?—speak.'

'And do you ask me that?' cried the Abbé Fouquet; 'ah! how can you put such aquestion—why I maintain a hundred men? Ah!'

'Why, yes, I do put that question to you. What have you to do with a hundred men?—answer.'

'Ingrate!' continued the abbé, more and more affected.

'Explain yourself.'

'Why, monsieur the superintendent, I only need one *valet de chambre*, for myself, and even if I were alone, could manage very well; but you, you who have so many enemies—a hundred men are not enough for me to defend you with. A hundred men!— you ought to have ten thousand. I maintain these men so that in public places, in assemblies, no voice may be raised against you; and without them, monsieur, you would be loaded with imprecations, you would be torn to pieces, you would not last a week; no, not a week, do you understand?'

'Ah! I did not know you were my champion to such an extent, monsieur l'abbé.'

'You doubt it?' cried the abbé. 'Listen, then, to what happened, no longer ago than yesterday, in the Rue de la Huchette.* A man was bargaining for a fowl.'

'Well, how could that injure me, abbé?'

'This way. The fowl was not fat. The purchaser refused to give eighteen sous for it, saying that he could not afford eighteen sous for the skin of a fowl from which M. Fouquet had sucked all the fat.'

'Go on.'

'The joke caused a deal of laughter,' continued the abbé; 'laughter at your expense, death to the devils! and the common people were delighted. The joker added, "Give me a fowl fed by M. Colbert, if you like! and I will pay all you ask." And immediately there was a clapping of hands. A frightful scandal! you understand; a scandal which forces a brother to hide his face.'

Fouquet coloured. 'And you hid it?' said the superintendent.

'No, for it so happened I had one of my men in the crowd; a new recruit from the provinces, one M. Menneville, whom I like very much. He made his way through the press, saying to the joker: "Hey, you scurvy joker, here's a thrust for Colbert!" "And one for Fouquet," replied the joker. Upon which they drew in front of the cook's shop, with a hedge of the curious round them, and five hundred as curious at the windows.'

'Well?' said Fouquet.

'Well, monsieur, my Menneville spitted the joker, to the great astonishment of the spectators, and said to the cook: "Take this goose, my friend, it is fatter than your fowl." That is the way, monsieur,' ended the abbé, triumphantly, 'in which I spend my revenues; I maintain the honour of the family, monsieur.' Fouquet hung his head. 'And I have a hundred as good as he,' continued the abbé.

'Very well,' said Fouquet, 'give the account to Gourville, and remain here this evening.'

'Shall we have supper?'

'Yes, there will be supper.'

'But your cashier's office is closed.'

'Gourville will open it for you. Leave us, monsieur l'abbé, leave us.'

'Then we are friends?' said the abbé, with a bow.

'Oh, yes, friends. Come, Gourville.'

'Are you going out? You will not stay to supper, then?'

'I shall be back in an hour; rest easy, abbé.' Then aside to Gourville—'Let my English horses be harnessed,' said he, 'and direct the coachman to stop at the Hôtel de Ville in Paris.'

LVI

M. DE LA FONTAINE'S WINE

CARRIAGES were already bringing the guests of Fouquet to Saint-Mandé; already the whole house was getting warm with the preparations for supper, when the superintendent launched his fleet horses upon the road to Paris, and going by the quays, in order to meet fewer people on the way, soon reached the Hôtel de Ville. It wanted a quarter to eight. Fouquet alighted at the corner of the Rue de Long-Pont,* and, on foot, directed his course towards the Place de Grève, accompanied by Gourville. As they passed the Place, they saw a man dressed in black and purple, of dignified mien, who was preparing to get into a hired carriage, and told the coachman to drive to Vincennes. He had before him a large hamper filled with bottles, which he had just purchased at the tavern with the sign of Our Lady.

'Eh, but! that is Vatel!* my major-domo!' said Fouquet to Gourville.

'Yes, monseigneur,' replied the latter.

'What can he have been doing at that tavern?'

'Buying wine, no doubt.'

'What! but wine for me, at a tavern?' said Fouquet. 'My cellar then must be in a miserable condition!' and he advanced towards the major-domo, who was arranging his bottles in the carriage, with the most minute care.

'Holà! Vatel,' said he, in the voice of a master.

'Take care, monseigneur!' said Gourville, 'you will be recognized.'

'What does it matter?—Vatel!'

The man dressed in black and purple turned round. He had a good and mild countenance, without expression—a mathematician minus the pride. A certain fire sparkled in the eyes of this personage, a rather sly smile played round his lips; but the observer might soon have remarked that the fire and the smile meant nothing, signified nothing. Vatel laughed like an absent man, and amused himself like a child. At the sound of his master's voice he turned round, exclaiming: 'Oh! monseigneur!'

'Yes, it is I. What the devil are you doing here, Vatel? Wine! You are buying wine at a tavern in the Place de Grève!'

'But, monseigneur,' said Vatel, quietly, after having darted a hostile glance at Gourville, 'why am I interfered with here? Is my cellar kept in bad order?'

'No, Vatel, no; but——'

'But what?' replied Vatel. Gourville touched Fouquet's elbow.

'Don't be angry, Vatel; I thought my cellar—your cellar—sufficiently well stocked for us to be able to dispense with recourse to that of Our Lady's tavern.'

'Eh, monsieur,' said Vatel, shrinking from monseigneur to monsieur with a degree of disdain: 'your cellar is so well stocked that when certain of your guests dine with you they have nothing to drink.'

Fouquet, in great surprise, looked at Gourville. 'What do you mean by that?'

'I mean that your butler had not wine for all tastes, monsieur; and that M. de la Fontaine, M. Pellisson, and M. Conrart,* do not drink when they come to the house—these gentleman do not like strong wine. What is to be done, then?'

'Well, and therefore?'

'Well, then, I have found here a *vin de Joigny*,* which they like. I know they come once a week to drink here. That is the reason I am making this provision.'

Fouquet had no more to say, he was convinced. Vatel, on his part, had much more to say, without doubt, and it was plain he was getting warm. 'It is just as if you would reproach me, monseigneur, for going to the Rue Planche-Mibray* myself to fetch the cider M. Loret drinks when he comes to dine at your house.'

'Loret drinks cider at my house!' cried Fouquet, laughing.

'Certainly he does, monsieur, and that is the reason why he dines there with pleasure.'

'Vatel,' cried Fouquet, pressing the hand of his major-domo, 'you are a man! I thank you, Vatel, for having understood that at my house M. de la Fontaine, M. Conrart, and M. Loret, are as great as dukes and peers, as great as princes, greater than myself. Vatel, you are a good servant, and I double your salary.'

Vatel did not even thank his master, he merely shrugged his shoulders a little, murmuring this proud sentiment: 'To be thanked for having done one's duty is humiliating.'

'He is right,' said Gourville, as he drew Fouquet's attention, by a gesture, to another point. He showed him a low-built tumbrel, drawn by two horses, upon which rocked two strong gibbets, bound together, back to back, by chains, whilst an archer, seated upon the cross-beam, suffered, as well as he could, with his head cast down, the comments of a hundred vagabonds, who guessed the destination of the gibbets, and were escorting them to the Hôtel de Ville. Fouquet started. 'It is decided, you see,' said Gourville.

'But it is not done,' replied Fouquet.

'Oh, do not flatter yourself, monseigneur; if they have thus lulled your friendship and suspicions—if things have gone so far, you will be able to undo nothing.'

'But I have not given my sanction.'

'M. de Lyonne has ratified for you.'

'I will go to the Louvre.'

'Oh, no, you will not.'

'Would you advise such baseness?' cried Fouquet, 'would you advise me to abandon my friends? would you advise me, whilst able to fight, to throw the arms I hold in my hand to the ground?'

'I do not advise you to do anything of the kind, monseigneur. Are you in a position to quit the post of superintendent at this moment?'

'No.'

'Well, if the king wishes to displace you——'

'He will displace me absent as well as present.'

'Yes, but you will not have insulted him.'

'Yes, but I shall have been base; now I am not willing that my friends should die; and they shall *not* die!'

'For that it is necessary you should go to the Louvre, is it?'

'Gourville!'

'Beware! once at the Louvre, you will be forced to defend your friends openly, that is to say, to make a profession of faith; or you will be forced to abandon them irrevocably.'

'Never!'

'Pardon me; the king will propose the alternative to you, rigorously, or else you will propose it to him yourself.'

'That is true.'

'That is the reason why conflict must be avoided. Let us return to Saint-Mandé, monseigneur.'

'Gourville, I will not stir from this place, where the crime is to be carried out, where my disgrace is to be accomplished; I will not stir, I say, till I have found some means of combating my enemies.'

'Monseigneur,' replied Gourville, 'you would excite my pity if I did not know you for one of the great minds of this world. You possess a hundred and fifty millions, you are equal to the king in position, and a hundred and fifty millions his superior in money. M. Colbert did even have the wit to have the will of Mazarin accepted. Now, when a man is the richest person in a kingdom, and will take the trouble to spend the money, if things are done he does not like, it is because he is a poor man. Let us return to Saint-Mandé, I say.'

'To consult with Pellisson?—we will.'

'No, monseigneur, to count your money.'

'So be it,' said Fouquet, with angry eyes; 'yes, yes, to Saint-Mandé!' He got into his carriage again, and Gourville with him. Upon their road, at the end of the Faubourg Saint-Antoine, they overtook the humble carriage of Vatel, who was quietly conveying home his *vin de Joigny*. The black horses, going at a swift pace, alarmed, as they passed, the timid hack of the major-domo, who, putting his head out at the window, cried, in a fright, 'Take care of my bottles!'

LVII

THE GALLERY OF SAINT-MANDÉ

FIFTY persons were waiting for the superintendent. He did not even take the time to place himself in the hands of his *valet de chambre* for a minute, but on arrival went straight into the principal drawing-room. There his friends were assembled in full chat. Supper was about to be served, but, above all, the Abbé Fouquet watched for the return of his brother, and was endeavouring to do the honours of the house in his absence. Upon the arrival of the superintendent, a murmur of joy and affection was heard; Fouquet, full of affability, good humour, and munificence, was beloved by his poets, his artists, and his men of business. His brow, upon which his little court read, as upon that of a god, all the movements of his soul, and thence drew rules of conduct—his brow, upon which affairs of state never impressed a wrinkle, was this evening paler than usual, and more than one friendly eye remarked that pallor. Fouquet placed himself at the head of the table, and presided gaily during supper. He recounted Vatel's secret mission to La Fontaine, he related the history of Menneville and the skinny fowl to Pellisson, in such a manner that all the table heard it. A tempest of laughter and jokes ensued, which was only checked by a serious and even melancholy gesture from Pellisson. The Abbé Fouquet, not being able to comprehend why his brother should have led the conversation in that direction, listened with all his ears, and sought in the countenance of Gourville, or in that of his brother, an explanation which nothing afforded him. Pellisson took up the matter: 'Did they mention M. Colbert, then?' said he.

'Why not?' replied Fouquet; 'if true, as it is said to be, that the king has made him his intendant?' Scarcely had Fouquet uttered these words, with a marked intention, than an explosion broke forth among the guests.

'The miser!' said one.

'The miserable little cur!' said another.

'The hypocrite!' said a third.

Pellisson exchanged a meaning look with Fouquet. 'Messieurs,' said he, 'in truth we are abusing a man whom no one knows: it is neither charitable nor reasonable; and here is monsieur le surintendant, who, I am sure, agrees with me.'

'Entirely,' replied Fouquet. 'Let Colbert's fat fowls alone; our business to-day is with the stuffed pheasants of M. Vatel.' This speech stopped the dark cloud which was beginning to throw its shade over the guests. Gourville succeeded so well in animating the poets with the *vin de Joigny*; the abbé, intelligent as a man who stands in need of his host's money, so enlivened the financiers and the noble lords, that, amidst the vapours of this joy and the noise of conversation, anxieties disappeared completely. The will of Cardinal Mazarin was the subject of the conversation at the second course and dessert; then Fouquet ordered bowls of sweetmeats and fountains of liquors to be carried into the salon adjoining the gallery. He led the way thither, conducting by the hand a lady, elected queen of the hour by his preference. The musicians then supped, and the promenades in the gallery and the gardens commenced, beneath a spring sky, mild and flower-scented. Pellisson then approached the superintendent, and said: 'Something troubles monseigneur?'

'Greatly,' replied the minister; 'ask Gourville to tell you what it is.' Pellisson, on turning round, found La Fontaine treading upon his heels. He was obliged to listen to a Latin verse, which the poet had composed upon Vatel.* La Fontaine had, for an hour, been scanning this verse in every corner, seeking some one to pour it out on advantageously. He thought he had caught Pellisson, but the latter escaped him; he turned towards Sorel,* who had, himself, just composed a quatrain in honour of the supper, and the Amphitryon.* La Fontaine in vain endeavoured to gain attention to his verses; Sorel wanted to obtain a hearing for his quatrain. He was obliged to give way to M. le Comte de Charost,* whose arm Fouquet had just taken. L'Abbé Fouquet perceived that the poet, absent-minded as usual, was about to follow the two talkers; and he interposed. La Fontaine seized upon him, and recited his verses. The abbé, who was quite innocent of Latin, nodded his head, in cadence, at every roll which La Fontaine impressed upon his body, according to the undulations of the dactyls and spondees. While this was going on, behind the confiture-basins, Fouquet related the event of the day to his son-in-law, M. de Charost. 'We will send the idle and useless to look at the fireworks,' said Pellisson to Gourville, 'whilst we converse here.'

'So be it,' said Gourville, addressing four words to Vatel. The latter then led towards the gardens the major part of the beaux, the ladies and the chatterers, whilst the men walked in the gallery, lighted by three hundred wax-lights, in the sight of all; the admirers of fireworks all ran away towards the garden. Gourville approached Fouquet, and said: 'Monsieur, we are here.'

'All?' said Fouquet.

'Yes—count.' The superintendent counted; there were eight persons. Pellisson and Gourville walked arm in arm, as if conversing upon vague and frivolous subjects. Sorel and two officers imitated them, in an opposite direction. The Abbé Fouquet walked alone. Fouquet, with M. de Charost, walked as if entirely absorbed in the conversation of his son-in-law. 'Messieurs,' said he, 'let no one of you raise his head as he walks, or appear to pay attention to me; continue walking, we are alone, listen to me.'

A perfect silence ensued, disturbed only by the distant cries of the joyous guests, from the groves where they watched the fireworks. It was a whimsical spectacle this, of these men walking in groups, as if each one was occupied about something, whilst lending attention really to only one amongst them, who, himself, seemed to be speaking only to his companion. 'Messieurs,' said Fouquet, 'you have, without doubt, remarked the absence of two of my friends this evening, who were with us on Wednesday. For God's sake, abbé, do not stop—it is not necessary to enable you to listen; walk on, carrying your head in a natural way, and as you have good eyes, place yourself at the window, and if any one returns towards the gallery, give us notice by coughing.'

The abbé obeyed.

'I have not observed their absence,' said Pellisson, who, at this moment, was turning his back to Fouquet, and walking the other way.

'I do not see M. Lyodot,' said Sorel, 'who pays me my pension.'*

'And I,' said the abbé, at the window, 'do not see M. d'Eymeris, who owes me eleven hundred livres from our last game of brelan.'*

'Sorel,' continued Fouquet, walking bent, and gloomily, 'you will never receive your pension again from M. Lyodot; and you, abbé, will never be paid your eleven hundred livres by M. d'Eymeris; for both are doomed to die.'

'To die!' exclaimed the whole assembly, stopped in their tracks, in spite of themselves, in the comedy they were playing, by that terrible word.

'Recover yourselves, messieurs,' said Fouquet, 'for perhaps, we are watched—I said: to die!'

'To die!' repeated Pellisson; 'what, the men I saw six days ago, full of health, gaiety, and the spirit of the future! What then is man, good God! that disease should thus bring him down all at once!'

'It is not a disease,' said Fouquet.

'Then there is a remedy,' said Sorel.

'No remedy. Messieurs de Lyodot and D'Eymeris are on the eve of their last day.'

'Of what are these gentlemen dying, then?' asked an officer.

'Ask of him who kills them,' replied Fouquet.

'Who kills them? Are they being killed, then?' cried the terrified chorus.

'They are doing better still; they are hanging them,' murmured Fouquet, in a sinister voice, which sounded like a funeral knell in that rich gallery, splendid with pictures, flowers, velvet, and gold. Involuntarily every one stopped; the abbé quitted his window; the first rockets of the fireworks began to mount above the trees. A prolonged cry from the gardens called the superintendent to enjoy the spectacle. He drew near to a window, and his friends placed themselves behind him, attentive to his least wish.

'Messieurs,' said he, 'M. Colbert has caused to be arrested and tried and will execute my two friends; what does it become me to do?'

'*Mordieu!*' exclaimed the abbé, the first one to speak, 'run M. Colbert through the body.'

'Monseigneur,' said Pellisson, 'you must speak to his majesty.'

'The king, my dear Pellisson, himself signed the order for the execution.'

'Well!' said the Comte de Charost, 'the execution must not take place, then; that is all.'

'Impossible,' said Gourville, 'unless we could bribe the jailers.'

'Or the governor,' said Fouquet.

'This night the prisoners might be allowed to escape.'

'Which of you will take charge of the business?'

'I,' said the abbé, 'will carry the money.'

'And I,' said Pellisson, 'will be the bearer of the words.'

'Words and money,' said Fouquet, 'five hundred thousand livres to the governor of the Conciergerie,* that is sufficient; nevertheless, it shall be a million, if necessary.'

'A million!' cried the abbé; 'why, for less than half, I would have half Paris sacked.'

'There must be no disorder,' said Pellisson. 'The governor being bought, the two prisoners escape; once clear of the fangs of the law, they will call together the enemies of Colbert, and prove to the king that his young justice, like all other monstrosities, is not infallible.'

'Go to Paris, then, Pellisson,' said Fouquet, 'and bring hither the two victims; to-morrow we shall see.'

Gourville gave Pellisson the five hundred thousand livres. 'Take care the wind does not carry you away,' said the abbé; 'what a responsibility. By God! Let me help you a little.'

'Silence!' said Fouquet, 'somebody is coming. Ah! the fireworks are producing a magical effect.' At this moment a shower of sparks fell rustling among the branches of the neighbouring trees. Pellisson and Gourville went out together by the door of the gallery; Fouquet descended to the garden with the five last plotters.

LVIII

EPICUREANS

As Fouquet was giving, or appearing to give, all his attention to the brilliant illuminations, the languishing music of the violins and oboes, the sparkling sheaves of the fireworks, which, inflaming the heavens with glowing reflections, picked out behind the trees the dark profile of the prison of Vincennes; as, we say, the superintendent was smiling on the ladies and the poets, the *fête* was every whit as gay as usual; and Vatel, whose restless, even jealous look, earnestly consulted the expression of Fouquet, did not appear dissatisfied with the welcome given to the ordering of the evening's entertainment. The fireworks over, the company dispersed about the gardens and beneath the marble porticos with the delightful liberty which reveals in the master of the house so much forgetfulness of greatness, so much courteous hospitality, so much magnificent carelessness. The poets wandered about, arm in arm, through the groves; some reclined upon beds of moss, to the great damage of velvet clothes and curled heads, into which little dried leaves and blades of grass insinuated themselves. The ladies, in small numbers, listened to the songs of the singers and the verses of the poets; others listened to the prose, spoken with much art, by men who were neither actors nor poets, but to whom youth and solitude gave an unaccustomed eloquence, which appeared to them better than everything else in the world. 'Why,' said La Fontaine, 'does not our master Epicurus descend into the garden? Epicurus* never abandoned his pupils; the master is wrong.'

'Monsieur,' said Conrart, 'you yourself are in the wrong persisting in decorating yourself with the name of an Epicurean; indeed, nothing here reminds me of the doctrine of the philosopher of Gargettus.'*

'Bah!' said La Fontaine, 'is it not written that Epicurus purchased a large garden and lived in it tranquilly with his friends?'

'That is true.'

'Well, has not M. Fouquet purchased a large garden at

Saint-Mandé, and do we not live here very tranquilly with him and his friends?'

'Yes, no doubt; unfortunately it is neither the garden nor the friends which constitute the resemblance. Now, what likeness is there between the doctrine of Epicurus and that of M. Fouquet?'

'This—pleasure gives happiness.'

'Next?'

'Well, I do not think we ought to consider ourselves unfortunate, for my part, at least. A good repast—*vin de Joigny*, which they have the delicacy to go and fetch for me from my favourite tavern—not one impertinence heard during a supper an hour long, in spite of the presence of ten millionaires and twenty poets.'

'I stop you there. You mentioned *vin de Joigny*, and a good repast; do you persist in that?'

'I persist—*antecho*, as they say at Port Royal.'*

'Then please to recollect that the great Epicurus lived, and made his pupils live, upon bread, vegetables, and water.'

'That is not certain,' said La Fontaine; 'and you appear to me to be confounding Epicurus with Pythagoras, my dear Conrart.'

'Remember, likewise, that the ancient philosopher was rather a bad friend of the gods and the magistrates.'*

'Oh! that is what I will not admit,' replied La Fontaine. 'Epicurus was like M. Fouquet.'

'Do not compare him to monsieur le surintendant,' said Conrart, in an agitated voice, 'or you would accredit the reports which are circulated concerning him and us.'

'What reports?'

'That we are bad Frenchmen, lukewarm with regard to the king, deaf to the law.'*

'I return, then, to my text,' said La Fontaine. 'Listen, Conrart, this is the morality of Epicurus, whom, besides, I consider, if I must tell you so, as a myth. Antiquity is mostly mythical. Jupiter, if we give a little attention to it, is life. Alcides is strength. The words are there to bear me out; Zeus, that is *zen*, to live. Alcides, that is, *alcé*, vigour.* Well, Epicurus, that is mild watchfulness, that is protection; now who watches better over the state, or who protects individuals better than M. Fouquet does?'

'You talk etymology and not morality; I say that we modern Epicureans make poor citizens.'

'Oh!' cried La Fontaine, 'if we become bad citizens, it is not through following the maxims of our master. Listen to one of his principal aphorisms.'

'I will.'

'Pray for good leaders.'

'Well?'

'Well! what does M. Fouquet say to us every day? "When shall we be governed?" Does he say so? Come, Conrart, be frank.'

'He says so, that is true.'

'Well, that is a doctrine of Epicurus.'

'Yes; but that is a little seditious, observe.'

'What! seditious to wish to be governed by good heads or leaders?'

'Certainly, when those who govern are bad.'

'Patience, I have a reply for all.'

'Even for what I have just said to you?'

'Listen! would you submit to those who govern ill? Oh! it is written: *Cacôs politeuousi*.* You grant me the text?'

'By God! I think so. Do you know you speak Greek as well as Aesop* did, my dear La Fontaine.'

'Is there any wickedness in that, my dear Conrart?'

'God forbid I should say so.'

'Then let us return to M. Fouquet. What did he repeat to us all the day? Was it not this? "What a pedant is that Mazarin! what an ass! what a leech! We must, however, submit to the fellow." Now, Conrart, did he say so, or did he not?'

'I confess that he said it, and even perhaps too often.'

'Like Epicurus, my friend, still like Epicurus; I repeat, we are Epicureans, and that is very amusing.'

'Yes; but I am afraid there will rise up, by the side of us, a sect like that of Epictetus;* you know him well; the philosopher of Hierapolis, he who called bread luxury, vegetables prodigality, and clear water drunkenness; he who, being beaten by his master, said to him, grumbling a little it is true, but without being angry. "I will lay a wager you have broken my leg!"—and who won his wager.'

'He was a fool, that fellow Epictetus.'

'Granted, but he might easily become the fashion by only changing his name into that of Colbert.'

'Bah!' replied La Fontaine, 'that is impossible. Never will you find Colbert in Epictetus.'

'You are right, I shall find—*coluber** there, at the most.'

'Ah! you are beaten, Conrart; you are reduced to a play upon words. M. Arnaud pretends that I have no logic; I have more than M. Nicole.'*

'Yes,' replied Conrart, 'you have logic, but you are a Jansenist.'*

This peroration was hailed with a boisterous shout of laughter; by degrees the promenaders had been attracted by the exclamations of the two disputants around the arbour under which they were arguing. The discussion had been religiously listened to, and Fouquet himself, scarcely able to suppress his laughter, had given an example of self-control. But with the climax of the scene he threw off all restraint, and laughed aloud. Everybody laughed as he did, and the two philosophers were saluted with unanimous felicitations. La Fontaine, however, was declared conqueror, on account of his profound erudition and his unchallengeable logic. Conrart obtained the compensation due to an unsuccessful combatant; he was praised for the sincerity of his intentions, and the purity of his conscience.

At the moment when this jollity was manifesting itself by the most lively demonstrations, when the ladies were reproaching the two adversaries with not having admitted women into the system of Epicurean happiness, Gourville was seen hastening from the other end of the garden, approaching Fouquet, and detaching him, by his presence alone, from the group. The superintendent preserved on his face the smile and character of carelessness; but scarcely was he out of sight than he threw off the mask.

'Well!' said he, eagerly, 'where is Pellisson! What is he doing?'

'Pellisson has returned from Paris.'

'Has he brought back the prisoners?'

'He has not even seen the governor of the prison.'

'What! did he not tell him he came from me?'

'He told him so, but the man sent him this reply: "If any one came to me from M. Fouquet, he would have a letter from M. Fouquet."'

'Oh!' cried the latter, 'if a letter is all he wants——'

'It is useless, monsieur!' said Pellisson, showing himself at the corner of the little wood, 'useless! Go yourself, and speak in your own name.'

'You are right. I will go in, as if to work; let the horses remain harnessed, Pellisson. Entertain my friends, Gourville.'

'One last word of advice, monseigneur,' replied the latter.

'Speak, Gourville.'

'Do not go to the governor save at the last minute; it is brave, but it is not wise. Excuse me, Monsieur Pellisson, if I am not of the same opinion as you; but take my advice, monseigneur, send again a message to him——he is a worthy man, but do not carry it yourself.'

'I will think of it,' said Fouquet; 'besides, we have all the night before us.'

'Do not reckon too much on time; were the hours we have twice as many as they are, they would not be too much,' replied Pellisson; 'it is never a fault to arrive too soon.'

'Adieu!' said the superintendent; 'come with me, Pellisson. Gourville, I commend my guests to your care.' And he set off. The Epicureans did not perceive that the head of the school had left them; the violins continued playing all night long.

LIX

A QUARTER OF AN HOUR'S DELAY

FOUQUET, on leaving his house for the second time that day, felt himself less heavy and less disturbed than might have been expected. He turned towards Pellisson, who was meditating in the corner of the carriage some good arguments against the violent proceedings of Colbert.

'My dear Pellisson,' said Fouquet, 'it is a great pity you are not a woman.'

'I think, on the contrary, it is very fortunate,' replied Pellisson, 'for, monseigneur, I am excessively ugly.'*

'Pellisson! Pellisson!' said the superintendent, laughing: 'You repeat too often, you are "ugly", not to leave people to believe that it gives you much pain.'

'In fact it does, monseigneur, much pain; there is no man more unfortunate than I: I was handsome, the small-pox rendered me hideous; I am deprived of a great means of attraction; now, I am your principal clerk, or something of that sort; I take great interest in your affairs, and if, at this moment, I were a pretty woman, I could render you an important service.'

'What?'

'I would go and find the governor of the Palais.* I would seduce him, for he is a gallant man, extravagantly partial to women; then I would get away our two prisoners.'

'I hope to be able to do so myself, although I am not a pretty woman,' replied Fouquet.

'Granted, monseigneur; but you are compromising yourself very much.'

'Oh!' cried Fouquet, suddenly, with one of those secret transports which the generous blood of youth, or the remembrance of some sweet emotion, infuses into the heart. 'Oh! I know a woman who will enact the personage we stand in need of, with the lieutenant-governor of the Conciergerie.'

'And, on my part, I know fifty, monseigneur; fifty trumpets, which will inform the universe of your generosity, of your devotion to your friends, and, consequently, will ruin you sooner or later in ruining themselves.'

'I do not speak of such women, Pellisson; I speak of a noble and beautiful creature who combines the intelligence and wit of her sex with the valour and coolness of ours; I speak of a woman, handsome enough to make the walls of a prison bow down to salute her, discreet enough to let no one suspect by whom she has been sent.'

'A treasure!' said Pellisson; 'you would make a famous present to monsieur the governor of the Conciergerie! By God! monseigneur, he might have his head cut off; but he would, before dying, have had such happiness as no man had enjoyed before him.'

'And I add,' said Fouquet, 'that the governor of the Palais would not have his head cut off, for he would get from me horses, to effect his escape, and five hundred thousand livres wherewith to live comfortably in England: I add, that this lady, my friend, would give him nothing but the horses and the money. Let us go and seek her, Pellisson.'

The superintendent reached forth his hand towards the gold and silken cord* placed in the interior of his carriage, but Pellisson stopped him. 'Monseigneur,' said he, 'you are going to waste as much time in seeking this lady as Columbus took to discover the new world. Now, we have but two hours in which we can possibly succeed; the governor once gone to bed, how shall we get at him without making a disturbance? When daylight dawns, how can we conceal our proceedings? Go, go yourself, monseigneur, and do not seek either woman or angel tonight.'

'But, my dear Pellisson, here we are before her door.'

'What! before the angel's door?'

'Why, yes!'

'This is the hotel of Madame de Bellière!'

'Hush!'

'Ah! Good Lord!' exclaimed Pellisson.

'What have you to say against her?'

'Nothing, alas! and it is that which causes my despair. Nothing, absolutely nothing. Why can I not, on the contrary, say ill enough of her to prevent your going to her?'

But Fouquet had already given orders to stop, and the carriage was motionless. 'Prevent me!' cried Fouquet; 'why, no power on earth should prevent my going to pay my compliments to Madame de Plessis-Bellière; besides, who knows that we shall not stand in need of her!'

'No, monseigneur, no!'

'But I do not wish you to wait for me, Pellisson,' replied Fouquet, sincerely courteous.

'The more reason I should, monseigneur; knowing that you are keeping me waiting, you will, perhaps, stay a shorter time. Take care! You see there is a carriage in the courtyard: she has some one with her.' Fouquet leant towards the steps of the carriage. 'One word more,' cried Pellisson; 'do not go to this lady till you have been to the governor, for Heaven's sake!'

'Eh! five minutes, Pellisson,' replied Fouquet, alighting at the steps of the hotel, leaving Pellisson in the carriage, in a very ill humour. Fouquet ran upstairs, gave his name to the footman, which excited an eagerness and a respect that showed the habit the mistress of the house had of honouring that name in her family. 'Monsieur le surintendant,' cried the marquise, advancing, very pale, to meet him; 'what an honour! what an unexpected pleasure!' said she. Then, in a low voice, 'Take care!' added the marquise, 'Marguerite Vanel is here!'

'Madame,' replied Fouquet, rather agitated, 'I came on business. One single word, and quickly, if you please!' And he entered the salon. Madame Vanel had risen, paler, more livid, than Envy herself. Fouquet in vain addressed her, with the most agreeable, most pacific salutation; she only replied by a terrible glance darted at the marquise and Fouquet. This keen glance of a jealous woman is a stiletto which pierces every cuirass; Marguerite Vanel plunged it straight into the hearts of the two confidants. She dropped a curtsy to *her friend*, a more profound one to Fouquet, and took leave, under pretence of having a number of visits to make, without the marquise trying to prevent her, or Fouquet, a prey to anxiety, thinking further about her. She was scarcely out of the room, and Fouquet left alone with the marquise, before he threw himself on his knees, without saying a word. 'I expected you,' said the marquise, with a tender sigh.

'Oh! no,' cried he, 'or you would have sent away that woman.'

'She has been here little more than half an hour, and I had no expectation she would come this evening.'

'You love me just a little, then, marquise?'

'That is not the question, now; it is of your danger; how are your affairs going on?'

'I am going this evening to get my friends out of the prisons of the Palais.'

'How will you do that?'

'By buying and bribing the governor.'

'He is a friend of mine; can I assist you, without injuring you?'

'Oh! marquise, it would be a signal service; but how can you be employed without your being compromised? Now, never shall my life, my power, or even my liberty, be purchased at the expense of a single tear from your eyes, or of one frown of pain upon your brow.'

'Monseigneur, no more such words, they bewilder me; I have been culpable in trying to serve you, without calculating the extent of what I was doing. I love you in reality, as a tender friend, and as a friend, I am grateful for your delicate attentions—but, alas!—alas! you will never find a mistress in me.'

'Marquise!' cried Fouquet, in a tone of despair; 'why not?'

'Because you are too much beloved,' said the young woman, in a low voice; 'because you are too much beloved by too many people—because the splendour of glory and fortune wound my eyes, whilst the darkness of sorrow attracts them; because, in short, I, who have rejected you in your proud magnificence; I who scarcely looked at you in your splendour, I came, like a mad woman, to throw myself, as it were, into your arms, when I saw misfortune hovering over your head. You understand me, now, monseigneur? Become happy again, that I may remain chaste in heart and in thought: your misfortune means my ruin.'

'Oh! madame,' said Fouquet, with an emotion he had never before felt; 'were I to fall to the lowest degree of human misery, and hear from your mouth that word which you now refuse me, that day, madame, you will be mistaken in your noble pride; that day you will fancy you are consoling the most unfortunate of men, and you will have said "I love you" to the most illustrious, the most ecstatic, the most triumphant of the happy beings of this world.'

He was still at her feet, kissing her hand, when Pellisson entered precipitately, crying, in very ill humour, 'Monseigneur! madame! for Heaven's sake! excuse me. Monseigneur, you have been here half an hour. Oh! do not both look at me so reproachfully. Madame, pray who is that lady who left your house soon after monseigneur came in?'

'Madame Vanel,' said Fouquet.

'Ha!' cried Pellisson 'I knew it.'

'Well! what then?'

'Why, she got into her carriage, looking deadly pale.'

'What consequence is that to me?'

'Yes, but what she said to her coachman is of consequence to you.'

'Kind Heaven!' cried the marquise, 'what was that?'

'To M. Colbert's!' said Pellisson, in a hoarse voice.

'Great God!—begone, begone, monseigneur!' replied the

marquise, pushing Fouquet out of the salon, whilst Pellisson dragged him by the hand.

'Am I, then, indeed,' said the superintendent, 'become a child, to be frightened by a shadow?'

'You are a giant,' said the marquise, 'whom a viper is trying to bite in the heel.'

Pellisson continued to drag Fouquet to the carriage. 'To the Palais at full speed!' cried Pellisson to the coachman. The horses set off like lightning; no obstacle relaxed their pace for an instant. But, at the arcade Saint-Jean,* as they were coming out upon the Place de Grève, a long file of horsemen, barring the narrow passage, stopped the carriage of the superintendent. There was no means of forcing this barrier; it was necessary to wait till the mounted archers of the watch, for it was they who stopped the way, had passed with the heavy carriage they were escorting, and which ascended rapidly towards the Place Baudoyer. Fouquet and Pellisson took no further account of this circumstance beyond deploring the minute's delay they had thus to submit to. They entered the habitation of the governor of the Palais five minutes after. That officer was still walking about in the front court. At the name of Fouquet, whispered in his ear by Pellisson, the governor eagerly approached the carriage, and, hat in his hand, was profuse in his attentions. 'What an honour for me, monseigneur,' said he.

'One word, monsieur le gouverneur, will you take the trouble to get into my carriage?' The officer placed himself opposite Fouquet in the coach.

'Monsieur,' said Fouquet, 'I have a service to ask of you.'

'Speak, monseigneur.'

'A service that will be compromising for you, monsieur, but which will assure to you forever my protection and my friendship.'

'Were it to cast myself into the fire for you, monseigneur, I would do it.'

'That is well,' said Fouquet; 'what I require is much more simple.'

'That being so, monseigneur, what is it?'

'To conduct me to the chamber of Messieurs Lyodot and D'Eymeris.'

'Will monseigneur have the kindness to say for what purpose?'

'I will tell you in their presence, monsieur; at the same time that I will give you ample means of easing the consequences of their escape.'

'Escape! Why, then, monseigneur does not know?'

'What?'

'That Messrs. Lyodot and D'Eymeris are no longer here.'

'Since when?' cried Fouquet, in great agitation.

'About a quarter of an hour.'

'Whither have they gone, then?'

'To Vincennes—to the prison.'

'Who took them from here?'

'An order from the king.'

'Oh! damn! damn!' exclaimed Fouquet, striking his forehead. 'Damn!' and without saying a single word more to the governor, he threw himself back in his carriage, despair in his heart, and death on his face.

'Well!' said Pellisson, with great anxiety.

'Our friends are lost. Colbert is conveying them to Vincennes. They crossed our very path under the arcade Saint-Jean.'

Pellisson, struck as by a thunderbolt, made no reply. With a single reproach he would have killed his master. 'Where is monseigneur going?' said the footman.

'Home—to Paris. You, Pellisson, return to Saint-Mandé, and bring the Abbé Fouquet to me within an hour. Begone!'

LX

PLAN OF BATTLE

THE night was already far advanced when the Abbé Fouquet joined his brother. Gourville had accompanied him. These three men, pale with dread of future events, resembled less three powers of the day than three conspirators, united by one single thought of violence. Fouquet walked for a long time, with his eyes fixed upon the floor, striking his hands one against the other. At length, taking courage, in the midst of a deep sigh:

'Abbé,' said he, 'you were speaking to me only to-day of a certain body of men you maintain!'

'Yes, monsieur,' replied the abbé.

'Tell me precisely who are these men?' The abbé hesitated.

'Come! no fear, I am not threatening you; tell me straight, for I am not joking.'

'Since you demand the truth, monseigneur, here it is:—I have a hundred and twenty friends or companions of pleasure, who are pledged to me as the thief is to the gallows.'

'And you think you can depend upon them?'

'Entirely.'

'And you will not compromise yourself?'

'My name will not even be mentioned.'

'And are they men of resolution?'

'They would burn Paris, if I promised them they should not be burnt in turn.'

'The thing I ask of you, abbé,' said Fouquet, wiping the sweat which fell from his brow, 'is to loose your hundred and twenty men upon the people I will point out to you, at a certain moment given—is it possible?'

'It will not be the first time such a thing has happened to them, monseigneur.'

'That is well: but would these bandits attack an armed force?'

'They are used to that.'

'Then get your hundred and twenty men together, abbé.'

'Directly. But where?'

'On the road to Vincennes, to-morrow, at two o'clock precisely.'

'To carry off Lyodot and D'Eymeris? There will be cut and thrust!'

'No doubt; are you afraid?'

'Not for myself, but for you.'

'Your men will know, then, what they have to do!'

'They are too intelligent not to guess. Now, a minister who organizes a fray against his king—exposes himself——'

'Of what importance is that to you, pray? Besides, if I fall, you fall with me.'

'It would then be more prudent, monsieur, not to stir in this affair, and leave the king to take this little satisfaction.'

'Think well of this, abbé, Lyodot and D'Eymeris at Vincennes are a prelude of ruin for my house. I repeat it—I arrested, you will be imprisoned—I imprisoned, you will be exiled.'

'Monsieur, I am at your orders; have you any to give me?'

'What I told you—I wish that, to-morrow, the two financiers of whom they mean to make examples, whilst there remain so many criminals unpunished, should be snatched from the fury of my enemies. Take your measures accordingly. Is this possible?'

'It is possible.'

'Describe your plan.'

'It is of rich simplicity. The ordinary guard at executions consists of twelve archers.'

'There will be a hundred to-morrow.'

'I reckon so. I even say more—there will be two hundred.'

'Then your hundred and twenty men will not be enough.'

'Pardon me. In every crowd composed of a hundred thousand spectators, there are ten thousand bandits or cutpurses—only they dare not take the initiative.'

'Well?'

'There will then be, to-morrow, in the Place de Grève, which I choose as my battle-field, ten thousand auxiliaries to my hundred and twenty men. The attack commenced by the latter, the others will finish it.'

'That all appears feasible. But what will be done with regard to the prisoners in the Place de Grève?'

'This; they must be thrust into some house—that will make a siege necessary to get them out again. And stop! here is another idea, more sublime still: certain houses have two exits—one onto the Place, and the other into the Rue de la Mortellerie, or la Vannerie, or la Tixeranderie.* The prisoners, entering by one door, will go out at another.'

'Yes; but work out a definite plan.'

'I am trying to do so.'

'And I,' cried Fouquet, 'I have found it. Listen to what has just occurred to me.'

'I am listening.'

Fouquet made a sign to Gourville, who appeared to understand. 'One of my friends lends me sometimes the keys of a house which he rents, Rue Baudoyer,* the spacious gardens of which extend behind a certain house of the Place de Grève.'

'That is the place for us,' said the abbé. 'What house?'

'A tavern, pretty well frequented, whose sign represents the Face of Our Lady.'

'I know it,' said the abbé.

'This tavern has windows opening upon the Place, a place of exit into the court, which must abut upon the gardens of my friend by a communicating door.'

'Good!' said the abbé.

'Enter by the tavern, take the prisoners in; defend the door while you enable them to escape by the garden and the Place Baudoyer.'

'That is all plain. Monsieur, you would make an excellent general, like monsieur le prince.'

'Have you understood me?'

'Perfectly well.'

'How much will it amount to, to make your bandits all drunk with wine, and to satisfy them with gold?'

'Oh, monsieur, what an expression! Oh! monsieur, if they heard you! some of them are very susceptible.'

'I mean to say they must be brought to the point where they cannot tell heaven from earth; for I shall to-morrow contend with the king; and when I fight I mean to conquer—please understand that.'

'It shall be done, monsieur. Give me your other ideas.'

'The rest is your business.'

'Then give me your purse.'

'Gourville, count a hundred thousand livres for the abbé.'

'Good! and do not count the cost, did you not say?'

'I did.'

'That is well.'

'Monseigneur,' objected Gourville, 'if this should be known, we should lose our heads.'

'Eh! Gourville,' replied Fouquet, purple with anger, 'you excite my pity. Speak for yourself, if you please. My head does not shake in that manner upon my shoulders. Now, abbé, is everything arranged?'

'Everything.'

'At two o'clock to-morrow.'

'At twelve, because it will be necessary to prime our men in a secret manner.'

'That is true; do not stint the innkeeper's wine.'

'I will spare neither his wine nor his house,' replied the abbé, with a sneering laugh. 'I have my plan, I tell you; leave me to set it in operation, and you shall see.'

'Where shall you be yourself?'

'Everywhere; nowhere.'

'And how shall I receive information?'

'By a courier, whose horse shall be kept in the garden of your friend. Incidentally, what is the name of your friend?'

Fouquet looked again at Gourville, who came to the rescue by saying, ['The name is immaterial.'

Fouquet went on,]* 'You should go with the abbé for a number of reasons. But you will find the house easily enough. At the front is the sign of the Face of Our Lady. The garden is behind; it is the only garden in the street.'

'Good, good! I will go and give notice to my men.'

'Accompany him, Gourville,' said Fouquet, 'and count him down the money. One moment, abbé—one moment, Gourville— what name will be given to this carrying off?'

'A very natural one, monsieur—the Riot.'

'The riot on account of what? For, if ever the people of Paris are disposed to pay their compliments to the king, it is when he hangs financiers.'

'I will manage that,' said the abbé.

'Yes; but you may manage it badly, and people will guess.'

'Not at all—not at all. I have another idea.'

'What is that?'

'My men shall cry out "*Colbert, vive Colbert!*" and shall throw themselves upon the prisoners as if they would tear them in pieces, and shall force them from the gibbets, as too mild a punishment.'

'Ah! that is an idea,' said Gourville. 'By God! monsieur l'abbé, what an imagination you have!'

'Monsieur, we are worthy of our family,' replied the abbé, proudly.

'Strange fellow,' murmured Fouquet. Then he added, 'It is ingenious. Carry it out, but shed no blood.'

Gourville and the abbé set off together, with their heads full of the planned riot. The superintendent laid himself down upon some cushions, half anticipating the sinister projects of the morrow, half dreaming of love.

LXI

THE TAVERN OF THE FACE OF OUR LADY

AT two o'clock the next day fifty thousand spectators had taken their position upon the Place, around the two gibbets which had been raised between the Quai de la Grève and the Quai Pelletier;* one close to the other, with their backs to the embankment of the river. In the morning also, all the sworn criers of the good city of Paris had traversed the quarters of the city, particularly the market areas and the suburbs, announcing with their hoarse and indefatigable voices the great justice done by the king upon two speculators, two thieves, leeches of the people. And these people, whose interests were so warmly looked after, in order not to fail in respect for their king, quitted shops, stalls, and workshops, to go and show a little gratitude to Louis XIV, absolutely like invited guests, who feared to commit an impoliteness in not repairing to the house of him who had invited them. According to the decree, which the criers read aloud and incorrectly, two tax-farmers, monopolists of money, dilapidators of the royal provisions, extortioners, and forgers, were about to undergo capital punishment on the Place de Grève, with their names blazoned over their heads. As to their names, the decree made no mention of them. The curiosity of the Parisians was at its height, and, as we have said, an immense crowd waited with feverish impatience the hour fixed for the execution. The news had already spread that the prisoners, transferred to the Château of Vincennes, would be conducted from that prison to the Place de Grève. Consequently, the Faubourg and the Rue Saint Antoine* were crowded; for the population of Paris in those days of great executions was divided into two categories: those who came to see the condemned pass—these were of timid and mild hearts, but philosophically curious—and those who wished to see the condemned die—these had hearts that hungered for sensation. On this day M. d'Artagnan received his last instructions from the king, and made his adieux to his friends, the number of whom was, at the moment, reduced to Planchet; then he traced the plan of his day, as every busy man whose moments are counted ought to do, because he appreciates their importance.

'My departure is to be,' said he, 'at break of day, three o'clock in the morning; I have then fifteen hours before me. Take from them the six hours of sleep which are indispensable for me—six; one hour for meals—seven; one hour for a farewell visit to Athos—eight; two hours for chance circumstances—total, ten. There are then five hours left. One hour to get my money—that is, to have payment refused by M. Fouquet; another hour to go and receive my money of M. Colbert, together with his questions and scowls; one hour to look over my clothes and arms, and get my boots cleaned. I have still two hours left. *Mordioux!* how rich I am!' And so saying, D'Artagnan felt a strange joy, a joy of youth, a perfume of those great and happy years of former times mount into his brain and intoxicate him. 'During these two hours I will go,' said the musketeer, 'and take my quarter's rent owing for the Face of Our Lady. That will be pleasant! Three hundred and seventy-five livres! *Mordioux!* but that is astonishing! If the poor man who has but one livre in his pocket, found a livre and twelve deniers,* that would be justice, that would be excellent; but never does such a god-send fall to the lot of the poor man. The rich man, on the contrary, makes himself money with his money, which he does not even spend. Here are three hundred and seventy-five livres which fall to me from heaven. I will go then to the Face of Our Lady, and drink a glass of Spanish wine with my tenant, which he cannot fail to offer me. But order must be observed, Monsieur d'Artagnan, order must be observed! Let us organize our time, then, and distribute the employment of it! Item 1, Athos; Item 2, the Face of Our Lady; Item 3, M. Fouquet; Item 4, M. Colbert; Item 5, supper; Item 6, clothes, boots, horse, portmanteau; Item 7 and last, sleep.'

In consequence of this arrangement, D'Artagnan went straight to the Comte de la Fère, to whom, modestly and ingenuously, he related a part of his fortunate adventures. Athos had not been without uneasiness on the subject of D'Artagnan's visit to the king; but few words sufficed for an explanation. Athos divined that Louis had charged D'Artagnan with some important mission, and did not even make an effort to draw the secret from him. He only recommended him to take care of himself, and offered discreetly to accompany him if that were desirable.

'But, my dear friend,' said D'Artagnan, 'I am going nowhere.'

'What! you come and bid me adieu, and are going nowhere?'

'Oh! yes, yes,' replied D'Artagnan, colouring a little, 'I am going to make an acquisition.'

'That is quite another thing. Then I change my formula. Instead of "Do not get yourself killed," I will say—"Do not get yourself robbed." '

'My friend, I will inform you if I set eyes on any property that pleases me, and shall expect you will favour me with your opinion.'

'Yes, yes,' said Athos, too delicate to permit himself even the consolation of a smile. Raoul imitated the paternal reserve. But D'Artagnan thought it would appear too mysterious to leave his friends under a pretext, without even telling them the route he was about to take.

'I have chosen Le Mans,'* said he to Athos. 'Is it a good country?'

'Excellent, my friend,' replied the count, without making him observe that Le Mans was in the same direction as La Touraine, and that by waiting two days, at most, he might travel with a friend. But D'Artagnan, more embarrassed than the count, dug, at every explanation, deeper into the mud, into which he sank by degrees. 'I shall set out to-morrow at day-break,' said he at last. 'Till that time, will you come with me, Raoul?'

'Yes, monsieur le chevalier,' said the young man, 'if monsieur le comte does not want me.'

'No, Raoul; I am to have an audience to-day with Monsieur, the king's brother; that is all I have to do.'

Raoul asked Grimaud for his sword, which the old man brought him immediately. 'Now then,' added D'Artagnan, opening his arms to Athos, 'adieu, my dear friend!' Athos held him in a long embrace, and the musketeer, who knew his discretion so well, murmured in his ear—'An affair of state,' to which Athos only replied by a pressure of the hand, still more significant. They then separated. Raoul took the arm of his old friend, who led him along the Rue Saint-Honoré. 'I am conducting you to the abode of the god Plutus,'* said D'Artagnan to the young man; 'prepare yourself. The whole day you will witness the piling-up of crowns. Heavens! how I am changed!'

'Oh! what numbers of people there are in the street!' said Raoul.

'Is there a procession to-day?' asked D'Artagnan of a passer-by.

'Monsieur, it is a hanging,' replied the man.

'What! a hanging at the Grève?' said D'Artagnan,

'Yes, monsieur.'

'The devil take the rogue who gets himself hung the day I want to go and collect my rent!' cried D'Artagnan. 'Raoul, did you ever see anybody hung?'

'Never, monsieur—thank God!'

'Oh! how young that sounds! If you were on guard in the trenches, as I was, and a spy!—But, pardon me, Raoul, I am rambling—you are quite right, it is a hideous sight to see a person hung! At what hour do they hang them, monsieur, if you please?'

'Monsieur,' replied the stranger respectfully, delighted at joining conversation with two men of the sword; 'it will take place about three o'clock.'

'Aha! it is now only half-past one; let us step out, we shall be there in time to pocket my three hundred and seventy-five livres, and get away before the arrival of the malefactor.'

'Malefactors, monsieur,' continued the good burgher; 'there are two of them.'

'Monsieur, I return you many thanks,' said D'Artagnan, who as he grew older, had become polite to a degree. Drawing Raoul along, he directed his course rapidly in the direction of La Grève. Without that great experience musketeers have of a crowd, to which were joined an irresistible strength of wrist and an uncommon suppleness of shoulders, our two travellers would not have arrived at their place of destination. They followed the line of the quay, which they had gained on quitting the Rue Saint-Honoré, where they left Athos. D'Artagnan went first; his elbow, his wrist, his shoulder formed three wedges which he knew how to insert with skill into the groups, to make them split and separate like firewood. He made use sometimes of the hilt of his sword as an additional help: introducing it between ribs that were too rebellious, making it take the part of a lever or crowbar, to separate husband from wife, uncle from nephew, and brother from brother. And all this was done so naturally, and with such gracious smiles, that people must have had ribs of bronze, not to cry thank you when the wrist made its play, or hearts of diamond not to be enchanted when such a bland smile enlivened the lips of the musketeer. Raoul, following his friend, cajoled the women who admired his looks, pushed back the men, who felt the rigidity of his muscles, and both opened, thanks to these manœuvres, the compact and muddy tide of the populace. They arrived in sight of the two gibbets, from which Raoul turned away his eyes in disgust. As for D'Artagnan, he did not even see them; his house with its gabled roof, its windows crowded with the curious, attracted and even absorbed all the attention he was capable of. He distinguished in the Place and around the houses a good number of musketeers on leave, who, some with women, others with friends, awaited the crowning ceremony. What rejoiced him above all was to see that his tenant, the innkeeper, was so busy he hardly knew which way to turn. Three lads could not supply the drinkers. They filled the shop, the chambers, and even the court. D'Artagnan called Raoul's attention to this concourse, adding: 'The fellow will have no excuse for not paying his rent. Look at those drinkers, Raoul, one would say they were jolly companions. *Mordioux!* why, there is no room anywhere!' D'Artagnan, however, contrived to catch hold of the master by the corner of his apron, and to make himself known to him.

'Ah, monsieur le chevalier,' said the innkeeper, half distracted, 'one minute if you please. I have here a hundred mad devils turning my cellar upside down.'

'The cellar, if you like, but not the money box.'

'Oh, monsieur, your thirty-seven and a half pistoles* are all counted out ready for you, upstairs in my chamber; but there are in that chamber thirty customers, who are emptying a keg of Port wine which I tapped for them this very morning. Give me a minute—only a minute?'

'So be it; so be it.'

'I will go,' said Raoul, in a low voice, to D'Artagnan; 'all this hilarity is vile!'

'Monsieur,' replied D'Artagnan, sternly, 'you will please to remain where you are. The soldier ought to familiarize himself with all kinds of spectacles. There are in the eye, when it is young, fibres which we must learn how to harden; and we are not truly generous and good save from the moment when the eye has become hardened, and the heart remains tender. Besides, my little Raoul, would you leave me alone here? That would be very wrong of you. Look, there is yonder in the court-yard a tree, and under the shade of that tree we shall breathe more freely than in this hot atmosphere of spilt wine.'

From the spot on which they had placed themselves the two new guests of the Face of Our Lady heard the ever-increasing hubbub of the tide of people, and missed neither a cry nor a gesture of the drinkers, at tables in the tavern, or disseminated in the chambers. If D'Artagnan had wished to place himself as a lookout for an expedition, he could not have succeeded better. The tree under which he and Raoul were seated covered them with its already thick foliage; it was a low, thick chestnut-tree, with sloping branches, that cast their shade over a table so dilapidated the drinkers had abandoned it. We said that from this post D'Artagnan saw everything. He observed the goings and comings of the waiters; the arrival of new drinkers; the welcome, sometimes friendly, sometimes hostile, given to the new-comers, by others already installed. He observed all this to amuse himself, for the thirty-seven and a half pistoles were a long time coming. Raoul recalled his attention to it. 'Monsieur,' said he, 'you do not hurry your tenant, and the condemned men will soon be here. There will then be such a press we shall not be able to get out.'

'You are right,' said the musketeer, 'Holloa! oh! somebody there! *Mordioux!*' But it was in vain he cried and knocked upon the wreck of the old table, which fell to pieces beneath his fist; nobody came. D'Artagnan was preparing to go and seek the innkeeper himself, to force him to a definite explanation, when the door of the court in which he was with Raoul, a door which communicated with the garden situated at the back, opened, and a man dressed as a cavalier, with his sword in the sheath, but not at his belt, crossed the court without closing the door; and having cast an oblique glance at D'Artagnan and his companion, directed his course towards the tavern itself, looking about in all directions with his eyes capable of piercing the walls of conscience. 'Humph!' said D'Artagnan, 'my tenants are communicating. That, no doubt, now, is some aficionado of hanging matters.' At the same moment, the cries and disturbance in the upper chambers ceased. Silence, under such circumstances, surprises more than a twofold increase of noise. D'Artagnan wished to see what was the cause of this sudden silence. He then perceived that the man, dressed as a cavalier, had just entered the principal chamber, and was haranguing the tipplers, who all listened to him with the greatest attention. D'Artagnan would perhaps have heard his speech but for the dominant noise of the crowd, which made a formidable accompaniment to the harangue of the orator. But it was soon finished, and all the people the tavern contained came out, one after the other, in little groups, so that there only remained six in the chamber; one of these six, the man with the sword, took the innkeeper aside, engaging him in more or less serious talk, whilst the others lit a great fire in the chimney-place—a circumstance rendered strange by the fine weather and the heat.

'It is very singular,' said D'Artagnan to Raoul, 'but I think I know those faces yonder.'

'Don't you think you can smell the smoke here?' said Raoul.

'I rather think I can smell a conspiracy,' replied D'Artagnan.

He had not finished speaking, when four of these men came down into the court, and without the appearance of any evil intent, mounted guard at the communicating door, casting, at intervals, glances at D'Artagnan, which signified many things.

'*Mordioux!*' said D'Artagnan, in a low voice, 'there is something going on. Have you a curious mind, Raoul?'

'According to the subject, chevalier.'

'Well, I am as curious as an old woman. Come a little more to the front; we shall get a better view of the place. I would lay a wager that view will be something curious.'

'But you know, monsieur le chevalier, that I am not willing to become a passive and indifferent spectator of the death of the two poor devils.'

'And I, then—do you think I am a savage? We will go in again, when it is time to do so. Come along!' And they made their way towards the front of the house, and placed themselves near the window, which, still more strangely than the rest, remained unoccupied. The two last drinkers, instead of looking out at this window, kept up the fire. On seeing D'Artagnan and his friend enter: 'Ah! ah! a reinforcement,' murmured they.

D'Artagnan jogged Raoul's elbow. 'Yes, my braves, a reinforcement,' said he; 'Hell's teeth! that's a famous fire. Who are you going to cook?'

The two men uttered a shout of jovial laughter, and, instead of answering, threw on more wood. D'Artagnan could not take his eyes off them.

'I suppose,' said one of the fire-makers, 'they sent you to tell us the time—did not they?'

'Without doubt they did,' said D'Artagnan, anxious to know what was going on; 'why should I be here else, if it were not for that?'

'Then place yourself at the window, if you please, and observe.' D'Artagnan smiled knowingly, made a sign to Raoul, and placed himself at the window.

LXII

VIVE COLBERT!

THE spectacle which the Grève now presented was a frightful one. The heads, levelled by the perspective, extended afar, thick and agitated as the ears of corn in a vast plain. From time to time a fresh report, or a distant rumour, made the heads turn and thousands of eyes flash. Now and then there were great movements. All those ears of corn bent, and became waves more agitated than those of the ocean, which rolled from the extremities to the centre, and beat, like the tides, against the hedge of archers who surrounded the gibbets. Then the handles of the halberds fell upon the heads and shoulders of the rash invaders;

at times, also, it was the steel as well as the wood, and, in that case, a large empty circle was formed around the guard; a space won at the expense of the extremities, which underwent, in their turn the oppression of the sudden movement, which drove them against the parapets of the Seine. From the window, which commanded a view of the whole Place, D'Artagnan saw, with interior satisfaction, that such of the musketeers and guards as found themselves involved in the crowd were able, with blows of their fists and the hilts of their swords, to keep room. He even remarked that they had succeeded, by that collective discipline which doubles the strength of the soldier, in getting together in one group to the amount of about fifty men; and that, with the exception of a dozen stragglers whom he still saw rolling here and there, the nucleus was complete, and within reach of his voice. But it was not only the musketeers and guards that drew the attention of D'Artagnan. Around the gibbets, and particularly at the entrances to the arcade of Saint-Jean, moved a noisy mass, a busy mass; daring, resolute faces were to be seen here and there, mingled with silly and indifferent faces; signals were exchanged, hands given and taken. D'Artagnan remarked among the groups, and those groups the most animated, the face of the cavalier whom he had seen enter by the communicating door from his garden, and who had gone upstairs to harangue the drinkers. That man was organizing troops and giving orders.

'*Mordioux!*' said D'Artagnan to himself, 'I was not deceived; I know that man—it is Menneville. What the devil is he doing here!'

A distant murmur, which became more distinct by degrees, stopped this reflection, and drew his attention another way. This murmur was occasioned by the arrival of the culprits; a strong picket of archers preceded them, and appeared at the angle of the arcade. The entire crowd now joined as if in one cry; all the cries united formed one immense howl. D'Artagnan saw Raoul was becoming pale, and he slapped him roughly on the shoulder. The men tending the fire turned round on hearing the great cry, and asked what was going on. 'The condemned men have arrived,' said D'Artagnan. 'That's well,' replied they, again replenishing the fire. D'Artagnan looked at them with much uneasiness; it was evident that these men who were making such a fire for no apparent purpose had some strange intentions. The condemned men appeared in the Place. They were walking, the executioner before them, whilst fifty archers formed a hedge on their right and their left. Both were dressed in black; they appeared pale, but firm. They looked impatiently over the people's heads, standing on tip-toe at every step. D'Artagnan remarked this. '*Mordioux!*' cried he, 'they are in a great hurry to get a sight of the gibbet!' Raoul drew back, without, however, having the power to leave the window. Even terror has its attractions.

'Death! Death!' cried fifty thousand voices.

'Yes; death!' howled a hundred frantic others, as if the great mass had given them the reply.

'String them up! Hang them high!' cried the crowd together; '*Vive le roi!*'

'Well,' said D'Artagnan, 'this is droll; I should have thought it was M. Colbert who had caused them to be hung.'

There was, at this moment, a great rolling movement in the crowd, which stopped for a moment the march of the condemned men. The people of bold and resolute aspect, whom D'Artagnan had observed, by dint of pressing, pushing, and lifting themselves up, had succeeded in almost touching the hedge of archers. The procession resumed its march. All at once, to cries of '*Vive Colbert!*', those men, of whom D'Artagnan never lost sight, fell upon the escort, which in vain endeavoured to stand against them. Behind these men was the crowd. Then commenced, amidst a frightful tumult, as frightful a confusion. This time, there was something more than cries of expectation or cries of joy, there were cries of pain. Halberds struck men down, swords ran them through, muskets were discharged at them. The confusion became then so great that D'Artagnan could no longer make out anything. Then, from this chaos, suddenly surged something like a visible intention, like an effort of will. The condemned men had been torn from the hands of the guards, and were being dragged towards the Face of Our Lady. Those who dragged them shouted, '*Vive Colbert!*' The people hesitated, not knowing which they ought to fall upon, the archers or the aggressors. What stopped the people was, that those who cried '*Vive Colbert!*' began to cry, at the same time,

'Not the rope! not the rope! the stake! the stake! burn the thieves! burn the extortioners!' This cry, shouted as with one voice, obtained enthusiastic success. The populace had come to witness an execution, and here was an opportunity offered them of performing one themselves. It was this that most tempted the populace: therefore, they immediately sided with the party of the aggressors against the archers, crying with the minority, which had become, thanks to them, the most solid majority. 'Yes, yes; burn the thieves! *Vive Colbert!*'

'*Mordioux!*' exclaimed D'Artagnan, 'this begins to look serious.'

One of the men who remained near the chimney approached the window, a firebrand in his hand. 'Ah, ah!' said he, 'it gets warm.' Then, turning to his companion, 'There is the signal,' added he; and he immediately applied the burning brand to the wainscoting. Now, the Face of Our Lady was not a very newly-built house; and therefore, did not require much entreating to take fire. In a second the boards began to crackle, and the flames arose sparkling to the ceiling. A howling from without replied to the shouts of the incendiaries. D'Artagnan, who had not seen what passed, being busy at the window, felt, at the same time, the smoke which choked him and the fire that scorched him. 'Zounds!' cried he, turning round, 'is the fire here? Are you drunk or mad, my masters?'

The two men looked at each other with an air of astonishment. 'In what?' asked they of D'Artagnan; 'was it not a thing agreed upon?'

'A thing agreed upon that you should burn my house!' vociferated D'Artagnan, snatching the brand from the hand of the incendiary, and striking him with it across the face. The second wanted to assist his comrade, but Raoul, seizing him by the middle, threw him out of the window, whilst D'Artagnan pushed his man down the stairs. Raoul, first disengaged, tore the burning wainscoting down, and threw it flaming into the chamber. At a glance, D'Artagnan saw there was nothing to be feared from the fire, and sprang to the window. The disorder was at its height. The air was filled with simultaneous cries of 'The stake!' 'Kill them!' 'String them up!' 'Burn them alive!' '*Vive Colbert!*' '*Vive le roi!*' The group which had forced the culprits from the hands of the archers had drawn close to the house, which appeared to be the goal towards which they dragged them. Menneville was at the head of this group, shouting louder than all the others, 'Burn them! burn them! *Vive Colbert!*' D'Artagnan began to comprehend what was meant. They wanted to burn the condemned men, and his house was to serve as a funeral pile.

'Halt, there!' cried he, sword in hand, and one foot upon the window. 'Menneville, what do you want to do?'

'Monsieur d'Artagnan,' cried the latter; 'give way, give way!'

'Burn them! burn the thieves! *Vive Colbert!*'

These cries exasperated D'Artagnan. '*Mordioux!*' said he. 'What! burn the poor devils who are only condemned to be hung? that is infamous!'

Before the door, however, the mass of anxious spectators, rolled back against the walls, had become more thick, and closed up the way. Menneville and his men, who were dragging along the culprits, were within ten paces of the door.

Menneville made a last effort. 'Make way! Make way!' cried he, pistol in hand.

'Burn them! burn them!' repeated the crowd. 'The Face of Our Lady is on fire! Burn the thieves! burn the monopolists in the Face of Our Lady!'

There now remained no doubt, it was plainly D'Artagnan's house that was their object. D'Artagnan remembered the old cry, always so effective from his mouth: 'Rally round, Musketeers!' shouted he, with the voice of a giant, with one of those voices which dominate over cannon, the sea, the tempest. 'Rally round, Musketeers!' And suspending himself by the arm from the balcony, he allowed himself to drop amidst the crowd, which began to draw back from a house that rained men. Raoul was on the ground as soon as he, both sword in hand. All the musketeers on the Place heard that challenging cry—all turned round at that cry, and recognized D'Artagnan. 'To the captain, to the captain!' cried they, in their turn. And the crowd opened before them as though before the prow of a vessel. At that moment D'Artagnan and Menneville found themselves face to face. 'Make way!' cried Menneville, seeing that he was within an arm's length of the door.

'No one passes here,' said D'Artagnan.

'Take that, then!' said Menneville, firing his pistol, almost within arm's-length. But before the cock fell, D'Artagnan had struck up Menneville's arm with the hilt of his sword, and passed the blade through his body.

'I told you plainly to keep yourself quiet,' said D'Artagnan to Menneville, who rolled at his feet.

'Make way!' cried the companions of Menneville, at first terrified, but soon recovering, when they found they had only to do with two men. But those two men were hundred-armed giants; the swords flew about in their hands like the burning blade of the archangel.* They pierce with its point, strike with the flat, cut with the edge; every stroke brings down a man. 'For the king!' cried D'Artagnan, to every man he struck at, that is to say, to every man that fell. This cry became the charging word for the musketeers, who, guided by it, joined D'Artagnan. Meanwhile the archers, recovering from the panic they had undergone, charge the aggressors in the rear, and regular as mill-strokes, overturn or knock down all who oppose them. The crowd, which sees swords gleaming, and drops of blood flying in the air—the crowd falls back and crushes itself. At length cries for mercy and of despair resound; that is, the farewell of the vanquished. The two condemned men are again in the hands of the archers. D'Artagnan approaches them, seeing them pale and sinking: 'Console yourselves, poor men,' said he, 'you will not undergo the frightful torture with which these wretches threatened you. The king has condemned you to be hung: you shall only be hung. Go on, hang them, and it will be over.'

There is no longer anything going on at the Face of Our Lady. The fire has been extinguished with two tuns of wine instead of water. The conspirators have fled by the garden. The archers are dragging the culprits to the gibbets. From this moment the affair did not occupy much time. The executioner, giving no thought to operating according to the rules of art, made such haste, that he dispatched the condemned men in a couple of minutes. In the meantime the people gathered around D'Artagnan—they congratulated, they cheered him. He wiped his brow, streaming with sweat, and his sword, streaming with blood. He shrugged his shoulders at seeing Menneville writhing at his feet in the last convulsions. And, while Raoul turned away his eyes in compassion, he pointed to the musketeers the gibbets laden with their melancholy fruit. 'Poor devils!' said he, 'I hope they died blessing me, for I saved them with great difficulty.' These words caught the ear of Menneville at the moment when he himself was breathing his last sigh. A dark, ironical smile flitted across his lips; he tried to reply, but the effort hastened the snapping of the chord of life—he expired.

'Oh! all this is very horrible!' murmured Raoul: 'let us begone, monsieur le chevalier.'

'You are not wounded?' asked D'Artagnan.

'Not at all; thank you.'

'That's well! Thou art a brave fellow, *mordioux!* The head of the father, and the arm of Porthos. Ah! if he had been here, good Porthos, you would have seen something worth looking at.' Then as if by way of remembrance—

'But where the devil can that brave Porthos be?' murmured D'Artagnan.

'Come, chevalier, pray come away,' urged Raoul.

'One minute, my friend; let me take my thirty-seven and a half pistoles, and I am at your service. The house is a good property,' added D'Artagnan, as he entered the Face of Our Lady, 'but decidedly, even if it were less profitable, I should prefer its being in another part of town.'

LXIII

HOW M. D'EYMERIS'S DIAMOND PASSED INTO THE HANDS OF M. D'ARTAGNAN

WHILST this violent, noisy, and bloody scene was passing on the Grève, several men, barricaded behind the gate which led to the garden, replaced their swords in their sheaths, assisted one among them to mount a ready saddled horse which was waiting in the garden, and like a flock of startled birds, fled in all directions, some climbing the walls, others rushing out at the gates with all the fury of a panic. He who mounted the horse, and gave him the spur so sharply that the animal was near leaping the wall, this horseman, we say, crossed the Place Baudoyer, passed like lightning before the crowd in the streets, riding against, running over, and knocking down all that came in his way, and, ten minutes after, arrived at the gates of the superintendent,* more out of breath than his horse. The Abbé Fouquet, at the clatter of the hoofs on the pavement, appeared at a window of the court, and before even the horseman had set foot to the ground, 'Well! Danicamp*?' cried he, leaning half out of the window.

'Well, it is all over,' replied the horseman.

'All over!' cried the abbé. 'Then they are saved?'

'No, monsieur,' replied the horseman, 'they are hung.'

'Hung!' repeated the abbé, turning pale. A side door suddenly opened, and Fouquet appeared in the chamber, pale, distracted, with lips half opened, breathing a cry of grief and anger. He stopped upon the threshold to listen to what was addressed from the court to the window.

'Miserable wretches!' said the abbé, 'you did not fight, then?'

'Like lions.'

'Say like cowards.'

'Monsieur!'

'A hundred men accustomed to war, sword in hand, are worth ten thousand archers in a surprise. Where is Menneville, that boaster, that braggart, who was to come back either dead or a conqueror.'

'Well, monsieur, he has kept his word. He is dead!'

'Dead! Who killed him?'

'A demon disguised as a man, a giant armed with ten flaming swords—a madman, who at one blow extinguished the fire, put down the riot, and caused a hundred musketeers to rise up out of the pavement of the Grève.'

Fouquet raised his brow, streaming with sweat, murmuring, 'Oh! Lyodot and D'Eymeris! dead! dead! dead! and I dishonoured.'

The abbé turned round, and perceiving his brother, despairing and pale, 'Come, come,' said he, 'it is a stroke of fate, monsieur; we must not lament thus. Our attempt has failed, because God——'

'Be silent, abbé! be silent!' cried Fouquet; 'your excuses are blasphemies. Order that man up here, and let him relate the details of this terrible event.'

'But, brother——'

'Obey, monsieur!'

The abbé made a sign, and in half a minute the man's step was heard upon the stairs. At the same time Gourville appeared behind Fouquet, like the guardian angel of the superintendent, pressing one finger on his lips so that he might remain attentive even amidst the bursts of his grief. The minister resumed all the serenity that human strength left at the disposal of a heart half broken with sorrow. Danicamp appeared. 'Make your report,' said Gourville.

'Monsieur,' replied the messenger, 'we received orders to carry off the prisoners, and to cry "*Vive Colbert!*" whilst carrying them off.'

'To burn them alive, was it not, abbé?' interrupted Gourville.

'Yes, yes, the order was given to Menneville. Menneville knew what was to be done, and Menneville is dead.'

This news appeared rather to reassure Gourville than to sadden him.

'Yes, certainly to burn them alive,' said the abbé, eagerly.

'Granted, monsieur, granted,' said the man, looking into the eyes and the faces of the two interlocutors, to ascertain what there was profitable or disadvantageous to himself in telling the truth.

'Now, proceed,' said Gourville.

'The prisoners,' cried Danicamp, 'were brought to the Grève, and the people, in a fury, insisted upon their being burnt instead of being hung.'

'And the people were right,' said the abbé. 'Go on.'

'But,' resumed the man, 'at the moment the archers were broken, at the moment the fire was set to one of the houses of the Place destined to serve as a funeral-pile for the guilty, this fury, this demon, this giant of whom I told you, and who, we had been informed, was the proprietor of the house in question, aided by a young man who accompanied him, threw out of the window those who kept up the fire, called to his assistance the musketeers who were in the crowd, leaped himself from the window of the first story into the Place, and plied his sword so desperately that the victory was restored to the archers, the prisoners were retaken, and Menneville killed. When once

recaptured, the condemned men were executed in three minutes.' Fouquet, in spite of his self-command, could not prevent
a deep groan escaping him.

'And this man, the proprietor of the house, what is his name?'
said the abbé.

'I cannot tell you, not having even been able to get sight of
him; my post had been appointed in the garden, and I remained
at my post: only the affair was related to me as I repeat it. I was
ordered, once the affair was at an end, to come at best speed and
announce to you the manner in which it finished. According to
this order, I set out, full gallop, and here I am.'

'Very well, monsieur, we have nothing else to ask of you,' said
the abbé, more and more dejected, in proportion as the moment
approached for finding himself alone with his brother.

'Have you been paid?' asked Gourville.

'Partly, monsieur,' replied Danicamp.

'Here are twenty pistoles. Begone, monsieur, and never forget
to defend, as this time has been done, the true interests of the
king.'

'Yes, monsieur,' said the man, bowing and pocketing the
money. After this he went out. Scarcely had the door closed
after him when Fouquet, who had remained motionless, advanced with a rapid step and stood between the abbé and
Gourville. Both of them at the same time opened their mouths
to speak to him. 'No excuses,' said he, 'no recriminations against
anybody. If I had not been a false friend I should not have
confided to any one the care of delivering Lyodot and D'Eymeris.
I alone am guilty; to me alone are reproaches and remorse due.
Leave me, abbé.'

'And yet, monsieur, you will not prevent me,' replied the
latter, 'from endeavouring to find out the name of the miserable
fellow who has intervened to the advantage of M. Colbert in this
so well-arranged affair; for, if it is good policy to love our friends
dearly, I do not believe that is bad which consists in obstinately
pursuing our enemies.'

'A truce to policy, abbé; begone, I beg of you, and do not let
me hear any more of you till I send for you; what we most need
are circumspection and silence. You have a terrible example
before you, gentlemen: no reprisals, I forbid them.'

'There are no orders,' grumbled the abbé, 'which will prevent me from avenging a family affront upon the guilty person.'

'And I,' cried Fouquet, in that imperative tone to which one feels there is nothing to reply, 'if you entertain one thought, one single thought, which is not the absolute expression of my will, I will have you cast into the Bastille two hours after that thought has manifested itself. Regulate your conduct accordingly, abbé.'

The abbé coloured and bowed. Fouquet made a sign to Gourville to follow him, and was already directing his steps towards his closet, when the usher announced with a loud voice: 'Monsieur le Chevalier d'Artagnan.'

'Who is he?' said Fouquet, negligently, to Gourville.

'An ex-lieutenant of his majesty's musketeers,' replied Gourville, in the same tone. Fouquet did not even take the trouble to reflect, and resumed his walk. 'I beg your pardon, monseigneur!' said Gourville, 'but I have remembered; this brave man has quitted the king's service, and probably comes to receive an instalment of some pension or other.'

'Devil take him!' said Fouquet, 'why does he choose his moment so ill?'

'Permit me then, monseigneur, to announce your refusal to him; for he is one of my acquaintance, and is a man whom, in our present circumstances, it would be better to have as a friend than an enemy.'

'Answer him as you please,' said Fouquet.

'Eh! by God!' said the abbé, still full of selfish spite; 'tell him there is no money, particularly for musketeers.'

But scarcely had the abbé uttered this imprudent speech, when the partly-open door was thrown back, and D'Artagnan appeared.

'Eh! Monsieur Fouquet,' said he, 'I was well aware there was no money for musketeers here. Therefore I did not come to obtain any, but to have it refused. That being done, receive my thanks. I give you good-day, and will go and seek it at M. Colbert's'. And he went out, making an easy bow.

'Gourville,' said Fouquet, 'run after that man and bring him back.' Gourville obeyed, and overtook D'Artagnan on the stairs.

D'Artagnan, hearing steps behind him, turned round and saw

Gourville. '*Mordioux!* my dear monsieur,' said he, 'these are sad lessons which you gentlemen of finance teach us; I come to M. Fouquet to receive a sum accorded by his majesty, and I am received like a mendicant who comes to ask charity, or a thief who comes to steal a piece of plate.'

'But you pronounced the name of M. Colbert, my dear M. d'Artagnan; you said you were going to M. Colbert's?'

'I certainly am going there, were it only to ask satisfaction of the people who try to burn houses, crying "*Vive Colbert!*"'

Gourville pricked up his ears. 'Oh, oh!' said he, 'you allude to what has just happened at the Grève?'

'Yes, certainly.'

'And how did that which has taken place concern you?'

'What! do you ask me whether it concerns me or does not concern me, if M. Colbert pleases to make a funeral-pile of my house?'

'So ho, *your* house—was it *your* house they wanted to burn!'

'By God, it was!'

'So the Face of Our Lady belongs to you, then.'

'It has done this week.'

'Well, then, are you the brave captain, are you the valiant blade who dispersed those who wished to burn the condemned men?'

'My dear Monsieur Gourville, put yourself in my place. I was an agent of the public force and a landlord, too. As a captain, it is my duty to have the orders of the king accomplished. As a proprietor, it is to my interest my house should not be burnt. I have at the same time attended to the laws of interest and duty in replacing Messrs. Lyodot and D'Eymeris in the hands of the archers.'

'Then it was you who threw the man out of the window?'

'It was I, myself,' replied D'Artagnan, modestly.

'And you who killed Menneville?'

'I had that misfortune,' said D'Artagnan, bowing like a man who is being congratulated.

'It was you then, in short, who caused the two condemned persons to be hung?'

'Instead of being burnt, yes, monsieur, and I am proud of it. I saved the poor devils from horrible tortures. Understand, my dear Monsieur de Gourville, that they wanted to burn them alive? It passes imagining!'

'Go, my dear Monsieur d'Artagnan, go,' said Gourville, anxious to spare Fouquet the sight of the man who had just caused him such profound grief.

'No,' said Fouquet, who had heard all from the door of the antechamber; 'not so; on the contrary, Monsieur d'Artagnan, come in.'

D'Artagnan wiped from the hilt of his sword a last bloody trace, which had escaped his notice, and returned. He then found himself face to face with these three men, whose countenances wore very different expressions. With the abbé it was anger, with Gourville stupor, with Fouquet it was dejection.

'I beg your pardon, monsieur le ministre,' said D'Artagnan, 'but my time is short; I have to go to the office of the intendant, to explain myself to Monsieur Colbert, and to receive my quarter's pension.'

'But, monsieur,' said Fouquet, 'there is money here.' D'Artagnan looked at the superintendent with astonishment. 'You have been answered inconsiderately, monsieur, I know, because I heard it,' said the minister; 'a man of your merit ought to be known by everybody.' D'Artagnan bowed. 'Have you an order?' added Fouquet.

'Yes, monsieur.'

'Give it me, I will pay you myself; come with me.' He made a sign to Gourville and the abbé, who remained in the chamber where they were. He led D'Artagnan into his cabinet. As soon as the door was shut, 'How much is due to you, monsieur?'

'Why, something like five thousand livres, monseigneur.'

'For arrears of pay?'

'For a quarter's pay.'

'A quarter consisting of five thousand livres!' said Fouquet, fixing upon the musketeer a searching look. 'Does the king, then, give you twenty thousand livres a year?'*

'Yes, monseigneur, twenty thousand livres a year. Do you think it is too much?'

'I?' cried Fouquet, and he smiled bitterly. 'If I had any knowledge of mankind, if I were—instead of being a frivolous, inconsequent, and vain spirit—of a prudent and reflective spirit; if, in a word, I had, as certain persons have known how, regulated my life, you would not receive twenty thousand livres a year, but a hundred thousand, and you would not belong to the king but to me.'

D'Artagnan coloured slightly. There is sometimes in the manner in which an eulogy is given, in the voice, in the affectionate tone, a poison so sweet, that the strongest mind is intoxicated by it. The superintendent terminated his speech by opening a drawer, and taking from it four wrapped cylinders, which he placed before D'Artagnan. The Gascon opened one. 'Gold!' said he.

'It will be less burdensome, monsieur.'

'But then, monsieur, these make twenty thousand livres.'

'No doubt they do.'

'But only five are due to me.'

'I wish to spare you the trouble of coming four times to my office.'

'You overwhelm me, monsieur.'

'I do only what I ought to do, monsieur le chevalier; and I hope you will not bear me any malice on account of the rude reception my brother gave you. He is of a sour, capricious disposition.'

'Monsieur,' said D'Artagnan, 'believe me, nothing would grieve me more than an excuse from you.'

'Therefore I will make no more, and will content myself with asking you a favour.'

'Oh, monsieur.'

Fouquet drew from his finger a ring worth about a thousand pistoles. 'Monsieur,' said he, 'this stone was given me by a friend of my childhood, by a man to whom you have rendered a great service.'

'A service—I?' said the musketeer; 'I have rendered a service to one of your friends?'

'You cannot have forgotten it, monsieur, for it dates this very day.'

'And that friend's name was——?'

'M. d'Eymeris.'

'One of the condemned men?'

'Yes, one of the victims. Well! Monsieur d'Artagnan, in return for the service you have rendered him, I beg you to accept this diamond. Do so for my sake.'

'Monsieur! you——'

'Accept it, I say. To-day is for me a day of mourning; here-after you will, perhaps, learn why; to-day I have lost one friend; well, I will try to get another.'

'But, Monsieur Fouquet——'

'Adieu! Monsieur d'Artagnan, adieu!' cried Fouquet, with much emotion; 'or rather, *au revoir*.' And the minister quitted the closet, leaving in the hands of the musketeer the ring and the twenty thousand livres.

'Oh!' said D'Artagnan, after a moment's dark reflection. 'How on earth am I to understand what this means? *Mordioux!* I can understand this much, only: he is a gentleman! I will go and explain matters to M. Colbert.' And he went out.

LXIV

OF THE NOTABLE DIFFERENCE D'ARTAGNAN FINDS BETWEEN MONSIEUR L'INTENDANT AND MONSIEUR LE SURINTENDANT

M. COLBERT resided in the Rue Neuve des Petits-Champs, in a house which had belonged to Beautru.* D'Artagnan's legs cleared the distance in less than a quarter of an hour. When he arrived at the residence of the new favourite, the court was full of archers and police, who came to congratulate him, or to excuse themselves, according to whether he should choose to praise or blame. The sentiment of flattery is instinctive with people of abject condition; they have the sense of it, as the wild animal has that of hearing and smell. These people, or their leader, understood that there was a pleasure to offer to M. Colbert, in rendering him an account of the fashion in which his name had been pronounced during the rash enterprise of the morning. D'Artagnan made his appearance just as the chief of the watch was giving his report. He stood close to the door, behind the archers. That officer took Colbert on one side, in spite of his resistance and the contraction of his bushy eyebrows.

'In case,' said he, 'you really desired, monsieur, that the people should do justice on the two traitors, it would have been wise to warn us of it; for, indeed, monsieur, in spite of our regret at displeasing you, or thwarting your views, we had our orders to execute.'

'Triple fool!' replied Colbert, furiously shaking his hair, thick and black as a mane; 'what are you telling me? What! that *I* could have had an idea of staging a riot! Are you mad or drunk?'

'But, monsieur, they cried "*Vive Colbert!*"' replied the trembling watch.

'A handful of conspirators——'

'No, no; a mass of people.'

'Ah! indeed,' said Colbert, expanding. 'A mass of people cried, "*Vive Colbert!*" Are you certain of what you say, monsieur?'

'All we had to do was to open our ears, or rather to close them, so terrible were the cries.'

'And this was from the people, the people of Paris?'

'Certainly, monsieur; only the people of Paris beat us.'

'Oh! very well,' continued Colbert, thoughtfully. 'Then you suppose it was the people alone who wished to burn the condemned men?'

'Oh! yes, monsieur.'

'That is quite another thing. You strongly resisted, then?'

'We had three of our men crushed to death, monsieur!'

'But you killed nobody yourselves?'

'Monsieur, a few of the rioters were left upon the square, and one among them who was not a common man.'

'Who was he?'

'A certain Menneville, upon whom the police have a long time had an eye.'

'Menneville!' cried Colbert, 'what, he who killed, in Rue de la Huchette, a worthy man who wanted a fat fowl?'

'Yes, monsieur; the same.'

'And did this Menneville also cry, "*Vive Colbert*"?'

'Louder than all the rest; like a madman.'

Colbert's brow grew dark and wrinkled. The glow of success and ambition which had lighted his face was extinguished, like the light of glow-worms we crush beneath the grass. 'Then you say,' resumed the disappointed intendant, 'that the initiative came from the people? Menneville was my enemy; I would have had him hung, and he knew it well. Menneville belonged to the Abbé Fouquet—the affair originated with Fouquet; does not everybody know that the condemned men were his friends from childhood?'

'That is true,' thought D'Artagnan, 'and thus are all my doubts cleared up. I repeat it, Monsieur Fouquet may be called what they please, but he is a very gentlemanly man.'

'And,' continued Colbert, 'are you quite sure Menneville is dead?'

D'Artagnan thought the time was come for him to make his appearance. 'Perfectly, monsieur' replied he, advancing suddenly.

'Oh! is that you, monsieur?' said Colbert.

'In person,' replied the musketeer with his deliberate tone; 'it appears that you had in Menneville a pretty enemy.'

'It was not I, monsieur, who had an enemy,' replied Colbert; 'it was the king.'

'Two-faced brute!' thought D'Artagnan, 'to think to play the great man and the hypocrite with me. Well,' continued he to Colbert, 'I am very happy to have rendered so good a service to the king; will you take upon you to tell his majesty, monsieur l'intendant?'

'What commission is this you give me, and what do you charge me to tell his majesty, monsieur? Be precise, if you please,' said Colbert, in a sharp voice, tuned beforehand to hostility.

'I give you no commission,' replied D'Artagnan, with that calmness which never abandons the banterer; 'I thought it would be easy for you to announce to his majesty that it was I who, being there by chance, did justice upon Menneville and restored things to order.'

Colbert opened his eyes and interrogated the chief of the watch with a look—'Ah! it is very true,' said the latter, 'that this gentleman saved us.'

'Why did you not tell me, monsieur, that you came to relate me this?' said Colbert with envy; 'everything is explained, and more favourably for you than for any body else.'

'You are in error, monsieur l'intendant, I did not at all come for the purpose of relating it to you.'

'It is an exploit, nevertheless.'

'Oh!' said the musketeer carelessly, 'constant habit blunts the mind.'

'To what do I owe the honour of your visit, then!'

'Simply to this: the king ordered me to come to you.'

'Ah!' said Colbert, recovering himself, when he saw D'Artagnan draw a paper from his pocket; 'it is to demand some money of me?'

'Precisely, Monsieur.'

'Have the goodness to wait, if you please, monsieur, till I have dispatched the report of the watch.'

D'Artagnan turned upon his heel, insolently enough, and finding himself face to face with Colbert, after his first turn, he bowed to him as a harlequin* would have done; then, after a second about-turn, he directed his steps towards the door in quick time. Colbert was struck with this pointed rudeness, to which he was not accustomed. In general, men of the sword, when they came to his office, had such a need of money, that though their feet seemed to take root in the marble, they never lost their patience. Was D'Artagnan going straight to the king? Would he go and describe his rough reception, or recount his exploit? This was a matter for grave consideration. At all events, the moment was badly chosen to send D'Artagnan away, whether he came from the king, or on his own account. The musketeer had rendered too great a service, and that too recently, for it to be already forgotten. Therefore Colbert thought it would be better to shake off his arrogance and call D'Artagnan back. 'Ho! Monsieur d'Artagnan,' cried Colbert, 'what! are you leaving me thus?'

D'Artagnan turned round: 'Why not?' said he, quietly, 'we have no more to say to each other, have we?'

'You have at least money to receive, as you have an order?'

'Who, I? Oh! not at all, my dear Monsieur Colbert.'

'But, monsieur, you have an order. And, in the same manner as you give a sword-thrust, when you are required, I, on my part, pay when an order is presented to me. Present yours.'

'It is useless, my dear Monsieur Colbert,' said D'Artagnan, who inwardly enjoyed this confusion in the ideas of Colbert; 'my order is paid.'

'Paid, by whom?'

'By monsieur le surintendant.'

Colbert grew pale.

'Explain yourself,' said he, in a choking voice—'if you are paid why do you show me that paper?'

'In consequence of the word "order" of which you spoke to me so prettily just now, dear M. Colbert; the king told me to take a quarter of the pension he is pleased to make me.'

'From me?' said Colbert.

'Not exactly. The king said to me: "Go to M. Fouquet; the superintendent will, perhaps, have no money, then you will go and draw it from M. Colbert."'

The countenance of M. Colbert brightened for a moment; but it was with his unfortunate physiognomy as with a stormy sky, sometimes radiant, sometimes dark as night, according as the lightning-gleams or the cloud passes. 'Eh! and was there any money in the superintendent's coffers?' asked he.

'Why, yes, he could not be badly off for money,' replied D'Artagnan—'it may be believed, since M. Fouquet, instead of paying me a quarter or five thousand livres——'

'A quarter or five thousand livres!' cried Colbert, struck, as Fouquet had been, with the generosity of the sum for a soldier's pension, 'why, that would be a pension of twenty thousand livres?'

'Exactly, M. Colbert. Heavens! you reckon like old Pythagoras; yes, twenty thousand livres.'

'Ten times the appointment of an intendant of finances. I beg to offer you my compliments,' said Colbert, with a vicious smile.

'Oh!' said D'Artagnan, 'the king apologized for giving me so little; but he promised to make it more hereafter, when he should be rich; but I must be gone, having much to do——'

'So, then, notwithstanding the expectation of the king, the superintendent paid you, did he?'

'In the same manner as, in opposition to the king's expectation, you refused to pay me.'

'I did not refuse, monsieur, I only begged you to wait. And you say that M. Fouquet paid you your five thousand livres?'

'Yes, as *you* might have done; but he did even better than that, M. Colbert.'

'And what did he do?'

'He politely counted me out the whole sum, saying, that for the king, his coffers were always full.'

'The whole sum! M. Fouquet has given you twenty thousand livres instead of five thousand?'

'Yes, monsieur.'

'And what for?'

'In order to spare me three visits to the money-chest of the superintendent, so that I have the twenty thousand livres in my pocket in good new coin. You see, then, that I am able to leave without standing in need of you, having come here only for form's sake.' And D'Artagnan slapped his hand upon his pocket, with a laugh which disclosed to Colbert thirty-two magnificent teeth, as white as the teeth of any twenty-five-year-old, and which seemed to say in their language: 'Serve up to us thirty-two little Colberts, and we will chew them willingly.' The serpent is as brave as the lion, the hawk as courageous as the eagle: that cannot be contested. There are no creatures that walk the earth, not even those animals we have labelled cowards, which will not show courage when required to defend themselves. Colbert was not frightened at the thirty-two teeth of D'Artagnan. He recovered, and suddenly, 'Monsieur,' said he, 'monsieur le surintendant has done what he had no right to do.'

'What do you mean by that?' replied D'Artagnan.

'I mean that your note—will you let me see your note, if you please?'

'Very willingly; here it is.'

Colbert seized the paper with an eagerness which the musketeer did not remark without uneasiness, and particularly without a certain degree of regret at having trusted him with it. 'Well, monsieur, the royal order says this: "At sight, I command that there be paid to M. d'Artagnan the sum of five thousand livres, forming a quarter of the pension I have made him."'

'So, in fact, it is written,' said D'Artagnan, affecting calmness.

'Very well; the king only owed you five thousand livres; why has more been given to you?'

'Because there was more; and M. Fouquet was willing to give me more; that does not concern anybody.'

'It is natural,' said Colbert, with a proud ease, 'that you should be ignorant of the usages of state-finance; but, monsieur, when you have a thousand livres to pay, what do you do?'

'I never have a thousand livres to pay,' replied D'Artagnan.

'Once more,' said Colbert, irritated—'once more, if you had any sum to pay, would you not pay what you owed?'

'That only proves one thing,' said D'Artagnan; 'and that is, that you have your particular customs in finance, and M. Fouquet has his own.'

'Mine, monsieur, are the correct ones.'

'I do not say they are not.'

'And you have accepted what was not due to you.'

D'Artagnan's eyes flashed. 'What is not due to me *yet*, you meant to say, M. Colbert; for if I had received what was not due to me at all, I should have committed a theft.'

Colbert made no reply to this subtlety. 'You then owe fifteen thousand livres to the public chest,' said he, carried away by his jealous ardour.

'Then you must give me credit for them,' replied D'Artagnan, with his imperceptible irony.

'Not at all, monsieur.'

'Well! what will you do, then? You will not take my gold from me, will you?'

'You must return it to my chest.'

'I! Oh! Monsieur Colbert, don't reckon upon that.'

'The king needs his money, monsieur.'

'And I, monsieur, I need the king's money.'

'That may be; but you must return this.'

'Not a *sou*. I have always understood that in matters of accounting, a good cashier never gives back or takes back.'

'Then, monsieur, we shall see what the king will say about it. I will show him this note, which proves that M. Fouquet not only pays what he does not owe, but that he does not even keep receipts for the sums that he has paid.'

'Ah! now I understand why you have taken that paper, M. Colbert!'

Colbert did not perceive all that there was of a threatening character in his name pronounced in a certain manner. 'You shall see hereafter what use I will make of it,' said he, holding up the paper in his fingers.

'Oh!' said D'Artagnan, snatching the paper from him with a rapid movement; 'I understand it perfectly well, M. Colbert; I do not need to wait and see.' And he crumpled up in his pocket the paper he had so cleverly seized.

'Monsieur, monsieur!' cried Colbert, 'this is violence!'

'Nonsense! You must not be particular about a soldier's manners!' replied D'Artagnan. 'I kiss your hands, my dear M. Colbert.' And he went out, laughing in the face of the future minister.

'That man, now,' muttered he, 'was about to grow quite friendly; it is a great pity I was obliged to cut his company so soon.'

LXV

PHILOSOPHY OF THE HEART AND MIND

FOR a man who had seen so many much more dangerous predicaments, the position of D'Artagnan with respect to M. Colbert was only comic. D'Artagnan, therefore, did not deny himself the satisfaction of laughing at the expense of monsieur l'intendant, all the way from the Rue des Petits-Champs to the Rue des Lombards. It was a great while since D'Artagnan had laughed so long together. He was still laughing when Planchet appeared, laughing likewise, at the door of his house; for Planchet, since the return of his patron, since the entrance of the English guineas, passed the greater part of his life in doing what D'Artagnan had only done from Rue Neuve des Petits-Champs to the Rue des Lombards.

'You are home, then, my dear master?' said Planchet.

'No, my friend,' replied the musketeer; 'I am off, and that quickly. I will sup with you, go to bed, sleep five hours, and at break of day leap into my saddle. Has my horse had an extra feed?'

'Eh! my dear master,' replied Planchet, 'you know very well that your horse is the jewel of the family; that my lads are caressing it all day, and cramming it with sugar, nuts, and biscuits. You ask me if he has had an extra feed of oats; you should ask if he has not had enough to burst him.'

'Very well, Planchet, that is all right. Now, then, I pass to what concerns me—my supper?'

'Ready. A smoking roast joint, white wine, crayfish, and fresh-gathered cherries.* All ready, my master.'

'You are a capital fellow, Planchet; come on, then, let us sup, and I will go to bed.'

During supper D'Artagnan observed that Planchet kept rubbing his forehead, as if to facilitate the issue of some idea closely pent within his brain. He looked with an air of kindness at this worthy companion of former adventures and misadventures, and, clinking glass against glass, 'Come, Planchet,' said he, 'let us see what it is that gives you so much trouble to bring forth. *Mordioux!* speak freely, and quickly.'

'Well, this is it,' replied Planchet: 'you appear to me to be going on some expedition or other.'

'I don't say that I am not.'

'Then you have some new idea?'

'That is possible, too, Planchet.'

'Then there will be fresh capital to be ventured? I will lay down fifty thousand livres upon the idea you are about to carry out.' And so saying, Planchet rubbed his hands one against the other with a rapidity evincing great delight.

'Planchet,' said D'Artagnan, 'there is but one misfortune.'

'And what is that?'

'That the idea is not mine. I can risk nothing upon it.'

These words drew a deep sigh from the heart of Planchet. Avarice is an ardent counsellor; she carries away her man, as Satan did Jesus, to the mountain, and when once she has shown to an unfortunate man all the kingdoms of the earth, she is able to repose herself, knowing full well that she has left her companion Envy to gnaw his heart. Planchet had tasted of riches easily acquired, and was never afterwards likely to stop in his desires; but as he had a good heart in spite of his covetousness, as he adored D'Artagnan, he could not refrain from making him a thousand recommendations, each more affectionate than the others. He would not have been sorry, nevertheless, to have caught a little hint of the secret his master concealed so well; tricks, snares, counsels and traps were all useless, D'Artagnan let nothing confidential escape him. The evening passed thus.

After supper the portmanteau occupied D'Artagnan, he took a turn to the stable, patted his horse, and examined its shoes and legs; then, having counted over his money, he went to bed, sleeping as if he was only twenty, because he had neither anxiety nor remorse; he closed his eyes five minutes after he had blown out his lamp. Many events might, however, have kept him awake. Thought boiled in his brain, conjectures abounded, and D'Artagnan was a great drawer of horoscopes; but, with that imperturbable phlegm which does more than genius for the fortune and happiness of men of action, he put off reflection till the next day, for fear, he said, not to be fresh when he wanted to be so.

The day came. The Rue des Lombards had its share of the caresses of Aurora of the rosy fingers, and D'Artagnan arose like Aurora. He did not awaken anybody, he placed his portmanteau under his arm, descended the stairs without making one of them creak, and without disturbing one of the sonorous snorings in every storey from the garret to the cellar, then, having saddled his horse, shut the stable and house doors, he set off, at a foot-pace, on his expedition to Brittany. He had done quite right not to trouble himself with all the political and diplomatic affairs which solicited his attention; for, in the morning, in freshness and mild twilight, his ideas developed themselves in purity and abundance. In the first place, he passed before the house of Fouquet, and tossed into a large gaping box the fortunate order which, the evening before, he had had so much trouble to recover from the hooked fingers of the intendant. Placed in an envelope, and addressed to Fouquet, it had not even been guessed at by Planchet, who in divination was equal to Calchas or the Pythian Apollo.* D'Artagnan thus returned the order to Fouquet, without compromising himself, and without having thenceforward any reproaches to make himself. When he had effected this proper restitution, 'Now,' said he to himself, 'let us inhale much morning air, much freedom from cares, much health, let us allow my mount Zephyr, whose flanks puff as if he needed to inhale the whole atmosphere, to breathe, and let us be very ingenious in our little calculations. It is time,' said D'Artagnan, 'to form a plan of campaign, and, according to the method of M. Turenne, who has a large head full of all sorts of good counsels, before the plan of the campaign it is advisable to draw a striking portrait of the generals to whom we are opposed. In the first place, M. Fouquet presents himself. What is M. Fouquet?— M. Fouquet,' replied D'Artagnan to himself, 'is a handsome man very much beloved by the women, a generous man very much beloved by the poets; a man of wit, much execrated by petitioners. Well, now I am neither woman, poet, nor petitioner: I neither love nor hate monsieur le surintendant. I find myself, therefore, in the same position in which M. de Turenne found himself when opposed to the Prince de Condé at Jargeau, Gien and the Faubourg Saint-Antoine.* He did not execrate monsieur le prince, it is true, but he obeyed the king. Monsieur le prince is an agreeable man, but the king is king. Turenne heaved a deep sigh, called Condé "My cousin", and swept away his army. Now what does the king wish?—That does not concern me. Now, what does M. Colbert wish?—Oh, that's another thing. M. Colbert wishes all that M. Fouquet does not wish. Then what does M. Fouquet wish?—Oh, that is serious. M. Fouquet wishes precisely for all which the king wishes.'

This monologue ended, D'Artagnan began to laugh, whilst making his whip whistle in the air. He was already on the high road, frightening the birds in the hedges, listening to the livres chinking and dancing in his leather pocket, at every step; and, let us confess it, every time that D'Artagnan found himself in such conditions, tenderness was not his dominant vice. 'Come,' said he, 'I cannot think the expedition a very dangerous one; and it will fall out with my voyage as with that play M. Monk took me to see in London, which was called, I think, "Much Ado about Nothing".'*

LXVI

THE JOURNEY

IT was perhaps the fiftieth time since the day on which we open this history, that this man, with a heart of bronze and muscles of steel, had left house and friends, everything, in short, to go in search of fortune and death. The one—that is to say, death—

had constantly retreated before him, as if afraid of him; the other—that is to say, fortune—for only a month past had really made an alliance with him. Although he was not a great philosopher, after the fashion of either Epicurus or Socrates, he was a powerful spirit, having knowledge of life, and endowed with thought. No one is as brave, as adventurous, or as skilful as D'Artagnan, without being at the same time inclined to be a dreamer. He had picked up, here and there, some scraps of M. de la Rochefoucault, worthy of being translated into Latin by MM. de Port Royal; and he had made a collection, *en passant*, in the society of Athos and Aramis, of many morsels of Seneca and Cicero, translated by them, and applied to the uses of common life.* That contempt of riches which our Gascon had observed as an article of faith during the thirty-five first years of his life, had for a long time been considered by him as the first article of the code of bravery. 'Item one,' said he, 'A man is brave because he has nothing. A man has nothing because he despises riches.' Therefore, with these principles, which, as we have said, had regulated the thirty-five first years of his life, D'Artagnan was no sooner possessed of riches, than he felt it necessary to ask himself if, in spite of his riches, he were still brave. To this, for any other but D'Artagnan, the events of the Place de Grève might have served as a reply. Many consciences would have been satisfied with them, but D'Artagnan was brave enough to ask himself sincerely and conscientiously if he were brave. Therefore to this:

'But it appears to me that I drew promptly enough, and cut and thrust pretty freely on the Place de Grève, to be satisfied of my bravery,' D'Artagnan had himself replied. 'Gently, captain, that is not an answer. I was brave that day, because they were burning my house, and there are a hundred, and even a thousand, to speak against one, that if those gentlemen of the riots had not formed that unlucky idea, their plan of attack would have succeeded, or, at least, it would not have been I who would have opposed myself to it. Now, what will be brought against me? I have no house to be burnt in Brittany; I have no treasure there that can be taken from me. No; but I have my skin; that precious skin of M. d'Artagnan, which to him is worth more than all the houses and all the treasures of the world. That skin to which I cling above everything, because it is, everything considered, the binding of a body which encloses a heart very warm and ready to fight, and, consequently, to live. Then, I do desire to live: and, in reality, I live much better, more completely, since I have become rich. Who the devil ever said that money spoiled life? Upon my soul, it is no such thing, on the contrary, it seems as if I absorbed a double quantity of air and sun. *Mordioux*, what will it be then, if I double that fortune; and if, instead of the switch I now hold in my hand, I should ever carry the baton of a marshal? Then I really don't know if there will be, from that moment, enough of air and sun for me. In fact, this is not a dream, who the devil would oppose it, if the king made me a Marshal of France, as his father, King Louis XIII, made a duke and constable of Albert de Luynes? Am I not as brave, and much more intelligent, than that imbecile de Vitry?* Ah! that's exactly what will prevent my advancement: I have too much wit. Luckily, if there is any justice in this world, fortune owes me many compensations. She owes me certainly, a recompense for all I did for Anne of Austria,* and an indemnification for all she has not done for me. Then, at the present, I am very well with a king, and with a king who has the appearance of determining to reign. May God keep him on that illustrious road! For, if he is resolved to reign, he will need me; and if he needs me, he will give me what he has promised me—warmth and light; so that I march, comparatively, now, as I marched formerly—from nothing to everything. Only the nothing of to-day is the everything of former days; there has only this little change taken place in my life. And now let us see! let us state the case of the heart, as I just now was speaking of it. But in truth, I only spoke of it from memory.' And the Gascon applied his hand to his breast, as if he were actually seeking the place where his heart was.

'Ah! wretch!' murmured he, smiling with bitterness. 'Ah! poor mortal species! You hoped, for an instant, that you had not a heart, and now you find you have one—bad courtier as you are—and even one of the most seditious. You have a heart which speaks to you in favour of M. Fouquet. And what is M. Fouquet, when the king is in question?—A conspirator, a real conspirator, who did not even give himself the trouble to conceal his being a conspirator; therefore, what a weapon would you not have against him, if his good grace, and his intelligence had not made a scabbard for that weapon. An armed revolt!— for, in fact, M. Fouquet has been guilty of an armed revolt. Thus, while the king vaguely suspects M. Fouquet of rebellion, I know it—I could prove that M. Fouquet had caused the blood of his majesty's subjects to be shed. Now, then, let us see. Knowing all that, and holding my tongue, what further would this heart wish in return for a kind action of M. Fouquet's, for an advance of fifteen thousand livres, for a diamond worth a thousand pistoles, for a smile in which there was as much bitterness as kindness?—I am saving his life.'

'Now, then, I hope,' continued the musketeer, 'that this imbecile of a heart is going to preserve silence, and so be fairly quits with M. Fouquet. Now, then, the king becomes my sun, and as my heart is quits with M. Fouquet, let him beware who places himself between me and my sun! Forward, for his majesty Louis XIV!—Forward!'

These reflections were the only impediments which were able to retard the progress of D'Artagnan. These reflections once made, he increased the speed of his horse. But, however perfect his mount Zephyr might be, it could not hold out at such a pace for ever. The day after they left Paris, D'Artagnan left his mount at Chartres in the good hands of an innkeeper with whom he had grown friendly. From that moment, the musketeer travelled on post-horses. By this mode of locomotion, he traversed the space separating Chartres from Châteaubriand.* In the last of these two cities, far enough from the coast to prevent any one guessing that D'Artagnan wished to reach the sea—far enough from Paris to prevent all suspicion of his being a messenger from Louis XIV, whom D'Artagnan had called his sun, without suspecting that he who was only at present a rather poor star in the heaven of royalty, would, one day, make that star his emblem;* the messenger of Louis XIV, we say, quitted the post and purchased a broken-down old nag—one of those animals which an officer of cavalry would never choose, for fear of being disgraced. Excepting the colour, this new acquisition recalled to the mind of D'Artagnan the famous yellow horse with which, or rather upon which, he had made his first appearance in the world.* Truth to say, from the moment he crossed this new steed, it was no longer D'Artagnan who was travelling—it was a good man clothed in an iron-grey jerkin and brown breeches, so that he looked a cross between priest and layman; that which brought him nearest to the churchman was, that D'Artagnan had placed on his head a skull-cap of threadbare velvet, and over the skull-cap, a large black hat; no more sword; a stick hung by a cord to his wrist; but to this, he promised himself, as an unexpected auxiliary, to add, upon occasion, a good dagger, ten inches long, concealed under his cloak. The nag purchased at Châteaubriand completed the metamorphosis; it was called, or rather D'Artagnan called it, Ferret.

'If I have changed Zephyr into Ferret,' said D'Artagnan, 'I must make some diminutive or other of my own name. So, instead of D'Artagnan, I will be Agnan, simply; that is a concession which I naturally owe to my grey coat, my round hat, and my old skull-cap.'

Monsieur d'Artagnan travelled, then, pretty easily upon Ferret, who trotted along alertly enough and, while keeping to a trot, still managed cheerfully about twelve leagues a day, upon four spindle-shanks, of which the practised eye of D'Artagnan had appreciated the strength and safety beneath the thick mass of hair which covered them. Jogging along, the traveller took notes, studied the country, which he traversed reserved and silent, ever seeking the most plausible pretext for reaching Belle-Isle-en-Mer, and for seeing everything without arousing suspicion. In this manner, he was enabled to convince himself of the importance the event assumed in proportion as he drew near to it. In this remote country, in this ancient duchy of Brittany, which was not France at that period, and is not so even now,* the people knew nothing of the king of France. They not only did not know him, but were unwilling to know him. One face—a single one—floated visibly for them upon the political current. Their ancient dukes no longer ruled them; government was a void—nothing more. In place of the sovereign duke, the seigneurs of parishes reigned without control; and, above these seigneurs, was God, who has never been forgotten in Brittany. Among these suzerains of châteaux and steeples, the most powerful, the richest, and the most popular, was M. Fouquet, seigneur

of Belle-Isle.* Even in the country, even within sight of that
mysterious isle, legends and traditions consecrate its wonders.
Not every one could go there: the isle, of an extent of six leagues
in length, and six in breadth, was a seigneurial property, which
the people had for a long time held in fear, covered as it was by
the name of Retz, so redoubtable in that country. Shortly after
the erection of this seignieury into a marquisate, Belle-Isle passed
to M. Fouquet. The celebrity of the isle did not date from
yesterday; its name, or rather its qualification, is traced back to
the remotest antiquity. The ancients called it Kalonèse,* from
two Greek words, signifying beautiful isle. Thus, at a distance of
eighteen hundred years, it had borne, in another idiom, the
same name it still bears. There was, then, something very particular about this property of M. Fouquet's, besides its position
of six leagues off the coast of France; a position which makes it
sovereign in its maritime solitude, like a majestic ship which
disdains roads, and proudly casts anchor in mid-ocean.

D'Artagnan learnt all this without appearing the least in the
world astonished. He also learnt that the best way to get intelligence was to go to La Roche-Bernard, a tolerably important
city at the mouth of the Vilaine.* Perhaps there he could embark; if not, crossing the salt marshes, he would repair to
Guérande or Le Croisic,* to wait for an opportunity to cross
over to Belle-Isle. He had discovered, besides, since his departure from Châteaubriand, that nothing would be impossible
for Ferret under the impulsion of M. Agnan, and nothing to
M. Agnan through the initiative of Ferret. He prepared, then,
to sup off a teal and a pie, in an inn at La Roche-Bernard, and
ordered to be brought from the cellar, to wash down these two
Breton dishes, some cider, which, the moment it touched his
lips, he perceived to be more Breton still.

LXVII

BEFORE taking his place at table, D'Artagnan acquired, as was
his custom, all the information he could; but it is an axiom of
curiosity, that every man who wishes to question well and fruit-
fully ought in the first place to lay himself open to questions.
D'Artagnan sought, then, with his usual skill, a promising questioner in the tavern at La Roche-Bernard. At the moment, there
were in the house, on the first storey, two travellers either preparing for supper, or at supper itself. D'Artagnan had seen their
horses in the stable, and their baggage in the hall. One travelled
with a lackey, undoubtedly a person of consideration; two Perche
mares, sleek, sound beasts, were suitable means of locomotion.
The other, a little fellow, a traveller of meagre appearance, wearing a dusty overcoat, dirty linen, and boots more worn by the
pavement than the stirrup, had come from Nantes with a cart
drawn by a horse so like Ferret in colour, that D'Artagnan
might have gone a hundred miles without finding a better match.
This cart contained divers large packets wrapped in pieces of old
cloth.

'That traveller yonder,' said D'Artagnan to himself, 'is the
man for my money. He will do, he suits me; I ought to do for
and suit him; M. Agnan, with the grey doublet and the rusty
skull-cap, is not unworthy of supping with the gentleman of the
old boots and still older horse.'

This said, D'Artagnan called the host, and asked him to send
his teal, pie, and cider up to the chamber of the gentleman of
modest exterior. He himself climbed, a plate in his hand, the
wooden staircase which led to the chamber, and began to knock
at the door.

'Come in!' said the stranger. D'Artagnan entered, with a sim-
per on his lips, his plate under his arm, his hat in one hand, his
candle in the other.

'Excuse me, monsieur,' said he, 'I am, as you are, a traveller;

I know no one in the hotel, and I have the bad habit of losing my spirits when I eat alone; so that my repast appears a bad one to me, and does not nourish me. Your face, which I saw just now, when you came down to have some oysters opened—your face pleased me much. Besides, I have observed you have a horse just like mine, and that the host, no doubt on account of that resemblance, has placed them side by side in the stable, where they appear to agree amazingly well together. I therefore, monsieur, do not see any reason why the masters should be separated when the horses are united. Accordingly, I am come to request the pleasure of being admitted to your table. My name is Agnan, at your service, monsieur, the unworthy steward of a rich seigneur, who wishes to purchase some salt-works* in this country, and sends me to examine his future acquisitions. In truth, monsieur, I should be well pleased if my countenance were as agreeable to you as yours is to me; for, upon my honour, I am at your service.'

The stranger, whom D'Artagnan saw for the first time—for before he had only caught a glimpse of him—the stranger had black and brilliant eyes, a sallow complexion, a brow a little wrinkled by the weight of fifty years, a pleasant enough face, but some cunning in his eye.

'One would say,' thought D'Artagnan, 'that this merry fellow has never exercised more than the upper part of his head, his eyes, and his brain. He must be a man of science: his mouth, nose, and chin signify absolutely nothing.'

'Monsieur,' replied the latter, with whose mind and person we have been making so free, 'you do me much honour; not that I am ever bored, for I have,' added he, smiling, 'a company which amuses me always; but, never mind that, I am very happy to receive you.' But when saying this, the man with the worn boots cast an uneasy look at his table, from which the oysters had disappeared, and upon which there was nothing left but a morsel of salt bacon.

'Monsieur,' D'Artagnan hastened to say, 'the host is bringing me up a pretty piece of roasted poultry and a superb pie.' D'Artagnan had read in the look of his companion, however rapidly it disappeared, the fear of an attack by a cadger: he divined justly. At this opening, the features of the man of modest exterior relaxed; and, as if he had been waiting for the moment for his entrance, as D'Artagnan spoke, the host appeared, bearing the announced dishes. The pie and the teal were added to the morsel of broiled bacon; D'Artagnan and his guest bowed, sat down opposite to each other, and, like two brothers, shared the bacon and the other dishes.

'Monsieur,' said D'Artagnan, 'you must confess that association is a wonderful thing.'

'How so?' replied the stranger, with his mouth full.

'Well, I will tell you,' replied D'Artagnan.

The stranger gave a short truce to the movement of his jaws, in order to hear the better.

'In the first place,' continued D'Artagnan, 'instead of one candle, which each of us had, we have two.'

'That is true!' said the stranger, struck with the extreme lucidity of the observation.

'Then I see that you eat my pie in preference, whilst I, in preference, eat your bacon.'

'That is true again.'

'And then, in addition to being better lighted and eating what we prefer, I place the pleasure of your company.'

'Truly, monsieur, you are very convivial,' said the stranger, cheerfully.

'Yes, monsieur; convivial, as all people are who carry nothing on their minds, or, for that matter in their heads. Oh! I can see it is quite another matter with you,' continued D'Artagnan; 'I can read in your eyes all sorts of genius.'

'Oh, monsieur!'

'Come, confess one thing.'

'What is that?'

'That you are a learned man.'

'By Jove! monsieur.'

'Am I right?'

'Almost.'

'Come, then!'

'I am an author.'

'There!' cried D'Artagnan, clapping his hands, 'I knew I could not be deceived! It is a miracle!'

'Monsieur——'

'What! shall I have the honour of passing the evening in the society of an author, of a celebrated author, perhaps?'

'Oh!' said the stranger, blushing, 'celebrated, monsieur, celebrated is not the word.'

'Modest!' cried D'Artagnan, transported, 'he is modest!' Then, turning towards the stranger, with a character of blunt good humour: 'But tell me at least the name of your works, monsieur; for you will please to observe you have not told me your name, and I have been forced to guess at your genius.'

'My name is Jupenet,* monsieur,' said the author.

'A fine name! a grand name! upon my honour; and I do not know why—pardon me the mistake, if it be one—but surely I have heard that name somewhere.'

'I have written verses,' said the poet, modestly.

'Ah! that is it, then; I have heard them read.'

'A tragedy.'

'I must have seen it performed.'

The poet blushed again, and said: 'I do not think that can be the case, for my verses have never been printed.'

'Well, then, it must have been the tragedy which informed me of your name.'

'You are again mistaken, for the actors of the Hôtel de Bourgogne* would have nothing to do with it,' said the poet, with a smile, the recipe of which certain sorts of pride alone know the secret. D'Artagnan bit his lips. 'Thus, then, you see, monsieur,' continued the poet, 'you are in error on my account, and that not being at all known to you, you have never heard tell of me.'

'Ah! that confounds me. That name, Jupenet, appears to me, nevertheless, a fine name, and quite as worthy of being known as those of Corneille, or Rotrou, or Garnier.* I hope, monsieur, you will have the goodness to repeat to me a part of your tragedy presently, by way of dessert, for instance. That would make a sweet pudding—*mordioux!* Ah! pardon me, monsieur, that was a little oath which escaped me, because it is a habit with my lord and master. I sometimes allow myself to usurp that little oath, as it seems in pretty good taste. I take this liberty only in his absence, please to observe, for you may understand that in his presence—but, in truth, monsieur, this cider is abominable; do you not think so? And besides, the pot is of such an irregular shape it will not stand on the table.'

'Suppose we were to make it level?'

'To be sure; but with what?'

'With this knife.'

'And the teal, with what shall we cut that up? Do you not, by chance, mean to touch the teal?'

'Certainly.'

'Well, then——'

'Wait.'

And the poet rummaged in his pocket, and drew out a piece of brass, oblong, quadrangular, about a twelfth of an inch thick, and an inch and a half in length. But scarcely had this little piece of brass seen the light, than the poet appeared to have committed an imprudence, and made a movement to put it back again in his pocket. D'Artagnan perceived this, for he was a man who missed nothing. He stretched forth his hand towards the piece of brass: 'Humph! what you hold in your hand is pretty; will you allow me to look at it?'

'Certainly,' said the poet, who appeared to have yielded too soon to a first impulse. 'Certainly, you may look at it: but it will be in vain for you to look at it,' added he, with a satisfied air; 'if I were not to tell you its use, you would never guess it.'

D'Artagnan had seized as an admission the hesitation of the poet, and his eagerness to conceal the piece of brass which a first movement had induced him to take out of his pocket. His attention, therefore once awakened on this point, he surrounded himself with a circumspection which gave him a superiority on all occasions. Besides, whatever M. Jupenet might say about it, by a simple inspection of the object, he perfectly well knew what it was. It was a piece of type as used in printing.

'Can you guess, now, what this is?' continued the poet.

'No,' said D'Artagnan, 'I have no idea.'

'Well, monsieur,' said M. Jupenet, 'this little piece of metal is a printing letter.'

'Bah!'

'A capital.'

'Stop, stop, stop,' said D'Artagnan, opening his eyes very innocently.

'Yes, monsieur, a capital; the first letter of my name.'

'And this is a letter, is it?'

'Yes, monsieur.'

'Well, I will confess one thing to you.'

'And what is that?'

'No, I will not, I was going to say something stupid.'

'No, no,' said Monsieur Jupenet, with a patronizing air.

'Well, then, I cannot comprehend, if that is a letter, how you can make a word.'

'A word?'

'Yes, a printed word.'

'Oh, that's very easy.'

'Let me see.'

'Does it interest you?'

'Enormously.'

'Well, I will explain the thing to you. Pay attention.'

'I am attending.'

'This is it.'

'Good.'

'Watch closely.'

'I am looking.' D'Artagnan, in fact, appeared absorbed in his observations. Jupenet drew from his pocket seven or eight other pieces of brass smaller than the first.

'Ah, ah,' said D'Artagnan.

'What!'

'You have, then, a whole printing-office in your pocket. Devil take it! that is curious indeed.'

'Is it not?'

'Good God, what a number of things we learn by travelling.'

'Your health!' said Jupenent, quite enchanted.

'And yours, *mordioux*, yours. But—an instant—not in this cider. It is an abominable drink, unworthy of a man who quenches his thirst at the Hippocrene* fountain—is not it so you call your fountain, you poets?'

'Yes, monsieur, our fountain is so called. That comes from two Greek words—*hippos*, which means a horse, and——'

'Monsieur,' interrupted D'Artagnan, 'you shall drink of a liquor which comes from one single French word, and is none the worse for that—from the word *grape*; this cider gives me the heartburn. Allow me to inquire of your host if there is not a good bottle of Beaugency, or of the Ceran* growth, at the back of the large bins in his cellar.'

The host, being sent for, immediately attended.

'Monsieur,' interrupted the poet, 'take care, we shall not have time to drink the wine, unless we make great haste, for I must take advantage of the tide to secure the boat.'

'What boat?' asked D'Artagnan.

'Why the boat which sets out for Belle-Isle!'

'Ah—for Belle-Isle,' said the musketeer, 'that is good.'

'Bah! you will have plenty of time, monsieur,' replied the inn-keeper, uncorking the bottle, 'the boat will not leave for an hour.'

'But who will give me notice?' said the poet.

'Your fellow-traveller,' replied the host.

'But I scarcely know him.'

'When you hear him departing, it will be time for you to go.'

'Is he going to Belle-Isle, likewise, then?'

'Yes.'

'The traveller who has a lackey?' asked D'Artagnan. 'He is some gentleman, no doubt?'

'I know nothing of him.'

'What!—know nothing of him?'

'No, all I know is, that he is drinking the same wine as you.'

'By God!—that is a great honour for us,' said D'Artagnan, filling his companion's glass whilst the host went out.

'So,' resumed the poet, returning to his dominant ideas, 'you never saw any printing done?'

'Never.'

'Well, then, take the letters thus, which compose the word, you see: V, O, and here is a U, an E and an M.' And he assembled the letters with a swiftness and skill which did not escape the eye of D'Artagnan.

'*Volume*,' said he, as he ended.

'Good!' said D'Artagnan; 'here are the letters got together; but how are they kept so?' And he poured out a second glass for the poet. M. Jupenet smiled like a man who has an answer for everything; then he pulled out—still from his pocket—a little metal ruler, composed of two parts, like a carpenter's rule, against which he put together, and in a line, the characters, holding them under his left thumb.

'And what do you call that little metal ruler?' said D'Artagnan, 'for, I suppose, all these things have names.'

'This is called a composing-stick,' said Jupenet; 'it is by the aid of this stick that the lines are formed.'

'Come, then, I was not mistaken in what I said; you have a press in your pocket,' said D'Artagnan, laughing with an air of such foolish simplicity that the poet was completely his dupe.

'No,' replied he; 'but I am too lazy to write, and when I have a verse in my head, I print it immediately. That is a labour spared.'

'*Mordioux!*' thought D'Artagnan to himself, 'this must be cleared up.' And under a pretext, which did not pose any problem to the musketeer, who was fertile in expedients, he left the table, went downstairs, ran to the shed under which stood the poet's little cart, and poked the point of his poniard into the stuff which enveloped one of the packages, which he found full of types, like those which the poet had in his pocket.

'Humph!' said D'Artagnan, 'I do not yet know whether M. Fouquet wishes to fortify Belle-Isle; but, at all events, here are some spiritual munitions for the castle.' Then, enchanted with his rich discovery, he ran upstairs again and resumed his place at the table.

D'Artagnan had learnt what he wished to know. He, however, remained, none the less, face to face with his partner, until the moment they heard from the next room symptoms of a person's being about to go out. The printer was immediately on foot; he had given orders for his horse to be got ready. His carriage was waiting at the door. The second traveller got into his saddle, in the courtyard, with his lackey. D'Artagnan followed Jupenet to the door; he embarked his cart and horse on board the boat. As to the opulent traveller, he did the same with his two horses and servant. But all the wit D'Artagnan employed in endeavouring to find out his name was wasted—he could learn nothing. Only he took such notice of his countenance, that it was impressed upon his mind forever. D'Artagnan had a great inclination to embark with the two travellers, but an interest, more powerful than curiosity—that of success—repelled him from the shore, and brought him back again to the tavern. He entered with a sigh, and went to bed directly in order to be ready early in the morning with fresh ideas and the sage counsel of sufficient sleep.

LXVIII

D'ARTAGNAN CONTINUES HIS INVESTIGATIONS

At daybreak D'Artagnan saddled Ferret, who had fared sumptuously all night, devouring the remainder of the oats and hay left by the other two horses. The musketeer sifted all he possibly could out of the innkeeper, who he found cunning, mistrustful, and devoted, body and soul, to M. Fouquet. In order not to awaken the suspicions of this man, he carried on his tale of being a probable purchaser of salt-works. To have embarked for Belle-Isle at Roche-Bernard, would have been to expose himself still further to comments which had, perhaps, been already made, and would be carried to the castle. Moreover, it was singular that the traveller and his lackey should have remained a mystery to D'Artagnan, in spite of all the questions addressed by him to the innkeeper, who appeared to know him perfectly well. The musketeer then made some enquiries concerning the salt-works, and took the road to the marshes, leaving the sea on his right, and penetrating into that vast and desolate plain which resembles a sea of mud, of which, here and there, a few crests of salt silver the undulations. Ferret walked admirably, on his little nervous legs, along the foot-wide causeways which separate the salt-works. D'Artagnan, aware of the consequences of a fall, which would result in a cold bath, allowed him to go as he liked, contenting himself with looking at, on the horizon, three steeples, that rose up like lance-blades from the bosom of the bare plain. Piriac,* the bourg of Batz and Le Croisic, exactly resembling each other, attracted and suspended his attention. If the traveller turned round, the better to make his observations, he saw on the other side a horizon of three other steeples, Guérande, Le Pouliguen, and Saint-Joachim, which, in their circumference, represented a set of skittles, of which he and Ferret were but the wandering ball. Piriac was the first little port on his right. He went thither, with the names of the principal salt-makers on his lips. At the moment he reached the little port of Piriac, five large barges, laden with stone, were leaving it. It appeared strange to D'Artagnan, that stones should be leaving a country where none are found. He had recourse to all the amenity of M. Agnan to learn from the people of the port the cause of this singular trade. An old fisherman replied to M. Agnan, that the stones very certainly did not come from Piriac or the marshes.

'Where do they come from, then?' asked the musketeer.

'Monsieur, they come from Nantes and Paimbœuf.'*

'Where are they going, then?'

'Monsieur, to Belle-Isle.'

'Ah! ah!' said D'Artagnan, in the same tone he had assumed to tell the printer that his character interested him; 'are they building at Belle-Isle, then?'

'Why, yes, monsieur, M. Fouquet has the walls of the castle repaired every year.'

'Is it in ruins, then?'

'It is old.'

'Thank you.'

'The fact is,' said D'Artagnan to himself, 'nothing is more natural; every proprietor has a right to repair his own property. It would be like telling me I was fortifying the Face of Our Lady, when I was simply obliged to make repairs. In honest truth, I believe false reports have been made to his majesty, and he is very likely to be wrong.'

'You must confess,' continued he then, aloud, and addressing the fisherman—for his role as a suspicious man was imposed upon him by the object of his mission—'you must confess, my dear monsieur, that these stones travel in a very curious fashion.'

'How so?' said the fisherman.

'They come from Nantes or Paimbœuf on the Loire, do they not?'

'With the tide.'

'That is convenient—I don't say it is not; but why do they not go straight from Saint-Nazaire* to Belle-Isle?'

'Eh! because the barges are fresh-water boats, and take the sea badly,' replied the fisherman.

'That is not sufficient reason.'

'Pardon me, monsieur, one may see that you have never been a sailor,' added the fisherman, not without contempt.

'Explain that to me, if you please, my good man. It appears to me that to come from Paimbœuf to Piriac, and go from Piriac to Belle-Isle, is as if we went from Roche-Bernard to Nantes, and from Nantes to Piriac.'

'By water that would be the nearest way,' replied the fisherman, imperturbably.

'But there is a bend in the river?'

The fisherman shook his head.

'The shortest road from one place to another is a straight line,' continued D'Artagnan.

'You forget the tide, monsieur.'

'Well! take the tide.'

'And the wind.'

'Well, and the wind.'

'Without doubt; the current of the Loire carries boats almost as far as Le Croisic. If they want to heave to a little, or refresh the crew, they come to Piriac along the coast; from Piriac they find another reverse current, which carries them two leagues and a half, to the Isle-Dumal.'

'Granted.'

'There the current of the Vilaine throws them upon another isle, the isle of Hoedic.'*

'I agree with that.'

'Well, monsieur, from that isle to Belle-Isle the way is quite straight. The sea, broken both above and below, passes like a canal—like a mirror between the two isles; the barges glide along upon it like ducks upon the Loire; that's how it is.'

'It does not signify,' said the obstinate M. Agnan; 'it is a long way round.'

'Ah! yes; but M. Fouquet will have it so,' replied the fisherman with finality, taking off his woollen cap at the enunciation of that respected name.

A look from D'Artagnan, a look as keen and piercing as a sword-blade, found nothing in the heart of the old man but simple confidence—on his features, nothing but satisfaction and disinterestedness. He said, 'M. Fouquet will have it so,' as he would have said, 'God has willed it.'

D'Artagnan had already advanced too far in this direction; besides, the barges being gone, there remained nothing at Piriac but a single boat—that of the old man, and it did not look fit for sea without great preparation. D'Artagnan therefore patted Ferret, who, as a new proof of his charming character, resumed his march with his feet in the salt marshes, and his nose to the dry wind, which bends the furze and the broom of this landscape. They reached Le Croisic about five o'clock.

If D'Artagnan had been a poet, it was a beautiful spectacle: at high tide the sea covers a beach a league or more wide which, at low tide, appears grey and desolate, strewn with polyps and seaweed, and pebbles sparse and white, like bones in some vast old cemetery. But the soldier, the politician, and the ambitious man, had no longer the sweet consolation of looking towards heaven, to read there a hope or a warning. A red sky signifies nothing to such people but wind and disturbance. White and fleecy clouds upon the azure only say that the sea will be smooth and peaceful. D'Artagnan found the sky blue, the breeze embalmed with saline perfumes, and he said: 'I will embark with the first tide, if it be but in a nutshell.'

At Le Croisic as at Piriac, he had remarked enormous heaps of stone lying along the shore. These gigantic walls, reduced at every tide by the barges for Belle-Isle, were, in the eyes of the musketeer, the consequence and the proof of what he had well divined at Piriac. Was it a wall that M. Fouquet was constructing? was it a fortification that he was erecting? To ascertain that, he must make fuller observations. D'Artagnan put Ferret into a stable; supped, went to bed, and on the morrow took a walk upon the port or rather upon the shingle. The entrance to the harbour at Le Croisic is fifty feet wide and there is a look-out which resembles an enormous sugarloaf on a dish. The flat strand is the dish. Hundreds of barrowsful of earth mixed with pebbles and shaped into a cone with paths winding round it make up both the sugarloaf and the look-out. It is so now, and it was so two hundred years ago, only the sugarloaf was not so large, and probably there were to be seen no trellises of lath around it, staked out like pretty railings along the passages that wind towards the little terrace. Upon the shingle lounged three or four fishermen talking about sardines and shrimps. D'Artagnan, with his eyes animated by rough gaiety, and a smile upon his lips, approached these fishermen.

'Any fishing going on to-day?' said he.

'Yes, monsieur,' replied one of them, 'we are only waiting for the tide.'

'Where do you fish, my friends?'

'Along the coasts, monsieur.'

'Which are the best coasts?'

'Ah, that is all according. Those around the isles, for example.'

'Yes, but they are a long way off, those isles, are they not?'

'Not very; four leagues.'

'Four leagues! That is quite a voyage.'

The fishermen laughed in M. Agnan's face.

'Hear me, then,' said the latter, with an air of simple stupidity; 'four leagues off you lose sight of land, do you not?'

'Why, not always.'

'Ah, it is a long way—too long, or else I would have asked you to take me aboard, and to show me what I have never seen.'

'What is that?'

'A live sea-fish.'

'Monsieur comes from inland?' said a fisherman.

'Yes, I come from Paris.'

The Breton shrugged his shoulders; then:

'Have you ever seen M. Fouquet in Paris?' asked he.

'Often,' replied D'Artagnan.

'Often!' repeated the fishermen, closing their circle round the Parisian. 'Do you know him?'

'A little; he is the intimate friend of my master.'

'Ah!' said the fisherman, in astonishment.

'And,' said D'Artagnan, 'I have seen all his châteaux of Saint Mandé, of Vaux, and his hotel in Paris.'

'Is that a fine place?'

'Superb.'

'It is not so fine a place as Belle-Isle,' said the fisherman.

'Bah!' cried M. d'Artagnan, breaking into a laugh so loud that he angered all his auditors.

'It is very plain you have never seen Belle-Isle,' said the most curious of the fishermen. 'Do you know that there are six leagues of it; and that there are such trees on it as cannot be equalled even at Nantes?'

'Trees out at sea!' cried D'Artagnan; 'well, I should like to see them.'

'That can be easily done; we are fishing at the Isle de Hoedic—come with us. From that place you will see, looking like Paradise, the black trees of Belle-Isle against the sky; you will see the white line of the castle, which cuts the horizon of the sea like a blade.'

'Oh,' said D'Artagnan, 'that must be very beautiful. But do you know there are a hundred turrets at M. Fouquet's château of Vaux?'

The Breton raised his head in profound admiration, but he was not convinced. 'A hundred turrets! Ah, that may be; but Belle-Isle is finer than that. Should you like to see Belle-Isle?'

'Is that possible?' asked D'Artagnan.

'Yes, with permission of the governor.'

'But I do not know the governor.'

'As you know M. Fouquet, you can tell your name.'

'Oh, my friends, I am not a gentleman.'

'Everybody enters Belle-Isle,' continued the fisherman in his strong, pure language, 'provided he means no harm to Belle-Isle or its master.'

A slight shudder crept over the body of the musketeer. 'That is true,' thought he. Then, recovering himself, 'If I were sure,' said he, 'not to be sea-sick.'

'What, upon *her*?' said the fisherman, pointing with pride to his pretty round-bottomed bark.

'Well, you almost persuade me,' cried M. Agnan; 'I will go and see Belle-Isle, but they will not admit me.'

'We shall enter, safe enough.'

'You! What for?'

'Why, monsieur! to sell fish to the corsairs.'

'Ha! Corsairs—what do you mean?'

'Well, I mean that M. Fouquet is having two corsairs built to chase the Dutch and the English, and we sell our fish to the crews of those little vessels.'

'Come, come!' said D'Artagnan to himself—'better and better. A printing-press, bastions, and corsairs! Well, M. Fouquet is not an enemy to be despised, as I presumed to fancy. He is worth the trouble of travelling to see him nearer.'

'We sail at half-past five,' said the fisherman gravely.

'I am quite ready, and I will not leave you now.' So D'Artagnan saw the fishermen haul their boats to meet the tide with a windlass. The sea rose; M. Agnan allowed himself to be hoisted on board, not without sporting a little fear and awkwardness, to the amusement of the young beach-urchins who watched him with their large intelligent eyes. He laid himself down upon a folded sail, not interfering with anything whilst the boat prepared for sea; and, with its large square sail, it was fairly out within two hours. The fishermen, who prosecuted their occupation as they proceeded, did not perceive that their passenger had not become pale, neither groaned nor suffered; that in spite of that horrible tossing and rolling of the bark, to which no hand imparted direction, the novice passenger had preserved his presence of mind and his appetite. They fished, and their fishing was sufficiently fortunate. To lines baited with prawn, soles came, frolicking, to bite. Two nets had already been broken by the immense weight of congers and haddocks; three sea-eels ploughed the hold with their slimy folds and their dying contortions. D'Artagnan brought them good luck; they told him so. The soldier found the occupation so pleasant, that he put his hand to the work—that is to say, to the lines—and uttered roars of joy and *mordioux* enough to have astonished his musketeers themselves, every time that a shock given to his line by the captured fish required the play of the muscles of his arm, and the employment of his best dexterity. The fun of the outing had made him forget his diplomatic mission. He was struggling with a very large conger, and holding fast with one hand to the side of the vessel, in order to seize with the other the gaping jowl of his antagonist, when the master said to him. 'Take care they don't see you from Belle-Isle!'

These words produced the same effect upon D'Artagnan as the hissing of the first bullet on a day of battle; he let go of both line and conger, which, dragging each other, returned again to the water. D'Artagnan perceived, within half a league at most, the blue, clear profile of the cliffs of Belle-Isle, dominated by the majestic whiteness of the castle. In the distance, the land with its forests and verdant plains; cattle on the grass. This was what first attracted the attention of the musketeer. The sun darted its rays of gold upon the sea, raising a shining mist round this enchanted isle. Little could be seen of it, owing to this dazzling light, but the salient points; every shadow was strongly marked, and striped with bands of darkness the luminous fields and walls. 'Eh! eh!' said D'Artagnan, at the aspect of those masses of black rocks, 'these are fortifications which do not stand in need of any engineer to render a landing difficult. How the devil can a landing be effected on that isle which God has defended so completely?'

'This way,' replied the skipper of the boat, changing the sail, and impressing upon the rudder a twist which turned the boat in the direction of a pretty little port, neat, semicircular, and newly battlemented.

'What the devil do I see yonder?' said D'Artagnan.

'You see Locmaria,'* replied the fisherman.

'Well, but there?'

'That is Bangor.'

'And further on?'

'Sauzon, and then Le Palais.'

'*Mordioux!* It is a world of its own. Ah! there are some soldiers.'

'There are seventeen hundred men in Belle-Isle, monsieur,' replied the fisherman, proudly. 'Do you know that the smallest garrison is of twenty companies of infantry?'

'*Mordioux!*' cried D'Artagnan, stamping with his foot. 'His majesty was right enough.'

They landed.

LXIX

IN WHICH THE READER, NO DOUBT, WILL BE AS ASTONISHED AS D'ARTAGNAN WAS TO MEET AN OLD ACQUAINTANCE

THERE is always something in a landing, if it be only from the smallest sea-boat—a trouble and a confusion which do not leave the mind the liberty which it needs in order to study at the first glance the new locality presented to it. The movable bridges, the agitated sailors, the noise of the water on the pebbles, the cries and importunities of those who wait upon the shores, are multiplied details of that sensation which is summed up in one single result—hesitation. It was not, then, till after standing several minutes on the shore that D'Artagnan saw upon the harbour, but more particularly in the interior of the isle, an immense number of workmen in motion. At his feet D'Artagnan recognized the five barges laden with rough stone he had seen leave the port of Piriac. The smaller stones were transported to the shore by means of a chain formed by twenty-five or thirty peasants. The large stones were loaded on trolleys which conveyed them in the same direction as the others, that is to say towards the works, of which D'Artagnan could as yet appreciate neither the strength nor the extent. Everywhere was to be seen an activity equal to that which Telemachus observed on his landing at Salentum.* D'Artagnan felt a strong inclination to penetrate into the interior; but he could not, under the penalty of exciting mistrust, exhibit too much curiosity. He advanced then little by little, scarcely going beyond the line formed by the fishermen on the beach, observing everything, saying nothing, and meeting all suspicion that might have been excited with a half-silly question or a polite bow. And yet, whilst his companions carried on their trade, giving or selling their fish to the workmen or the inhabitants of the city, D'Artagnan had gained ground by degrees, and, reassured by the little attention paid to him, he began to cast an intelligent and confident look upon the men and things that appeared before his eyes. And his very first glance fell on certain earthworks about which the eye of a soldier could not be mistaken. At the two extremities of the harbour, in order that their fires should converge upon the great axis of the ellipse formed by the basin, in the first place two batteries had been raised, evidently destined to receive flank pieces, for D'Artagnan saw the workmen finishing the platform and making ready the demi-circumference in wood upon which the wheels of the guns might turn to embrace every direction over the epaulement.* By the side of each of these batteries other workmen were strengthening gabions filled with earth, the lining of another battery. The latter had embrasures, and the overseer of the works called successively men who, with cords, tied the fascines and cut the lozenges and right angles of turfs destined to retain the matting of the embrasures. To judge by the activity displayed in these works, already so far advanced, they might be considered as finished: they were not yet furnished with their cannons, but the platforms had their housings and their beams all prepared; the earth, beaten carefully, was consolidated; and supposing guns to be already on the island, in less than two or three days the port might be completely armed. What astonished D'Artagnan, when he turned his eyes from the coast batteries to the fortifications of the town, was to see that Belle-Isle was defended by an entirely new system, of which he had often heard the Comte de la Fère speak as a wonderful advance, but of which he had as yet never seen the application. These fortifications belonged neither to the Dutch method of Marollais, nor to the French method of the Chevalier Antoine de Ville, but to the system of Manesson Mallet,* a skilful engineer, who about six or eight years previously had quitted the service of Portugal to enter that of France. The works had this peculiarity, that instead of rising above the ground, as did the ancient ramparts designed to defend a city from escalades, they, on the contrary, sank into it; and what created the height of the walls was the depth of the ditches. It did not take long to make D'Artagnan perceive the superiority of such a system, which gives no advantage to cannon. Besides, as the ditches were lower than, or on a level with, the sea, they could be instantly flooded by means of subterranean sluices. Otherwise, the works were almost complete, and a group of workmen, receiving orders from a man who appeared to be the co-ordinator of the works, were occupied in placing the last stones. A bridge of planks, thrown over the ditches for the greater convenience of the manœuvres of the barrows, joined the interior to the exterior. With an air of simple curiosity, D'Artagnan asked if he might be permitted to cross the bridge, and he was told that no order prevented it. Consequently he crossed the bridge, and advanced towards the group.

This group was superintended by the man whom D'Artagnan had already remarked, and who appeared to be the engineer-in-chief. A plan was lying open before him upon a large stone forming a table, and at some paces from him a crane was in action. This engineer, who by his evident importance first attracted the attention of D'Artagnan, wore a jerkin, which, from its sumptuousness, was scarcely in harmony with the work he was employed in, that rather necessitated the costume of a master-mason than of a noble. He was a man of immense stature and great square shoulders, and wore a hat covered with feathers. He gesticulated in the most majestic manner, and appeared, for D'Artagnan only saw his back, to be scolding the workmen for their idleness and want of strength.

D'Artagnan continued to draw nearer. At that moment the man with the feathers ceased to gesticulate, and, with his hands placed upon his knees, was following, half-bent, the effort of six workmen to raise a block of hewn stone to the top of a piece of timber destined to support that stone, so that the cord of the crane might be passed under it. The six men, all on one side of the stone, united their efforts to raise it to eight or ten inches from the ground, sweating and blowing, whilst a seventh got ready, as soon as there should be daylight enough beneath it, to slide in the roller that was to support it. But the stone had already twice escaped from their hands before gaining a sufficient height for the roller to be introduced. There is no need to say that every time the stone escaped them, they bounded quickly backwards, to keep their feet from being crushed by the stone as it fell back. Every time, the stone, abandoned by them, sunk deeper into the damp earth, which rendered the operation more and more difficult. A third effort was followed by no better success, but with progressive discouragement. And yet, when the six men were bent towards the stone, the man with the feathers had himself, with a powerful voice, given the word of command, 'Heave!' which regulates manœuvres of strength. Then he drew himself up.

'Oh! oh!' said he, 'what is all this about? Have I to do with men of straw? Devil take it! stand on one side, and you shall see how this is to be done.'

'Hell's teeth!' said D'Artagnan, 'is he going to try to lift that rock? that would be a sight worth seeing.'

The workmen, as commanded by the engineer, drew back with their ears down, and shaking their heads, with the exception of the one who held the plank, who prepared to perform the office. The man with the feathers went up to the stone, stooped, slipped his hands under the face lying upon the ground, stiffened his Herculean muscles, and, without a strain, with a slow motion, like that of a machine, he lifted the end of the rock a foot from the ground. The workman who held the plank profited by the space thus given him, and slipped the roller under the stone.

'That's the way,' said the giant, not letting the rock fall again, but placing it upon its support.

'*Mordioux!*' cried D'Artagnan, 'I know but one man capable of such a feat of strength.'

'Who's that?' cried the colossus, turning round.

'Porthos!' murmured D'Artagnan, seized with stupor, 'Porthos at Belle-Isle!'

On his part, the man with the feathers fixed his eyes upon the disguised lieutenant, and, in spite of his metamorphosis, recognized him. 'D'Artagnan!' cried he; and the colour mounted to his face. 'Hush!' said he to D'Artagnan.

'Hush!' in his turn, said the musketeer. In fact, if Porthos had just been discovered by D'Artagnan, D'Artagnan had just been discovered by Porthos. The interest of the particular secret of each struck them both at the same instant. Nevertheless, the first movement of the two men was to throw their arms round each other. What they wished to conceal from the bystanders, was not their friendship, but their names. But, after the embrace, came reflection.

'What the devil brings Porthos to Belle-Isle, lifting stones?' said D'Artagnan; only D'Artagnan uttered that question in a low voice. Less strong in diplomacy than his friend, Porthos thought aloud.

'How the devil did you come to Belle-Isle?' asked he of D'Artagnan; 'and what are you doing here?' It was necessary to reply without hesitation. To hesitate in his answer to Porthos would have been a check, for which the self-love of D'Artagnan would never have consoled itself.

'Confound it! my friend, I am at Belle-Isle because *you* are.'

'Ah, bah!' said Porthos, visibly stupefied with the argument, and seeking to account for it to himself, with the felicity of deduction we know to be peculiar to him.

'It's true,' continued D'Artagnan, unwilling to give his friend time to recollect himself, 'I have been to see you at Pierrefonds.'

'Indeed!'

'Yes.'

'And you did not find me there?'

'No, but I found Mouston.'*

'Is he well?'

'Very!'

'Good, but Mouston did not tell you I was here.'

'Why should he *not*? Have I, perchance, deserved to lose his confidence?'

'No; but he did not know.'

'Well; that is a reason at least that does not offend my self-love.'

'Then, how did you manage to find me?'

'My dear friend, a great noble, like you, always leaves traces behind him on his passage; and I should think but poorly of myself, if I were not sharp enough to follow the traces of my friends.' This explanation, flattering as it was, did not entirely satisfy Porthos.

'But I left no traces behind me, for I came here disguised,' said Porthos.

'Ah! You came disguised, did you?' said D'Artagnan.

'Yes.'

'And how?'

'As a miller.'

'And do you think a great noble, like you, Porthos, can affect common manners so as to deceive people?'

'Well, I swear to you, my friend, that I played my part so well that *everybody* was deceived.'

'Indeed! so well, that I have not discovered and joined you?'

'Yes; but *how* did you discover and join me?'

'Stop a bit. I was going to tell you how. Do you imagine Mouston——?'

'Ah! it was that fellow, Mouston,' said Porthos, gathering up those two triumphant arches which served him for eyebrows.

'But stop, I tell you—it was no fault of Mouston's, because he was ignorant of where you were.'

'I know he was; and that is why I am in such haste to understand——'

'Oh! how impatient you are, Porthos.'

'When I do not comprehend, I am terrible.'

'Well, you will understand. Aramis wrote to you at Pierrefonds, did he not?'

'Yes.'

'And he told you to come before the equinox.'

'That is true.'

'Well! that is it,' said D'Artagnan, hoping that this reason would mystify Porthos. Porthos appeared to give himself up to a violent mental labour.

'Yes, yes,' said he, 'I understand. As Aramis told me to come before the equinox, you have understood that that was to join him. You then inquired where Aramis was, saying to yourself, "Where Aramis is, there Porthos will be." You have learnt that Aramis was in Brittany, and you said to yourself, "Porthos is in Brittany."'

'Exactly. In good truth, Porthos, I cannot tell why you have not turned conjuror. So you understand that, arriving at Roche-Bernard, I heard of the splendid fortifications going on at Belle-Isle. The account raised my curiosity, I embarked in a fishing-boat, without dreaming that you were here: I came, and I saw a monstrous fine fellow lifting a stone Ajax* could not have stirred. I cried out, "Nobody but the Baron de Bracieux* could have performed such a feat of strength." You heard me, you turned round, you recognized me, we embraced; and, by God! if you like, my dear friend, we will embrace again.'

'Ah! now all is explained,' said Porthos; and he embraced D'Artagnan with so much friendship as to deprive the musketeer of his breath for five minutes.

'Why, you are stronger than ever,' said D'Artagnan, 'and still, happily, in your *arms*.' Porthos saluted D'Artagnan with a gracious smile. During the five minutes D'Artagnan spent recovering his breath, he reflected that he had a very difficult role to play. It was necessary that he always should question and never reply. By the time his respiration returned to normal, he had fixed his plans for the campaign.

LXX

WHEREIN THE IDEAS OF D'ARTAGNAN, AT FIRST STRANGELY CLOUDED, BEGIN TO CLEAR A LITTLE

D'ARTAGNAN immediately took the offensive. 'Now that I have told you all, dear friend, or rather now you have guessed all, tell me what you are doing here, covered with dust and mud?'

Porthos wiped his brow, and looked around him with pride. 'Why, it appears,' said he, 'that you may see what I am doing here.'

'No doubt, no doubt, you lift great stones.'

'Oh! to show these idle fellows what a *man* is,' said Porthos, with contempt. 'But you understand——'

'Yes, that it is not your place to lift stones, although there are many whose place it is, who cannot lift them as you do. It was that which made me ask you, just now. What are you doing here, baron?'

'I am studying topography, chevalier.'

'You are studying topography?'

'Yes; but you—what are you doing in that common dress?'

D'Artagnan perceived he had committed a fault in giving expression to his astonishment. Porthos had taken advantage of it, to retort with a question. 'Why,' said he, 'you know I am a bourgeois, in fact; my dress, then, has nothing astonishing in it, since it conforms with my condition.'

'Nonsense! you are a musketeer.'

'You are wrong, my friend; I have given in my resignation.'

'Bah!'

'It's true.'

'And have you abandoned the service?'

'I have left it.'

'You have abandoned the king?'

'Quite.'

Porthos raised his arms towards heaven, like a man who has heard extraordinary news. 'Well, that *does* confound me,' said he.

'It is nevertheless true.'

'And what led you to form such a resolution?'

'The king displeased me. Mazarin had sickened me for a long time, as you know; so I threw my hand in and got out.'

'But Mazarin is dead.'

'I know that well enough, dammit! Only, at the period of his death, my resignation had been given in and accepted two months. Then, feeling myself free, I set off for Pierrefonds, to see my friend Porthos. I had heard talk of the happy division you had made of your time, and I wished, for a fortnight, to divide mine after your fashion.'

'My friend, you know that it is not for a fortnight my house is open to you; it is for a year—for ten years—for life.'

'Thank you, Porthos.'

'Ah! but perhaps you need money—do you?' said Porthos, making something like fifty louis chink in his pocket. 'In that case, you know——'

'No, thank you; I am not in need of anything. I placed my savings with Planchet, who pays me the interest of them.'

'Your savings?'

'Yes, to be sure,' said D'Artagnan: 'why should I not put by my savings, as well as another, Porthos?'

'Oh, there is no reason why; on the contrary, I always suspected you—that is to say, Aramis always suspected you to have savings. For my own part, d'ye see, I take no concern about the management of my household; but I presume the savings of a musketeer must be small.'

'No doubt, relative to yourself, Porthos, who are a millionaire; but you shall judge. I had laid by twenty-five thousand livres.'

'That's pretty well,' said Porthos, with an affable air.

'And,' continued D'Artagnan, 'on the twenty-eighth of last month* I added to it two hundred thousand livres more.'

Porthos opened his large eyes, which eloquently demanded of the musketeer, Where the devil did you steal such a sum as that, my dear friend? 'Two hundred thousand livres!' cried he, at length.

'Yes; which, with the twenty-five I had, and twenty thousand I have about me, complete the sum of two hundred and forty-five thousand livres.'

'But tell me, whence comes this fortune?'

'I will tell you all about it presently, dear friend; but as you have, in the first place, many things to tell me yourself, let us have my recital in its proper order.'

'Bravo!' said Porthos; 'then we are both rich. But what can I have to relate to you?'

'You have to relate to me how Aramis came to be appointed——'

'Ah! bishop of Vannes.'

'That's it,' said D'Artagnan, 'bishop of Vannes. Dear Aramis! do you know how he succeeded so well?'

'Yes, yes; and he does not mean to stop there.'

'What! do you mean he will not be contented with purple stockings, and that he wants a red hat?'*

'Hush! that is *promised* him.'

'Bah! by the king?'

'By somebody more powerful than the king.'

'Ah! the devil! Porthos: what incredible things you tell me, my friend!'

'Why incredible? Is there not *always* somebody in France more powerful than the king?'

'Oh, yes; in the time of King Louis XIII it was Cardinal Richelieu; in the time of the Regency it was Cardinal Mazarin. In the time of Louis XIV it is M——'

'Go on.'

'It is M. Fouquet.'

'Jove! you have hit it the first time.'

'So, then, I suppose it is M. Fouquet who has promised Aramis the red hat?'

Porthos assumed an air of reserve. 'Dear friend,' said he, 'God preserve me from meddling with the affairs of others, above all from revealing secrets it may be to their interest to keep. When you see Aramis, he will tell you all he thinks he ought to tell you.'

'You are right, Porthos; and you are a padlock for secrets. But, to revert to yourself?'

'Yes,' said Porthos.

'You said just now you came hither to study topography?'

'I did so.'

'By God! my friend, what fine things you will do!'

'How do you mean?'

'Why, these fortifications are admirable.'

'Is that your opinion?'

'Decidedly it is. In truth, to anything but a regular siege, Belle-Isle is absolutely impregnable.'

Porthos rubbed his hands. 'That is my opinion,' said he.

'But who the devil has fortified this paltry little place in this manner?'

Porthos drew himself up proudly: 'Did not I tell you who?'

'No.'

'Do you not suspect?'

'No; all I can say is that he is a man who has studied all the systems, and who appears to me to have hit on the best.'

'Hush!' said Porthos; 'consider my modesty, my dear D'Artagnan.'

'In truth,' replied the musketeer, 'can it be you—who—oh!'

'Pray—my dear friend——'

'You who have imagined, traced, and combined these bastions, these redans, these curtains, these half-moons;* and are preparing that covered way?'

'I beg you——'

'You who have built that lunette with its retiring angles and its salient angles?'

'My friend——'

'You who have given that inclination to the openings of your embrasures, by means of which you so effectively protect the men who serve the guns!'

'Eh! By Jove! yes.'

'Oh! Porthos, Porthos! I must bow down before you—I must admire you! But you have always concealed from us this superb, this incomparable genius. I hope, my dear friend, you will show me all this in detail?'

'Nothing more easy. Here lies my original sketch, my plan.'

'Show it me.' Porthos led D'Artagnan towards the stone that served him for a table, and upon which the plan was spread. At the foot of the plan was written, in the formidable writing of Porthos, writing of which we have already had occasion to speak:

'Instead of making use of the square or rectangle, as has been done to this time, you will suppose your place enclosed in a regular hexagon, this polygon having the advantage of offering more angles than the quadrilateral. Every side of your hexagon, of which you will determine the length in proportion to the dimensions taken upon the spot, will be divided into two parts, and upon the middle point you will elevate a perpendicular towards the centre of the polygon, which will equal in length the sixth part of the side. By the extremities of each side of the polygon, you will trace two diagonals, which will cut the perpendicular. These will form the precise lines of your defence.'

'The devil!' said D'Artagnan, stopping at this point of the demonstration; 'why, this is a complete system, Porthos.'

'Entirely,' said Porthos. 'Continue.'

'No; I have read enough; but, since it is you, my dear Porthos, who direct the works, what need have you of setting down your system so formally in writing?'

'Oh! my dear friend, death!'

'How! death?'

'Why, we are all mortal, are we not?'

'That is true,' said D'Artagnan; 'you have a reply for everything, my friend.' And he replaced the plan upon the stone.

But however short the time he had the plan in his hands, D'Artagnan had been able to distinguish, under the enormous writing of Porthos, a much more delicate hand, which reminded him of certain letters to Marie Michon,* with which he had been acquainted in his youth. Only the India-rubber had passed and repassed so often over this writing that it might have escaped a less practiced eye than that of our musketeer.

'Bravo! my friend, bravo!' said D'Artagnan.

'And now you know all that you want to know, do you not?' said Porthos, wheeling about.

'*Mordioux!* yes, only do me one last favour, dear friend?'

'Speak, I am master here.'

'Do me the pleasure to tell me the name of that gentleman who is walking yonder.'

'Where, there?'

'Behind the soldiers.'

'Followed by a lackey?'

'Exactly.'

'In company with a mean sort of fellow, dressed in black?'

'Yes, I mean him.'

'That is M. Gétard.'*

'And who is Gétard, my friend?'

'He is the architect of the house.'

'Of what house?'

'Of M. Fouquet's house.'

'Ah! ah!' cried D'Artagnan, 'you are of the household of M. Fouquet, then, Porthos?'

'I! what do you mean by that?' said the topographer, blushing to the top of his ears.

'Why, you say the house, when speaking of Belle-Isle, as if you were speaking of the château of Pierrefonds.'

Porthos bit his lips. 'Belle-Isle, my friend,' said he, 'belongs to M. Fouquet, does it not?'

'Yes, I believe so.'

'As Pierrefonds belongs to me?'

'I told you I believed so; there are no two ways about *that*.'

'Did you ever see a man there who is accustomed to walk about with a ruler in his hand?'

'No; but I might have seen him there, if he really walked there.'

'Well, that gentleman is M. Boulingrin.'*

'Who is M. Boulingrin?'

'Now we are coming to it. If, when this gentleman is walking with a ruler in his hand, any one should ask me, "Who is M. Boulingrin?" I should reply: "He is the architect of the house." Well! M. Gétard is the Boulingrin of M. Fouquet. But he has nothing to do with the fortifications, which are my department alone; do you understand? mine, absolutely mine.'

'Ah! Porthos,' cried D'Artagnan, letting his arms fall as a conquered man gives up his sword; 'ah! my friend, you are not only a Herculean topographer, you are, still further, a dialectician of the first water.'

'Is it not powerfully reasoned?' said Porthos: and he puffed and blew like the conger which D'Artagnan had let slip from his hand.

'And now,' said D'Artagnan, 'that shabby-looking man, who accompanies M. Gétard, is he also of the household of M. Fouquet?'

'Oh! yes,' said Porthos, with contempt; 'it is one M. Jupenet, or Juponet,* a sort of poet.'

'Who is to come to establish himself here?'

'I believe so.'

'I thought M. Fouquet had poets enough, yonder—Scudéry, Loret, Pellisson, La Fontaine?* If I must tell you the truth, Porthos, that poet disgraces you.'

'Eh!—my friend; but what saves us is that he is not here as a poet.'

'As what, then, is he?'

'As printer. And you make me remember, I have a word to say to the pedant.'

'Say it, then.'

Porthos made a sign to Jupenet, who remembered D'Artagnan perfectly, and did not care to come nearer; which naturally produced another sign from Porthos. This was so imperative, he was obliged to obey. So he approached. 'Come hither!' said Porthos. 'You only landed yesterday, and you have begun your tricks already.'

'How so, monsieur le baron?' asked Jupenet, trembling.

'Your press was groaning all night, monsieur,' said Porthos, 'and you prevented my sleeping, devil take you!'

'Monsieur——' objected Jupenet, timidly.

'You have nothing yet to print: therefore you have no occasion to set your press going. What did you print last night?'

'Monsieur, a light poem of my own composition.'

'Light! no, no, monsieur; the press groaned pitifully beneath it. Let it not happen again. Do you understand?'

'Yes, monsieur.'

'You promise?'

'I do, monsieur!'

'Very well; this time I pardon you. Adieu!'

The poet retreated as humbly as he had approached.

'Well, now we have combed that fellow's head, let us breakfast.'

'Yes,' replied D'Artagnan, 'let us breakfast.'

'Only,' said Porthos, 'I beg you to observe, my friend, that we have only two hours for our repast.'

'A shame! We will try to make two hours suffice. But why have you only two hours?'

'Because it is high tide at one o'clock, and, with the tide, I am going to Vannes. But, as I shall return to-morrow, my dear friend, you can stay here; you shall be master; I have a good cook and a good cellar.'

'No,' interrupted D'Artagnan, 'better than that.'

'What?'

'You are going to Vannes, you say?'

'To a certainty.'

'To see Aramis?'

'Yes.'

'Well! I came from Paris on purpose to see Aramis.'

'That's true.'

'I will go with you then.'

'Do; that's the thing.'

'Only, I ought to have seen Aramis first, and you after. But man proposes, and God disposes. I have begun with you, and will finish with Aramis.'

'Very well!'

'And in how many hours can you go from here to Vannes?'

'Oh! six hours. Three hours by sea to Sarzeau,* three hours by road from Sarzeau to Vannes.'

'How convenient that is! Being so near to the bishopric, do you often go to Vannes?'

'Yes; once a week. But, stop till I get my plan.'

Porthos picked up his plan, folded it carefully, and engulfed it in his large pocket.

'Good!' said D'Artagnan aside; 'I think I now know the real engineer who is fortifying Belle-Isle.'

Two hours after, at high tide, Porthos and D'Artagnan set out for Sarzeau.

LXXI

A PROCESSION AT VANNES

THE passage from Belle-Isle to Sarzeau was made rapidly enough, thanks to one of those little corsairs of which D'Artagnan had been told during his voyage, and which, shaped for fast sailing and destined for the chase, were sheltered at that time in the roadstead of Locmaria,* where one of them, with a quarter of its war-crew, performed duty between Belle-Isle and the continent. D'Artagnan had an opportunity of convincing himself that Porthos, though engineer and topographer, was not deeply versed in affairs of state. In another, his perfect ignorance might have passed for well-informed dissimulation. But D'Artagnan knew too well all the inner recesses of his Porthos, not to find a secret if there were one there; like those regular, fastidious old bachelors, who know how to find, with their eyes shut, each book on the shelves of their library and each piece of linen in their wardrobe. So if he had discovered nothing, our cunning D'Artagnan, in rolling and unrolling his Porthos, it was because, in truth, there was nothing to be found.

'So be it,' said D'Artagnan; 'I shall get to know more at Vannes in half an hour, than Porthos has discovered at Belle-Isle in two months. Only, in order that I may find out something, it is important that Porthos should not make use of the only stratagem I leave at his disposal. He must not warn Aramis of my arrival.' All the care of the musketeer was then, for the moment, confined to watching Porthos. And let us hasten to say, Porthos did not deserve all this mistrust. Porthos thought no evil. Perhaps, on first seeing him, D'Artagnan had inspired him with a little suspicion; but almost immediately D'Artagnan had reconquered in that good and brave heart the place he had always occupied, and not the least cloud darkened the large eye of Porthos, fixed from time to time with tenderness on his friend.

On landing, Porthos enquired if his horses were waiting, and soon perceived them at the crossing of the road that winds round Sarzeau, and which, without passing through that little city, leads towards Vannes. These horses were two in number, one for M. de Vallon, and one for his equerry; for Porthos had an equerry, since Mouston was only able to use a carriage as a means of locomotion. D'Artagnan expected that Porthos would propose to send forward his equerry upon one horse to bring back another, and he—D'Artagnan—had made up his mind to oppose this proposition. But nothing D'Artagnan had expected happened. Porthos simply told the equerry to dismount and await his return at Sarzeau, whilst D'Artagnan would ride his horse; which was arranged.

'Eh! but you have grown foresighted, my dear Porthos,' said D'Artagnan to his friend, when he found himself in the saddle, upon the equerry's horse.

'Yes; but this is a kindness on the part of Aramis. I have not my stud here, and Aramis has placed his stables at my disposal.'

'Good horses for bishop's horses, *mordioux!*' said D'Artagnan. 'It is true, Aramis is a bishop of a peculiar kind.'

'He is a holy man!' replied Porthos, in an almost sing-song voice, and with his eyes raised towards heaven.

'Then he is much changed,' said D'Artagnan; 'you and I have known him passably profane.'

'Grace has touched him,'* said Porthos.

'Bravo,' said D'Artagnan, 'that only increases my desire to see my dear old friend.' And he spurred his horse, which sprang into a canter.

'By God!' said Porthos, 'if we go on at this rate, we shall only take one hour instead of two.'

'To go how far, do you say, Porthos?'

'Four leagues and a half.'

'Then we shall make good time.'

'I could have taken you by the canal, but the devil take rowers and boat-horses! The first are like tortoises; the second like snails; and when a man is able to put a good horse between his knees, that horse is better than rowers or any other means of locomotion.'

'You are right; you above all, Porthos, who always look magnificent on horseback.'

'Rather heavy, my friend; I was weighed the other day.'

'And what do you weigh?'

'Three hundredweight!' said Porthos, proudly.

'Bravo!'

'So you see, I am forced to choose horses whose loins are straight and wide, otherwise I break them down in two hours.'

'Yes, giant's horses you must have, must you not?'

'You are very polite, my friend,' replied the engineer, with affectionate majesty.

'As a case in point,' replied D'Artagnan, 'your horse seems to be in a sweat already.'

'Confound it! It is hot! Ah, ah! do you see Vannes now?'

'Yes, perfectly. It looks a handsome city.'

'Charming, according to Aramis, at least; but I think it black; but black seems to be considered handsome by artists, I regret to say.'

'Why so, Porthos?'

'Because I have lately had my château of Pierrefonds, which was grey with age, plastered white.'

'Humph!' said D'Artagnan, 'and white is more cheerful.'

'Yes, but it is not so noble, so Aramis tells me. Fortunately there are dealers in black as well as white. I will have Pierrefonds replastered in black; that's all there is to it. If grey is handsome, you understand, my friend, black must be superb.'

'To be sure!' said D'Artagnan, 'that appears logical.'

'Were you never at Vannes, D'Artagnan?'

'Never.'

'Then you know nothing of the city?'

'Nothing.'

'Well, look!' said Porthos, raising himself in his stirrups, which made the fore-quarters of his horse bend sadly—'do you see that corner, in the sun, yonder?'

'Yes, I see it plainly.'

'Well that is the cathedral.'

'Which is called?'

'Saint-Pierre.* Now look again—in the faubourg on the left, do you see another cross?'

'Perfectly well.'

'That is Saint Patern, the parish preferred by Aramis.'

'Indeed!'

'Without doubt. Saint Patern, you see, passes for having been the first bishop of Vannes. It is true that Aramis claims he was not. But he is so learned that that may be only a paro—a para——'

'A paradox,' said D'Artagnan.

'Precisely; thank you! my tongue trips, I am so hot.'

'My friend,' said D'Artagnan, 'continue your interesting description, I beg. What is that large white building with many windows?'

'Oh! that is the college of the Jesuits. *Pardieu!* you have an apt hand. Do you see, close to the college, a large house with steeples, turrets, built in a handsome Gothic style, as that fool, M. Gétard, says?'

'Yes, that is plainly to be seen. Well?'

'Well, that is where Aramis resides.'

'What! does he not reside at the Bishop's Palace?'

'No; that is in ruins. Also the palace is in the city, and Aramis prefers the lower town. That is why, as I told you, he is partial to Saint Patern; Saint Patern is in the lower town. Besides, there are in the lower town a mall, a tennis-court, and a house of Dominicans. Look, that where the handsome steeple rises to the heavens.'

'Well?'

'Next, you see the lower town is like a separate city, it has its own walls, towers, and ditches; that is where the quay is too, and the boats dock at the quay. If our little corsair did not draw eight feet of water, we could have come full sail up to Aramis's windows.'

'Porthos, Porthos,' cried D'Artagnan, 'you are a well of knowledge, a spring of ingenious and profound reflections. Porthos, you no longer surprise me, you confound me.'

'Here we are,' said Porthos, turning the conversation with his usual modesty.

'And high time we were,' thought D'Artagnan, 'for Aramis's horse is melting away like a steed of ice.'

They entered almost at the same instant the lower town; but scarcely had they gone a hundred paces when they were surprised to find the streets strewn with leaves and flowers. Against the old walls of Vannes hung the oldest and the strangest tapestries of France. From over balconies fell long white sheets decorated with bouquets. The streets were deserted; it was plain the entire population was assembled at one point. The blinds were closed, and the breeze penetrated into the houses under the hangings, which cast long black shadows on the walls. Suddenly, at the corner of a street, chants struck the ears of the newly arrived travellers. A crowd in holiday garb appeared through the clouds of incense which mounted to the heavens in blue wreaths, and clouds of rose-leaves fluttered as high as the first stories. Above all heads were to be seen the cross and banners, the sacred symbols of religion. Then, beneath these crosses and banners, as if protected by them, walked a group of young girls clothed in white, crowned with corn-flowers. At the two sides of the street, enclosing the cortège, marched the guards of the garrison, carrying bouquets in the barrels of their muskets and on the points of their lances. It was a religious procession.

Whilst D'Artagnan and Porthos were looking on with critical glances, which disguised an extreme impatience to get forward, a magnificent canopy approached preceded by a hundred Jesuits and a hundred Dominicans, and escorted by two archdeacons, a treasurer, a penitent and twelve canons. A singer with a thundering voice—a man certainly picked out from all the voices of France, as was the drum-major of the imperial guard from all the giants of the empire—escorted by four other chanters, who appeared to be there only to serve him as an accompaniment, made the air resound, and the windows of the houses rattle. Under the canopy appeared a pale and noble countenance, with black eyes, black hair streaked with threads of white, a delicate, compressed mouth, a prominent and angular chin. His head, full of grace and majesty, was covered by the bishop's mitre, a head-dress which gave it, in addition to the character of sovereignty, that of asceticism and evangelic meditation.

'Aramis!' cried the musketeer, involuntarily, as this lofty countenance passed before him. The prelate started at the sound of the voice. He raised his large black eyes, with their long lashes, and turned them without hesitation towards the spot whence the exclamation proceeded. At a glance, he saw Porthos and D'Artagnan close to him. On his part, D'Artagnan, thanks to the keenness of his sight, had seen all, seized all. The full portrait of the prelate had entered his memory, never to leave it. One thing had particularly struck D'Artagnan. On seeing him, Aramis had coloured, then he had concentrated under his eyelids the fire of the look of the master, and the indefinable affection of the friend. It was evident that Aramis had asked himself this question: 'Why is D'Artagnan with Porthos, and what does he want at Vannes?' Aramis comprehended all that was passing in the mind of D'Artagnan, on turning his look upon him again, and seeing that he had not lowered his eyes. He knew the acuteness and intelligence of his friend; he feared to let him guess the secret of his blush and his astonishment. He was still the same Aramis, always having a secret to conceal.* Therefore to put an end to his inquisitorial glance, which had to be expunged at any price, as a general silences a troublesome enemy battery, Aramis stretched forth his beautiful white hand, upon which sparkled the amethyst of the pastoral ring; he cut the air with sign of the cross and poured out his benediction upon his two friends. Perhaps, thoughtful and absent, D'Artagnan, impious in spite of himself, might not have bent beneath this holy benediction; but Porthos saw his hesitation, and laying his friendly hand upon the back of his companion, he crushed him down towards the earth. D'Artagnan was forced to give way; indeed, he was little short of being flat on the ground. In the meantime Aramis had passed. D'Artagnan, like Antaeus,* had only touched the ground, and he turned towards Porthos, almost angry. But there was no mistaking the intention of the brave Hercules; it was a feeling of religious propriety that had prompted him. Besides, speech, with Porthos, instead of disguising his thought, always completed it.

'It is very polite of him,' said he, 'to have given his benediction to us alone. Decidedly, he is a holy man, and a brave man.' Less convinced than Porthos, D'Artagnan made no reply.

'Observe, my friend,' continued Porthos, 'he has seen us; and, instead of continuing to walk on at the steady pace of the procession, as he did just now—see, what a hurry he is in; do you see how the column is increasing its speed? He is eager to join us and embrace us, is dear Aramis.'

'That is true,' replied D'Artagnan, aloud. Then to himself: 'It is equally true, he has seen me, the fox, and will have time to prepare himself to receive me.'

But the procession had passed; the road was free. D'Artagnan and Porthos walked straight up to the Bishop's Palace, which was surrounded by a large crowd anxious to see the prelate return. D'Artagnan observed that this crowd was composed principally of citizens and military men. He recognized in the nature of these supporters the wiliness of his friend. Aramis was not the man to seek for vain popularity. He cared very little for being beloved by people who could be of no service to him. Women, children, and old men, that is to say, the procession of ordinary bishops, was not the procession for him.

Ten minutes after the two friends had crossed the threshold of the palace, Aramis returned like a triumphant conqueror; the soldiers presented arms to him as to a superior; the citizens bowed to him as to a friend and a patron, rather than as a head of the Church. There was something in Aramis resembling those Roman senators who had their doors always surrounded by clients. At the foot of the steps, he had a conference of half a minute with a Jesuit, who, in order to speak to him more secretly, passed his head under the canopy. He then re-entered his palace; the doors closed slowly, and the crowd melted away, whilst chants and prayers were still resounding abroad. It was a magnificent day. Earthly perfumes were mingled with the perfumes of the air and the sea. The city breathed happiness, joy, and strength. D'Artagnan felt something like the presence of an invisible hand which had, all-powerfully, created this strength, this joy, this happiness, and spread perfumes everywhere.

'Oh! oh!' said he, 'Porthos has got fat; but Aramis is grown taller!'

LXXII

HIS GRACE THE BISHOP OF VANNES

PORTHOS and D'Artagnan had entered the bishop's residence by a private door, as his personal friends. Of course, Porthos served D'Artagnan as guide. The worthy baron behaved everywhere rather as if he were at home. Nevertheless, whether it was a tacit acknowledgment of the sanctity of the personage of Aramis and his character, or the habit of respecting him who imposed upon him morally, a worthy habit which had always made Porthos a model soldier and an excellent companion; for all these reasons, say we, Porthos preserved in the palace of His Grace the Bishop of Vannes a sort of reserve which D'Artagnan remarked at once, in the attitude he took with respect to the valets and officers. And yet this reserve did not go so far as to prevent his asking questions. Porthos questioned. They learned that His Grace had just returned to his apartment and was changing into less formal apparel, less majestic than he had appeared with his flock. After a quarter of an hour, which D'Artagnan and Porthos spent looking mutually at each other with the white of their eyes, and turning their thumbs in all the different evolutions which go from north to south, a door of the chamber opened and His Grace appeared, dressed in the undress of a prelate. Aramis carried his head high, like a man accustomed to command: his purple robe was tucked up on one side, and his white hand was on his hip. He had retained the fine moustache, and the lengthened *royale* of the time of Louis XIII. He exhaled, on entering, that delicate perfume which, among elegant men and women of high fashion, never changes, and appears to be incorporated in the person, of which it has become the natural emanation. But in his case, the perfume had retained something of the religious sublimity of incense. It no longer intoxicated, it penetrated; it no longer inspired desire, it inspired respect. Aramis, on entering the chamber, did not hesitate an instant; and without pronouncing one word, which, whatever it might be, would have been cold on such an occasion, he went straight up to the musketeer, so well disguised under the costume of M. Agnan, and pressed him in his arms with a tenderness which the most distrustful could not have suspected of coldness or affectation.

D'Artagnan, on his part, embraced him with equal ardour. Porthos pressed the delicate hand of Aramis in his immense hands, and D'Artagnan remarked that His Grace gave him his left hand, probably from habit, seeing that Porthos already ten times had been near injuring his fingers covered with rings, by pounding his flesh in the vice of his fist. Wary of the pain, Aramis was cautious, and only presented flesh to be bruised, and not fingers to be crushed against gold or the sharp angles of diamonds.

Between two embraces, Aramis looked D'Artagnan in the face, offered him a chair, sitting down himself in the shade, observing that the light fell full upon the face of his interlocutor. This manœuvre, familiar to diplomats and women, is very much like the advantage of the guard which, according to their skill or habit, combatants endeavour to take on the ground at a duel. D'Artagnan was not the dupe of this tactic; but he did not appear to perceive it. He felt himself caught; but, precisely because he was caught, he felt himself on the road to discovery, and it mattered little to him, old condottiere as he was, to be beaten in appearance, provided he drew from his assumed defeat the advantages of victory. Aramis began the conversation.

'Ah! dear friend! my good D'Artagnan,' said he, 'what a delightful surprise!'

'It is a surprise, my reverend companion,' said D'Artagnan, 'which is an effect of our old friendship. I have come seeking you, as I always have sought you when I had any grand enterprise to propose to you, or some hours of liberty to give you.'

'Ah! indeed,' said Aramis, unruffled, 'you have been seeking me?'

'Eh! yes, he has been seeking you, Aramis,' said Porthos, 'and the proof is that he tracked me down at Belle-Isle. That is friendship, is it not?'

'Ah! yes,' said Aramis, 'at Belle-Isle! certainly!'

'Good!' said D'Artagnan; 'there is my booby Porthos, without thinking of it, has fired the first cannon of attack.'

'At Belle-Isle!' said Aramis, 'in that out-of-the-way place! That is kind, indeed!'

'And it was I who told him you were at Vannes,' continued Porthos, in the same tone.

D'Artagnan armed his mouth with a finesse almost ironical.

'Yes, I knew, but I wanted to see,' replied he.

'To see what?'

'If our old friendship still held out; if, on seeing each other, our hearts, hardened as they are by age, would still give the old cry of joy, which salutes the coming of a friend.'

'Well, and you must have been satisfied,' said Aramis.

'So-so.'

'How is that?'

'Yes, Porthos said hush! and you——'

'Well! and I?'

'And you gave me your benediction.'

'What did you expect, my friend?' said Aramis, smiling; 'that is the most precious thing that a poor prelate, like me, has to give.'

'Indeed, my dear friend!'

'Doubtless.'

'And yet they say at Paris that the bishopric of Vannes is one of the best in France.'

'Ah! you are now speaking of temporal wealth,' said Aramis, casually.

'To be sure, I wish to speak of that; I set great store by it.'

'In that case, let me speak of it,' said Aramis, with a smile.

'You own yourself to be one of the richest prelates in France?'

'My friend, since you ask me to give you an account, I will tell you that the bishopric of Vannes is worth about twenty thousand livres a year, neither more nor less. It is a diocese which contains a hundred and sixty parishes.'

'That is very pretty,' said D'Artagnan.

'It is superb!' said Porthos.

'And yet,' resumed D'Artagnan, casting his eyes over Aramis, 'you don't mean to bury yourself here forever?'

'Pardon me. I do not admit the word *bury*.'

'But it seems to me, that at this distance from Paris a man is buried, or nearly so.'

'My friend, I am getting old,' said Aramis; 'the noise and bustle of a city no longer suit me. At fifty-seven* we ought to seek calm and meditation. I have found them here. What is there more beautiful, and stern at the same time, than old Armorica?* I find here, dear D'Artagnan, all that is opposite to what I formerly loved, and that is what must happen at the end of life, which is opposite to the beginning. A little of my old pleasure of former times still comes to greet me here, now and then, without diverting me from the road of salvation. I am still of this world, and yet, every step that I take brings me nearer to God.'

'Eloquent, wise, and discreet; you are an accomplished prelate, Aramis, and I offer you my congratulations.'

'But,' said Aramis, smiling, 'you did not come here only for the purpose of paying me compliments. Speak; what brings you hither? May it be that, in some fashion or other, you want me?'

'Thank God, no, my friend,' said D'Artagnan, 'it is nothing of that kind. I am rich and free.'

'Rich!' exclaimed Aramis.

'Yes, rich for me; not for you, or Porthos, understand. I have an income of about fifteen thousand livres.'

Aramis looked at him suspiciously. He could not believe—
particularly on seeing his friend in such humble guise—that he
had made so large a fortune. Then D'Artagnan, seeing that the
hour for explanations had come, related the history of his English adventures. During the recital he saw ten times the eyes of
the prelate sparkle, and his slender fingers work convulsively. As
to Porthos, it was not admiration he manifested for D'Artagnan;
it was enthusiasm, it was delirium. When D'Artagnan had
finished, 'Well!' said Aramis.

'Well!' said D'Artagnan, 'you see, then, I have in England
friends and property, in France a treasure. If your heart tells
you so, I offer them to you. That is what I came here for.'

However firm was his look, he could not this time meet the
gaze of Aramis. He allowed, therefore, his eye to stray upon
Porthos—like the sword which yields to too powerful a pressure, and seeks another road.

'At all events,' said the bishop, 'you have assumed a singular
travelling costume, old friend.'

'Frightful! I know it is. You may understand why I would not
travel as a cavalier or a noble: since I became rich, I am miserly.'

'And you say, then, you came to Belle-Isle?' said Aramis,
without transition.

'Yes,' replied D'Artagnan; 'I knew I should find you and
Porthos there.'

'Find me!' cried Aramis. 'Me! for the last year past I have not
once crossed the sea.'

'Oh,' said D'Artagnan, 'I should never have supposed you
were such a stay-at-home.'

'Ah, dear friend, I must tell you that I am no longer the
Aramis of old. Riding on horseback is unpleasant to me; the sea
fatigues me. I am a poor, ailing priest, always complaining,
always grumbling, and inclined to the austerities which appear
to accord with old age—preliminary parleyings with death. I
linger, my dear D'Artagnan, I linger.'

'Well, that is all the better, my friend, for we shall probably
be neighbours soon.'

'Ah!' said Aramis, with a degree of surprise he did not even
seek to dissemble. 'You, my neighbour?'

'*Mordioux!* yes.'

'How so?'

'I am about to purchase some very profitable salt-works, which are situated between Piriac and Le Croisic. Imagine, my friend, a clear profit of twelve per cent. Never any slack trade, never any unprofitable expenses; the ocean, faithful and regular, brings every twelve hours its tribute to my coffers. I am the first Parisian who has dreamt of such a speculation. Do not say anything about it, I beg of you, and in a short time we will communicate on the matter. I am to have three leagues of country for thirty thousand livres.'

Aramis darted a look at Porthos, as if to ask if all this were true, if some snare were not concealed beneath this outward indifference. But soon, as if ashamed of having consulted this poor auxiliary, he collected all his forces for a fresh assault and new defence. 'I heard that you had had some difference with the court, but that you had come out of it as you know how to get through everything, D'Artagnan, with the honours of war.'

'I?' said the musketeer, with a burst of laughter that did not conceal his embarrassment: for, from these words, Aramis was not unlikely to be acquainted with his last dealings with the king. 'I? Oh, tell me all about that, pray, Aramis!'

'Yes, it was related to me, a poor bishop, lost in the middle of this sandy heath, that the king had taken you as the confidant of his amours.'

'With whom?'

'With Mademoiselle de Mancini.'

D'Artagnan breathed freely again. 'Ah! I don't say no to that,' replied he.

'It appears that the king took you, one morning, over the bridge of Blois* to talk with his lady-love.'

'That's true,' said D'Artagnan. 'And you know that, do you? Well, then, you must know that the same day I gave in my resignation!'

'What, sincerely?'

'Nothing more so.'

'It was after that, then, that you went to the Comte de la Fère's?'

'Yes.'

'Afterwards to me?'

'Yes.'

'And then Porthos?'

'Yes.'

'Was it in order to pay us a simple visit?'

'No, I did not know you were engaged, and I wished to take you with me into England.'

'Yes, I understand; and then you executed alone, wonderful man that you are, what you wanted to propose to us all four. I suspected you had something to do with that famous restoration, when I learned that you had been seen at King Charles's receptions, and that he appeared to treat you like a friend, or rather, like a person to whom he was under an obligation.'

'But how the devil did you learn all that?' asked D'Artagnan, who began to fear that the enquiries of Aramis had extended further than he wished.

'Dear D'Artagnan,' said the prelate, 'my friendship resembles, in a degree, the solicitude of that night watch whom we have in the little tower on the jetty, at the extremity of the quay. That brave man, every night, lights a lantern to direct the boats that come from sea. He is concealed in his sentry-box, and the fishermen do not see him; but he follows them with interest; he senses their coming; he calls them; he draws them into the way to the port. I resemble this watcher: from time to time some news reaches me, and recalls to my remembrance all those I loved. Then I follow the friends of old days over the stormy ocean of the world, I, a poor watcher, to whom God has kindly given the shelter of a sentry-box.'

'Well, what did I do when I came from England?'

'Ah! there,' replied Aramis, 'you get beyond my depth. I know nothing of you since your return. D'Artagnan, my eyes are dim. I regretted you did not think of me. I wept over your forgetfulness. I was wrong. I see you again, and it is a great day, a great, great day, I assure you, solemnly! How is Athos?'

'Very well, thank you.'

'And our young pupil, Raoul?'

'He seems to have inherited the skill of his father, Athos, and the strength of his tutor, Porthos.'

'And on what occasion have you been able to judge of that?'

'Eh! on the eve of my departure from Paris.'

'Indeed! tell me all about it!'

'Yes; there was an execution at the Place de la Grève, and in consequence of that execution, a riot. We happened, by accident, to be in the riot; and in this riot we were obliged to have recourse to our swords. And he did wonders.'

'Bah! what did he do?'

'Why, in the first place, he threw a man out of the window, as he would have flung a spool of wound cotton.'

'Come, that's pretty well,' said Porthos.

'Then he drew, and cut and thrust away, as we fellows used to do in the good old times.'

'And what was the cause of this riot?' said Porthos.

D'Artagnan remarked upon the face of Aramis a complete indifference to this question from Porthos. 'Why,' said he, fixing his eyes upon Aramis, 'on account of two tax-farmers, friends of M. Fouquet, whom the king forced to disgorge their plunder, and then hanged them.'

A scarcely perceptible contraction of the prelate's brow showed that he had heard D'Artagnan's reply. 'Oh, oh!' said Porthos; 'and what were the names of these friends of M. Fouquet?'

'MM. d'Eymeris and Lyodot,' said D'Artagnan. 'Do you know those names, Aramis?'

'No,' said the prelate, disdainfully; 'they sound like the names of financiers.'

'Exactly; so they were.'

'Oh! M. Fouquet allows his friends to be hanged, then,' said Porthos.

'And why not?' said Aramis.

'Why, it seems to me——'

'If these culprits were hanged, it was by order of the king. Now M. Fouquet, although superintendent of finances, has not, I believe, the right of life and death.'

'That may be,' said Porthos; 'but in the place of M. Fouquet——'

Aramis was afraid Porthos was about to say something awkward, so interrupted him. 'Come, D'Artagnan,' said he; 'this is quite enough about other people, let us talk a little about you.'

'Of me you know all that I can tell you. On the contrary, let me hear a little about you, Aramis.'

'I have told you, my friend. There is nothing of Aramis left in me.'

'Nor of the Abbé d'Herblay even?'

'No, not even of him. You see a man whom Providence has taken by the hand, whom he has conducted to a position that he could never have dared even to hope for.'

'Providence?' asked D'Artagnan.

'Yes.'

'Well, that is strange! I was told it was M. Fouquet.'

'Who told you that?' cried Aramis, without being able, with all the power of his will, to prevent the colour rising to his cheeks.

'Why, Bazin.'

'The fool!'

'I do not say he is a man of genius, it is true; but he told me so; and after him, I repeat it to you.'

'I have never seen M. Fouquet,' replied Aramis, with a look as pure and calm as that of a virgin who has never told a lie.

'Well, but if you had seen him and known him, there is no harm in that,' replied D'Artagnan. 'M. Fouquet is a very good sort of a man.'

'Humph!'

'A great politician.' Aramis made a gesture of indifference.

'An all-powerful minister.'

'I only hold to the king and the pope.'

'Listen then,' said D'Artagnan, in the most natural tone imaginable. 'I said that because everybody here swears by M. Fouquet. The plain is M. Fouquet's; the salt-works I am about to buy are M. Fouquet's; the island in which Porthos studies topography is M. Fouquet's; the garrison is M. Fouquet's; the galleys are M. Fouquet's. I confess, then, that nothing would have surprised me in your enfeoffment, or rather in that of your diocese, to M. Fouquet. He is a different master from the king, that is all; but quite as powerful as Louis.'

'Thank God! I am not vassal to anybody; I belong to nobody, and am entirely my own master,' replied Aramis, who, during this conversation, followed with his eye every gesture of D'Artagnan, every glance of Porthos. But D'Artagnan was impassive and Porthos motionless; the thrusts aimed so skilfully were parried by an able adversary; not one hit the mark. Nevertheless, both began to feel the fatigue of such a contest, and the announcement of supper was well received by everybody. Supper changed the course of conversation. Besides, they felt that, upon their guard as each one had been, they could neither of them boast of having the advantage. Porthos had understood nothing of what had been meant. He had held himself motionless, because Aramis had made him a sign not to stir. Supper, for him, was nothing but supper; but that was quite enough for Porthos. The supper, then, went off very well. D'Artagnan was in high spirits. Aramis exceeded himself in affability. Porthos ate like old Pelops.* Their talk was of war, finance, the arts, and love. Aramis feigned astonishment at every word of politics D'Artagnan risked. This long series of surprises increased the mistrust of D'Artagnan, as the persistent indifference of D'Artagnan provoked the suspicions of Aramis. At length D'Artagnan, deliberately, uttered the name of Colbert: he had reserved that stroke for the last.

'Who is this Colbert?' asked the bishop.

'Oh! come,' said D'Artagnan to himself, 'this is too much! We must be careful, *mordioux!* we must be careful.'

And he then gave Aramis all the information respecting M. Colbert he could desire. The supper, or rather, the conversation, was prolonged till one o'clock in the morning between D'Artagnan and Aramis. At ten o'clock precisely, Porthos had fallen asleep in his chair and snored like an organ. At midnight he woke up and they sent him to bed. 'Hum!' said he, 'I was near falling asleep; but that was all very interesting you were talking about.'

At one o'clock Aramis conducted D'Artagnan to the chamber destined for him, which was the best in the episcopal residence. Two servants were placed at his command. 'To-morrow, at eight o'clock,' said he, taking leave of D'Artagnan, 'we will take, if agreeable to you, a ride on horseback with Porthos.'

'At eight o'clock!' said D'Artagnan; 'so late?'

'You know that I require seven hours' sleep,' said Aramis.

'That is true.'

'Good-night, dear friend!' And he embraced the musketeer cordially.

D'Artagnan allowed him to depart; then, as soon as the door was closed, 'Good!' cried he, 'at five o'clock I will be up and about.'

This determination being made, he went to bed and quietly 'put two and two together', as people say.

LXXIII

IN WHICH PORTHOS BEGINS TO BE SORRY FOR HAVING COME WITH D'ARTAGNAN

SCARCELY had D'Artagnan extinguished his taper, when Aramis, who had watched through his curtains the last glimmer of light in his friend's apartment, traversed the corridor on tiptoe, and went to Porthos's room. The giant, who had been in bed nearly an hour and a half, lay grandly stretched out on the down bed. He was in that happy calm of the first sleep, which, with Porthos, resisted the noise of bells or the report of cannon; his head was rocked by the gentle cradling which reminds us of the soothing movement of a ship. In a moment Porthos would have begun to dream. The door of the chamber opened softly under the delicate pressure of the hand of Aramis. The bishop approached the sleeper. A thick carpet deadened the sound of his steps, besides which Porthos snored in a manner to drown all noise. He laid one hand on his shoulder—'Rouse yourself,' said he, 'wake up, my dear Porthos.' The voice of Aramis was soft and kind, but it conveyed more than a notification—it conveyed an order. His hand was light, but it indicated a danger. Porthos heard the voice and felt the hand of Aramis, even in the depth of his sleep. He started up. 'Who goes there?' cried he, in his giant's voice.

'Hush! hush! It is I,' said Aramis.

'You, my friend? And what the devil do you wake me for?'

'To tell you that you must set off directly.'

'Set off?'

'Yes.'

'Where for?'

'For Paris.'

Porthos sat up in his bed, and then sank back again, fixing his great eyes in agitation upon Aramis.

'For Paris?'

'Yes.'

'A hundred leagues?' said he.

'A hundred and four,' replied the bishop.

'Oh God!' sighed Porthos, lying down again, like children who argue with their nurse to gain an hour or two more sleep.

'Thirty hours' riding,' said Aramis, firmly. 'You know there are good relays.'

Porthos pushed out one leg, allowing a groan to escape him.

'Come, come! my friend,' insisted the prelate with a hint of impatience.

Porthos drew the other leg out of the bed. 'And is it absolutely necessary that I should go, at once?'

'Very necessary.'

Porthos got upon his feet, and began to shake both walls and floors with steps like a marble statue.

'Hush! hush! for the love of Heaven, my dear Porthos!' said Aramis, 'you will wake somebody.'

'Ah! that's true,' replied Porthos, in a voice of thunder, 'I forgot that; but don't worry, I am on my guard.' And so saying, he let fall a belt loaded with his sword and pistols, and a purse, from which the crowns escaped with a prolonged jingling. This noise made the blood of Aramis boil, whilst it drew from Porthos a formidable burst of laughter. 'Now that's funny!' said he, in the same voice.

'Not so loud, Porthos, not so loud.'

'True, true!' and he lowered his voice a half-note.

'I was going to say,' continued Porthos, 'that it is funny that we are never so slow as when we are in a hurry, and never make so much noise as when we wish to be silent.'

'Yes, that is true; but let us give the proverb the lie, Porthos; let us make haste, and hold our tongue.'

'You see I am doing my best,' said Porthos, putting on his breeches.

'Very well.'

'This is something urgent?'

'It is more than that, it is serious, Porthos.'

'Oh, oh!'

'D'Artagnan has questioned you, has he not?'

'Questioned me?'

'Yes, at Belle-Isle?'

'Not the least in the world.'

'Are you sure of that, Porthos?'

'*Parbleu!*'

'It is impossible. Try to remember.'

'He asked me what I was doing, and I told him—studying topography. I would have made use of another word which you employed one day.'

'"Castrametation"?'*

'Yes, that's it; but I never could recollect it.'

'All the better. What more did he ask you?'

'Who M. Gétard was.'

'Next?'

'Who M. Jupenet was.'

'He did not happen to see our plan of fortifications, did he?'

'Yes.'

'The devil he did!'

'But don't be alarmed, I had rubbed out your writing, with India-rubber. It was impossible for him to suppose you had given me any advice in those works.'

'Ay; but our friend has phenomenally keen eyes.'

'What are you afraid of?'

'I fear that everything is discovered, Porthos; the matter is, then, to prevent a great misfortune. I have given orders to my servants to close all the gates and doors. D'Artagnan will not be able to get out before daybreak. Your horse is ready saddled; you will gain the first relay; by five o'clock in the morning, you will have covered fifteen leagues. Come!'

Aramis than assisted Porthos to dress, piece by piece, with as much speed as the most skilful *valet de chambre* could have done. Porthos, half stupefied, let him do as he liked, and apologized profusely. When he was ready, Aramis took him by the hand, and led him, making him place his foot carefully on every step of the stairs, preventing him bumping into door-frames, turning him this way and that, as if Aramis had been the giant and Porthos the dwarf. Soul set fire to and animated matter. A horse was waiting, ready saddled, in the courtyard. Porthos mounted. Then Aramis himself took the horse by the bridle, and led him over horse-droppings spread in the yard, with the evident intention of suppressing noise. He, at the same time, held tight the horse's nose, to prevent him neighing. When arrived at the outer gate, drawing Porthos towards him, who was going off without even asking him what for: 'Now, friend Porthos, now; ride for all you are worth, till you get to Paris,' whispered he in his ears; 'eat on horseback, drink on horseback, sleep on horseback, but waste not a minute.'

'That's enough; I will not stop.'

'Deliver this letter to M. Fouquet; cost what it may, he must have it to-morrow before mid-day.'

'He shall.'

'And do not forget *one* thing, my friend.'

'What is that?'

'That your dukedom rides on this.'

'Oh! oh!' said Porthos, with his eyes sparkling; 'I will do it in twenty-four hours, in that case.'

'Try.'

'Then let go the bridle—and forward, Goliath!'

Aramis did let go, not the bridle, but the horse's nose. Porthos released his hand, clapped spurs to his horse, which set off at a gallop. As long as he could distinguish Porthos through the darkness, Aramis followed him with his eyes: when he was completely out of sight, he re-entered the yard. Nothing had stirred in D'Artagnan's apartment. The *valet* placed on watch at the door had neither seen any light, nor heard any noise. Aramis closed his door carefully, sent the lackey to bed, and quickly sought his own. D'Artagnan really suspected nothing; therefore he thought he had gained everything, when he awoke in the morning, about half-past four. He ran to the window in his shirt. The window looked out upon the court. Day was dawning. The court was deserted; the fowls, even, had not left their roosts. Not a servant appeared. Every door was closed.

'Good! all is still,' said D'Artagnan to himself. 'Never mind: I am up first in the house. Let us dress; that will be so much done.' And D'Artagnan dressed himself. But, this time, he endeavoured not to give to the costume of M. Agnan the look of shop-keeperish, even clerical severity he had affected before; he managed, by drawing his belt tighter, by buttoning his clothes in a different fashion, and by putting on his hat a little on one side, to restore to his person a little of that military swagger, the absence of which had surprised Aramis. This being done, he made free, or affected to make free with his host, and entered his chamber without ceremony. Aramis was asleep or feigned to be so. A large book lay open upon his night-desk, a wax-light was still burning in its silver sconce. This was more than enough to prove to D'Artagnan the undisturbed peace of the prelate's night, and the good sense of his waking early. The musketeer did to the bishop precisely as the bishop had done to Porthos—he tapped him on the shoulder. Evidently Aramis pretended to sleep; for, instead of waking suddenly, he who slept so lightly required a repetition of the summons.

'Ah! ah! is that you?' said he, stretching his arms. 'What an agreeable surprise! Sleep had made me forget I had the happiness of having you here. What o'clock is it?'

'I do not know,' said D'Artagnan, a little embarrassed. 'Early, I believe. But, you know, that devil of a habit of waking with the day, sticks to me still.'

'Do you want us to go out so soon?' asked Aramis. 'It appears to me to be very early.'

'Just as you like.'

'I thought we had agreed not to get on horseback before eight.'

'Possibly; but I had so great a wish to see you, that I said to myself, the sooner the better.'

'And my seven hours' sleep!' said Aramis: 'take care; I had reckoned upon them, and what I lose of them I must make up.'

'But it seems to me that, formerly, you were less of a sleeper than that, dear friend; your blood was alive, and you were never to be found in bed.'

'And it is exactly on account of what you tell me, that I am so fond of being there now.'

'Then you confess, that it is not for the sake of sleeping, that you have put me off till eight o'clock.'

'I have been afraid you would laugh at me, if I told you the truth.'

'Tell me, notwithstanding.'

'Well, from six to eight, I am accustomed to perform my devotions.'

'Your devotions?'

'Yes.'

'I did not believe a bishop's exercises were so severe.'

'A bishop, my friend, must sacrifice more to appearance than a simple cleric.'

'*Mordioux!* Aramis, that is a word which reconciles me with your greatness. To appearances! That is a musketeer's word, in good truth! Long live appearances, Aramis!'

'Instead of congratulating me upon it, pardon me, D'Artagnan. It is a very mundane word which I had allowed to escape me.'

'Must I leave you, then?'

'I want time to collect my thoughts, my friend, and for my usual prayers.'

'Well, I leave you to them; but on account of that poor pagan, D'Artagnan, abridge them for once, I beg; I thirst to talk with you.'

'Well, D'Artagnan, I promise you that within an hour and a half——'

'An hour and a half of devotions! Ah! my friend, be as reasonable with me as you can. Let me have the best bargain possible.'

Aramis began to laugh.

'Still agreeable, still young, still gay,' said he. 'You have come into my diocese to set me quarrelling with divine grace.'

'Bah!'

'And you know well that I was never able to resist your seductions; you will cost me my salvation, D'Artagnan.'

D'Artagnan bit his lips.

'Well,' said he, 'I will take the sin on my own head, favour me with one simple Christian sign of the cross, favour me with one pater, and we will part.'

'Hush!' said Aramis, 'we are already no longer alone, I hear visitors coming up.'

'Well, dismiss them.'

'Impossible; I made an appointment with them yesterday; it is the principal of the college of the Jesuits, and the superior of the Dominicans.'

'Your staff? Well, so be it!'

'What are you going to do?'

'I will go and wake Porthos, and remain in his company till you have finished the conference.'

Aramis did not stir, his brow remained unbent, he betrayed himself by no gesture or word; 'Go,' said he, as D'Artagnan advanced to the door.

'By the way, do you know where Porthos sleeps?'

'No, but I will enquire.'

'Take the corridor, and open the second door on the left.'

'Thank you! *au revoir*.' And D'Artagnan departed in the direction pointed out by Aramis.

Ten minutes had not passed away when he came back. He found Aramis seated between the superior of the Dominicans and the principal of the college of the Jesuits, exactly in the same situation as he had found him formerly in the inn at Crèvecœur.* This company did not at all scare the musketeer.

'What is it?' said Aramis, quietly. 'You have apparently something to say to me, my friend.'

'It is,' replied D'Artagnan, fixing his eyes upon Aramis, 'it is that Porthos is not in his apartment.'

'Indeed,' said Aramis, calmly; 'are you sure?'

'By God! I have just come from his chamber.'

'Where can he be, then?'

'That is what I am asking *you*.'

'And have not you enquired?'

'Yes, I have.'

'And what answer did you get?'

'That Porthos, often walking out in a morning, without saying anything, had probably gone out.'

'What did you do, then.'

'I went to the stables,' replied D'Artagnan, casually.

'What to do?'

'To see if Porthos had departed on horseback.'

'And?' interrogated the bishop.

'Well, there is a horse missing, stall No. 3, Goliath.'

All this dialogue, it may be easily understood, was not exempt from a degree of suspicion on the part of the musketeer, and perfect composure on the part of Aramis.

'Oh! I guess how it is,' said Aramis, after having considered for a moment, 'Porthos is gone out to give us a surprise.'

'A surprise?'

'Yes; the canal which goes from Vannes to the sea abounds in teal and snipe; that is Porthos's favourite sport, and he will bring us back a dozen for breakfast.'

'Do you think so?' said D'Artagnan.

'I am sure of it. Where else can he be? I would lay a wager he took a gun with him.'

'Well, that is possible,' said D'Artagnan.

'Do one thing, my friend. Get on horseback, and join him.'

'You are right,' said D'Artagnan, 'I will.'

'Shall I go with you?'

'No, thank you; Porthos is a rather noticeable man: I will enquire as I go along.'

'Will you take an arquebus?'

'Thank you.'

'Order what horse you like to be saddled.'

'The one I rode yesterday, on coming from Belle-Isle.'

'So be it: use the horse as your own.'

Aramis rang, and gave orders to have the horse M. d'Artagnan had chosen saddled.

D'Artagnan followed the servant charged with the execution of this order. When arrived at the door, the servant drew on one side to allow M. d'Artagnan to pass; and at that moment he caught the eye of his master. A knitting of the brow gave the intelligent spy to understand that all should be given to D'Artagnan he wished. D'Artagnan got into the saddle, and Aramis heard the steps of his horse on the pavement. An instant after, the servant returned.

'Well?' asked the bishop.

'Monseigneur, he has followed the course of the canal, and is going towards the sea,' said the servant.

'Good!' said Aramis.

In fact, D'Artagnan, dismissing all suspicion, hastened towards the ocean, constantly hoping to see in the dunes, or on the beach, the colossal figure of Porthos. He persisted in fancying he could trace a horse's steps in every puddle. Sometimes he imagined he heard the report of a gun. This illusion lasted three hours; during two of which he went forward in search of his friend—in the last he returned to the house.

'We must have crossed,' said he, 'and I shall find them waiting for me at table.'

D'Artagnan was mistaken. He no more found Porthos at the palace than he had found him on the sea-shore. Aramis was waiting for him at the top of the stairs, looking very much concerned.

'Did my people not find you, my dear D'Artagnan?' cried he, as soon as he caught sight of the musketeer.

'No; did you send any one after me?'

'I am deeply concerned, my friend, deeply, to have induced you to make such a useless search; but, about seven o'clock, the almoner of Saint Patern came here. He had met Du Vallon, who was going away, and who, being unwilling to disturb anybody at the palace, had charged him to tell me that, fearing M. Gétard would play him some ill turn in his absence, he was going to take advantage of the morning tide to make a tour to Belle-Isle.'

'But tell me, Goliath has not crossed the four leagues of sea, I should think.'

'There are full six,' said Aramis.

'That makes it less probable still.'

'Therefore, my friend,' said Aramis, with one of his blandest smiles, 'Goliath is in the stable, well pleased, I will answer for it, that Porthos is no longer on his back.' In fact, the horse had been brought back from the relay by the direction of the prelate, who missed no detail. D'Artagnan appeared as well satisfied as possible with the explanation. He began behaving with a dissimulation which agreed perfectly with the suspicions that arose more and more strongly in his mind. He breakfasted between the Jesuit and Aramis, having the Dominican in front of him, and smiling particularly at the Dominican, whose jolly fat face pleased him much. The repast was long and sumptuous; excellent Spanish wine, fine Morbihan oysters, exquisite fish from the mouth of the Loire, enormous prawns from Paimbœuf, and delicious game from the downs, constituted the principal part of it. D'Artagnan ate much, and drank but little. Aramis drank nothing but water. After the repast,

'You offered me an arquebus,' said D'Artagnan.

'I did.'

'Lend it me, then.'

'Are you going shooting?'

'Whilst waiting for Porthos, it is the best thing I can do, I think.'

'Take which you like from the gun-room.'

'Will you not come with me?'

'I would with great pleasure; but, alas! my friend, sporting is forbidden to bishops.'

'Ah!' said D'Artagnan, 'I did not know that.'

'Besides,' continued Aramis, 'I shall be busy till mid-day.'

'I shall go alone, then?' said D'Artagnan.

'I am sorry to say you must; but come back to dinner.'

'By God! the food at your house is too good to make me think of not coming back.' And thereupon D'Artagnan quitted his host, bowed to the guests, and took his arquebus; but, instead of shooting, went straight to the little port of Vannes. He looked in vain to observe if anybody saw him; he could discern neither a suspicious thing nor person. He engaged a little fishing-boat for twenty-five livres, and set off at half-past eleven, convinced that he had not been followed; and that was true, he had not been followed; but a Jesuit brother, placed in the top of the steeple of his church, had not, since the morning, by the help of an excellent glass, lost sight of one of his steps. At three-quarters past eleven, Aramis was informed that D'Artagnan was sailing towards Belle-Isle. The voyage was rapid; a good north-north-east wind drove him towards the isle. As he approached, his eyes were constantly fixed upon the coast. He looked to see if, upon the shore or upon the fortifications, the brilliant dress and vast stature of Porthos should stand out against a slightly clouded sky; but his search was vain. He landed without having seen anything; and learnt from the first soldier interrogated by him, that M. du Vallon had not yet returned from Vannes. Then, without wasting an instant, D'Artagnan ordered his little boat to put its head towards Sarzeau. We know that the wind changes with the different hours of the day. The breeze had veered from the north-north-east to the south-east; the wind, then, was almost as good for the return to Sarzeau, as it had been for the voyage to Belle-Isle. In three hours D'Artagnan had reached the mainland; two hours more sufficed for his ride to Vannes. In spite of the rapidity of his passage, what D'Artagnan endured of impatience and anger during that short passage, the deck alone of the vessel, upon which he stamped backwards and forwards for three hours, could testify. He made but one bound from the quay whereon he landed to the Bishop's Palace. He thought to terrify Aramis by the promptitude of his return; he wished to reproach him with his duplicity, and yet with reserve; but with sufficient spirit, nevertheless, to make him feel all the consequences of it, and force from him a part of his secret. He hoped, in short—thanks to that heat of expression which is to secrets what the charge with the bayonet is to redoubts—to bring the mysterious Aramis to some admission or other. But he found, in the vestibule of the palace, the *valet de chambre*, who barred his way, while smiling upon him with a stupid air.

'Monseigneur?' cried D'Artagnan, endeavouring to put him aside with his hand. Moved for an instant, the valet resumed his station.

'Monseigneur?' said he.

'Yes, to be sure; do you not know me, fool?'

'Yes; you are the Chevalier d'Artagnan.'

'Then let me pass.'

'It is no use.'

'Why no use?'

'Because His Grace is not at home.'

'What! His Grace is not at home? where is he then?'

'Gone.'

'Gone?'

'Yes.'

'Whither?'

'I don't know; but, perhaps he tells monsieur le chevalier.'

'And how? where? in what fashion?'

'In this letter, which he gave me for monsieur le chevalier.' And the *valet de chambre* drew a letter from his pocket.

'Give it me, then, you rogue,' said D'Artagnan, snatching it from his hand. 'Oh, yes,' continued he, at the first line, 'yes, I understand;' and he read:

DEAR FRIEND—An affair of the most urgent nature calls me to a distant parish of my diocese. I hoped to see you again before I set out; but I lose that hope in thinking that you are going, no doubt, to remain two or three days at Belle-Isle, with our dear Porthos. Amuse yourself as well as you can; but do not attempt to hold out against him at table. This is a counsel I might have given even to Athos, in his most brilliant and best days. Adieu, dear friend; believe that I regret greatly not having better, and for a longer time, profited by your excellent company.

'*Mordioux!*' cried D'Artagnan. 'I have been tricked. Ah! blockhead, brute, triple fool that I am! But those laugh best who laugh last. Oh, duped, duped like a monkey who has been given an empty nutshell!' And with a hearty blow bestowed upon the nose of the smirking *valet de chambre*, he made all haste out of the Bishop's Palace. Ferret, however good a trotter, was not equal to present circumstances. D'Artagnan, therefore took a post-horse, and chose a mount which he soon caused to demonstrate, with good spurs and a light hand, that deer are not the swiftest animals in nature.

LXXIV

IN WHICH D'ARTAGNAN MAKES ALL SPEED, PORTHOS SNORES, AND ARAMIS COUNSELS

ABOUT thirty to thirty-five hours after the events we have just related, as M. Fouquet, according to his custom, having forbidden his door, was working in the closet of his house at Saint Mandé, with which we are already acquainted, a carriage, drawn by four horses steaming with sweat, entered the court at full gallop. This carriage was, probably, expected; for three or four lackeys hastened to the door, which they opened. While M. Fouquet rose from his desk and ran to the window, a man got painfully out of the carriage, descending with difficulty the three steps of the door, leaning upon the shoulders of the lackeys. He had scarcely uttered his name, when the valet upon whom he was not leaning sprang up the steps of the house, and disappeared into the vestibule. This man went to inform his master;

but he had no occasion to knock at the door: Fouquet was standing on the threshold.

'Monseigneur, the Bishop of Vannes,' said he.

'Very well!' replied his master.

Then, leaning over the banister of the staircase, of which Aramis was beginning to ascend the first steps,

'Ah, dear friend!' said he, 'you, so soon!'

'Yes; I, myself, monsieur! but bruised, battered, as you see.'

'Oh! my poor friend,' said Fouquet, presenting him his arm, on which Aramis leant, whilst the servants drew back respectfully.

'Bah!' replied Aramis, 'it is nothing, since I am here; the principal thing was that I should *get* here, and here I am.'

'Speak quickly,' said Fouquet, closing the door of the cabinet behind Aramis and himself.

'Are we alone?'

'Yes, perfectly.'

'No one observes us?—no one can hear us?'

'Be satisfied; nobody.'

'Is M. du Vallon arrived?'

'Yes.'

'And you have received my letter?'

'Yes. The affair is serious, apparently, since it necessitates your attendance in Paris, at a moment when your presence was so urgent elsewhere.'

'You are right, it could not be more serious.'

'Thank you! thank you! What is it about? But, for God's sake! before anything else, take time to breathe, dear friend. You are so pale, you frighten me.'

'I am really in great pain. But, for Heaven's sake, think nothing about me. Did M. du Vallon tell you nothing, when he delivered the letter to you?'

'No; I heard a great noise; I went to the window; I saw at the foot of the steps a horseman the size of an equestrian statue; I went down, he held the letter out to me, and his horse fell down dead.'

'But he?'

'He fell with the horse; he was lifted, and carried to an apartment. Having read the letter, I went up to him, in hopes of obtaining more ample information; but he was asleep, and, so deeply, that it was impossible to wake him. I took pity on him; I gave orders that his boots should be cut from off his legs, and that he should be left undisturbed.'

'So far well; now, this is the question in hand, monseigneur. You have seen M. d'Artagnan in Paris, have you not?'

'Yes, and think him a man of intelligence, and even a man of heart; although he did bring about the death of our dear friends, Lyodot and D'Eymeris.'

'Alas! yes, I heard of that. At Tours I met the courier who was bringing me the letter from Gourville, and the dispatches from Pellisson. Have you seriously reflected on that event, monsieur?'

'Yes.'

'And in it you perceived a direct attack upon your sovereignty?'

'And do you believe it to be so?'

'Oh, yes, I think so.'

'Well, I must confess, that sad idea occurred to me likewise.'

'Do not blind yourself, monsieur, in the name of Heaven! Listen attentively to me—I return to D'Artagnan.'

'I am all attention.'

'In what circumstances did you see him?'

'He came here for money.'

'With what kind of order?'

'With an order from the king.'

'Direct?'

'Signed by his majesty.'

'There, then! Well, D'Artagnan has been to Belle-Isle; he was disguised; he came in the character of some sort of a steward, charged by his master to purchase salt-works. Now, D'Artagnan has no other master but the king; he came, then, sent by the king. He saw Porthos.'

'Who is Porthos?'

'I beg your pardon, I made a mistake. He saw M. du Vallon at Belle-Isle; and he knows, as well as you and I do, that Belle-Isle is fortified.'

'And you think that the king sent him there?' said Fouquet, pensively.

'I certainly do.'

'And D'Artagnan, in the hands of the king, is a dangerous instrument?'

'The most dangerous imaginable.'

'Then I formed a correct opinion of him at the first glance.'

'How so?'

'I wished to have him in my service.'

'If you judged him to be the bravest, the most acute, and the most adroit man in France, you judged correctly.'

'He must be had then, at any price.'

'D'Artagnan?'

'Is not that your opinion?'

'It may be my opinion, but you will never get him.'

'Why?'

'Because we have allowed the time to go by. He was dissatisfied with the court, we should have profited by that; since then, he has passed into England; there he powerfully assisted in the restoration, there he made a fortune, and, after all that, he returned to the service of the king. Well, if he has returned to the service of the king, it is because he is well paid in that service.'

'We will pay him even better, that is all.'

'Oh! monsieur, excuse me; D'Artagnan has a high respect for his word, and where that is once engaged he keeps it.'

'What do you conclude, then?' said Fouquet, with great inquietude.

'At present, the principal thing is to parry a dangerous blow.'

'And how is it to be parried?'

'Listen. D'Artagnan will come and render an account to the king of his mission.'

'Oh, we have time enough to think about that.'

'How so?'

'You are much in advance of him, I presume?'

'Nearly ten hours.'

'Well, in ten hours——'

Aramis shook his pale head. 'Look at these clouds which flit across the heavens; at these swallows which cut the air. D'Artagnan moves more quickly than the clouds or the birds; D'Artagnan is the wind which carries them.'

'A strange man!'

'I tell you, he is superhuman, monsieur. He is of my own age, and I have known him these five-and-thirty years.'

'Well?'

'Well, listen to my calculation, monsieur. I sent M. du Vallon off to you two hours after midnight. M. du Vallon was eight hours in advance of me; when did M. du Vallon arrive?'

'About four hours ago.'

'You see, then, that I gained four upon him; and yet Porthos is a staunch horseman, and he has left on the road eight dead horses, whose bodies I came to successively. I rode post fifty leagues; but I have the gout, the gravel, and what else I know not; so that fatigue kills me. I was obliged to dismount at Tours; since then, rolling along in a carriage, half-dead, sometimes overturned, thrown against the sides and the back of the carriage, always with four spirited horses at full gallop, I have arrived—arrived, gaining four hours upon Porthos; but, see you, D'Artagnan does not weigh three hundredweight, as Porthos does; D'Artagnan has not the gout and gravel, as I have; he is not a horseman, he is a centaur.* D'Artagnan, mark you, set out for Belle-Isle when I set out for Paris; and D'Artagnan, notwithstanding my ten hours' advance, D'Artagnan will arrive within two hours after me.'

'But what of accidents?'

'He never meets with accidents.'

'Horses may fail him.'

'He will run as fast as a horse.'

'Good God! what a man!'

'Yes, he is a man whom I love and admire. I love him because he is good, great, and loyal; I admire him because he represents in my eyes the culminating point of human power; but, whilst loving and admiring him, I fear him, and am on my guard against him.* Now then, I summarize, monsieur; in two hours D'Artagnan will be here; forestall him. Go to the Louvre, and see the king before he sees D'Artagnan.'

'What shall I say to the king?'

'Nothing; give him Belle-Isle.'

'Oh! Monsieur d'Herblay! Monsieur d'Herblay,' cried Fouquet, 'what plans crushed all at once!'

'After one plan that has failed, there is always another that may lead to fortune; we should never despair. Go, monsieur, and go at once.'

'But that garrison, so carefully chosen, the king will change it directly.'

'That garrison, monsieur, was the king's when it entered Belle-Isle; it is yours now; it is the same with all garrisons after a fortnight's occupation. Let things go on, monsieur. Do you see any disadvantage in having an army at the end of a year, instead of two regiments? Do you not see that your garrison of to-day will generate support for you at La Rochelle, Nantes, Bordeaux, Toulouse—in short, wherever they may be sent to? Go to the king, monsieur; go; time flies, and D'Artagnan, while we are wasting time, is flying, like an arrow, along the high-road.'

'Monsieur d'Herblay, you know that each word from you is a seed which fructifies in my thoughts. I will go to the Louvre.'

'Instantly, will you not?'

'I only ask time to change my dress.'

'Remember that D'Artagnan has no need to pass through St. Mandé; but will go straight to the Louvre; that is cutting off an hour from the advantage that yet remains to us.'

'D'Artagnan may have everything, but he does not have my English horses. I shall be at the Louvre in twenty-five minutes.' And, without losing a second, Fouquet gave orders for his departure.

Aramis had only time to say to him, 'Return as quickly as you go: for I shall await you impatiently.'

Five minutes later the superintendent was flying along the road to Paris. During this time, Aramis asked to be shown the chamber in which Porthos was sleeping. At the door of Fouquet's cabinet he was embraced by Pellisson, who had just heard of his arrival, and had left his office to see him. Aramis received, with that friendly dignity which he knew so well how to assume, his respectful earnest embrace: but all at once stopping on the landing-place, 'What is that I hear up yonder?'

There was, in fact, a hoarse, growling kind of noise, like the roar of a hungry tiger, or an impatient lion. 'Oh, that is nothing,' said Pellisson, smiling.

'Well; but——'

'It is M. du Vallon snoring.'

'Ah! true,' said Aramis: 'I had forgotten. No one but he is capable of making such a noise. Allow me, Pellisson, to enquire if he needs anything.'

'And you will permit me to accompany you?'

'Oh, certainly;' and both entered the chamber. Porthos was stretched upon the bed; his face was purple rather than red; his eyes were swollen; his mouth was wide open. The roaring which escaped from the deep cavities of his chest made the glass of the windows rattle. To those well-developed and clearly defined muscles starting from his face, to his hair matted with sweat, to the energetic heaving of his chin and shoulders, it was imposs-ible to refuse a certain degree of admiration. Strength carried to this point is semi-divine. The Herculean legs and feet of Porthos had, by swelling, burst his stockings; all the strength of his huge body was converted into the solidity of stone. Porthos moved no more than does the giant of granite which reclines upon the plains of Agrigentum.* According to Pellisson's orders, his boots had been cut off, for no human power could have pulled them off. Four lackeys had tried in vain, pulling at them as they would have pulled capstans; and yet all this did not awaken him. They had hacked off his boots in fragments, and his legs had fallen back upon the bed. They then cut off the rest of his clothes, carried him to a bath, in which they let him soak a considerable time. They then put on him clean linen, and placed him in a well-warmed bed—the whole with efforts and pains which might have roused a dead man, but which did not make Porthos open an eye, or interrupt for a second the formidable pitch of his snoring. Aramis wished on his part, with his restless nature, armed with extraordinary courage, to outbrave fatigue, and employ himself with Gourville and Pellisson, but he fainted in the chair in which he had insisted on waiting. He was carried into the adjoining room, where the repose of bed soon soothed his failing brain.

In the meantime Fouquet was hastening to the Louvre, at the best speed of his English horses. The king was at work with Colbert. All at once the king became thoughtful. The two sentences of death he had signed on mounting his throne sometimes recurred to his memory: they were two black spots which he saw with his eyes open; two spots of blood which he saw when his eyes were closed. 'Monsieur,' said he rather sharply to the intendant; 'it sometimes seems to me that those two men you made me condemn were not very great culprits.'

'Sire, they were picked out from the herd of tax-farmers and financiers, which wanted culling.'

'Picked out by whom?'

'By necessity, sire,' replied Colbert, coldly.

'Necessity!—a great word,' murmured the young king.

'A great goddess, sire.'

'They were devoted friends of the superintendent, were they not?'

'Yes, sire; friends who would have given up their lives for Monsieur Fouquet.'

'They have given them, monsieur,' said the king.

'That is true; but, happily, unavailingly—which was not their intention.'

'How much money had these men fraudulently obtained?'

'Ten millions, perhaps; of which six have been confiscated.'

'And is that money in my coffers?' said the king with a certain air of distaste.

'It is there, sire: but this confiscation, whilst threatening M. Fouquet, has not touched him.'

'You conclude, then, M. Colbert——'

'That if M. Fouquet has raised against your majesty a troop of factious rioters to extricate his friends from punishment, he will raise an army when he has in turn to extricate *himself* from punishment.'

The king darted at his confidant one of those looks which

resemble the blinding fire of a flash of lightning, one of those looks which illuminate the darkness of the basest consciences. 'I am astonished,' said he, 'that, thinking such things of M. Fouquet, you did not come to give me your counsels thereupon.'

'Counsels upon what, sire?'

'Tell me, in the first place, clearly and precisely, what you think, M. Colbert.'

'Upon what subject, sire?'

'Upon the conduct of M. Fouquet.'

'I think, sire, that M. Fouquet, not satisfied with attracting all the money to himself, as M. Mazarin did, and by that means depriving your majesty of one part of your power, still wishes to attract to himself all the friends of easy life and pleasure—of what idlers call poetry, and politicians, corruption.* I think that, by having subjects of your majesty in his pay, he trespasses upon the royal prerogative, and cannot, if this continues so, be long in placing your majesty among the weak and the obscure.'

'How would you describe all these projects, M. Colbert?'

'The projects of M. Fouquet, sire?'

'Yes.'

'They are called crimes of treason.'

'And what is done to criminals guilty of treason?'

'They are arrested, tried, and punished.'

'You are quite sure that M. Fouquet has conceived the idea of the crime you impute to him?'

'I can say more, sire; there is even a beginning to the execution of it.'

'Well, then, I return to that which I was saying, M. Colbert.'

'And you were saying, sire?'

'Give me counsel.'

'Pardon me, sire; but, in the first place, I have something to add.'

'Speak—what?'

'An evident, palpable, material proof of treason.'

'And what is that?'

'I have just learnt that M. Fouquet is fortifying Belle-Isle.'

'Ah, indeed!'

'Yes, sire.'

'Are you sure?'

'Perfectly. Do you know, sire, what soldiers there are in Belle-Isle?'

'No, I do not. Do you?'

'I am ignorant, likewise, sire; I should therefore propose to your majesty to send somebody to Belle-Isle.'

'Who?'

'Me, for instance.'

'And what would you do at Belle-Isle?'

'Inform myself whether, after the example of the ancient feudal lords, M. Fouquet was battlementing his walls.'

'And with what purpose could he do that?'

'With the purpose of defending himself some day against his king.'

'But, if it be thus, M. Colbert,' said Louis, 'we must immediately do as you say: M. Fouquet must be arrested.'

'That is impossible.'

'I thought I had already told you, monsieur, that I suppressed that word in my service.'

'The service of your majesty cannot prevent M. Fouquet from being his superintendent of finance.'

'Well?'

'And, in consequence of holding that post, he has for him all the parliament,* as he has all the army by his largesses, literature by his favours, and the aristocracy by his gifts.'

'That is to say, then, that I can do nothing against M. Fouquet?'

'Absolutely nothing—at least at present, sire.'

'You are a sterile counsellor, M. Colbert.'

'Oh, no, sire; for I will not confine myself to pointing out the peril to your majesty.'

'Come, then, where shall we begin to undermine this Colossus; let us see;' and his majesty began to laugh bitterly.

'He has grown great by money: kill him by money, sire.'

'If I were to deprive him of his office?'

'A bad tactic, sire.'

'The good—the good, then?'

'Ruin him, sire, that is the way.'

'But how?'

'Occasions will not be wanting; take advantage of all occasions.'

'Point them out to me.'

'Here is one to begin with. His royal highness Monsieur is about to be married: his nuptials must be magnificent. That is a good occasion for your majesty to demand a million of M. Fouquet. M. Fouquet, who pays twenty thousand livres down when he need not pay more than five thousand, will easily find that million when your majesty demands it.'

'That is very well; I *will* demand it,' said Louis.

'If your majesty will sign the order, I will have the money got together myself.' And Colbert pushed a paper before the king, and presented a pen to him.

At that moment the usher opened the door and announced monsieur le surintendant. Louis turned pale. Colbert let the pen fall, and drew back from the king, over whom he extended his black wings like an evil spirit. The superintendent made his entrance like a man of the court, to whom a single glance was sufficient to enable him to take in the situation. That situation was not very encouraging for Fouquet, whatever might be his consciousness of strength. The small black eye of Colbert, dilated by envy, and the limpid eye of Louis XIV inflamed by anger, signalled some pressing danger. Courtiers are, with regard to court rumours, like old soldiers, who distinguish through the blasts of wind and bluster of leaves the sound of the distant steps of an armed troop. They can, after having listened, tell pretty nearly how many men are marching, how many arms resound, how many cannons roll. Fouquet had then only to question the silence which his arrival had produced: he found it big with menacing revelations. The king allowed him time enough to advance as far as the middle of the chamber. His adolescent modesty drew from him a momentary forbearance. Fouquet boldly seized the opportunity.

'Sire,' said he, 'I was impatient to see your majesty.'

'What for?' asked Louis.

'To announce some good news to you.'

Colbert, minus grandeur of person and largeness of heart, resembled Fouquet in many points. He had the same shrewdness, the same knowledge of men; moreover, that great power of self-control which gives to hypocrites time to reflect, and gather themselves up to take a spring. He guessed that Fouquet was going to meet head on the blow he was about to deal him. His eyes glittered ominously.

'What news?' asked the king. Fouquet placed a roll of papers on the table.

'Let your majesty have the goodness to cast your eyes over this work,' said he. The king slowly unfolded the paper.

'Plans?' said he.

'Yes, sire.'

'And what are these plans?'

'A new fortification, sire.'

'Ah, ah!' said the king, 'you amuse yourself with tactics and strategies then, M. Fouquet?'

'I occupy myself with everything that may be useful to the reign of your majesty,' replied Fouquet.

'Beautifully drawn!' said the king, looking at the design.

'Your majesty understands, without doubt,' said Fouquet, bending over the paper; 'here is the circle of the walls, here are the forts, there the advanced works.'

'And what do I see here, monsieur?'

'The sea.'

'The sea all round?'

'Yes, sire.'

'And what is, then, the name of this place of which you show me the plan?'

'Sire, it is Belle-Isle-en-Mer,' replied Fouquet with simplicity.

At this word, at this name, Colbert made so marked a movement, that the king turned round to enforce the necessity for prudence. Fouquet did not appear to be the least in the world concerned by the movement of Colbert, or the king's signal.

'Monsieur,' continued Louis, 'you have then fortified Belle-Isle?'

'Yes, sire; and I have brought the plan and the accounts to your majesty,' replied Fouquet; 'I have expended sixteen hundred thousand livres in this operation.'

'What to do?' replied Louis, coldly, having taken the initiative from a sly look from the intendant.

'For an aim very easy to grasp,' replied Fouquet. 'Your majesty was on cool terms with Great Britain.'

'Yes; but since the restoration of King Charles II I have formed an alliance with him.'

'A month since, sire, your majesty has truly said; but it is more than six months since the fortifications of Belle-Isle were begun.'

'Then they have become useless.'

'Sire, fortifications are never useless. I fortified Belle-Isle against MM. Monk and Lambert and all those London citizens who were playing at soldiers. Belle-Isle will be ready fortified against the Dutch, against whom either England or your majesty cannot fail to make war.'

The king was again silent, and looked askance at Colbert. 'Belle-Isle, I believe,' added Louis, 'is yours, M. Fouquet?'

'No, sire.'

'Whose then?'

'Your majesty's.'*

Colbert was seized with as much terror as if a gulf had opened beneath his feet. Louis started with admiration, either at the genius or the devotion of Fouquet.

'Explain yourself, monsieur,' said he.

'Nothing more easy, sire; Belle-Isle is one of my estates; I have fortified it at my own expense. But as nothing in the world can oppose a subject making an humble present to his king, I offer your majesty the proprietorship of the estate, of which you will leave me the usufruct. Belle-Isle, as a place of war, ought to be occupied by the king. Your majesty will be able, henceforth, to keep a safe garrison there.'

Colbert felt almost as though he were sinking down upon the floor. To keep himself from falling, he was obliged to hold by the columns of the wainscoting.

'This is a piece of great skill in the art of war that you have exhibited here, monsieur,' said Louis.

'Sire, the initiative did not come from me,' replied Fouquet; 'many officers have inspired me with it. The plans themselves have been made by one of the most distinguished engineers.'

'His name?'

'M. du Vallon.'

'M. du Vallon?' resumed Louis; 'I do not know him. It is much to be lamented, M. Colbert,' continued he, 'that I do not know the names of the men of talent who do honour to my reign.' And while saying these words he turned towards Colbert. The latter felt crushed, the sweat flowed from his brow, no word presented itself to his lips, he suffered the torments of martyr-dom. 'You will recollect that name,' added Louis XIV.

Colbert bowed, but was paler than his ruffles of Flemish lace. Fouquet continued:

'The masonries are of Roman concrete; the architects mixed it for me after the best accounts of antiquity.'

'And the cannon?' asked Louis.

'Oh! sire, that is your majesty's business; it did not become me to place cannon in my own house, unless your majesty had told me it was yours.'

Louis began to oscillate, undetermined between the hatred which this so powerful man inspired him with, and the pity he felt for the other, so cast down, who seemed to him a poor version of the former. But the consciousness of his kingly duty prevailed over the feelings of the man, and he stretched out his finger to the paper.

'It must have cost you a great deal of money to carry these plans into execution,' said he.

'I believe I had the honour of telling your majesty the amount.'

'Repeat it if you please, I have forgotten it.'

'Sixteen hundred thousand livres.'

'Sixteen hundred thousand livres! you are enormously rich, monsieur.'

'It is your majesty who is rich, since Belle-Isle is yours.'

'Yes, thank you; but however rich I may be, M. Fou-quet——' The king stopped.

'Well, sire?' asked the superintendent.

'I foresee the moment when I shall need money.'

'You, sire?—And at what moment, then?'

'To-morrow, for example.'

'Will your majesty do me the honour to explain yourself?'

'My brother is going to marry the English princess.'

'Well?—sire.'

'Well, I ought to give the bride a reception worthy of the granddaughter of Henry IV.'

'That is but just, sire.'

'Then I shall need money.'

'No doubt.'

'I shall want——' Louis hesitated. The sum he was going to

demand was the same that he had been obliged to refuse Charles
II. He turned towards Colbert, that he might give the blow.

'I shall need, to-morrow——' repeated he, looking at Colbert.

'A million,' said the latter, bluntly: delighted to take his
revenge.

Fouquet turned his back upon the intendant to listen to the
king. He did not turn round, but waited till the king repeated,
or rather murmured, 'A million.'

'Oh! sire,' replied Fouquet disdainfully, 'a million! What will
your majesty do with a million?'

'It appears to me, nevertheless——' said Louis XIV.

'That is not more than is spent at the nuptials of one of the
most petty princes of Germany.'

'Monsieur!'

'Your majesty must have two millions at least. The horses
alone would run away with five hundred thousand livres. I shall
have the honour of sending your majesty sixteen hundred thousand livres this evening.'

'How,' said the king, 'sixteen hundred thousand livres?'

'Look, sire,' replied Fouquet, without even turning towards
Colbert, 'I know that the sum lacks four hundred thousand
livres of the two millions. But this gentleman' (pointing over his
shoulder to Colbert, who if possible, became paler, behind him)
'has in his coffers nine hundred thousand livres of mine.'

The king turned round to look at Colbert.

'But——' said the latter.

'Monsieur,' continued Fouquet, still speaking indirectly to
Colbert, 'monsieur received, a week ago, sixteen hundred thousand livres; he has paid a hundred thousand livres to the guards,
sixty-four thousand livres to the hospitals, twenty-five thousand
to the Swiss,* a hundred and thirty thousand for provisions, a
thousand for arms, ten thousand for general expenses; I do not
err, then, in reckoning upon nine hundred thousand livres that
are left.'* Then turning towards Colbert, like a disdainful head
of office towards his inferior, 'Take care, monsieur,' said he,
'that those nine hundred thousand livres be remitted to his
majesty this evening, in gold.'

'But,' said the king, 'that will make two millions five hundred
thousand livres.'

'Sire, the five hundred thousand livres over will serve as pocket money for his Royal Highness. You understand, Monsieur Colbert, this evening before eight o'clock.'

And with these words, bowing respectfully to the king, the superintendent made his exit backwards, without honouring with a single look the envious man, whose head he had just half-shaved.

Colbert tore his ruffles to pieces in his rage, and bit his lips till they bled.

Fouquet had not passed the door of the closet, when an usher, pushing by him, exclaimed: 'A courier from Brittany for his majesty.'

'M. d'Herblay was right,' murmured Fouquet, pulling out his watch; 'an hour and fifty-five minutes. Just in time!'*

LXXVI

IN WHICH D'ARTAGNAN AT LAST GETS HIS HANDS ON HIS CAPTAIN'S COMMISSION

THE reader will guess whom the usher preceded in announcing the courier from Brittany. This messenger was easily recognized. It was D'Artagnan, his clothes dusty, his face inflamed, his hair dripping with sweat, his legs stiff; he lifted his feet painfully at every step, on which resounded the clink of his blood-stained spurs. He perceived in the doorway he was passing through the superintendent coming out. Fouquet bowed with a smile to him who, an hour before, was bringing him ruin and death. D'Artagnan found in his goodness of heart, and in his inexhaustible vigour of body, enough presence of mind to remember the kind reception of this man; he bowed then, also, much more from benevolence and compassion, than from respect. He felt upon his lips the word which had so many times been repeated to the Duc de Guise: 'Fly.'* But to pronounce that word would have been to betray his cause; to speak that word in the closet of the king, and before an usher, would have been to ruin himself uselessly, and could save nobody. So D'Artagnan contented himself with bowing to Fouquet, and entered. At this moment the king was hovering between the astonishment the last words of Fouquet had given him, and his pleasure at the return of D'Artagnan. Without being a courtier, D'Artagnan had a glance as sure and as rapid as if he had been one. He read, on his entrance, devouring humiliation on the countenance of Colbert. He even heard the king say these words to him:

'Ah! Monsieur Colbert; so you have nine hundred thousand livres to hand?' Colbert, choked, bowed but made no reply. All this scene entered into the mind of D'Artagnan, by the eyes and ears at once.

The first word of Louis to his musketeer, as if he wished it to contrast with what he was saying at the moment, was a kind 'good day'. His second was to send away Colbert. The latter left the king's cabinet, pallid and tottering, whilst D'Artagnan twisted up the ends of his moustache.

'I love to see one of my servants in such disarray,' said the king, admiring the martial stains upon the clothes of his envoy.

'I thought, sire, my presence at the Louvre was sufficiently urgent to excuse my presenting myself thus before you.'

'You bring me great news, then, monsieur.'

'Sire, the thing is this, in two words: Belle-Isle is fortified, admirably fortified; Belle-Isle has a double enceinte, a citadel, two detached forts; its harbour contains three corsairs; and the side batteries only await their cannon.'

'I know all that, monsieur,' replied the king.

'What! your majesty knows all that?' replied the musketeer, stupefied.

'I have the plan of the fortifications of Belle-Isle,' said the king.

'Your majesty has the plan?'

'Here it is.'

'That is it indeed, sire: I saw one just like it when I was there.' D'Artagnan's brow became clouded.

'Ah! I understand all. Your majesty did not trust to me alone, but sent some other person,' said he, in a reproachful tone.

'Of what importance is the manner, monsieur, in which I have learnt what I know, provided I know it?'

'Sire, sire,' said the musketeer, without seeking even to disguise his dissatisfaction; 'but I must be permitted to say to your majesty, that it is not worth while to make me use such speed, to risk twenty times the breaking of my neck, to salute me on my arrival with such intelligence. Sire, when people are not trusted, or are deemed insufficient, they should scarcely be employed.' And D'Artagnan, with a movement perfectly military, stamped with his foot, and left upon the floor dust stained with blood. The king looked at him, inwardly enjoying his first triumph.

'Monsieur,' said he, after a minute, 'not only is Belle-Isle known to me, but, still further, Belle-Isle is mine.'

'That is well! that is well, sire, I ask but one thing more,' replied D'Artagnan—'My discharge.'

'What! your discharge?'

'Without doubt I am too proud to eat the bread of the king without earning it, or rather by gaining it badly. My discharge, sire!'

'Oh, oh!'

'I ask for my discharge, or I will take it.'

'You are angry, monsieur?'

'I have reason, *mordioux!* Thirty-two hours in the saddle, I ride night and day, I perform prodigies of speed, I arrive stiff as the corpse of a man who has been hung—and another arrives before me! Come, sire, I am a fool!—My discharge, sire!'

'Monsieur d'Artagnan,' said Louis, leaning his white hand upon the dusty arm of the musketeer, 'what I tell you will not at all affect that which I promised you. A king's word given must be kept.' And the king going straight to his table, opened a drawer, and took out a folded paper. 'Here is your commission of captain of musketeers; you have earned it, Monsieur d'Artagnan.'

D'Artagnan opened the paper eagerly, and scanned it twice. He could scarcely believe his eyes.

'And this commission is given you,' continued the king, 'not only on account of your journey to Belle-Isle, but, moreover, for your brave intervention at the Place de Grève. There, likewise, you served me valiantly.'

'Ah, ah!' said D'Artagnan, without his self-command being able to prevent a blush from mounting to his eyes—'you know that also, sire?'

'Yes, I know it.'

The king possessed a piercing glance and infallible judgment, when it was his object to read men's minds. 'You have something to say,' said he to the musketeer, 'something to say which you do not say. Come, speak freely, monsieur: you know that I told you, once for all, that you are to be always quite frank with me.'

'Well, sire! what I have to say is this, that I would prefer being made captain of musketeers for having charged a battery at the head of my company or taken a city, than for causing two wretches to be hung.'

'Is this quite true that you tell me?'

'And why should your majesty suspect me of dissimulation, I ask?'

'Because I know you well, monsieur; you cannot repent of having drawn your sword for me.'

'Well, in that your majesty is deceived, and greatly; yes, I do repent of having drawn my sword on account of the results that action produced; the poor men who were hung, sire, were neither your enemies nor mine; and they could not defend themselves.'

The king preserved silence for a moment. 'And your companion, M. d'Artagnan, does he partake of your repentance?'

'My companion?'

'Yes, you were not alone, I have been told.'

'Alone, where?'

'At the Place de Grève.'

'No, sire, no,' said D'Artagnan, blushing at the idea that the king might have a suspicion that he, D'Artagnan, had wished to attract to himself all the glory that belonged to Raoul; 'no, *mordioux!* and as your majesty says, I had a companion, and a good companion, too.'

'A young man?'

'Yes, sire; a young man. Oh! your majesty must accept my compliments, you are as well informed of things out of doors as things within. It is M. Colbert who makes all these fine reports to the king.'

'M. Colbert has said nothing but good of you, M. d'Artagnan, and he would have met with a bad reception if he had come to tell me anything else.'

'That is fortunate!'

'But he also said much good of that young man.'

'And with justice,' said the musketeer.

'In short, it appears that this young man is a fire-eater,' said Louis, in order to sharpen the sentiment which he mistook for envy.

'A fire-eater! Yes, sire,' repeated D'Artagnan, delighted on his part to direct the king's attention to Raoul.

'Do you not know his name?'

'Well, I think——'

'You know him then?'

'I have known him nearly five-and-twenty years, sire.'

'Why, he is scarcely twenty-five years old!' cried the king.

'Well, sire! I have known him ever since he was born,* that is all.'

'Do you affirm that?'

'Sire,' said D'Artagnan, 'your majesty questions me with a mistrust in which I recognize another character than your own. M. Colbert, who has so well informed you, has he not forgotten to tell you that this young man is the son of my most intimate friend?'

'The Vicomte de Bragelonne?'

'Certainly, sire. The father of the Vicomte de Bragelonne is M. le Comte de la Fère, who so powerfully assisted in the restoration of King Charles II. Bragelonne comes of a valiant race, sire.'

'Then he is the son of that nobleman who came to me, or rather to M. Mazarin, on the part of king Charles II, to offer me his alliance?'

'Exactly, sire.'

'And the Comte de la Fère is a great soldier, say you?'

'Sire, he is a man who has drawn his sword more times for the king, your father, than there are, at present, months in the happy life of your majesty.'

It was Louis XIV who now bit his lip.

'That is well, M. d'Artagnan, very well! And M. le Comte de la Fère is your friend, you say?'

'For about forty years;* yes, sire. Your majesty may see that I do not speak to you of yesterday.'

'Should you be glad to see this young man, M. d'Artagnan?'

'Delighted, sire.'

The king touched his bell, and an usher appeared. 'Call M. de Bragelonne,' said the king.

'Ah! ah! he is here?' said D'Artagnan.

'He is on guard to-day, at the Louvre, with the company of the gentlemen of monsieur le prince.'

The king had scarcely ceased speaking, when Raoul presented himself, and, on seeing D'Artagnan, smiled on him with that charming smile which is only found upon the lips of youth.

'Come, come,' said D'Artagnan, familiarly, to Raoul, 'the king will allow you to embrace me; only tell his majesty you thank him.'

Raoul bowed so gracefully, that Louis, to whom all superior qualities were pleasing when they did not overshadow his own, admired his beauty, strength and modesty.

'Monsieur,' said the king, addressing Raoul, 'I have asked monsieur le prince to be kind enough to give you up to me; I have received his reply, and you belong to me from this morning. Monsieur le prince was a good master, but I hope you will not lose by the exchange.'

'Yes, yes, Raoul, be satisfied; the king has some good points,' said D'Artagnan, who had fathomed the character of Louis, and played on his self-love, within certain limits; always observing, be it understood, the proprieties, and flattering, even when he appeared to be bantering.

'Sire,' said Bragelonne, with a voice soft and musical, and with the natural and easy elocution he inherited from his father; 'Sire, it is not from this day that I belong to your majesty.'

'Oh! no, I know,' said the king; 'you mean your action on the Grève. That day, you were truly mine, monsieur.'

'Sire, it is not of that day, I would speak; it would not become me to refer to so paltry a service in the presence of such a man as M. d'Artagnan. I would speak of a circumstance which created an epoch in my life, and which led me, from the age of sixteen, to the devoted service of your majesty.'

'Ah! ah!' said the king, 'what was that circumstance? Tell me, monsieur.'

'This is it, sire. When I was setting out on my first campaign, that is to say, to join the army of monsieur le prince, M. le

Comte de la Fère came to conduct me as far as Saint-Denis, where the remains of King Louis XIII wait, upon the lowest steps of the mausoleum, a successor, whom God will not send him, I hope, for many years. Then he made me swear upon the ashes of our masters, to serve royalty represented by you— incarnate in you, sire—to serve it in word, in thought, and in action. I swore, and God and the dead were witnesses to my oath.* During ten years, sire, I have not so often as I desired had occasion to keep it. I am a soldier of your majesty, and nothing else; and, on calling me nearer to you, I do not change my master, I only change my garrison.'

Raoul was silent, and bowed. Louis still listened after he had done speaking.

'*Mordioux!*' cried D'Artagnan, 'that was well spoken! was it not, your majesty? A good race! a noble race!'

'Yes,' murmured the agitated king, without, however, daring to show his emotion which had no other cause than contact with this man of so intrinsically noble a character. 'Yes, monsieur, you say truly: wherever you were, you were the king's. But in changing your garrison, believe me you will find advancement of which you are worthy.'

Raoul saw that this ended what the king had to say to him. And with the perfect tact which characterized his refined nature, he bowed and retired.

'Is there anything else, monsieur, of which you have to inform me?' said the king, when he found himself again alone with D'Artagnan.

'Yes, sire, and I kept that news for the last, for it is sad, and will clothe European royalty in mourning.'

'What do you tell me?'

'Sire, in passing through Blois, a word, a sad word, echoed from the palace, struck my ear.'

'In truth, you terrify me, M. d'Artagnan.'

'Sire, this word was pronounced to me by a groom, who wore a black band on his arm.'

'My uncle, Gaston of Orléans, perhaps?'

'Sire, he has rendered his last sigh.'*

'And I was not told of it!' cried the king, whose royal susceptibility saw an insult in his not having been informed.

'Oh! do not be angry, sire,' said D'Artagnan; 'neither the couriers of Paris, nor the couriers of the whole world, can travel with your servant; the courier from Blois will not be here these two hours, and he rides well, I assure you, seeing that I only passed him on the further side of Orléans.'

'My uncle Gaston,' murmured Louis, pressing his hand to his brow, and comprising in those three words all that his memory recalled of that symbol of opposing sentiments.

'Eh! yes, sire, it is thus,' said D'Artagnan, philosophically replying to the royal thought, 'it is thus the past flies away.'

'That is true, monsieur, that is true; but there remains for us, thank God! the future; and we will try to make it not too dark.'

'I feel confidence in your majesty on that head,' said D'Artagnan, bowing, 'and now——'

'You are right, monsieur; I had forgotten the hundred leagues you have just ridden. Go, monsieur, take care of one of the best of soldiers, I mean yourself, and when you have reposed a little, come and place yourself at my disposal.'

'Sire, absent or present, I am always yours.'

D'Artagnan bowed and retired. Then, as if he had only come from Fontainebleau, he quickly traversed the Louvre to rejoin Bragelonne.

LXXVII

A LOVER AND HIS MISTRESS

WHILE the wax-lights were burning in the castle of Blois, around the inanimate body of Gaston of Orléans, that last representative of the past; while the citizens of the city were thinking out his epitaph, which was far from being a panegyric; while madame the dowager, no longer remembering that in her young days she had loved that senseless corpse to such a degree as to fly her father's palace* for his sake, was making, within twenty paces of the funeral apartment, her little calculations of interest and her little sacrifices of pride; other interests and other prides were in agitation in all the parts of the castle into which a living soul could penetrate. Neither the lugubrious sounds of the bells, nor

the voices of the chanters, nor the splendour of the wax-lights
through the windows, nor the preparations for the funeral, had
power to divert the attention of two persons, placed at a window
of the inner court—a window that we are acquainted with, and
which lighted a chamber forming part of what were called the
little apartments. For the rest, a joyous beam of the sun, for the
sun appeared to care little for the loss France had just suffered;
a sunbeam, we say, descended upon them, drawing perfumes
from the neighbouring flowers, and animating the walls themselves. These two persons, so occupied, not by the death of the
duke, but by the conversation which was the consequence of
that death, were a young woman and a young man. The latter
personage, a man of from twenty-five to twenty-six years of age,
with an expression now lively now downcast, making good use
of two large eyes, shaded with long eyelashes, was short of
stature and dark of skin; he smiled with an enormous, but well-
furnished mouth, and his pointed chin, which appeared to enjoy
a mobility nature does not ordinarily grant to that portion of the
countenance, leant from time to time very lovingly towards his
companion, who, we must say, did not always draw back so
rapidly as strict propriety had a right to require. The young
girl—we know her, for we have already seen her, at that very
same window, by the light of that same sun—the young girl
presented a singular mixture of shyness and reflection; she was
charming when she laughed, beautiful when she became serious;
but, let us hasten to say, she was more frequently charming than
beautiful. These two appeared to have attained the culminating
point of a discussion—half-bantering, half-serious.

'Now, Monsieur Malicorne,' said the young girl, 'does it, at
length, please you that we should talk reasonably?'

'You believe that that is very easy, Mademoiselle Aure,' replied the young man. 'To do what we like, when we can only do
what we are able——'

'Good! there he is embroiled in complications.'

'Who, I?'

'Yes, you; quit that lawyer's logic, my dear.'

'Another impossibility.'

'Clerk,* I am Mademoiselle de Montalais.'

'Demoiselle, I am Monsieur Malicorne.'

'Alas, I know it well, and you overwhelm me by your rank; so I will say no more to you.'

'Well, no, I don't overwhelm you: say what you have to tell me—say it, I insist upon it.'

'Well, I obey you.'

'That is truly fortunate.'

'Monsieur is dead.'

'Ah, heavens! there's news! And where do you come from, to be able to tell us that?'

'I come from Orléans, mademoiselle.'

'And is that all the news you bring?'

'Ah, no; I am come to tell you that Madame Henrietta of England is coming to marry the king's brother.'

'Indeed, Malicorne, you are insupportable with your news of the last century. Now, mind, if you persist in this bad habit of laughing at people, I will have you turned out.'

'Oh!'

'Yes: for really you exasperate me.'

'There, there. Patience, mademoiselle.'

'You want to make yourself important; I know well enough why. Go!'

'Tell me, and I will answer you frankly, yes, if the thing be true.'

'You know that I am anxious to be appointed a lady of honour, which I have been foolish enough to ask of you, and you do not use your credit.'

'Who, I?' Malicorne cast down his eyes, joined his hands, and assumed his sullen air. 'And what credit can a poor lawyer's clerk have, pray?'

'Your father has not twenty thousand livres a year for nothing, M. Malicorne.'

'A provincial fortune, Mademoiselle de Montalais.'

'Your father is not in the secrets of monsieur le prince for nothing.'

'An advantage which is confined to lending monseigneur money.'

'In a word, you are not the most cunning young fellow in the province for nothing.'

'You flatter me!'

'Who, I?'

'Yes, you.'

'How so?'

'Since I maintain that I have no credit, and you maintain I have.'

'Well, then—my appointment?'

'Well—your appointment?'

'Shall I have it, or shall I not?'

'You shall have it.'

'Yes, but when?'

'When you like.'

'Where is it, then?'

'In my pocket.'

'What—in your pocket?'

'Yes.'

And, with a smile, Malicorne drew from his pocket a letter, upon which mademoiselle seized as on a prey, and which she read eagerly. As she read, her face brightened.

'Malicorne,' cried she after having read it, 'In truth, you are a good lad.'

'Why, mademoiselle?'

'Because you might have been paid for this letter, and you have not.' And she burst into a loud laugh, thinking to put the clerk out of countenance; but Malicorne sustained the attack bravely.

'I do not understand you,' said he. It was now Montalais who was disconcerted in her turn. 'I have declared my sentiments to you,' continued Malicorne. 'You have told me three times, laughing all the while, that you did not love me; you have embraced me once without laughing, and that is all I want.'

'All?' said the proud and coquettish Montalais, in a tone through which wounded pride was visible.

'Absolutely all, mademoiselle,' replied Malicorne.

'Ah!'—And this monosyllable indicated as much anger as the young man might have expected gratitude. He shook his head quietly.

'Listen, Montalais,' said he, without heeding whether that familiarity pleased his mistress or not; 'let us not quarrel about it.'

'And why not?'

'Because during the year I have known you, you might have had me turned out of doors twenty times if I did not please you.'

'Indeed; and on what account should I have had you turned out?'

'Because I had been sufficiently impertinent for that.'

'Oh, that—yes, that's true.'

'You see plainly that you are forced to admit it,' said Malicorne.

'Monsieur Malicorne!'

'Don't let us be angry; if you have allowed me to stay, then it has not been without cause.'

'It is not, at least, because I love you,' cried Montalais.

'Granted. I will even say that, at this moment, I am certain that you hate me.'

'Oh, you have never spoken so truly.'

'Well, for my part I detest you.'

'Ah, I'll bear it in mind.'

'Do so. You find me brutal and foolish; for my part I find you have a harsh voice, and your face is too often distorted with anger. At this moment you would allow yourself to be thrown out of that window rather than allow me to kiss the tip of your finger; I would jump from the top of the balcony rather than touch the hem of your robe. But, in five minutes, you will love me, and I shall adore you. Oh, it is just so.'

'I doubt it.'

'And I swear it.'

'Coxcomb!'

'And then, that is not the true reason. You stand in need of me, Aure, and I of you. When it pleases you to be gay, I make you laugh; when it suits me to be loving, I look at you. I have given you an appointment as lady of honour which you wished for; you will give me, presently, something I wish for.'

'I will?'

'Yes, you will; but, at this moment, my dear Aure, I declare to you that I wish for absolutely nothing, so be at ease.'

'You are a frightful man, Malicorne; I was going to rejoice at getting this appointment, and thus you quench my joy.'

'Good; there is no time lost—you will rejoice when I am gone.'

'Go, then; and after——'

'So be it; but, in the first place, a piece of advice.'

'What is it?'

'Resume your good humour—you are ugly when you sulk.'

'Brute!'

'Come, let us tell the truth to each other, while we are about it.'

'Oh, Malicorne! Hard-hearted man!'

'Oh, Montalais! Ungrateful girl!'

The young man leant with his elbow upon the window-frame; Montalais took a book and opened it. Malicorne stood up, brushed his hat with his sleeve, smoothed down his black doublet; Montalais, though pretending to read, looked at him out of the corner of her eye.

'Good!' cried she, furious; 'he has assumed his respectful air—and he will sulk for a week.'

'A fortnight, mademoiselle,' said Malicorne, bowing.

Montalais lifted up her little doubled fist. 'Monster!' said she; 'oh! that I were a man!'

'What would you do to me?'

'I would strangle you.'

'Ah! very well, then,' said Malicorne; 'I believe I begin to want something.'

'And what do you want, Monsieur Demon? That I should lose my soul from anger?'

Malicorne was rolling his hat respectfully between his fingers; but, all at once, he let fall his hat, seized the young girl by the shoulders, pulled her towards him, and sealed her mouth with two lips that were very warm, for a man pretending to so much indifference. Aure would have cried out, but the cry was stifled in the kiss. Agitated and, apparently, angry, the young girl pushed Malicorne against the wall.

'Good!' said Malicorne, philosophically, 'that's enough for six weeks. Adieu, mademoiselle, accept my very humble salutation.' And he made three steps towards the door.

'Well! no—you shall not go!' cried Montalais, stamping with her little foot. 'Stay where you are! I order you!'

'You order me?'

'Yes; am I not mistress here?'

'Of my heart and soul, without doubt.'

'A pretty property! The soul is foolish and the heart dry.'

'Beware, Montalais, I know you,' said Malicorne; 'you are going to fall in love with your humble servant.'

'Well, yes!' said, she, hanging round his neck with childish indolence, rather than with loving abandonment. 'Well, yes! for I must thank you at least.'

'And for what?'

'For my appointment; is it not my whole future?'

'And mine.'

Montalais looked at him.

'It is frightful,' said she, 'that I can never guess whether you are speaking seriously or not.'

'I cannot speak more seriously. I was going to Paris—you are going there—*we* are going there.'

'And so it was for that motive only you have served me; selfish fellow!'

'What would you have me say, Aure? I cannot live without you.'

'Well! in truth, it is just so with me; you are, nevertheless, it must be confessed, a very hard-hearted young man.'

'Aure, my dear Aure, take care! if you take to calling names again, you know the effect they produce upon me, and I shall adore you.' And so saying, Malicorne drew the young girl a second time towards him. But at that instant a step sounded on the staircase. The young people were so close that they would have been surprised in each other's arms, if Montalais had not violently pushed Malicorne against the door, just then opening. A loud cry, followed by angry reproaches, immediately resounded. It was Madame de Saint-Rémy who uttered the cry and the angry words. The unfortunate Malicorne almost crushed her between the wall and the door she was coming in at.

'It is that good-for-nothing again!' cried the old lady. 'Always here!'

'Ah, madame!' replied Malicorne, in a respectful tone; 'it is one interminable week since I was here.'

LXXVIII

IN WHICH WE AT LENGTH SEE THE TRUE HEROINE OF THIS HISTORY REAPPEAR

BEHIND Madame de Saint-Rémy stood Mademoiselle de la Vallière. She heard the explosion of maternal anger, and as she divined the cause of it, she entered the chamber trembling, and perceived the unfortunate Malicorne, whose woeful countenance might have softened or set laughing whoever observed it coolly. He had promptly entrenched himself behind a large chair, as if to avoid the first attacks of Madame de Saint-Rémy; he had no hopes of prevailing with words, for she spoke louder than he, and without stopping; but he reckoned upon the eloquence of his gestures. The old lady would neither listen to nor see anything; Malicorne had long been one of her antipathies. But her anger was too great not to overflow from Malicorne to his accomplice. Montalais had her turn.

'And you, mademoiselle; you may be certain I shall inform madame of what is going on in the apartment of one of her ladies of honour.'

'Oh, dear mother!' cried Mademoiselle de la Vallière, 'for mercy's sake, spare——'

'Hold your tongue, mademoiselle, and do not trouble yourself to intercede for unworthy people; that a young maid of honour like you should be subjected to a bad example is, certainly, a misfortune great enough: but that you should sanction it by your indulgence is what I will not allow.'

'But in truth,' said Montalais, rebelling again, 'I do not know under what pretext you treat me thus. I am doing no harm, I think?'

'And that great good-for-nothing, mademoiselle,' resumed Madame de Saint-Rémy, pointing to Malicorne, 'is he here to do any good, I ask you?'

'He is neither here for good nor harm, madame; he comes to see me, that is all.'

'It is all very well! all very well!' said the old lady. 'Her royal highness shall be informed of it, and she will judge.'

'At all events, I do not see why,' replied Montalais, 'it should be forbidden M. Malicorne to have intentions towards me, if his intentions are honourable.'

'Honourable intentions with such a face!' cried Madame de Saint-Rémy.

'I thank you in the name of my face, madame,' said Malicorne.

'Come, daughter, come,' continued Madame de Saint-Rémy; 'we will go and inform madame that at the very moment she is weeping for her husband, at the moment when we are all weeping for a master in this old castle of Blois, the abode of grief, there are people who amuse themselves with flirtations!'

'Oh!' cried both the accused, with one voice.

'A maid of honour! a maid of honour!' cried the old lady, lifting her hands towards heaven.

'Well! it is there you are mistaken, madame,' said Montalais, highly exasperated; 'I am no longer a maid of honour, of madame's at least.'

'Have you given in your resignation, mademoiselle? That is well! I cannot but applaud such a determination, and I do applaud it.'

'I do not give in my resignation, madame; I take another service—that is all.'

'In the bourgeoisie or in the *robe*?'* asked Madame de Saint-Rémy, disdainfully.

'Please to learn, madame, that I am not a girl to serve in either; and that instead of the miserable court at which you vegetate, I am going to reside in a court which is almost royal.'

'Ha, ha! a royal court,' said Madame de Saint-Rémy, forcing a laugh; 'a royal court! What think you of that, my daughter?'

And she turned round towards Mademoiselle de la Vallière, whom she would by main force have dragged away from Montalais, and who, instead of obeying the impulse of Madame de Saint-Rémy, looked first at her mother and then at Montalais with her beautiful conciliatory eyes.

'I did not say a royal court, madame,' replied Montalais; 'because Madame Henrietta of England, who is about to become the wife of His Royal Highness Monsieur,* is not a queen. I said *almost* royal, and I spoke correctly, since she will be sister-in-law to the king.'

A thunderbolt falling upon the castle of Blois would not have astonished Madame de Saint-Rémy more than the last sentence of Montalais.

'What do you say? Her Royal Highness Madame Henrietta?' stammered out the old lady.

'I say I am going to belong to her household, as maid of honour; that is what I say.'

'As maid of honour!' cried, at the same time, Madame de Saint-Rémy with despair, and Mademoiselle de la Vallière with delight.

'Yes, madame, as maid of honour.'

The old lady's head sank down as if the blow had been too severe for her. But, almost immediately recovering herself, she launched a last projectile at her adversary.

'Oh! oh!' said she; 'I have heard of many of these sorts of promises before, which often lead people to flatter themselves with wild hopes, and, at the last moment, when the time comes to keep the promises, and have the hopes realized, they are surprised to see the great credit upon which they reckoned vanish like smoke.'

'Oh! madame, the credit of my protector is incontestable, and his promises are as good as deeds.'

'And would it be indiscreet to ask you the name of this powerful protector?'

'Oh! good heavens! no! it is that gentleman there,' said Montalais, pointing to Malicorne, who, during this scene, had preserved the most imperturbable coolness, and the most comic dignity.

'Monsieur!' cried Madame de Saint-Rémy, with an explosion of hilarity, 'monsieur is your protector! Is the man whose credit is so powerful, and whose promises are as good as deeds, Monsieur Malicorne!'

Malicorne bowed.

As to Montalais, as her sole reply, she drew the letter of appointment from her pocket, and showed it to the old lady.

'Here is the proof,' said she.

At once all was over. As soon as she had cast a rapid glance over the wonderful letter, the good lady clasped her hands, an unspeakable expression of envy and despair spread over her face, and she was obliged to sit down to avoid fainting. Montalais was not malicious enough to rejoice extravagantly at her victory, or to overwhelm the conquered enemy, particularly when that enemy was the mother of her friend; she enjoyed, but did not abuse, her triumph. Malicorne was less generous; he assumed noble poses in his armchair, and stretched himself out with a familiarity which, two hours earlier, would have drawn upon him threats of a caning.

'Maid of honour to the young madame!' repeated Madame de Saint-Rémy, still but half convinced.

'Yes, madame, and through the protection of M. Malicorne, moreover.'

'It is incredible!' repeated the old lady: 'is it not incredible, Louise?' But Louise did not reply; she was sitting, thoughtful, almost sad; passing one hand over her beautiful brow, she sighed heavily.

'Well, monsieur,' said Madame de Saint-Rémy, all at once, 'how did you manage to obtain this post?'

'I asked for it, madame.'

'Of whom?'

'One of my friends.'

'And have you friends sufficiently powerful at court to give you such proofs of their credit?'

'It appears so.'

'And may one ask the name of these friends?'

'I did not say I had many friends, madame, I said I had one friend.'

'And that friend is called?'

'Really, madame, you go too far! When one has a friend as powerful as mine, we do not publish his name in that fashion, in open day, in order that he may be stolen from us.'

'You are right, monsieur, to be silent as to this name; for I think it would be pretty difficult for you to tell it.'

'At all events,' said Montalais, 'if the friend does not exist, the letter does, and that cuts short the question.'

'Then, I conceive,' said Madame de Saint-Rémy, with the gracious smile of a cat who is going to scratch, 'when I found monsieur here just now——'

'Well?'

'He brought you the letter.'

'Exactly, madame; you have guessed correctly.'

'Well, then, nothing can be more moral or proper.'

'I think so, madame.'

'And I have been wrong, as it appears, in reproaching you, mademoiselle.'

'Very wrong, madame; but I am so accustomed to your reproaches, that I pardon you these.'

'In that case, let us begone, Louise; we have nothing to do but to retire. Well!'

'Madame!' said La Vallière, starting, 'did you speak?'

'You do not appear to be listening, my child.'

'No, madame, I was thinking.'

'About what?'

'A thousand things.'

'You bear me no ill-will, at least, Louise?' cried Montalais, pressing her hand.

'And why should I, my dear Aure?' replied the girl, in a voice soft as a flute.

'Why!' resumed Madame de Saint-Rémy; 'if she did bear you a little ill-will, poor girl, she could not be much blamed.'

'And why should she bear me ill-will, good gracious?'

'It appears to me that she is of as good a family, and as pretty as you.'

'Mother! mother!' cried Louise.

'Prettier a hundred times, madame—not of a better family; but that does not tell me why Louise should bear me ill-will.'

'Do you think it will be very amusing for her to be buried alive at Blois, when you are going to shine at Paris?'

'But, madame, it is not I who prevent Louise following me thither; on the contrary, I should certainly be most happy if she came there.'

'But it appears that M. Malicorne, who is all-powerful at court——'

'Ah! too bad, madame,' said Malicorne, 'everyone for himself in this poor world.'

'Malicorne! Malicorne!' said Montalais. Then turning towards the young man:

'Occupy Madame de Saint-Rémy, either in disputing with

her, or making it up with her; I must speak to Louise.' And, at the same time, a soft pressure of the hand recompensed Malicorne for his future obedience. Malicorne went grumbling towards Madame Saint-Rémy, whilst Montalais said to her friend, throwing one arm around her neck:

'What is the matter? Tell *me*. Is it true that you would not love me if I were to shine, as your mother says?'

'Oh, no!' said the young girl, with difficulty restraining her tears; 'on the contrary, I rejoice at your good fortune.'

'Rejoice! why, I think you are ready to cry!'

'Do people never weep except from envy?'

'Oh! yes, I understand; I am going to Paris and that word Paris recalls to your mind a certain cavalier——'

'Aure!'

'A certain cavalier who formerly lived near Blois, and who now resides at Paris.'

'In truth, I do not know what ails me, but I feel heavy-hearted.'

'Weep, then, weep, as you cannot give me a smile!'

Louise raised her sweet face, which the tears, rolling down one after the other, lit like diamonds.

'Come, confess,' said Montalais.

'What shall I confess?'

'What makes you weep; people don't weep without cause. I am your friend; whatever you would wish me to do, I will do. Malicorne is more powerful than you would think. Do you wish to go to Paris?'

'Alas!' sighed Louise.

'Do you wish to come to Paris?'

'To remain here alone, in this old castle, I who have enjoyed the pleasure of listening to your songs, of pressing your hand, of running about the park with you. Oh! how bored I shall be! how quickly I shall die!'

'Do you wish to come to Paris?'

Louise breathed another sigh.

'You do not answer me.'

'What do you want me to reply?'

'Yes or no; it is not very difficult, I think.'

'Oh! you are very fortunate, Montalais!'

'That is to say you would like to be in my place.'

Louise was silent.

'Little obstinate thing!' said Montalais; 'did ever anyone keep her secrets from her friend so? But confess that you would like to come to Paris; confess that you are dying with the wish to see Raoul again!'

'I cannot confess that.'

'Then you are wrong.'

'In what way?'

'Because—— Do you see this letter?'

'To be sure I do.'

'Well, I could have got you a similar one.'

'By whose means?'

'Malicorne's.'

'Aure, are you telling the truth? Is that possible?'

'Malicorne is there; and what he has done for me, he surely can for you.'

Malicorne had heard his name pronounced twice; he was delighted at having an opportunity of coming to a conclusion with Madame de Saint-Rémy, and he turned round:

'What is the question, mademoiselle?'

'Come here, Malicorne,' said Montalais, with an imperious gesture. Malicorne obeyed.

'A letter like this,' said Montalais.

'How so?'

'A letter like this; that is plain enough.'

'But——'

'I want one—I must have one!'

'Oh! oh! you must have one!'

'Yes.'

'It is impossible, is it not, M. Malicorne?' said Louise, with her sweet soft voice.

'If it is for *you*, mademoiselle——'

'For me. Yes, Monsieur Malicorne, it *would* be for me.'

'And if Mademoiselle de Montalais asks it at the same time——'

'Mademoiselle de Montalais does not ask, she requires it.'

'Well! we will endeavour to obey you, mademoiselle.'

'And you will have her appointed?'

'We will try.'

'No evasive answers, Louise de la Vallière shall be maid of honour to Madame Henrietta within a week.'

'How you talk!'

'Within a week, or else——'

'Well! or else?'

'You may take back your letter, Monsieur Malicorne; I will not leave my friend.'

'Dear Montalais!'

'All right. Keep your letter; Mademoiselle de la Vallière shall be a maid of honour.'

'Is that true?'

'Quite true.'

'I may then hope to go to Paris?'

'Depend upon it.'

'Oh! Monsieur Malicorne, what joy!' cried Louise, clapping her hands, and bounding with pleasure.

'Little dissembler!' said Montalais, 'try again to make me believe you are not in love with Raoul.'

Louise blushed like a rose in June, but instead of replying, she ran and embraced her mother. 'Madame,' said she, 'do you know that M. Malicorne is going to have me appointed maid of honour?'

'M. Malicorne is a prince in disguise,' replied the old lady, 'he is all-powerful, it seems.'

'Should you also like to be maid of honour?' asked Malicorne of Madame de Saint-Rémy. 'While I am about it, I might as well get everybody appointed.'

And upon that he went away, leaving the poor lady quite disconcerted.

'Humph!' murmured Malicorne as he descended the stairs—'Humph! there goes another thousand livres! but I must get through as well as I can; my friend Manicamp* does nothing for nothing.'

LXXIX

MALICORNE AND MANICAMP

THE introduction of these two new personages into this history, and that mysterious link between names and characters, merit some attention on the part of both historian and reader. We will then enter into some details concerning Messieurs Malicorne and Manicamp. Malicorne, we know, had made the journey to Orléans in search of the letter of appointment for Mademoiselle de Montalais, the arrival of which had produced such a strong feeling at the castle of Blois. At that moment, M. de Manicamp was at Orléans. A singular personage was this M. de Manicamp; a very intelligent young fellow, always poor, always needy, although he dipped his hand freely into the purse of M. le Comte de Guiche, one of the best-furnished purses of the period. M. le Comte de Guiche had had, as the companion of his boyhood, this de Manicamp, a poor gentleman, vassal-born, of the house of Gramont. M. de Manicamp, with his tact and talent, had created himself an income in the opulent family of the celebrated marshal. From his childhood he had, with calculation beyond his age, lent his name and complaisance to the follies of the Comte de Guiche. If his noble companion had stolen some fruit destined for Madame la Maréchale, if he had broken a mirror, or put out a dog's eye, Manicamp declared himself guilty of the crime committed, and received the punishment, which was not made the milder for falling on the innocent. But this was the way this system of abnegation was paid for: instead of wearing such cheap clothes as his family fortunes entitled him to, he was able to appear brilliant, superb, like a young noble with fifty thousand livres a year. It was not that he was mean in character or humble in spirit; no, he was a philosopher, or rather he had the indifference, the apathy, the obstinacy which prevent a man from attaching any value to worldly success. His sole ambition was to spend money. But, in this respect, the worthy M. de Manicamp was a bottomless pit. Three or four times every year he drained the Comte de Guiche, and when the Comte de Guiche was thoroughly drained, when he had turned out his pockets and his purse before him, when he declared that it would be at least a fortnight before paternal munificence would refill those pockets and that purse, Manicamp lost all his energy, he went to bed, remained there, ate nothing and sold his handsome clothes, on the grounds that, remaining in bed, he did not need them. During this prostration of mind and strength, the purse of the Comte de Guiche was getting full again, and when once filled, overflowed into that of De Manicamp, who bought new clothes, dressed himself again, and recommenced the same life he had followed before. This mania of selling his new clothes for a quarter of what they were worth, had rendered our hero sufficiently celebrated in Orléans, a city where, in general, we should be puzzled to say why he came to pass his days of penitence. Provincial rakes with six hundred livres a year shared the fragments of his opulence.

Among the admirers of these splendid toilettes, our friend Malicorne was conspicuous; he was the son of a syndic* of the city, of whom M. de Condé, always needy as a Condé, often borrowed money at enormous interest. M. Malicorne kept the paternal money-chest; that is to say, that in those times of easy morals, he had made for himself, by following the example of his father, and lending at high interest for short terms, a revenue of eighteen hundred livres, without reckoning six hundred livres furnished by the generosity of the syndic; so that Malicorne was the king of the younger element at Orléans, having two thousand four hundred livres to scatter, squander, and waste on follies of every kind. But, quite contrary to Manicamp, Malicorne was terribly ambitious. He loved from ambition: he spent money out of ambition: and he would have ruined himself for ambition. Malicorne had determined to rise, at whatever price it might cost, and for this, at whatever price it did cost, he had given himself a mistress and a friend. The mistress, Mademoiselle de Montalais, was cruel, as regarded love; but she was of a noble family, and that was sufficient for Malicorne. The friend had little or no friendship, but he was the favourite of the Comte de Guiche, himself the friend of Monsieur, the king's brother; and that was sufficient for Malicorne. Only, in the chapter of charges, Mademoiselle de Montalais cost per annum: Ribbons, gloves, and sweets, a thousand livres. De Manicamp cost—money lent, never returned—from twelve to fifteen hundred livres per annum. So that there was nothing left for Malicorne. Ah! yes, we are mistaken; there was left the paternal coffer. He employed a mode of proceeding, upon which he preserved the most profound secrecy, and which consisted in advancing to himself, from the coffers of the syndic, half a dozen years' profits, that is to say, fifteen thousand livres, swearing to himself—observe, quite to himself—to repay this deficiency as soon as an opportunity should present itself. The opportunity was expected to be the acquisition of a good post in the household of Monsieur, when that household would be established at the period of his marriage. This juncture had arrived, and the household was about to be established. A good post in the family of a prince of the blood, when it is given by the credit, and on the recommendation, of a friend like the Comte de Guiche, is worth at least twelve thousand livres per annum; and by the means which M. Malicorne had taken to make his revenues fructify, twelve thousand livres might rise to twenty thousand. Then, when once an incumbent of this post, he would marry Mademoiselle de Montalais. Mademoiselle de Montalais, of a half noble family, would not only bring a dowry, but would ennoble Malicorne. But, in order that Mademoiselle de Montalais, who had not a large marriage portion, although an only daughter, should be suitably dowered, it was necessary that she should belong to some great princess, as generous as the dowager Madame was covetous. And in order that the wife should not be of one party whilst the husband belonged to the other, a situation which presents serious disadvantages, particularly with characters like those of the future consorts—Malicorne had imagined the idea of making the central point of union the household of Monsieur, the king's brother. Mademoiselle de Montalais would be maid of honour to Madame. M. Malicorne would be officer to Monsieur.

It is obvious the plan was formed by a clear head; it is also obvious that it had been bravely executed. Malicorne had asked Manicamp to ask the Comte de Guiche for a letter of appointment as maid of honour; and the Comte de Guiche had asked for this letter from Monsieur, who had signed it without hesitation. The forward plan of Malicorne—for we may well suppose that the combinations of a mind as active as his were not confined to the present, but extended to the future—the forward plan of Malicorne, we say, was this: To obtain entrance into the household of Madame Henrietta for a woman devoted to himself, who was intelligent, young, handsome, and intriguing; to learn, by means of this woman, all the feminine secrets of the young household; while he, Malicorne, and his friend Manicamp, should, between them, know all the male secrets of the young community. It was by these means that a rapid and splendid fortune might be acquired at one and the same time. Malicorne was a vile name;* he who bore it had too much wit to conceal this truth from himself; but an estate might be purchased; and Malicorne of some place, or even De Malicorne itself, for short, would ring more nobly on the ear.

It was not improbable that a most aristocratic origin might be hunted up by the heralds for this name of Malicorne; might it not come from some estate where a bull with deadly horns had caused some great misfortune, and baptized the soil with the blood it had spilt? True, this plan presented itself bristling with difficulties: but the greatest of all was Mademoiselle de Montalais herself. Capricious, moody, close, giddy, free, prudish, a virgin armed with claws, Erigone* stained with grapes, she sometimes overturned, with a single dash of her white fingers, or with a single puff from her laughing lips, the edifice which had exhausted Malicorne's patience for a month.

Love apart, Malicorne was happy; but this love, which he could not help feeling, he had the strength to conceal with care; persuaded that at the least relaxation of the ties by which he had bound his Protean female,* the demon would overthrow him and laugh at him. He humbled his mistress by disdaining her. Burning with desire, when she advanced to tempt him, he had the art to appear as cold as ice, persuaded that if he opened his arms, she would run away laughing at him. On her side, Montalais believed she did not love Malicorne; while, on the contrary, in reality she did. Malicorne repeated to her so often his protestation of indifference, that she ended up, sometimes, by believing him; and then she believed she detested Malicorne. If she tried to bring him back by coquetry, Malicorne played the coquette better than she could. But what made Montalais hold to Malicorne in an indissoluble fashion, was that Malicorne always came cram full of fresh news from the court and the city; that Malicorne always brought to Blois a fashion, a secret, a perfume; that Malicorne never asked for a meeting, but, on the contrary, had to be begged to receive the favours he burned to obtain. On her side, Montalais was no miser with stories. By her means, Malicorne learnt all that passed at Blois, in the family of the dowager Madame; and he related to Manicamp tales that made him ready to die with laughing, which the latter, out of idleness, took ready-made to M. de Guiche, who carried them to Monsieur.

Such, in two words, was the web of petty interests and petty conspiracies which united Blois with Orléans, and Orléans with Paris; and which was about to bring into the last named city, where she was to produce so great a revolution, the poor little La Vallière, who was far from suspecting, as she returned joyfully, leaning on the arm of her mother, what strange future awaited her. As to that good man, Malicorne—we speak of the syndic of Orléans—he did not see more clearly into the present than others did into the future; and had no suspicion as he walked, every day, between three and five o'clock, after his dinner, upon the Place Sainte-Catherine,* in his grey coat, cut after the fashion of Louis XIII, and his cloth shoes with great knots of ribbon, that it was he who was paying for all those bursts of laughter, all those stolen kisses, all those whisperings, all those little keepsakes, and all those bubble projects which formed a chain of forty-five leagues in length, from the castle at Blois to the Palais Royal.

LXXX

MANICAMP AND MALICORNE

MALICORNE, then, left Blois, as we have said, and went to find his friend Manicamp, then in temporary retreat in the city of Orléans. It was just at the moment when that young nobleman was employed in selling the last decent clothing he had left. He had, a fortnight before, extorted from the Comte de Guiche a hundred pistoles, all he had, to assist in equipping him properly to go and meet Madame, on her arrival at Le Havre. He had drawn from Malicorne, three days before, fifty pistoles, the cost of the appointment obtained for Montalais. He had then no expectation of anything else, having exhausted all his resources, with the exception of selling a handsome suit of cloth and satin, embroidered and laced with gold, which had been the admiration of the court. But to be able to sell this suit, the last he had left—as we have been forced to confess to the reader—Manicamp had been obliged to take to his bed. No more fire, no more pocket-money, no more walking-money, nothing but sleep to take the place of repasts, companies and balls. It has been said—'He who sleeps, dines'; but it has never been said—He who sleeps, plays—or, He who sleeps, dances. Manicamp, reduced to this extremity of neither playing nor dancing, for a week at least, was, consequently, very sad; he was expecting a money-lender, and saw Malicorne enter. A cry of distress escaped him.

'Eh! what!' said he, in a tone which nothing can describe, 'you again, dear friend?'

'Humph! you are not very polite!' said Malicorne.

'Ay, but look, I was expecting money, and, instead of money, I see *you*.'

'And suppose I brought you some money?'

'Oh! that would be quite another thing. You are very welcome, my dear friend!'

And he held out his hand, not for the hand of Malicorne, but for the purse. Malicorne pretended to be mistaken, and gave him his hand.

'And the money?' said Manicamp.

'My dear friend, if you wish to have it, earn it.'

'What must be done for it?'

'Earn it, by God!'

'How?'

'Oh! it is tiresome, I warn you.'

'The devil!'

'You must get out of bed, and go immediately to M. le Comte de Guiche.'

'I get up!' said Manicamp, stretching himself in his bed, complacently, 'oh, no, thank you!'

'You have sold all your clothes?'

'No, I have one suit left, the handsomest even, but I expect a purchaser.'

'And breeches?'

'Well, if you look, you will see them on that chair.'

'Very well! since you have breeches and a doublet left, put your legs into the first and your back into the other; have a horse saddled, and set off.'

'Not I.'

'And why not?'

'Devil take it! don't you know, then, that M. de Guiche is at Étampes?'*

'No, I thought he was at Paris. You will then only have fifteen leagues to go, instead of thirty.'

'You are a wonderfully clever fellow! If I were to ride fifteen leagues in these clothes, they would never be fit to put on again; and, instead of selling them for thirty pistoles, I should be obliged to take fifteen.'

'Sell them for what you like, but I must have a second letter of appointment for a maid of honour.'

'Good! for whom? Is Montalais doubled then?'

'You wretch! It is you who are doubled. You swallow up two fortunes—mine, and that of M. le Comte de Guiche.'

'You should say that of M. le Comte de Guiche and yours.'

'That is true; honour where it is due; but I return to my letter.'

'And you are wrong.'

'How?'

'My friend, there will only be twelve maids of honour for madame; I have already obtained for you what twelve hundred women are trying for, and for that I was forced to employ all my diplomacy.'

'Oh! yes, I know you have been quite heroic, my dear friend.'

'We know what we are about,' said Manicamp.

'To whom do you say that? When I am king, I promise you one thing.'

'What? To call yourself Malicorne the First?'

'No; to make you superintendent of my finances; but that is not the question now.'

'Unfortunately.'

'The present affair is to procure for me a second place of maid of honour.'

'My friend, if you were to promise me a ticket to heaven, I would decline to disturb myself at this moment.'

Malicorne chinked the money in his pocket.

'There are twenty pistoles here,' said Malicorne.

'And what would I do with twenty pistoles?'

'Well!' said Malicorne, a little angrily, 'suppose I were to add them to the five hundred you already owe me?'

'You are right,' replied Manicamp, stretching out his hand again, 'and from that point of view I can accept them. Hand over.'

'One moment, what the devil! it is not only holding out your hand that will do; if I give you the twenty pistoles, shall I have my letter?'

'To be sure you shall.'

'Soon?'

'To-day.'

'Oh! take care! Monsieur de Manicamp; you undertake much, and I do not ask that. Thirty leagues in a day is too much, you would kill yourself.'

'I think nothing impossible when obliging a friend.'

'You are quite heroic.'

'Where are the twenty pistoles?'

'Here they are,' said Malicorne, showing them.

'Good.'

'Yes, but my dear M. Manicamp, they will go on post-horses alone!'

'No, no, make yourself easy on that score.'

'Pardon me. Why, it is fifteen leagues from this place to Étampes?'

'Fourteen.'

'Well! fourteen be it; fourteen leagues make seven posts; at twenty sous the post, seven livres; seven livres per courier, fourteen; as many for coming back, twenty-eight! as much for bed and supper, that makes sixty livres that this venture would cost.'

Manicamp stretched himself like a serpent in his bed, and fixing his two great eyes upon Malicorne, 'You are right,' said he; 'I could not return before to-morrow;' and he took the twenty pistoles.

'Now, then, be off!'

'Well, as I cannot be back before to-morrow, we have time.'

'Time for what?'

'Time for a hand of cards.'

'What are the stakes?'

'Your twenty pistoles, *pardieu!*'

'No; you always win at cards.'

'How about a wager, then?'

'What have you got to put up against my twenty?'

'Another twenty.'

'And what form is this wager to take?'

'This. We have said it was fourteen leagues to Étampes?'

'Yes.'

'And fourteen leagues back?'

'Yes.'

'Well; for these twenty-eight leagues you cannot allow less than fourteen hours?'

'That is agreed.'

'One hour to find the Comte de Guiche.'

'Go on.'

'And an hour to persuade him to write a letter to monsieur.'

'Just so.'

'Sixteen hours in all?'

'You reckon as well as M. Colbert.'

'It is now twelve o'clock.'

'Half-past.'

'Ah!—you have a fine watch!'

'What were you saying?' said Malicorne, putting his watch quickly back into his fob.

'Ah! true; I was offering to lay you twenty pistoles against these you have lent me, that you will have the Comte de Guiche's letter in——'

'How soon?'

'In eight hours.'

'Have you a winged horse, then?'

'That is no matter. Will you bet?'

'I shall have the Comte's letter in eight hours?'

'Yes.'

'In my hand?'

'In your hand.'

'Well, be it so; I agree,' said Malicorne, curious to know how this seller of clothes would manage it.

'Is it agreed?'

'It is.'

'Pass me the pen, ink, and paper.'

'Here they are.'

'Thank you.'

Manicamp raised himself with a sigh, and leaning on his left elbow, in his best hand, traced the following lines:

'Good for an order for a place of maid of honour to Madame, which M. le Comte de Guiche will take upon him to obtain at sight.

'DE MANICAMP.'

This painful task accomplished, he laid himself down in bed again.

'Well!' asked Malicorne, 'what does this mean?'

'That means that if you are in a hurry to have the letter from the Comte de Guiche for Monsieur, I have won my wager.'

'How the devil is that?'

'It is transparent enough, I think; you take that paper.'

'Well?'

'And you set out instead of me.'

'Ah!'

'You put your horses to their best speed.'

'Good!'

'In six hours you will be at Étampes; in seven hours you have the letter from the comte, and I shall have won my wager without stirring from my bed, which suits me and you too, at the same time, I am very sure.'

'Decidedly, Manicamp, you are a great man.'

'I know.'

'I am to start then for Étampes?'

'Directly.'

'I am to go to the Comte de Guiche with this order?'

'He will give you a similar one for Monsieur.'

'Then I go to Paris.'

'You will present the order from the Comte de Guiche to Monsieur.'

'Monsieur will approve?'

'Instantly.'

'And I shall have my letter?'

'You will.'

'Ah!'

'Well, I hope I have behaved nicely?'

'Adorably.'

'Thank you.'

'You do as you please, then, with the Comte de Guiche, Manicamp?'

'Except make money of him—everything.'

'Pity! the exception is annoying; but then, if instead of asking him for money, you were to ask——'

'What?'

'Something important.'

'What do you call important?'

'Well! suppose one of your friends asked you for a favour?'

'I would not do it.'

'Selfish fellow!'

'Or at least I would ask him what service he would render me in exchange.'

'Ah! that, perhaps, is fair. Well, that friend is speaking to you.'

'What, you, Malicorne?'

'Yes; I.'

'Ah! ah! you are rich, then?'

'I have still fifty pistoles left.'

'Exactly the sum I need. Where are those fifty pistoles?'

'Here,' said Malicorne, tapping his pocket.

'Then speak, my friend; what do you want?'

Malicorne took up the pen, ink, and paper again, and presented them all to Manicamp. 'Write!' said he.

'Dictate!'

'An order for a position in the household of Monsieur.'

'Oh!' said Manicamp, laying down the pen, 'a position in the household of Monsieur for fifty pistoles?'

'You mistook me, my friend; you did not hear plainly.'

'What did you say, then?'

'I said five hundred.'

'And the five hundred?'

'Here they are.'

Manicamp devoured the money with his eyes; but this time Malicorne held it at a distance.

'Eh! what do you say to that? Five hundred pistoles.'

'I say it is cheap, my friend,' said Manicamp, taking up the pen again, 'and you exhaust my credit. Dictate.'

Malicorne dictated:

'An order for a position of gentleman to Monsieur, which my friend the Comte de Guiche will obtain for my friend Malicorne.'

'There you are,' said Manicamp.

'Pardon me, you have forgotten to sign.'

'Ah! that is true. The five hundred pistoles?'

'Here are two hundred and fifty of them.'

'And the other two hundred and fifty?'

'When I have my letter.'

Manicamp made a face.

'In that case give me the recommendation back again.'

'What to do?'

'To add two words to it.'

'Two words?'

'Yes; two words only.'

'What are they?'

'"In haste".'

Malicorne returned the recommendation; Manicamp added the words.

'Good,' said Malicorne, taking back the paper.

Manicamp began to count out the pistoles.

'There are twenty missing,' said he.

'How so?'

'The twenty I have won.'

'How?'

'By laying that you would have the letter from the Comte De Guiche in eight hours.'

'Ah! that's fair,' and he gave him the twenty pistoles.

Manicamp began to scoop up his gold by handfuls, and pour it in cascades upon his bed.

'This second appointment,' murmured Malicorne, whilst drying his paper, 'at the first glance, appears to cost me more than the first, but——' He stopped, took up the pen in his turn, and wrote to Montalais:

MADEMOISELLE—Announce to your friend that her commission will not be long before it arrives; I am setting out to get it signed: that will be twenty-eight leagues I shall have gone for the love of you.

Then with his sardonic smile, taking up the interrupted sentence: 'This place,' said he, 'at the first glance, appears to cost more than the first; but—the benefit will be, I hope, in proportion with the expense, and Mademoiselle de la Vallière will yield a bigger return than Mademoiselle de Montalais, or else—or else my name is not Malicorne. Farewell, Manicamp,' and he left the room.

LXXXI

THE COURTYARD OF THE HÔTEL GRAMMONT

ON Malicorne's arrival at Orléans, he was informed that the Comte de Guiche had just set out for Paris. Malicorne rested himself for a couple of hours, and then prepared to continue his journey. He reached Paris during the night, and alighted at a small hotel, where, in his previous journeys to the capital, he had been accustomed to put up, and at eight o'clock the next morning presented himself at the Hôtel Grammont.* Malicorne arrived just in time, for the Comte de Guiche was on the point of taking leave of Monsieur before setting out for Le Havre, where the principal members of the French nobility had gone to await Madame's arrival from England. Malicorne pronounced the name of Manicamp, and was immediately admitted. He found the Comte de Guiche in the courtyard of the Hôtel Grammont, inspecting his horses, which his trainers and equerries were passing in review before him. The count, in the presence of his tradespeople and of his servants, was engaged in praising or blaming, as the case seemed to deserve, the equipment, horses, and harness that were being submitted to him;

when, in the midst of this important occupation, the name of Manicamp was announced.

'Manicamp!' he exclaimed: 'let him enter by all means.' And he advanced a few steps toward the door.

Malicorne slipped through the half-open door, and looking at the Comte de Guiche, who was surprised to see a face he did not recognize, instead of the one he expected, said: 'Forgive me, monsieur le comte, but I believe a mistake has been made. M. Manicamp himself was announced to you, instead of which it is only an envoy from him.'

'Ah!' exclaimed De Guiche, coldly; 'and what do you bring me?'

'A letter, monsieur le comte.' Malicorne handed him the first document, and narrowly watched the count's face, who, as he read it, began to laugh.

'What!' he exclaimed, 'another maid of honour? Are all the maids of honour in France, then, under his protection?'

Malicorne bowed.

'Why does he not come himself?' he inquired.

'He is confined to his bed.'

'The deuce! he has no money then, I suppose,' said De Guiche, shrugging his shoulders. 'What does he do with his money?'

Malicorne made a gesture, to indicate that upon this subject he was as ignorant as the count himself. 'Why does he not make use of his credit, then?' continued De Guiche.

'With regard to that, I think——'

'What?'

'That Manicamp has credit with no one but yourself, monsieur le comte.'

'He will not be at Le Havre, then?' Whereupon Malicorne made another movement.

'But everyone will be there.'

'I trust, monsieur le comte, that he will not neglect so excellent an opportunity.'

'He should be at Paris by this time.'

'He will take the direct road perhaps, to make up for lost time.'

'Where is he now?'

'At Orléans.'

'Monsieur,' said De Guiche, 'you seem to me a man of very good taste.'

Malicorne was wearing some of Manicamp's clothes. He bowed in return, saying, 'You do me a very great honour, monsieur le comte.'

'Whom have I the pleasure of addressing?'

'My name is Malicorne, monsieur.'

'M. de Malicorne, what do you think of these pistol-holsters?'

Malicorne was a man of great readiness, and immediately understood the position of affairs. Besides, the 'de' which had been prefixed to his name raised him to the rank of the person with whom he was conversing. He looked at the holsters with the air of a connoisseur, and said, without hesitation: 'Somewhat heavy, monsieur.'

'You see,' said De Guiche to the saddler, 'this gentleman, who understands these matters well, thinks the holsters heavy, a complaint I had already made.' The saddler was full of excuses.

'What do you think,' asked de Guiche, 'of this horse, which I have just purchased?'

'To look at it, it seems perfect, monsieur le comte; but I must mount it before I give you my opinion.'

'Do so, M. de Malicorne, and ride him round the court two or three times.'

The courtyard of the hotel was so arranged, that whenever there was any occasion for it, it could be used as a riding-school. Malicorne, with perfect ease, arranged the bridle and snaffle-reins, placed his left hand on the horse's mane, and, with his foot in the stirrup, raised himself and seated himself in the saddle. At first, he made the horse walk the whole circuit of the courtyard at a foot-pace; next at a trot; lastly at a gallop. He then drew up close to the count, dismounted, and threw the bridle to a groom standing by. 'Well,' said the count, 'what do you think of it, M. de Malicorne?'

'This horse, monsieur le comte, is of the Mecklenburg breed. In looking whether the bit suited his mouth, I saw that he was rising seven, the very age when the training of a horse intended for a charger should commence. The fore-hand is light. A horse which holds its head high, it is said, never tires his rider's hand. The withers are rather low. The drooping of the hind-quarters would almost make me doubt the purity of its German breed, and I think there is English blood in him. He stands well on his legs, but he trots high, and may cut himself, which requires attention to be paid to his shoeing. He is biddable; and as I made him turn round and change his feet, I found him quick and ready in doing so.'

'Well said, M. de Malicorne,' exclaimed the comte; 'you are a judge of horses, I perceive;' then, turning towards him again, he continued, 'you are most becomingly dressed, M. de Malicorne. That is not a provincial cut, I presume. Such a style of dress is not to be met with at Tours or Orléans.'

'No, monsieur le comte; my clothes were made at Paris.'

'There is no doubt about that. But let us resume our own affair. Manicamp wishes for the appointment of a second maid of honour.'

'You see what he has written, monsieur le comte.'

'For whom was the first appointment?'

Malicorne felt the colour rise in his face as he answered hurriedly.

'A charming maid of honour, Mademoiselle de Montalais.'

'Ah, ah! you are acquainted with her?'

'We are affianced, or nearly so.'

'That is quite another thing, then; a thousand compliments,' exclaimed De Guiche, upon whose lips a courtier's jest was already fitting, but to whom the word 'affianced', addressed by Malicorne with respect to Mademoiselle de Montalais, recalled the respect due to women.

'And for whom is the second appointment intended?' asked De Guiche; 'is it for any one to whom Manicamp may happen to be affianced? In that case I pity her, poor girl! for she will have a sad fellow for a husband.'

'No, monsieur le comte; the second appointment is for Mademoiselle de la Baume le Blanc de la Vallière.'

'Someone new,' said De Guiche.

'New? yes, monsieur,' said Malicorne, smiling in his turn.

'Very well. I will speak to Monsieur about it. By the by, she is of gentle birth?'

'She belongs to a very good family, and is maid of honour to Madame.'

'That's all right, then. Will you accompany me to Monsieur?'

'Most certainly, if I may be permitted the honour.'

'Have you your carriage?'

'No; I came here on horseback.'

'Dressed as you are?'

'No, monsieur; I posted from Orléans, and I changed my travelling suit for the one I have on, in order to present myself to you.'

'True, you already told me you had come from Orléans;' saying which he crumpled Manicamp's letter in his hand, and thrust it in his pocket.

'I beg your pardon,' said Malicorne, timidly; 'but I do not think you have read all.'

'Not read all, do you say?'

'No; there were two letters in the same envelope.'

'Oh! are you sure?'

'Quite sure.'

'Let us look, then,' said the count, as he opened the letter again.

'Ah! you are right,' he said, opening the paper which he had not yet read.

'I suspected it,' he continued—'another application for an appointment under Monsieur. This Manicamp is a regular vampire: he is carrying on a trade in it.'

'No, monsieur le comte, he wishes to make a present of it.'

'To whom?'

'To myself, monsieur.'

'Why did you not say so at once, my dear M. Mauvaisecorne?'

'Malicorne, monsieur le comte.'

'Forgive me; it is the Latin that bothers me—that terrible mine of etymologies. Why the deuce are young men of family taught Latin? *Mala* and *mauvaise*—you understand it is the same thing. You will forgive me, I trust, M. de Malicorne.'

'Your kindness affects me much, monsieur: but it is a reason why I should make you acquainted with one circumstance without any delay.'

'What is it?'

'That I was not born a gentleman. I am not without courage, and not altogether deficient in ability; but my name is Malicorne simply.'

'You appear to me, monsieur,' exclaimed the count, looking at the astute face of his companion, 'to be a most agreeable man. Your face pleases me, M. Malicorne, and you must possess some indisputably excellent qualities to have pleased that egotistical Manicamp. Be candid and tell me whether you are not some saint descended upon the earth.'

'Why so?'

'For the simple reason that he is prepared to give you something for nothing. Most unlike him. Did you not say that he intended to make you a present of some appointment in the king's household?'

'I beg your pardon, count; but, if I succeed in obtaining the appointment, you, and not he, will have bestowed it on me.'

'Besides, he will not have given it to you for nothing, I suppose. Stay, I have it; there is a Malicorne at Orléans, who lends money to the prince.'

'I think that must be my father, monsieur.'

'Ah! the prince has the father, and that terrible dragon of a Manicamp has the son. Take care, monsieur; I know him. He will fleece you completely.'

'The only difference is, that I lend without interest,' said Malicorne, smiling.

'I was correct in saying you were either a saint or very much resembled one. M. Malicorne, you shall have the post you want, or I will forfeit my good name.'

'Ah! monsieur le comte, what a debt of gratitude shall I not owe you?' said Malicorne, transported.

'Let us go to the prince, my dear M. Malicorne.' And De Guiche proceeded toward the door, desiring Malicorne to follow him. At the very moment they were about to cross the threshold, a young man appeared on the other side. He was from twenty-four to twenty-five years of age, of pale complexion, bright eyes, and brown hair and eyebrows. 'Good-day,' he said, suddenly, almost pushing De Guiche back into the courtyard again.

'Is that you, De Wardes?*—What! and booted, spurred and whip in hand, too?'

'The most befitting costume for a man about to set off for Le Havre. There will be no one left in Paris to-morrow.' And hereupon he saluted Malicorne with great ceremony, whose handsome dress gave him the appearance of a prince.

'M. Malicorne,' said De Guiche to his friend. De Wardes bowed.

'M. de Wardes,' said Guiche to Malicorne, who bowed in return. 'By the by, De Wardes,' continued De Guiche, 'you who are so well acquainted with these matters, can you tell us, probably, what appointments are still vacant at the court; or rather in the prince's household?'

'In the prince's household,' said De Wardes, looking up with an air of consideration, 'let me see—the appointment of the master of the horse is vacant, I believe.'

'Oh,' said Malicorne, 'there is no question of such a post as that, monsieur; my ambition is not nearly so exalted.'

De Wardes had a more penetrating observation than De Guiche, and fathomed Malicorne immediately. 'The fact is,' he said, looking at him from head to foot, 'a man must be either a duke or a peer to fill that post.'

'All I solicit,' said Malicorne, 'is a very humble appointment; I am of little importance, and I do not rank myself above my position.'

'M. Malicorne, whom you see here,' said De Guiche to De Wardes, 'is a very excellent fellow, whose only misfortune is that of not being of gentle birth. As far as I am concerned, you know, I attach little value to those who have but gentle birth to boast of.'

'Assuredly,' said De Wardes; 'but will you allow me to remark, my dear count, that, without rank of some sort, one can hardly hope to belong to his royal highness's household.'

'You are right,' said the count, 'court etiquette is absolute. The devil!—I never so much as gave it a thought.'

'Alas! a sad misfortune for me, monsieur le comte,' said Malicorne, changing colour.

'Yet not without remedy, I hope,' returned De Guiche.

'The remedy is found easily enough,' exclaimed De Wardes; 'you can be created a gentleman. His Eminence the Cardinal Mazarin did nothing else from morning till night.'

'Hush, hush, De Wardes,' said the count; 'no jests of that kind; it ill becomes us to turn such matters into ridicule. Letters of nobility, it is true, are purchasable;* but that is a sufficient misfortune without the nobles themselves laughing at it.'

'Upon my word, De Guiche, you're quite a Puritan, as the English say.'

At this moment the Vicomte de Bragelonne was announced by one of the servants in the courtyard, in precisely the same manner as he would have done in a room.

'Come here, my dear Raoul. What! you, too, booted and spurred? You are setting off, then?'

Bragelonne approached the group of young men, and saluted them with that quiet and serious manner peculiar to him. His bow was principally addressed to De Wardes, with whom he was unacquainted, and whose features, on his perceiving Raoul, had assumed a strange sternness of expression. 'I have come, De Guiche,' he said, 'to ask your companionship. We set off for Le Havre, I presume.'

'This is admirable—delightful. We shall have a most enjoyable journey. M. Malicorne, M. Bragelonne—ah! M. de Wardes, let me present you.' The young men saluted each other coolly. Their very natures seemed, from the beginning, disposed to take exception to each other. De Wardes was pliant, subtle, full of dissimulation; Raoul was calm, grave, and upright. 'Decide between us—between De Wardes and myself, Raoul.'

'Upon what subject?'

'Upon the subject of noble birth.'

'Who can be better informed on that subject than a De Gramont?'*

'No compliments; it is your opinion I ask.'

'At least, inform me of the subject under discussion.'

'De Wardes asserts that the distribution of titles is abused; I, on the contrary, maintain that a title is useless to the man on whom it is bestowed.'

'And you are correct,' said Bragelonne, quietly.

'But, monsieur le vicomte,' interrupted De Wardes, with a kind of obstinacy, 'I affirm that it is I who am correct.'

'What was your opinion, monsieur?'

'I was saying that everything is done in France at the present moment, to humiliate men of good family.'

'And by whom?'

'By the king himself. He surrounds himself with people who cannot show four quarterings.'*

'Nonsense,' said De Guiche; 'where could you possibly have seen that, De Wardes?'

'One example will suffice,' he returned, directing his look fully upon Raoul.

'State it then.'

'Do you know who has just been nominated captain-general of the musketeers—an appointment more valuable than a peerage; for it gives precedence over all the marshals of France?'

Raoul's colour mounted in his face; for he saw the object De Wardes had in view. 'No; who has been appointed? In any case it must have been very recently, for the appointment was vacant a week ago; a proof of which is, that the king refused Monsieur, who solicited the post for one of his protégés.'

'Well, the king refused it to Monsieur's protégé, in order to bestow it upon the Chevalier d'Artagnan, a younger brother of some Gascon family,* who has been trailing his sword in the antechambers for the last thirty years.'

'Forgive me if I interrupt you,' said Raoul, darting a glance full of severity at De Wardes: 'but you give me the impression of being unacquainted with the gentleman of whom you are speaking.'

'I not acquainted with M. d'Artagnan? Can you tell me, monsieur, who does *not* know him?'

'Those who *do* know him, monsieur,' replied Raoul, with still greater calmness and sternness of manner, 'are in the habit of saying, that if he is not as good a gentleman as the king—which is not his fault—he is the equal of all the kings of the earth in courage and loyalty. Such is my opinion, monsieur; and I thank heaven I have known M. d'Artagnan from my birth.'*

De Wardes was about to reply, when De Guiche interrupted him.

LXXXII

THE PORTRAIT OF MADAME

THE discussion was turning unpleasant. De Guiche perfectly understood the whole matter, for there was in Bragelonne's face a look instinctively hostile, while in that of De Wardes there was something like a determination to offend. Without inquiring into the different feelings which prompted his two friends, De Guiche resolved to ward off the blow which he felt was on the point of being dealt by one of them, and perhaps by both. 'Gentlemen,' he said, 'we must take our leave of each other, I must pay a visit to Monsieur. You, De Wardes, will accompany me to the Louvre, and you, Raoul, will remain here in charge; and as all that is done here is under your advice, you will bestow the last glance upon my preparations for departure.'

Raoul, with the air of one who neither seeks nor fears a quarrel, bowed his head in token of assent, and seated himself upon a bench in the sun. 'That is well,' said De Guiche, 'remain where you are, Raoul, and tell them to show you the two horses I have just purchased; you will give me your opinion, for I only bought them on condition that you ratified the purchase. By the by, I have to beg your pardon for having omitted to enquire after the Comte de la Fère.' While pronouncing these latter words, he closely observed De Wardes, in order to perceive what effect the name of Raoul's father would produce upon him. 'I thank you,' answered the young man, 'the count is very well.' A gleam of deep hatred passed into De Wardes's eyes. De Guiche, who appeared not to notice the foreboding expression, went up to Raoul, and grasping him by the hand, said, 'It is agreed, then, Bragelonne, is it not, that you will rejoin us in the courtyard of the Palais Royal?' He then signed to De Wardes to follow him, who had been engaged in balancing himself first on one foot, then on the other. 'We are going,' said he, 'come, M. Malicorne.' This name made Raoul start; for it seemed that he had already heard it pronounced before, but he could not remember on what occasion. While he was trying to recall it half-dreamily, yet half-irritated at his conversation with De Wardes, the three young men set out on their way towards the Palais Royal, where Monsieur was residing. Malicorne learned two things; the first, that the young men had something to say to each other; and the second, that he ought not to walk in the same line with them; and therefore he walked behind. 'Are you mad?' said De Guiche to his companion, as soon as they had left the Hôtel de Grammont; 'you attack M. d'Artagnan, and that, too, before Raoul.'

'Well,' said De Wardes, 'what of it?'

'What do you mean by "what of it?"'

'Certainly, is there any ban on attacking M. d'Artagnan?'

'But you know very well that M. d'Artagnan was one of those celebrated and terrible four men who were called the musketeers.'

'That they may be: but I do not perceive why, on that account, I should be forbidden to hate M. d'Artagnan.'

'What cause has he given you?'

'Me! personally, none.'

'Why hate him, therefore?'

'Ask my dead father that question.'

'Really, my dear De Wardes, you surprise me. M. d'Artagnan is not one to leave unsettled any enmity he may have to incur, without completely clearing his account. Your father, I have heard, on his side, carried matters with a high hand. Moreover, there are no enmities so bitter that they cannot be washed away by blood, by a good sword-thrust honourably given.'

'Listen to me, my dear De Guiche, this inveterate dislike existed between my father and M. d'Artagnan, and when I was a small child, he acquainted me with the reason for it, and, as forming part of my inheritance, I regard it as a particular legacy bestowed upon me.'

'And does this hatred concern M. d'Artagnan alone?'

'As for that, M. d'Artagnan was so intimately associated with his three friends, that some portion of the full measure of my hatred falls to their lot, and that hatred is of such a nature, whenever the opportunity occurs, they shall have no occasion to complain of their allowance.'

De Guiche had kept his eyes fixed on De Wardes, and shuddered at the bitter manner in which the young man smiled. Something like a presentiment flashed across his mind; he knew that the time had passed when nobles fought duels; but that the feeling of hatred treasured up in the mind, instead of being diffused abroad, was still hatred all the same; that a smile was sometimes as full of meaning as a threat; and, in a word, that to the fathers who had hated with their hearts and fought with their arms, would now succeed sons, who would indeed hate with their hearts, but would no longer combat their enemies save by means of intrigue or treachery. As, therefore, it certainly was not Raoul whom he could suspect either of intrigue or treachery, it was for Raoul that De Guiche trembled. However, while these gloomy forebodings cast a shade of anxiety over De Guiche's countenance, De Wardes had resumed the entire mastery over himself.

'At all events,' he observed, 'I have no personal ill-will towards M. de Bragelonne; I do not know him even.'

'In any case,' said De Guiche, with a certain amount of severity in his tone of voice, 'do not forget one circumstance, that Raoul is my most intimate friend;' a remark at which De Wardes bowed.

The conversation terminated there, although De Guiche tried his utmost to draw out his secret from him; but, doubtless, De Wardes had determined to say nothing further, and he remained impenetrable. De Guiche therefore promised himself a more satisfactory result with Raoul. In the mean time they had reached the Palais Royal, which was surrounded by a crowd of lookers-on. The household belonging to Monsieur awaited his command to mount their horses, in order to form part of the escort of the ambassadors, to whom had been entrusted the care of bringing the young princess to Paris. The brilliant display of horses, arms, and rich liveries, afforded some compensation in those times, thanks to the kindly feelings of the people,* and to the traditions of deep devotion to their sovereigns, for the enormous expenses charged upon the taxes. Mazarin had said: 'Let them sing, provided they pay;' while Louis XIV's motto was, 'Let them look.' Sight had replaced the voice; the people could still look, but they were no longer allowed to sing. De Guiche left De Wardes and Malicorne at the foot of the grand staircase, while he himself, who shared the favour and good graces of Monsieur with the Chevalier de Lorraine,* who always smiled at him most affectionately, though he could not endure him, went straight to the prince's apartments, whom he found engaged in admiring himself in the glass, and rouging his face. In a corner of the closet, the Chevalier de Lorraine was extended full length upon some cushions, having just had his long hair curled, with which he was playing in the same manner a woman would have done. The prince turned round as the count entered, and perceiving who it was, said: 'Ah! is that you, Guiche? come here and tell me the truth.'

'You know, my lord, it is one of my defects to speak the truth.'

'You will hardly believe, De Guiche, how that wicked chevalier has annoyed me.'

The chevalier shrugged his shoulders.

'Why, he claims,' continued the prince, 'that Mademoiselle Henrietta is better looking as a woman than I am as a man.'*

'Do not forget, my lord,' said De Guiche, frowning slightly, 'you require me to speak the truth.'

'Certainly,' said the prince, tremblingly.

'Well, and I shall tell it you.'

'Do not be in a hurry, Guiche,' exclaimed the prince, 'you have plenty of time; look at me attentively, and try to recollect Madame. Besides, her portrait is here. Look at it.' And he held out to him a miniature of the finest possible execution. De Guiche took it, and looked at it for a long time attentively.

'Upon my honour, my lord, this is indeed a most lovely face.'

'But look at me, count, look at *me*,' said the prince, endeavouring to direct upon himself the attention of the count, who was completely absorbed in contemplation of the portrait.

'It is wonderful,' murmured Guiche.

'Really, one would almost imagine you had never seen the young lady before.'

'It is true, my lord, I have seen her, but it was five years ago; there is a great difference between a child twelve years old and a girl of seventeen.'*

'Well, what is your opinion?'

'My opinion is that the portrait must be flattering, my lord.'

'Of that,' said the prince triumphantly, 'there can be no doubt; but let us suppose that it is not, what would your opinion be?'

'My lord, that your highness is exceedingly happy to have so charming a bride.'

'Very well, that is your opinion of her, but of me?'

'My opinion, my lord, is that you are too handsome for a man.'

The Chevalier de Lorraine burst out laughing. The prince understood how severe towards himself this opinion of the Comte de Guiche was, and he looked somewhat displeased, saying, 'My friends are not over indulgent.' De Guiche looked at the portrait again, and, after lengthy contemplation, returned it with apparent unwillingness, saying, 'Most decidedly, my lord, I should rather prefer to look ten times at your highness, than to look at Madame once again.' It seemed as if the chevalier had detected some mystery in these words, which were incomprehensible to the prince, for he exclaimed: 'Very well, get married yourself.' Monsieur continued rouging himself, and when he had finished, looked at the portrait again, once more turned to admire himself in the glass, and smiled, and no doubt was satisfied with the comparison. 'You are very kind to have come,' he said to Guiche, 'I feared you would leave without bidding me adieu.'

'Your highness knows me too well to believe me capable of so great a disrespect.'

'Besides, I suppose you have something to ask from me before leaving Paris?'

'Your highness has indeed guessed correctly, for I have a request to make.'

'Very good, what is it?'

The Chevalier de Lorraine immediately displayed the greatest attention, for he regarded every favour conferred upon another as a theft committed against himself. And, as Guiche hesitated, the prince said: 'If it be money, nothing could be more opportune, for I am in funds; the superintendent of finances has sent me 500,000 pistoles.'

'I thank your highness; but it is not an affair of money.'

'What is it, then? Tell me.'

'The appointment of a maid of honour.'

'Oh! oh! Guiche, what a protector you have become of young ladies,' said the prince, 'you never speak of anyone else now.'

The Chevalier de Lorraine smiled, for he knew very well that nothing displeased the prince more than to show any interest in ladies. 'My lord,' said the Comte, 'it is not I who am directly interested in the lady of whom I have just spoken; I am acting on behalf of one of my friends.'

'Ah! that is different; what is the name of the young lady in whom your friend is interested?'

'Mlle de la Baume le Blanc de la Vallière; she is already maid of honour to the dowager princess.'

'Why, she is lame,' said the Chevalier de Lorraine, stretching himself on his cushions.

'Lame,' repeated the prince, 'and Madame to have her constantly before her eyes? Most certainly not, it may be dangerous for her when in an interesting condition.'

The Chevalier de Lorraine burst out laughing.

'Chevalier,' said Guiche, 'your conduct is ungenerous; while I am soliciting a favour, you do me all the mischief you can.'

'Forgive me, comte,' said the Chevalier de Lorraine, somewhat uneasy at the tone in which Guiche had made his remark, 'but I had no intention of doing so, and I begin to believe that I have mistaken one young lady for another.'

'There is no doubt of it, monsieur; and I do not hesitate to declare that such is the case.'

'Do you attach much importance to it, Guiche?' inquired the prince.

'I do, my lord.'

'Well, you shall have it; but ask me for no more appointments, for there are none to give away.'

'Ah!' exclaimed the chevalier, 'midday already, that is the hour fixed for the departure.'

'You dismiss me, monsieur?' inquired Guiche.

'Really, count, you treat me very ill to-day,' replied the chevalier.

'For heaven's sake, count, for heaven's sake, chevalier,' said Monsieur, 'do you not see how you are distressing me?'

'Your highness's signature?' said Guiche.

'Take a blank appointment from that drawer, and give it to me.' Guiche handed the prince the document indicated, and at the same time presented him with a pen already dipped in ink; whereupon the prince signed. 'Here,' he said returning him the appointment, 'but I give it on one condition.'

'Name it.'

'That you make friends with the chevalier.'

'Willingly,' said Guiche. And he held out his hand to the chevalier with an indifference amounting to contempt.

'Adieu, count,' said the chevalier, without seeming in any way to have noticed the count's slight; 'adieu, and bring us back a princess who will not talk with her own portrait too much.'

'Yes, set off and lose no time. By the by, who accompany you?'

'Bragelonne and De Wardes.'

'Both excellent and fearless companions.'

'Too fearless,' said the chevalier; 'endeavour to bring them both back, count.'

'A bad heart, bad!' murmured De Guiche; 'he scents mischief everywhere, and sooner than anything else.' And taking leave of the prince, he quitted the apartment. As soon as he reached the vestibule, he waved in the air the paper which the prince had signed. Malicorne hurried forward, and received it, trembling with delight. When, however, he held it in his hand, Guiche observed that he still awaited something further.

'Patience, monsieur,' he said; 'the Chevalier de Lorraine was there, and I feared an utter failure if I asked too much at once. Wait until I return. Adieu.'

'Adieu, monsieur le comte; a thousand thanks,' said Malicorne.

'Send Manicamp to me. By the way, monsieur, is it true that Mlle de la Vallière is lame?' As he said this a horse drew up behind him, and on turning round he noticed that Bragelonne, who had just at that moment entered the courtyard, turned suddenly pale. The poor lover had heard the remark, which, however, was not the case with Malicorne, for he was already beyond the reach of the count's voice.

'Why is Louise's name spoken of here?' said Raoul to himself; 'oh! let not De Wardes, who stands smiling yonder, even say a word about her in my presence.'

'Now, gentlemen,' exclaimed the Comte de Guiche, 'prepare to start.'

At this moment the prince, who had completed his toilette, appeared at the window, and was immediately saluted by the acclamations of all who composed the escort, and ten minutes afterwards, banners, scarves, and feathers were fluttering and waving in the air, as the cavalcade galloped away.

LXXXIII

LE HAVRE

THIS brilliant and animated company, the members of which were inspired by various feelings, arrived at Le Havre four days after their departure from Paris. It was about five o'clock in the afternoon, and no intelligence had yet been received of Madame.* They were soon engaged in quest of apartments; but the greatest confusion immediately ensued among the masters, and violent quarrels among their attendants. In the midst of this disorder, the Comte de Guiche fancied he recognized Manicamp. It was, indeed, Manicamp himself; but as Malicorne had taken possession of his very best costume, he had not been able to get any other than a suit of purple velvet, trimmed with silver. Guiche recognized him as much by his dress as by his features, for he had very frequently seen Manicamp in his purple suit, which was his last resource. Manicamp presented himself to the count under an arch of torches, which set in a blaze, rather than illuminated, the gate by which Le Havre is entered, and which is situated close to the tower of Francis I.* The count, remarking the woe-begone expression on Manicamp's face, could not resist laughing. 'Well, my poor Manicamp,' he exclaimed, 'how purple you look; are you in mourning?'

'Yes,' replied Manicamp; 'I am in mourning.'

'For whom, or for what?'

'For my blue-and-gold suit, which has disappeared, and in the place of which I could find nothing but this; and I was even obliged to economize, from necessity, to get it back.'

'Indeed?'

'It is singular you should be astonished at that, since you leave me without any money.'

'At all events, here you are, and that is the principal thing.'

'By the most horrible roads.'

'Where are you lodging?'

'Lodging?'

'Yes!'

'I am not lodging anywhere.'

De Guiche began to laugh. 'Well,' said he, 'where do you intend to lodge?'

'In the same place you do.'

'But I don't know, myself.'

'What do you mean by saying you don't know?'

'Why should I know where I am to stay?'

'Have you not retained a hotel?'

'I?'

'Yes, you or the prince.'

'Neither of us has thought of it. Le Havre is of considerable size, I imagine; and provided I can get a stable for a dozen horses, and a suitable house in a good part of town——'

'Certainly, there are some very excellent houses.'

'Well then——'

'But not for us.'

'What do you mean by saying not for us?—for whom, then?'

'For the English, of course.'

'For the English?'

'Yes; the houses are all taken.'

'By whom?'

'By the Duke of Buckingham.'

'I beg your pardon?' said Guiche, whose attention this name had awakened.

'Yes, by the Duke of Buckingham. His Grace was preceded by a courier, who arrived here three days ago, and immediately retained all the houses fit for habitation the town possesses.'

'Come, come, Manicamp, let us understand each other.'

'Well, what I have told you is clear enough, it seems to me.'

'But surely Buckingham does not occupy the whole of Le Havre?'

'He certainly does not occupy it, since he has not yet arrived; but, once disembarked, he will occupy it.'

'Oh! oh!'

'It is quite clear you are not acquainted with the English; they have a mania for monopolizing everything.'*

'That may be; but a man who has the whole of one house, is satisfied with it, and does not require two.'

'Yes, but two men?'

'Be it so: for two men, two houses, or four or six, or ten, if you like; but there are a hundred houses at Havre.'

'Yes, and all the hundred are let.'

'Impossible!'

'What an obstinate fellow you are. I tell you Buckingham has hired all the houses surrounding the one which the queen dowager of England and the princess her daughter will inhabit.'

'He is singular enough, indeed,' said De Wardes, caressing his horse's neck.

'Such is the case, however, monsieur.'

'You are quite sure of it, Monsieur de Manicamp?' and as he put this question, he looked slyly at De Guiche, as though to interrogate him upon the degree of confidence to be placed in his friend's state of mind. During this discussion the night had closed in, and the torches, pages, attendants, squires, horses, and carriages blocked the gate and filled the empty area before it; the torches were reflected in the harbour, which the rising tide was gradually filling, while on the other side of the jetty might be noticed groups of curious lookers-on, consisting of sailors and townspeople, who seemed anxious to miss nothing of the spectacle. Amidst all this hesitation of purpose, Bragelonne, as though a perfect stranger to the scene, remained on his horse somewhat to the rear of Guiche, and watched the rays of light reflected on the water, inhaling with rapture the sea breezes, and listening to the waves which noisily broke upon the shore and on the beach, tossing the spray into the air with a noise that echoed in the distance. 'But,' exclaimed De Guiche, 'what is Buckingham's motive for providing such a supply of lodgings?'

'Yes, yes,' said De Wardes; 'what reason has he?'

'A very excellent one,' replied Manicamp.

'You know what it is, then?'

'I fancy I do.'

'Tell us, then.'

'Bend your head down towards me.'

'What! may it not be spoken except in private?'

'You shall judge of that yourself?'

'Very well.' De Guiche bent down.

'Love,' said Manicamp.

'I do not understand you at all.'

'Say rather, you cannot understand me *yet*.'

'Explain yourself.'

'Very well; it is quite certain, count, that his royal highness will be the most unfortunate of husbands.'

'What do you mean?'

'The Duke of Buckingham——'

'It is a name of ill omen* to princes of the house of France.'

'And so the duke is madly in love with Madame, so the rumour runs, and will have no one approach her but himself.'

De Guiche coloured. 'Thank you, thank you,' said he to Manicamp, grasping his hand. Then, recovering himself, added, 'Whatever you do, Manicamp, be careful that this project of Buckingham's is not made known to any Frenchman here; for, if so, many a sword would be unsheathed in this country that does not fear English steel.'

'But after all,' said Manicamp, 'I have had no satisfactory proof given me of the love in question, and it may be no more than an idle tale.'

'No, no,' said De Guiche, 'it must be the truth;' and despite his command over himself, he clenched his teeth.*

'Well,' said Manicamp, 'after all, what does it matter to you? What does it matter to me whether the prince is to be what the late king was? Buckingham the father for the queen, Buckingham the son for the princess.'

'Manicamp! Manicamp!'

'It is a fact, or at least, everybody says so.'

'Silence!' cried the count.

'But why silence?' said De Wardes; 'it is a highly creditable circumstance for the French nation. Are not you of my opinion, Monsieur de Bragelonne?'

'To what circumstance do you allude?' inquired De Bragelonne with an abstracted air.

'That the English should render homage to the beauty of our queens and our princesses.'

'Forgive me, but I have not been paying attention to what has passed; will you oblige me by explaining.'

'There is no doubt it was necessary that Buckingham the father should come to Paris in order that his majesty, King Louis XIII, should perceive that his wife was one of the most beautiful women of the French court; and it seems necessary, at the present time, that Buckingham the son should consecrate, by the devotion of his worship, the beauty of a princess who has French blood in her veins. The fact of having inspired a passion on the other side of the Channel will henceforth confer a title to beauty on this.'

'Sir,' replied De Bragelonne, 'I do not like to hear such matters treated so lightly. Gentlemen like ourselves should be careful guardians of the honour of our queens and our princesses. If we jest at them, what will our servants do?'

'How am I to understand that?' said De Wardes, whose ears tingled at the remark.

'In any way you choose, monsieur,' replied De Bragelonne, coldly.

'Bragelonne, Bragelonne,' murmured De Guiche.

'M. de Wardes,' exclaimed Manicamp, noticing that the young man had spurred his horse close to the side of Raoul.

'Gentlemen, gentlemen,' said De Guiche, 'do not set such an example in public, in the street too. De Wardes, you are wrong.'

'Wrong; in what way, may I ask?'

'You are wrong, monsieur, because you are always speaking ill of some one or something,' replied Raoul, with undisturbed composure.

'Let it pass, Raoul,' said De Guiche, in an undertone.

'Pray do not think of fighting, gentlemen!' said Manicamp, 'before you have rested yourselves; for in that case you will not be able to do much.'

'Come,' said De Guiche, 'forward, gentlemen!' and breaking through the horses and attendants, he cleared the way for himself towards the centre of the square, through the crowd, followed by the whole cavalcade. A large gateway looking out upon a courtyard was open; Guiche entered the courtyard, and Bragelonne, De Wardes, Manicamp, and three or four other gentlemen, followed him. A sort of council of war was held, and the means to be employed for saving the dignity of the embassy were deliberated upon. Bragelonne was of opinion that the right of priority should be respected, while De Wardes suggested that the town should be sacked. This latter proposition appearing to Manicamp rather premature, he proposed instead that they should first rest themselves. This was the wisest thing to do, but, unhappily, to follow his advice, two things were lacking; namely, a house and beds. De Guiche reflected for a while, and then said aloud, 'Let him who loves me, follow me!'

'The attendants also?' enquired a page who had approached the group.

'Everyone,' exclaimed the impetuous young man. 'Manicamp, show us the way to the house intended for her Royal Highness's residence.'

Without in any way divining the count's project, his friends followed him, accompanied by a crowd of people, whose acclamations and delight seemed a happy omen for the success of that project with which they were yet unacquainted. The wind was blowing strongly from the harbour, moaning in fitful gusts.

LXXXIV

AT SEA

THE following day was somewhat calmer, although the gale still continued. The sun had, however, risen through a bank of orange clouds, tingeing with its cheerful rays the crests of the black waves. Watch was impatiently kept from the different look-outs. Towards eleven o'clock in the morning a ship, with sails full set, was signalled as in view; two others followed at the distance of about half a knot. They approached like arrows shot from the bow of a skilful archer; and yet the sea ran so high that their speed was as nothing compared to the rolling of the billows in which the vessels were plunging first in one direction and then in another. The English fleet was soon recognized by the line of the ships, and by the colour of their pennants; the one which had the princess on board carried the admiral's flag and preceded the others.

The rumour now spread that the princess was arriving. The whole French court ran to the harbour, while the quays and

jetties were soon covered by crowds of people. Two hours afterwards, the other vessels had overtaken the flagship, and the
three, not venturing perhaps to enter the narrow entrance of the
harbour, cast anchor between Le Havre and La Hève.* When
the manœuvre had been completed, the vessel which bore the
admiral saluted France by twelve discharges of cannon, which
were returned, discharge for discharge, from the fort of Francis
I. Immediately afterwards a hundred boats were launched—they
were covered with the richest stuffs, and intended for the con-
veyance of the different members of the French nobility to the
vessels at anchor. But when it was observed that even inside
the harbour the boats were tossed to and fro, and that beyond
the jetty the waves rose mountains high, dashing upon the shore
with a terrible uproar, it was readily understood that not one of
those frail boats would be able with safety to reach a fourth part
of the distance between the shore and the vessels at anchor. A
pilot-boat, however, notwithstanding the wind and the sea, was
getting ready to leave the harbour for the purpose of placing
itself at the admiral's disposal.

De Guiche, who had been looking among the different boats
for one stronger than the others, which might offer a chance of
reaching the English vessels, perceived the pilot-boat getting
ready to start, said to Raoul: 'Do you not think, Raoul, that
intelligent and vigorous men, as we are, ought to be ashamed to
retreat before the brute strength of wind and waves?'

'That is precisely the very reflection I was silently making to
myself,' replied Bragelonne.

'Shall we get into that boat, then, and push off? Will you
come, De Wardes?'

'Take care, or you will get drowned,' said Manicamp.

'And for no purpose,' said De Wardes, 'for with the wind in
your teeth, as it will be, you will never reach the vessels.'

'You refuse, then?'

'Assuredly I do; I would willingly risk and lose my life in an
encounter against men,' he said, glancing at Bragelonne, 'but as
to fighting with oars against waves, I have no taste for that.'

'And for myself,' said Manicamp, 'even were I to succeed in
reaching the ships, I should not be indifferent to the loss of the
only good dress which I have left—salt water would ruin it.'

'You, then, refuse also?' exclaimed De Guiche.

'Decidedly I do; I beg you to understand that most distinctly.'

'But,' exclaimed De Guiche, 'look, De Wardes—look, Mani-camp—look yonder, the princesses are looking at us from the poop of the admiral's vessel.'

'An additional reason, my dear fellow, why we should not make ourselves ridiculous by being drowned while they look on.'

'Is that your last word, Manicamp?'

'Yes.'

'And yours, De Wardes?'

'Yes.'

'Then I go alone.'

'Not so,' said Raoul, 'for I shall accompany you; I thought it was understood I should do so.'

The fact is, that Raoul, uninfluenced by devotion, measuring the risk they ran, saw how imminent the danger was, but he willingly allowed himself to accept a peril which De Wardes had declined.

The boat was about to set off when De Guiche called to the pilot. 'Stay,' said he: 'we require two places in your boat;' and wrapping five or six pistoles in paper, he threw them from the quay into the boat.

'It seems you are not afraid of salt water, young gentlemen.'

'We are afraid of nothing,' replied De Guiche.

'Come along, then.'

The pilot approached the side of the boat, and the two young men, one after the other, with equal alacrity, jumped into the boat. 'Courage, my men,' said De Guiche; 'I have twenty pistoles left in this purse, and as soon as we reach the admiral's vessel they shall be yours.' The sailors bent themselves to their oars, and the boat bounded over the crest of the waves. The interest taken in this hazardous expedition was universal; the whole population of Le Havre hurried towards the jetties and every eye was directed towards the little boat; at one moment it flew suspended on the crest of the foaming waves, then suddenly glided downwards towards the bottom of a raging abyss, where it seemed utterly lost. After an hour's struggling with the waves, it reached the spot where the admiral's vessel was anchored, from the side of which two boats had already been dispatched to their aid. Upon the quarter-deck of the flag-ship, sheltered by a canopy of velvet and ermine, which was suspended by stout supports, Henrietta, the queen-dowager, and the young princess—with the admiral, the Duke of Norfolk,* standing beside them—watched with alarm this frail boat, at one moment tossed to the heavens, and the next buried beneath the waves, and against whose dark sail the noble figures of the two French gentlemen stood forth in relief like two luminous apparitions. The crew, leaning against the bulwarks and clinging to the shrouds, cheered the courage of the two daring young men, the skill of the pilot, and the strength of the sailors. They were received at the side of the vessel by a shout of triumph. The Duke of Norfolk, a handsome young man, from twenty-six to twenty-eight years of age, advanced to meet them. De Guiche and Bragelonne lightly mounted the ladder on the starboard side, and, conducted by the Duke of Norfolk, who resumed his place near them, they approached to offer their homage to the princesses. Respect, and yet more, a certain apprehension, for which he could not account, had hitherto restrained the Comte de Guiche from looking at Madame attentively, who, however, had observed him immediately, and had asked her mother, 'Is not that Monsieur* in the boat yonder?' Madame Henrietta, who knew Monsieur better than her daughter did, smiled at the mistake her vanity had led her into, and had answered, 'No; it is only M. de Guiche, his favourite.' The princess, at this reply, was constrained to check an instinctive tenderness of feeling which the courage displayed by the count had awakened. At the very moment the princess had put this question to her mother, De Guiche had, at last, summoned courage to raise his eyes towards her and could compare the original with the portrait he had so lately seen. No sooner had he seen her pale face, her eyes so full of animation, her beautiful nut-brown hair, her expressive lips, and her every gesture, which, while betokening royal descent, seemed to thank and to encourage him at one and the same time, than he was, for a moment, so overcome that had it not been for Raoul, on whose arm he leant, he would have fallen. His friend's amazed look, and the encouraging gesture of the queen, restored Guiche to his self-possession. In a few words he explained his mission, explained in what way he had become the envoy of his royal highness; and saluted, according to their rank and the reception they gave him, the admiral and several of the English noblemen who were grouped around the princesses.

Raoul was then presented, and was most graciously received; the share that the Comte de la Fère had had in the restoration of Charles II was known to all; and, more than that, it was the count who had been charged with the negotiation of the marriage, by means of which the grand-daughter of Henry IV was now returning to France. Raoul spoke English perfectly, and constituted himself his friend's interpreter with the young English noblemen, who were indifferently acquainted with the French language. At this moment a young man came forward, of extremely handsome features, and whose dress and arms were remarkable for their extravagance of material. He approached the princesses, who were engaged in conversation with the Duke of Norfolk, and, in a voice which ill concealed his impatience, said, 'It is time now to disembark, your Royal Highness.' The younger of the princesses rose from her seat at this remark, and was about to take the hand which the young nobleman extended to her, with an eagerness which arose from a variety of motives, when the admiral intervened between them, observing: 'A moment, if you please, my lord; it is not possible for ladies to disembark just now, the sea is too rough; it is probable the wind may abate before sunset, and the landing will not be effected, therefore, until this evening.'

'Allow me to observe, my lord,' said Buckingham, with an irritation of manner which he did not seek to disguise, 'you detain these ladies, and you have no right to do so. One of them, unhappily, now belongs to France, and you perceive that France claims them by the voice of her ambassadors;' and at the same moment he indicated Raoul and Guiche, whom he saluted.

'I cannot suppose that these gentlemen intend to expose the lives of their Royal Highnesses,' replied the admiral.

'These gentlemen,' retorted Buckingham, 'arrived here safely, notwithstanding the wind; allow me to believe that the danger will not be greater for their Royal Highnesses, when the wind will be in their favour.'

'These envoys have shown how great their courage is,' said

the admiral. 'You may have observed that there was a great number of persons on shore who did *not* venture to accompany them. Moreover, the desire which they had to show their respect with the least possible delay to Madame and her illustrious mother, induced them to brave the sea, which is very tempestuous to-day, even for sailors. These gentlemen, however, whom I recommend as an example for my officers to follow, can hardly be so for these ladies.'

Madame glanced at the Comte de Guiche, and perceived that his face was burning with confusion. This look had escaped Buckingham, who had eyes for nothing but Norfolk, of whom he was evidently very jealous; he seemed anxious to remove the princesses from the deck of a vessel where the admiral reigned supreme. 'In that case,' returned Buckingham. 'I appeal to Madame herself.'

'And I, my lord,' retorted the admiral, 'I appeal to my own conscience, and to my own sense of responsibility. I have undertaken to convey Madame safe and sound to France, and I shall keep my promise.'

'But, sir——' continued Buckingham.

'My lord, permit me to remind you that I command here.'

'Are you aware what you are saying, my lord?' replied Buckingham, haughtily.

'Perfectly so; I therefore repeat it: I alone command here, all yield obedience to me; the sea and the winds, the ships and men too.' This remark was made in a dignified and authoritative manner. Raoul observed its effect upon Buckingham, who trembled with anger from head to foot, and leaned against one of the poles of the tent to prevent himself falling; his eyes became suffused with blood, and the hand which he did not need for his support wandered towards the hilt of his sword.

'My lord,' said the queen, 'permit me to observe that I agree in every particular with the Duke of Norfolk; if the heavens, instead of being clouded as they are at the present moment, were perfectly serene and propitious, we can still afford to bestow a few hours upon the officer who has conducted us so successfully, and with such extreme attention, to the French coast, where he is to take leave of us.'

Buckingham, instead of replying, seemed to seek counsel from the expression of Madame's face. She, however half-concealed beneath the thick curtains of the velvet and gold which sheltered her, had not heard the discussion, having been occupied in watching the Comte de Guiche, who was conversing with Raoul. This was a fresh misfortune for Buckingham, who fancied he perceived in Madame Henrietta's look a deeper feeling than that of curiosity. He withdrew, almost tottering in his gait, and nearly stumbled against the mainmast of the ship.

'The duke has not acquired a steady footing yet,' said the queen-mother, in French, 'and that may possibly be his reason for wishing to find himself on firm land again.'

The young man overheard this remark, turned suddenly pale, and, letting his hands fall in great discouragement by his side, drew aside, mingling in one sigh his old affection and his new hatreds. The admiral, however, without taking any further notice of the duke's ill-humour, led the princesses into the quarter-deck cabin, where dinner had been served with a magnificence worthy in every respect of his guests. The admiral seated himself at the right hand of the princess, and placed the Comte de Guiche on her left. This was the place Buckingham usually occupied; and when he entered the cabin, how profound was his unhappiness to see himself banished by etiquette from the presence of his sovereign, to a position inferior to that which, by rank, he was entitled to. De Guiche, on the other hand, paler still perhaps from happiness than his rival was from anger, seated himself tremblingly next the princess, whose silken robe, as it lightly touched him, caused a tremor of mingled regret and happiness to pass through his whole frame. The repast finished, Buckingham darted forward to hand Madame Henrietta from the table; but this time it was De Guiche's turn to give the duke a lesson. 'Have the goodness, my lord, from this moment,' said he, 'not to interpose between her royal highness and myself. From this moment, indeed, her royal highness belongs to France, and when she deigns to honour me by touching my hand, it is the hand of Monsieur, the brother of the king of France, she touches.'

And saying this, he presented his hand to Madame Henrietta with such marked deference, and at the same time, with such nobility, that a murmur of admiration rose from the English, while a groan of despair escaped from Buckingham's lips. Raoul, who loved, understood it all. He fixed upon his friend one of those profound looks which a bosom friend or mother can alone extend, either as protector or guardian, over the one who is about to stray from the right path. Towards two o'clock in the afternoon the sun shone forth anew, the wind subsided, the sea became smooth as a crystal mirror, and the fog, which had shrouded the coast, disappeared like a veil withdrawn from before it. The smiling hills of France appeared in full view, with their numerous white houses rendered more conspicuous by the bright green of the trees or the clear blue sky.

LXXXV

THE TENTS

THE admiral, as we have seen, was determined to pay no further attention to Buckingham's threatening glances and bad temper. In fact, from the moment they left England, he had gradually accustomed himself to his behaviour. De Guiche had not yet in any way remarked the animosity which appeared to influence that young nobleman against him, but he felt, instinctively, that there could be no sympathy between himself and the favourite of Charles II.* The queen-mother, with greater experience and calmer judgment, perceived the exact position of affairs, and, as she discerned its danger, was prepared to meet it, whenever the proper moment should arrive. Quiet had been everywhere restored, except in Buckingham's heart; he, in his impatience, addressed himself to the princess, in a low voice: 'For Heaven's sake, madame, I implore you to hasten your disembarkation. Do you not perceive how that insolent Duke of Norfolk is killing me with his attentions and devotions to you?'

Henrietta heard this remark; she smiled, and without turning her head towards him, but giving only to the tone of her voice that inflection of gentle reproach and quiet provocation which women and princesses so well know how to assume, she murmured, 'I have already hinted, my lord, that you must have taken leave of your senses.'

Not a single detail escaped Raoul's attention; he heard both Buckingham's entreaty and the princess's reply; he observed Buckingham retire, heard his deep sigh, and saw him pass his hand across his face. He understood everything, and trembled as he reflected on the position of affairs, and the state of the minds of those about him. At last the admiral, with studied delay, gave the last orders for the departure of the boats. Buckingham heard the directions given with such an exhibition of delight that a stranger would really imagine the young man's reason was affected. As the Duke of Norfolk gave his commands, a large boat or barge, decked with flags, and capable of holding about twenty rowers and fifteen passengers, was slowly lowered from the side of the admiral's vessel. The barge was carpeted with velvet and decorated with coverings embroidered with the arms of England, and with garlands of flowers; for, at that time, ornamentation was by no means forgotten in these political pageants. No sooner was this truly royal boat afloat, and the rowers held their oars uplifted, awaiting, like soldiers presenting arms, the embarkation of the princess, than Buckingham ran forward to the ladder in order to take his place. His progress was, however, halted by the queen. 'My lord,' she said, 'it is hardly becoming that you should allow my daughter and myself to land without having previously ascertained that our apartments are properly prepared. I beg your lordship to be good enough to precede us ashore, and to give directions that everything be in proper order on our arrival.'

This was a fresh disappointment for the duke, and, still more so, since it was so unexpected. He hesitated, coloured violently, but could not reply. He had thought he might be able to keep near Madame during the passage to the shore, and, by this means, to enjoy to the very last moment the brief period fortune still kept for him. The order, however, was explicit; and the admiral, who heard it given, immediately called out, 'Launch the ship's pinnace.' His directions were executed with the promptness which distinguishes every manœuvre on board a man-of-war.

Buckingham, in utter hopelessness, cast a look of despair at the princess, of supplication towards the queen, and directed a glance full of anger towards the admiral. The princess pretended not to notice him, while the queen turned aside her head, and the admiral laughed outright, at the sound of which Buckingham seemed ready to spring upon him. The queen-mother rose, and with a tone of authority, said, 'Pray set off, sir.'

The young duke hesitated, looked around him, and with a last effort, half-choked by contending emotions, said, 'And you, gentlemen, M. de Guiche and M. de Bragelonne, do not you accompany me?'

De Guiche bowed and said, 'Both M. de Bragelonne and myself await her majesty's orders; whatever the commands she imposes on us, we shall obey them.' Saying this, he looked towards the princess, who cast down her eyes.

'Your grace will remember,' said the queen, 'that M. de Guiche is here to represent Monsieur; it is he who will do the honours of France, as you have done those of England; his presence cannot be dispensed with; besides, we owe him this small favour for the courage he displayed in venturing to seek us in such a terrible stress of weather.'

Buckingham opened his lips, as if he were about to speak, but, whether thoughts or expressions failed him, not a syllable escaped them, and turning away, as though out of his mind, he leapt from the vessel into the pinnace. The sailors were just in time to catch hold of him to steady themselves; for his weight and the rebound had almost upset the boat.

'His grace cannot be in his senses,' said the admiral aloud to Raoul.

'I am uneasy on the duke's account,' replied Bragelonne.

While the boat was advancing towards the shore, the duke kept his eyes immovably fixed upon the admiral's ship, like a miser torn away from his coffers, or a mother separated from her child, about to be led away to death. No one, however, acknowledged his signals, his frowns, or his pitiful gestures. In very anguish of mind, he sank down in the boat, burying his hands in his hair, whilst the boat, impelled by the exertions of the merry sailors, flew over the waves. On his arrival he was in such a state of apathy that, had he not been received at the harbour by the messenger whom he had directed to precede him, he would hardly have had strength to ask his way. Having once, however, reached the house which had been set apart for

him, he shut himself up, like Achilles in his tent.* The barge
bearing the princesses quitted the admiral's vessel at the very
moment Buckingham landed. It was followed by another boat
filled with officers, courtiers, and zealous friends. Great numbers of the inhabitants of Le Havre, having embarked in fishing-
cobles and boats of every description, set off to meet the royal
barge. The cannon from the forts fired salutes, which were
returned by the flag-ship and the two other vessels, and the
flashes from the open mouths of the cannon floated in white
smoke over the waves, and disappeared in the clear blue sky.

The princess landed at the decorated quay. Bands playing gay
music greeted her arrival, and accompanied every step she took.
During the time she was passing through the centre of the town,
and treading beneath her delicate feet the rich carpets and the
gay flowers which had been strewn upon the ground, De Guiche
and Raoul, escaping from their English friends, hurried through
the town and hastened rapidly towards the place intended for
the residence of Madame.

'Let us hurry forward,' said Raoul to De Guiche, 'for, if I
read Buckingham's character aright, he will create some disturbance, when he learns the result of our deliberations of yesterday.'

'Never fear,' said De Guiche, 'De Wardes is there, who is
determination itself, while Manicamp is the very soul of
gentleness.'

De Guiche was not, however, the less diligent on that account, and five minutes afterwards they were within sight of the
Hôtel de Ville. The first thing which struck them was the number
of people assembled in the square. 'Excellent,' said De Guiche;
'our apartments, I see, are prepared.'

In fact, in front of the Hôtel de Ville, upon the wide square
before it, eight tents had been raised, surmounted by the flags
of France and England united. The hotel was surrounded by
tents, as by a girdle of variegated colours; ten pages and a dozen
mounted troopers, who had been given to the ambassadors as an
escort, mounted guard outside the tents. It had a singularly
curious effect, almost fairy-like in its appearance. These tents
had been constructed during the night-time. Fitted up, within
and without, with the richest materials that De Guiche had been
able to procure in Le Havre, they completely encircled the Hôtel

de Ville. The only passage which led to the steps of the hotel, and which was not enclosed by the silken barricade, was guarded by two tents, resembling two pavilions, the doorways of both of which opened towards the entrance. These two tents were intended for De Guiche and Raoul; in whose absence they were to be occupied, that of De Guiche by De Wardes, and that of Raoul by Manicamp. Surrounding these two tents, and the six others, a hundred officers, gentlemen, and pages, dazzling in their display of silk and gold, thronged like bees buzzing about a hive. Every one of them, their swords by their sides, was ready to obey the slightest sign either of De Guiche or Bragelonne, the leaders of the embassy.

At the very moment the two young men appeared at the end of one of the streets leading to the square, they perceived, crossing the square at full gallop, a young man on horseback, whose costume was of surprising richness. He pushed hastily through the crowd of curious lookers-on, and, at the sight of these unexpected erections, uttered a cry of anger and dismay. It was Buckingham, who had awakened from his stupor, in order to adorn himself with a costume perfectly dazzling in its beauty, and to await the arrival of the princess and the queen-mother at the Hôtel de Ville. At the entrance to the tents, the soldiers barred his passage, and his further progress was halted. Buckingham, raging to no avail, raised his whip; but his arm was seized by a couple of officers. Of the two guardians of the tent, only one was there. De Wardes was inside the Hôtel de Ville, engaged in attending to the execution of some orders given by De Guiche. At the noise made by Buckingham, Manicamp, who was indolently reclining upon the cushions at the doorway of one of the tents, rose with his usual indifference, and, perceiving that the disturbance continued, made his appearance from underneath the curtains. 'What is the matter?' he said, in a gentle tone of voice, 'and who is it making this disturbance?'

It so happened that, at the moment he began to speak, silence had just been restored, and, although his voice was very soft and gentle in its tone, every one heard his question. Buckingham turned round, and looked at the tall thin figure, and the listless expression of countenance of his questioner. Probably the personal appearance of Manicamp, who was dressed very plainly, did not inspire him with much respect, for he replied disdainfully, 'Who may you be, monsieur?'

Manicamp, leaning on the arm of a gigantic trooper, as firm as the pillar of a cathedral, replied in his usual tranquil tone of voice, 'And *you*, monsieur?'

'I, monsieur, am the Duke of Buckingham; I have hired all the houses which surround the Hôtel de Ville, where I have business to transact; and as these houses are let, they belong to me, and, as I hired them in order to preserve the right of free access to the Hôtel de Ville, you are not justified in preventing me passing to it.'

'But who prevents you passing, monsieur?' inquired Manicamp.

'Your sentinels.'

'Because you wish to pass on horseback, and orders have been given to let only persons on foot pass.'

'No one has any right to give orders here, except myself,' said Buckingham.

'On what grounds?' inquired Manicamp, with his soft tone. 'Will you do me the favour to explain this enigma to me?'

'Because, as I have already told you, I have hired all the houses looking on the square.'

'We are very well aware of that, since nothing but the square itself has been left for us.'

'You are mistaken, monsieur; the square belongs to me, as well as the houses in it.'

'Forgive me, monsieur, but you are mistaken there. In *our* country, we say, the highway belongs to the king, therefore this square is his majesty's; and, consequently, as we are the king's ambassadors, the square belongs to us.'

'I have already asked you who you are, monsieur,' exclaimed Buckingham, exasperated at the coolness of his interlocutor.

'My name is Manicamp,' replied the young man, in a voice, whose tones were as harmonious and sweet as the notes of an Aeolian harp.*

Buckingham shrugged his shoulders contemptuously, and said, 'When I hired these houses which surround the Hôtel de Ville, the square was unoccupied: this slum of yours obstructs my view; I hereby order it to be removed.'

A hoarse and angry murmur ran through the crowd of listeners at these words. De Guiche arrived at this moment; he pushed through the crowd which separated him from Buckingham, and, followed by Raoul, arrived on the scene of action from one side, just as De Wardes came up from the other. 'Pardon me, my lord; but if you have any complaint to make, have the goodness to address it to me, inasmuch as it was I who supplied the plans for the construction of these tents.'

'Moreover, I would beg you to observe, monsieur, that the term "slum" is a highly objectionable one!' added Manicamp, graciously.

'You were saying, monsieur—' continued De Guiche.

'I was saying, monsieur le comte,' resumed Buckingham, in a tone of anger more marked than ever, although in some measure moderated by the presence of an equal, 'I was saying, that it is impossible these tents can remain where they are.'

'Impossible?' exclaimed De Guiche, 'and why?'

'Because I object to them.'

A movement of impatience escaped De Guiche, but a warning glance from Raoul restrained him.

'You should the less object to them, monsieur, on account of the abuse of priority you have permitted yourself to exercise.'

'Abuse!'

'Most assuredly. You commission a messenger, who hires in your name the whole of the town of Le Havre, without considering the members of the French court, who would be sure to arrive here to meet Madame. Your Grace will admit that this is hardly friendly conduct in the representative of a friendly nation.'

'The right of possession belongs to him who is first on the ground.'

'Not in France, monsieur.'

'Why not in France?'

'Because France is a country where courtesy is observed.'

'Which means?' exclaimed Buckingham, in so violent a manner that those who were present drew back, expecting an immediate collision.

'Which means, monsieur,' replied De Guiche, now rather pale, 'that I caused these tents to be raised as lodgings for myself and my friends, as a shelter for the ambassadors of France, as the only place of refuge which your exactions have left us in the town; and that I, and those who are with me, shall remain in them, at least, until an authority more powerful, and more supreme, than your own shall dismiss me from them.'

'In other words, until we are ejected, as the lawyers say,' observed Manicamp, blandly.

'I know an authority, monsieur, which I trust is such as you will respect,' said Buckingham, placing his hand on his sword.

At this moment, and as the goddess of Discord, inflaming all minds, was about to direct their swords against each other, Raoul gently placed his hand on Buckingham's shoulder. 'One word, my lord,' he said.

'First, I demand my right,' exclaimed the fiery young man.

'It is precisely upon that point I wish to have the honour of addressing a word to you.'

'Very well, monsieur, but let your remarks be brief.'

'One question is all I ask; you can hardly expect me to be briefer.'

'Speak, monsieur, I am listening.'

'Are you, or is the Duke of Orléans, going to marry the grand-daughter of Henry IV?'

'What do you mean?' exclaimed Buckingham, retreating a few steps, bewildered.

'Have the goodness to answer me,' persisted Raoul tranquilly.

'Do you mean to mock me, monsieur?' inquired Buckingham.

'Your question is a sufficient answer for me. You admit, then, that it is not you who are going to marry the princess?'

'You know it perfectly well, monsieur.'

'I beg your pardon, but your conduct has been such as to leave it not altogether certain.'

'Proceed, monsieur, what do you mean to convey?'

Raoul approached the duke. 'Are you aware, my lord,' he said, lowering his voice, 'that your extravagances very much resemble the excesses of jealousy? Such jealous outbursts, with respect to any woman, are not becoming in one who is neither her lover nor her husband; and I am sure you will admit that my remark applies with still greater force, when the lady in question is a princess of the blood royal!'

'Monsieur,' exclaimed Buckingham, 'do you mean to insult Madame Henrietta?'

'Be careful, my lord,' replied Bragelonne, coldly, 'for it is you who insult her. A little while since, when on board the admiral's ship, you wearied the queen, and exhausted the admiral's patience. I was watching, my lord; and, at first, I concluded you were not in possession of your senses, but I have since surmised the real significance of your folly.'

'Monsieur!' exclaimed Buckingham.

'One moment more, for I have yet another word to add. I trust I am the only one of my companions who have guessed it.'

'Are you aware, monsieur,' said Buckingham, trembling with mingled feelings of anger and uneasiness, 'are you aware that you are using language to me which requires to be checked?'

'Weigh your words well, my lord,' said Raoul, haughtily; 'my nature is not such that its vivacities need checking; whilst you, on the contrary, are descended from a race whose passions are suspected by all true Frenchmen; I repeat, therefore, for the second time, have a care!'

'A care for what, may I ask? Do you presume to threaten me?'

'I am the son of the Comte de la Fère, my lord, and I never threaten, because I strike first. Therefore, understand me well, the threat that I hold out to you is this—'

Buckingham clenched his hands, but Raoul continued, as though he had not observed the gesture. 'At the very first word, beyond the respect and deference due to her royal highness, which you permit yourself to use towards her . . . Be patient, my lord, for I am perfectly so.'

'You?'

'Undoubtedly. So long as madame remained on English territory, I held my peace; but from the very moment she stepped on French ground, and now that we have welcomed her in the name of the prince, I warn you, that at the first mark of disrespect which you, in your insane attachment, exhibit towards the royal house of France, I shall have one of two courses to follow; either I declare, in the presence of every one, the madness with which you are now affected, and I have you ignominiously ordered back to England; or if you prefer, I will run my dagger through your throat in the presence of all here. This second alternative seems to me the least disagreeable, and I think I shall hold to it.'

Buckingham had become paler than the lace collar around his neck. 'M. de Bragelonne,' he said, 'is it, indeed, a gentleman who is speaking to me?'

'Yes; only the gentleman is speaking to a madman. Get a grip on yourself, my lord, and he will address quite different language to you.'

'But, M. de Bragelonne,' murmured the duke, in a strangled voice, putting his hand to his neck, 'Do you not see I am choking?'

'If your death were to take place at this moment, my lord,' replied Raoul, with unruffled composure, 'I should, indeed, regard it as a great happiness, for this circumstance would prevent all kinds of malicious comment; not alone about yourself, but also about those illustrious persons whom your devotion is compromising in so absurd a manner.'

'You are right, you are right,' said the young man, almost beside himself. 'Yes, yes: better to die, than to suffer as I do at this moment.' And he grasped a beautiful dagger, the handle of which was inlaid with precious stones; and which he half drew from his breast.

Raoul thrust his hand aside. 'Be careful what you do,' he said; 'if you do not kill yourself, you commit a ridiculous action; and if you were to kill yourself, you sprinkle blood upon the marriage gown of the princess of England.'

Buckingham remained a minute gasping for breath; during this interval, his lips quivered, his fingers worked convulsively, and his eyes wandered as though in delirium. Then suddenly, he said, 'M. de Bragelonne, I know nowhere a nobler mind than yours; you are, indeed, a worthy son of the most perfect gentleman that ever lived. Keep your tents.' And he threw his arms round Raoul's neck. All who were present, astounded at this conduct, which was the very reverse of what was expected, considering the violence of the one adversary, and the determination of the other, began immediately to clap their hands, and a thousand cheers and joyful shouts arose from all sides. De Guiche, in his turn, embraced Buckingham somewhat against his inclination; but, at all events, he did embrace him. This was the signal for French and English to do the same; and they who, until that moment, had looked at each other nervously, fraternized on the spot. In the meantime, the procession of the princess arrived, and had it not been for Bragelonne, two armies would have been engaged together in conflict, and blood have been shed upon the flowers with which the ground was covered. At the appearance, however, of the banners borne at the head of the procession, complete order was restored.

LXXXVI

NIGHT

CONCORD returned to its place amidst the tents. English and French rivalled each other in their devotion and courteous attention to the illustrious travellers. The English forwarded to the French baskets of flowers, of which they had made a plentiful provision to greet the arrival of the young princess; the French in return invited the English to a supper, which was to be given the next day. Congratulations were poured in upon the princess everywhere during her journey. From the respect paid her on all sides, she seemed like a queen; and from the adoration with which she was treated by two or three, she appeared an object of worship. The queen-mother gave the French the most affectionate reception. France was her native country,* and she had suffered too much unhappiness in England for England to have made her forget France. She taught her daughter, then, by her own affection for it, to love a country where they had both been hospitably received, and where a brilliant future opened before them. After the public entry was over, and the spectators in the streets had partially dispersed, and the sound of the music and cheering of the crowd could be heard only in the distance; when the night had closed in, wrapping, with its star-covered mantle, the sea, the harbour, the town, and the surrounding country, De Guiche, still excited by the great events of the day, returned to his tent, and seated himself upon one of the stools with so profound an expression of distress that Bragelonne kept his eyes fixed on him until he heard him sigh, and then approached him. The count had thrown himself back on his seat, leaning his shoulders against the partition of the tent, and remained thus, his face buried in his hands with heaving chest and restless limbs.

'You are suffering?' asked Raoul.

'Cruelly.'

'Bodily, I suppose?'

'Yes; bodily.'

'This has indeed been a harassing day,' continued the young man, his eyes fixed upon his friend.

'Yes; a night's rest will probably restore me.'

'Shall I leave you?'

'No; I wish to talk to you.'

'You shall not speak to me, Guiche, until you have first answered my questions.'

'Proceed, then.'

'You will be frank with me?'

'I always am.'

'Can you imagine why Buckingham has been so violent?'

'I have my suspicions.'

'Because he is in love with Madame, is it not?'

'One could almost swear to it, to observe him.'

'You are mistaken; there is nothing of the kind.'

'It is you who are mistaken, Raoul; I have read his distress in his eyes, in his every gesture and action the whole day.'

'You are a poet, my dear count, and find subjects for your muse everywhere.'

'I can perceive love clearly enough.'

'Where it does not exist.'

'No, where it does exist.'

'Do you not think you are deceiving yourself, Guiche?'

'I am convinced of what I say,' said the count.

'Now, tell me, count,' said Raoul, fixing a penetrating look on him, 'what has happened to make you so clear-sighted?'

Guiche hesitated for a moment, and then answered, 'Self-love, I suppose.'

'Self-love is a pedantic word, Guiche.'

'What do you mean?'

'I mean that, generally, you are less out of spirits than seems to be the case this evening.'

'I am tired.'

'Listen to me, Guiche; we have been campaigners together;*
we have been on horseback for eighteen hours at a time, and our
horses dying from exhaustion, or hunger, have fallen beneath
us, and yet we have laughed at our mishaps. Believe me, it is not
fatigue that saddens you to-night.'

'It is anger, then.'

'Anger?'

'The anger I felt this evening.'

'The mad conduct of the Duke of Buckingham, do you mean?'

'Of course; is it not vexatious for us, the representatives of
our sovereign master, to witness the devotion of an Englishman
to our future mistress, the second lady in point of rank in the
kingdom?'

'Yes, you are right; but I do not think any danger is to be
apprehended from Buckingham.'

'No; still, he is intrusive. Did he not, on his arrival here,
almost succeed in creating a disturbance between the English
and ourselves; and, had it not been for you, for your admirable
coolness, for your singular decision of character, swords would
have been drawn in the very streets of the town.'

'You observe, however, that he has changed his tactics.'

'Yes, certainly; but this is the very thing that amazes me so
much. You spoke to him in a low tone of voice, what did you say
to him? You think he loves her; you admit that such a passion
does not give way readily. He does not love her, then!' De
Guiche pronounced the latter words with so marked an expression that Raoul raised his head. The noble character of the
young man's countenance expressed a displeasure which could
easily be read.

'What I said to him, count,' replied Raoul, 'I will repeat to
you. Listen to me. I said, "You look with wistful feelings, and
most injurious desire, upon the sister of your prince—her to
whom you are not affianced, who is not, who can never be
anything to you; you outrage those who, like ourselves, have
come to seek a young lady to escort her to her husband."'

'You spoke to him in that manner?' asked Guiche, colouring.

'In those very terms; I even added more. "How would you
regard us," I said, "if you were to see among us a man mad
enough, disloyal enough, to entertain other than sentiments of

the most perfect respect for a princess who is the destined wife of our master?"'

These words were so applicable to De Guiche that he turned pale, and, overcome by a sudden agitation, was barely able to stretch out one hand mechanically towards Raoul, as he covered his eyes and face with the other.

'But,' continued Raoul, not interrupted by this movement of his friend, 'Heaven be praised, the French, who are pronounced to be thoughtless and indiscreet, reckless even, are capable of bringing a calm and sound judgment to bear on matters of such high importance. "So," I added, "Learn, my lord, that we gentlemen of France devote ourselves to our sovereigns by sacrificing to them our affections as well as our fortunes and our lives: and whenever it may chance to happen that the tempter suggests one of those vile thoughts that set the heart on fire, we extinguish the flame, even if it has to be done by shedding our blood for the purpose. Thus it is that the honour of three is saved: our country's, our master's, and our own. It is thus that we act, your grace; it is thus that every man of honour ought to act." In this manner, my dear Guiche,' continued Raoul, 'I addressed the Duke of Buckingham; and he admitted I was right and resigned himself unresistingly to my arguments.'

De Guiche, who had hitherto sat leaning forward while Raoul was speaking, drew himself up, his eyes glancing proudly; he seized Raoul's hand, his face, which had been as cold as ice, seemed on fire. 'And you spoke magnificently,' he said, in a half-choking voice; 'you are indeed a friend, Raoul. But now, I entreat you, leave me to myself.'

'Do you wish it!'

'Yes; I need rest. Many things have agitated me to-day, both in mind and body; when you return to-morrow I shall no longer be the same man.'

'I leave you, then,' said Raoul, as he withdrew. The count advanced a step towards his friend, and clasped him warmly in his arms. But in this friendly pressure Raoul could detect the nervous agitation of a great internal conflict.

The night was clear, starlit, and splendid; the tempest had passed away, and the sweet influences of the evening had restored life, peace, and security everywhere. A few fleecy clouds were floating in the heavens, and indicated from their appearance a continuance of beautiful weather, tempered by a gentle breeze from the east. Upon the large square in front of the hotel, the shadows of the tents, intersected by the golden moonbeams, formed as it were a huge mosaic of jet and yellow flagstones. Soon, however, the entire town was wrapped in slumber; a feeble light still glimmered in Madame's apartment, which looked out upon the square, and the soft rays from the expiring lamp seemed to be the image of the calm sleep of a young girl, hardly yet aware of life's anxieties, and in whom the flame of life sinks placidly as sleep steals over the body. Bragelonne quitted the tent with the slow and measured step of a man curious to observe, but anxious not to be seen. Sheltered behind the thick curtains of his own tent, surveying with a glance the whole square, he noticed that, after a few moments' pause, the curtains of De Guiche's tent shook, and then were drawn partially aside. Behind them he could perceive the shadow of De Guiche, his eyes glittering in the obscurity, fastened ardently upon the princess's sitting apartment, which was partially lighted by the lamp in the inner room. The soft light which illumined the windows was the count's star. The fervent aspirations of his nature could be read in his eyes. Raoul, concealed in the shadows, divined the many passionate thoughts that established, between the tent of the young ambassador and the balcony of the princess, a mysterious and magical bond of sympathy—a bond created by thoughts imprinted with so much strength and persistence of will, that they must have caused happy and loving dreams to alight upon the perfumed couch on which the count, with the eyes of his soul, gazed so eagerly. But De Guiche and Raoul were not the only watchers. The window of one of the houses looking on the square was opened too, the casement of the house where Buckingham resided. By the aid of the rays of light which issued from this latter, the profile of the duke could be distinctly seen, as he indolently reclined upon the carved balcony with its velvet hangings; he also was breathing in the direction of the princess's apartment his prayers and the wild visions of his love.

Raoul could not resist smiling, as, thinking of Madame, he said to himself, 'Hers is, indeed, a heart well besieged;' and then added, compassionately, as he thought of Monsieur, 'and he is a husband well threatened too; it is a good thing for him that he is a prince of such high rank, that he has an army to guard what is his.' Bragelonne watched for some time the conduct of the two lovers, listened to the loud and uncivil slumbers of Manicamp, who snored as imperiously as though he was wearing his blue and gold, instead of his purple suit.

Then he turned towards the night breeze, which bore towards him, he seemed to think, the distant song of the nightingale; and, after having laid in a due provision of melancholy, another nocturnal malady, he retired to rest thinking, with regard to his own love affair, that perhaps four or even a larger number of eyes, quite as ardent as those of De Guiche and Buckingham, were coveting his own idol in the château at Blois. 'And Mademoiselle de Montalais is by no means a very conscientious garrison,' said he to himself, sighing aloud.

LXXXVII

FROM LE HAVRE TO PARIS

THE next day the celebrations took place, accompanied by all the pomp and animation that the resources of the town and the cheerful disposition of men's minds could supply. During the last few hours spent in Le Havre, every preparation for the departure had been made. After Madame had taken leave of the English fleet, and, once again, had saluted the country in saluting its flags, she entered her carriage, surrounded by a brilliant escort. De Guiche had hoped that the Duke of Buckingham would accompany the admiral to England; but Buckingham succeeded in demonstrating to the queen that there would be great impropriety in allowing Madame to proceed to Paris, almost unprotected. As soon as it had been settled that Buckingham was to accompany Madame,* the young duke selected a corps of gentlemen and officers to form part of his own suite, so that it was almost an army that now set out towards Paris, scattering gold, and exciting the liveliest demonstrations as they passed through the different towns and villages on the route. The weather was very fine. France is a beautiful country, especially along the

route by which the procession passed. Spring cast its flowers
and its perfumed foliage on their path. Normandy, with its vast
variety of vegetation, its blue skies and silver rivers, displayed
itself in all the loveliness of a paradise to the new sister of the
king. Celebrations and brilliant displays received them everywhere along the line of march. De Guiche and Buckingham
forgot everything; De Guiche in his anxiety to prevent any fresh
attempts on the part of the duke, and Buckingham, in his desire
to awaken in the heart of the princess a softer remembrance of
the country to which the recollection of many happy days belonged. But, alas! the poor duke could tell that the image of that
country so cherished by himself became, from day to day, fainter
in Madame's mind, in exact proportion as her affection for
France became more deeply engraved on her heart. In fact, it
was not difficult to perceive that his most devoted attention
awakened no acknowledgment, and that the grace with which he
rode one of his most fiery horses was wasted, for it was only
casually and by the merest accident that the princess's eyes were
turned towards him. In vain did he try, in order to attract one of
those looks, which were thrown carelessly around, or bestowed
elsewhere, to produce in the animal he rode its greatest display
of strength, speed, temper, and address; in vain did he, by
exciting his horse almost to madness, spur him, at the risk of
dashing himself in pieces against the trees, or of rolling in the
ditches, over the gates and barriers which they passed, or down
the steep slopes of the hills. Madame, whose attention had been
aroused by the noise, turned her head for a moment to observe
the cause of it, and then, slightly smiling, again entered into
conversation with her faithful guardians, Raoul and De Guiche,
who were quietly riding at her carriage doors. Buckingham felt
himself a prey to all the tortures of jealousy; an unknown, un-
familiar anguish glided through his veins, and laid siege to
his heart; and then, as if to show that he knew the folly of his
conduct, and that he wished to correct, by the humblest submission, his flights of absurdity, he mastered his horse, and compelled him, reeking with sweat and flecked with foam, to champ
his bit close beside the carriage, amidst the crowd of courtiers.
Occasionally he obtained a word from Madame as a recompense,
and yet her speech seemed almost a reproach.

'It is well, my lord,' she said, 'now you are reasonable.'

Or from Raoul, 'Your grace is killing your horse.'

Buckingham listened patiently to Raoul's remarks, for he instinctively felt, without having had any proof that such was the case, that Raoul checked the display of De Guiche's feelings, and that, had it not been for Raoul, some mad act or proceeding, either of the count, or of Buckingham himself, would have brought about an open break, or a disturbance—perhaps even exile itself. From the moment of that excited conversation the two young men had held in front of the tents at Le Havre, when Raoul made the duke see the impropriety of his conduct, Buckingham felt himself attracted towards Raoul almost in spite of himself. He often entered into conversation with him, and it was nearly always to talk to him either of his father or of D'Artagnan, their mutual friend, in whose praise Buckingham was nearly as enthusiastic as Raoul. Raoul endeavoured, as much as possible, to make the conversation turn upon this subject in De Wardes' presence, who had, during the whole journey, been exceedingly angered by the superior position taken by Bragelonne, and especially by his influence over De Guiche. De Wardes had that keen and merciless shrewdness most evil natures possess; he had immediately remarked De Guiche's melancholy, and divined the nature of his regard for the princess. Instead, however, of treating the subject with the same reserve which Raoul practised; instead of regarding with the respect which was their due the obligations and duties of society, De Wardes resolutely attacked in the count the ever-sounding chord of youthful audacity and pride. It happened one evening, during a halt at Mantes,* that while De Guiche and De Wardes were leaning against a barrier, engaged in conversation, Buckingham and Raoul were also talking together as they walked up and down. Manicamp was engaged in devoted attendance on the princess, who already treated him without reserve, on account of his versatile fancy, frank courtesy of manner, and conciliatory disposition.

'Confess,' said De Wardes, 'that you are really ill, and that your pedagogue of a friend has not succeeded in curing you.'

'I do not understand you,' said the count.

'Yet it is easy enough; you are dying of love.'

'You are mad, De Wardes.'

'Madness it would be, I admit, if Madame were really indifferent to your suffering; but she takes so much notice of it, observes it to such an extent, that she compromises herself, and I tremble lest, on our arrival at Paris, M. de Bragelonne may not denounce both of you.'

'For shame, De Wardes, again attacking De Bragelonne.'

'Come, come, a truce to child's play,' replied the count's evil genius, in an undertone; 'you know as well as I do what I mean. Besides, you must have observed how the princess's glance softens as she looks at you; you can tell, by the very inflection of her voice, what pleasure she takes in listening to you, and can feel how thoroughly she appreciates the verses you recite to her. You cannot deny, too, that every morning she tells you how indifferently she slept the previous night.'

'True, De Wardes, quite true: but what good is there in your telling me all this?'

'Is it not important to know the exact state of affairs?'

'No, no; not when I am a witness of things that are enough to drive a man mad.'

'Stay, stay,' said De Wardes; 'look, she calls you—do you understand? Profit by the occasion, while your pedagogue is absent.'

De Guiche could not resist; an invincible attraction drew him towards the princess. De Wardes smiled as he saw him withdraw.

'You are mistaken, monsieur,' said Raoul, suddenly stepping across the barrier against which the previous moment the two friends had been leaning. 'The pedagogue is here, and has overheard you.'

De Wardes, at the sound of Raoul's voice, which he recognized without having occasion to look at him, half drew his sword.

'Put up your sword,' said Raoul; 'you know perfectly well that, until our journey is at an end, every demonstration of that nature is useless. Why do you distil into the heart of the man you term your friend all the bitterness that infects your own? As for myself, you wish to arouse a feeling of deep dislike against a man of honour—my father's friend, and my own; and as for the count, you wish him to love one who is destined for your master. Really, monsieur, I should regard you as a coward, and a traitor too, if I did not, with greater justice, regard you as a madman.'

'Monsieur,' exclaimed De Wardes, exasperated, 'I was mistaken, I find, in terming you a pedagogue. The tone you adopt, and the style which is peculiarly your own, is that of a Jesuit, and not of a gentleman. Please do not use, whenever I am present, this style I complain of, and the tone also. I hate M. d'Artagnan because he was guilty of a cowardly act towards my father.'

'You lie, monsieur,' said Raoul, coolly.

'You call me a liar, monsieur?' exclaimed De Wardes.

'Why not, since what you assert is untrue?'

'You give me the lie and will not draw your sword?'

'I have resolved, monsieur, not to kill you until Madame shall have been delivered safely into her husband's hands.'

'Kill me! Believe me, monsieur, your schoolmaster's rod does not kill so easily.'

'No,' replied Raoul, sternly, 'but M. d'Artagnan's sword kills; and, not only do I possess his sword, but he has himself taught me how to use it; and with that sword, when a befitting time arrives, I will avenge his name—a name you have dishonoured.'

'Take care, monsieur,' exclaimed De Wardes; 'if you do not immediately give me satisfaction, I will avail myself of every means to revenge myself.'

'Indeed, monsieur,' said Buckingham, suddenly, appearing upon the scene of action, 'that is a threat which smacks of assassination, and therefore, ill becomes a gentleman.'

'What did you say, my lord?' said De Wardes, turning round towards him.

'I said, monsieur, that the words you have just spoken are displeasing to my English ears.'

'Very well, monsieur, if what you say is true,' exclaimed De Wardes, thoroughly incensed, 'I at least find in you one who will not escape me. Understand my words as you like.'

'I take them in the manner they cannot but be understood,' replied Buckingham, with that haughty tone which characterized him, and which, even in ordinary conversation, gave a tone of defiance to everything he said; 'M. de Bragelonne is my friend, you insult M. de Bragelonne, and you shall give me satisfaction for that insult.'

De Wardes cast a look upon De Bragelonne, who, faithful to the character he had assumed, remained calm and unmoved, even after the duke's defiance.

'It would seem that I did not insult M. de Bragelonne, since M. de Bragelonne, who carries a sword by his side, does not consider himself insulted.'

'At all events you insult some one.'

'Yes, I insulted M. d'Artagnan,' resumed De Wardes, who had observed that this was the only means of stinging Raoul, so as to awaken his anger.

'That, then,' said Buckingham, 'is another matter.'

'Precisely so,' said De Wardes; 'it is the province of M. d'Artagnan's friends to defend him.'

'I am entirely of your opinion,' replied the duke, who had regained all his coolness of manner: 'if M. de Bragelonne were offended, I could not reasonably be expected to espouse his quarrel, since he is himself here; but when you say that it is a quarrel of M. d'Artagnan——'

'You will of course leave me to deal with the matter,' said De Wardes.

'Nay, on the contrary, for I draw my sword,' said Buckingham, unsheathing it as he spoke; 'for if M. d'Artagnan injured your father, he rendered, or at least did all that he could to render, a great service to mine.'*

De Wardes was thunderstruck.

'M. d'Artagnan,' continued Buckingham, 'is the bravest gentleman I know. I shall be delighted, as I owe him many personal obligations, to settle them with you, by crossing my sword with yours.' At the same moment Buckingham drew his sword gracefully from its scabbard, saluted Raoul, and put himself on guard.

De Wardes advanced a step to meet him.

'Stay gentlemen,' said Raoul, advancing towards them, and placing his own drawn sword between the combatants, 'the affair is hardly worth the trouble of blood being shed almost in the presence of the princess. M. de Wardes speaks ill of M. d'Artagnan, with whom he is not even acquainted.'

'What, monsieur,' said De Wardes, setting his teeth hard

together, and resting the point of his sword on the toe of his boot, 'do you assert that I do not know M. d'Artagnan?'

'Certainly not; you do not know him,' replied Raoul, coldly, 'and you are even not aware where he is to be found.'

'Not know where he is?'

'Such must be the case, since you fix your quarrel with him upon strangers, instead of seeking M. d'Artagnan where he is to be found.' De Wardes turned pale. 'Well, monsieur,' continued Raoul. 'I will tell you where M. d'Artagnan is: he is now in Paris; when on duty he is to be met with at the Louvre—when not on duty, in the Rue des Lombards. M. d'Artagnan can be easily discovered at either of those two places. Having, therefore, as you assert, so many causes of complaint against him, show your courage in seeking him out, and afford him an opportunity of giving you that satisfaction you seem to ask of every one but of himself.' De Wardes passed his hand across his forehead, which was covered with perspiration. 'For shame, M. de Wardes! so quarrelsome a disposition is hardly becoming after the publication of the edicts against duels.* Pray think of that; the king will be incensed at our disobedience, particularly at such a time—and his majesty will be in the right.'

'Excuses,' murmured De Wardes; 'mere pretexts.'

'Really, M. de Wardes,' resumed Raoul, 'such remarks are the idlest bluster. You know very well that the Duke of Buckingham is a man of undoubted courage, who has already fought ten duels, and will probably fight eleven.* His name alone is significant enough. As far as I am concerned, you are well aware that I can fight also. I fought at Lens, at Bléneau, at the Dunes* in front of the artillery, a hundred paces in front of the line, while you—I say this parenthetically—were a hundred paces behind it. True it is, that on that occasion there was far too great a concourse of persons present for your courage to be observed, and on that account perhaps, you did not reveal it; while here, it would be a display, and would excite remark—you wish that others should talk about you, in what manner you do not care. Do not depend upon me, M. de Wardes, to assist you in your designs, for I shall certainly not afford you that pleasure.'

'Sensibly observed,' said Buckingham, putting up his sword, 'and I ask your forgiveness, M. de Bragelonne, for having allowed myself to yield to a first impulse.'

De Wardes, however, on the contrary, perfectly furious, bounded forward and raised his sword, threateningly, against Raoul, who had scarcely time to put himself in a posture of defence.

'Take care, monsieur,' said Bragelonne, tranquilly, 'or you will put out one of my eyes.'

'You will not fight, then?' said De Wardes.

'Not at this moment; but this I promise to do: immediately on our arrival at Paris I will conduct you to M. d'Artagnan, to whom you shall detail all the causes of complaint you have against him. M. d'Artagnan will solicit the king's permission to measure swords with you. The king will give his consent, and when you have received the sword-thrust in due course, you will consider, in a calmer frame of mind, the precepts of the Gospel, which enjoin forgetfulness of injuries.'

'Ah!' exclaimed De Wardes, furious at this imperturbable coolness, 'one can clearly see you are half a bastard, M. de Bragelonne.'

Raoul became as pale as death; his eyes flashed lightning, causing De Wardes involuntarily to fall back. Buckingham, also, who had perceived their expression, threw himself between the two adversaries, whom he had expected to see leap on each other. De Wardes had reserved this injury for the last; he clasped his sword firmly in his hand, and awaited the encounter. 'You are right, monsieur,' said Raoul, mastering his emotion, 'I am only acquainted with my father's name; but I know too well that the Comte de la Fère is too upright and honourable a man to allow me to fear for a single moment that there is, as you insinuate, any stain upon my birth. My ignorance, therefore, of my mother's name* is a misfortune for me, and not a reproach. You are deficient in loyalty of conduct; you are wanting in courtesy, in reproaching me with misfortune. It matters little, however, the insult has been given, and I consider myself insulted accordingly. It is quite understood, then, that after you shall have received satisfaction from M. d'Artagnan, you will settle your quarrel with me.'

'I admire your prudence, monsieur,' replied De Wardes with a bitter smile; 'a little while ago you promised me a sword-thrust from M. d'Artagnan, and now, after I shall have received his, you offer me one from yourself.'

'Do not disturb yourself,' replied Raoul, with concentrated anger; 'in all affairs of that nature, M. d'Artagnan is exceedingly skilful, and I will beg him as a favour to treat you as he did your father;* in other words, to spare your life at least, so as to leave me the pleasure, after your recovery, of killing you outright; for you have the heart of a viper, M. de Wardes, and in very truth, too many precautions cannot be taken against you.'

'I shall take my precautions against you,' said De Wardes, 'be assured of it.'

'Allow me, monsieur,' said Buckingham, 'to translate your remark by a piece of advice I am about to give M. de Bragelonne; M. de Bragelonne, wear a breastplate.'

De Wardes clenched his hands. 'Ah!' said he, 'you two gentlemen intend to wait until you have taken that precaution before you measure your swords against mine.'

'Very well, monsieur,' said Raoul, 'since you positively will have it so, let us settle the affair now.' And, drawing his sword he advanced towards De Wardes.

'What are you going to do?' said Buckingham.

'Be easy,' said Raoul, 'it will not take long.'

De Wardes placed himself on his guard; their swords crossed. De Wardes flew upon Raoul with such impetuosity, that at the first clashing of the steel blades Buckingham clearly saw that Raoul was only trifling with his adversary. Buckingham stepped aside, and watched the combat. Raoul was as calm as if he were handling a foil, instead of a sword; having retreated a step, he parried three or four fierce thrusts which De Wardes made at him, caught the sword of the latter within his own, and sent it flying twenty paces the other side of the barrier. Then as De Wardes stood disarmed and astounded at his defeat, Raoul sheathed his sword, seized him by the collar and the waist-band, and hurled his adversary to the other end of the barrier, trembling and mad with rage.

'We shall meet again,' murmured De Wardes, rising from the ground and picking up his sword.

'I have done nothing for the last hour,' said Raoul, 'but say the same thing.' Then, turning towards the duke, he said, 'I entreat you to be silent about this affair; I am ashamed to have gone so far, but my anger carried me away, and I ask your forgiveness for it; forget it, too.'

'Dear viscount,' said the duke, pressing within his own the vigorous and valiant hand of his companion, 'allow me, on the contrary, to remember it, and to look after your safety; that man is dangerous—he will kill you.'

'My father,' replied Raoul, 'lived for twenty years under the menace of a much more formidable enemy,* and he still lives.'

'Your father had good friends, viscount.'

'Yes,' sighed Raoul, 'such friends, indeed, that none are now left like them.'*

'Do not say that, I beg, at the very moment I offer you my friendship;' and Buckingham opened his arms to embrace Raoul, who delightedly received the proffered alliance. 'In my family,' added Buckingham, 'you are aware, M. de Bragelonne, we die to save our friends.'

'I know it well, duke,' replied Raoul.

LXXXVIII

AN ACCOUNT OF WHAT THE CHEVALIER DE LORRAINE THOUGHT OF MADAME

NOTHING further interrupted the journey. Under a pretext that was little remarked, M. de Wardes went forward in advance of the others. He took Manicamp with him, for his equable and dreamy disposition acted as a counterpoise to his own. It is a subject of remark, that quarrelsome and restless characters invariably seek the companionship of gentle, timorous dispositions, as if the former sought, in the contrast, a repose for their own ill humour, and the latter a protection for their weakness. Buckingham and Bragelonne, admitting De Guiche into their friendship, in concert with him, sang the praises of the princess during the whole of the journey. Bragelonne had, however, insisted that their three voices should be in concert, instead of singing in solo parts, as De Guiche and his rival seemed to have acquired a dangerous habit of doing. This style of harmony pleased the queen-mother exceedingly, but it was not perhaps so agreeable to the young princess, who was an incarnation of coquetry, and who, without any fear as far as her own voice was concerned, was only too eager to throw herself into the most

dangerous arias. She possessed one of those fearless and in-
cautious dispositions that find gratification in an excess of sens-
itiveness of feeling, and for whom, also, danger has a certain
fascination.* And so her glances, her smiles, her toilette, an
inexhaustible armoury of offensive weapons, were showered on
the three young men with overwhelming force; and from her
well-stored arsenal issued glances, kindly recognitions, and a
thousand other little charming attentions which were intended
to strike at long range the gentlemen who formed the escort, the
townspeople, the officers of the different cities she passed through,
pages, populace, and servants; it was wholesale slaughter, a general rout. By the time Madame arrived at Paris, she had reduced
to slavery about a hundred thousand lovers, and brought in her
train to Paris half a dozen men who were almost mad about her,
and two who were, indeed, literally out of their minds. Raoul
was the only person who divined the power of this woman's
attraction, and, as his heart was already engaged, he arrived in
the capital full of indifference and distrust. Occasionally during
the journey he conversed with the queen of England about the
power of fascination which Madame possessed, and the mother,
whom so many misfortunes and deceptions had taught experience, replied: 'Henrietta was sure to be illustrious in one way or
another, whether born in a palace or born in obscurity; for she
is a woman of great imagination, capricious, and self-willed.' De
Wardes and Manicamp, in their self-appointed roles as couriers,
had announced the princess's arrival. The procession was met at
Nanterre* by a brilliant escort of horsemen and carriages. It was
Monsieur himself, followed by the Chevalier de Lorraine and by
his favourites, the latter being themselves followed by a portion
of the king's military household, who had arrived to meet his
affianced bride. At St. Germain, the princess and her mother
had changed their heavy travelling coach, somewhat the worse
for the journey, for a light, richly decorated carriage drawn by
six horses with white and gold harness. Seated in this open
carriage, as though upon a throne, and beneath a parasol of
embroidered silk, fringed with feathers, sat the young and lovely
princess, on whose beaming face were reflected the softened
rose-tints which suited her delicate skin to perfection. Monsieur, on reaching the carriage, was struck by her beauty; he

showed his admiration in so marked a manner that the Chevalier de Lorraine shrugged his shoulders as he listened to his compliments, while Buckingham and De Guiche were almost heartbroken. After the usual courtesies had been rendered, and the ceremony completed, the procession slowly resumed the road to Paris. The presentations had been carelessly made, and Buckingham, with the rest of the English gentlemen, had been introduced to Monsieur, from whom they had received but very indifferent attention. But, during their progress, as he observed that the duke devoted himself with his accustomed earnestness to the carriage-door, he asked the Chevalier de Lorraine, his inseparable companion, 'Who is that horseman?'

'He was presented to your highness a short while ago; it is the handsome Duke of Buckingham.'

'Ah, yes, I remember.'

'Madame's knight,' added the favourite, with an inflection of the voice which envious minds can alone give to the simplest phrases.

'What do you say?' replied the prince.

'I said "Madame's knight".'

'Has she a recognized knight, then?'

'One would think you could judge of that for yourself; look, only, how they are laughing and flirting. All three of them.'

'What do you mean by all three?'

'Do you not see that De Guiche is one of the party?'

'Yes, I see. But what does that prove?'

'That Madame has two admirers instead of one.'

'You poison the simplest thing!'

'I poison nothing. Ah! your royal highness's mind is perverted. The honours of the kingdom of France are being paid to your wife and you are not satisfied.'

The Duke of Orléans dreaded the satirical humour of the Chevalier de Lorraine whenever it reached a certain degree of bitterness, and he changed the conversation abruptly. 'The princess is pretty,' said he, very negligently, as if he were speaking of a stranger.

'Yes,' replied the chevalier, in the same tone.

'You say "yes" like a "no". She has very beautiful black eyes.'

'Yes, but small.'

'That is so, but they are brilliant. She is tall, and of a good figure.'

'I fancy she stoops a little, my lord.'

'I do not deny it. She has a noble air.'

'Yes, but her face is thin.'

'I thought her teeth beautiful.'

'They can easily be seen, for her mouth is large enough. Decidedly, I was wrong, my lord; you are certainly handsomer than your wife.'

'But do you think me as handsome as Buckingham?'

'Certainly, and he thinks so, too; for look, my lord, he is redoubling his attentions to Madame to prevent your effacing the impression he has made.'

Monsieur made a movement of impatience, but as he noticed a smile of triumph pass across the chevalier's lips, he drew up his horse to a foot-pace. 'Why,' said he, 'should I speculate further about my cousin? Do I not already know her? Were we not brought up together? Did I not see her at the Louvre when she was a child?'

'A great change has taken place in her since then, prince. At the time you allude to, she was somewhat less brilliant, and scarcely so proud, either. One evening, particularly, you may remember, my lord, the king refused to dance with her, because he thought her plain and badly dressed!'

These words made the Duke of Orléans frown. It was by no means flattering for him to marry a princess of whom, when young, the king had not thought much. He would probably have answered, but at this moment De Guiche quitted the carriage to join the prince. He had remarked the prince and the chevalier together, and full of anxious attention; he seemed to try and guess the nature of the remarks which they had just exchanged. The chevalier, whether he had some treacherous object in view, or from imprudence, did not take the trouble to dissimulate, but said, 'Count, you're a man of excellent taste.'

'Thank you for the compliment,' replied De Guiche; 'but why do you say that?'

'I appeal to His Highness.'

'No doubt of it,' said Monsieur; 'and Guiche knows perfectly well that I regard him as a most consummate cavalier.'

'Well, since that is decided, I resume. You have been in the princess's society, count, for the last week, have you not?'

'Yes,' replied De Guiche, colouring in spite of himself.

'Well then, tell us frankly, what do you think of her personal appearance?'

'Of her personal appearance?' returned De Guiche, stupefied.

'Yes; of her appearance, of her mind, of herself, in fact.'

Astounded by this question, De Guiche hesitated answering.

'Come, come, De Guiche,' resumed the chevalier, laughingly, 'tell us your opinion frankly: the prince commands it.'

'Yes, yes,' said the prince, 'be frank.'

De Guiche stammered out a few unintelligible words.

'I am perfectly well aware,' returned Monsieur, 'that the subject is a delicate one, but you know you can tell me everything. What do you think of her?'

In order to avoid betraying his real thoughts, De Guiche had recourse to the only defence which a man taken by surprise really has, and accordingly told an untruth. 'I do not find Madame,' he said, 'either good or bad looking, yet rather good than bad looking.'

'What! count,' exclaimed the chevalier, 'you who went into such ecstasies and uttered so many exclamations at the sight of her portrait.'

De Guiche coloured violently. Fortunately his horse, which was slightly restive, enabled him by a sudden plunge to conceal his agitation. 'What portrait?' he murmured, joining them again. The chevalier had not taken his eyes off him.

'Yes, the portrait. Was not the miniature a good likeness?'

'I do not remember. I had forgotten the portrait; it quite escaped my recollection.'

'And yet it made a very marked impression upon you,' said the chevalier.

'That is not unlikely.'

'Is she witty, at all events?' inquired the duke.

'I believe so, my lord.'

'Is M. de Buckingham witty too?' said the chevalier.

'I do not know.'

'My own opinion is, that he must be,' replied the chevalier, 'for he makes Madame laugh, and she seems to take no little pleasure in his society, which never happens to a clever woman when in the company of a booby.'

'Of course, then, he must be clever,' said De Guiche, simply.

At this moment Raoul arrived opportunely, seeing that De Guiche was pressed by his dangerous questioner, to whom he addressed a remark, and in that way changed the conversation. The entry to Paris was brilliant and joyous.

The king, in honour of his brother, had directed that the festivities should be on a scale of the greatest possible magnificence. Madame and her mother alighted at the Louvre, where during their exile they had so gloomily submitted to obscurity, misery, and privations of every description. That palace, which had been so inhospitable a residence for the unhappy daughter of Henry IV, the naked walls, the uneven floors, the ceilings matted with cobwebs, the vast dilapidated chimney-places, the cold hearths on which the charity extended to them by parliament hardly permitted a fire to glow,* was completely altered in appearance. The richest hangings and the thickest carpets, glistening flagstones, and pictures, with their richly-gilded frames; in every direction could be seen candelabra, mirrors, and furniture and fittings of the most sumptuous character; in every direction were guards of the proudest military bearing with floating plumes, crowds of attendants and courtiers in the antechambers and upon the staircases. The courtyards, where the grass had formerly been allowed to grow wild, as if the ungrateful Mazarin had thought it a good idea to let the Parisians perceive that solitude and disorder were, with misery and despair, the fit accompaniments of fallen monarchy—the immense courtyards, formerly silent and desolate, were now all thronged with courtiers whose horses were pacing and prancing to and fro. The carriages were filled with young and beautiful women, who awaited the opportunity of saluting, as she passed, the daughter of that daughter of France who, during her widowhood and exile, had sometimes gone without wood for her fire, and bread for her table, whom the meanest attendants at the château had treated with indifference and contempt. And so, Madame Henrietta once more returned to the Louvre, with her heart more swollen with bitter recollections than her daughter's, whose disposition was fickle and forgetful, with triumph and delight.

She knew only too well that this brilliant reception was offered to the happy mother of a king restored to his throne, a throne second to none in Europe, whereas the worse than indifferent reception she had before met with was offered to her, the daughter of Henry IV, as a punishment for having been unfortunate. After the princesses had been installed in their apartments and had rested, the gentlemen who had formed their escort, having, in like manner, recovered from their fatigue, resumed their accustomed habits and occupations. Raoul began by setting off to see his father, who had left for Blois. He then tried to see M. d'Artagnan, who, however, being engaged in the organization of a military household for the king, could not be found anywhere. Bragelonne next sought out De Guiche, but the count was occupied in a long conference with his tailors and with Manicamp, which consumed his whole time. With the Duke of Buckingham he fared still worse, for the duke was purchasing horses, horses galore, and diamonds in abundance. He monopolized every embroiderer, jeweller, and tailor that Paris could boast of. Between De Guiche and himself a vigorous contest ensued, invariably a courteous one, in which, to ensure success, the duke was ready to spend a million; while Marshal de Gramont had only allowed his son 60,000 francs. So Buckingham laughed and spent his money. Guiche groaned in despair, and would have shown it more violently, had it not been for the advice De Bragelonne gave him.

'A million!' repeated De Guiche daily; 'I must submit. Why will not the marshal advance me a portion of my inheritance?'

'Because you would throw it away,' said Raoul.

'What can that matter to him? If I am to die of it, I shall die of it, and then I shall need nothing further.'

'But what need is there to die?' said Raoul.

'I do not wish to be bested in elegance by an Englishman.'

'My dear count,' said Manicamp, 'elegance is not a costly commodity, it is only a very difficult accomplishment.'

'Yes, but difficult things cost a good deal of money, and I have only got 60,000 francs.'

'A very embarrassing state of things, truly,' said De Wardes; 'even if you spent as much as Buckingham, there is only 940,000 francs difference.'

'Where am I to find them?'

'Get into debt.'

'I am in debt already.'

'A greater reason for getting further in.'

Advice like this resulted in De Guiche becoming excited to such an extent that he committed extravagances where Buckingham only incurred expenses. The rumour of this prodigality warmed the hearts of all the shopkeepers in Paris; from the residence of the Duke of Buckingham to that of the Comte de Gramont nothing but miracles were attempted. While all this was going on, Madame was resting herself, and Bragelonne was engaged in writing to Mademoiselle de la Vallière. He had already dispatched four letters, and not an answer to any one of them had been received, when, on the very morning fixed for the marriage ceremony, which was to take place in the chapel at the Palais Royal,* Raoul, who was dressing, heard his valet announce M. de Malicorne. 'What can this Malicorne want with me?' thought Raoul; and then said to his valet, 'Let him wait.'

'He is a gentleman from Blois,' said the valet.

'Admit him at once,' said Raoul, eagerly.

Malicorne entered as brilliant as a star, and wearing a superb sword at his side. After having saluted Raoul most gracefully, he said: 'M. de Bragelonne, I am the bearer of a thousand compliments from a lady to you.'

Raoul coloured. 'From a lady,' said he, 'from a lady at Blois?'

'Yes, monsieur; from Mademoiselle de Montalais.'

'Thank you, monsieur; I recollect you now,' said Raoul. 'And what does Mademoiselle de Montalais require of me?'

Malicorne drew four letters from his pocket, which he offered to Raoul.

'My own letters, is it possible?' he said, turning pale; 'my letters, and the seals unbroken?'

'Monsieur, your letters did not find, at Blois, the person to whom they were addressed, and so they are now returned to you.'

'Mademoiselle de la Vallière has left Blois, then?' exclaimed Raoul.

'A week ago.'

'Where is she, then?'

'In Paris.'

'How was it known that these letters were from me?'

'Mademoiselle de Montalais recognized your handwriting and your seal,' said Malicorne.

Raoul coloured and smiled. 'Mademoiselle de Montalais is exceedingly obliging,' he said; 'she is always kind and charming.'

'Always, monsieur.'

'Surely she could give me some precise information about Mademoiselle de la Vallière. I could never find her in this immense city.'

Malicorne drew another packet from his pocket. 'You may possibly find in this letter what you are anxious to learn.'

Raoul hurriedly broke the seal. The writing was that of Mademoiselle Aure, and inclosed were these words: 'Paris, Palais Royal. The day of the nuptial blessing.'

'What does this mean?' inquired Raoul of Malicorne; 'you probably know?'

'I do, monsieur.'

'For pity's sake, tell me, then.'

'Impossible, monsieur.'

'Why so?'

'Because Mademoiselle Aure has forbidden me to do so.'

Raoul looked at his strange visitor, and remained silent for a moment; then he went on: 'At least, tell me whether it is fortunate or unfortunate.'

'That you will see.'

'You are very severe in your reservations.'

'Will you grant me a favour, monsieur?' said Malicorne.

'In exchange for what you refuse me?'

'Precisely.'

'What is it?'

'I have the greatest desire to see the ceremony, and I have no ticket to admit me, in spite of all the steps I have taken to secure one. Could you get me admitted?'

'Certainly.'

'Do me this kindness, then, I beg you.'

'Most willingly, monsieur; come with me.'

'I am exceedingly indebted to you, monsieur,' said Malicorne.

'I thought you were a friend of M. de Manicamp.'

'I am, monsieur; but this morning I was with him as he was dressing, and I let a bottle of blacking fall over his new suit, and he flew at me sword in hand, so that I was obliged to make my escape. That is the reason I could not ask him for a ticket. He would have killed me.'

'I can well believe it,' laughed Raoul. 'I know Manicamp is capable of killing a man who has been unfortunate enough to commit the crime you have to reproach yourself with, but I will repair the mischief as far as you are concerned. I will but fasten my cloak, and shall then be ready to serve you, not only as a guide, but as your introducer, too.'

LXXXIX

A SURPRISE FOR RAOUL

MADAME's marriage was celebrated in the chapel of the Palais Royal, in the presence of a crowd of courtiers, who had been most scrupulously selected. However, notwithstanding the marked favour which an invitation indicated, Raoul, faithful to his promise to Malicorne, who was so anxious to witness the ceremony, obtained admission for him. After he had fulfilled this engagement, Raoul approached De Guiche, who, as if in contrast with his magnificent costume, exhibited a countenance so utterly dejected that the Duke of Buckingham was the only one present who could compete with him as far as pallor and discomfiture were concerned.

'Take care, count,' said Raoul, approaching his friend, and preparing to support him at the moment the archbishop blessed the married couple. In fact, the Prince of Condé was attentively scrutinizing these two images of desolation, standing like caryatides on either side of the nave of the church. The count, after that, kept a more careful watch over himself.

At the end of the ceremony, the king and queen processed towards the grand reception-room, where Madame and her suite were to be presented to them. It was remarked that the king, who had seemed more than surprised at his sister-in-law's appearance, was most flattering in his compliments to her. Again, it was remarked that the queen-mother, fixing a long and thoughtful gaze upon Buckingham, leaned towards Madame de Motteville as though to ask her, 'Do you not see how much he resembles his father?' and finally it was remarked that Monsieur watched everybody, and seemed rather cross. After the reception of the princess and ambassadors, Monsieur solicited the king's permission to present to him as well as to Madame the persons belonging to their new household.

'Are you aware, vicomte,' enquired the Prince de Condé of Raoul, 'whether the household has been selected by a person of taste, and whether there are any faces worth looking at?'

'I have not the slightest idea, monseigneur,' replied Raoul.

'You affect ignorance, surely.'

'In what way, monseigneur?'

'You are a friend of De Guiche, who is one of the friends of the prince.'

'That may be so, monseigneur; but the matter having no interest whatever for me, I never questioned De Guiche on the subject; and De Guiche, never having been questioned, did not communicate any particulars to me.'

'But Manicamp?'

'It is true I saw Manicamp at Le Havre, and during the journey here, but I was no more inquisitive with him than I had been towards De Guiche. Besides, is it likely that Manicamp should know anything of such matters? for he is a person of only secondary importance.'

'My dear vicomte, do you not know better than that?' said the prince; 'why, it is these persons of secondary importance who, on such occasions, have all the influence; and the truth is, that nearly everything has been done through Manicamp's presentations to De Guiche, and through De Guiche to Monsieur.'

'I assure you, monseigneur, I was not aware of that,' said Raoul, 'and what your highness does me the honour to impart is perfectly new to me.'

'I believe you, although it seems incredible; besides we shall not have long to wait. See, the flying squadron is advancing, as good Queen Catherine* used to say. Ah! ah! what pretty faces!'

A bevy of young girls at this moment entered the salon,

conducted by Madame de Navailles,* and to Manicamp's credit
be it said, if indeed he had taken that part in their selection
which the Prince de Condé assigned him, it was a display calculated to dazzle those who, like the prince, could appreciate every
character and style of beauty. A young, fair-complexioned girl,
between twenty and one-and-twenty years of age, whose large
blue eyes flashed, as she opened them, in the most dazzling
manner, walked at the head of the group and was the first
presented.

'Mademoiselle de Tonnay-Charente,'* said Madame de
Navailles to Monsieur, who, as he saluted his wife, repeated,
'Mademoiselle de Tonnay-Charente.'

'Ah! ah!' said the Prince de Condé to Raoul, '*she* is present-
able enough.'

'Yes,' said Raoul, 'but has she not a somewhat haughty style?'

'Bah! we know these airs very well, vicomte; three months
hence she will be tame enough. But look, there, indeed, is a
pretty face.'

'Yes,' said Raoul, 'and one I am acquainted with.'

'Mademoiselle Aure de Montalais,' said Madame de Navailles.
The name and Christian name were carefully repeated by
Monsieur.

'Great heavens!' exclaimed Raoul, fixing his bewildered gaze
upon the entrance-doorway.

'What's the matter?' inquired the prince; 'was it Mademoiselle Aure de Montalais who made you utter such a "Great
heavens"?'

'No, monseigneur, no,' replied Raoul, pale and trembling.

'Well, then, if it be not Mademoiselle Aure de Montalais, it is
that pretty blonde who follows her. What beautiful eyes! She is
rather thin, but has fascinations without number.'

'Mademoiselle de la Baume le Blanc de la Vallière!' said
Madame de Navailles; and, as this name resounded through his
whole being, a cloud seemed to rise from his breast to his eyes,
so that he neither saw nor heard anything more; and the prince,
finding him nothing more than a mere echo which remained
deaf to his banter, moved forward for a closer view of the beautiful girls whom his first glance had picked out.

'Louise here! Louise a maid of honour to Madame!'

murmured Raoul, and his eyes, which did not suffice to satisfy his reason, wandered from Louise to Montalais. The latter had already shrugged off her assumed timidity, which she only needed for the presentation and for her curtsies.

Mademoiselle de Montalais, from the corner of the room to which she had retired, was looking with no small confidence at the different persons present; and, noticing Raoul, she amused herself with the profound astonishment which her own and her friend's presence there caused the unhappy lover. Her waggish and malicious look, which Raoul tried to avoid meeting, and which yet he sought inquiringly from time to time, placed him on the rack. As for Louise, whether from natural timidity, or some other reason for which Raoul could not account, she kept her eyes constantly cast down; intimidated, dazzled, and with impeded respiration, she withdrew herself as much as possible aside, unaffected even by the nudges Montalais gave her with her elbow. The whole scene was a puzzle for Raoul, the key to which he would have given anything to obtain. But no one was there who could assist him, not even Malicorne; who, a little uneasy at finding himself in the presence of so many persons of good birth, and not a little discouraged by Montalais's bantering glances, had described a circle, and by degrees succeeded in getting to within a few paces of the prince, behind the group of maids of honour, and nearly within reach of Mademoiselle Aure's voice, she being the planet around which he, as her attendant satellite, seemed constrained to gravitate. As he recovered his self-possession, Raoul fancied he recognized voices on his right hand that were familiar to him, and he perceived De Wardes, De Guiche, and the Chevalier de Lorraine, conversing together. It is true they were talking in tones so low that the sound of their words could hardly be heard in the vast apartment. To speak in that manner from any particular place without bending down, or turning round, or looking at the person with whom one may be engaged in conversation, is a talent that cannot be immediately acquired by newcomers. Long study is needed for such conversations, which, without a look, gesture, or movement of the head, seem like the conversation of a group of statues. In fact, in the king's and the queen's grand assemblies, while their majesties were speaking, and while every one present seemed to be listening in the midst of the most profound silence, some of these noiseless conversations took place, in which adulation was not the prevailing feature. But Raoul was one among others exceedingly clever in this art, so much a matter of etiquette, and from the movement of the lips he was often able to guess the sense of the words.

'Who is Montalais?' inquired De Wardes, 'and this La Vallière? What country-town have we had sent here?'

'Montalais?' said the chevalier, 'oh, I know her; she is a good sort of a girl, whom we shall find amusing enough. La Vallière is a charming girl, slightly lame.'

'Ah! bah!' said De Wardes.

'Do not be absurd, De Wardes, there are some very revealing and ingenious Latin axioms about lame ladies.'

'Gentlemen, gentlemen,' said De Guiche, looking at Raoul with uneasiness, 'be a little careful, I entreat you.'

But the uneasiness of the count, in appearance at least, was not needed. Raoul had preserved the firmest and most indifferent countenance, although he had not missed a word that passed. He seemed to keep an account of the insolence and licence of the two speakers in order to settle matters with them at the earliest opportunity.

De Wardes seemed to guess what was passing in his mind, and continued:

'Who are these young ladies' lovers?'

'Montalais's lover?' said the chevalier.

'Yes, Montalais first.'

'You, I, or De Guiche—whoever likes, in fact.'

'And the other?'

'Mademoiselle de la Vallière?'

'Yes.'

'Take care, gentlemen,' exclaimed De Guiche, anxious to put a stop to De Wardes's reply; 'take care, Madame is listening to us.'

Raoul thrust his hand up to the wrist into his doublet in great agitation. But the very malignity which he saw was excited against these poor girls made him take a serious resolution. 'Poor Louise,' he thought, 'has come here only with an honourable object in view, and under honourable protection; and I must learn what that object is which she has in view, and who it is that protects her.' And following Malicorne's manœuvre, he made his way toward the group of the maids of honour. The presentations were soon over. The king, who had done nothing but look at and admire Madame, shortly afterwards left the reception-room, accompanied by the two queens. The Chevalier de Lorraine resumed his place beside Monsieur, and, as he accompanied him, insinuated a few drops of the venom he had collected during the last hour, while looking at some of the faces in the court, and suspecting that some of their hearts might be happy. A few of the persons present followed the king as he quitted the apartment; but such of the courtiers as assumed an independence of character, and professed gallant conduct, began to approach the ladies of the court. The prince paid his compliments to Mademoiselle de Tonnay-Charente, Buckingham devoted himself to Madame Chalais and Mademoiselle de Lafayette,* whom Madame had already distinguished by her notice, and whom she held in high regard. As for the Comte de Guiche, who had abandoned Monsieur as soon as he could approach Madame alone, he conversed, with great animation, with Madame de Valentinois, and with Mesdames de Créquy and de Châtillon.*

Amid these varied political and amorous interests, Malicorne was anxious to gain Montalais's attention; but the latter preferred talking with Raoul, even if it were only to amuse herself with his innumerable questions and his astonishment. Raoul had gone directly to Mademoiselle de la Vallière, and had saluted her with the profoundest respect, at which Louise blushed, and could not say a word. Montalais, however, hurried to her assistance.

'Well, monsieur le vicomte, here we are, you see.'

'I do, indeed, see you,' said Raoul, smiling, 'and it is exactly because you are here that I wish to ask for some explanation.'

Malicorne approached the group with his most fascinating smile.

'Go away, Malicorne; really you are exceedingly indiscreet.' At this remark Malicorne bit his lips and retired a few steps, without making any reply. His smile, however, changed its expression, and from its former frankness, became mocking in its expression.

'You wished for an explanation, M. Raoul?' inquired Montalais.

'It is surely worth one, I think; Mademoiselle de la Vallière a maid of honour to Madame!'

'Why should not she be a maid of honour, as well as myself?' inquired Montalais.

'Pray, accept my compliments, young ladies,' said Raoul, who fancied he perceived they were not disposed to answer him in a direct manner.

'Your remark was not made in a very complimentary manner, vicomte.'

'Mine?'

'Certainly; I appeal to Louise.'

'M. de Bragelonne probably thinks the position is above my condition,' said Louise, hesitatingly.

'Assuredly not,' replied Raoul, eagerly; 'you know very well that such is not my feeling; were you called upon to occupy a queen's throne, I should not be surprised; how much greater reason, then, such a position as this? The only circumstance that amazes me is, that I should have learned it only to-day, and that by the merest accident.'

'That is true,' replied Montalais, with her usual giddiness; 'you know nothing about it, and there is no reason you should. M. de Bragelonne wrote several letters to you, but your mother was the only person who remained behind at Blois, and it was necessary to prevent these letters falling into her hands; I intercepted them, and returned them to M. Raoul, so that he believed you were still at Blois while you were here in Paris, and had no idea whatever, indeed, how high you had risen in rank.'

'Did you not inform M. Raoul, as I begged you to do?'

'Why should I? to give him an opportunity of making some of his severe remarks and moral reflections, and to undo what we had so much trouble in effecting? Certainly not.'

'Am I so very severe, then?' said Raoul, inquiringly.

'Besides,' said Montalais, 'it is sufficient to say that it suited me. I was about to set off for Paris—you were away; Louise was weeping her eyes out; interpret that as you please; I begged a friend, a protector of mine, who had obtained the appointment for me, to solicit one for Louise; the appointment arrived. Louise left in order to get her costume prepared; as I had my own ready, I remained behind; I received your letters, and returned them to you, adding a few words, promising you a surprise. Your surprise stands before you, monsieur, and seems to be a fair one enough; you have nothing more to ask. Come, M. Malicorne, it is now time to leave these young people together: they have many things to talk about; give me your hand; I trust that you appreciate the honour conferred upon you, M. Malicorne.'

'Forgive me,' said Raoul, detaining the giddy girl, and giving to his voice an intonation, the gravity of which contrasted with that of Montalais; 'forgive me, but may I enquire the name of the protector you speak of? For if protection be extended towards you, Mademoiselle Montalais—for which, indeed, so many reasons exist,' added Raoul, bowing, 'I do not see that the same reasons exist why Mademoiselle de la Vallière should be similarly cared for.'

'But, M. Raoul,' said Louise, innocently, 'there is no difference in the matter, and I do not see why I should not tell it you myself; it was M. Malicorne who obtained it for me.'

Raoul remained for a moment almost stunned, asking himself if they were trifling with him; he then turned round to question Malicorne, but he had been hurried away by Montalais, and was already at some distance from them. Mademoiselle de la Vallière attempted to follow her friend, but Raoul, with gentle authority, detained her.

'Louise, one word, I beg.'

'But, M. Raoul,' said Louise, blushing, 'we are alone. Everyone has left. They will become anxious, and will be looking for us.'

'Fear nothing,' said the young man, smiling, 'we are neither of us of sufficient importance for our absence to be remarked.'

'But I have my duty to perform, M. Raoul.'

'Do not be alarmed, I am acquainted with these usages of the court; you will not be on duty until to-morrow: a few minutes are at your disposal, which will enable you to give me the information I am about to have the honour to ask you for.'

'How serious you are, M. Raoul!' said Louise.

'Because the circumstances are serious. Are you listening?'

'I am listening: I would only repeat, monsieur, that we are quite alone.'

'You are right,' said Raoul, and, offering her his hand, he led the young girl into the gallery adjoining the reception-room, the windows of which looked out upon the courtyard. Everyone was hurrying towards the middle window, which had a balcony outside, from which all the details of the slow and formal preparations for departure could be seen. Raoul opened one of the side windows, and then, being alone with Louise, said to her: 'You know, Louise, that from my childhood* I have regarded you as my sister, as one who has been the confidante of all my troubles, to whom I have entrusted all my hopes.'

'Yes, M. Raoul,' she answered softly; 'yes, M. Raoul, I know that.'

'You used, on your side, to show the same friendship towards me, and had the same confidence in me; why have you not, on this occasion, been my friend—why have you shown suspicion of me?'

Mademoiselle de la Vallière did not answer. 'I fondly thought you loved me,' said Raoul, whose voice became more and more agitated; 'I fondly thought you consented to all the plans we had, together, laid down for our own happiness, at the time when we wandered up and down the walks at Cour-Cheverny,* under the avenue of poplar trees leading to Blois. You do not answer me, Louise. Is it possible,' he inquired, breathing with difficulty, 'that you no longer love me?'

'I did not say so,' replied Louise, softly.

'Oh! tell me the truth, I implore you. All my hopes in life are centred in you. I chose you for your gentle and simple tastes. Do not let yourself be dazzled, Louise, now that you are in the midst of a court where all that is pure too soon becomes corrupt—where all that is young too soon grows old. Louise, close your ears, so as not to hear what may be said; shut your eyes, so as not to see the examples before you; shut your lips, that you may not inhale the corrupting influences about you. Without falsehood or subterfuge, Louise, am I to believe what Mademoiselle de Montalais said? Louise, did you come to Paris because I was no longer at Blois?'

La Vallière blushed and concealed her face in her hands.

'Yes, it was so, then!' exclaimed Raoul, delightedly; 'that was, then, your reason for coming here. I love you as I never yet loved you. Thanks, Louise, for this devotion; but measures must be taken to place you beyond all insult, to shield you from every snare. Louise, a maid of honour, in the court of a young princess in these days of free manners and inconstant affections—a maid of honour is placed as an object of attack without having any means of defence afforded her; this state of things cannot continue; you must be married in order to be respected.'

'Married?'

'Yes, here is my hand, Louise: will you place yours within it?'

'But your father?'

'My father leaves me perfectly free.'

'Yet——'

'I understand your scruples, Louise; I will consult my father.'

'Reflect, M. Raoul; wait.'

'Wait! it is impossible. To reflect, Louise, when *you* are concerned, would be insulting—give me your hand, dear Louise; I am my own master. My father will consent, I know; give me your hand, do not keep me waiting like this. One word in answer, one word only; if not, I shall begin to think that, to change you for ever, nothing more was needed than a single step in the palace, a single breath of favour, a smile from the queen, a look from the king.'

Raoul had no sooner pronounced this latter word, than La Vallière became as pale as death, no doubt from fear at seeing the young man grow angry. With a movement as rapid as thought, she placed both her hands in those of Raoul, and then fled, without adding a syllable; disappearing without casting a look behind her. Raoul felt his whole frame tremble at the contact of her hand; he received the compact as a solemn bargain wrung by affection from her child-like timidity.

XC

THE CONSENT OF ATHOS

RAOUL left the Palais Royal full of ideas that admitted no delay in execution. He mounted his horse in the courtyard, and followed the road to Blois, while the marriage festivities of Monsieur and the princess of England were being joyously celebrated by the courtiers, much to the despair of De Guiche and Buckingham. Raoul wasted no time on the road, and in sixteen hours he arrived at Blois. As he travelled along, he marshalled his arguments in the most becoming manner. Fever also is an argument that cannot be answered, and Raoul had an attack. Athos was in his study, making additions to his memoirs,* when Raoul entered, accompanied by Grimaud. Keen-sighted and shrewd, a mere glance at his son told him that something extraordinary had befallen him.

'You seem to come on a matter of importance,' said he to Raoul, after he had embraced him, pointing to a seat.

'Yes, monsieur,' replied the young man; 'and I entreat you to give me the same kind attention that has never yet failed me.'

'Speak, Raoul.'

'I present the case to you, monsieur, without preamble, for that would be unworthy of you. Mademoiselle de la Vallière is in Paris as one of Madame's maids of honour. I have pondered deeply on the matter; I love Mademoiselle de la Vallière above everything; and it is not proper to leave her in a position where her reputation, her virtue even, may be assailed. It is my wish, therefore, to marry her, monsieur, and I have come to ask for your consent to my marriage.'

While this communication was being made to him, Athos maintained the profoundest silence and reserve. Raoul, who had begun his address with an assumption of self-possession, finished it by allowing a manifest emotion to escape him at every word. Athos fixed upon Bragelonne a searching look, overshadowed indeed by a hint of regret.

'You have reflected well upon it?' he inquired.

'Yes, monsieur.'

'I believe you are already acquainted with my views respecting this alliance?'

'Yes, monsieur,' replied Raoul, in a low voice; 'but you added, that if I persisted——'

'You do persist then?'

Bragelonne stammered out an almost unintelligible assent.

'Your passion,' continued Athos, tranquilly, 'must indeed be very great, since, notwithstanding my distaste for this union, you persist in wishing it.'

Raoul passed his trembling hand across his forehead to remove the perspiration that collected there. Athos looked at him, and his heart was touched by pity. He rose and said,

'It is no matter. My own personal feelings are not to be taken into consideration since yours are concerned; you need my assistance; I am ready to give it. Tell me what you want.'

'Your kind indulgence, first of all, monsieur,' said Raoul, taking hold of his hand.

'You have mistaken my feelings, Raoul, I have more than mere indulgence for you in my heart.'

Raoul kissed as devotedly as a lover could have done the hand he held in his own.

'Come, come,' said Athos, 'I am quite ready; what do you wish me to sign?'

'Nothing whatever, monsieur, only it would be very kind if you would take the trouble to write to the king, to whom I belong, and solicit his majesty's permission for me to marry Mademoiselle de la Vallière.'

'Well thought, Raoul! After, or rather before myself, you have a master to consult, that master being the king; it is loyal in you to submit yourself voluntarily to this double proof; I will grant your request without delay, Raoul.'

The count approached the window, and, leaning out, called to Grimaud, who showed his head from an arbour covered with jasmine, which he was occupied in trimming.

'My horses, Grimaud,' continued the count.

'Why this order, monsieur?' inquired Raoul.

'We shall set off in a few hours.'

'Where?'

'For Paris.'

'Paris, monsieur?'

'Is not the king at Paris?'

'Certainly.'

'Well, ought we not to go there?'

'Yes, monsieur,' said Raoul, almost alarmed by this kindness. 'I do not ask you to put yourself to such inconvenience, and a letter merely——'

'You mistake my position, Raoul; it is not respectful that a simple gentleman, such as I am, should write to his sovereign. I wish to speak, I ought to speak, to the king, and I will do so. We will go together, Raoul.'

'You overpower me with your kindness, monsieur.'

'How do you think his majesty is inclined?'

'Towards me, monsieur?'

'Yes.'

'Excellently well disposed.'

'His majesty told you so?' continued the count.

'With his own lips.'

'On what occasion?'

'Upon the recommendation of M. d'Artagnan, I believe, and on account of an affair in the Place de Grève, when I had the honour to draw my sword in the king's service. I have reason to believe that, vanity apart, I stand well with his majesty.'

'So much the better.'

'But I entreat you, monsieur,' pursued Raoul, 'not to maintain towards me your present grave and serious manner. Do not make me bitterly regret having heeded feelings stronger than anything else.'

'That is the second time you have said so, Raoul; it was quite unnecessary; you require my formal consent, and you have it. We need say no more on the subject, therefore. Come and see my new plantations, Raoul.'

The young man knew very well that, after the expression of his father's wish, no opportunity of discussion was left him. He bowed his head, and followed his father into the garden. Athos unhurriedly pointed out to him the grafts, the cuttings, and the avenues he was planting. This perfect repose of manner disconcerted Raoul extremely; the affection with which his own heart was filled seemed so great that the whole world could hardly contain it. How, then, could his father's heart remain void, and closed to its influence? Bragelonne, therefore, collecting all his courage, suddenly exclaimed,

'It is impossible, monsieur, you can have any reason to reject Mademoiselle de la Vallière! In Heaven's name, she is so good, so gentle and pure, that your mind, so shrewd in its insights, ought to value her accordingly. Does any secret repugnance, or any hereditary conflict, exist between you and her family?'

'Look, Raoul, at that beautiful lily of the valley,' said Athos;

'observe how the shade and the damp situation suit it, particularly the shadow which that sycamore-tree casts over it, so that the warmth, and not the blazing heat of the sun, filters through its leaves.'

Raoul stopped, bit his lips, and then, with the blood mantling in his face, he said, courageously, 'One word of explanation, I beg, monsieur. You cannot forget that your son is a man.'

'In that case,' replied Athos, drawing himself up with sternness, 'prove to me that you are a man, for you do not show yourself a son. I begged you to wait the opportunity of forming an illustrious alliance. I would have obtained a wife for you from the first ranks of the rich nobility. I wish you to be distinguished by the splendour which glory and fortune confer, for nobility of descent you have already.'

'Monsieur,' exclaimed Raoul, carried away by a first impulse. 'I was reproached the other day for not knowing who my mother was.'

Athos turned pale; then, knitting his brows like the greatest of all the heathen deities: 'I am waiting to learn the reply you made,' he demanded, in an imperious manner.

'Forgive me! oh, forgive me,' murmured the young man, sinking at once from the lofty tone he had assumed.

'What is your reply, monsieur?' inquired the count, stamping his feet upon the ground.

'Monsieur, my sword was in my hand immediately, my adversary placed himself on guard, I struck his sword over the palisade, and threw him after it.'

'Why did you suffer him to live?'

'The king has prohibited duelling, and, at that moment, I was an ambassador of the king.'

'Very well,' said Athos, 'but all the more reason why I should see his majesty.'

'What do you intend to ask him?'

'Authority to draw my sword against the man who has inflicted this injury upon me.'

'If I did not act as I ought to have done, I beg you to forgive me.'

'Did I reproach you, Raoul?'

'Still, the permission you are going to ask from the king?'

'I will implore his majesty to sign your marriage-contract, but on one condition.'

'Are conditions necessary with me, monsieur? Command, and you shall be obeyed.'

'On one condition, I repeat,' continued Athos; 'that you tell me the name of the man who spoke of your mother in that way.'

'What need is there that you should know his name? The offence was directed against myself, and the permission once obtained from his majesty, to revenge it is my affair.'

'Tell me his name, monsieur.'

'I will not allow you to expose yourself.'

'Do you take me for a Don Diego?* His name, I say.'

'You insist upon it?'

'I demand it.'

'The Vicomte de Wardes.'

'Very well,' said Athos, tranquilly, 'I know him. But our horses are ready, I see; and, instead of delaying our departure for a couple of hours, we will set off at once. Come, monsieur.'

XCI

MONSIEUR BECOMES JEALOUS OF THE DUKE OF BUCKINGHAM

WHILE the Comte de la Fère was proceeding on his way to Paris, accompanied by Raoul, the Palais Royal was the theatre wherein a scene of what Molière would have called excellent comedy, was being performed. Four days had elapsed since his marriage, and Monsieur, having breakfasted very hurriedly, passed into his antechamber, scowling and out of temper. The repast had not been over-agreeable.* Madame had had breakfast served in her own apartment, and Monsieur had breakfasted almost alone: the Chevalier de Lorraine and Manicamp were the only persons present at the meal, which lasted three-quarters of an hour without a single syllable having been uttered. Manicamp, who was less intimate with his royal highness than the Chevalier de Lorraine, vainly endeavoured to detect, from the expression of the prince's face, what had made him so ill-humoured. The

Chevalier de Lorraine, who had no occasion to speculate about anything, inasmuch as he knew everything, ate his breakfast with that extraordinary appetite which the troubles of one's friends only stimulates, and enjoyed at the same time both Monsieur's ill-humour and the vexation of Manicamp. He seemed delighted, while he went on eating, to detain the prince, who was very impatient to move, still at table. Monsieur at times repented the power which he had permitted the Chevalier de Lorraine to acquire over him, and which exempted the latter from any observance of etiquette towards him. Monsieur was now in one of those moods, but he feared as much as he liked the chevalier, and contented himself with nursing his anger without showing it. Every now and then Monsieur raised his eyes to the ceiling, then lowered them towards the slices of pâté which the chevalier was attacking, and finally, not wishing to betray his resentment, he gesticulated in a manner which Harlequin might have envied. At last, however, Monsieur could control himself no longer, and at the dessert, rising from the table in excessive wrath, as we have related, he left the Chevalier de Lorraine to finish his breakfast as he pleased. Seeing Monsieur rise from the table, Manicamp, napkin in hand, rose also. Monsieur ran rather than walked, towards the antechamber, where, finding an usher in attendance, he gave him whispered instructions. Then, turning back again, but avoiding passing through the breakfast apartment, he crossed several rooms, with the intention of seeking the queen-mother in her oratory, where she usually spent the day.

It was about ten o'clock in the morning. Anne of Austria was engaged in writing as Monsieur entered. The queen-mother was extremely attached to her son, for he was handsome in person and amiable in disposition. He was, in fact, more affectionate, and it might be, more effeminate than the king. He pleased his mother by those trifling sympathizing attentions all women are glad to receive. Anne of Austria, who would have been rejoiced to have had a daughter, almost found in this, her favourite son, the attentions, solicitude, and playful manners of a child of twelve years of age. All the time he spent with his mother he employed in admiring her arms, in giving his opinion upon her cosmetics, and recipes for compounding essences, in which she was very particular: and then, too, he kissed her hands and cheeks in the most childlike and loving way, and had always some sweetmeats to offer her, or some new fashion to recommend. Anne of Austria loved the king, or rather the regal power in her eldest son; Louis XIV represented legitimacy by divine right.* With the king, her character was that of the queen-mother, with Philip she was simply a mother. He knew that, of all places of refuge, a mother's heart is the most compassionate and surest. When still a child, he always fled there for refuge when he and his brother quarrelled, sometimes when he had struck him, which constituted the crime of high treason on his part, after certain engagements with hands and nails, in which the king and his rebellious subject indulged in their night-shirts over the right to a disputed bed, having their servant Laporte as umpire—Philip, having won, but terrified by his victory, used to flee to his mother to obtain reinforcements from her, or at least the assurance of forgiveness, which Louis XIV granted with difficulty, and after an interval. Anne, from this habit of peaceable intervention, succeeded in arranging the disagreements between her sons, and in sharing, at the same time, all their secrets. The king, jealous of that maternal solicitude which was bestowed particularly upon his brother, felt disposed to show towards Anne of Austria more submission and attachment than his character really dictated. Anne of Austria had adopted this line of conduct especially towards the young queen. In this manner she ruled with almost despotic sway over the royal household, and she was already preparing her batteries to govern with the same absolute authority the household of her second son. Anne experienced a feeling of pride whenever she saw anyone enter her apartment with a tragic face, pale cheeks, or red eyes, gathering from appearances that assistance was required either by the weakest or the most rebellious. She was writing, we have said, when Monsieur entered her oratory, not with red eyes or pale cheeks, but restless, out of temper, and angry. With an absent air he kissed his mother's hands, and sat himself down before receiving her permission to do so. Considering the strict rules of etiquette established at the court of Anne of Austria, this neglect of customary civilities was a sign of preoccupation, especially on Philip's part, who, of his own

accord, observed a respect towards her of a rather exaggerated
character. If, therefore, he so strikingly failed in this regard,
there must be a serious cause for it.

'What is the matter, Philip?' inquired Anne of Austria, turning towards her son.

'A good many things,' murmured the prince, in a doleful
voice.

'You look like a man who has a great deal to do,' said the
queen, laying down her pen. Philip frowned, but did not reply.
'Among the various subjects which occupy your mind,' said
Anne of Austria, 'there must surely be one that absorbs it more
than others.'

'One indeed has occupied me more than any other.'

'Well, what is it? I am listening.'

Philip opened his mouth as if to express all the troubles his
mind was filled with, and which he seemed to be waiting only
for an opportunity of declaring. But he suddenly became silent,
and a sigh alone expressed all that his heart was overflowing
with.

'Come, Philip, show a little firmness,' said the queen-mother.
'When one has to complain of anything, it is generally an individual who is the cause of it. Am I not right?'

'I do not say no, madame.'

'Whom do you wish to speak about? Come, take courage.'

'In fact, madame, what I might possibly have to say must be
kept a profound secret; for when a lady is involved——'

'Ah! you are speaking of Madame, then?' inquired the queen-
mother, with a feeling of the liveliest curiosity.

'Yes.'

'Well, then, if you wish to speak of Madame, do not hesitate
to do so. I am your mother, and she is a stranger to me. Yet, as
she is my daughter-in-law, rest assured I shall be interested,
even were it for your own sake alone, in hearing all you may
have to say about her.'

'Pray tell me, madame, in your turn, whether you have not
noticed anything?'

'Noticed anything? Philip? Your words almost frighten me,
from their want of meaning. What do you mean: anything?'

'Madame is pretty, certainly.'

'No doubt of it.'

'Yet not altogether beautiful.'

'No, but as she grows older, she will probably become strikingly beautiful. You must have noticed the change which a few years have already made in her. Her beauty will improve more and more; she is now only sixteen years of age.* At fifteen I was, myself, very thin; but even as she is at present, Madame is very pretty.'

'And consequently others have noticed it.'

'Undoubtedly, for a woman of ordinary rank is noticed—and with still greater reason a princess.'

'She has been well brought up, I imagine?'

'Madame Henriette, her mother, is a woman rather cold in manner, slightly pretentious, but full of noble thoughts. The princess's education may have been neglected, but her principles, I believe, are good. Such at least was the opinion I formed of her when she resided in France; but she afterwards returned to England, and I am ignorant of what may have occurred there.'

'What do you mean?'

'Simply that there are some heads naturally giddy, which are easily turned by good fortune.'

'That is the very word, madame. I think the princess rather giddy.'

'We must not exaggerate, Philip; she is clever and witty, and has a certain coquetry very natural in a young woman; but this defect in persons of high rank and position, is a great advantage at a court. A princess with a hint of coquetry usually forms a brilliant court around her; her smile stimulates emulation, arouses wit, and even courage; the nobles, too, fight better for a prince whose wife is beautiful.'

'Thank you extremely, madame,' said Philip, with some temper; 'you really have drawn some very alarming pictures for me.'

'In what way?' asked the queen, with pretended simplicity.

'You know, madame,' said Philip, dolefully, 'whether I had or had not a very great dislike to getting married.'

'Now, indeed, you alarm me. You have some serious cause of complaint against Madame.'

'I do not say it is serious exactly.'

'In that case, then, throw aside your doleful looks. If you

show yourself to others in your present state, people will take
you for a very unhappy husband.'

'The fact is,' replied Philip, 'I am not altogether satisfied as a
husband, and I shall not be sorry if others know it.'

'For shame, Philip.'

'Well, then, madame, I will tell you frankly that I do not
understand the life I am required to lead.'

'Explain yourself.'

'My wife does not seem to belong to me; she is always leaving
me for some reason or another. In the mornings there are visits,
correspondence, and clothes; in the evenings, balls and concerts.'

'You are jealous, Philip.'

'I! Heaven forbid. Let others act the part of a jealous husband, not I. But I *am* angry.'

'All these things you reproach your wife with are perfectly
innocent, and, so long as you have nothing of greater importance——'

'Yet, listen; without being very blamable, a woman can excite
a good deal of uneasiness. Certain visitors may be received,
certain preferences shown, which expose young women to remark, and which are enough to drive out of their senses even
those husbands who are least disposed to be jealous.'

'Ah! now we are coming to the real point at last, and not
without some difficulty. You speak of frequent visits, and certain preferences—very good; for the last hour we have been
beating about the bush, and at last you have broached the true
question.'

'Well then, yes——'

'This is more serious than I thought. It is possible, then, that
Madame can have given you grounds for these complaints against
her?'

'Precisely so.'

'What, your wife, married only four days ago, prefers some
other person to yourself! Take care, Philip, you exaggerate your
grievances; in wishing to prove everything, you prove nothing.'

The prince, bewildered by his mother's serious manner, wished
to reply, but he could only stammer out unintelligible words.

'You take it back, then?' said Anne of Austria. 'I prefer it, as
it is an acknowledgment of your error.'

'No!' exclaimed Philip, 'I do not take it back, and I will prove all I asserted. I spoke of preference and of visits, did I not? Well, listen.'

Anne of Austria prepared herself to listen, with that love of gossip which the best woman living and the best mother, were she a queen even, always finds in being drawn into the petty squabbles of a household.

'Well,' said Philip, 'tell me one thing.'

'What is that?'

'Why does my wife retain an English court about her?' said Philip, as he crossed his arms and looked his mother steadily in the face, as if he were convinced that she could not answer the question.

'For a very simple reason,' returned Anne of Austria; 'because the English are her countrymen, because they have expended large sums in order to accompany her to France, and because it would be hardly polite—not politic certainly—to dismiss abruptly those members of the English nobility who have not shrunk from any devotion or from any sacrifice.'

'A wonderful sacrifice indeed,' returned Philip, 'to desert a wretched country to come to a beautiful one, where a greater effect can be produced for a guinea than can be procured elsewhere for four! Extraordinary devotion, really, to travel a hundred leagues in company with a woman one is in love with?'

'In love, Philip! think what you are saying. Who is in love with Madame?'

'The Duke of Buckingham. Perhaps you will defend him, too?'

Anne of Austria blushed and smiled at the same time. The name of the Duke of Buckingham recalled certain recollections of a very tender and melancholy nature.* 'The Duke of Buckingham?' she murmured.

'Yes; one of those armchair soldiers——'

'The Buckinghams are loyal and brave,' said Anne of Austria, courageously.

'This is too much; my own mother takes the part of my wife's lover against me,' exclaimed Philip, incensed to such an extent that his weak character was affected almost to tears.

'Philip, my son,' exclaimed Anne of Austria, 'such an expression is unworthy of you. Your wife has no lover; and, had she one, it would not be the Duke of Buckingham. The members of that family, I repeat, are loyal and discreet, and the rights of hospitality are sure to be respected by them.'

'The Duke of Buckingham is an Englishman, madame,' said Philip, 'and may I ask if the English so very religiously respect what belongs to princes of France?'

Anne blushed a second time, and turned aside under the pretext of taking her pen from her desk again, but in reality to conceal her confusion from her son. 'Really, Philip,' she said, 'you seem to discover expressions for the purpose of hurting me, and your anger blinds you while it alarms me; reflect a little.'

'There is no need for reflection, madame. I can see with my own eyes.'

'Well, and what do you see?'

'That Buckingham never quits my wife. He presumes to make presents to her, and she ventures to accept them. Yesterday she was talking about violet-scented sachets; well, our French perfumers, as you know very well, madame, for you have over and over again asked for it without success—our French perfumers, I say, have never been able to procure this scent.* The duke, however, wore about him a sachet which smelled of violets, and I am sure that the one my wife has came from him.'

'Indeed, monsieur,' said Anne of Austria, 'you build your pyramids on needle points; be careful. What harm, I ask you, can there be in a man giving to his countrywoman a recipe for a new fragrance? These strange ideas, I protest, painfully recall your father to me; he who so frequently and so unjustly made me suffer.'*

'The Duke of Buckingham's father was probably more reserved and more respectful than his son,' said Philip, thoughtlessly, not perceiving how deeply he had wounded his mother's feelings. The queen turned pale, and pressed her clenched hands upon her bosom; but, recovering herself immediately, she said, 'You came here with some intention or another, I suppose?'

'Certainly.'

'What was it?'

'I came, madame, intending to complain energetically, and to inform you that I will not submit to such behaviour from the Duke of Buckingham.'

'What do you intend to do, then?'

'I shall complain to the king.'

'And what do you expect the king to reply?'

'So be it,' said Monsieur, with an expression of stern determination on his countenance, which offered a singular contrast to its usual gentleness. 'Very well. I will defend myself!'

'What do you call defending yourself?' inquired Anne of Austria, in alarm.

'I will have the Duke of Buckingham leave the princess, I will have him leave France, and I will see that my wishes are intimated to him.'

'You will intimate nothing of the kind, Philip,' said the queen, 'for if you act in that manner, and violate hospitality to that extent, I will invoke the severity of the king against you.'

'Do you threaten me, madame?' exclaimed Philip, almost in tears; 'do you threaten me in the midst of my grievances?'

'I do not threaten you; I only place an obstacle in the path of your hasty anger. I maintain, that, to adopt towards the Duke of Buckingham, or any other Englishman, any rigorous measure— to take even a discourteous step towards him, would be to plunge France and England into the most disastrous quarrel. Can it be possible that a prince of the blood, the brother of the king of France, does not know how to hide an injury, even did it exist in reality, where political necessity requires it?' Philip made a movement. 'Besides,' continued the queen, 'the injury is neither true nor possible, and it is merely a matter of foolish jealousy.'

'Madame, I know what I know.'

'Whatever you may know, I can only advise you to be patient.'

'I am not patient by disposition, madame.'

The queen rose, full of severity, and with an icy ceremonious manner. 'Explain what you really require, monsieur,' she said.

'I do not require anything, madame; I simply express what I desire. If the Duke of Buckingham does not, of his own accord, discontinue his visits to my apartments I shall forbid him entrance.'

'That is a point you will refer to the king,' said Anne of Austria, her heart swelling as she spoke, and her voice trembling with emotion.

'But, madame,' exclaimed Philip, striking his hands together, 'act as my mother and not as the queen, since I speak to you as a son; it is simply a matter of a few minutes' conversation between the duke and myself.'

'It is that very conversation I forbid,' said the queen, resuming her authority, 'because it is unworthy of you.'

'Be it so; I will not appear in the matter, but I shall intimate my will to Madame.'

'Oh!' said the queen-mother, with a melancholy arising from reflection, 'never tyrannize over a wife—never behave too haughtily or imperiously towards her. A woman unwillingly convinced is unconvinced.'

'What is to be done, then?—I will consult my friends about it.'

'Yes, your double-dealing advisers, your Chevalier de Lorraine—your De Wardes. Entrust the conduct of this affair to me. You wish the Duke of Buckingham to leave, do you not?'

'As soon as possible, madame.'

'Send the duke to me, then; smile upon your wife, behave to her, to the king, to every one, as usual. But follow no advice but mine. Alas! I too well know what any household comes to, that is troubled by advisers.'

'You shall be obeyed, madame.'

'And you will be satisfied at the result. Send the duke to me.'

'That will not be difficult.'

'Where do you suppose him to be?'

'At my wife's door, whose *levée* he is probably awaiting.'

'Very well,' said Anne of Austria, calmly. 'Be good enough to tell the duke, that I shall be charmed if he would call on me.'

Philip kissed his mother's hand, and set out to find the Duke of Buckingham.

XCII

FOR EVER!

THE Duke of Buckingham, obedient to the queen-mother's invitation, presented himself in her apartments half an hour after the departure of the Duc d'Orléans. When his name was announced by the gentleman-usher in attendance, the queen, who was sitting with her elbow resting on a table, and her head buried in her hands, rose, and smilingly received the graceful and respectful salutation which the duke addressed to her. Anne of Austria was still beautiful. It is well known that at her then somewhat advanced age,* her long auburn hair, perfectly formed hands, and bright ruby lips, were still the admiration of all who saw her. On the present occasion, abandoned entirely to a memory which evoked all the past in her heart, she looked almost as beautiful as in the days of her youth, when her palace was open to the visits of the Duke of Buckingham's father, then a young and impassioned man, as well as an unfortunate prince, who lived for her alone, and died with her name upon his lips.* Anne of Austria fixed upon Buckingham a look so tender in its expression, that it denoted, not only the indulgence of maternal affection, but a gentleness of expression like the coquetry of a woman who loves.

'Your majesty,' said Buckingham, respectfully, 'desired to speak to me.'

'Yes, duke,' said the queen, in English; 'will you be good enough to sit down?'

The favour which Anne of Austria thus extended to the young man, and the welcome sound of the language of a country from which the duke had been estranged since his stay in France, deeply affected him. He immediately conjectured that the queen had a request to make of him. After having abandoned the few first moments to the irrepressible emotions he experienced, the queen resumed the smiling air with which she had received him. 'What do you think of France?' she said, in French.

'It is a lovely country, madame,' replied the duke.

'Had you ever seen it before?'

'Once only, madame.'

'But, like all true Englishmen, you prefer England?'

'I prefer my own native land to France,' replied the duke; 'but if your majesty were to ask me which of the two cities, London or Paris, I should prefer as a residence, I should be forced to answer, Paris.'

Anne of Austria observed the ardent manner with which these words had been pronounced. 'I am told, my lord, you have rich possessions in your own country, and that you live in a splendid and time-honoured palace.'

'It was my father's residence,' replied Buckingham, casting down his eyes.

'Those are indeed great advantages, and they are also precious memories,' replied the queen, alluding, in spite of herself, to recollections from which it is impossible voluntarily to detach oneself.

'In fact,' said the duke, yielding to the melancholy influence of this opening conversation, 'sensitive persons live as much in the past or the future, as in the present.'

'That is very true,' said the queen, in a low tone of voice. 'It follows, then, my lord,' she added, 'that you, who are a man of feeling, will soon leave France in order to shut yourself up with your wealth and your relics of the past.'

Buckingham raised his head and said, 'I think not, madame.'

'What do you mean?'

'On the contrary, I think of leaving England in order to take up my residence in France.'

It was now Anne of Austria's turn to show surprise. 'Why?' she said. 'Are you not in favour with the new king?'

'Perfectly so, madame, for his majesty's kindness to me is unbounded.'

'It cannot,' said the queen, 'be because your fortune has diminished, for it is said to be enormous.'

'My income, madame, has never been so large.'

'There is some secret cause, then?'

'No, madame,' said Buckingham, eagerly, 'there is nothing secret in my reason for this determination. I prefer residence in France; I like a court so distinguished by its refinement and courtesy; I like the amusements, somewhat serious in their nature, which are not the amusements of my own country, but are met with in France.'

Anne of Austria smiled shrewdly. 'Amusements of a serious nature?' she said. 'Has your grace well reflected on their seriousness?' The duke hesitated. 'There is no amusement so serious,' continued the queen, 'as to prevent a man of your rank——'

'Your majesty seems to insist greatly on that point,' interrupted the duke.

'Do you think so, my lord?'

'If you will forgive me for saying so, it is the second time you have vaunted the attractions of England at the expense of the delight which all experience who live in France.'

Anne of Austria approached the young man, and placing her beautiful hand upon his shoulder, which trembled at the touch, said, 'Believe me, monsieur, nothing can equal living in one's own native country. I have very frequently had occasion to regret Spain. I have lived long, my lord, very long for a woman, and I confess to you, that not a year has passed I have not regretted Spain.'

'Not one year, madame?' said the young duke, coldly, 'Not one of those years when you reigned Queen of Beauty—as you still are, indeed?'

'A truce to flattery, duke, for I am old enough to be your mother.' She emphasized these latter words in a manner, and with a gentleness, which penetrated Buckingham's heart. 'Yes,' she said, 'I am old enough to be your mother; and for that reason, I will give you a word of advice.'

'That advice being that I should return to London?' he exclaimed.

'Yes, my lord.'

The duke clasped his hands with a gesture of alarm, which did not fail to produce its effect upon the queen, already disposed to softer feelings by the tenderness of her own recollections. 'It must be so,' she added.

'What!' he again exclaimed, 'am I seriously told that I must leave—that I must exile myself—that I am to flee at once?'

'Exile yourself, did you say? One would fancy France was your native country.'

'Madame, the country of those who love is the country of those whom they love.'

'Not another word, my lord; you forget to whom you speak.'

Buckingham threw himself on his knees. 'Madame, you are the source of intelligence, of goodness, and of compassion; you are the first person in this kingdom, not only by your rank, but the first person in the world on account of your angelic nature. I have said nothing, madame. Have I, indeed, said anything you should answer with such a cruel remark? What have I betrayed?'

'You have betrayed yourself,' said the queen, in a low tone of voice.

'I have said nothing—I know nothing.'

'You forget you have spoken and thought in the presence of a woman; and besides——'

'Besides,' said the duke, 'no one knows you are listening to me.'

'On the contrary, it is known; you have all the faults and all the qualities of youth.'

'I have been betrayed or denounced, then?'

'By whom?'

'By those infernally sharp-eyed observers at Le Havre who read my heart like an open book.'

'I do not know whom you mean.'

'M. de Bragelonne, for instance.'

'I know the name without being acquainted with the person to whom it belongs. M. de Bragelonne has said nothing.'

'Who can it be, then? If any one, madame, had had the boldness to notice in me that which I do not myself wish to see——'

'What would you do, duke?'

'There are secrets which kill those who discover them.'

'He, then, who has discovered your secret, madman that you are, still lives: and, what is more, you will not slay him, for he is armed on all sides—he is a husband, a jealous man—he is the second gentleman in France—he is my son, the Duc d'Orléans.'

The duke turned pale as death. 'You are very cruel, madame,' he said.

'You see, Buckingham,' said Anne of Austria, sadly, 'how you pass from one extreme to another, and fight with shadows, when it would seem so easy to remain at peace with yourself.'

'If we fight, madame, we die on the field of battle,' replied the young man, gently, abandoning himself to the blackest gloom.

Anne ran towards him and took him by the hand. 'Villiers,' she said, in English, with a vehemence of tone which nothing could resist, 'what is it you ask? Do you ask a mother to sacrifice her son: a queen to consent to the dishonour of her house? Child that you are, do not dream of it. What! in order to spare your tears am I to commit these crimes? Villiers! you speak of the dead; the dead, at least, were full of respect and submission; they resigned themselves to an order of exile; they carried their despair away with them in their hearts, like a priceless possession, because their despair was caused by the woman they loved, and because death, that promise of peace, was like a gift or a favour conferred upon them.'

Buckingham rose, his features distorted, and his hands pressed against his heart. 'You are right, madame,' he said, 'but those of whom you speak had received their order of exile from the lips of the one whom they loved; they were not driven away; they were entreated to leave, and were not mocked.'

'No,' murmured Anne of Austria, 'they were not forgotten. But who says you are driven away, or that you are exiled? Who says that your devotion will not be remembered? I do not speak on any one's behalf but my own, when I tell you to leave. Do me this kindness—grant me this favour; let me, for this also, be indebted to one of your name.'

'It is for your sake, then, madame?'

'For mine alone.'

'No one whom I shall leave behind me will venture to mock—no prince even who shall say, "I required it." '

'Listen to me, duke,' and hereupon the dignified features of the queen assumed a solemn expression. 'I swear to you that no one commands in this matter but myself. I swear to you that, not only shall no one either laugh or boast in any way, but no one even shall fail in the respect due to your rank. Rely upon me, duke, as I rely upon you.'

'You do not explain yourself, madame; my heart is full of bitterness, and I am in utter despair; no consolation, however gentle and affectionate, can afford me relief.'

'Do you remember your mother,* duke?' replied the queen, with a winning smile.

'Very slightly, madame; yet I remember how she used to cover me with her caresses and her tears whenever I wept.'

'Villiers,' murmured the queen, passing her arm round the young man's neck, 'look upon me as your mother, and believe that no one shall ever make my son weep.'

'I thank you, madame,' said the young man, affected and

almost choked by his emotion; 'I feel there is indeed still room in my heart for a gentler and nobler sentiment than love.'

The queen-mother looked at him and pressed his hand. 'Go,' she said.

'When must I leave? Command me.'

'At any time that may suit you, my lord,' resumed the queen; 'you will choose your own day of departure. Instead, however, of setting off to-day, as you would doubtless wish to do, or to-morrow, as others may have expected, leave the day after to-morrow, in the evening; but announce to-day that it is your wish to leave.'

'My wish?' murmured the young duke.

'Yes, duke.'

'And shall I never return to France?'

Anne of Austria reflected for a moment, seemingly absorbed in sad and serious thought. 'It would be a consolation for me,' she said, 'if you were to return on the day when I shall be carried to my final resting-place at Saint-Denis beside the king,* my husband.'

'Who made you suffer so much!' said Buckingham.

'Who was king of France,' replied the queen.

'Madame, you are goodness itself; the tide of prosperity is setting in on you; your cup brims over with happiness, and many long years are yet before you.'

'In that case you will not come for some time, then,' said the queen, endeavouring to smile.

'I shall not return,' said Buckingham, 'young as I am. Death does not reckon by years; it is impartial; some die young, some reach old age.'

'I will not harbour any sorrowful ideas, duke. Let me comfort you; return in two years. I perceive from your face that the very idea which saddens you so much now, will have disappeared before six months have passed, and will be not only dead but forgotten in the period of absence I have assigned you.'

'I think you judged me better a little while ago, madame,' replied the young man, 'when you said that time is powerless against members of the family of Buckingham.'

'Silence,' said the queen, kissing the duke upon the forehead with an affection she could not restrain. 'Go, go; spare me and forget yourself no longer. I am the queen; you are the subject of the king of England; King Charles awaits your return. Adieu, Villiers—farewell.'

'For ever!' replied the young man, and he fled, trying to master his emotion.

Anne leaned her head upon her hands, and then looking at herself in the glass, murmured, 'It has been truly said, that a woman who has truly loved is always young, and that the bloom of the girl she was at twenty ever lies concealed in some secret cloister of her heart.'

[The story continues in *Louise de la Vallière*]

LIST OF HISTORICAL CHARACTERS

ANCRE: see Concini.

ANJOU: see Orléans.

ANNE OF AUSTRIA: Anne of Austria (1601–66), daughter of Philip III of Spain and a member of the Spanish Habsburg family, married Louis XIII in 1615. She remained aloof from the intrigues of Marie de' Medici, the Queen Regent, but actively opposed Richelieu, who set out to destroy Austro-Spanish influence on French policy. She was loyally supported by her 'Spanish entourage', the members of which were steadily eliminated by Richelieu. After Louis's death in 1643, she ruled as Regent during the minority of Louis XIV, working closely with Mazarin, who was almost certainly her lover and possibly her husband. With his help, she defended the interests of the Crown during both the Parliamentary and Aristocratic phases of the Fronde (1648–53). Thereafter she played a lesser political role, and her influence over Louis declined after he took personal control of government after 1661. She died of breast cancer in 1666.

D'AUBIGNÉ: Agrippa d'Aubigné (1552–1630), soldier and diplomat in the Protestant cause, historian and poet. Grandfather of Françoise, the future Madame de Maintenon.

BASSOMPIERRE: François de Bassompierre (1579–1646), Marshal of France, For intriguing against Richelieu, he was consigned to the Bastille in 1631, where he remained until the cardinal's death in 1642.

BEAUFORT: François de Vendôme (1616–69), Duc de Beaufort, grandson of Henri IV and his mistress Gabrielle d'Estrées. Jailed at Vincennes in 1643 for plotting with Madame de Chevreuse against Mazarin, he escaped on Whit Sunday 1648. For his role in the defence of Paris against the *parlement*'s forces under Condé he was acknowledged by the people as 'King of Les Halles'. In 1653 he made his peace with the king, and later served with honour in the Mediterranean, where he died at the siege of Candia.

BELLEGARDE: Roger de Saint-Lary et de Termes (1562–1646), Duc de Bellegarde, Governor of Burgundy.

BELLIÈRE: see Plessis-Bellière.

BERNOUIN: first *valet de chambre* to Mazarin.

BOILEAU: Nicolas Boileau-Despréaux (1636–1711), poet, critic, and principal theorist of French classicism.

BRÉGY: Charlotte Saumaize de Chazan (1618–93) was named one of Anne of Austria's ladies-in-waiting on her marriage to the Comte de Brégy in 1637.

BRÉGY: Nicolas de Flesselles, Comte de Brégy, privy councillor and diplomat: he was ambassador to Portugal and Sweden (1644–8) and then to Holland. In the 1650s he served in the French army in Piedmont. His long-suffering wife developed a distaste for marriage which became part of the 'preciosity' movement. It was said that she was loved by Mazarin. She sued for separation, but after an interminable series of lawsuits she was ordered to return to her husband in 1659. A man of no morals and considerable self-importance, Brégy was well known for his boasting and bravado.

BRETEUIL: Louis Le Tonnelier de Breteuil (1609–85) held a number of offices before becoming Intendant of Paris in 1653. He was later appointed controller of finances with Le Tellier (q.v.) and Hervart (q.v.). He was named privy councillor in 1666 when Colbert became Controller-General.

BRIENNE: Henri-Auguste de Loménie (1595–1666), Comte de Brienne. An experienced diplomat, he was appointed by Mazarin in 1643 as secretary of state at the Foreign Office. He sold his office to Hugues de Lionne in 1663.

BRIENNE: Louis-Henri de Loménie (1635–98), Comte de Brienne, son of Henri-Auguste. He had entered the Foreign Office in 1651 through the influence of his father: the same year he became a secretary of state. In 1663 Louis XIV requested his resignation. His *Mémoires*, first published in 1720 and reissued in 1828 and 1838, were one of Dumas's sources of information on the background to the period.

BUCKINGHAM: George Villiers (1592–1628), first Duke of Buckingham. *The Three Musketeers* chronicles, in exaggeratedly romantic terms, the course of the impossible, requited love he felt for Anne of Austria. A favourite of Charles I, he acquired great wealth and popularity, and he wielded enormous political power, not always wisely.

BUCKINGHAM: George Villiers (1627–87), second Duke of Buckingham, was, after the assassination of his father, brought up with the children of Charles I. During the civil war, he lost his estates, fought at Worcester with Charles, emigrated, and returned secretly to marry the daughter of Thomas Fairfax, to whom his estates had been given. They were returned to him after the Restoration, and for 25 years he was the wildest of the rakes at court. He had his father's charm and unpredictability but not his effectiveness. Thus, when Charles crossed from Scotland into England in 1651 on his way to defeat at Worcester,

Buckingham, though very inexperienced, demanded command of the army. When Charles refused, he sulked and refused to change his shirt. As one of the rakes in the entourage of Charles II, he was unpredictable, inflammable, and bisexual. Though he continued to exert great influence on the king, his excesses and intrigues led him to see the inside of the Tower on four occasions.

CATHERINE DE' MEDICI: Catherine de' Medici (1519–89), queen of Henri II.

CHALAIS: Anne-Marie de la Trémouille (1642–1722), Mme de Chalais, daughter of the Duc de Noirmoutiers. Sometime mistress of the Comte de Guiche (q.v.).

CHALAIS: Henri de Talleyrand (1599–1626), Comte de Chalais, plotted with Madame de Chevreuse against the life of Richelieu. He failed, and in August 1626 was beheaded, not by the regular executioner but by an unskilled volunteer who required thirty attempts to complete his task.

CHARLES I: Charles Stuart (1600–49), King of England, was executed at Whitehall on 30 January 1649.

CHARLES II: Charles Stuart (1630–85) fled to France in 1646 by way of Scilly and Jersey. He remained on the Continent but, after the death of his father, accepted the terms of the Scottish commissioners and returned to Scotland, where he was crowned at Scone in January 1651. He marched on England, was routed by Cromwell at Worcester on 3 September 1651, and, after six perilous weeks as a fugitive, returned to France in October, where he remained for three years until he was made *persona non grata* by the treaty signed by Mazarin and Cromwell in 1655. He spent almost two years in Cologne and a further three in the Low Countries, constantly seeking money for his lavish life-style and support for his campaign to regain his throne. In June 1659, he travelled to the Pyrenees to ask both Spain and France for help. The Spaniards received him civilly but Mazarin refused to see him and he returned empty-handed to Holland. Finally, with Monk's support, the monarchy was restored and he entered London on 29 May 1661.

CHAROST: Louis-Armand de Béthune-Charost (1640–1717) was Fouquet's son-in-law. His father, Louis de Béthune de Charost (1605–81), was raised to a dukedom in 1671. In 1657 Louis-Armand married Marie (b. 1640), daughter of Louise Fourché (d. 1641), first wife of Nicolas Fouquet.

CHÂTILLON: Isabelle Angélique de Montmorency-Bouteville (d. 1695), widow of Gaspard de Coligny (1620–49), Duc de Châtillon, who was killed at the battle of Charenton in 1649. She was well known for her amorous intrigues and may have been mistress in 1651 to Charles II. She remarried in 1664 and became the Duchess of Mecklenbourg.

CHEVREUSE: Claude de Lorraine (1578–1657), Duc de Chevreuse.

CHEVREUSE: Marie-Aimé de Rohan-Montbazon (1600–79), widow of the Duc de Luynes, married the Duc de Chevreuse in 1622. She was one of Anne of Austria's 'frivolous' friends and ran through many lovers, most of whom, like Chalais (q.v.), she involved in her plots to unseat Richelieu. Louis XIII exiled her, but she regularly returned to court, where she continued her intrigues. She abetted Buckingham's plans to invade France in 1628 and was again banished, first to Poitou and later to the château-prison at Loches, 40 km south-east of Tours. In 1637 she escaped and fled to Spain and thence to England, where she was caught up in the English Civil War and briefly imprisoned on the Isle of Wight. She lived in Belgium until she was allowed to return to France in 1643 by Mazarin, whom she opposed. She was again exiled for her intrigues, and eventually settled in Brussels, where she continued to side with the enemies of Mazarin. She returned to France after the Amnesty of Rueil on 12 April 1649. She continued to be active throughout the Fronde, though her scheming partnership with Laigues (q.v.) continued on a reduced scale. Dumas makes her the mother of Raoul.

CINQ-MARS: Henri Coeffier d'Effiat, Marquis de Cinq-Mars, executed in 1642 for conspiring against Richelieu with Madame de Chevreuse.

COADJUTOR: see Retz.

COLBERT: Édouard-François Colbert, brother of Louis's finance minister.

COLBERT: Jean-Baptiste Colbert (1619–83), the son of a minor royal official in Picardy and an agent of Richelieu. As a young man, Colbert was placed with a Parisian notary named Chapelain. Through his cousin, Colbert de Saint-Pouange, he was employed in 1640 by Des Noyers, Secretary of State for War. In 1642 he became principal clerk to Le Tellier (q.v.), Saint-Pouange's brother-in-law, and his secretary in 1649. When Mazarin's intendant died in 1655, Colbert succeeded him. In 1658 he purchased the barony of Seignelay and thus entered the aristocracy. Mazarin entrusted him with increasingly important responsibilities and, on his death-bed, recommended him to Louis XIV: 'I owe you everything, but I pay my debt to your majesty in giving you Colbert.' In 1661 he became Louis's chief minister and immediately began introducing the reforms which were necessary after the maladministration of Fouquet (q.v.). In 1661 revenues amounted to 82 millions but took 52 millions to collect; within a decade, the figures were 104 and 27 million. Among other measures, Colbert forced the tax-farmers to restore Crown revenues which they had appropriated. His economic policies were accompanied by administrative reforms and a determination to develop every aspect of national life. Dumas did not care for him, and usually portrays him as ruthless and personally uncouth. Even so, he gives a fair estimate of Colbert's achievements in *Twenty Years After* (World's Classics, p. 466).

COLBERT: Jean-Baptiste Colbert, sieur de Saint-Pouange, was an official in various government services before becoming *intendant* of Metz and later of other parts of Flanders. He was cousin to Colbert, and helped him at the start of his career.

CONCINI: Concino Concini, a Florentine adventurer who, abetted by his wife, Laure Galigaï, acquired great power through his influence over Marie de' Medici, wife of Henri IV and regent of France during the minority of Louis XIII, who made him Maréchal d'Ancre. He died on 24 April 1617 when resisting the king's order for his arrest. He was shot on the Pont du Louvre by the Marquis de Vitry (q.v.), Captain of the King's Guard. After Concini's death, Louis XIII assumed royal power and successfully resisted the Medici's challenge to his authority.

CONDÉ: Claire-Clémence de Maille-Brézé (*c*.1620–94), Princesse de Condé, wife of 'Monsieur le Prince'.

CONDÉ: Louis de Bourbon (1621–86), Duc d'Enghien, became Prince de Condé on the death of his father in 1646. Known as 'Monsieur le Prince' and 'Condé the Great', he fought with valour at the battles of Rocroi (1643), Nördlingen (1645), and Lens (1648). In the autumn of 1648, he threw his military skills behind the royal cause. Believing he had been insufficiently rewarded for his efforts, he reacted with such arrogance that he alienated both the queen and Mazarin. In 1650 he was jailed at Vincennes. In 1651 the political situation had changed and Mazarin was forced to release him. He thereupon raised an army to rescue the young king from his advisers. He failed, refused to accept the peace of 1653, went over to Spain, and took part in all the campaigns against France. He was rehabilitated in 1659, and retired to his estate at Chantilly. Recalled to service in 1668, he fought his last battle in 1674.

CONRART: Valentin Conrart (1603–75), first secretary of the French Academy created by Richelieu in 1635, and occasional poet—so occasional that Boileau went out of his way to admire his 'prudent silence'.

CRÉQUI: Mme de Créqui, wife of François Créqui (d. 1687), who was made director of France's galleys in 1661, and Marshal of France in 1668. She enjoyed a reputation for great virtue.

CROMWELL: Oliver Cromwell (1599–1658) was a moderate compared with the extreme fundamentalists who surrounded him. Dumas viewed him as a cynical manipulator and ranked him alongside Richelieu and Mazarin.

DANGEAU: Philippe, Marquis de Dangeau (1638–1720), an assiduous courtier renowned for his wit and author of a detailed *Journal* chronicling life at court from 1684 onwards.

FELTON: John Felton (1595–1628), the Puritan zealot who murdered the Duke of Buckingham at Portsmouth in 1628. In Dumas's version of events (*The Three Musketeers*, ch. 59), Felton was goaded to his act by Milady.

FOUQUET: A protégé of Mazarin, Nicolas Fouquet (1615–80) was still, in 1661, Superintendent of France's finances and the master of vast wealth acquired through abuse of power. He built the magnificent château at Vaux (1658) and was a generous patron of art and literature. He was admired for his munificent style of management, but resented by sections of the court and the bourgeoisie for his unashamed corruption. It has been argued that Louis turned against him out of jealousy for his wealth, but it is more likely that he feared the influence of Fouquet, who, in 1658, acquired the Breton island of Belle-Île from which he might have led a campaign against the throne at a time when Louis had yet to command the obedience of all the provinces of France. A cabal was formed to ruin him. Fouquet was arrested by Charles de Batz (the real d'Artagnan) in September 1661 and, after his trial, was escorted (also by d'Artagnan) to the prison of Pignerol in the Savoy, where he remained until his death in 1680. Dumas, himself a reckless man who admired lavish style, gives him a noble and sympathetic persona. It was Fouquet who appointed Aramis Bishop of Vannes and promised him a cardinal's hat. On his instructions, Aramis fortified Belle-Île, using the skills of Porthos, who remained ignorant of his plans. Exploiting his position as Vicar-General of the Jesuits, Aramis was prepared to throw the inexhaustible resources of the order behind his protector against the wily Colbert, who, by means of purloined letters, had amassed enough evidence to convince the king of his corruption. Dumas viewed Fouquet as a dashing Cavalier who possessed all the flair and imagination he found lacking in the grim and devious Roundhead, Colbert.

FOUQUET: Basile Fouquet (1622–80), brother of Nicolas, was an abbé with devious talents whom Mazarin placed at the head of his secret service. He had a hand in many of the political intrigues of the 1640s and 1650s, and his plotting helped his brother to acquire high office. He turned against Fouquet after about 1657 and quarrelled publicly with him in January 1661. After Fouquet's fall, he was exiled. After Fouquet's trial in 1664, according to Courtilz de Sandras (*Memoirs of d'Artagnan*, iii. 163 ff.), he pretended to be mad to escape a fate similar to his brother's. Fouquet's judgement of him ('a fellow without a heart, without ideas; a devourer of wealth', p. 396) was shared by many.

FOUQUET: Marie-Madeleine (d. 1716), daughter of François de Castille, a counsellor in the Paris *parlement*, who brought him a dowry of 2 million livres, was the second, and very retiring wife of Nicolas Fouquet.

GONDI: see Retz.

GOURVILLE: Jean Hérault de Gourville (1625–1703) was a *frondeur* before becoming Fouquet's agent. After the arrest of Fouquet in September 1661, he was sentenced to death, but escaped to Brussels, where he lived on money not entirely honestly come by.

GRAMONT: Antoine de Gramont (1604–78), Comte de Guiche, later Duc de Gramont, was made Marshal of France in 1641. Father of Raoul's friend, the Comte de Guiche (q.v.).

GUÉNAUD: François Guénaud (*c.*1590–1667), professor in the Faculty of Medicine in Paris and principal doctor to Anne of Austria. He used antinomy as an emetic, in ways which Boileau (*Satires* iv. 32) considered lethal. He was the *bête noire* of Guy Patin (1601–72), the greatest medical man of his day. Molière lampooned Guénaud, who figures as Macroton in *L'Amour médecin* (1665).

GUICHE: Armand de Gramont (1637–73), Comte de Guiche, a soldier and a man of considerable charm who enjoyed amorous intrigues with both men and women. He was part of the entourage of Philippe d'Orléans. Dumas makes him Raoul's closest friend.

GUISE: Henri de Lorraine (1614–64), Duc de Guise.

HAUTEFORT: Marie de Hautefort (1616–91), Maréchale de Schomberg, a favourite of Louis XIII and an ally of Anne of Austria. She was dismissed, temporarily, from court in 1639.

HENRY IV: Henry IV (1553–1610), grandfather of Louis XIV, had revived French fortunes abroad and at home ended the religious strife of the sixteenth century.

HENRIETTA: Henrietta-Anne Stuart (1644–70), youngest daughter of Charles I and Henrietta-Maria. She was left at Exeter when her mother fled to France, but her governess, Lady Dalkeith, dressed as a beggar-woman, smuggled her to France in 1646, where her mother brought her up as a Catholic. Clever and beautiful, she became Duchess of Orléans ('Madame') when she married Philippe, brother to Louis XIV, on 31 March 1661. Philippe's homosexuality and jealousy made their marriage unsuccessful. In 1670 Louis XIV sent her to England, where she persuaded Charles II, her brother, to sign the Treaty of Dover. On her return to France, she died of poison.

HENRIETTA-MARIA OF ENGLAND: Henrietta-Maria (1609–69), younger sister of Louis XIII, had married Charles of England by proxy in 1625. The marriage had been arranged by Buckingham. After the Rebellion, she parted from Charles in 1644 and escaped to France, whence she observed events in England with alarm. She was not well received, especially after the death of Charles I, when she lived in near destitution. She remained in France until October 1660, when she returned briefly to London with Henrietta. She spent the years 1662–5 in England (Pepys called her 'a very little, plain old woman') and died of an overdose of opiate in her château at Colombes. Her remains were buried at Saint-Denis.

HERVART: Barthélemy Hervart (d. 1676), a German Protestant banker. He had financed Louis XIII's military campaigns and, in the first phase of the Fronde, persuaded the army of Turenne (then declaring against Mazarin) not to follow his lead. 'M. Hervart has saved the state and kept His Majesty's crown on his head,' declared the grateful Mazarin, who made him Intendant of Finances and, in 1656, Comptroller-General. When Louis returned from Brittany in September 1661, after the arrest of Fouquet, he asked Hervart for money and was given 2 millions. Hervart, a friend of La Fontaine, was 'one of the greatest milords in Paris and had a most splendid mansion there' (Courtilz, *Memoirs of d'Artagnan*, iii. 165).

JUXON: William Juxon (1582–63) became Bishop of London in 1633. He ministered to the king in his last moments at Whitehall and it was to him that Charles spoke the word 'Remember!'

LA BAUME LE BLANC: Laurent de la Baume le Blanc (1611–51), seigneur de la Vallière, soldier and administrator, married Françoise de la Coutelaye in 1640, mother of his three children. See La Vallière and Saint-Rémy.

LA FAYETTE: Marie-Madeleine Pioche de la Vergne (1634–93), Comtesse de la Fayette, separated from her husband and settled in Paris in 1659. She was an intimate of the circle of Henrietta (later

Duchess of Orléans) and wrote an account of her life, *Histoire de Madame Henriette d'Angleterre* (published posthumously in 1720), on which Dumas drew heavily. She is remembered as a novelist, her masterpiece being *La Princesse de Clèves* (1678), written in a formal, ceremonial style, which shows that duty and happiness are not compatible. She is usually credited as the pioneer of the *roman d'analyse*—the psychological novel—to which the French have remained addicted.

LA FONTAINE: Jean de la Fontaine (1621–95), known primarily as the author of the *Fables* (1668–94) and various collections of *Tales* which appeared between 1664 and his death.

LAIGUES: Geoffroy, Marquis de Laigues (1614–74), former captain of guards to Gaston d'Orléans, who fought in the campaigns of the 1640s and distinguished himself at the battle of Lens (1648). His association with Madame de Chevreuse dated from the Fronde (see *Twenty Years After*), in which he took an prominent part.

LAMBERT: John Lambert (1619–83) trained as a lawyer, but became one of the great soliders of the Civil War. He fought at Marston Moor and rose rapidly. He fought at Dunbar and pursued Charles to Worcester. He was prominent in installing Cromwell as Lord Protector, but subsequently turned against him. He led the disaffected soldiers who opposed Richard Cromwell, and was regarded as head of the extreme Republican party. By October 1659, after dismissing the remnants of the 'Rump' Parliament, he headed a 'Committee of Safety' which more or less governed the country. He was outmanoeuvred by Monk in the spring of 1661. He was sent to the Tower, jailed in 1662, and banished to Guernsey.

LAPORTE: Pierre de la Porte (1603–80) entered the service of Anne of Austria in 1621. He enabled her to correspond with the Spanish court, and for his 'treasons' was imprisoned by Richelieu in 1637. He returned to favour when Anne became Regent in 1643. He served the queen loyally and was made Louis XIV's *valet de chambre* in 1645, a position which he used to undermine the influence of Mazarin. His *Memoirs*, first published in 1755, were one of Dumas's major sources.

LA ROCHEFOUCAULD: François (1613–80), Prince de Marcillac, later Duc de la Rochefoucauld, author of the cynical *Maximes* (1665) and of *Memoirs* (first published 1662) on which Dumas drew when researching the period. He chivalrously helped Madame de Chevreuse to escape from France in 1637. The Duchesse de Longueville was his mistress between 1646 and 1652.

LA VALLIÈRE: Françoise-Louise de la Baume le Blanc (1644–1710), later known as the Duchesse de la Vallière, was born near Amboise.

She was part of the entourage of the Duchess of Orléans at Blois and moved with her to Paris after the death of Gaston d'Orléans (q.v.). In 1661, the Duchesse de Choisy proposed her as lady-of-honour to Henrietta d'Orléans with a pension of 100 livres and the privilege of living at the Tuileries. There she caught the attention of the king. She was his mistress between 1661 and 1667 and bore him four children. No great beauty and slightly lame, she attracted Louis by the sweetness of her face and manners. After being replaced by Madame de Montespan, she retired from court life in 1670 and took the veil in 1674.

LE TELLIER: Michel Le Tellier (1603–85) was Secretary of State for War between 1643 and 1666.

LEVEN: Alexander Leslie, created Earl of Leven in 1640, was commander of the Scots forces which finally deserted Charles's cause in 1646. He bought Montrose in 1650 and, after treating him with the greatest contempt, had him hanged at Edinburgh on 21 May 1651.

LIONNE: Hugues de Lionne (1611–71), seigneur de Berny, diplomat and ambassador. Mazarin appointed him first as Minister, then, in June 1659, Secretary of State for foreign affairs. Lionne was instrumental in concluding the Treaty of the Pyrenees in 1659 and, as a skilful negotiator, played a crucial role in the military campaigns of Louis XIV in the 1660s.

LONGUEVILLE: Anne-Geneviève de Bourbon-Condé (1619–79), Duchesse de Longueville. She was sister to Condé (q.v.) and mistress of La Rochefoucauld (q.v.) during the Fronde.

LORET: Jean Loret (1600–65), the author of a weekly verse gazette which commented on public events and people. He supported Fouquet and, after his arrest, spoke in his defence. For his pains, Colbert stopped his small pension. However, Fouquet, from prison, arranged for a sum of money to be paid to him anonymously.

LORRAINE: Philippe (1643–1702), called the Chevalier de Lorraine because he had been intended to join the Order of Malta. Later known as Prince Philippe, he was for many years the favourite of Philippe d'Orléans, who ensured he was given military and ecclesiastical preferment.

LOUIS XIII: Louis de Bourbon (1601–43), 'Louis the Just', became king of France and Navarre in 1610 on the assassination of his father, Henri IV. He survived the revolt led by his mother the Regent, Marie de' Medici, and appointed Richelieu as his Prime Minister in 1624.

LOUIS XIV: Louis (1638–1715) succeeded to the throne on the death of his father, Louis XIII, in 1643. During his minority, France was ruled by Anne of Austria, who appointed Gaston d'Orléans

Lieutenant-Governor of the Kingdom and Mazarin as her first minister. Thanks to Mazarin, the monarchy survived the civil wars of the Fronde (1648–52) not only intact but considerably strengthened. Even after he came of age, Louis continued to be dominated by Mazarin, who negotiated his marriage with the Spanish Infanta in June 1660. But when Mazarin died in March 1661, Louis made it clear that he intended to rule personally. Abetted by Colbert, he removed his corrupt finance minister Fouquet in September and the following year declared that henceforth he was to be known as the Sun King.

LUYNES: Charles (1578–1621), Marquis d'Albert, Duc de Luynes, was an intimate of Louis XIII. He was instrumental in turning the king against Concini (q.v.), who was murdered in 1617. Subsequently, he acquired high office as Constable of Normandy. But in 1621 he failed to halt the Protestants at Montauban and, growing increasingly unpopular, he was disgraced. In 1617 he married Marie de Rohan, the future Duchesse de Chevreuse (q.v.).

LUYNES: Louis-Charles d'Albert (1620–90), Duc de Luynes, son of Madame de Chevreuse by her first marriage.

MALICORNE: Germain Texier (1626–94), Baron de Malicorne. Dumas makes him the son of a lawyer, an intriguer with lofty ambitions. In fact, Malicorne was a squire of the Duc de Guise by 1648 and already the lover of Mlle de Pons. In 1665 he married a daughter of Saint-Rémy (q.v.) by his first marriage.

MANCINI: the family name of Mazarin's numerous nieces and nephews. Hortense (1646–99) married the Duke of La Meilleraie, a great-nephew of Richelieu: the couple took the title of Duke and Duchess de Richelieu. Louis fell in love with Marie (1640–1715) in 1658, but instead made a political marriage with the Infanta of Spain. Olympe (1639–1708) married the Duke of Soissons in 1657 and later became Louis's mistress.

MANICAMP: Louis de Madallan de Lesparre (c.1628–1708) fought his first campaign in 1646 and served under Condé at Lens (1648) and elsewhere. His *seigneurie* at Manicamp in the Soissonnais was made into a *comté* in 1693 and his son, Roger-Constant (1691–1723), was known as the Comte de Manicamp. However, of the historical Louis de Madallan (who lost an arm at Charenton in 1652), Dumas retains only the name.

MARCILLAC: see La Rochefoucauld.

MARIE DE' MEDICI: Marie de' Medici (1573–1642), mother of Louis XIII. As Regent, she opposed her son's assumption of royal power in 1617 and her supporters attempted to start a civil war: to the disappointment of her followers, she submitted to Louis in 1619 and rejoined the court. When she failed to win Richelieu to her cause, she tried to undermine his influence with the king, was imprisoned at Compiègne, but escaped to Brussels in 1631. In 1641 she was in London, but finally settled in Cologne in circumstances so reduced that she died, so it was said, in a hayloft.

MAZARIN: The Italian-born Giulio Mazarini (1602–61), a soldier and diplomat in the service of the Pope, who sent him to France to negotiate with Richelieu in 1630. Richelieu retained him to defend French interests in Italy. He was sent to the French court as papal legate in 1634, became Richelieu's protégé, and in 1639, on entering the service of the King of France, was naturalized French. In 1641 he was made cardinal through the influence of Richelieu, who, shortly before his death, recommended him as his successor. Though personally unpopular, he made himself indispensable to the Queen Regent. Mazarin was her lover and may (as Dumas believed) have been secretly married to her: though a cardinal, he was not an ordained priest. His power aroused the envy of the nobility, his demands for increased taxes alienated the middle class, and his foreign origins were a focus for popular resentment. He was generally considered to be excessively avaricious and self-serving: estimates of his private fortune on his death range from 13 to 40 million livres. His diplomatic skills were very great. He furthered French interests in southern Germany by the Treaty of Westphalia which ended the Thirty Years War in 1648, and secured the alliance of Cromwell. At home, he survived the Fronde and so strengthened the French throne that Louis XIV's creation of the modern French nation owed a great deal to him. He brokered the marriage of Louis XIV with the Spanish Infanta in 1660. He died at the Château de Vincennes on 9 March 1661, more, it was reported, a philosopher than a Christian, though the priest who attended his last moments affirmed that he died in the true faith.

MICHON, MARIE: the name by which Madame de Chevreuse is known in *The Three Musketeers*.

MONK: George Monk (1608–70) was a career soldier who saw active service on the Continent between 1625 and 1640 when he threw in with the anti-royalists. Taken prisoner in 1644, he spent two years in the Tower. After signing the Covenant, he served under Cromwell at Dunbar and in 1654 was sent back to Scotland as governor. When the disorder which followed the departure of both Cromwells degenerated into the political chaos of the autumn of 1659, he decided to intervene. On 1 January 1660 he crossed the Tweed with 6,000 men, and in five weeks reached London unopposed. He kept his motives secret and allied himself with no party, though the Republicans offered him the Protectorate. His own preference for the return of the Stuarts was confirmed by the rising tide of popular opinion. On 23 May 1660 he was at Dover to meet Charles, who made him Duke of Albemarle and gave him the highest offices in the state. He withdrew soon after from political life, but continued to serve Charles as a naval commander in engagements against the Dutch.

'MONSIEUR': the court title of the king's brother: it was given to Gaston d'Orléans until his death in 1660, and thereafter to Philippe d'Anjou, who succeeded him as Duke of Orléans.

'MONSIEUR LE PRINCE': that is, Condé.

MONTALAIS: Nicole-Anne-Constance de Montalais, whom Dumas calls 'Aure', was lady-in-waiting at the court of Gaston d'Orléans at Blois, and a companion to Louise de la Vallière. In 1661 she was attached to the retinue of Henrietta, Duchess of Orléans, to whom she was presented by Mlle de Montpensier. She had a taste for intrigue and was involved in the 'Spanish letter' affair of 1664. Her sister, Françoise de Montalais, married Jean de Bueil, Comte de Marans, in 1660; Mme de Sévigné did not care for her.

MONTESPAN: Françoise-Athénaïs de Rochechouart de Mortemart (1641–1707) was born at the château de Tonnay-Charente. A maid of honour at the wedding of Philippe d'Orléans and Henrietta in March 1661, she married the complaisant Duc de Montespan et d'Antin in 1663. As Mme de Montespan, she was to oust Louise de la Vallière from the affections of Louis XIV by 1667.

MONTMORENCY: Henri, Duc de Montmorency, was executed for treason in 1632.

MONTPENSIER: see Orléans, Anne-Marie-Louise.

MONTROSE: James Graham (1612–50), Marquis of Montrose, at first an opponent of the king, but by June 1640 an ardent royalist. In 1644 he rallied the clans, but his victorious Scottish campaign ended with his defeat by Lesley at Philiphaugh in 1645. Failing to raise the Highlands, he escaped to Norway in 1646. He was in Holland when, on 5 February 1649, he heard of the execution of Charles I. He launched an invasion of Scotland, but few rallied to his cause. His small army was massacred on 27 April 1650 and he was captured by Macleod of Assynt, who sold him to Leslie, Earl of Leven. Leslie treated him with great contempt before hanging him at Edinburgh on 21 May.

MOTTEVILLE: Françoise Bertaut (1621–89) married Nicolas Langlois, seigneur de Motteville, in 1639, by which time she was a trusted member of the Queen's 'Spanish' entourage. Her *Memoirs*, first published in 1723 and reprinted in 1824 and 1838, were extensively used by Dumas for the background to the period.

NAVAILLES: Suzanne de Baudéan (d. 1700), Duchess of Navailles, married Philippe de Montaut de Bénac, Duke of Navailles, in 1651. In 1661 he was governor of Le Havre. She was appointed lady-in-waiting to the queen, but was disgraced in 1664.

NOIRMOUTIERS: Louis de la Trémouille (1612–66), Duke of Noirmoutiers.

ORLÉANS: Anne-Marie-Louise d'Orléans (1627–93), Duchess of Montpensier, daughter of Gaston d'Orléans, known as 'la Grande Mademoiselle'. In 1681 she was secretly married to the Duc de Lauzun.

ORLÉANS: Gaston-Jean-Baptiste de France, Duke of Orléans (1608–60), younger brother of Louis XIII, known as 'Monsieur', had regularly participated in the intrigues mounted against Richelieu. On the accession of Louis XIV in 1643, he was appointed Lieutenant-Governor of the Kingdom. He supported Anne of Austria during the first Fronde, but after the second was exiled to Blois in 1652. He was reconciled with Louis at the end of 1659 and received him at Chambord and Blois in January 1660. In *The Man in the Iron Mask* (World's Classics edition, p. 190), Aramis judged him to be 'void of courage and honesty', a verdict echoed by contemporaries like Retz, who remarked that Orléans 'had everything a gentleman should have, except courage'.

ORLÉANS: Henri d'Orléans (1595–1663) was the husband of Madame de Longueville, Condé's sister.

ORLÉANS: Marguerite de Lorraine (1613–72), Duchess of Orléans, wife of Gaston, known as 'Madame' and, after his death, as the 'Dowager Madame'.

ORLÉANS: Philippe (1640–1701), second son of Louis XIII and Anne of Austria, and brother to Louis XIV, was Duke of Anjou until the death of Gaston, his uncle, in February 1660, when he inherited the title Duke of Orléans. Married Henrietta of England on 31 March 1661. His homosexuality ensured that the marriage was not happy.

PELLISSON: Paul Pellisson (1624–93) was part of Fouquet's literary entourage. After Fouquet's arrest, he wrote spiritedly in his defence and spent five years in the Bastille before regaining favour by his appointment as Historiographer Royal.

PLESSIS: see Plessis-Bellière.

PLESSIS-BELLIÈRE: Suzanne de Bruc (1608–1705), wife of Jacques de Rougé, Marquis de Plessis-Bellière, who died in action at Naples in 1654. She remained close to Fouquet throughout the 1650s. It was she, not Mme Fouquet, who organized the Superintendent's cultural gatherings, which could be serious but were often playful: when her parrot died in 1653, Fouquet and his entourage wrote verses to mark its passing.

PRIDE: Thomas Pride (d. 1658), a former drayman, rose through the ranks during the Civil Wars. When, in 1648, the House of Commons seemed inclined to reach a settlement with the king, Colonel Pride was charged by the army to silence its royalist elements who had rejected the call for Charles to be brought to trial. On 6–7 December 1648, he arrested 60 uncooperative members of Parliament. To 'Pride's Purge' were added a further 96 exclusions, which left the 'Rump' Parliament, consisting of 53 members, to try the king. Pride was one of his judges and signed his death-warrant. He died in 1658, but after the Restoration his body was dug up and hanged with Cromwell's at Tyburn.

RACAN: Honoré de Bueil, Marquis de Racan (1589–1670), a member of the French Academy, known as an elegiac and pastoral poet.

RAIS or RETZ: Gilles de Retz (1404–40) fought with Joan of Arc but was remembered in Brittany, where he had estates, for necromancy and for kidnapping and murdering children. He was the model for Bluebeard in the collection of fairy-tales published in 1697 by Charles Perrault (1628–1703).

RETZ: Jean-François-Paul de Gondi (1613–79) was named coadjutor to his uncle the first Archbishop of Paris in 1643. A leading figure in opposing Mazarin in the first Fronde, he rallied to the queen's party in the second. He became Cardinal de Retz in 1652. Dumas knew his *Memoirs* (1662), which had been reprinted in 1837.

RICHELIEU: Armand-Jean du Plessis (1585–1642) was Bishop of Luçon before being appointed Cardinal in 1622. He was named Head of the Royal Council in 1624 and became the most powerful man in France during the reign of Louis XIII. An admirer of Machiavelli, he played a crucial role in maintaining France as a great international power and in creating the highly centralized state which Louis XIV was to inherit and further strengthen. It was against the wily and ruthless 'Red Duke' (so called because of his cardinal's robes and his Dukedom of Richelieu) that d'Artagnan and his comrades had had waged an epic struggle of wits in *The Three Musketeers*.

ROCHESTER: John Wilmot (1647–80), Earl of Rochester, travelled in France and Italy before making his mark as the wittiest reprobate in Charles's court. Excessively dissolute, witty, crude, and self-destructive, he died of alcoholism and syphilis at the age of 33, but not before undergoing a religious conversion. Nevertheless, he managed to find time to leave his mark as a satirical versifier. Horace Walpole remarked that his poems 'have much more obscenity than wit, more wit than poetry, and more poetry than politeness'.

ROTROU: Jean Rotrou (1609–50), author of tragedies.

SAINT-RÉMY, MME DE: Françoise Le Prévôt de la Coutelaye, who became Mme de Saint-Rémy on her third marriage in 1655. Her first husband was Besnard, Councillor at the *parlement* of Rennes. Her second, Laurent de la Baume le Blanc (q.v.), was the lord of the manor of La Vallière at Reugny, 10 km west of Amboise, and owner of a town house at Tours, where Louise was born on 6 August 1644. When her second husband died in 1654, she married Saint-Rémy, first chamberlain to Gaston.

SAINT-RÉMY: Jacques de Couravel, Marquis de Saint-Rémy, was appointed principal chamberlain to Gaston d'Orléans at Blois on 6 March 1655, the year in which he married Louise's mother, Françoise de la Coutelaye. After Gaston's death in February 1660 he moved to Paris, where he continued in his functions in the household of Philippe, the new Duke of Orléans.

SCHOMBERG: Charles de Schomberg (1601–56), Duc d'Halluin, second husband of Marie de Hautefort (q.v.).

SCUDÉRY: Georges de Scudéry (1601–67), author, with his sister Madeleine (1607–1701), of two influential novels in the 'precious' style: *Artamène, ou le Grand Cyrus* (1649–53) and *Clélie* (1654–60).

SOREL: Charles Sorel (1597–1674), enemy of the fashionable pastoral mode and author of the *Histoire comique de Francion* (1622), an early picaresque novel of 'low life'.

TONNAY-CHARENTE: see Montespan.

TRÉMOUILLE: see Noirmoutiers.

TRÉVILLE: Arnaud-Jean du Peyrer (1598–1672), Comte de Troisvilles (pronounced and usually written Tréville), was a Gascon career soldier like d'Artagnan. His courage and loyalty were admired by Louis XIII, who appointed him Captain-Lieutenant of his Musketeers in 1634. In 1642 he was exiled for his opposition to Richelieu, and when Mazarin disbanded the Musketeers in 1646 he retired to Foix as its governor. In *The Three Musketeers*, which makes the main characters about 10 years older than their historical counterparts, it is in Tréville's office in 1625 that Dumas, following Courtilz de Sandras's pseudo-*Memoirs of d'Artagnan* (i. 13), arranges the first meeting between d'Artagnan, Athos, Porthos, and Aramis.

TURENNE: Henri de la Tour d'Auvergne (1611–75), Vicomte de Turenne, Marshal of France. Drawn into the Fronde against Mazarin by Madame de Longueville, he rallied to the Court party in 1651, assuming command of the royal forces against Condé. Known was 'le Grand Turenne', he was one of the greatest military commanders of his century.

VALENTINOIS: Catherine-Charlotte de Gramont (1639–78), sister to the Comte de Guiche, married Louis de Grimaldi, Duke of Valentinois, Prince of Monaco, in 1660. She was not reckoned to be chaste, even by the broadest standards. Mme Sévigné speaks of her often as the Princesse de Monaco.

VANEL: According to Courtilz's *Vie de Colbert* (1695), Colbert paid his attentions to 'Anne-Marguerite Vanel, wife of Jean Coiffier, of the Audit Office, a dainty and extremely pretty young woman with a lively and very witty turn of mind'. Courtilz adds that her permanent brightness wearied Colbert, who passed her on to his brother. Coiffier received his appointment in 1654. Anne-Marguerite's father was Claude Vanel (d. 1687), a magistrate in the Paris *parlement* and later chief financial steward to Philippe, Duke of Orléans.

VENDÔME: see Beaufort.

VILLIERS: see Buckingham.

VITRY: Nicolas de l'Hôpital (1581–1644), Marquis de Vitry. Louis XIII's Captain of Guards, he was made Marshal of France on the day he shot Concini (q.v.). Vitry was sent to the Bastille in 1637 for abusing his position as Governor of Provence. He was released on the death of Richelieu in 1642.

WARDES: François-René Crespin du Bec (1620–88), Marquis de Vardes, captain of the Cent-Suisses, well known for his intrigues. He was bold, scheming, and a consummate liar, though Mme de Motteville nevertheless found him 'charming' (*Memoirs*, iv. 279). His wife Nicolaï died in 1660, an event which scarcely interrupted the flow of liaisons and plots. Implicated in the 'Spanish letter' affair of 1664, he was banished to Aigues-Mortes, of which he had been appointed governor in 1660, where he remained for seventeen years.

WILMOT: see Rochester.

EXPLANATORY NOTES

[† indicates that fuller details will be found in the List of Historical Characters]

7 *Blois*: on the Loire, 181 km south-west of Paris and 60 km from Orléans. It was in the château there that the Duc de Guise was murdered by Henri III's guards in 1588; Dumas had told the tale in *The Forty-Five Guardsmen* (1847). Dumas had visited Blois 'and its bloodstained château' in August 1830, when, immediately after the Revolution in Paris, he had been sent by Lafayette to promote the National Guard in the Vendée.

Monsieur: that is, Gaston of Orléans,† who had been exiled to Blois as a punishment for his role in the Fronde. His presence is anachronistic: he died on 2 February 1660. In this chapter Dumas brings together a number of historical events which occurred in 1659 and 1660.

8 *Louis XIV*: see List of Historical Characters. His father Louis XIII and Gaston d'Orléans were sons of Henri IV (1553–1610), who had ended the religious wars of the sixteenth century and began the work of unifying the French nation which was to be continued by Richelieu, Mazarin, and Louis XIV.

Castle of the States: the States-General had been held in the château in 1576 and 1588.

a little excitement: Dumas repeats the charge, made in *Twenty Years After* (World's Classics, p. 47), that Gaston was responsible for the deaths of Chalais† (1626), Montmorency† (1632), and Cinq-Mars† (1642), who had been executed for plotting with the Spanish party against Richelieu.

Mazarin: Cardinal Richelieu, Head of the Royal Council (Prime Minister) since 1624, nominated Mazarin† as his successor on his death in 1642.

Beuvron . . . Cheverny . . . Chambord: the Beuvron flows westwards through the Sologne into the Loire at Candé, 13 km west of Blois, Cheverny, with its château, is 13 km south-east of Blois, and Chambord 18 km due east: the celebrated château there was built in the reign (1515–47) of François I.

buskins: laced half-boots strapped or laced to the ankle and lower part of the leg.

9 *halberds*: a medieval weapon consisting of a broad blade with sharp edges ending in a sharp point and mounted on a handle 5 to 7 feet long. Overtaken as a weapon of war by the musket, halberds with richly decorated blades continued in ceremonial use into the seventeenth century, when they were carried by palace guards.

Madame: Marguerite, Duchess d'Orléans,[†] wife of Gaston. After his death, she was known as the Dowager Madame.

10 *Montalais*: for Montalais (and Louise de la Vallière and Madame de Saint-Rémy, later in the paragraph), see the List of Historical Characters. Dumas, who confusingly calls Montalais 'Aure' and 'Françoise', took his view of her from Mme de la Fayette: see following note.

11 *Monsieur Raoul*: Dumas's source for the love of Raoul for Louise was Mme de la Fayette's *Histoire de Madame Henriette d'Angleterre* (published posthumously in 1720). 'Madame was attended by a young person named Montalais who, though possessing naturally quick wit, also had a mind given to intrigue and scheming: nor could it be said that her conduct was directed by good sense and reason. She had lived in no court other than that of the Dowager Madame at Blois whose maid-of-honour she had been. This lack of experience of society together with her gallant habits equipped her perfectly to play the role of confidante. She had already been the confidante of La Vallière at Blois, where a man named Bragelonne had been in love with her. A handful of letters had been exchanged; Mme de Saint-Rémy had got wind of the affair. In the event, matters did not progress very far. But the King grew very jealous. La Vallière [. . .] unburdened herself to Montalais [. . .]. Eventually, the King forgave her. Montalais manœuvred in such a way that she acquired the confidence of the King. He questioned her several times about the Bragelonne matter, with which he knew that she was acquainted, but Montalais being a more proficient liar than La Vallière, he became easy in his mind after speaking to her. Even so, he was extremely put out that he might not be the first man La Vallière had loved; he even feared that she still adored Bragelonne. In short, he felt all the anxiety and delicate sentiment of a man in love [. . .]. La Vallière's lack of wit prevented her, though mistress to the king, from taking full advantage of the credit given her by such passionate devotion which another in her place would have put to good advantage' (Mme de la Fayette, *Œuvres complètes*, Paris, 1992, pp. 458, 462). The Bragelonne in question has been identified as Jean de Bragelonne, a councillor at the *parlement* at Rennes, though it seems more likely that he was

connected to one of several Bragelonnes in the service of Gaston d'Orléans: Jérôme (1588–1658) (whose son François (1626–1703), seigneur de Hauteville, was Captain-Lieutenant of Gendarmes to Gaston); or, as seems most likely, Jacques (d. 1679), Chevalier de Bragelonne, chief steward of Gaston's household.

12 *Mary de Medici*: Marie de' Medici,[†] having failed in her bid to prolong her Regency, was exiled to Blois in 1617. She escaped on 21 February 1619 through a window by means of a ladder. She was the mother of six children by Henri IV: Louis (who succeeded his father), Gaston, Nicolas (who died in infancy), Elizabeth (later Queen of Spain), Christine-Marie (later Duchess of Savoie), and Henrietta-Maria (later queen of Charles I of England).

13 *Monsieur le Prince*: Raoul is attached to the household of the Prince de Condé.[†]

15 *a young man*: Raoul is entirely Dumas's invention. Though he will display dashing courage later on, his character has the dreamy, almost feminine sensitivity which makes him more a hero of Dumas's Romantic times than of the seventeenth century. The circumstances of his conception are related in *Twenty Years After* (chs. 10 and 22), where, however, he is slightly older: born in 1633, he took part in the battle of Lens (1648). Here, Dumas makes him a few years younger (it is 1660, which makes his date of birth 1635 or 1636).

16 *M. de Saint-Rémy*: Jacques de Couravel, Marquis de Saint-Rémy.[†]

Rocroi and Lens: two of Condé's most famous victories, the first over the Spaniards in 1643, and the second which led to the Peace of Westphalia in 1648.

17 *Paimbœuf and Saint-Nazaire*: ports at the mouth of the Loire: the first on the left bank, and the second on the right bank.

19 *sister-in-law*: that is, Anne of Austria,[†] widow of Louis XIII and mother of Louis XIV. Dumas pre-dates the cancer which was to kill her in 1666: it did not declare itself until 1664.

20 *for the frontiers*: Mazarin worked hard to repair the troubled relationship between France and Spain. The Treaty of the Pyrenees was signed on 7 November 1659 and, to cement it, Mazarin negotiated the marriage of Louis XIV to the Infanta, Maria-Theresa, daughter of Philip IV (1605–65) of Spain. They were married at Saint-Jean-de-Luz on 9 June 1660.

Vendôme or Romorantin: equidistant from Blois, Vendôme lies to the north of the Loire and Romorantin to the south.

Beaugency: on the Loire, 25 km downstream from Orléans and 31 upstream from Blois. D'Artagnan had a particular taste for the white wine produced in this area.

21 *Meung*: Meung-sur-Loire, 6 km upstream from Beaugency. It was there that the young d'Artagnan, riding his yellow horse, first encountered Milady and Rochefort in ch. 1 of *The Three Musketeers*.

M. Le Cardinal: that is, Mazarin.

Brouage: Mazarin had 7 nieces, all of whom he presented at court. Louis fell in love with Olympe Mancini[†] in 1656. Hortense[†] became Duchesse de Mazarin. Louis was first attracted to Marie[†] in 1658, a development which Mazarin viewed with mixed feelings, since it posed a threat to his policy of reconciliation with Spain. Putting politics above the interests of his family, Mazarin urged the king to set duty before love: 'I entreat you, for the sake of your good name, your happiness, for the service of God and for the good of your country.' It was for this reason that he decided to remove his nieces (and Marie in particular) from circulation by sending them to Brouage, on the Atlantic coast south of La Rochelle, then a sizeable port but now silted up. To reach Brouage, their route lay along the Loire, though Mazarin took measures to separate both parties. But Dumas again bends the facts for dramatic purposes. Marie de Mancini, accompanied by two of her sisters, left Paris for Brouage on 22 June 1659. Mazarin left 4 days later, and Louis shortly after.

Vive de Roi!: Gaston, who coveted the throne of France, had the misfortune to live under two kings: his brother Louis XIII and his nephew Louis XIV. Here, Dumas judges him less harshly than in *Twenty Years After*: see List of Historical Characters.

22 *my father*: Raoul is the son of Athos, who, after the adventures described in *The Three Musketeers*, had taken the title of the Comte de la Fère.

24 *awkwardness of movement*: she limped as the result of a badly set leg broken in an accident when she was young; Dumas tells the story in *Twenty Years After* (World's Classics, pp. 133, 149).

Mademoiselle de Hautefort: Marie d'Hautefort,[†] one of Anne of Austria's faithful 'Spanish' entourage, was instrumental in arranging the escape of Madame de Chevreuse[†] in October 1637: see *Twenty Years After* (World's Classics, p. 196). Louis XIII, a jealous lover, one day surprised Mlle de Hautefort holding a letter. 'He wanted to see it; she refused. Finally, he tried to snatch it from her. Knowing what sort of man he was, she slipped it into her bodice and said: "If you want it, you'll have to take it!" Do you know what he did? He took the fire-tongs from the hearth, fearing to touch the pretty woman's bosom.' (Tallemant des Réaux, *Historiettes*, Pléiade, 1960, i. 338). There are several versions of this story and a variant, which Dumas recounts elsewhere. In October 1637, Séguier, Keeper of the Seals and Chancellor, was ordered to search the queen's apartments, and if necessary her person, for evidence of her intelligence with Spain. Séguier searched the queen's rooms but balked at ransacking the royal bosom.

24 *his way to Poitiers*: the main road through France from Paris to Spain, where Louis was to meet the Infanta, lay through Orléans, Blois, Poitiers, Angoulême, Bordeaux, and Bayonne.

25 *Mesdemoiselles de Mancini*: Mazarin's nieces: see List of Historical Characters.

26 *Mazarino Mazarini*: Dumas reminds us frequently (by reference to his accent) of Mazarin's Italian origins, which were frequently held against him and had been exploited during the Fronde by his political opponents, who either wrote or paid for the large number of songs and satires known collectively as the 'Mazarinades'. As we have seen, Mazarin did not attempt to make Marie Queen of France, though many believed this was his ambition; see below, pp. 109–11.

Don Luis de Haro: Luis Méndez de Haro (1599–1661), Duke of Carpio, one of the most capable Spanish ministers during the *ancien régime*. Haro, first minister to Philip of Spain, met Mazarin on neutral ground at the Île des Faisans, at the foot of the Pyrenees, which belonged to neither nation, and negotiated the marriage. 'These two splendid courts appeared in their full lustre among those savage mountains' (David Hume, *History of Great Britain* (London, 1789 edn.), x. 340) and Philip ceremonially betrothed his daughter to Louis. The exiled Charles II was in attendance; Philip received him civilly, but Mazarin refused to see him (ibid. 341). In Chs. 6–11, Dumas transfers Charles's rebuff to Blois, nine months later.

27 *M. Malicorne*: see List of Historical Characters.

29 *invented the post*: Louis XI (1423–83) overcame aristocratic opposition and laid the foundation for a united French nation. He encouraged the spread of printing, established twelve universities, and, in 1464, to promote better communications, created a system of relays and staging posts which was a distant forerunner of the postal service, which Paris would see only in the 1760s.

30 *and knows it*: see *Twenty Years After* (World's Classics, p. 129), where Bragelonne is said to be at three gun-shots distance from La Vallière: 'a large white house, slate roof, built on an eminence, shaded by enormous sycamores'. Later (p. 114 below), it is 'a handsome white-and-red house', a half-hour's gallop from Blois. Louise hailed from La Vallière, a fifteenth-century manor near Reugny, 10 km north-west of Amboise. But there was no estate of Bragelonne. According to the epilogue of *The Three Musketeers*, Athos had retired to 'a small property in the Roussillon' which he had just inherited. Subsequently he was left the estate of La Fère from a 'near relative' named Bragelonne (*Twenty Years After*, World's Classics, p. 352).

31 *reconciliation with the court*: Condé,† a major player in the Fronde, had long remained opposed to Mazarin and the court, and had returned to the fold only in late 1659, after duly expressing contrition for his past conduct: he saw the king at Chambord in January 1660 and the royal party dined at Blois the following day. Here again, Dumas condenses events. Throughout the saga, Athos, Comte de la Fère, remains true to his belief in the absolute authority of all monarchs. Though politically inactive in the years following *Twenty Years After*, he could scarcely have approved of Condé's conduct.

vaults of Saint-Denis: in ch. 24 of *Twenty Years After*, Athos teaches Raoul to love monarchy by showing him the shrine of French kings at Saint-Denis, then a village outside the walls of Paris, named after the third-century saint of that name who was buried there. An abbey was built over the tomb in 626 by Dagobert I, who was interred in its church. Thereafter it became the mausoleum of the kings of France. The practice, begun in the thirteenth century, of erecting monuments over the royal tombs, was discontinued after the Renaissance: Bourbon coffins were placed in the crypt without memorial.

Turenne: during the Fronde, 'le Grand Turenne'† had begun as an opponent of Mazarin but settled his differences with the court party in 1651, and defeated Condé at a crucial engagement in the Faubourg Saint-Antoine in 1652. It was his success at the Battle of the Dunes in 1658 which paved the way for the Treaty of the Pyrenees which brought peace between France and Spain in 1659. Raoul fought with Condé at Lens (August 1648), but must have left his service that autumn when Condé defied Mazarin, who (in Athos's view) defended the king against the nobility. In other words, Raoul had served under Turenne for far longer than he had been attached to Condé. Dumas here bends the facts to suit the needs of the tale he tells, since Condé is to have a greater role in the events which follow than Turenne.

32 *the name of Athos*: Athos is the oldest of the Musketeers. His birth and past are shrouded in mystery in *The Three Musketeers*, where they are part of the plot. A little more is revealed in *Twenty Years After*, where we learn (p. 137) that his mother had been maid of honour to Marie de' Medici, a sure indication of his noble birth and of his family's standing. Though susceptible to the charms of dominant women (he was Milady's first husband, and Raoul is the result of his affair with the scheming Mme de Chevreuse), Athos has a very other-wordly image. The manuscript book of the next sentence probably contains his memoirs: in the preface to *The Three Musketeers*, Dumas claims (according to a familiar literary convention) to be no more than the editor of a work by the Comte de la Fère discovered in an archive.

34 *to understand that*: Athos's opposition to Louise is explained by his wish to see Raoul in a position to serve the monarchy, a role he could carry out only by making an illustrious marriage.

Grimaud: a man of few words and infinite resource (in *Twenty Years After*, chs. 18–25, he played a central role in Beaufort's escape from Vincennes in 1648), who had been Athos's servant since *The Three Musketeers*.

35 *royale*: a style in beards begun by Louis XIII, more easily recognized in English as a Vandyke.

Cropoli: the character of Cropoli and his household is an instance of Dumas's occasional comic invention.

36 *Castle of the States*: see note to p. 8. Dumas's description of Blois is recalled from his visit in 1830.

37 *to strangle*: Catherine de' Medici (1519–89), wife of Henri II, mother to three French kings. Many tales survive of her ruthless ambition and Dumas made good use of them in novels such as *La Reine Margot*.

Maréchal d'Ancre: that is, Concino Concini,[†] killed on the Pont du Louvre by order of Louis XIII on 24 April 1617.

Mary de Medici: see note to p. 12.

38 *the Raphaels and the Caracci*: only in the ironical sense a 'rival' of Raphael Santi (1483–1520) and the Caracci, a family of Italian painters who founded the Bolognese school in the late sixteenth century. Dumas probably has in mind Annibale Caracci (1560–1609), an admirer of Raphael.

la Maréchale d'Ancre: Leonora Dori, known as Laure Galigaï, wife of Concino Concini.[†] She was believed to have exerted an evil influence over the queen, and was tried for witchcraft and executed on 8 July 1617. Her house, situated in what is now the Rue de Tournon, was pillaged (but not burned) in September 1616, before the murder of her husband.

39 *Bronzino*: Angiolo Bronzino (1503–72), portraitist and poet, born in Florence, is 'a god among painters'. Pittrino is 'an ultramontane artist' because he hailed from the 'further' side of the Alps.

Albani: Francesco Albani (1578–1660), a member of the Bolognese school who had studied under Ludovico Caracci (1555–1619). He specialized in idyllic scenes from ancient mythology populated by Venuses, Galateas, and angels' heads.

Anacreontically: the work of Anacreon (560–478 BC), a Greek lyric poet, survives only in fragments. The sixty or so 'Anacreontic Odes', which are attributed to him, were in fact written much later. They celebrate love and wine with great delicacy of grace and expression.

échevin: until the end of the *ancien régime*, the various trades and avocations (builders, printers, bakers, etc.) were carried out under the auspices of organized guilds. Elected officers (*échevins* and *syndics*) oversaw work, regulated corporate life, and dealt with the State and other bodies.

oubliettes: the oubliette was a windowless, subterranean dungeon with an opening at the top used for prisoners condemned to be 'forgotten'. The castle at Pierrefonds, owned by Porthos, was equipped with deep, narrow oubliettes built into the walls and reached below moat-level. They are illustrated in Viollet-le-duc's *Dictionnaire d'architecture* (1853–69). Those at Blois were even grimmer. In 1830, Dumas had seen 'the oubliettes of Catherine de Medici which were 80 feet deep, with sides bristling with razor-sharp steel blades and spikes pointed like the tips of lances, which were so numerous and so artistically arranged in spirals that a man falling, though one of God's creatures, losing a limb or a slice of flesh with every impact as he went, would be a shapeless lump of meat when he reached the bottom. The next day, quicklime was thrown after him to prevent his remains going bad' (*La Revue des deux mondes*, Jan. 1831).

41 *Rama*: the city built by Baasha, King of Israel 'to the intent that he might let none go out or come in to Asa king of Judah' (II

Chronicles 16: 1). Jeremiah (31: 15) foretold the weeping at Rama which followed Herod's slaughter of the innocents (Matthew 2: 18).

41 *and the white*: if Dumas's social egalitarianism shows through here, so does a view of the superiority of 'the white race' shortly to be publicized by Gobineau (1816–82) in his influential *Essai* (1853–5) on 'the inequality of the human races'. It is one of the rare occasions when Dumas, grandson of a West Indian slave, refers to this issue, favouring the view of 'racial aristocracy'.

42 *a physiognomist*: the 'science' of physiognomy held that facial traits provided a sure guide to character. It was developed into a rigorous system by Johann-Caspar Lavater (1741–1801). Dumas probably did not believe the theory but, as a novelist, found it useful. In his descriptions of people, he regularly exploits 'physiognomy'.

45 *pistoles*: the *pistole* was worth 10 livres, the *louis* 24, and the *écu*, or crown, 3 livres.

a Jew: the medieval kings of France had persistently persecuted the Jews: from the eleventh to the fourteenth century, they were massacred, dispossessed, exiled, and recalled many times. In 1394 they were again banished, but by the sixteenth century had returned to certain parts of France. While canon law forbade the charging of interest on money-lending, Jewish law forbade only the taking of interest from coreligionists. By the Renaissance the Jews had a monopoly of usury, and were tolerated by Louis XIV, who needed them as essential cogs in the financial system.

47 *Parry*: readers of *Twenty Years After* will recall the devotion of 'Parry' to Charles I. The character is an invention of Dumas, who, however, may have had in mind Sir Thomas Parry (d. 1560), who during Mary's reign was one of the Protestants allowed to attend upon the Princess Elizabeth when she was confined at Hatfield. He remained one of Elizabeth's favourites. He was knighted on her accession and became controller of her household in November 1558. Parry was the principal promoter of Dudley's marriage to the queen.

48 *musketeers*: the Musketeers were formed in 1622 as a 100-strong élite section of the royal bodyguard and served the king, who was their captain. Their commander had the rank of 'Captain-Lieutenant', a post held by Tréville[†] between 1634 and 1642. The Musketeers were disbanded in 1646 and did not reform until 1657, when Mazarin appointed the Duke of Nevers, a nephew, Captain-Lieutenant. They formed a company of 150 men, were paid 35

sous a day (20 sous to a livre), and wore a sky-blue surtout decorated with a silver cross. They were known as 'Grey Musketeers' after the colour of their horses. In 1660, a second company of 'Black Musketeers' was created. Both followed the king into battle and saw service in the siege wars of the period.

queen-mother: that is, Anne of Austria.[†]

Dangeau: see List of Historical Characters.

gorget and buff-coat: the gorget was originally a piece of armour protecting the throat; when chain-mail and armour were abandoned, it survived as an ornament or as the badge of an officer on duty. The buff-jerkin, worn under armour, survived as the buff-coat which replaced metal armour: it was thick enough to stop a blade or a bullet. In ceremonial versions, buff-coats were richly embroidered with coloured silks.

50 *ten years*: in fact, Charles had spent a decade working for the restoration of the English monarchy in a variety of ways, and his presence at Blois (a transposition of his unsuccessful visit to Mazarin in 1659: see note to p. 26) was but one of the many steps he had taken. Dumas gives it prominence for dramatic reasons.

the general: that is General Monk,[†] later Duke of Albemarle.

51 *Tenby*: on the South Welsh coast near Pembroke. Parry's escape, like the character, is an invention, Dumas probably remembered the town as the place from which the future Henry VII had fled to Brittany in 1471.

his minister: that is, Mazarin, who amassed a considerable fortune in the service of the king; see Chs. 10 and 45.

52 *public charity*: Henrietta-Maria,[†] wife of Charles I and sister to Louis XIII, had left England in 1644 and remained in France. Her presence was, at times, a political embarrassment, and while she lived in reduced circumstances her situation was not as pathetic as Charles claims here. She had three sons and three daughters. The daughter mentioned here is probably Henrietta-Anne[†] (1644–70), who was to marry Philippe d'Orléans,[†] brother of Louis XIV. Her two other sons were James (1633–1701), Duke of York (later James II), and Henry (1639–60), Duke of Gloucester.

53 *assassination and treachery*: see notes to pp. 7 and 61. Henri's crown passed to Henri IV,[†] King of Navarre, and first of the kings of the senior Bourbon line, in 1593.

five feet two inches: the French foot ('le pied de roi') was the equivalent of 12.8 English inches. In British terms, Louis measured

5 feet 6 inches, which was about average for the period. Charles II, at 6 feet 2, was considered very tall. Elsewhere in the saga, Dumas tells us that d'Artagnan also measured 5 feet 6, while Porthos, the 'giant', was 6 feet 4.

55 *a good stomach from nature*: like Richelieu, who had suffered agonies from piles, Mazarin was not a man of robust constitution.

a true Lorrainer: the Duchess of Orléans was Marguerite de Lorraine before her marriage to Gaston in 1632.

56 *Auricule*: the name (from the Latin *auricula*, ear) was chosen by Dumas as appropriate for a music mistress.

57 *in that word*: because Louis is in love with Marie de Mancini.

ten-year-old fashions: when Louis passed through Blois in March 1659, the backwardness of Gaston's court was much remarked. 'The ladies', said Mme de Montpensier (*Mémoires*, iii. 376), 'were dressed like the dinner-tables: unfashionably.'

58 *Marquis de la Vallière*: that is, Laurent de la Baume le Blanc,† seigneur de la Vallière.

daube truffée: braised beef with truffles. Truffles are also served with the *dinde* (turkey) mentioned in the next paragraph.

table of Jupiter: Olympus was the home of the gods, presided over by Jupiter, father of Diana the Huntress who vowed she would never marry. Venus was the goddess of beauty. Alcmena, wife of Amphitryon, was seduced by Jupiter and became the mother of Hercules. Io was also loved by Jupiter, who changed her into a heifer.

61 *in the States*: the States-General, held in Blois in 1588, brought together representatives from the provincial States, composed of members of the three 'orders' (clergy, nobility, and 'third estate'), and constituted the nearest equivalent to a national assembly that was possible in an absolute monarchy. The States-General, first convened in 1302, met at irregular intervals—and not at all between 1614 and 1789.

stab of the poniard: the States-General of 1588 were notable for their violence: Henri III defeated the League, formed by the Duc de Guise in 1576 to protect Catholic interests, and ultimately to unseat the king. The Duc de Guise was murdered on 23 December 1588. In 1830, on his visit to the château, Dumas had been rather sceptical of the graphic details provided by the guide.

62 *blood of Concini*: see note to p. 37.

not customary with him: Dumas takes care to show that Louis, who will turn himself into an autocratic monarch after the death of Mazarin, is as yet uncertain of his authority, dominated still by the greater power of the cardinal.

63 *Lieutenant*: the Captain of the Musketeers was the king, who had only a ceremonial role. The commanding officer of the company had the rank of Captain-Lieutenant (see note to p. 48). In 1661, this officer was a nephew of Mazarin who took no interest in his duties and left all the work to Charles de Batz, the original d'Artagnan. Dumas's d'Artagnan, though clearly the *de facto* commanding officer, has only the rank of Lieutenant, a matter which is of perpetual concern to him: see note to p. 105. Dumas later (p. 377) adds to the confusion by allowing Louis to make d'Artagnan 'Captain-General', a rank superior to that of Marshal of France; there was no such grade in the Musketeers.

his guards: in 1623 Richelieu had formed his own body of guards, who, on his death, transferred their loyalty to Mazarin.

65 *musket*: the musket was introduced into the French army in about 1575, being lighter and more accurate than the harquebus which it replaced. In 1660 the musket was still a matchlock (flintlocks appeared towards the end of the century) and was heavy: for firing, a forked rest was required.

67 *The day——*: 30 January 1649, when Charles I was executed at Whitehall. The role played by the Musketeers in events is chronicled in *Twenty Years After*, chs. 57–70.

68 *our house*: that is, the House of Stuart.

Laporte: La Porte† was in the habit of reading out extracts from Mézeray's *Histoire de France* (1643–51) with a view to teaching him to respect strong kings and despise weak monarchs who relied on ministers like Mazarin.

69 *Scone*: Charles arrived in Paris in April 1646 and spent two years there. In summer of 1648, part of the Parliamentary fleet mutinied and sailed to Helvœtsluys. Charles rushed to the Dutch Republic and led an unsuccessful expedition to the Thames. He returned to the Dutch, who soon wearied of his haughty manner: though penniless, he expected to be treated liked royalty. He moved on to France in 1649, where he was not well received: Louis XIV and his mother, obliged to flee Paris as the Fronde approached, had no money to spare for Charles and his hangers-on. In 1650 he accepted the conditions laid down by the Scottish commissioners,

and landed at the mouth of the Spey on 23 June. He was crowned
at Scone on 1 January 1651.

69 *was my wish*: in order to reclaim his father's crown, but also because he took badly to the Covenant (the founding document of
Presbyterianism), which was imposed on him, especially when the
Scots demanded that it be extended to all England. Ever since
Voltaire's *Lettres philosophiques* (1734), the French had been familiar with a view of poor Charles subjected to a regime of prayers,
fasting and six sermons day. But it was for political reasons that he
made an unsuccessful attempt to flee before deciding to remain
and make the best of the situation. Cromwell 'returned upon us' at
Dunbar on 3 September 1650, when the Scots were defeated.

Montrose: the Marquis of Montrose† was hung in Edinburgh by
Leslie, Earl of Leven† on 21 May. His remains were gathered and
buried in 1662.

entered England: in August 1651, Charles marched into England at
the head of 10,000 men. He was routed by Cromwell at Worcester
on 3 September, a day which marked the anniversary of Cromwell's
victory a year earlier.

Protector: Dumas anticipates. Cromwell† was not declared Protector until December 1653, over two years after the defeat of Charles
at Worcester.

a romance: Charles, joining up with Wilmot, wandered for six
weeks, with a price of £1,000 on his head, hiding in the oak at
Boscobel, riding diguised as a serving man, lurking around Stone-
henge: many stories are told of his adventures. To reach Mrs
Norton's safe house, near Bristol, he 'personated a servant', and a
groom who recognized him was sworn to secrecy. Failing to find a
ship, he 'intrusted himself to Colonel Windham, of Dorsetshire',
but there were constant perils. 'The sagacity of a smith, who
remarked that his horse's shoes had been made in the north, not in
the west, as he pretended, once detected him; and he narrowly
escaped' (Hume, *History*, x. 201–4). Charles survived because he
was protected by the Catholic gentry and clergy, of whom the
'court chaplain' was one.

70 *Brighelmsted*: Dumas's attempt at Brightelmstone, the former name
of Brighton (which superseded it in the nineteenth century). Charles
embarked at Shoreham on 15 October 1651, arriving at Fécamp
the next day. Thereafter he remained on the Continent, where he
continued to promote his cause. In June 1659, he travelled to
Fuenterrabía in Spain (just across the border from Hendaye) where

the French and Spanish had gathered to negotiate the Treaty of the Pyrenees and the marriage of Louis with the Infanta. He attempted to enlist their support. The Spaniards received him civilly but Mazarin closed his door. Dumas turns Charles's visit to Mazarin in 1659 into his journey to Blois in 'May 1660'.

everything is changed there: Mazarin's treaty with Cromwell, then Lord Protector, was signed in October 1655. After his death on 3 September 1658, Cromwell was succeeded by his son Richard (1626–1712), who was unable to contain the anarchy which broke out after the death of the Protector: as Dumas indicates, England was politically weak but militarily strong. Richard left office on 22 April 1659 and retired into private life.

Lambert and Monk: that is, John Lambert[†] and George Monk.[†]

71 *arms of royalty*: after a decade of Civil War, the tide of popular opinion was already beginning to turn to thoughts of restoration.

I possess nothing: Mazarin had kept a tight rein on the royal purse-strings and, as Prime Minister, controlled expenditure. The details Louis gives of his treatment are confirmed by the *Memoirs* of La Porte.[†]

72 *M. de Retz*: Paul de Gondi, Cardinal de Retz,[†] had been one of the leading figures in the Fronde. Dumas regularly took Mazarin to task for leaving the welfare of the exiled English queen to others: see *Twenty Years After* (World's Classics, p. 137).

grandson of Henri IV: Charles's mother, Henrietta-Maria,[†] was the daughter of Henri IV.[†]

73 *four French gentlemen*: the attempt made by Dumas's four comrades to save Charles I against impossible odds is told in *Twenty Years After* (chs. 57–70).

with a haughtiness: another glimpse of the authority which lies just beneath the surface of the young King of France.

74 *Gascon accent*: d'Artagnan hailed from Gascony, the part of south-west France situated between the Atlantic coast, the Garonne, and the western Pyrenees. Gascons, who had supported Henri IV and continued to be prominent at the court of Louis XIII, were traditionally fiery and given to acts of bravado known as 'gasconnades'. It is this aspect of d'Artagnan's 'Gascon' character which Dumas exploits. Save for a few exclamations (such as *Mordioux!* (= 'Mort de dieu', 'God's death/S'death')), he makes no attempt to flavour d'Artagnan's speech with his accent. In *The Three Musketeers* (World's Classics, pp. 87 and 471), Athos comments on his 'patois',

which was strong enough to enable Richelieu to recognize him through a hedge. In *Twenty Years After* (World's Classics, p. 84), his accent was still strong enough to prevent his being mistaken for another in the dark. Charles de Batz-Castelmore, on whom the character is based, was born near Tarbes and never lost his accent, which is detectable in his surviving letters, the spelling of which is appalling even by seventeenth-century standards.

74 *Bernouin*: see List of Historical Characters.

75 *Brienne*: Henri-Auguste de Loménie de Brienne.†

    M. Guénaud: François Guénaud,† first physician to Anne of Austria.

    Colbert: Jean-Baptiste Colbert,† Mazarin's confidant and protégé.

78 *Leyden jar or a voltaic battery*: the jar, a form of condenser, was developed by three Dutchmen at Leiden in 1745, and Volta did not perfect his battery until 1800.

79 *find Jews*: see note to p. 45.

83 *even on the scaffold*: before he was beheaded, Charles I's last word, 'Remember!', was addressed to Bishop Juxon.† In *Twenty Years After* (ch. 70), it was intended for Athos, who crouched beneath the scaffold.

    treaty with Cromwell: the trade treaty, which also promised non-aggression (and included a secret clause expelling James, Charles's brother, from France), was concluded in October 1655. Charles, who was paid an allowance by Mazarin (who delayed his departure until agreement with Cromwell was certain), had left Paris for Germany on 30 June 1654.

84 *brother-in-law*: Charles I had married Henrietta-Maria, the sister of Louis XIII, and was thus Louis's uncle by marriage.

    Rump Parliament: in late 1648, when the Long Parliament (which had first met in 1640) proved unwilling to order the execution of Charles I, Cromwell sent two regiments to the House of Commons, under command of Thomas Pride.† On 6–7 December 1648, Pride arrested 60 uncooperative members of Parliament and ordered a further hundred or so home: the remaining 53 were left to try the king. Those who escaped 'Pride's Purge' constitutued the 'Rump' Parliament. When it created difficulties in 1653, Cromwell had dissolved it. In 1659 it was revived by the army's leaders, who sought a body which, though seemingly constitutional, would do their bidding. In October the military again expelled the Rump for interfering in military affairs. When Monk declared himself in favour of restoring it (against calls for a free parliament), it reconvened on 26 December and pursued extreme republican policies. But by the end of February 1660 it finally lost the battle of wills with Monk.

war with Holland: it was in fact Louis's ambition to expand France's frontiers into the Spanish Netherlands which led to war with both Spain and the Dutch Republic. Louis invoked the Law of Devolution (which gave inheritance rights to the female line), and argued that Spain's territories in the Low Countries (then nominally governed by the absentee Don Juan, a bastard son of Philip IV) should revert to the Queen of France, formerly the Infanta. By 1667, Charleroi, Tournai, and Lille had become French, and in 1672 Louis invaded Dutch territory by land and sea: the episode forms the background to Dumas's *The Black Tulip* (1850).

Mazarinades: the name more frequently given to the enormous number of satirical songs and pamphlets which chronicled the failings and 'political tricks' of the Cardinal.

85 *let Holland do so*: as the political climate grew increasingly favourable to him, Charles, who was installed in Brussels, travelled to Holland on 4 April 1660 and the same day signed the Declaration of Breda, which set out the terms for the restoration of the monarchy.

brave brewer: Oliver Cromwell† trained as a lawyer, but did not practise. Robert Cromwell (d. 1617), the Lord Protector's father, owned land on which there was a small brewery.

triple brass: Horace (*Odes*, II. i. 9.) pictures the first sailor ever to put to sea with a heart of oak and girt with 'triple-plated bronze' (*aes triplex*).

86 *burns his nightcap*: Dumas always refers favourably to Louis XI (1423–83), who, though autocratic and cruel, nevertheless laid the foundation for the unified modern state on which the seventeenth century was to build. Louis meant that problems were to be faced afresh each day.

a marvel of depth and tenacity: the estimate of Monk† which Dumas puts in Mazarin's mouth is not altogether overstated. Monk was a gruff, canny, professional soldier who played his cards close to his chest. Historians still argue about his motives for his return to royalism: was he convinced early in 1659 that the monarchy should be restored for the good of the country—and of himself—or was his opinion formed by the politicking which clearly sickened him as the year drew to its close?

86 *Piscina*: Mazarin was born at Piscina in the Abruzzi. His father, Pietro Mazarini (1576–1654), was a minor Sicilian noble, born at Palermo, though Mazarin's enemies said that he was a hatter or a fisherman.

Monsieur le Prince: Beaufort,[†] Retz,[†] and Condé[†] ('Monsieur le Prince') had all opposed Mazarin at various times before, during, and after the Fronde.

velvet cap: that is, his cardinal's skull-cap.

Satan has twisted: Dante, *Hell*, xx. 10–24: 'So twisted that the tears their eyes did weep / Fell down the spine, nor left the haunches dry' (Plumptre's translation).

87 *dispersing it*: on reaching London in February, Monk continued to avoid offending the Rump, though without giving it his support. See note to p. 83.

to leave France: that is, by the terms of the treaty of 1655; see note to p. 83. This was why Charles travelled to Spain and not France to seek an interview with Mazarin in 1659.

companion of my childhood: when the adolescent Charles arrived in France in 1646, he remained in Paris and was a familiar of the royal court.

89 *Duc de Guise*: see note to p. 61.

90 *the Louvre*: the Louvre was the palace of the French kings. Begun in 1204, building continued sporadically through successive reigns and was not finished until Napoleon III implemented a decree of 1848 which voted funds for its completion. Although Louis XIV added the colonnade facing Saint-Germain-de-l'Auxerrois, he chose Versailles as his royal residence. Work on developing what had been one of Louis XIII's hunting-lodges there began in 1661.

91 *over thirty years*: though *The Three Musketeers* begins in 1625, d'Artagnan was not accepted into the Musketeers until the end of the adventure, in 1628. In the saga, his service is continuous. In reality, the Musketeers were disbanded between 1646 and 1657.

92 *facing the sun*: Dumas's descriptions of his characters are usually perfunctory and conventional. He is much more successful in presenting them, as here, symbolically. D'Artagnan is noble and untamed; Louis was to transform himself into the Sun King.

93 *Callot*: Jacques Callot (1592–1635), engraver and painter, known for his realistic representation of seventeenth-century manners. Dumas may have in mind the eighteen plates which show 'The Miseries of War'.

94 *valid*: Louis pleaded with Anne (see p. 98) who opposed the match. Her wish was that Louis should marry the Infanta and thus renew the links between France and Spain. According to Mme de Motteville (*Mémoires*, iv. 163), Anne prevented Louis from corresponding with Marie. The reigning pope was Alexander VII (1655–67). The chapter is based on two meetings with Marie: their farewell on 22 June 1659, and a reunion at Saint-Jean-d'Angély on 10 August.

97 *so much to say*: Dumas links nature and love in a way which reflects the pathetic fallacy of the Romantic Age. The seventeenth century found nature tolerable only when disciplined in formal gardens.

99 *fierce and disdainful*: see Virgil, *Aeneid* vi. 467–71, where Dido's anger blazed and Aeneas' words have no more effect on her than on a block of Parian marble. She refuses to forgive him for subordinating their love to his duty as ruler of the Trojans; even in Hades, where he sees her, her spirit will not relent.

100 *yet I depart*: by June 1659, Mazarin's plans to make peace with Spain were far advanced and Louis said a tearful farewell to Marie: 'not content to hear him swear the sincerest feelings for her, she would rather have received a more positive expression of his love in the form of action which his rank authorized him to take. She took him to task on this score and, seeing him shed tears as she stepped into her coach, observed that he wept and was not master to have it otherwise [. . .]. Still weeping, he allowed her to leave, promising however that he would never agree to the Spanish marriage and would not give up his plan to marry her [. . .]. The King saw Mlle de Mancini again at Saint-Jean-d'Angély [between La Rochelle and Cognac, on 10 August]. In the few moments he spent with her, he seemed more in love with her than ever and he repeated his promise to remain true. Time, absence and other considerations led him finally to break his promise' (Mme de la Fayette, op. cit. 445).

101 *energy*: a quality more prized in Dumas's day than in the seventeenth century.

102 *the old one*: Dumas enables his heroes to age very convincingly. Basically, they do not change and they are as effective as ever. But d'Artagnan and Athos are particularly given to commenting unfavourably on the new generation which falls short of the 'old' standards of honour, courage, and comradeship. Raoul turns out to be limp and over-sensitive, and de Wardes—sneaky rather than evil—is no more than a pale shadow of the two great villains who

had previously tested the Musketeers: Milady in *The Three Mus-keteers* and her son Mordaunt in *Twenty Years After*. To some extent, Dumas (who was 45 in 1847) compares the younger gen-eration who had grown up during the bourgeois reign of Louis-Philippe with the fiery, full-blooded men with whom he had fought for the political and literary revolution of 1830.

103 *below my value*: while d'Artagnan is committed to an an ideal of service to king and country, he is in no doubt of his own worth. He had many times been promised preferment (by Richelieu, Anne of Austria, Mazarin) but was still underpaid and still in the ranks. His comrades had done better. Athos, as we have seen, has re-joined the nobility; Porthos, thanks to a good marriage, is a wealthy landowner; and Aramis has risen in the Church. Beneath d'Artagnan's bluff good humour lies a seam of bitterness.

104 *secret archives*: d'Artagnan's services to the crown are to be found only in the Musketeer saga: Charles de Batz-Castelmore, the his-torical d'Artagnan, was a minor figure in history.

Tasso's or Ariosto's epics: *Jerusalem Delivered*, by Torquato Tasso (1544–95), and *Orlando furioso*, by Ludovico Ariosto (1474–1533).

M. de Richelieu: Richelieu, though outmanœuvred by d'Artagnan, had rewarded him with a commission in the Musketeers in ch. 67 of *The Three Musketeers*. D'Artagnan had not only saved Bucking-ham[†] in the affair of the diamond studs (chs. 10–23) but also tried to warn him against the assassin Felton (ch. 59). Though he had no hand in freeing Beaufort[†] from Vincennes (*Twenty Years After*, chs. 18–25), he had given Beaufort and Retz[†] sterling support during the Fronde and ensured that the latter's interests were furthered by forcing Mazarin to sign the Treaty of Rueil (chs. 93–5). Anne of Austria had thanked him twice: once for retrieving the studs and once for his part in the Fronde (*Twenty Years After*, World's Classics, p. 773): on both occasions she rewarded him with a diamond ring.

105 *regency*: Anne of Austria was regent during the minority of Louis XIV. D'Artagnan refers to his exploits in *Twenty Years After*, which not only describes the Musketeers' attempt to save Charles I but also their role in the civil war of the Fronde in 1649–50.

marshals of France: on d'Artagnan's promotions, see next note. Anne remarked that the Captain-Lieutenancy 'is one of the chief military posts connected with the King's house' (*Twenty Years After*, p. 769), for the man who held it was close to the king.

the commission himself: d'Artagnan received his commission as a Musketeer from Richelieu in 1628. He was still a lieutenant in 1649 (*Twenty Years After*, p. 29). It was in fact Anne of Austria who signed his commission as Captain-Lieutenant, to fill the post left vacant by Tréville† (ibid., p. 769): even so, Mazarin still had authority to rescind the appointment and had done so. D'Artagnan's ambition was still (as it had been in 1650) to be appointed Marshal of France (*Twenty Years After*, p. 787).

106 *fifty-four years of age*: Dumas makes d'Artagnan, born in 1606, slightly older than Charles de Batz-Castelmore, who was born in about 1615.

Henri IV: Henri was from the Béarn, a region situated south-west of Gascony. Dumas noted earlier (p. 74) that d'Artagnan is a Gascon.

107 *lives of my family*: for the way in which d'Artagnan saved Louis from the prying mob, see *Twenty Years After*, ch. 54.

108 *death is behind it*: another sentiment more readily associated with the Romantics than with the seventeenth century.

111 *the exiles*: that is, Mazarin's nieces, exiled to Brouage.

114 *Lazarus*: Luke 16: 24.

116 *at his last moments?*: Grimaud had played a vital supporting role in the Musketeers' efforts to rescue Charles I: see *Twenty Years After*, chs. 66–70.

117 *stadtholder of Holland*: William (1650–1702), Charles II's nephew, was the son of William II of Orange and Mary, eldest daughter of Charles I. The Act of Exclusion of 1654 debarred any member of the House of Orange from becoming Stadtholder, the supreme office which gave command of the army and of all branches of government. The Dutch Republic was ruled by Jan De Witt. It was not until the murder of the De Witt brothers in 1672 that William was proclaimed Stadtholder: see *The Black Tulip*. In 1689, William became King of England.

119 *the route to exile*: Dumas's chronology is now completely out of step with history. Only six days have elapsed since Chapter 1 ('the middle of the month of May, in the year 1660'), and yet many of the events which are still ongoing had in reality already occurred. While Louis's marriage with the Infanta (9 June 1660) is still two weeks off, his love for Marie de Mancini began and ended in 1659; Monk crossed the Tweed on 1 January 1660; and Charles landed at Dover on 4 May 1660, two weeks before he now sets off to go

into exile in Holland. In fact, in the early months of 1660, Charles was based at Brussels, but moved to Breda on 4 April.

120 *ascended the scaffold*: on 30 January 1649. For Athos's role in events, see *Twenty Years After*, ch. 70.

His name?: the executioner was Mordaunt, son of Milady, who died 'a violent death' in *Twenty Years After*, ch. 77.

121 *castle of Newcastle*: see *Twenty Years After*, p. 598. The 'castle' will subsequently become an abbey, and both, like Charles's million, are convenient inventions.

122 *encamped there*: Monk crossed into England at the Tweed on 1 January 1660 and marched directly to London, which he reached five weeks later. Dumas's grasp of English history was as weak as his geography: he will situate Newcastle on the Tweed.

123 *your aunt*: that is, Anne of Austria.† Athos refers to events in the two previous instalments of the saga.

126 *Melun*: 56 km south-east of Paris.

127 *the fourth day*: by Dumas's chronology it is now still May and will be for some time: see p. 133.

Bazin: Aramis's servant since the days of *The Three Musketeers*.

the Trojans: *Iliad*, xvii. The death of Patroclus, slain by Hector, revived Achilles' determination and turned the fortunes of the field in favour of the Greeks. When Hector was dead, Patroclus was buried with full honours.

Chevalier d'Herblay: even as a young man, Aramis had shown an interest in theological matters: he then intended to join the Lazarists. But it is at a Jesuit monastery that d'Artagnan finds him in *Twenty Years After* (chs. 9–10), where he is known as the abbé d'Herblay. D'Artagnan's reference to the Vicar-General is intended as a jibe at Aramis's long-standing ambition for preferment.

128 *Bishop of Vannes*: in Brittany. He was appointed in April (p. 129). Charles de Rosmadec had been Bishop of Vannes since 1647. He was not known to Fouquet.

Monsieur Fouquet: Nicolas Fouquet,† the all-powerful finance minister, abused his position to create an enormous personal fortune. Work had begun on his magnificent château at Vaux-le-Vicomte, 6 km from Melun, in 1654.

129 *in verse*: in *The Three Musketeers*, Aramis wrote verses, including a poem made up of words of one syllable. D'Artagnan pokes similar fun at his versifying in *Twenty Years After* (World's Classics, p. 93).

132 *powerful personages in the kingdom*: from the beginning of the saga, Aramis, the most secretive of Dumas's quartet, maintains mysterious relationships with powerful political figures—notably Mme de Chevreuse,† Mme de Longueville,† and, now, Fouquet.

133 *Vicar-General d'Herblay*: so d'Artagnan's jest (p. 127) has turned out to be less fanciful than he imagined. The General of the Society of Jesus (founded in 1534 by Ignatius Loyola) is elected by a congregation of professed members and holds office for life. A German named Nickel was Vicar-General between 1652 and 1664.

its ruin: the splendour of Fouquet's château at Vaux-le-Vicomte was taken by Louis as incontrovertible evidence that public moneys had been diverted into its construction. It was after the fête given at Vaux in August 1661 that the king decided to have Fouquet arrested.

Pierrefonds: at the end of *The Three Musketeers*, Porthos, the amiable giant, marries Mme Coquenard, widow of a wealthy lawyer. By 1648, she is dead and his estates comprise 'that of Vallon at Corbeil, that of Bracieux in the Soissonnais, and that of Pierrefonds in Valois' (*Twenty Years After*, World's Classics, p. 242). Dumas gives a number of contradictory locations for Porthos's scattered properties. If Vallon is usually placed near Corbeil (between Evry and Melun), Bracieux is said to be near Meaux or situated in the Loire valley, though most frequently it is placed near Villers-Cotterêts: 'four leagues from that town', as d'Artagnan is informed (ibid. 106). On the other hand, Pierrefonds, between Villers-Cotterêts and Compiègne, was real enough. Its twelfth century castle was largely demolished at the end of the sixteenth for the shelter it had given to Catholic extremists. It was bought by Napoleon in 1813 and renovated by Viollet-le-duc in 1862.

Nanteuil-le-Haudoin and Crépy: Dumas, who knew the area, gives us only the last part of d'Artagnan's itinerary. Nanteuil is only 12 km from Crépy-en-Valois, which is 17 km from Pierrefonds.

Louis of Orléans: Louis XII (1462–1515).

to our readers: in *Twenty Years After*, ch. 12.

134 *poussa*: a kelly; a round-bellied figure, weighted at the base, which, when pushed, returns to the vertical position.

Mousqueton: Porthos's indolent servant since the start of the saga.

136 *Carmelite*: one of the four main mendicant orders, the Order of Our Lady of Mount Carmel, founded in Palestine in the twelfth century, entered France during the reign of Louis IX (1214–70).

137 *Racan*: Honoré de Bueil (1589–1670), Marquis de Racan, remembered for his versions of the pastoral: Dumas anticipates his death by a decade.

the cestus: a form of boxing practised by Greeks and Romans. It was a glove loaded with lead or iron which was strapped to the hands and forearms of boxers to make their punches more telling.

138 *M. du Vallon*: Porthos's full title is Monsieur du Vallon de Bracieux de Pierrefonds.

139 *the Equinox*: Dumas overlooks the fact that it is now near the end of May and that the Equinox (21 March) has passed.

140 *Rue des Lombards*: then known for its apothecaries and confectioners. The street still exists: it crosses the Boulevard de Sébastopol and ends at the church of Saint-Merri in the 4th *arrondissement*.

Planchet: d'Artagnan's resourceful servant since the beginning of the saga. After *The Three Musketeers*, he bought a grocer's shop, which is now given a name.

143 *usury*: with certain exceptions, the practice of usury was forbidden by Church law (see note to p. 45). The charging of interest on money-loans continued to be debated throughout the eighteenth century and into the nineteenth, when Ruskin, among others, spoke against it.

meetings: that is, duels: Planchet defends his honour against accusations that he is an usurer. Duels had been forbidden during the reign of Henri III (1574–89). Louis XIII renewed the ban in 1617, and during the next ten years a number of high-ranking duellists were decapitated. Richelieu enforced the ban, as did Louis XIV and his successors in the eighteenth century, when various attempts were made to regulate the wearing of swords. The ban was justified on several grounds. The Crown could not afford to lose good fighting men in petty squabbles, but, more important, the duelling code was based on an ideal of aristocratic honour which transcended royal authority and which it therefore challenged. Even so, duelling—a form of natural justice which took precedence over the king's law—outlived the *ancien régime* and continued in France in various forms until the end of the nineteenth century.

145 *Mordaunt*: see *Twenty Years After*, ch. 77.

146 *Duke of York*: the future James II (1633–1701).

now styled: but only by royalists, of whom d'Artagnan is one.

heart of a king: though history would suggest that, as a judge of kings, d'Artagnan seems to be badly mistaken, the final instalment of the saga, *The Man in the Iron Mask*, will prove him right.

149 *Palais Royal*: see *Twenty Years After*, ch. 81.

Rumps and Barebones: on the Rump parliaments, see note to p. 84. The Barebone Parliament (named after Praise-God Barebone, a prominent member with strong views) was convened by Cromwell in 1653 to draw up a new constitution.

150 *Nescio vos*: 'I know you not': the close of the parable of the ten virgins (Matthew 25: 12).

151 *living bear*: in La Fontaine's 'The Bear and the Two Friends' (*Fables*, V. 20), the two friends sell the bearskin before they have caught the bear.

153 *Rue Tiquetonne*: d'Artagnan's hotel, an invention, was situated at the western end of the present Rue Tiquetonne, which links the Rue Montmartre and the Rue Saint-Denis in the 2nd *arrondissement*. At the end of *Twenty Years After* (World's Classics, p. 788), he asks for a room on the first floor as befits a commander of musketeers.

154 *M. Coquenard*: the miserly lawyer of *The Three Musketeers* (ch. 32), whose widow (and money) Porthos had married: see note to p. 133.

155 *form and principle*: a rare personal comment from Dumas, who despised the materialism of his own bourgeois era.

157 *disciple of Pythagoras*: Pythagoras (582–c.500 BC), philosopher and mathematician. Obedience, silence, and abstinence were observed by his followers.

a hanging offence: originally an ecclesiastical offence, bigamy was made a felony in England by the statute of 1604. Smuggling was to attract the attention of the English by the end of the century, and Dumas, a great admirer of Walter Scott, might have remembered the vigorous methods used by excisemen (in *Redgauntlet*) to bring smugglers to book.

158 *guards*: that is, members of the bodyguard formed by Richelieu in 1623: see note to p. 63. In *The Three Musketeers*, Dumas makes much of the rivalry between Musketeers and Guards.

Bergues and Saint Omer: Bergues is 8 km inland from Dunkirk and 30 km north-east of St-Omer.

159 *true French hearts*: anti-English feeling was as strong in Dumas's day (though Anglophobia alternated with periodic bouts of Anglomania) as it was in 1660.

160 *Don Quixote*: Cervantes's novel (1605) was first translated into French in 1619.

intra pectus: 'in their hearts'.

161 *potent fluid*: Dumas seems to have in mind something like adrenalin.

fourth time: d'Artagnan had travelled to England to retrieve the diamond studs in *The Three Musketeers*, and to Newcastle to support Charles I in *Twenty Years After*. For his third journey, Dumas may have in mind the presence of Charles de Batz-Castelmore at the battle of Newbury, or the missions which involved carrying Mazarin's dispatches of Cromwell between 1648 and as late as 1654: see Courtilz de Sandras, *Memoirs of d'Artagnan*, ii. 304.

more than once a day: yet another instance of Dumas's projection of the Romantic viewpoint into the affairs of the seventeenth century.

162 *Meung*: see *The Three Musketeers*, ch. 1.

164 *Cyclops*: the Cyclops of Mount Etna were one-eyed giants who made the thunderbolts fired by Zeus. In the *Iliad* Polyphemus, a Cyclops, son of Neptune, imprisoned the companions of Ulysses, who released them by blinding him.

Quos ego . . .: *Aeneid*, i. 135; when Aeolus, king of the winds, unleashes a furious tempest without his consent, Neptune calls them to order in a speech including these words. The stormy waves subside as quickly—to carry on the Virgilian metaphor—as 'an angry crowd is calmed by a wise orator'.

166 *pirates of Tunis*: Tunisia, ruled by Turkey between 1575 and 1702, was a centre for the corsairs who, operating on the Barbary Coast, preyed upon the ships of the Christian powers.

Ponantais: a word used by Mediterranean peoples for the Atlantic Ocean: it is the opposite of the Levant.

galleys: galleys, usually manned by captives or criminals, were in general use in the Mediterranean until the northern nations took the lead in sailing-ships. Corsair galleys were rowed by Christian prisoners. French convict galleys were gradually replaced from 1748 by the *bagne*, a land-based prison, though they continued in use until the 1830s: see *The Count of Monte Cristo* (World's Classics, p. 109). St Vincent de Paul (1576–1660), appointed Almoner-General of the galleys in 1619, did much to improve the lot of the prisoners: it is said that in 1622 he took the place of a galley-slave as a way of winning him to the faith.

Breskens: a port situated at the mouth of the Scheldt, on the left bank downstream from Antwerp.

167 *Newkerke Street*: Dumas was to visit The Hague in May 1849 for the coronation of William III. Before then, his knowledge of Holland and its history was sketchy. Here he mentions two of its famous landmarks. When he wrote *The Black Tulip* in 1850, he knew that the De Witt brothers were buried on 21 August 1672 in the Nieuwe Kerk.

stadtholder of Holland: there was no Stadtholder in 1660 (see note to p. 117) and William II of Nassau had died in 1650. Charles had long been living at Brussels. When it became clear that the political mood of England had changed, he travelled north to Breda in Holland (about 60 km short of The Hague), where he signed the Declaration on 4 April 1660 and received many emissaries: see note to p. 85.

Scheveningen: then a fishing village about 3 km north of The Hague.

168 *the Archipelago*: the islands of the Aegean Sea, between Greece and Turkey.

badly governed: by the autumn of 1659, the power of the military outstripped the authority of Parliament: in October, the French ambassador wrote that 'there is now no government in England'.

169 *Peter Wentworth*: Pepys records that in the autumn of 1659, twenty-two members had been refused entrance to the Commons. Wentworth was the family name of the Fairfaxes, father and son, who served the crown loyally. Perhaps Dumas has in mind Peter Wentworth (1530–96), who was sent to the Tower by Elizabeth for his fierce defence of parliamentary liberties.

his seat: in the autumn of 1656 'a motion in form was made by Alderman Pack, one of the city members, for investing the protector with the dignity of king'. The matter was debated in April 1657 and Cromwell accepted that there were excellent practical reasons to justify such a step. Lambert was opposed to the move. 'But how to bring over the soldiers to the same way of thinking was the question. The office of king had been painted to them in such horrible colours, that there were no hopes of reconciling them suddenly to it, even though bestowed upon their general, to whom they were so much devoted . . . Cromwell, after the agony and perplexity of long doubt, was at last obliged to refuse the crown' (Hume, *History*, x. 296–300).

enemies of each other: on 17 October, Lambert† expelled the Rump and headed a 'Committee of Safety' which ruled autocratically: this presented Monk† with a pretext to heed calls to restore a 'lawful' Parliament. Dumas, as was his habit, reduces a complex political situation to a conflict between two men, but, as Hume wrote, 'a rivalship had long subsisted between Monk and Lambert' (Hume, *History*, x. 345). Monk kept all sides guessing: as late as 18 January 1660, Pepys noted: 'All the world is at a loss to think what Monk will do.' Charles's supporters found his motives as much a mystery as any one else.

169 *pacified Scotland*: after distinguishing himself at Dunbar, he had been sent back to Scotland as governor in 1654. He succeeded, as Dumas says, in establishing order.

eleven thousand old soldiers: Lambert had begun assembling his forces at Newcastle in November, though even as he did so, other parts of the army were declaring for the Parliament. At the end of 1659, the Common Council of London wrote to Monk asking him to restore a free and full Parliament. On New Year's Day 1660, he crossed the Tweed with 6,000 men.

170 *constituted power*: writing in the months which preceded the Revolution of 1848, Dumas, who at other times respects the 'people and its sacred rights' (e.g. his romantic defence of the brave Scots on p. 171), here launches a broadside at the unstable 'populace'.

near Newcastle: Coldstream is on the Tweed, some 60 miles north of Newcastle, which is on the Tyne. But though invisible to each other, their proximity produced the effects which Dumas notes.

never lies: but historians repeat themselves and historical novelists make the most of their opportunities: the story of Monk's sheep is a local legend.

171 *fragment of tobacco*: Monk was a habitual chewer of tobacco.

172 *Newcastle Abbey*: the abbey, which Dumas situates on the Tweed, was a convenient fiction.

early in June: the chronology of Dumas's story requires this date. But these events at Newcastle took place in the first days of 1660.

Austerlitz: where Napoleon overcame the Austrians and Russians on 2 December 1805.

173 *Picard*: Picardy, one of the old French provinces, is the part of north-eastern France between Normandy and the Belgian frontier.

174 *my lord*: the use of the title is to be explained not only by d'Artagnan's limited English. During the interregnum, the title was retained by those with a right to it, extended as a courtesy, and also given to republican officers and their dependants.

176 *hard-featured*: Charles was 6 feet 2 inches tall, with sallow features which made him look more Spanish than English.

great facility: during the early part of his career, Monk had seen service in Cadiz, had taken part in Buckingham's attempt to raise the siege of La Rochelle, and had been a soldier in the Low Countries.

178 *Digby*: Francis Digby, son of Lord Bristol; died at the battle of Solebay in 1672. Spithead is an invented name.

181 *Newcastle*: references to the diamond studs affair in *The Three Musketeers* and Athos's mission to save Charles I in *Twenty Years After*. Dumas nowhere offers an account of Athos's 'pleasure trip' to Scotland.

182 *Holy Ghost*: Charles I made Athos a Knight of the Garter a few days before his death in *Twenty Years After* (World's Classics, p. 503). For his part in arranging an end to the first Fronde in 1650 (ibid., pp. 773–4), Anne of Austria made him a Chevalier of the Ordre du Saint-Esprit. The Ordre du Saint-Esprit, the *ancien régime*'s highest chivalric order, was founded in 1578: abolished in 1791, it was revived during the Restoration and finally disappeared in 1830.

183 *by the Scots*: after Naseby, Charles joined the Scottish army at Newark in 1646. There the Scots kept him a virtual prisoner. When the Scots retreated to Newcastle, he was obliged to go with them. Accepting Cromwell's promise that arrears of 2 millions would be paid, they handed Charles over in 1647 to the English commissioners.

186 *felucca*: long, narrow and light, the felucca had both sail and oars, but was better suited to the Mediterranean than to the North Sea. It was in such a boat that the Musketeers planned their escape to France in *Twenty Years After* (ch. 74).

in pace: 'Here lies the body of the venerable Peter William Scott, honourable canon of the Abbey of Newcastle. He departed this life on the fourteenth day of February in the year of our Lord 1208. May he rest in peace.' There was no such man.

190 *singular voice*: that is, Athos is struck by d'Artagnan's Gascon accent.

Menneville: the character is an invention, but Dumas gives him the name of Mademoiselle de Menneville, lady-in-waiting to Anne of Austria, who was at one time Fouquet's mistress.

196 *'Here lies Charles I'*: Charles was buried on 7 February 1649 in St George's Chapel at Windsor.

200 *third king of my race*: more properly, monarchs: Mary Stuart, daughter of James V of Scotland, was executed by Elizabeth I in 1587. Charles I was beheaded in 1649.

211 *hoys*: the hoy was a lighter, rigged like a sloop, which carried passengers and goods from port to port along the coast, or did heavy work, such as carrying provisions out to ships and weighing anchors.

according to Virgil: Claude Schopp has traced the allusion to Caesar's *Commentaries*, ii. 10–17.

212 *king of England*: Charles continued to be thought of as king by the many royalists who supported his cause at home and abroad. He never lived in a 'humble residence' attended by one faithful retainer, but in a large circle of loyalists and hangers-on, the numbers of which swelled dramatically in the months preceding the Restoration. He and his brothers were wined and dined at The Hague.

218 *in less than six weeks*: if it is still 'early June', Charles will be restored towards the end of July 1660. In fact, he landed at Dover on May 25 and entered London four days later.

220 *a king his kingdom*: Dumas, one of nature's swashbucklers, chooses to pass silently over the months of careful manœuvring which led to the meeting at Dover when Charles insisted on addressing Monk as 'Father'. Real kings, in Dumas's world, decide these matters at a glance.

221 *nom de guerre*: it was not unusual that, on entering the army, younger sons should adopt *noms de guerre* to avoid confusion with an elder brother. Dumas mistakenly believed that all four Musketeers had followed this practice and that their professional names concealed 'illustrious persons' (see Introduction, p. xv). After *The Three Musketeers*, all save d'Artagnan leave the Musketeers and revert to what appear to be their family names: Athos as the Comte de la Fère, Aramis as the Abbé d'Herblay, and Porthos as Monsieur du Vallon, later as Monsieur du Vallon de Bracieux, and later still as the Baron du Vallon de Bracieux de Pierrefonds.

225 *Hollands gin*: gin, made from malt or unmalted barley or other grain. The name is an abbreviated form of the French *genièvre* (juniper) with which it is flavoured. It was associated especially with Schiedam and known as 'Schiedam' or 'Hollands' gin. It was generally drunk in some diluted form.

228 *by Saint Patrick*: Monk had signed the Covenant, though he was far from being a fundamentalist. It was probably his service in

Ireland, rather than any religious motive, which leads him to tolerate the use of the name of a Catholic saint in this way.

232 *patron saint*: on the contrary, Monk's Puritan allies regarded saints
as enshrining popish idolatry.

circumvallations: the art of fortifying a place, either for defence
or attack, consisting of a rampart and a trench surrounding the
besieged place or force.

a week for consideration: negotiations between Monk and Lambert
had broken off on 24 December 1659. This allows for Dumas's
week, though Monk had yet to move his army across the Tweed.

233 *from Lambert to Monk*: Lambert's support declined rapidly. Pepys
speaks on 4 January 1660 of 'letters from the North that brought
certain news that my Lord Lambert his forces were all forsaking
him, and that he did now declare for Parliament himself'. On
5 January the Parliament ordered Monk to London, where he
arrived with 400 men on 3 February. On 20 April he dissolved
the Rump, and on 1 May presented to Parliament the Declaration
of Breda in which Charles stated his terms and his intention
to reoccupy his throne within 40 days.

military party: Lambert returned to London but was outmanœuvred
by Monk. He was tried for treason after the Restoration, reprieved,
and banished to Guernsey, where he lived in confinement for the
rest of his life.

Barnet: 'Monk continued his march with few interruptions till he
reached St. Albans. He there sent a message to the parliament;
desiring them to remove from London those regiments, which,
though they now professed to return to their duty, had so lately
offered violence to that assembly.' The House was 'perplexed' and
some regiments refused to yield, but 'for want of leaders, the
soldiers were at last [. . .] obliged to submit. Monk with his army
took quarters in Westminster [on 3 February]' (Hume, *History*, x.
353–4).

234 *six weeks*: the 'forty days' of the Declaration of Breda.

235 *mother and sister*: that is, James, Duke of York (later James II) and
Henry (1639–60), Duke of Gloucester. His mother was Henrietta-
Maria, queen to Charles I, and his sister Henrietta-Anne (1644–
70), later Duchess of Orléans.

and nonsense: Dumas judges the English revolution harshly, taking
no account, for instance, of the success of English foreign policy at
this time. Cf. Hume (*History*, x. 372–3): 'No people could undergo

a change more sudden and entire in their manners than the English during this period. From tranquillity, concord, submission, sobriety, they passed in an instant to a state of faction, fanaticism, rebellion and almost frenzy [. . .]. "Your friends, the Cavaliers," said a parliamentarian to a Royalist, "are very dissolute and debauched." "True," replied the Royalist, "they have the infirmities of men: but your friends, the Roundheads, have the vices of devils, tyranny, rebellion, and spiritual pride."'

238 *vanity*: Ecclesiastes 1: 2.

240 *La Rochelle*: that is, the siege of 1628: see *The Three Musketeers*, ch. 29.

241 *La Fère*: Athos lives on his estate at Bragelonne. But this seems to suggest that La Fère is elsewhere (perhaps in the Roussillon: see note to p. 30). Yet it is to La Fère, near Blois, that he speaks of returning on p. 281.

242 *31st of January*: that is, in 1649, the day following the death of Charles I. The masked executioner was Mordaunt, son of Milady (see *Twenty Years After*, chs. 70–1). But Dumas forgets that the tavern they had rooms not at the Hartshorn but at the Bedford (World's Classics, p. 562).

244 *meanness of Henry IV?*: d'Aubigné† was a staunch Huguenot and a not uncritical supporter of Henri IV. Dumas refers to an autobiographical memoir first published in 1729.

245 *Gaston*: that is, Gaston d'Orléans.† Henriette is Henrietta-Maria, queen to Charles I.

the Luynes, the Bellegardes, and the Bassompierres: see List of Historical Characters.

247 *holy court water*: that is, blessings in the form of preferment.

248 *Duke of Albemarle*: Monk was given his peerage on July 7: Dumas's chronology has caught up with history.

249 *nine o'clock*: Dumas forgets that Charles was to see Monk at nine: see p. 247.

250 *Golden Fleece*: a chivalric order first awarded at Bruges in 1429, which was subsequently adopted by both Austria and Spain as their highest order of chivalry.

his marriage: Louis solemnly married the Infanta, daughter of Philip of Spain, at St-Jean-de-Luz on 6 June 1660. Again, Dumas's chronology slips.

viceroy of Ireland and of Scotland: Monk was appointed Lord-Lieutenant of Ireland in August.

253 *head*: another careless slip: it is hardly likely that coins bearing the head of Charles II could have been minted so quickly.

254 *security business*: the image of British inventive ingenuity is a product of the eighteenth century. D'Artagnan's locksmith is the fruit of Dumas's invention.

a mark: the French standard mark weighed 244.75 grammes.

255 *Fabricius*: Gaius Fabricius Luscinus, Roman consul (*fl.* 280 BC) renowned for the simplicity of his life-style and his incorruptibility. Pyrrhus tried vainly to buy him with gifts.

256 *six days*: travellers went on taking a week to travel from London to Paris until the beginning of the nineteenth century. Such details were of interest to Dumas's audience, only recently introduced to the railway.

257 *grande supercilium*: 'lofty brow, arrogance'.

Lady Henrietta: Henrietta-Anne,[†] youngest daughter of Charles I and later Duchess of Orléans.

258 *Rochester*: John Wilmot, Earl of Rochester,[†] was then just 13 years of age and not yet the 'jester with both sexes' (p. 260) that he would become.

Buckingham: George Villiers, second Duke of Buckingham.[†] Dumas had much admired the dashing style of the first duke[†] in *The Three Musketeers*. After his father's murder by Felton in 1628, he was brought up with Charles, over whom he exerted great influence. But, though charming, he was weak and wayward, and rather older than Dumas suggests in the next chapter.

259 *we know this young princess*: we met her, not at the Louvre, but in the Carmelite convent in the Rue Saint-Jacques in *Twenty Years After* (ch. 38).

the coadjutor: that is, Paul de Gondi, Cardinal de Retz.[†]

power and wealth: Mary Stuart escaped from Loch Leven Castle in 1568 with very much these thoughts in mind.

early chapters of this history: the diamond studs affair occupies chs. 10–23 of *The Three Musketeers*, and the events leading up to Buckingham's murder chs. 49–59.

260 *my mother*: that is, the Queen-Mother of England.

truly in love: Charles's mother left Paris for London on 20 October 1660, taking Henrietta with her. 'The Duke of Buckingham, son of the Buckingham who was decapitated [*sic*], young, handsome and well-proportioned, was at that time extremely attached to her sister the Princess Royal [i.e. Marie, who died in December] who was then in London. But whatever his feelings for her, he was quite unable to resist the Princess of England [i.e. Henrietta], and the Duke fell so passionately in love with her that it might be said that he took leave of his senses' (Madame de la Fayette, op. cit., p. 448). The chapters which follow are a virtuoso orchestration of this brief version of events.

264　*too late*: in *The Three Musketeers* (ch. 59), d'Artagnan had attempted to warn Buckingham against the threat on his life engineered by Milady.

267　*a Goliath, a Nebuchadnezzar, or a Holofernes:* examples of powerful enemies. David faced Goliath armed with a sling. Nebuchadnezzar waged war against Egypt and Judea: he took Jerusalem (597 BC) and destroyed the temple ten years later. When Holofernes, a general of Nebuchadnezzar, was besieging Bethulia, he fell in love with Judith, who made him drunk and, when he wasn't looking, cut off his head.

　　to Boulogne: Dumas may be thinking of Courtilz's pseudo-*Memoirs of d'Artagnan* (i, ch. 13), where Mazarin, in about 1650, orders the Musketeer to drown an English agent.

　　te absolvo: 'I absolve you', from the Confession.

268　*Buckingham*: Anne of Austria loved Buckingham in 1626, but was never his mistress. It was said that she married Mazarin during the 1640s. While there is no evidence to prove that she did, Dumas tended to believe that the rumour was true.

　　accinction: the action of 'girding on' (weapons, armour, etc.).

270　*a gnat like me*: La Fontaine, *Fables*, ii. 9: 'The Lion and the Gnat'. The gnat, despised by the lion, demonstrates its power by biting the lord of the jungle to madness.

　　Fabius and Hannibal: Fabius Cunctator (*c*.275–203 BC), famous for the delaying tactics which prevented the Carthaginian Hannibal (247–183 BC) from forcing a confrontation in battle.

272　*Boulogne*: but d'Artagnan had told his men to wait for him at Calais on p. 224.

274　*Irus*: if Job epitomizes boil-filled misery, Irus is the mythological incarnation of poverty. He was a beggar in Ithaca who ran errands for Penelope's suitors. When Ulysses returned, dressed in rags, Irus tried to prevent him from entering the city. Ulysses dealt with him promptly. But while Job believes the voice of God in the whirlwind, repents, and is given 'twice as much as he had before' (Job 42: 10), Irus clearly missed his chance of fortune which a warmer welcome to Ulysses would surely have earned him.

280 *our neighbours?*: Dumas, with a teasing wink, owns up to his invention of the story.

281 *fourth day*: by following the chronology of historical events, the time must now be late autumn 1660, though only days have passed since the return of Monk and Charles to London.

Bracieux: the village of Bracieux is situated about 10 km from Blois, between Chambord and Cheverny, on the left bank of the Beuvron. It is distinct from the Bracieux ('in the Soissonnais', east of Paris) which forms part of Porthos's estate: see note to p. 133.

282 *Nimrod and Apollo*: Nimrod was 'a mighty hunter before the Lord' (Genesis 10: 9), and Apollo, in Greek mythology, was not only the sun god but god of the muses and of song. The best-known rail is perhaps the corncrake.

Louis XIII: Louis 'the Just' was a keen hunter.

283 *Rue Saint Honoré*: runs westward, from the Rue de la Ferronnerie, parallel to the Seine, between the Louvre and the Palais Royal.

Saint-Merri: the church of Saint-Merri, situated at the junction of the Rue des Lombards and the Rue Saint Martin.

284 *cost us all so dear*: a reference to *The Three Musketeers* (ch. 42), where Milady sends a gift of poisoned wine to the Musketeers.

287 *Palais Royal*: Richelieu had acquired land near the Louvre, then the royal palace, and on it built a residence, completed in 1636, which was known as the 'Palais-Cardinal'. In 1639, he made a gift of it to Louis XIII, after which it was known as the Palais Royal.

her husband: Anne's daughter-in-law was the Infanta, Queen of France since June 1660. 'Her husband' is Louis XIV.

Comtesse de Soissons: Mazarin, who was already gravely ill, is here assisted by his niece, Olympe, who became Countess of Soissons in 1657.

288 *providing that they paid*: during his 'night round' in *Twenty Years After* (World's Classics, p. 19), Mazarin overheard one of the many satirical songs aimed against him. 'They sing; they will pay,' he remarked.

Duc d'Anjou: on Philippe and his favourites, the Chevalier de Lorraine and the Comte de Guiche, see the List of Historical

Characters. In fact, Philippe became Duke of Orléans on the death of his uncle Gaston in January 1660: in Dumas's chronology, Gaston was alive in May 1660, when the tale opens, and his death has yet to be announced. Though Dumas plays down the effeminacy of his 'favourites', he does not attempt to hide it.

289 *the other third*: an anecdote picked up from the *Memoirs* of La Porte.[†]

Rocroi: the famous victory by Condé over the Spanish infantry in 1643. In the Middle Ages, a reiter was a mounted German soldier in the service of France. Later, reiters fought for the Huguenots.

293 *diavolo*: Dumas occasionally reminds us of Mazarin's Italian origins by putting expressions like this (and a few lines further on, *per Giove*, 'by Jove') into his mouth.

Naxos: in Greek, *potamos* means a river, Naxos is the largest of the Cyclades.

Rueil: the two men had last met in the spring of 1649 after d'Artagnan and Porthos had taken Mazarin prisoner at Rueil. See *Twenty Years After*, chs. 90–6.

295 *friends!*: after a decade of opposition to Mazarin, Condé settled his difference with the Crown in December 1659.

296 *highest merit*: Athos had been recruited by Tréville[†] in 1624 or 1625. On his voyages to England, see note to p. 181.

299 *Place de Grève*: the Place de Grève had been in use as a place of public execution since 1310: the guillotine was first used there in April 1792. Called the Place de l'Hôtel-de-Ville since 1806, the site is on the right bank of the Seine, opposite the Pont d'Arcole.

a parliament: during the *ancien régime*, the thirteen French *parlements* were essentially lawcourts, though they had the right (which the Paris *parlement* tested during the Fronde and several times in the following century) to give an opinion on any matter submitted to them by the king.

301 *Henrietta Stuart*: 'The Princess of England possessed the art of pleasing to the highest degree. What are called grace and charm informed her whole person, her actions and her mind, and never was princess so well fitted to be loved by women and adored by men. As she grew, so her beauty increased, so that, when the marriage of the King [with the Infanta, in June 1660] was over, that between Monsieur [i.e. Philippe] and Henrietta was decided' (Madame de la Fayette, op. cit., p. 448).

M. le Prince: that is, Condé.[†] Dumas's description of him a few lines on, if tending towards caricature, reflects contemporary views of his eagle glance and hawk nose.

306   *to obtain a reputation*: François Guénault:[†] see Boileau, *Satires*, iv. 32 and vi. 68.

scarcely fifty-two: Mazarin was born in 1602, which makes him 58. On p. 315, Dumas silently corrects his age.

309   *than Louis XIV*: Colbert[†] was nearly twenty years older than the king. The portrait which follows is accurate in essentials but reveals Dumas's distaste for the man (whom he thought unattractive) and for his accounting profession. Dumas, who had himself come from nowhere, shows no particular sympathy for Colbert, whose origins were lower-middle-class; he was not, as was said, the son of a draper from Reims. Dumas's version of events is based on the first pages of Courtilz's *Vie de Colbert* (1695).

313   *Théatin*: a religious order founded in Italy in 1524 by the Bishop of Chieti (Theate), later Pope Paul IV, which professed poverty. Mazarin had welcomed them to Paris and, when he died, left them 300,000 livres. He was regularly confessed by a Theatin brother.

314   *fisherman*: see note to p. 86.

Chronicle of Haolander: there is no such chronicle. Perhaps a memory of one of the many satirical pamphlets directed against Mazarin.

Bounet: probably Thomas Bonnet, author of *Recherches curieuses . . . sur . . . monseigneur l'éminentissime cardinal Jules Mazarin* (Paris, 1645; new edn. 1660).

315   *thirty-one years ago*: that is, Dumas has silently moved the time forward to 1661: it seems now to be about mid-February.

Casal: Casal or Casale Monferrato, on the Po. Louis XIII and Richelieu came through the pass above Susa held by the Duke of Savoy and relieved Casal, which was besieged by Savoyard and Spanish forces. D'Artagnan too had fought at Susa: see *Twenty Years After* (World's Classics, p. 23). An arquebusade was a volley of fire from the arquebusiers, who were armed with the cumbersome, match-firing ancestor of the musket.

the French and the Spaniards: that is, by negotiating the Treaty of the Pyrenees (1659) and cementing it with the marriage of Louis to the Infanta.

monsieur le prince: Condé,[†] who was by now rehabilitated.

315 *Beaufort*: Mazarin had sent Beaufort[†] to the Château at Vincennes in 1643, from which he escaped on Whit Sunday 1648 with, according to *Twenty Years After*, a little help from Athos and Grimaud.

316 *certain relations*: that Mazarin had married Anne of Austria. See note to p. 268.

Cambrai: Mazarin was accused of many vile deeds by pamphleteers. Though France had claims on the area around Cambrai, he could hardly have 'sold' it to the Spanish, except in the sense of using it as a pawn to negotiate with. The town had been taken by the Spaniards in 1595, and was returned to France by the treaty of Nijmegen in 1678.

written pamphlets: Mazarin was not a pamphleteer, though many of the anti-Mazarinades were published under his name.

317 *have the bishopric at Metz*: that is, the income from this and the other livings which are listed. St-Denis (see note to p. 31), which housed the remains of the French kings, and Cluny, a Benedictine abbey near Mâcon, were two of the richest abbeys in France.

318 *How well you reckon*: for his calculations to be correct, the rate of interest on an annual investment of 2 millions would need to be in the region of 20% a year, not 50%, to produce 'a further twenty millions in ten years'.

in 1644: see note to p. 313.

320 *restitution of a part*: the suggestion that Mazarin should make a gift of his money to Louis was made by Colbert on 3 March 1661. Estimates of Mazarin's fortune vary from 13 to 40 millions. Dumas, who liked large sums, prefers the higher estimate.

322 *where he was born*: on the Palais Royal, see note to p. 287. The Palais Mazarin was built on the left bank of the Seine opposite the Louvre. Louis XIV was born at Saint-Germain-en-Laye, 20 km west of Paris. He would not be satisfied with either: work began on the construction of Versailles in 1661.

323 *bushy eyebrows*: portraits of Colbert do not suggest that he was unusually well endowed in the eyebrow department. Perhaps a 'physiognomical' clue to his character, or maybe a reference to Virgil (*Eclogues*, viii. 33–4): 'loathe [. . .] my shaggy eyebrows and long beard'.

324 *Saint Simon*: Louis de Rouvroy (1675–1755) Duc de Saint-Simon, wrote his frank *Memoirs* between 1740 and 1750. They cover the period 1692 to the early 1720s and were not published, by royal command, during the *ancien régime*.

326 *sorrow in her countenance*: because she had been close, perhaps even secretly married, to Mazarin. The cancer mentioned a few lines on did not become apparent until 1664: see notes to pp. 268 and 19.

328 *Vaux to the Louvre*: Fouquet's château was at Vaux, near Melun, 56 km from Paris. See note to p. 128.

329 *for the people*: this argument was much used by the early champions of capitalism in the next century: the luxury of the privileged few stimulated 'the circulation of wealth'. That is, the demand for rich clothes, furniture, mansions, and other luxury goods provided work for those who would otherwise have had none.

Limousin, Perche, and Normandy: all three provinces, still called by their old feudal names, were famous for their horses. The Limousin was the area around Limoges, and the Perche was situated 150 km west of Paris.

331 *tell me as much*: Marie-Antoinette (1755–93), last queen of France during the *ancien régime*.

332 *Vincennes*: 7 km up river from the centre of Paris. The château of Vincennes had been one of the residences of French kings since its construction in the fourteenth century. It was fortified and contained a prison. Mazarin had gone there in early February. He was given the last rites on 7 March.

materialist: though a cardinal, Mazarin never took his vows. He outwardly observed religion but seems to have had small faith, though it is unlikely that he was a materialist. Materialists believed that the world was composed, not of two substances (matter, which was gross, and spirit, which was divine), but of matter alone. The implication of this view is that the cosmos is made entirely of matter and therefore there is no God.

334 *powder*: probably one of Guénault's[†] emetic preparations which Boileau claimed were lethal.

335 *Pantaloon*: a figure from the *commedia dell'arte* sometimes represented as a mean, coughing, lecherous old man.

ten long poems: an echo of Boileau's famous line (*Art poétique*, ii. 94): 'A sonnet without blemish is the equal of a long poem.'

339 *reproach Molière*: at the end of *Don Juan* (1665), Scapin, the Don's servant, is left complaining that he has not been paid. Boileau (*Art poétique*, iii. 399–400) thought the moment vulgar and said he preferred the Molière of *Le Misanthrope*.

340 *M. Colbert*: Mazarin's last words of advice are well attested: see Colbert.[†]

341 *Augustus*: Suetonius tells (*The Twelve Caesars*, ii. 99) how the dying Augustus called for a mirror, had his hair combed, and asked his friends if he had played the farce of life creditably.

last remedy: another of Guénault's emetics.

342 *Saint-Nicolas-des-Champs*: the curé's church was situated in the Rue Saint-Martin at its present junction with the Rue Réaumur.

Titian: one of the mythological canvases of Titian (1477–1576).

entering the room: on the morning of 9 March, 'the king called the nurse and as he got quietly out of bed gave her an unspeaking look, enquiring if the Cardinal was dead. This he did so as not to wake the Queen [Anne] or frighten her with the ghastly thought of death which is always most frightful' (Mme de Motteville, *Memoirs*, iv. 254).

343 *hundred Swiss*: Swiss mercenaries served in the armies of various European countries, but especially in France: the last Swiss regiments were disbanded in 1830. Colbert refers to the Swiss who formed the Palace Guard, in existence since medieval times.

346 *thirteen millions*: at his death, Mazarin's fortune was estimated at between 18 and 40 million livres. The account of his wealth on pp. 317–18 is based on the *Memoirs* of Brienne (ii. ch. 16), though the Théatin reaches the higher figure by some suspect arithmetic. The figure of 13 millions, which are 'not known' (pp. 313, 322), represents moneys which Mazarin had hidden in various places and are sometimes included in the higher estimates of his personal fortune.

348 *and Letellier*: Fouquet,[†] the Superintendent of Finances, Hugues de Lionne,[†] Secretary of State for Foreign Affairs, and Michel Le Tellier,[†] Secretary of State for War, were the three most powerful men in the kingdom.

You may go: 'On learning that the Cardinal was no more, [the King] dressed and summoned his ministers, Chancellor Le Tellier, Superintendant Fouquet, and M. de Brienne. He informed them that henceforth they were to send no letters without first speaking to him, saying that he did not wish that persons who asked his favour should apply to anyone but himself' (Mme de Motteville, *Memoirs*, iv. 254). Louis had begun as he meant to go on.

350 *Hervart*: while Breteuil[†] and Hervart[†] were real, Marin is an invention.

farmers-general: France had yet to acquire a civil service, the functions of which were, in theory, discharged by the nobility (who were similarly expected to staff the army) in exchange for their considerable privileges. However, to ease the financial plight of many aristocrats, it was made possible for public offices to be bought and sold like any other form of property. The 'farmers-general' (or 'tax-farmers'), drawn increasingly from the ranks of the rich upper middle classes, collected all levies due to the king. However, they generally managed to collect more than the levels of taxation stipulated by the Crown and were allowed to keep the difference, as a recognition of their trouble and the expense involved. It was a corrupt system which, in spite of Colbert's reforms, was to continue until 1789.

351 *set out for Paris*: Henrietta-Maria had travelled to London with Princess Henrietta in October 1660: see note to p. 260. 'The Queen of England was daily pressed by letters from Monsieur [Philippe d'Orléans] to return to France and enact his marriage, which he gave every indication of desiring most ardently. And so she was forced to leave England, though the season was unkind and rude' (Mme de la Fayette, op. cit., p. 448). She left London with Henrietta on 2 January 1661.

Belle-Isle-en-Mer: Belle-Île, west of Saint-Nazaire, outside Quiberon Bay. The island had belonged to the Abbey of Sainte-Croix at Quimperlé before passing into the Gondi family. It was bought in 1658 by Fouquet on instructions from Mazarin. Fouquet, viewing it as a safe refuge against any reversal of his fortunes, fortified it with 200 cannon.

354 *into Spain*: for the marriage of Louis XIV in June 1660.

356 *two years*: it is now March 1661, for Mazarin is only recently dead. Dumas seems to suggest that Raoul, who has been fighting the king's wars, has not seen her since the time they corresponded briefly in what is now dated as about 1658 or 1659 when Louise (born in August 1644) was 14 or 15. But Raoul has not been away from her for two years, for they spoke at Blois in 'May 1660' (Ch. 3).

357 *spoken ill . . . of women*: Athos may be the soul of gallantry, but the Pauline view of women expressed by Aramis in *The Three Musketeers* (World's Classics, p. 86: 'Woman was created for our destruction') is echoed throughout the male-dominated saga. Women find happiness in 'trifles', 'feelings', and 'mysteries'. When (like Milady or, in a lesser way, Montalais) they do not, they are considered beyond the pale.

358 *Rue des Arcis*: then part of the southern end of the Rue Saint-Martin.

359 *la Place Baudoyer*: the Place Baudoyer still exists: it flanks the eastern side of the annexe to the Hôtel de Ville in the fourth *arrondissement*.

very small hat: that is, d'Artagnan no longer has the wide-brimmed hat worn by Musketeers.

Pont Marie: links the Île Saint-Louis with the right bank of the Seine. Begun in 1613, it was first opened to traffic in 1635. In 1658 a flood had destroyed two of its arches, which had been replaced with wooden structures.

the cornet: the cavalry's equivalent of the ensign: the officer of the lowest commissioned rank who was entrusted with the flag displayed when the King of France was with his regiment. It was white or white embroidered with fleur-de-lis in gold.

360 *Francis II*: François (1544–60) became King of France in 1559. He was the adolescent, sickly husband of Mary Queen of Scots, niece of the powerful Guise family, under whose influence his reign saw harsh persecution of the Protestants: the Huguenot conspiracy at Amboise in 1560 cost 1,200 Protestant lives. To this ineffectual king, d'Artagnan adds Charles IV (1294–1328), last of the Capetian monarchs, and Henri III (1551–89), who ordered the murder of Guise in 1588.

361 *and Ireland*: that is, General Monk.†

362 *Rue de la Mortellerie*: the street is now the Rue de l'Hôtel de Ville. It got its name from its association with the mortar-makers who once traded there.

twenty pistoles: public executions, held on the Place de Grève, were visible from d'Artagnan's windows. Rooms in private houses which provided grandstand seats were hired out to spectators all through the *ancien régime*.

Saint Gervais and Saint Protais: the church, devoted to two brothers martyred by Nero, occupied the site of the first parish church on the right bank of the Seine. Work started in 1213 on a larger structure, which was not consecrated until 1420. This in turn gave way to another church begun in 1494: the façade, begun in 1616, was not completed until 1657.

363 *Croesus*: king (*c*.563–548 BC) of Lydia, famed for his wealth, which he derived from the gold-bearing bed of the Pactolus river.

M. Godard: the name is an invention.

Rue de la Vannerie: a street then located on part of what is now the Place de l'Hôtel de Ville.

you little Aramis!: d'Artagnan teases Raoul, who, however, is no dark horse like Aramis. Of the Musketeers, Aramis was the most successful with women. He had maintained mysterious contacts with 'Marie Michon', the pseudonym of Mme de Chevreuse,† in *The Three Musketeers*, and with Mme de Longueville† in *Twenty Years After*.

city of Troy: the city of Priam, last king of Troy and father of Hector, was besieged by the Greeks in the *Iliad*.

364 *verses at Fontainebleau*: the royal palace at Fontainebleau, near Melun, was built for François I. D'Artagnan (who imagines that Louis still pines for Marie de Mancini) casts him as one of the swooning poets in the entourage of Fouquet, a well-known patron of the arts.

house of Austria: Anne was the daughter of Philip III of Spain, and a Spanish Habsburg. The reign of Louis XIII had been marked by the intrigues of the 'Spanish Party' which centred upon her. D'Artagnan, who had served her in *The Three Musketeers*, was well acquainted with Spanish intrigues.

sols: plural of *sol*, an archaic form of *sou*, of which there were 20 to the livre.

366 *the other a fox*: that is, Richelieu and Mazarin. Dumas is never happier than when reducing complex characters to simple types.

Louis le Juste: Louis XIII was known as 'the Just'.

369 *Monsieur de Friedisch*: as we have seen earlier, the Swiss Guards were mainly German-speaking.

not far: the direct route was from the Rue des Lombards, along the Rue de la Ferronnerie and into the Rue St-Honoré.

370 *fire of the Huguenots*: a reference to *The Three Musketeers* (ch. 46) in which d'Artagnan and his three friends dashingly have breakfast on the Bastion of St-Gervais within range of Protestant guns during the siege of La Rochelle in 1628.

375 *the Châtelet*: criminal justice was administered from the Châtelet on the right bank of the Seine near the Pont-au-Change. It began as a fortress in 1130 and was demolished in 1802.

377 *captain of the musketeers*: made captain in 1649 by Mazarin, who was in no position to refuse (see *Twenty Years After*, ch. 94), the Cardinal had demoted him again 'as soon as peace was made' after the Fronde: see p. 105.

378 *those of my father*: *The Three Musketeers* had made much of the enmity between the King's Musketeers and the Guards who had served first Richelieu and then Mazarin: see note to p. 63.

379 *king's orders*: among the chivalric orders in royal gift were notably the Ordre du Saint-Esprit (see note to p. 182) and the Ordre de St-Michel, founded in 1469.

381 *lodge at the Louvre*: by tradition, the Musketeers had no barracks but found lodgings near the king's palace. However, as captain, d'Artagnan is required to be quartered near the king for instant service.

383 *Saint-Mandé*: now part of Paris's eastern suburb, Saint-Mandé, in the Bois de Vincennes, was in 1661 a small rural community dominated by the country house where Fouquet's literary entourage and political associates met regularly.

    the masters had dined: dinner was normally served in the early afternoon. Supper was taken in the evening.

385 *Ariadne*: the daughter of Minos who gave Theseus the thread which enabled him to escape from the labyrinth after slaying the Minotaur.

    subterranean passage: there was a communicating tunnel in Fouquet's town house (see note to p. 438), but not at Saint-Mandé. But Dumas was not a man to waste a good subterranean passage.

    la Marquise de Bellière: the Marquise de Plessis-Bellière.[†]

387 *my wife*: Fouquet's first wife died in 1640. In 1651, he married Marie-Madeleine de Castille (see Fouquet[†]).

388 *Madame Vanel*: Anne-Marguerite Vanel,[†] former mistress of Fouquet.

390 *d'Eymeris*: though Colbert later forced the tax-farmers to make restitution, no financier was tried in this dramatic manner in the summer of 1661. Given the power wielded by Fouquet, such a move would have been extremely dangerous to Louis. D'Eymeris, Lyodot, and de Vanin are inventions.

392 *De Vanin, indif.*: while d'Eymeris and Lyodot are classed as friends of M. F(ouquet), the Superintendent was 'indifferent' to the fate of de Vanin; see p. 390.

    d'Hautemont and de la Vallette: inventions, like d'Eymeris, Lyodot, and de Vanin.

394 *Gourville*: Jean Hérault de Gourville.[†]

395 *as it is with meteors*: although an age of reason, the belief that meteors, comets, and other celestial manifestations foretold of coming disasters was still widespread. In 1682, Pierre Bayle, a precursor of the *philosophes* of the Enlightenment, published his *Pensées sur la comète* which demonstrated that such a view is rooted not in reality but in superstition.

executioner of Paris: the executioner was considered to be an untouchable and holders of the office were not allowed to live within the city walls. In 1666 the executioner was paid as follows: branding (5 livres), cutting out a tongue (10 livres), hanging (20 livres), decapitation (30 livres), burning at the stake (40 livres). For reasons that are unclear, the rewards had grown smaller by 1686: hanging (10 livres, plus 4 livres for gibbet and rope), burning (10 livres, plus 10 livres for wood), etc.

Hôtel de Ville: begun in 1533 and completed in 1623, the Hôtel de Ville was the administrative centre of Paris.

396 *my brother*: Basile Fouquet.[†]

397 *M. de Bregi*: Nicolas de Flesselles, Comte de Brégy.[†]

399 *Rue de la Huchette*: in the Latin Quarter. It ran parallel to the Seine from just south of the Pont St-Michel to the Rue Saint-Jacques.

400 *Rue de Long-Pont*: on the line of the present Rue de Brosse. It ran from the Quai de Gesvres across the Rue de la Mortellerie into the Place St-Gervais.

Vatel: Fouquet's steward, who organized the fête at Vaux-le-Vicomte in August 1661 which was Fouquet's most magnificent—and final—extravagance. Vatel's professional standards were legendary. In 1671, as Condé's chief steward, he was responsible for a ceremonial supper for Louis XIV: there was not enough meat and the firework display was ruined by mist. For failing in his duty, he committed suicide.

401 *and M. Conrart*: Fouquet, who inspired great loyalty in his supporters, surrounded himself with administrators, writers, and artists who formed a coterie known as 'the Epicureans'. On these writers, and Loret a few paragraphs further on, see the List of Historical Characters.

vin de Joigny: Joigny, in Burgundy.

Rue Planche-Mibray: this street, which no longer exists, was a continuation of the Rue des Arcis (or des Assis) and led onto the

Pont Notre-Dame which linked the right bank of the Seine to the Île de la Cité.

405 *upon Vatel*: La Fontaine wrote (and translated) some Latin verse, but no poem to Vatel appears to have survived.

Sorel: Charles Sorel,[†] novelist.

Amphitryon: that is, Fouquet. Amphitryon was a king of Tiryns whose wife was visited by Zeus disguised as her husband: she became the mother of Hercules. The story has been told many times, and notably in 1668 by Molière who showed Amphitryon presiding over a banquet. Hence the name has come to mean a generous host.

Comte de Charost: Louis-Armand de Béthune-Charost.[†]

406 *my pension*: that is, Lyodot was his patron.

407 *brelan*: an old game in which the winning hand held three cards of the same denomination.

408 *Conciergerie*: a prison inside the Palais de Justice on the Île de la Cité. So called because it was originally the house of the concierge of the Royal Palace. During the French Revolution, Marie-Antoinette, Danton, Robespierre, and many other famous prisoners were held there.

409 *Epicurus*: Epicurus (341–270 BC), born at Samos, taught that pleasure is the greatest human good, defining it as the cultivation of the mind and the practice of virtue. His philosophy is not the hedonism which is evoked by the word 'Epicurean', and his disciples, according to his teaching, lived frugally. Fouquet's followers shared ideals which lay somewhere between these two extreme views. Interest in his ideas had been revived by Gassendi, a free-thinker, who had published a Life of Epicurus in 1647.

Gargettus: according to Lucretius (98–55 BC), whose *De rerum naturae* was greatly endebted to him, Epicurus was born at Gargettus in Attica.

410 *Port Royal*: originally a convent, founded in 1204, near Chevreuse (30 km south-west of Paris). Port-Royal transferred to the capital in 1625. In 1636, it began moving towards Jansenism (see note to p. 412). Among the Port-Royal faithful were a number of the century's most able moral philosophers and logicians—Nicole, Arnauld, and Pascal (who withdrew to Chevreuse in 1654); Racine was a pupil of the school which they founded. It taught a method of rational argument based on Cartesian principles. Port-Royal was closed by Louis XIV in 1709 and the building demolished in 1710.

Dumas uses the Greek *antecho*, which can mean 'I stand my ground', though Latin (perhaps *antiquo* 'I reject') would be more appropriate to the tradition of disputation.

and the magistrates: Epicurus' teachings argued that the test of ethical truth was the pleasure/pain principle, a notion which challenged the authority of both ecclesiastical and civil powers.

deaf to the law: an echo of the rumours circulating in the early summer against Fouquet and his influence.

vigour: among early attempts to explain the role played by the figures of ancient mythologies was the recourse to etymology. It was thought that the names given to the gods were clues to what they originally represented.

411 *Cacôs politeuousi*: 'they govern badly'.

Aesop: the Greek fabulist (7th–6th centuries BC), one of La Fontaine's principal sources for his *Fables*.

Epictetus: philosopher (*c*. AD 60–140), born at Hierapolis in Phrygia, who developed a system based on the Stoic principles. The anecdote of his broken leg is often quoted as an illustration of his teaching.

412 *coluber*: another attempt at etymological derivation; the word is Latin for 'snake'. Colbert's coat of arms featured a serpent.

M. Nicole: Pierre Nicole (1625–95) and Antoine Arnauld (1612–94) published the *Logique de Port-Royal* in 1662.

Jansenist: a believer in the doctrine formulated by Cornelius Jansen (1585–1638), Bishop of Ypres, in his *Augustinus* (1640), which, from a reading of Saint Augustine, advanced an austere view of divine grace, predestination, and free will against the Pelagian belief that salvation may be achieved through good works. Fiercely opposed by the Jesuits, Jansenism was finally declared heretical by Rome in 1713.

413 *excessively ugly*: though an intelligent and learned man (he was a member of the French Academy), Pellisson,[†] badly disfigured by smallpox, was famous for his ugliness. His mouth was very wide, his lips very thin, his teeth were black, and he seemed to have no neck. Lignières wrote of him: 'The Face of Pellisson / Is horrid to behold / Yet though his features / Are like some outlandish creature's / His face has charms for Sappho. / But ask not why they go well together: / They are two birds of a feather.' 'Sappho' was the name adopted in fashionable, 'precious' circles by Mlle de Scudéry, who was generally considered to be rather more than

plain. Their relationship was platonic only. Boileau (*Satires*, viii. 209) commented that Fouquet's gold went some way to compensate Pellisson for his unfortunate appearance.

414 *Palais*: that is, the Conciergerie prison in the old Royal Palace.

415 *gold and silken cord*: the check cord, by which passengers communicated with the coachman.

418 *arcade Saint-Jean*: the colonnade on the north side of the church of Saint-Jean-en-Grève.

421 *Tixeranderie*: the Rue de la Tissanderie (*sic*), which disappeared beneath the Rue de Rivoli in the nineteenth century, began on the southern side of the Cimetière St-Jean-en-Grève and ran west along the northern end of the Place de Grève before becoming the Rue de la Coutellerie, part of which which still exists. The Rue de la Vannerie, parallel to the Seine, entered the Place from the west and led out of it as the Rue de la Mortellerie (now the Rue de l'Hôtel de Ville).

422 *Rue Baudoyer*: an error for Place (or Porte) Baudoyer.

423 *went on*: the passage in square brackets is a suggested reading; the text is corrupt at this point.

424 *and the Quai Pelletier*: now the Quai de Gesvres and the Quai de l'Hôtel de Ville, on the right bank of the Seine. The place of execution was situated just opposite the end of the present Pont d'Arcole.

Rue Saint Antoine: the Faubourg Saint-Antoine lay outside the city's eastern wall. The Bastille was located at the Porte Saint-Antoine, and Rue Saint-Antoine led west before turning into a maze of streets on the eastern side of the Place de Grève.

425 *twelve deniers*: a *denier* was one 240th part of a livre. But Dumas here seems to be thinking of the *sou*, of which there were twenty to the livre.

426 *Le Mans*: 203 km south-west of Paris, just north of Touraine.

427 *Plutus*: in Greek mythology, the god of riches.

428 *thirty-seven and a half pistoles*: this makes, at 10 livres to the pistole, d'Artagnan's 375 livres.

436 *the archangel*: Michael, prince of the celestial armies, who was commanded by God to drive the rebel angels out of heaven. In Christian art, he is usually shown winged, clad in armour, and bears a shield and a lance or sword with which he slays a dragon.

438 *gates of the superintendent*: Fouquet's town house, which he had
acquired in 1659 from his brother, François, Bishop of Agde, was
situated on the site of the present no. 374, Rue St-Honoré, near
the Place Vendôme. A tunnel connected his house to no. 263
opposite, which he used as stores, kitchens, and stables.

Danicamp: one of Dumas's invented characters.

443 *twenty thousand livres a year*: Fouquet's surprise is well founded.
In 1660, a sub-lieutenant's pay was 1,000 livres, while that of a full
colonel was 6,000.

445 *Beautru*: Colbert bought a house in the Rue des Petits Champs
which still exists (it separates the Palais Royal and the Bibliothèque
Nationale), but not until 1665. The house was built by Guillaume
Beautru (1588–1669) in the 1630s. Between 1661 and 1669, Colbert
built a number of houses near by, in the Rue Vivienne.

448 *a harlequin*: Harlequin was a stock character from the *commedia
dell'arte*. By tradition he wore a black mask and a costume made of
multicoloured patches in the shape of diamonds.

453 *fresh-gathered cherries*: in spite of this reference to ripe cherries, the
time of the action is still suspended between the death of Mazarin
(9 March 1661) and the marriage of Philippe d'Orléans and
Henrietta of England, which will take place on 31 March 1661.

454 *Pythian Apollo*: Calchas was a soothsayer who advised Agamemnon
during the siege of Troy: on his counsel, Iphigenia was sacrificed
and the wooden horse constructed. In French, Calchas is a byword
for confidence in expectations. The oracles of Apollo (slayer of the
Python of Mount Parnassus) were delivered at Delphi.

455 *and the Faubourg Saint-Antoine*: in 1652, during the last phase of
the Fronde, Turenne faced Condé at Jargeau (near Orléans) and
Bléneau (at Gien, near Montargis) and finally overcame him in the
Faubourg Saint-Antoine on 2 July.

'Much Ado About Nothing': it hardly seems likely that Monk should
have taken d'Artagnan to the theatre. This is a reflection of the
awe in which Dumas's generation held Shakespeare.

456 *uses of common life*: Dumas allows d'Artagnan a smattering of learn-
ing but makes him essentially 'a dreamer', that is an instinctive
Romantic hero who relies on his native wit more than on books.
Among these masters, Epicurus (see note to p. 409) and Seneca
(AD 2–65) rank as stoics and La Rochefoucauld† as a cynic.
Socrates (470–399 BC) was a master of dialectical argument and
Cicero (106–43 BC) a fierce defender of integrity in public life. The

'gentlemen' of Port-Royal (see note to p. 410) could not have translated La Rochefoucauld's *Maximes*, which were not published in Paris until 1665.

457 *de Vitry*: both Luynes[†] and Vitry[†] were well rewarded for the roles they had played in the murder of Concini[†] in 1617.

all I did for Anne of Austria: from the diamond studs affair in *The Three Musketeers* to the taming of Mazarin at Rueil in *Twenty Years After*.

458 *Chartres from Châteaubriand*: about 250 km. Châteaubriant is 55 km south of Rennes.

his emblem: another reminder that Louis will be known as the Sun King.

459 *in the world*: it was on this mount that d'Artagnan had ridden from his home near Tarbes to Meung in *The Three Musketeers*. Its 'strange coat and eccentric gait' are described in the first chapter (World's Classics, p. 4).

even now: Brittany, one of the old provinces of France, was an independent duchy until it was joined to the French Crown by the marriage of Charles VIII and Anne of Brittany in 1491. It became fully French in 1532 during the reign of François I. However, Bretons remained geographically, culturally, and linguistically apart, and peasant revolts against the rule of Paris occurred at intervals, and notably in 1675. In Dumas's day, relations with Paris were still uneasy.

460 *seigneur of Belle-Isle*: see note to p. 351. The Retz mentioned a few lines further on is not the cardinal of that name but Gilles de Retz.[†]

Kalonèse: that is, *kalos* (beautiful) and *nesos* (island).

the Vilaine: the Vilaine rises near Laval, flows through Rennes, Redon, and the Morbihan and joins the Atlantic at La Roche-Bernard, 40 km south-east of Vannes, then known for the ships built there.

Guérande or Le Croisic: Guérande, a medieval fortified town, 6 km north of La Baule. Le Croisic lies on the southern arm of the salt marshes for which the Guérande Peninsula is well known; in the seventeenth century it was a busy fishing port.

462 *salt-works*: the extraction of salt by evaporation from the marshes, was a thriving business. During the *ancien régime*, salt was subject to a tax (*la gabelle*). But Guérande salt, because it was covered by an ancient privilege, was exempt of the levy, and circulated freely

throughout Brittany and was regularly exchanged, in neighbouring regions, for cereals and other produce, a practice which was illegal but lucrative. D'Artagnan's ploy is eminently plausible.

464 *Jupenet*: the character is an invention, but Fouquet did employ printers like Jupenet.

Hôtel de Bourgogne: since the time of the Renaissance, the former residence of the dukes of Burgundy had been home to successive troupes of actors who had the monopoly of staging plays, a privilege bitterly resented by other companies, who were obliged to restrict their activities to touring the provinces. In 1600 Mondory's players boldly set up in the Théâtre du Marais, and in 1658 Molière moved into the Petit-Bourbon and thence, in 1661, to the Palais Royal. When Louis XIV merged rival troupes into the Comédie-Française in 1680, the Hôtel de Bourgogne (now no. 29, Rue Étienne-Marcel in the 2nd *arrondissement*) became for a century the home of the Comédie-Italienne.

Corneille, or Rotrou, or Garnier: Pierre Corneille (1606–84), Jean de Rotrou (1609–50), and Robert Garnier (1544–90) represented the tragic tradition prior to the arrival of Racine.

466 *Hippocrene*: a spring on Mount Helicon which appeared when Pegasus, the winged horse, struck the rock with a hoof. It was consecrated to the Muses, and those who have drunk of its waters are said to be true poets.

467 *Ceran*: probably Serrant, an Anjou white. Beaugency was d'Artagnan's favourite wine.

469 *Piriac*: Piriac-sur-mer, on the tip of the northern promontory of the Guérande pensinsula. Batz, on the southern side, is 4 km east of Le Croisic. The steeples d'Artagnan sees a few lines later belong to Le Pouliguen (4 km east of Batz), Guérande to the north, and Saint-Joachim some 20 km east across the flat lands between the Vilaine and the Loire known as the Grande Brière.

470 *Nantes and Paimbœuf*: ports at the mouth of the Loire.

Saint-Nazaire: upstream from Paimbœuf on the northern bank of the Loire.

471 *Hoedic*: the uninhabited Île Dumet (*sic*) lies about 10 km off Piriac. The Île de Hoedic, slightly larger, is some 25 km west of Piriac, two-thirds of the way to Belle-Île.

476 *Locmaria*: boats landed then, as they do now, at Le Palais. Dumas here mentions the main settlements on the island: Locmaria in the east, Sauzon to the west, and Bangor which lies between them.

477 *Salentum*: in Book VIII of *Télémaque* (1699), a novel written by Fénelon (1651–1715) for the instruction of the Dauphin, Telemachus arrives at Salentum, in Calabria, guided by Mentor, who teaches the king, Idomeneus, how men should be governed.

epaulement: in fortification, the epaulement was a mass of earth or other material designed to protect artillery both at the front and on either flank. Gabions were empty cylindrical baskets, between 20 and 70 inches in height, which were filled with earth and used to safeguard defenders against enemy fire. Fascines were bundles of sticks bound at both ends and in the middle and used for filling ditches, strengthening ramparts, and raising mortar-batteries. The escalade, mentioned on p. 478, was an attack mounted on a besieged place by means of ladders.

478 *Mallet*: Alain Manesson Mallet (1630–1706) served the King of Portugal as a military engineer before returning to teach mathematics to Louis XIV's pages; his *Travaux de Mars, ou l'Art de la Guerre* did not appear until 1671. Samuel Marolois (*sic*), a French mathematician who lived much of his life in Holland, published *Fortifications, ou architecture militaire* in 1615. In 1648, Antoine, Chevalier de Ville (1596–1656), who had learned his knowledge of fortification from Jean Érard (d. 1620), was given the task of fortifying the towns ceded to France by the Peace of Westphalia; he had written *Les Fortifications* in 1629 and followed it with accounts of sieges, including Corbie (1637) and Hesdin (1639). But the most celebrated military engineer was the Comte de Pagan (1604–65), who lost an eye at the siege of Montauban. His *Traité des fortifications* was published in 1645.

481 *Mouston*: Porthos's servant had answered to 'Mousqueton' ('little musket')—this is how d'Artagnan addressed him on p. 134 above— until *Twenty Years After* (World's Classics, p. 120), when he let it be known that Mouston was a more dignified name for the steward of such an important master. Unfortunately, the word suggests 'small fly' or 'gnat' and is less dignified than he thinks.

482 *Ajax*: Ajax, son of Telamon, sailed against Troy. Homer ranked him next to Achilles as the most courageous of the Greeks.

Baron de Bracieux: for his part in the Fronde, Porthos had been made a baron by Anne of Austria (see *Twenty Years After*, World's Classics, p. 770). Bracieux was the name of one of his estates (see note to p. 133).

484 *twenty-eighth of last month*: Dumas's chronology is again uncertain in spite of this apparently specific indication. Since, in historical

terms, the royal wedding still lies in the future (31 March 1661), 'last month' presumably means February, though the cherry season has passed (p. 453).

485 *red hat*: Aramis, who already wears a bishop's purple, has designs on a cardinal's hat.

486 *half-moons*: in fortification, a redan consisted of two parapets of earth in the form of a V, the apex of which was pointed at the enemy: it was unprotected at the rear. A curtain was the section of a rampart between two bastions, redans, or gates; it was surmounted by a parapet behind which the defenders stood to fire on the covered way and, if applicable, into the moat. The covered way was a trench protected by an embankment: the most important of the outworks, it provided cover for troops falling back after an unsuccessful sortie. A half-moon was an outwork consisting of two faces forming a salient angle, the entrance to which was in the form of a crescent. A lunette was a half-hexagonal detached work presenting a salient angle to the enemy; it was used to protect bridges or, as here, the curtain of field-works.

487 *Marie Michon*: Aramis's secret contact at court in the first Musketeer adventure: for the crucial letter which he wrote to her, see *The Three Musketeers*, ch. 48. The name hid the identity of Madame de Chevreuse.†

488 *Gétard*: an invented character.

Boulingrin: Porthos's architect is also invention, as the name (a phonetic rendering of Bowling-green) is perhaps intended to suggest.

489 *Juponet*: the diminutive suggests 'little skirt, petticoat'.

La Fontaine: for all these writers, see the List of Historical Characters.

490 *Sarzeau*: in the Golfe du Morbihan, 22 km from Vannes.

491 *Locmaria*: that is, off Locmaria at the eastern end of the island.

492 *Grace has touched him*: Porthos is being playful. To be touched by divine grace was the hope of every Jansenist. But, as we know, Aramis is a high-ranking Jesuit.

493 *Saint-Pierre*: the Cathedral of St Pierre was begun the in the thirteenth century. The Church of St Patern, rebuilt in the eighteenth century, lay outside the old city walls. Dumas's description of Vannes is based on memories of a visit in the summer of 1830.

496 *a secret to conceal*: of the quartet, Aramis has been, from the start, the most guarded and the least accessible.

496 *Antaeus*: a giant, son of Poseidon, who challenged all strangers to wrestle with him. Hercules, perceiving that Antaeus's vigour increased each time he touched the earth, his mother, lifted him up and so succeeded in crushing him.

500 *at fifty-seven*: Dumas's Aramis, born in 1604, suffers from a variety of ailments (see p. 522). The date of birth of Henri d'Aramitz, on whom the character is very distantly based, is not known, though he was probably about ten years younger.

Armorica: the name of that part of ancient Gaul which subsequently became Brittany.

502 *the bridge of Blois*: see above, Ch. 13.

506 *Pelops*: Dumas's splendid grasp of the Greek myths here lets him down. Pelops was killed by his father, Tantalus, who served him as a dish for the gods. Only Ceres, distracted by grief for her dead daughter, tasted the ghastly meal. Jupiter restored Pelops to life and gave him an ivory shoulder to replace the limb eaten by Ceres.

509 *Castrametation*: the art of laying out a camp.

513 *inn at Crèvecœur*: see *The Three Musketeers*, ch. 26.

522 *a centaur*: the half-man, half-horse of Greek mythology.

against him: again, it is clear that whatever their political differences, the comrades remain united in spirit: see *Twenty Years After* (World's Classics, p. 534), where, after a moment of tension, the four friends forget their quarrels and are 'reunited and harmonious'.

524 *Agrigentum*: a Greek city on the south coast of Sicily, largely demolished by the Cathaginians in 405 BC. In his travel book, *Le Speronare* (1841), Dumas records a visit to modern Girgenti, where he saw the reassembled remnants of a large caryatid, four times life-sized, lying on its side, the most striking remains of the temple which had been destroyed by earthquake.

526 *corruption*: Dumas's position in this matter is clear: he is with poetry and Cavaliers against politics and Roundheads.

527 *all the parliament*: again Dumas telescopes history. Mazarin is dead (9 March) and Philippe will marry Henrietta on 31 March. Events unfolded as follows. Colbert provided evidence of Fouquet's long-standing mismanagement. On 4 May 1661, Louis decided that he would rule France himself. But he could not dismiss the superintendent, who was strong enough to lead a revolt from his impregnable base at Belle-Île. Thus Fouquet continued in office for some months. He brokered the marriage of Charles II with a Portuguese

princess, bought back Dunkirk, and in June was working to put the Duc d'Enghien on the Polish throne. In early August, Louis persuaded Fouquet, still expecting to succeed Mazarin, to resign his post as *procureur-général* which had made him answerable only to the Paris parliament, which, hoping to be protected by the superintendent of finances, was favourable to him. Fouquet agreed and sold the office for 1.4 million livres, which he gave to the king. On 17 August, Louis visited Saint-Mandé and was shocked that a subject should outshine a king; it is possible that Fouquet took liberties with Louise de la Vallière to which Louis took exception. After the *fête de Vaux*, Louis lured Fouquet to Nantes, where he was arrested on 5 September. His trial continued until 1664, when the former superintendent was jailed for life.

530 *Your majesty's*: on Belle-Île, see note to p. 351. Fouquet never gave the Island to Louis. On 5 September, Louis sent troops to Belle-Île. When news of Fouquet's downfall became known, the garrison surrendered. But Belle-Île remained Fouquet's property.

532 *hospitals . . . Swiss*: during the *ancien régime*, the *hôpital* was a multi-purpose instituion, having a role as prison, poor-house, asylum, and hospital. The Swiss are the German-speaking guards, who were employed mostly for ceremonial duties.

that are left: Colbert must indeed be startled by Fouquet's aplomb, for he fails to notice that these figures do not add up.

533 *Just in time!*: Aramis reckons Vannes to be 104 leagues (1 league was about 4 km) from Saint-Mandé and estimates that a mounted rider, with good changes of horse, can cover the distance in 30 hours (p. 508): ordinary mortals (see p. 57) needed 5 days to travel the 181 km separating Blois from Paris, though Raoul manages it in 16 hours (p. 638). Porthos left Vannes at about 2 a.m. and arrives at 8 p.m., which makes 42 hours. Aramis, travelling partly by coach, leaves at about 8 a.m. and arrives at midnight, which makes 40 hours. D'Artagnan wakes early, but after Porthos has set out. At 11.30 a.m. he sails to Belle-Île and back, then returns to Vannes about 8 hours later (pp. 516–17). This means that he set out at approximately 9 p.m. If he arrives 1 hour and 55 minutes after Aramis, then he has covered the distance in 29 hours (d'Artagnan says 32, p. 535) at an average speed of nearly 10 miles an hour. However, Aramis arrives at Fouquet's house 'thirty to thirty-five hours' (p. 518) after d'Artagnan leaves Vannes: which should make the time now between 3 and 7 o'clock in the morning. Dumas's computations are as cavalier as his heroes. Even d'Artagnan

in his youth could only manage 60 leagues in 40 hours: see *The Three Musketeers* (World's Classics, p. 191).

533 '*Fly*': the Duc de Guise, assassinated at Blois in 1588, was warned that his life was in danger.

537 *since he was born*: according to *Twenty Years After* (World's Classics, p. 132), d'Artagnan first met Raoul (then aged 15) in 1648.

about forty years: they first met—or rather crossed swords—in 1625: see *The Three Musketeers* (World's Classics, pp. 35–6).

539 *to my oath*: see note to p. 31.

rendered his last sigh: again, the dates are confused and time is going backwards, not forwards. Mazarin died on 9 March 1661. Gaston died in January 1660.

540 *father's palace*: Gaston d'Orléans married Marguerite de Lorraine at Nancy in 1632. Almost imediately, his brother, Louis XIII, attacked Lorraine, an independent duchy, and Gaston fled to Brussels. Marguerite escaped six months later and joined him. Their marriage was not recognized in France until after the death of Richelieu. Lorraine was ceded to Louis XV's brother-in-law, Stanislas Leszczynski, exiled king of Poland, in 1738. On his death, Lorraine became French.

541 *Clerk*: Dumas makes Malicorne† (if he is '25 or 26', he was born in about 1635) the son of a well-to-do lawyer and merchant at Orléans who was Condé's legal adviser and banker (p. 556). The links between the historical Malicorne and Dumas's character are very distant.

548 *or the robe*: according to the caste system, which would be even more strictly enforced by the requirements of Louis XIV's court, the clergy and the nobility made up first and second Estates, the middle classes and the labouring poor constituting the 'Tiers État'. But as the aristocracy (debarred by custom from engaging in trade or business) grew poorer, arranged marriages with well-to-do middle-class girls grew more frequent, thus ennobling bourgeois families in exchange for money. But the middle classes could also achieve their ambition of 'living nobly' by contributing to the royal coffers or buying state offices (sometimes created for the purpose). The *anobli* had the right to a title and the distinctive *robe* which indicated that the wearer was a member of a *parlement*. Well into the eighteenth century, the members of the *robe* were despised as upstarts not only by the ancient families of the *noblesse d'épée* (the

sword indicating their traditional military role) but also by members of the middle classes who had yet to be ennobled.

Monsieur: Philippe d'Orléans.

554 *Manicamp*: see List of Historical Characters. 'Manicamp' is one of the characters Dumas invents as part of the gilded entourage of Guiche.† If Malicorne is self-seeking on the Balzacian model, Manicamp personifies that other Romantic ideal: the languid dandy, à la Musset and Baudelaire (who, before his family cramped his style, would order a dozen suits at a time and then never wear them).

556 *syndic*: see note to p. 39.

558 *a vile name*: mainly because of the association of *corne* ('horn') with cuckoldry, a subject which has always been considered more amusing by Latin peoples than by Angles, Saxons, and Teutons.

Erigone: a daughter of Icarius who hanged herself when she heard that her father had been killed: she was made into the constellation Virgo. Before this starry promotion, however, Bacchus had deceived her by changing himself into bunch of grapes.

Protean female: Proteus had received the gift of prophecy from his father, Poseidon. But he was not always in an oracular mood and, to evade those who questioned him, assumed different shapes at will. The adjective has come to mean 'having many forms'.

559 *Place Sainte-Catherine*: demolished during the French Revolution.

561 *Étampes*: 50 km south-west of Paris.

567 *Hôtel Grammont*: some time after 1637, Antoine de Gramont (*sic*) bought the Hôtel de Clèves in the Rue d'Autriche (now Rue de l'Oratoire). Louis XIV bought and demolished it in 1667. The marshal moved into a house formerly occupied by Monnerot, a disgraced tax-farmer, and his family lived in it for three generations. It was on the site of the present Rue de Gramont.

572 *De Wardes*: in the pseudo-*Memoirs of d'Artagnan* (i, chs. 6–7), Courtilz tells how an English noblewoman, called simply Milady, becomes infatuated with the wealthy Marquis de Wardes, 'one of the handsomest noblemen of the court'. According to Courtilz (iii. 54–9), de Wardes was the brother of Antoine, Comte de Moret, who was killed at the siege of Gravelines in 1658. De Wardes became a favourite of Louis XIV and might have gone far had he not fallen under the influence of the Comtesse de Soissons (i.e. Olympe Mancini), who sought to avenge her sister, Marie, cruelly abandoned by the king. From the details he supplies (iii. 247, 257),

it is clear the Courtilz had in mind François-René Crespin du Bec, Marquis de Vardes,[†] who serves as the basis for two characters in the saga. Dumas had seized on the character, who, though too young to figure in the events described in *The Three Musketeers*, is present there as the treacherous de Wardes, who, aged 25 in 1627, is a loyal servant of Richelieu and a cousin to the Rochefort who insulted d'Artagnan at Meung. He stands in the path of d'Artagnan as he speeds to England to retrieve the diamond studs, and is left for dead at Calais in ch. 20—though he survived and lived long enough to poison his son's mind against d'Artagnan: see *Louise de la Vallière*, ch. 2. The same historical figure now reappears as his own son and plays a role much closer to his real, intriguing self. It is interesting to note that while Dumas attributes hereditary evil to the offspring of his villains (Mordaunt, son of Milady, is as wicked as she in *Twenty Years After*), the same does not apply in the case of Raoul, who, though he inherits Athos's honour and dignity, lacks his dash, flair, and effectiveness.

574 *are purchasable*: see note to p. 548.

De Gramont: the family name of the Dukes de Guiche.[†]

575 *four quarterings*: that is, are not pure-blooded aristocrats.

some Gascon family: de Wardes's example is not chosen at random: he holds d'Artagnan responsible for the death of his father. Yet if this is so, then he is older than '24 or 25' (p. 572). The encounter at Calais took place in 1626, and de Wardes seems to have died of his wounds quickly, but not before speaking (p. 577) of his hatred for d'Artagnan, whom he had met only once, at Calais.

from my birth: see note to p. 537.

578 *of the people*: Dumas compares his own materialistic times with a somewhat rose-tinted view of the relationship of subjects to their king in 'the good old days'.

Lorraine: on the Chevalier de Lorraine, see the List of Historical Characters.

579 *than I am as a man*: Dumas prudently expresses as femininity the well-attested homosexuality of both Philippe d'Orléans and the Chevalier de Lorraine.

of seventeen: Henrietta was born in 1644.

583 *Madame*: that is, Queen Henrietta-Maria of England. Pepys records events as follows: 'This day [11 Jan 1661] comes news . . . from Portsmouth that Princess Henrietta is fallen sick of the meazles on board the *London*, after the Queen and she was under sail. And so

was forced to come back into Portsmouth harbour; and in their way, by negligence of the pilot, run upon the Horse sand. The Queen and she continued aboard, and do not intend to come on shore till she sees what will become of the young Princess.' 27 January: 'Before I rose, letters come to me from Portsmouth, telling me that the Princess is now well and my Lord Sandwich set sail with the Queen and her yesterday from thence to France.' On 7 February, he reports that Buckingham and Sandwich fell out at Le Havre over cards. The account of events given by Mme de La Fayette (op. cit. 449) is altogether more dramatic. The English court accompanied Henrietta and Henrietta-Maria on the first day of their journey to Portsmouth, where Buckingham, unable to 'bring himself to be parted from the Princess of England, asked permission of the King to journey to France'. The carelessness of the pilot becomes a great peril, and Buckingham, already fearful for the Princess's life, is beside himself when she falls ill with measles. 'Her illness was extremely dangerous. The Duke of Buckingham behaved like a madman plunged into despair during those moments when he believed her very life was threatened. At the last, when she was well enough to brave the sea and make towards Le Havre, he became so excessively jealous of the attentions which the English Admiral showed for the Princess that he would grow angry with him for no reason, and the Queen, fearing lest some serious disorder should result, commanded the Duke of Buckingham to proceed directly to Paris while she remained some while in Le Havre to allow her daughter to regain her strength. When she was completely well again, she travelled to Paris. Monsieur [Philippe d'Orléans] sallied forth to meet her with all the attentions imaginable and continued until his marriage to show her a consideration which lacked nothing except love. But the miracle which lit a flame in the heart of this Prince was within the reach of no woman of flesh and blood. The Comte de Guiche was at that time his favourite.'

Francis I: the entrance to the port was marked by two towers, the larger of which was decorated with a statue of François I.

584 *monopolizing everything*: a belief even more strongly held in Dumas's day.

586 *a name of ill omen*: a reference not only to the foreign policy of the first Duke of Buckingham, which led to the siege of La Rochelle in 1628, but also to the rumours that Buckingham had supplanted Louis XIII in the affections of Anne of Austria.

586 *clenched his teeth*: according to Mme de la Fayette (op. cit. 449), Guiche was then in love not with Henrietta but with Mme de Chalais.† 'She was extremely attractive but was not beautiful. He sought her out, followed her wherever she went. In a word, it was a passion so public and so open that few believed that it could be requited by her who caused it, and it was thought that if indeed there was some intimacy between them, then she would have required him to behave more circumspectly. But what is certain was that if he were not loved truly he was not hated either, and that she looked upon his love without anger.' It was not until July 1661 that Guiche turned his attentions to Henrietta (ibid. 453).

589 *and La Hève*: that is, they heave to facing the beach which runs north from the port and ends in the rocky Cap de la Hève on which stands Ste-Adresse.

591 *Norfolk*: the admiral commanding the *London* was in fact Sir Edward Montagu, Earl of Sandwich (1625–72). It was he who had brought the Queen from France in October 1660, and he would escort her back to England again in July 1662.

Monsieur: that is, Philippe d'Orléans. After her marriage, Henrietta was known, according to the convention, as Madame.

595 *favourite of Charles II*: Charles, who had been brought up with Buckingham, remained under his influence. Pepys states roundly on 27 November 1667 that the King had 'become a slave to the Duke of Buckingham'.

598 *like Achilles in his tent*: in Book I of the *Iliad*, Achilles withdrew to his tent after quarrelling with Agamemnon.

600 *Aeolean harp*: Aeolus was the ruler and god of the winds, which he kept in a cave. An Aeolian harp is a simple instrument of 8 or 10 strings stretched over a sounding-box, which produces lulling harmonies when placed in a current of wind. It is said to have been invented by St Dunstan.

605 *her native country*: Henrietta-Maria, wife of Charles I, was the sister of Louis XIII.

607 *campaigners together*: that is, in the campaigns at home during the Fronde and abroad after it had ended. They first served together at Lens in 1648 (see *Twenty Years After*, World's Classics, p. 487). For other battles, see p. 616 below.

610 *accompany Madame*: Dumas blithely ignores, for dramatic pruposes, Mme de La Fayette's statement that Queen Henrietta-Maria,

wishing to avoid trouble, ordered Buckingham to ride on ahead to Paris: see note to p. 583.

612 *Mantes*: their route lies through Rouen and Mantes, which is 60 km from Paris.

615 *a great service to mine*: a reference not to the diamond studs affair but to d'Artagnan's valiant but vain attempt to warn Buckingham, through Lord de Winter, of Milady's murderous intentions: see *The Three Musketeers*, ch. 59.

616 *edicts against duels*: see note to p. 143.

probably fight eleven: Buckingham's most notorious duel was a three-a-side affair fought over his mistress, Lady Shrewsbury: see Pepys, 17 January 1668.

at Lens, at Bléneau, at the Dunes: the battle of Lens was fought in August 1648, Bléneau in April 1652, and the battle of the Dunes in June 1658 when Turenne, besieging Dunkirk, defeated the Spaniards commanded by Don Juan of Austria and Condé.

617 *my mother's name*: Raoul is the son of Athos and Mme de Chevreuse. The circumstances of his conception are given in chs. 10 and 22 of *Twenty Years After*.

618 *as he did your father*: at Calais where he was treacherously attacked by de Wardes in 1626, d'Artagnan did not kill his man, but left him for dead.

619 *a much more formidable enemy*: Raoul is thinking of the vendetta begun by Milady in *The Three Musketeers*, which was carried on by her son Mordaunt in *Twenty Years After*.

like them: yet another indirect expression of Dumas's nostalgia for the idealistic generation of 1830, which in 20 years had given way to the spirit of base materialism and political opportunism which the Revolution of 1848 would only confirm.

620 *certain fascination*: Henrietta's beauty and sharp mind made a great impression on the French court, and Dumas is right in saying that she had a taste for excitement. Towards the end of her short life, she was involved in politics and died, in mysterious circumstances, of poison.

Nanterre: the retinue passed through Nanterre, north-west of Paris, and arrived in the capital on 20 February. The St Germain mentioned a few lines later is St-Germain-en-Laye.

624 *fire to glow*: Henrietta-Maria had fled to France in 1644, where she had been somewhat coolly received by Mazarin, not only because of his meanness (to which Dumas always draws attention)

but because her presence was on occasions a source of political embarrassment to France's relations with England. Dumas always exaggerates her privations.

626 *Palais Royal*: 'the marriage of Monsieur [Philippe d'Orléans] took place during Lent, without ceremonial, in the Chapel of the Palais-Royal' (Madame de la Fayette, op. cit. 450), on 31 March 1661. The court was still in mourning for Mazarin and was not quite the sumptuous affair described by Dumas in the next chapter.

629 *good Queen Catherine*: Catherine de' Medici.[†]

630 *Madame de Navailles*: the Duchess of Navailles,[†] wife of the then governor of Le Havre.

Tonnay-Charente: later Mme de Montespan.[†]

633 *Mademoiselle de Lafayette*: on Madame de Chalais, see note to p. 586. Madame de la Fayette[†] (*sic*) was an intimate of the queen and wrote an account of her life on which Dumas drew for key episodes of his novel.

and de Châtillon: Dumas's sources is again Madame de la Fayette (op. cit. 451): 'Madame de Valentinois,[†] sister to the Comte de Guiche, who was well liked by Monsieur for her brother's sake but also her own (for he was as fond of her as his inclination allowed him to be fond of any woman), was one of the female company with which he chose to surround himself. Mesdames de Créqui[†] and de Châtillon[†] and Mademoiselle de Tonnay-Charente[†] were honoured to see Madame frequently, as were others to whom she had shown signs of favour before she was married.'

636 *from my childhood*: see note to p. 11.

Cour-Cheverny: a village near the château at Cheverny.

638 *his memoirs*: see note to p. 32.

642 *Don Diego*: a reference to the father of Le Cid, who, in the first act of Corneille's play (1637), asks his son to avenge the insult done to his honour.

over-agreeable: the chapter develops a brief moment of Mme de La Fayette's *Histoire de Madame Henriette d'Angleterre* (op. cit. 450). Buckingham's attentiveness had been plain even before the marriage was celebrated: 'Monsieur soon became aware of it, and it was on this occasion that Madame Henrietta first became acquainted with the constitutional jealousy of which he was later to give her so many proofs. She observed his downcast looks, and, as she cared nothing for the Duke of Buckingham, who, although most charming, has all too often known what it is not to be loved, she spoke to her mother the Queen [Henrietta-Maria], who made it her business to straighten Monsieur's crooked thoughts and to make him realize that the Duke's love was an absurd matter of no consequence. This did not displease Monsieur, yet he was not entirely satisfied. He spoke of it to his mother the Queen [Anne], who felt some sympathy for the passion of the Duke, which reminded her of the love which his father had long ago shown to her. She insisted that the matter should not be made public, but took the view that the Duke should be given to understand, when he had continued at the French court some while longer, that his presence was necessary in England. And this was what was decided and acted upon.'

644 *divine right*: a political theory, upon which the French monarchy was built, which stated that the authority of kings came directly from God. As the Pope was God's earthly representative in spiritual matters, so monarchs were the temporal lieutenants of the Almighty. The doctrine had been challenged during the Renaissance, but the *ancien régime* continued as an absolutist state until the French Revolution.

646 *sixteen years of age*: Henrietta was born at Exeter in 1644.

648 *melancholy nature*: Anne recalls her feelings for Buckingham, which he had shared in 1626. These feelings form the background to the first part of *The Three Musketeers*.

649 *procure this scent*: Dumas may well be right, but the flower-farmers of the Alpes-Maritimes, for example, used the traditional process of *enfleurage* with flowers which yield little essential oil. Blossoms were spread each day on layers of fatty material: after three weeks, the remaining grease was melted and a scented oil obtained. Alternatively, blossoms were macerated in oil, new ones being added to concentrate the perfume. Jonquil and violet required *enfleurage* followed by maceration. Alcohol, added to the resulting oils, extracted the odour.

made me suffer: Anne's protracted infertility (she was married in 1615 but her first child was not born until 1638) was one source of conjugal tension, as was Louis's all-consuming passion for hunting. Her own 'Spanish' intrigues, however, hardly helped matters.

652 *somewhat advanced age*: Anne, born in 1601, was 60.

her name on his lips: in *The Three Musketeers* (World's Classics, p. 117), Buckingham is a lover 'of adventure and romance'. Historians have judged him more severely. His policies made him unpopular at home, while abroad he increased tensions between

England and France. But Dumas casts him in the dashing, romantic mould: for a smile from Anne, he will mortgage his country's interests. His last words were of her (ibid. 541–2).

656 *your mother*: George Villiers, first Duke of Buckingham, married Katherine Manners, daughter of the Earl of Rutland and richest heiress in the kingdom, in 1620. After his assassination in 1628, she married Randall Macdonnell, Earl of Antrim.

657 *beside the king*: see note to p. 31.

American Literature

British and Irish Literature

Children's Literature

Classics and Ancient Literature

Colonial Literature

Eastern Literature

European Literature

History

Medieval Literature

Oxford English Drama

Poetry

Philosophy

Politics

Religion

The Oxford Shakespeare

A complete list of Oxford Paperbacks, including Oxford World's Classics, Oxford Shakespeare, Oxford Drama, and Oxford Paperback Reference, is available in the UK from the Academic Division Publicity Department, Oxford University Press, Great Clarendon Street, Oxford OX2 6DP.

In the USA, complete lists are available from the Paperbacks Marketing Manager, Oxford University Press, 198 Madison Avenue, New York, NY 10016.

Oxford Paperbacks are available from all good bookshops. In case of difficulty, customers in the UK can order direct from Oxford University Press Bookshop, Freepost, 116 High Street, Oxford OX1 4BR, enclosing full payment. Please add 10 per cent of published price for postage and packing.